SURFEIT OF
DEATH AND THE DANCING FOOTMAN
COLOUR SCHEME

Dame Ngaio Marsh was born in New Zealand in 1895 and died in February 1982. She wrote over 30 detective novels and many of her stories have theatrical settings, for Ngaio Marsh's real passion was the theatre. Both actress and producer, she almost single-handedly revived the New Zealand public's interest in the theatre. It was for this work that she received what she called her 'damery' in 1966.

'The finest writer in the English language of the pure, classical puzzle whodunit. Among the crime queens, Ngaio Marsh stands out as an Empress.' *The Sun*

'Ngaio Marsh transforms the detective story from a mere puzzle into a novel.' *Daily Express*

'Her work is as nearly flawless as makes no odds. Character, plot, wit, good writing, and sound technique.' *Sunday Times*

'She writes better than Christie!' *New York Times*

'Brilliantly readable ... first class detection.' *Observer*

'Still, quite simply, the greatest exponent of the classical English detective story.' *Daily Telegraph*

'Read just one of Ngaio Marsh's novels and you've got to read them all ...' *Daily Mail*

BY THE SAME AUTHOR

A Man Lay Dead
Enter a Murderer
The Nursing Home Murder
Death in Ecstasy
Vintage Murder
Artists in Crime
Death in a White Tie
Overture to Death
Death at the Bar
Surfeit of Lampreys
Death and the Dancing Footman
Colour Scheme
Died in the Wool
Final Curtain
Swing, Brother, Swing
Opening Night
Spinsters in Jeopardy
Scales of Justice
Off With His Head
Singing in the Shrouds
False Scent
Hand in Glove
Dead Water
Death at the Dolphin
Clutch of Constables
When in Rome
Tied up in Tinsel
Black As He's Painted
Last Ditch
Grave Mistake
Photo-Finish
Light Thickens
Black Beech and Honeydew (autobiography)

NGAIO MARSH

Surfeit of Lampreys

Death and the Dancing Footman

Colour Scheme

AND

A Fool About Money

HARPER

HARPER
an Imprint of HarperCollins*Publishers*
77-85 Fulham Palace Road
Hammersmith, London W6 8JB
www.harpercollins.co.uk

This omnibus edition 2015
2

Surfeit of Lampreys first published in Great Britain by Collins 1941
Death and the Dancing Footman first published in Great Britain by Collins 1942
Colour Scheme first published in Great Britain by Collins 1943
A Fool About Money first published in Great Britain in *Death on the Air and Other Stories* by HarperCollins*Publishers* 1995

Ngaio Marsh asserts the moral right to
be identified as the author of these works

Copyright © Ngaio Marsh Ltd 1941, 1942, 1943
A Fool About Money copyright © Ngaio Marsh (Jersey) Ltd 1989

ISBN 978 0 00 732872 7

All rights reserved. No part of this publication may be
reproduced, stored in a retrieval system, or transmitted,
in any form or by any means, electronic, mechanical,
photocopying, recording or otherwise, without the prior
permission of the publishers.

Mixed Sources
Product group from well-managed
forests and other controlled sources
www.fsc.org Cert no. SW-COC-1806
© 1996 Forest Stewardship Council

FSC is a non-profit international organisation established to promote the
responsible management of the world's forests. Products carrying the FSC
label are independently certified to assure consumers that they come
from forests that are managed to meet the social, economic and
ecological needs of present and future generations.

Find out more about HarperCollins and the environment at
www.harpercollins.co.uk/green

CONTENTS

Surfeit of Lampreys
1

Death and the Dancing Footman
283

Colour Scheme
579

BONUS STORY:
A Fool About Money
841

Surfeit of Lampreys

For
SIR HUGH & LADY ACLAND
with my love
For the one since he has helped me so
often with my stories and for the other
since she likes stories about London

Contents

1	Prelude in New Zealand	5
2	Arrival in London	16
3	Preparation for a Charade	28
4	Uncle G.	42
5	Mike Puts the Pot On	54
6	Catastrophe	66
7	Death of a Peer	77
8	Alleyn Meets the Lampreys	90
9	Two, Two, the Lily-White Boys	105
10	Statement from a Small Boy	120
11	Conversation Piece	135
12	According to the Widow	148
13	The Sanity of Lady Wutherwood	162
14	Perjury By Roberta	182
15	Entrance of Mr Bathgate	200
16	Night Thickens	214
17	Mr Fox Finds an Effigy	229
18	Scene By Candlelight	249
19	Severed Hand	263
20	Preparation for Poverty	272

Characters in the Story

Roberta Grey
Lord Charles Lamprey
Lady Charles Lamprey
Henry Lamprey — *Their eldest son*
Friede Lamprey (Frid) — *Their elder daughter*
Colin and Stephen Lamprey — *Twins. Their second and third sons*
Patricia Lamprey (Patch) — *Their second daughter*
Michael Lamprey (Mike) — *Their youngest son*
Mrs Burnaby (Nanny) — *Their nurse*
Baskett — *Their butler*
Cora Blackburn — *Their parlour-maid*
A Ship's Passenger
Stamford — *A commissionaire*
The Lady Katherine Lobe — *Aunt to Lord Charles*
Gabriel, Marquis of Wutherwood
  and Rune (Uncle G.). — *Elder brother to Lord Charles*
Violet, Marchioness of Wutherwood
  and Rune (Aunt V.). — *His wife*
Giggle — *Their chauffeur*
Tinkerton — *Lady Wutherwood's maid*
Dr Kantripp — *The Lampreys' doctor*
Sir Matthew Cairnstock — *A brain specialist*
Dr Curtis — *Police surgeon*
Detective-Inspector Fox } *Of the Central Branch, Criminal*
Chief Detective-Inspector } *Investigation Department*
  Alleyn
Detective-Sergeant Bailey — *A finger-print expert*
Detective-Sergeant Thompson — *A photographic expert*
Police-Constable Martin
Police-Constable Gibson
A Police Constable who has read *Macbeth*
Detective-Sergeant Campbell — *On duty at 24 Brummell St*
Nigel Bathgate — *Watson to Mr Alleyn*
Mrs Moffatt — *Housekeeper at 24 Brummell Street*
Moffatt — *Her husband*
Mr Rattisbon — *Solicitor*
A Nurse

CHAPTER 1

Prelude in New Zealand

Roberta Grey first met the Lampreys in New Zealand. She was at school with Frid Lamprey. All the other Lampreys went to school in England, Henry, the twins, and Michael, to Eton; Patch to an expensive girls' school near Tonbridge. In the New Zealand days, Patch and Mike were too little for school. They had Nanny and, later on, a governess. But when the time came for Frid to be bundled off to England there was a major financial crisis and she became a boarder at Te Moana Collegiate School for Girls. Long after they had returned to England the family still said that Frid spoke with a New Zealand accent, which was nonsense.

In after years Roberta was to find a pleasant irony in the thought that she owed her friendship with the family to one of those financial crises. It must have been a really bad one because it was at about that time that Lady Charles Lamprey suddenly got rid of all her English servants and bought the washing machine that afterwards, on the afternoon it broke loose from its mooring, so nearly killed Nanny and Patch. Not long after Frid went to board at Te Moana an old aunt of Lord Charles's died, and the Lampreys were rich again, and all the servants came back, so that on Roberta's first visit Deepacres seemed very grand indeed. In New Zealand the Lampreys were a remarkable family. Titles are rare in New Zealand and the younger sons of marquises are practically non-existent.

In two years' time Roberta was to remember with nostalgic vividness, that first visit. It took place during the half-term weekend, when the boarders at Te Moana were allowed to go home. Two days beforehand, Frid asked Roberta if she would spend the half-term at Deepacres.

There were long-distance telephone calls between Deepacres and Roberta's parents.

Frid said: 'Do come, Robin darling, such fun,' in a vague, kind voice.

She had no idea, of course, that for Roberta the invitation broke like a fabulous rocket, that her mother, when Lady Charles Lamprey telephoned, was thrown into a frenzy of sewing that lasted until two o'clock in the morning, that Roberta's father bicycled four miles before eight o'clock in order to leave at Te Moana a strange parcel, a letter of instruction on behaviour, and five shillings to give the housemaid. Frid always sympathized when Roberta said her people were poor, as though they were all in the same boat, but the poverty of the Lampreys, as Roberta was to discover, was a queer and baffling condition understood by nobody, not even their creditors, and certainly not by poor Lord Charles with his eyeglass, his smile, and his vagueness.

It was almost dark when the car arrived at Te Moana. Roberta was made shy by the discovery of Lady Charles in the front seat beside the chauffeur, and of Henry, dark and exquisite, in the back one. But the family charm was equal to more than the awkwardness of a child of fourteen. Roberta yielded to it in three minutes and it held her captive ever afterwards.

The thirty-mile drive up to the mountains was like a dream. Afterwards, Roberta remembered that they all sang an old song about building a stairway to Paradise, and that she felt as though she floated up the stairway as she sang. The surface of the road changed from tar to shingle, stones banged against the underneath of the car, the foothills came closer and salutary drifts of mountain air were blown in at the window. It was quite dark when they began to climb the winding outer drive of Deepacres. Roberta smelt native bush, cold mountain water and wet loam. The car stopped, and Henry, groaning, got out and opened the gate. That was to be Roberta's clearest picture of Henry, struggling with the gate, screwing up his face in the glare of the headlights. The drive up to Deepacres seemed very long indeed. When at last they came out on a wide gravelled platform before the house, something of Roberta's shyness returned.

Long after the Lampreys had gone to England Roberta would sometimes dream that she returned to Deepacres. It was always at night. In her dream the door stood open, the light streamed down the steps. Baskett was in the entrance with a young footman whose name Roberta, in her dreams, had forgotten. The smell of blue-gum fires, of the oil that Lady Charles burnt in the drawing-room, and of cabbage-tree bloom would come out through the open door to greet her. There, in the drawing-room, as on that first night, she would see the family. Patch and Mike had been allowed to stay up; the twins, Stephen and Colin, that week arrived from England, were collapsed in armchairs. Henry lay on the hearthrug with his shining head propped against his mother's knee. Lord Charles would be gently amused at something he had been reading in a month-old *Spectator*. Always he put it down out of politeness to Roberta. The beginning of the dream never varied, or the feeling of enchantment.

The Lampreys appeared, on that first night, to scintillate with polish, and the most entrancing worldly-wisdom. Their family jokes seemed then the very quintessence of wit. When she grew up Roberta had still to remind herself that the Lampreys were funny but, with the exception of Henry, not witty. Perhaps they were too kind to be wits. Their jokes depended too much on the inconsequent family manner to survive quotation. But on that first night Roberta was rapturously uncritical. In retrospect she saw them as a very young family. Henry, the eldest, was eighteen. The twins, removed from Eton during the last crisis, were sixteen, Frid fourteen, Patricia ten, and little Michael was four. Lady Charles – Roberta never could remember when she first began to call her Chariot – was thirty-seven, and it was her birthday. Her husband had given her the wonderful dressing-case that appeared later, in the first financial crisis after Roberta met them. There were many parcels arrived that day from England, and Lady Charles opened them in a vague pleased manner, saying of each one that it was 'great fun', or 'charming', and exclaiming from time to time: 'How kind of Aunt M.!' 'How kind of George!' 'How kind of the Gabriels!' The Gabriels had sent her a bracelet and she looked up from the cards and said: 'Charlie, it's from both of them. They must have patched it up.'

'The bracelet, darling?' asked Henry.

'No, the quarrel. Charlie, I suppose that, after all, Violet can't be going to divorce him.'

'They'll have six odious sons, Imogen' said Lord Charles, 'and I shall never, never have any money. How she can put up with Gabriel! Of course she's mad.'

'I understand Gabriel had her locked up in a nursing-home last year, but evidently she's loose again.'

'Gabriel's our uncle,' explained smiling at Roberta. 'He's a revolting man.'

'I don't think he's so bad,' murmured Lady Charles, trying on the bracelet.

'Mummy, he's the *End*,' said Frid, and the twins groaned in unison from the sofa. 'The *End*,' they said and Colin added: 'Last, loathsomest, lousiest, execrable, apart.'

'Doesn't scan,' said Frid.

'Mummy,' asked Patch who was under the piano with Mike, 'who's lousy? Is it Uncle Gabriel?'

'Not really, darling,' said Lady Charles, who had opened another parcel. 'Oh, Charlie, *look!* It's from Auntie Kit. She's knitted it herself, of course. What can it be?'

'Dear Aunt Kit!' said Henry. And to Roberta: 'She wears buttoned-up boots and talks in a whisper.'

'She's Mummy's second cousin and Daddy's aunt. Mummy and Daddy are relations in a weird sort of way,' said Frid.

'Which may explain many things,' added Henry, looking hard at Frid.

'Once,' said Colin, 'Aunt Kit got locked up in a railway lavatory for sixteen hours because nobody could hear her whispering: "Let me out, if you please, let me out!" '

'And of course she was too polite to hammer or kick,' added Stephen.

Patch burst out laughing and Mike, too little to know why, broke into a charming baby's laugh to keep her company.

'It's a hat,' said Lady Charles and put it on the top of her head.

'It's a tea-cosy,' said Frid. 'How common of Auntie Kit.'

Nanny came in. She was the quintessence of all nannies, opinionated, faithful, illogical, exasperating, and admirable. She stood just inside the door and said:

'Good evening, m'lady. Patricia, Michael. Come along.'

'Oh Nanny,' said Patch and Mike. 'It's not time. Oh *Nanny!*'

Lady Charles said: 'Look what Lady Katherine has sent me, Nanny. It's a hat.'

'It's a hot-water bottle cover, m'lady,' said Nanny. 'Patricia and Michael, say goodnight and come along.'

II

It was the first of many visits. Roberta spent the winter holidays at Deepacres and when the long summer holidays came she was there again. The affections of an only child of fourteen are as concentrated as they are vehement. All her life Roberta was to put her emotional eggs in one basket. At fourteen, with appalling simplicity, she gave her heart to the Lampreys. It was, however, not merely an attachment of adolescence. She never grew out of it, and though, when they met again after a long interval, she could look at them with detachment, she was unable to feel detached. She wanted no other friends. Their grandeur, and in their queer way the Lampreys were very grand for New Zealand, had little to do with their attraction for Roberta. If the crash that was so often averted had ever fallen upon them they would have carried their glamour into some tumbledown house in England or New Zealand, and Roberta would still have adored them.

By the end of two years she knew them very well indeed. Lady Charles, always vague about ages, used to talk to Roberta with extraordinary frankness about family affairs. At first Roberta was both flattered and bewildered by these confidences. She would listen aghast to stories of imminent disaster, of the immediate necessity for a thousand pounds, of the impossibility of the Lampreys keeping their heads above water, and she would agree that Lady Charles must economize by no longer taking *Punch* and *The Tatler*, and that they could all do without table-napkins. It seemed a splendid strategic move for the Lampreys to buy a second and cheaper car in order to make less use of the Rolls-Royce. When, on the day the new car arrived, they all went for a picnic in both cars, Roberta and Lady Charles exchanged satisfied glances.

'Stealth is my plan,' cried Lady Charles as she and Roberta talked together by the picnic fire. 'I shall wean poor Charlie gradually from the large car. You see it quite amuses him, already, to drive that common little horror.'

Unfortunately, it also amused Henry and the twins to drive the large car.

'They must have *some* fun,' said Lady Charles, and to make up she bought no new clothes for herself. She was always eager to deny herself, and so gaily and lightly that only Henry and Roberta noticed what she was up to. Dent, her maid, who was friendly with a pawnbroker, made expeditions to the nearest town with pieces of Lady Charles's jewellery, and as she had a great deal of jewellery this was an admirable source of income.

'Robin,' said Henry to Roberta, 'what has become of Mummy's emerald star?'

Roberta looked extremely uncomfortable.

'Has she popped it?' asked Henry, then added: 'You needn't tell me. I know she has.'

For twenty minutes Henry was thoughtful and he was particularly attentive to his mother that evening. He told his father that she was overtired and suggested that she should be given champagne with her dinner. After making this suggestion Henry caught Roberta's eye and suddenly he grinned. Roberta liked Henry best of all the Lampreys. He had the gift of detachment. They all knew that they were funny, they even knew they were peculiar and rather gloried in it, but only Henry had the faculty of seeing the family in perspective, only Henry could look a little ruefully at their habits, only Henry would recognize the futility of their economic gestures. He too, fell into the habit of confiding in Roberta. He would discuss his friends with her and occasionally his love affairs. By the time Henry was twenty he had had three vague love affairs. He also liked to discuss the family with Roberta. On the very afternoon when the great blow fell, Henry and Roberta had walked up through the bush above Deepacres and had come out on the lower slope of Little Mount Silver. The real name for Deepacres was Mount Silver Station but Lord Charles on a vaguely nostalgic impulse had re-christened it after the Lampreys' estate in Kent. From where they lay in the warm tussock, Henry and Roberta looked across forty miles of plains. Behind them rose the mountains, Little Mount Silver, Big Mount Silver, the Giant Thumb Range, and behind that, the back-country, reaching in cold sharpness away to the west coast. All through the summer the mountain air came down to meet the warmth of the plains and Roberta, scenting it, knew contentment. This was her country.

'Nice, isn't it?' she said, tugging at a clump of tussock.

'Very pleasant,' said Henry.

'But not as good as England?'

'Well, I suppose England's my country,' said Henry.

'If I was there expect I'd feel the same about New Zealand.'

'I expect so. But you're only once removed from England, and we're not New Zealand at all. Strangers in a strange land and making pretty considerable fools of ourselves. There's a financial crisis brewing, Roberta.'

'Again!' cried Roberta in alarm.

'Again, and it seems to be a snorter.'

Henry rolled over on his back and stared at the sky.

'We're hopeless,' he said to Roberta. 'We live by windfalls and they won't go on for ever. What will happen to us, Roberta?'

'Charlot,' said Roberta, 'thinks you might have a poultry farm.'

'She and Daddy both think so,' said Henry. 'What will happen? We'll order masses of hens, and I can't tell you how much I dislike the sensation of feathers, we'll build expensive modern chicken-houses, we'll buy poultrified garments for ourselves, and for six months we'll all be eaten up with the zeal of the chicken-house and then we'll employ someone to do the work and we won't have paid for the outlay.'

'Well,' said Roberta unhappily, 'why don't you say so?'

'Because I'm like the rest of my family,' said Henry. 'What do you think of us, Robin? You're such a composed little person with your smooth head and your watchfulness.'

'That sounds smug and beastly.'

'It isn't meant to. You've got a sort of Jane Eyreishness about you. You'll grow up into a Jane Eyre, I dare say, if you grow at all. Don't you sometimes think we're pretty hopeless?'

'I like you.'

'I know. But you must criticize a little. What's to be done? What, for instance, ought I to do?'

'I suppose,' said Roberta, 'you ought to get a job.'

'What sort of a job? What can I do in New Zealand or anywhere else for the matter of that?'

'Ought you to have a profession?'

'What sort of profession?'

'Well,' said Roberta helplessly, 'what would you like?'

'I'm sick at the sight of blood so I couldn't be a doctor.

I lose my temper when I argue, so I couldn't be a lawyer, and I hate the poor, so I couldn't be a parson.'

'Wasn't there some idea of your managing Deepacres?'

'A sheep farmer?'

'Well – a run-holder. Deepacres is a biggish run, isn't it?'

'Too big for the Lampreys. Poor Daddy! When we first got here he became so excessively New Zealand. I believe he used sheep-dip on his hair and shall I ever forget him with the dogs! He bought four, I think they cost twenty pounds each. He used to sit on his horse and whistle so unsuccessfully that even the horse couldn't have heard him and the dogs all lay down and went to sleep and the sheep stood in serried ranks and gazed at him in mild surprise. Then he tried swearing and screaming but he lost his voice in less than no time. We should never have come out here.'

'I can't understand why you did.'

'In a vague sort of way I fancy we were shooting the moon. I was at Eton and really didn't know anything about it, until they whizzed me away to the ship.'

'I suppose you'll all go back to England,' said Roberta unhappily.

'When Uncle Gabriel dies. Unless, of course, Aunt G. has any young.'

'But isn't she past it?'

'You'd think so, but it would be just like the Gabriels. I wish I could work that Chinese Mandarin trick and say in my head, "Uncle G. has left us!" and be sure that he would instantly fall down dead.'

'Henry!'

'Well, my dear, if you *knew* him. He's the most revolting old gentleman. How Daddy ever came to have such a brother! He's mean and hideous and spiteful and ought to have been dead ages ago. There were two uncles between him and Daddy but they were both killed in the Great War. I understand that they were rather nice, and at any rate they had no sons, which is the great thing in their favour.'

'Henry, I get so muddled. What is your Uncle Gabriel's name?'

'Gabriel.'

'No, I mean his title and everything.'

'Oh. Well, he's the Marquis of Wutherwood and Rune. While my grandfather was alive Uncle G. was Lord Rune, the Earl of Rune. That's the eldest son's title, you see. Daddy is just a younger son.'

'And when your Uncle G. dies your father will be Lord Wutherwood and you'll be Lord Rune?'

'Yes, I shall, if the old pig ever does die.'

'Well, then there'd be a job for you. You could go into the House of Lords.'

'No; I couldn't. Poor Daddy would do that. He could bring in a bill about sheep-dip if peers are allowed to bring in bills. I rather think they only squash them, but I'm not sure.'

'You wouldn't care about being a politician, I suppose?'

'No,' said Henry sadly, 'I'm afraid I wouldn't.' He looked thoughtfully at Roberta and shook his head. 'The only thing I seem to have any inclination for is writing nonsense-rhymes and playing cricket and I'm terribly bad at both. I adore dressing-up, of course, but only in funny noses and false beards, and we all like doing that, even Daddy, so I don't imagine it indicates the stage as a career. I suppose I shall have to try and win the heart of an ugly heiress. I can't hope to fascinate a pretty one.'

'Oh,' cried Roberta in a fury, 'don't pretend to be so *feeble!*'

'I'm not pretending, alas.'

'And don't be so affected. Alas!'

'But it's true, Robin. We are feeble. We're museum pieces. Carryovers from another age. Two generations ago we didn't bother about what we would do when we grew up. We went into regiments, or politics, and lived on large estates. The younger sons had younger sons' compartments and either fitted them nicely, or else went raffishly to the dogs and were hauled back by the head of the family. Everything was all ready for us from the moment we were born.'

Henry paused, wagged his head sadly and continued:

'Now look at us! My papa is really an amiable dilettante. So, I suppose, would I be if I could go back into the setting, but you can't do that without money. Our trouble is that we go on behaving in the grand leisured manner without the necessary backing. It's very dishonest of us, but we're conditioned to it. We're the victims of inherited behaviourism.'

'I don't know what that means.'

'Nor do I but *didn't* it sound grand?'

'I think that perhaps you got it a bit wrong.'

'Do you?' asked Henry anxiously. 'Anyway, Robin, we shan't last long at this rate. A dreadful time is coming when we shall be obliged to do something to justify our existence. Make money or speeches or something. When the last of the money goes we'll be for it. The ones with brains and energy may survive but they'll be starting from a long way behind scratch. They say that if you want a job in the city it's wise to speak with an accent and pretend you've been to a board school. A hollow mockery, because you've found out the moment you have to do sums or write letters.'

'But,' said Robin, 'your sort of education – '

'Suits me. It's an admirable preparation for almost everything except an honest job of work.'

'I don't think that's true.'

'Don't you? Perhaps you're right and it's just our family that's mad of itself without any excuse.'

'You're a nice family. I love every one of you.'

'Darling Robin.' Henry reached out a hand and patted her. 'Don't be too fond of us.'

'My mother,' said Robin, 'says you've all got such a tremendous amount of charm.'

'Does she?' To Robin's surprise Henry's face became faintly pink. 'Well,' he said, 'perhaps if your mother is right, *that* may tide us over until Uncle G. pops off. Something has got to do it. Are there bums in New Zealand?'

'What do you mean? Don't be common.'

'My innocent old Robin Grey! A bum is a gentleman in a bowler hat who comes to stay until you pay your bills.'

'Henry! How awful!'

'Frightful,' agreed Henry who was watching a hawk.

'I mean how shaming.'

'You soon get used to them. I remember one who made me a catapult when I was home for the holidays. That was the time Uncle G. paid up.'

'But aren't you ever – ever – '

Roberta felt herself go scarlet and was silent.

'Ashamed of ourselves?'

'Well – '

'Listen,' said Henry. 'I can hear voices.'

It was Frid and the twins. They were coming up the bush track and seemed to be in a state of excitement. In a moment they began shouting:

'Henry! Where are you-oou? Henry!'

'Hallo!' Henry shouted.

The manuka scrub on the edge of the bush was agitated and presently three Lampreys scrambled out into the open. The twins had been riding and still wore their beautiful English jodhpurs. Frid, on the contrary, was dressed in a bathing suit.

'I say, what do you think?' they cried.

'What?'

'Such a thrill! Daddy's got a marvellous offer for Deepacres,' panted Frid.

'We'll be able to pay our bills,' added Colin. And they all shouted together: 'And we're going back to England.'

CHAPTER 2

Arrival in London

Now that the last trunk was closed and had been dragged away by an impatient steward, the cabin seemed to have lost all its character. Surveying it by lamplight, for it was still long before dawn, Roberta felt that she had relinquished her ownership and was only there on sufferance. Odd scraps of paper lay about the floor, the wardrobe door stood open, across the dressing-table lay a trail of spilt powder. The unfamiliar black dress and overcoat in which she would go ashore hung on the peg inside the door and seemed to move stealthily, and of their own accord, from side to side. The ship still creaked with that pleasing air of absorption in its own progress. Outside in the dark the lonely sea still foamed past the porthole, and footsteps still thudded on the deck above Roberta's head. But all these dear and familiar sounds only added to her feeling of desolation. The voyage was over. Already the ship was astir with agitated passengers. Slowly the blackness outside turned to grey. For the last time she watched the solemn procession of the horizon, and the dawn-light on cold ruffles of foam.

She put on the black dress and, for the hundredth time, wondered if it was the right sort of garment in which to land. It had a white collar and there was a white cockade in her hat so perhaps she would not look too obviously in mourning.

'I've come thirteen thousand miles,' thought Roberta. 'Half-way round the world. Now I'm near the top of the world. These are northern seas and those fading stars are the stars of northern skies.'

She leant out of the porthole and the sound of the sea surged up into her ears. A cold dawn-wind blew her hair back. She looked forward and saw a string of pale lights strung like a necklace across a wan greyness. Her heart thumped violently, for this was her first sight of England. For a long time she leant out of the porthole. Gulls now swooped and mewed round the ship. Afar off she heard the hollow sound of a siren. Filled with the strange inertia that is sometimes born of excitement Roberta could not make up her mind to go up on deck. At last a bugle sounded for the preposterously early breakfast. Roberta opened her bulging handbag, and with a good deal of difficulty extracted the two New Zealand pound notes she meant to give her stewardess. It seemed a large tip but it would represent only thirty English shillings. The stewardess was waiting in the corridor. The steward was there too and the bath steward. Roberta was obliged to return to her cabin and grope again in her bag.

Breakfast was a strange hurried affair with everybody wearing unfamiliar clothes and exchanging addresses. Roberta felt there was no sense of conviction in the plans the passengers made to sustain the friendships they had formed, but she too gave addresses to one or two people and wrote theirs on the back of a menu card. She then joined in the passport queue and in her excitement kept taking her landing papers out of her bag and putting them back again. Through the portholes she saw funnels, sides of tall ships, and finally buildings that seemed quite close to hand. She had her passport stamped and went up to B. deck where the familiar notices looked blankly at her. Already the hatches were opened and the winches uncovered. She stood apart from the other passengers and like them gazed forward. The shore was now quite close and there were many other ships near at hand. Stewards, pallid in their undervests, leant out of portholes to stare at the big liner. Roberta heard a passenger say, 'Good old Thames.' She heard names that were strange yet familiar: Gravesend, Tilbury, Greenhithe.

'Nearly over, now, Miss Grey,' said a voice at her elbow. An elderly man with whom she had been vaguely friendly leant on the rail beside her.

'Yes,' said Roberta. 'Almost over.'

'This is your first sight of London?'

'Yes.'

'That must be a strange sensation. I can't imagine it. I'm a cockney, you see.' He turned and looked down at her. Perhaps he thought she looked rather small and young for he said:

'Someone coming to meet you?'

'At the station, not at the boat. An aunt. I've never met her.'

'I hope she's a nice aunt.'

'I do too. She's my father's sister.'

'You'll be able to break the ice by telling her that you recognized her at once from her likeness to your father – ' He broke off abruptly. 'I'm sorry,' he said. 'I've said something that's . . . I'm sorry.'

'It's all right,' said Roberta, and because he looked so genuinely sorry she added: 'I haven't got quite used to talking ordinarily about them yet. My father and mother, I mean. I've got to get used to it, of course.'

'Both?' said her companion compassionately.

'Yes. In a motor accident. I'm going to live with this aunt.'

'Well,' he said, 'I can only repeat that I do hope she's a nice aunt.'

Roberta smiled at him and wished, though he was kind, that he would go away. A steward came along the deck carrying letters.

'Here's the mail from the pilot boat,' said her companion.

Roberta didn't know whether to expect a letter or not. The steward gave her two and a wireless message. She opened the wireless first and in another second her companion heard her give a little cry. He looked up from his own letter. Roberta's dark eyes shone and her whole face seemed to have come brilliantly to life.

'Good news?'

'*Oh yes! Yes.* It's from my greatest friends. I'm to stay with them first. They're coming to the ship. My aunt's ill or something and I'm to go to them.'

'That's good news?'

'It's splendid news. I knew them in New Zealand, you see, but I haven't seen them for years.'

Roberta no longer wished that he would go away. She was so excited that she felt she must speak of her good fortune.

'I wrote and told them I was coming but the letter went by air-mail on the day I sailed.' She looked at her letters. 'This one's from Charlot.'

She opened it with shaking fingers. Lady Charles's writing was like herself, at once, thin, elegant and generous.

'Darling Robin,' Roberta read, 'we are all so excited. As soon as your letter came I rang up your Kentish aunt and asked if we might have you first. She says we may for one night only which is measly but you must come back soon. She sounds quite nice. Henry and Frid will meet you at the wharf. We are so glad, darling. There's only a box for you to sleep in but you won't mind that. Best love from us all. Charlot.'

The wireless said: 'Aunt ill so we are allowed to keep you for a month. Hurrah darling so glad aunt not seriously ill so everything splendid love Charlot.'

The second was from Roberta's aunt.

'My dearest Roberta,' it said, 'I am so grieved and vexed that I am unable to welcome you to Dear Old England but alas, my dear, I am prostrated with such *dreadful sciatica* that my doctor insists on a visit to a very special nursing home!! So expensive and worrying for poor me and I would at *whatever cost to myself,* have defied him if it had not been for your friend Lady Charles Lamprey, who rang me up from London which was quite an excitement in *my hum-drum life* to ask when you arrived and on hearing of my dilemma very kindly offered to take you for a *month or more*. At first I suggested *one night* but I know your dear father and mother thought very highly of Lady Charles Lamprey and now I feel I may with a clear conscience accept her offer. This letter will, I am assured, reach you while you are still on your ship. I am so *distressed* that this happened but all's well that ends well, and I'm afraid you will find life in a Kentish village *very quiet* after the gaiety and *grandeurs* of your London friends!!! Well, my dear, Welcome to England and believe me I shall look forward to our meeting as soon as ever I return!

With much love,

Your affectionate

AUNT HILDA

PS – I have written a little note to Lady Charles Lamprey. By the way I hope that is the *correct* way to address her! Should it perhaps be Lady *Imogen* Lamprey? I seem to remember she was The Hon. or was it Lady, Imogen Ringle. I do hope I have not committed a *faux pas!* I think her husband is the Lord Charles Lamprey who was at Oxford with dear old Uncle George Alton who afterwards became rector of Lumpington-Parva but I don't suppose he would remember. Aunt H.

PPS – On second thoughts he would be *much too young*! – A.H.'

Roberta grinned and then laughed outright. She looked up to find her fellow-passenger smiling at her.

'Everything as it should be?' he asked.

'Lovely,' said Roberta.

II

As the distance lessened between wharf and ship the communal life that had bound the passengers together for five weeks dwindled and fell away. Already they appeared to be strangers to each other and their last conversations grew more and more desultory and unreal. To Roberta the ship herself seemed to lose familiarity. Roberta had time even in her excitement to feel as if she was only there on sufferance and because she had so much enjoyed her first long voyage she was now aware of a brief melancholy. But only a ditch of dirty water remained and on the wharf a crowd waited behind a barrier. Isolated individuals had begun to flutter handkerchiefs. Roberta's eyes searched diligently among the closely packed people and she had decided that neither Henry nor Frid was there, when suddenly she saw them, standing apart from the others and waving with that vague sideways sweep of the Lampreys. Henry looked much as she remembered him but four years had made an enormous difference to Frid. Instead of a shapeless schoolgirl Roberta saw a post-debutante, a young woman of twenty who looked as if every inch of herself and her clothes had been subjected to a sort of intensive manicuring. How smart Frid was and how beautifully painted; and how different they both looked from any one else on the wharf. Henry was bare-headed and Roberta, accustomed to the close-cropped New Zealand heads, thought his hair rather long. But he looked nice, smiling up at her. She could see that he and Frid were having a joke. Roberta waved violently and in sudden embarrassment, looked away. Lines had been flung to men on the wharf. With an imperative rattle, gang-planks were thrown out and five men in bowler hats walked up the nearest one.

'We won't be allowed ashore just yet,' said her friend. 'There's always a delay. Good Lord, what on earth are those two people doing down there? They must be demented! Look!'

He pointed at Henry and Frid who thrust out their tongues, rolled their eyes, beat the air with their hands and stamped rhythmically.

'Extraordinary!' he ejaculated. 'Who can they be?'

'They are my friends,' said Roberta. 'They're doing a haka.'

'A what?'

'A Maori war-dance. It's to welcome me. They're completely mad.'

'Oh,' said her friend, 'yes. Very funny.'

Roberta got behind him and did a few haka movements. A lot of the passengers were watching Henry and Frid and most of the people on the wharf. When they had finished their haka they turned their backs to the ship and bent their heads.

'What are they doing now?' Roberta's friend asked.

'I don't know,' she answered nervously.

The barrier was lifted and the crowd on the wharf moved towards the gangways. For a moment or two Roberta lost sight of the Lampreys. The people round her began laughing and pointing, and presently she saw her friends coming on board. They now wore papier-mâché noses and false beards and they gesticulated excitedly.

'They must be characters,' said her acquaintance doubtfully.

The passengers all hurried towards the head of the gang-plank and Roberta was submerged among people much taller than herself. Her heart thumped, she saw nothing but the backs of overcoats and heard only confused cries of greeting. Suddenly she found herself in somebody's arms. False beards and noses were pressed against her cheeks, she smelt Frid's scent and the stuff Henry put on his hair.

'Hallo, darling,' cried the Lampreys.

'Did you like our haka?' asked Frid. 'I wanted us to wear Maori mats and be painted brown but Henry wanted to be bearded so we compromised. It's such fun you've come.'

'Tell me,' said Henry solemnly, 'what do you think of dear old England?'

'Did you have a nice voyage?' asked Frid anxiously.

'Were you sick?'

'Shall we go now?'

'Or do you want to kiss the captain?'

'Come on,' said Frid. 'Let's go. Henry says we've got to bribe the customs so that they'll take you first.'

'Do be quiet, Frid,' said Henry, 'it's all a secret and you don't call it a bribe. Have you got any money, Robin? I'm afraid we haven't.'

'Yes, of course,' said Roberta. 'How much?'

'Ten bob. I'll do it. It doesn't matter so much if I'm arrested.'

'You'd better take off your beard,' said Frid.

The rest of the morning was a dream. There was a long wait in the customs shed where Roberta kept re-meeting all the passengers to whom she had said goodbye. There was a trundling of luggage to a large car where a chauffeur waited. Roberta instantly felt apologetic about the size of her cabin trunk. She found it quite impossible to readjust herself to these rapidly changing events. She was only vaguely aware of a broad and slovenly street, of buildings that seemed incredibly drab, of ever-increasing traffic. When Henry and Frid told her that this was the East End and murmured about Limehouse and Poplar, Roberta was only vaguely disappointed that the places were so much less romantic than their associations, that the squalor held no suggestion of illicit glamour, that the street, Henry said it was the Commercial Road, looked so precisely like its name. When they came into the City and Henry and Frid pointed uncertainly to the Mansion House or suggested she should look at the dome of St Paul's, Roberta obediently stared out of the windows but nothing she saw seemed real. It was as if she lay on an unfamiliar beach and breaker after breaker rolled over her head. The noise of London bemused her more than the noise of the sea. Her mind was limp, she heard herself talking and wondered at the coherence of the sentences.

'Here's Fleet Street,' said Henry. 'Do you remember "up the Hill of Ludgate, down the Hill of Fleet"?'

'Yes,' murmured Roberta, 'yes. Fleet Street.'

'We've miles to go still,' said Frid. 'Robin, did you know I *am* going to be an actress?'

'She might have guessed,' said Henry, 'by the way you walk. Did you notice her walk, Robin? She sort of paws the ground. When she comes into the room she shuts the door behind her and leans against it.'

Frid grinned. 'I do it beautifully,' she said. 'It's second nature to me.'

'She goes to a frightful place inhabited by young men in mufflers who run their hands through their hair and tell Frid she's marvellous.'

'It's a dramatic school,' Frid explained. 'The young men are very intelligent. All of them say I'm going to be a good actress.'

'We'll be passing the Law Courts in a minute,' said Henry.

Scarlet omnibuses sailed past like ships. Inside them were pale people who looked at once alert, tired, and preoccupied. In a traffic jam a dark-blue car came so close alongside that the men in the back seat were only a few inches away from Roberta and the Lampreys.

'That's one of the new police cars, Frid,' said Henry.

'How do you know?'

'Well, I know it is. I expect those enormous men are Big Fours.'

'I wish they'd move on,' said Frid. 'I wouldn't be surprised if we fell into their hands one of these days.'

'Why?' asked Roberta.

'Well, the twins were saying at breakfast yesterday that they thought the only thing to be done was for them to turn crooks and be another lot of Mayfair boys.'

'It was rather a good idea, really,' said Henry. 'You see Colin said he'd steal some incredibly rich dowager's jewels and Stephen would establish his alibi at the Ritz or somewhere. Nobody can tell them apart, you know.'

'And then, you know,' added Frid, 'if one of them was arrested they'd each say it was the other and as one of them must be innocent, they'd have to let both of them go.'

'From which,' said Henry, 'you will have gathered we are in the midst of a financial crisis.' Roberta started at the sound of that familiar phrase.

'Oh, *no!*' she said.

'Oh, yes,' said Henry, 'and what's more it's a snorter. Everybody seems to be furious with us.'

'Mummy's going to pop the pearls this afternoon,' added Frid, 'on her way to the manicurist.'

'She's never done *that* before,' said Henry. 'This is the Strand, Robin. That church is either St Clemence Dane or St Mary le Strand and the next one is whatever that one isn't. We'd better explain about the crisis, I suppose.'

'I wish you would,' said Roberta. In her bemused condition the Lampreys' affairs struck a friendly and recognizable note. She could think sharply about their debts but she could scarcely so much as gape at the London she had greatly longed to see. It was as if her powers of receptivity were half anaesthetized and would respond only to familiar impressions. She listened attentively to a long recital of how Lord Charles had invested a great deal of the money he still mysteriously possessed in something called San Domingoes and how it had almost immediately disappeared. She heard of a strange venture in which Lord Charles planned to open a jewellery business in the City, run on some sort of commission basis, with Henry and the twins as salesmen. 'And at least,' said Frid, 'there would have been Mummy's things that she got out of pawn when Cousin Ruth died. It would have been better to sell than to pop them, don't you think?' This project, it appeared, had depended on somebody called Sir David Stein who had recently committed suicide, leaving Lord Charles with an empty office and a ten years' lease on his hands.

'And so now,' said Henry, 'we appear to be sunk. That's Charing Cross Station. We thought we would take you to a play tonight, Robin.'

'And we can dance afterwards,' said Frid. 'Colin's in love with a girl in the play so I expect he'll want her to come whizzing on with us, which is rather a bore. Have you asked Mary to come, Henry?'

'No,' said Henry. 'We've only got five seats and the twins both want to come and anyway I want to dance with Robin, and Colin's actress isn't coming.'

'Well, Stephen could take Mary off your hands.'

'He doesn't like her.'

'Mary is Henry's girl,' explained Frid. 'Only vaguely, though.'

'Well, she's quite nice really,' said Henry.

'Charming, darling,' said Frid handsomely.

Roberta suddenly felt rather desolate. She stared out of the window and only half-listened to Henry who seemed to think he ought to point out places of interest.

'This is Trafalgar Square,' said Henry. 'Isn't that thing in the middle too monstrous? Lions, you see, at each corner, but of course you've met them in photographs.'

'That building over there is the Tate Gallery,' said Frid.

'She means the National Gallery, Robin. I suppose you will want to see one or two sights, won't you?'

'Well, I suppose I ought to.'

'Patch and Mike are at home for the holidays,' said Frid. 'It will be good for them to take Robin to some sights.'

'Perhaps I could look some out for myself,' Roberta suggested with diffidence.

'You'll find it difficult to begin,' Henry told her. 'There's something so cold-blooded about girding up your loins and going out to find a sight. I'll come to one occasionally if you like. It may not be so bad once the plunge is taken. We are getting a very public-spirited family, Robin. The twins and I are territorials. I can't tell you how much we dislike it but we stiffened our upper lips and bit on the bullets and when the war comes we know what we have to do. In the meantime, of course, I've got to get a job, now we're sunk.'

'We're not definitely sunk until Uncle G. has spoken,' Frid pointed out.

'Uncle G.!' Robin exclaimed. 'I'd almost forgotten about him. He's always sounded like a myth.'

'It's to be hoped he doesn't behave like one,' said Henry. 'He's coming to see us tomorrow. Daddy has sent him an SOS I can't tell you how awful he is.'

'Aunt V. is worse,' said Frid gloomily. 'Let's face it, Aunt V. is worse. And they're both coming in order to go into a huddle with Daddy and Mummy about finance. We hope to sting Uncle G. for two thousand.'

'It'll all come to Daddy when they're dead, you see, Robin. They've no young of their own.'

'I thought,' said Roberta, 'that they were separated.'

'Oh, they're always flying apart and coming together again,' said Frid. 'They're together at the moment. Aunt V. has taken up witchcraft.'

'What!'

'Witchcraft,' said Henry. 'It's quite true. She's a witch. She belongs to a little black-magic club somewhere.'

'I don't believe you!'

'You may as well, because it's true. She started by taking up with a clergyman in Devon who had discovered an evil place on Dartmoor. It seems that he told Aunt V. that he thought he might as well sprinkle some holy water on this evil place but when he went there, the holy water was dashed out of his hands by an unseen power. He lent Aunt V. some books about black magic and instead of being horrified she took the wrong turning and thought it sounded fun. I understand she goes to the black mass and everything.'

'How can you possibly know?'

'Her maid, Miss Tinkerton, told Nancy. Tinkerton says Aunt V. is far gone in black magic. They have meetings at Deepacres. The real Deepacres, you know, in Kent. Aunt V. is always buying books about witchcraft, and she's got a lot of very queer friends. They've all got names like Olga and Sonia and Boris. Aunt V. is half-Rumanian, you know,' said Frid.

'Half-Hungarian, you mean,' corrected Henry.

'Well, all central-European anyway. Her name isn't Violet at all.'

'What is it?' asked Roberta.

'Something Uncle G. could neither spell nor pronounce so he called her Violet. A thousand years ago he picked her up in Budapest at an embassy. She's a very sinister sort of woman and quite insane. Probably the witchcraft is a throw-back to a gypsy ancestress of sorts. Of course Uncle G.'s simply furious about it, not being a warlock.'

'Naturally,' said Frid. 'I suppose he's afraid she might put a spell on him.'

'I wouldn't put it past her,' said Henry. 'She's a really evil old thing. She gives me absolute horrors. She's like a white toad. I'll bet you anything you like that under her clothes she's all cold and damp.'

'Shut up,' said Frid. 'All the same I wouldn't be surprised if you were right. Henry, do let's stop somewhere and have breakfast. I'm ravenous and I'm sure Robin must be.'

'It'll have to be Angelo's,' said Henry. 'He'll let us chalk it up.'

'I've got some money,' said Roberta rather shyly.

'No, no!' cried Frid. 'Angelo's *much* too dear to pay cash. We'll put it down to Henry's account and I've got enough for a tip, I think.'

'It may not be open,' said Henry. 'What's the time? The day seems all peculiar with this early start. Look, Robin, we're coming into Piccadilly Circus.'

Roberta stared past the chauffeur and, through the windscreen of the car, she had her first sight of Eros.

In the thoughts of those who have never visited them all great cities are represented by symbols; New York by a skyline, Paris by a river and an arch, Vienna by a river and a song, Berlin by a single street. But to British colonials the symbol of London is more homely than any of these. It is a small figure perched slantways above a roundabout, an elegant Victorian god with a Grecian name – Eros of Piccadilly Circus. When they come to London, colonials orientate themselves by Piccadilly Circus. All their adventures start from there. It is under the bow of Eros that to many a colonial has come that first warmth of realization that says to him: 'This is London.' It is here at the place which he learns, with a rare touch of insolence, to call the hub of the universe, that the colonial wakes from the trance of arrival, finds his feet on London paving stones, and is suddenly happy.

So it was for Roberta. From the Lampreys' car she saw the roundabout of Piccadilly, the great sailing buses, the sea of faces, the traffic of the Circus, and she felt a kind of realization stir in her heart.

'It's not so very big,' said Roberta.

'Quite small, really,' said Henry.

'I don't mean it's not thrilling,' said Roberta. 'It is. I . . . I feel as if I'd like to be . . . sort of inside it.'

'I know,' agreed Henry. 'Let's nip out, Frid, and walk round the corner to Angelo's.'

He said to the chauffeur: 'Pick us up in twenty minutes, will you Mayling?'

'Here's a jam,' said Frid. 'Now's our chance. Come on.'

Henry opened the door and took Roberta's hand. She scrambled out. The voyage, the ship, and the sea all slid away into remoteness. A new experience took Roberta and the sounds that are London engulfed her.

CHAPTER 3

Preparation for a Charade

The Lampreys lived in two flats which occupied the entire top storey of a building known as Pleasaunce Court Mansions. Pleasaunce Court is merely a short street connecting Cadogan Square with Lennox Gardens and the block of flats stands on the corner. To Roberta the outside seemed forbidding but the entrance hall had lately been redecorated and was more friendly. Pale green walls, a thick carpet, heavy armchairs and an enormous fire gave an impression of light and luxury. The firelight flickered on the chromium steel of a lift-cage in the centre of the hall and on a slotted framework that held the names of the flat owners. Roberta read the top one: 'No. 25 & 26, Lord and Lady Charles Lamprey. In.' Henry followed her gaze, crossed quickly to the board and moved a chromium steel tab.

' "Lord and Lady Charles Lamprey. Out," I fancy,' muttered Henry.

'Oh, are they!' cried Roberta. 'Are they away?'

'No,' said Henry. 'Ssh!'

'Ssh!' said Frid.

They moved their heads slightly in the direction of the door. A small man wearing a bowler hat stood on the pavement outside and appeared to consult an envelope in his hands. He looked up at the front of the flats and then approached the steps.

'Into the lift!' Henry muttered and opened the doors. Roberta in a state of extreme bewilderment entered the lift. A porter, heavily smart in a dark-green uniform and several medals, came out of an office.

'Hallo, Stamford,' said Henry. 'Good morning to you. Mayling's got some luggage out there in the car.'

'I'll attend to it, sir,' said the porter.

'Thank you so much,' murmured the Lampreys politely, and Henry added, 'his lordship is away this morning, Stamford.'

'Indeed, sir?' said the porter. 'Thank you, sir.'

'Up we go,' said Henry.

The porter shut them in, Henry pressed a button, and with a metallic sigh the lift took them to the top of the building.

'Stamford doesn't work the lift,' explained Henry, 'he's only for show and to look after the service flats downstairs.'

In three days, photographs of the Pleasaunce Court lift would appear in six illustrated papers and in the files of the criminal investigation department. It would be lit by flash lamps, sealed, dusted with powder, measured and described. It would be discussed by several millions of people. It was about to become famous. To Roberta it seemed very smart and she did not notice that, like the entrance hall, it had been modernized. The old liftman's apparatus, a handle projecting from a cylindrical casing, was still there but above it was a row of buttons with the Lampreys' floor, the fourth, at the top. They came out on a well-lit landing with two light green doors numbered 25 and 26. Henry pushed number 25 open and Roberta crossed a threshold into the past. The sensation of Deepacres, of that still-recurrent dream came upon her so poignantly that she caught her breath. Here was the very scent of Deepacres, of the scented oil Lady Charles burnt in the drawing-room, of Turkish cigarettes, of cut flowers and of moss. Our sense of smell works both consciously and subconsciously. About many households is an individual pleasantness of which human noses are only half aware and which is so subtle that it cannot be traced to one source. The Lampreys' house smell, while it might suggest burning cedarwood, scented oil, and hot-house flowers, was made up of these things and of something more, something that to Roberta seemed the very scent of their characters. It carried her back through four years and, while the pleasure of this experience was still new, she saw in the entrance hall some of their old possessions: a table, a steel engraving, a green Chinese elephant. It was with the strangest feeling of familiarity that she heard Lady Charles's voice crying:

'Is that old Robin Grey?'

Roberta ran through the doorway into her arms.

They were all there, in a long white drawing-room with crackling fires at each end and a great gaiety of flowers. Lady Charles, thinner than ever, was not properly up and had bundled herself into a red silk dressing-gown. She wore a net over her grey curls. Her husband stood beside her in his well-remembered morning attitude, a newspaper dangling from his hand, his glass in his eye, and his thin colourless hair brushed across his head. He beamed with pale myopic eyes at Roberta and inclined his head forward with an obedient air, ready for her kiss. The twins, with shining blond heads and solemn smiles, also kissed her. Patch, an overgrown schoolgirl in a puppy-fat condition, nearly knocked her over, and Mike, eleven years old, looked relieved when Roberta merely shook his hand.

'Such fun, darling,' said all the Lampreys in their soft voices. 'Such fun to see you.'

Presently they were all sitting before the fire, with Chariot in her chair, and Henry in his old place on the hearthrug and the twins collapsed on the sofa. Patch hurled herself on to the arm of Robin's chair, and Frid stood in an elegant attitude before the fire, and Lord Charles wandered vaguely about the room.

'Dear me,' said Henry, 'I feel like Uriah Heep. It's as good as the chiming of old bellses to see Robin Grey in the flesh.'

The twins murmured agreeably and Colin said: 'You haven't grown much.'

'I know,' said Roberta. 'I'm a pygmy.'

'A nice pygmy,' said Chariot.

'Do you think she's pretty?' asked Frid. 'I do.'

'Not exactly pretty,' said Stephen. 'I'd call her attractive.'

'Really!' said Lord Charles mildly. 'Does Robin, who I must say looks delightful, enjoy a public dissection of her charms?'

'Yes,' said Roberta. 'From the family, I do.'

'Of course she does,' shouted Patch dealing Roberta a violent buffet across the shoulders.

'What do you think of *me?*' asked Frid, striking an attitude. 'Aren't I quite, quite lovely?'

'Don't tell her she is,' said Colin. 'The girl's a nymphomaniac.'

'Darling!' murmured Lady Charles.

'My dear Colin,' said his father, 'it really would be a good idea if you stick to the words you understand.'

'Well,' Frid reasoned, 'you may thank your lucky stars I am so lovely. After all, looks go a long way on the stage. I may have to keep you all, and in the near future, too.'

'Apropos,' said Henry, 'I fancy there's a bum downstairs, chaps.'

'Oh *no!*' cried the Lampreys.

'The signs are ominous. I told Stamford you were out, Daddy.'

'Then I suppose I'd better stay in,' muttered Lord Charles. 'Who can it be this time? Not Smith & Weekly's again, surely? I wrote them an admirable letter explaining that – '

'Circumstances over which we had no control,' suggested Stephen.

'I put it better than that, Stephen.'

'Mike,' said Lady Charles, 'be an angel and run out on the landing. If you see a little man – '

'In a bowler,' said Henry and Frid.

'Yes, of course in a bowler. If you see him, don't say anything but just come and tell Mummy, darling, will you?'

'Right oh,' said Mike politely. 'Is he a bum, Mummy?'

'We think so but it's nothing to worry about. Do hurry, Mikey, darling.'

Mike grinned disarmingly and began to hop out of the room on one leg.

'I can hop for miles,' he said.

'Well, run quietly for a change.'

Mike gave a Red-Indian call and began to crawl out. The twins rose in a menacing fashion. He uttered a shrill yelp and ran.

'Isn't he Heaven?' Lady Charles asked Roberta.

'There's the lift!' Colin ejaculated.

'It'll only be Mike t-taking a run down and up,' said Stephen. 'I understand that Mike's playing with the lift is rather unpopular.'

'I bet it's the bum,' said Colin. 'Has Baskett been warned? I mean he may just lavishly show him in.'

'If Baskett doesn't know a bailiff's man,' said Lord Charles warmly, 'after having lived with us for fifteen years, he is a stupider fellow than I take him for.'

'There's the bell!' cried Lady Charles.

'It's all right,' said Henry. 'It'll only be Robin's luggage.'

'Thank Heaven! Robin, darling, you'd like to see your room, wouldn't you? Frid, darling, show Robin her room. It's too tiny and absurd, darling, but you won't mind, will you? Actually it was meant for a hall, but Mike and Patch turned it into a sort of railway station, so we're delighted to have it made sane again. I really must dress myself but I can't resist waiting to hear the worst about the bum.'

'Here's Mike,' said Frid.

Mike came back, still hopping on one leg, and singing:

> 'Hallelujah, I'm a bum!
> Hallelujah, bum again!
> Hallelujah, give us a hand up to – '

'Shut up,' said Stephen and Colin. 'What do you mean? Is he there?'

'Nope,' whispered Mike. 'Only *her* luggage.'

'Don't say "her",' said Stephen.

Mike began to hop up and down in front of the twins singing:

> 'Two, two the lily white boys
> Clothed all in green, oh.'

Colin took him by the shoulders and Stephen seized his heels. They swung him to and fro and flung him, screaming with pleasure, on the sofa.

'Lily white boys!' yelled Mike. 'I bet she doesn't know which is which. Do you?' He looked engagingly at Roberta.

'Do you – Robin?'

The twins turned to her, and raised their eyebrows.

'Do you?' they asked.

'I do when you speak,' said Roberta.

'I hardly stammer at all, now,' said Stephen.

'I know, but your voices are different, Stephen. And even if you didn't speak I'd only have to look behind your ears.'

'Oh,' said Mike, 'it's not fair. She knows the secret. Stephen's old mole. Old moledy Stephen doesn't wash behind his ears, yah, yah, yah!'

'Let's go to your room,' said Frid. 'Mike's turning mad dog, and the scare seems to be over.'

II

Roberta liked her room which was in 26. As Lady Charles had told her it was really the entrance hall but a heavy curtain had been hung across it making a passage, through which the others would have to go to reach the real passage and their bedrooms. Frid showed her the rest of 26 which was all bedrooms with Nanny Burnaby living in the ex-kitchen where she could make the cups of Ovaltine that she still forced the Lampreys to drink before they went to bed. Nanny was sitting by the electric stove which she had converted into a sort of bureau. Her hair had turned much greyer. Her face was netted over with lines as if, thought Roberta, each good or ill deed of the young Lampreys had left its sign on that one face alone. She had been playing patience and received Roberta exactly as if four days instead of four years had gone by since their last meeting.

'Nanny,' said Frid, 'things are gloomy. We're up the spout again and there's liable to be a bum at any moment.'

'Some folk will do anything,' said Nanny darkly.

'Well, I know, but I suppose they rather want their money.'

'Well, his lordship had better pay them and be done with it.'

'I'm afraid we haven't got any money at the moment, Nan.'

'Nonsense,' said Nanny.

She looked at Roberta and said, 'You don't grow much, Miss Robin.'

'No, Nanny. I rather think I've finished. I'm twenty now, you know.'

'Same age as Miss Frid and look how she's shot up. You need nourishing.'

'Nan,' said Frid. 'Uncle Gabriel's coming tomorrow.'

'Hm'm,' said Nanny.

'We hope he'll pull us out of the soup.'

'So he ought to with his own flesh and blood in need.'

Henry looked in at the door. By the singular scowl Nanny gave him, Roberta saw that he was still the favourite.

'Hallo, Mrs Burnaby,' he said. 'Have you heard the news? We're in the soup.'

'It's not the first time, Mr Henry, and it won't be the last. His lordship's brother will have to attend to it.'

Henry looked fixedly at his old nurse. 'If he doesn't,' he said, 'I think we'll really go bust.'

Nanny's hands, big-jointed with rheumatism, made a quick involuntary movement.

'You'll be all right, Nan,' added Henry. 'We fixed you up with an annuity, didn't we?'

'I'm not thinking of that, Mr Henry.'

'No. No, I don't suppose you are. I was, though.'

Nanny put on a pair of thick-lens spectacles and advanced upon Henry.

'You put your tongue out,' she ordered.

'Why on earth?'

'Do as you're told, Mr Henry.'

Henry put out his tongue.

'I thought so. Come to me before you go to bed this evening. You're bilious.'

'What utter rot.'

'You've always shown your liver in your spirits.'

'Nanny!'

'Talking a lot of rubbish about matters that are beyond your understanding. His other lordship will soon send certain people about their business.'

'Meaning us?'

'Stuff and nonsense. You know what I mean. Miss Robin, you'd better take a glass of milk with your lunch. You're over-excited.'

'Yes, Nanny,' said Roberta.

Nanny returned to her game of patience.

'The audience is over,' said Henry.

'I'd better unpack,' said Roberta.

'Leave out your pressings,' said Nanny. 'I'll do 'em.'

'Thank you, Nanny,' said Roberta and went to her room.

Now she was alone. The floor beneath her feet seemed unstable as though the sea, after five weeks' domination, was not easily to be forgotten. It was strange to feel this physical reminder of an experience already so remote. Roberta unpacked. The clothes that she had bought in New Zealand no longer pleased her but she was too much preoccupied by the affairs of the Lampreys to be much concerned with her own. During the last four years Roberta had passed through adolescence into womanhood. The emotional phases proper to those years had been interrupted by tragedy. Two months ago when the languors and propulsions of adolescence had not yet quite abated, Roberta's parents had been killed, and a kind of frost had closed about her emotions so that at first, though she felt the pain of her loss, it was with her reason rather than with her heart. Later, when the thaw came, she found that something unexpected had happened to her. Her affections, which had been easily and lightly bestowed, had crystallized, and she found herself indifferent to the greater number of her friends. With this discovery came another; that in four years her heart was still with an incredible family now half the world away. Her thought returned to Deepacres and she wanted the Lampreys. More than any one else in the world she wanted them. They might be scatter-brained, unstable, reprehensible, but they suited Roberta and she supposed she suited them. When her father's sister wrote to suggest that Roberta should come to England and live with her, Roberta was glad to go because, by the same mail, came a letter from Lady Charles Lamprey that awoke all her old love for the family. When it became certain that she would see them again she grew apprehensive lest they should find her an awkward carryover from their colonial days, but as soon as she saw Henry and Frid on the wharf she had felt safer, and now, as she put the last of her un-smart garments in a drawer that already contained several pieces of a toy railway, she was visited by the odd idea that it was she who had grown so much older and that the young Lampreys had merely grown taller.

'Otherwise,' thought Roberta, 'they haven't changed a bit.'

The door opened and Lady Charles came in. She was now dressed. Her grey hair shone in a mass of small curls, her thin face was delicately powdered, and she looked and smelt delightful.

'How's old Robin Grey?' she asked.

'Very happy.'

Lady Charles turned on the electric heater, drew up a chair, sat in it, folded her short skirt back over her knees and lit a cigarette. Roberta recognized, with a warm sense of familiarity, the signs of an impending gossip.

'I hope you won't be too uncomfortable, darling,' said Lady Charles.

'I'm in Heaven, Charlot, darling.'

'We do so wish we could have you for a long time. What are your plans?'

'Well,' said Roberta, 'my aunt has offered very nicely to have me as a sort of companion, but I think I want a job, a real job, I mean. So if she agrees, I'm going to try for a secretaryship in a shop, or failing that, an office. I've learnt shorthand and typing.'

'We must see what we can do. But of course you *must* have *some* fun first.'

'I'd love some fun but I've only got a tiny bit of money. About £200 a year. So I've got to start soon.'

'I must say I do think money's *awful*,' said Lady Charles. 'Here are we, practically playing mouth-organs and selling matches, and all because poor darling Charlie doesn't happen to have a head for sums. I'm so dreadfully worried, Robin. It's so hard for the children.'

'Hard for you, too.'

'Well, if we go bankrupt it'll be rather uncomfortable. Charlie won't be allowed on a racecourse for one thing. There's one comfort, he *has* paid his bookmaker. There's something so second-rate about not paying your bookmaker and the things they do to you are too shaming.'

'What sort of things?'

'I think they call out your name at Sandown and beat with a hammer to draw everybody's attention. Or is that only if you are a mason? At any rate we needn't dwell on it because it's almost the only thing that is *not* likely to happen to us.'

'But, Charlot, you've got over other fences.'

'Nothing like this. This isn't a fence; it's a mountain.'

'How did it all happen?'

'My dear, how does one run into debt? It simply occurs, bit by bit. And you know, Robin, I have made such enormous efforts. We've lived like anchorites and put down one thing after another. The children have been wonderful about it. The twins and Henry have answered any number of advertisements and have never given up the idea that they must get a job. And they've been so good about their fun, enjoying quite *cheap* things like driving about England and staying at second-rate hotels and going to Ostend for a little cheap gamble instead of the Riviera where all their friends are. And Frid was so good-natured about her coming-out. No ball; only dinner and cocktail parties which we ran on *sixpence*. And now she's going to this drama school and working so hard with the most appalling people. Of course the whole thing is the business of Charlie and the jewels. Don't ask me to tell you the complete story, it's too grim and involved for words to convey. The gist of it is that poor Charlie was to have this office in the City with buyers in the East and at places like the Galle Face Hotel at Colombo. He was in partnership with a Sir David Stein, who seemed a rather nice second-rate little man, we thought. Well, it appears that they had a great orgy of paper-signing and no sooner was that over than Sir David blew out his brains.'

'Why?'

'It seems he was in deep water and one of his chief interests had crashed quite suddenly. It turned out that Charlie had to meet a frightful lot of bills because he was Sir David's partner. So many, that we hadn't any money left to pay our own bills which had been mounting up a bit, anyhow. And there's no more coming in for six months. So there you are. Well, we must simply keep our heads and take the right line with Gabriel. Charlie wrote him a really charming telegram, just *right*, do you know? We took great trouble with it. Gabriel is at Deepacres and he hates coming up to London so we rather hoped he'd simply realize he couldn't let Charlie go bust and would send him a cheque. However, he telegraphed back: "Arriving Friday, six o'clock. Wutherwood," which has thrown us all into rather a fever.'

'Do you think it'll be all right?' asked Roberta.

'Well, it's simply *so* crucial that we're not thinking at all. Never jump your fences till you meet them. But I'm terribly anxious that we should take the right *line* with Gabriel. It's a bore that Charlie loathes him so whole-heartedly.'

'I didn't think he ever loathed anybody,' said Roberta.

'Well, as far as he can, he hates Gabriel. Gabriel has always been rather beastly to him and thinks he's extravagant. Gabriel himself is a miser.'

'Oh dear!'

'I know. Still he's a snob and I really don't believe he'll allow his brother to go bankrupt. He'd *crawl* with horror at the publicity. What we've got to do is decide on the *line* to take with Gabriel when he gets here. I thought the first thing was to consider his comfort. He likes a special kind of sherry, almost unprocurable, I understand, but Baskett is going to hunt for it. And he likes early Chinese pottery. Deepacres is full of leering goddesses and dragons. Well, by a great stroke of luck, one of the things poor Charlie bought with an eye to business is a small blue pot which was most frightfully expensive and which, in a mad moment, he paid for. I had the really brilliant idea of letting Mike give it to Gabriel. Mike has quite charming manners when he tries.'

'But, Charlot, if this pot is so valuable, couldn't you sell it?'

'I suppose we could, but how? And, anyway, my cunning tells me that it's much better to invest it as a sweetener for Gabriel. We've got to be diplomatic. Suppose the pot is worth a hundred pounds? My dear, we want two thousand. Why not use the pot as a sprat to catch a mackerel?'

'Yes,' said Roberta dubiously, 'but may he not think it looks a bit lavish to be giving away valuable pots?'

'Oh, no,' said Lady Charles with an air of dismissal, 'he'll be delighted. And anyway if he flings it back in poor little Mike's face, we've still *got* the pot.'

'True,' said Roberta, but she felt that there was a flaw somewhere in Lady Charles's logic.

'We'll all be in the drawing-room when he comes,' continued Lady Charles, 'and I thought perhaps we might have some charades.'

'What!'

'I know it sounds mad, Robin, but you see he *knows* we're rather mad and it's no good pretending we're not. And we're all good at charades, you can't deny it.'

Roberta remembered the charades in New Zealand, particularly one that presented the Garden of Eden. Lord Charles, with his glass in his eye, and an umbrella over his head to suggest the heat of the day, had enacted Adam. Henry was the serpent and the twins, angels. Frid had entered into the spirit of the part of Eve and had worn almost nothing but a brassière and a brown paper fig-leaf. Lady Charles had found one of the false beards that the Lampreys could always be depended upon to produce and had made a particularly irritable Deity. Patch had been the apple tree.

'Does he like charades?' asked Roberta.

'I don't suppose he ever sees any, which is all to the good. We'll make him feel gay. That's poor Gabriel's trouble. He's never gay enough.'

There was a tap at the door and Henry looked in.

'I thought you might like a good laugh,' said Henry. 'The bum has come up the back stairs and caught poor old Daddy. He's sitting in the kitchen with Baskett and the maids.'

'Oh, *no*!' said his mother.

'His name is Mr Grumble,' said Henry.

III

During lunch Lady Charles developed her theory of the way in which Lord Wutherwood – and Rune – was to be received and entertained. The family, with the exception of Henry, entered warmly into the discussion. Henry seemed to be more than usually vague and rather dispirited. Roberta, to her discomfiture, repeatedly caught his eye. Henry stared at her with an expression which she was unable to interpret until it occurred to her that he looked not at but through her. Roberta became less self-conscious and listened more attentively to the rest of the family. With every turn of their preposterous conversation her four years of separation from them seemed to diminish and Roberta felt herself slip, as of old, into an attitude of mind that half-accepted the mad logic of their scheming. They discussed the suitability of a charade, Lady Charles and her children with passionate enthusiasm. Lord Charles with an air of critical detachment. Roberta wondered what Lord Charles really felt about the crisis and whether she merely imagined that he wore a faintly troubled air. His face was at no time an expressive one. It was a pale oval face. Short-sighted eyes that looked dimly friendly, a colourless moustache and an oddly youthful mouth added nothing to its distinction, and yet it had distinction of a gentle kind. His voice was pitched rather high and he had a trick of letting his sentences die away while he opened his eyes widely and stroked the top of his head. Roberts realized that though she liked him very much she had not the smallest inkling as to what sort of thoughts went on in his mind. He was an exceedingly remote individual.

'Well, anyway,' Frid was saying, 'we can but try. Let's fill him up with sherry and do a charade. How about Lady Godiva? Henry the palfrey, Daddy the horrid husband, one of the twins Peeping Tom, and the rest of you the nice-minded populace.'

'If you think I'm going to curvet round the drawing-room with you sitting on my back in the rude nude – ' Henry began.

'Your hair's not long enough, Frid,' said Patch.

'I didn't say *I'd* be Lady Godiva.'

'Well, you can hardly expect Mummy to undress,' said Colin, 'and anyway you meant yourself.'

'Don't be an ass, darling,' said Lady Charles, 'of course we can't do Lady Godiva. Uncle G. would be horrified.'

'He might mistake it for a Witches' Sabbath,' said Henry, 'and think we were making fun of Aunt V.'

'If Frid rode on you, I expect he would,' said Patch.

'Why?' asked Mike. 'What do witches ride on, Daddy?'

Lord Charles gave his high-pitched laugh. Henry stared thoughtfully at Patch.

'If that wasn't rude,' he said, 'it would be almost funny.'

'Well, why not do a Witches' Sabbath?' asked Stephen. 'Uncle G. hates Aunt V. being a witch. I dare say it would be a great success. It would show we were on his side. We needn't make it too obvious, you know. It could be a word charade. Ipswich for instance.'

'How would you do Ips?' asked Colin.

'Patch could waggle hers,' said Henry.

'You are *beastly*, Henry,' stormed Patch. 'It's foul of you to say I'm fat. Mummy!'

'Never mind, darling, it's only puppy-fat. I think you're just right.'

'We could do Dulwich,' said Stephen. 'The first syllable could be a weekend at Deepacres. Everybody yawning.'

'That would be *really* rude,' said his mother seriously.

'It wouldn't be far wrong,' said Lord Charles.

'I know, Charlie, but it would never do. Don't let's get all wild and silly about it. Let's just think sensibly of a good funny charade. Not too vulgar and not insulting.'

There followed a long silence broken by Frid.

'I know,' Frid cried, 'we'll just be ourselves with bums in the house. It could be a breakfast scene with Baskett coming in to say: "A person to see you, m'lord." You wouldn't mind, would you, Baskett?'

With that smile demanded by the infinite courtesy of service, Baskett offered Frid cheese. Roberta wondered suddenly if Baskett thought the Lampreys as funny as she did. Frid hurried on with her plan.

'It really would be a good idea, Mummy. You see, Baskett could bring in the bum, and we could all plead with him and Daddy could say all the things he really wants Uncle G. to hear. Robin could do the bum, she'd look Heaven in a bowler and a muffler. It would seem sort of gay and gallant at the same time.'

'What would be the word?' asked Patch.

'Bumptious?'

'The second syllable's impossible,' Colin objected.

'Bumboat?'

'Too obvious.'

'Well, bumpkin. The second syllable could be about relations. We could actually have Uncle G. in it. Robin could be Uncle G. His coat and hat and umbrella will be in the hall ready to hand. We'd all plead with her and say:

"Your own kith and *kin*, Gabriel, dear fellow, your own kith and *kin*." '

'Yes, that's all very well,' said Stephen, 'but you've forgotten *the* "p".'

'It could be silent as in – '

'That will do, Frid,' said Lord Charles.

CHAPTER 4

Uncle G.

On the morning after her arrival Roberta woke to see a ray of thin London sunshine slanting across the counterpane. A maid in a print dress had drawn the curtains and put a tray on the bedside table. Dream and reality mixed themselves in Roberta's thoughts. As she grew wide-awake she began to count over the wonderful events of the night that was past. In the hour before dawn she had been driven through London. She had seen jets from hose-pipes splayed fan-wise over deserted streets, she had heard the jingle of milk carts and seen the strange silhouette made by roofs and chimney pots against a thinning sky. She had heard Big Ben tell four of a spring morning and the clocks of Chelsea answer him. Before that she had danced in a room so full of shadows, abrupt lights, relentless music, and people, that the memory was as confused as a dream. She had danced with Colin and Stephen and Henry. Colin had played the fool, pretended he was a Russian, and spoken broken English. Stephen with his quick stutter had talked incessantly and complimented Roberta on her dancing. She had danced most often with Henry who was more silent than the twins. He said so little that Roberta, in a sudden panic had wondered if he merely danced with her out of a sense of hospitality and regretted the absence of the person called Mary. In those strange surroundings Henry had become remote, a sophisticated grandee with a white waistcoat, and a gardenia in his coat. Yet, when she danced with him, behind all her bewilderment Roberta had been aware of a deep satisfaction. Now, lying still in her bed, she called back the events of the night and so potently that though her eyes were still open she had no thought for the sunlight on her counterpane but anxiously examined the picture of herself and Henry. There they were, moving together among a shadowy company of dancers. He did not wait to see if Stephen or Colin would ask her to dance, but himself asked her quickly and danced on until long after the others had gone back to their table. There was a sort of protective decisiveness in his manner that pleased and embarrassed Roberta. Perhaps, after all, he was only worried about the financial crisis. 'Heaven knows,' thought Roberta, 'it's enough to worry anybody but a Lamprey into a thousand fits.' She realized that the crisis lay like a nasty taste behind the savour of her own enjoyment. It was not discussed during that dazzling evening until they got home. Creeping into the flat in the half-light, they found Nanny's Thermos of Ovaltine and sat drinking it round the heater in Roberta's room. Henry laughed unexpectedly and said: 'Well, chaps, we may not be here much longer.'

Frid, very elegant and pale, struck a tragic attitude and said: 'The last night in the old home. Pause for sobs.' There was a brief silence broken by Stephen.

'Uncle Gabriel,' Stephen said, 'has s-simply g-got to stump up.'

'What if he won't?' Colin had asked.

'We'll bribe Aunt V. to bewitch him,' said Frid. She pulled her cloak over her head, crouched down, and crooked her fingers and croaked:

> 'Weary sen'nights, nine times nine,
> Shall he dwindle peak and pine.'

The twins instantly turned themselves into witches and circled with Frid round the heater.

> 'Double, double, toil and trouble,
> Fire burn and cauldron bubble.'

'Shut up,' said Henry. 'I thought you said it was unlucky to quote *Macbeth?*'

'If we gave Aunt V. the ingredients for a charm,' said Colin, 'I expect she'd be only too pleased to make Uncle G. dwindle peak and pine.'

'They're awkward things to beat up in a hurry,' said Frid.

Stephen said: 'I wonder what Aunt V.'s friends d-do about it. It must be rather dull to be witches if you can't cast murrains on cattle or give your husband warts.'

'I wish,' Roberta cried, 'that you'd tell me the truth about your Aunt V. and not go rambling on about her being a witch.'

'Poor Robin,' Henry said. 'It does sound very silly, but as an actual fact, and if her mind is to be believed, Aunt V. has taken up some sort of black magic I imagine it boils down to reading histories of witchcraft and turning tables. In my opinion Aunt V. is simply dotty.'

'Well,' Frid said, 'let's go to bed, anyway.' She kissed the air near Roberta's cheek and drifted to the door. 'Come on, twins,' she added.

The twins kissed Roberta and wandered after Frid.

Henry stood in the doorway.

'Sleep well,' he said.

'Thank you, Henry,' said Roberta. 'It was a lovely party.'

'For once,' said Henry, 'I thought so too. Goodnight, Robin.'

Roberta, as she watched the sun on her counterpane, reviewed this final scene several times, and felt happy.

II

The visit of Lord Wutherwood was prejudiced from the start by the arrival of Lady Katherine Lobe. Lady Katherine was a maiden aunt of Lord Charles. She was extremely poor and lived in a small house at Hammersmith. There she was surrounded by photographs of the Lamprey children to whom she was passionately devoted. Being poor herself, she spent the greater part of her life in working for the still-poorer members of her parish. She wore nondescript garments; hats that seemed to have no connection with her head, and grey fabric gloves. She was extremely deaf and spoke in a toneless whispering manner, with kind smiles, and with many anxious looks into the faces of the people she addressed. But for all her diffidence there was a core of determination in Lady Katherine. In her likes and dislikes she was immovable. Nothing would reconcile her to a person of whom she disapproved, and unfortunately she disapproved most strongly of her nephew Wutherwood, who, for his part, refused to meet her. At Christmas she invariably wrote him a letter on the subject of goodwill towards men, pointing out his shortcomings under this heading and enclosing a blank promise to pay yearly a large sum to one of her charities. Lord Wutherwood's only reply to these communications was an irritable tearing across of the enclosures. For his younger brother Lady Katherine had the warmest affection. Occasionally she would travel in a bus up to the West End in order to visit the Lampreys and beg, with a gentle persistence, for their old clothes or force them to buy tickets for charitable entertainments. They were always warned by letter of these visits, but on this occasion Lady Charles, agitated by the crisis, had forgotten to open the note, and the only warning she had was Baskett's announcement, at six o'clock in the evening, of Lady Katherine's arrival.

The Lampreys and Roberta had assembled in the drawing-room to await the arrival of Lord Wutherwood. They were unnaturally silent. Even Mike had caught the feeling of tension. He stood by the wireless and turned the control knob as rapidly as possible until told to stop, when he flung himself moodily full length on the hearthrug and kicked his feet together.

'There's the lift,' cried Lady Charles suddenly. 'Mike, stay where you are and jump up. Remember to shake hands with Uncle Gabriel. Sprinkle some "sirs" through your conversation, for Heaven's sake, and when I nod to you, you are to give him the pot.'

'Mike'll break it,' said Patch.

'I won't,' shouted Mike indignantly.

'And remember,' continued his mother, 'if I suggest a charade you're all to go out and come back quietly and do one. Then, when you've finished, go out again so that Daddy can talk to Uncle Gabriel. And remember – '

'Can't we listen?' asked Patch.

'We'll probably hear Uncle G. all over the flat,' said Henry.

'And remember not to mention witchcraft. Uncle G. hates it.'

'Ssh!'

'Can't we be talking?' Frid suggested. 'You'd think there was a corpse in the flat.'

'If you can think of anything to say, say it,' said her father gloomily.

Frid began to speak in a high voice. 'Aren't those flowers over there *too* marvellous?' she asked. Nobody answered her. In the distance a bell rang. Baskett was heard to walk across the hall.

'Lovely, darling,' said Lady Charles violently. She appealed mutely to the children who stared in apprehension at the door and grimaced at each other. Lady Charles turned to Roberta.

'Robin, darling, do tell us about your voyage home. Did you have fun?'

'Yes,' said Roberta, whose heart was now thumping against her ribs. 'Yes. We had a fancy-dress ball.'

Lady Charles and Frid laughed musically. The door opened and Baskett came in.

'Lady Katherine Lobe, m'lady,' said Baskett.

'Good God!' said Lord Charles.

Lady Katherine came in. She walked with short steps and peered amiably through the cigarette smoke.

'Imogen, darling,' she whispered.

'Aunt Kit!'

The Lampreys kept their heads admirably. They told Lady Katherine how delighted they were to see her and seated her by the fire. They introduced Roberta to her, and teased her gently about her lame ducks, and with panic-stricken glances at each other, asked her to remove her raincoat.

'So nice to see you all,' whispered Lady Katherine. 'Such luck for me to find the whole family. And there's Michael home for the holidays and grown enormously. Patricia too. And the twins. Don't speak twins, and let me see if I can guess. This is Stephen, isn't it?'

'Yes, Aunt Kit,' said Colin.

'There! I knew I was right. You got my note, Imogen, darling?'

'Yes, Aunt Kit. We're so pleased,' said Charlot.

'Yes. I wondered if you had got it because you all looked quite surprised when I walked in. So I wondered.'

'We thought you were Uncle Gabriel,' shouted Mike.

'What dear?'

'Uncle Gabriel.'

Lady Katherine passed a grey fabric finger across her lips. 'Is Gabriel coming, Charles?'

'Yes, Aunt Kit,' said Lord Charles. And as she merely gazed dimly at him he added loudly: 'He's coming to see me on business.'

'We're going to have some charades,' bawled Mike.

'I'm very glad,' said Lady Katherine emphatically. 'I wish to see Gabriel. I have written to him several times but no response did I get. It's about our Fresh Air Fund. A day in the country for a hundred children and a fortnight in private homes for Twenty Sickly Mites. I want Gabriel to take six.'

'Six Sickly Mites?' asked Henry.

'What, dear?'

'Do you want Uncle Gabriel to take six sickly mites at Deepacres?'

'It's the least he can do. I'm afraid Gabriel is inclined to be too self-centred, Charles. He's a very wealthy man and he should think of other people more than he does. Your mama always said so. And I hear the most disquieting news of Violet. It appears that she has taken up spiritualism and sits in the dark with a set of very second-rate sort of people.'

'Not spiritualism, darling,' said Charlot. 'Black magic.'

'What, dear?'

'Magic.'

'Oh. Oh, I see. That's entirely different. I suppose she does it to entertain their house-parties. But that doesn't alter the fact that both Violet and Gabriel are getting rather self-centred. It would be an excellent thing for both of them if they adopted two children.'

'For mercy's sake, Aunt Kit,' cried Charlot, 'don't suggest that to Gabriel.'

'Don't suggest anything,' said Lord Charles. 'I implore you, Aunt Kit, not to tackle Gabriel this afternoon. You see – ' he peered anxiously at his watch and broke off. 'Good God, Immy,' he whispered to his wife, 'we must do something. She'll infuriate him. Take her to your room.'

'Under what pretext?' muttered Charlot.

'Think of something.'

'Aunt Kit, would you like to see my bedroom?'

'What, dear?'

'It's no good, Mummy,' said Frid. 'Better tell her we're bust.'

'I think so,' said Lord Charles. He bent his legs and brought his face close to his aunt's.

'Aunt Kit,' he shouted. 'I'm in difficulties.'

'Are you, dear?'

'I've no money.'

'What?'

'There's a bum in the house,' yelled Patch.

'Be quiet, Patch,' said Henry. His father continued. 'I've asked Gabriel to lend me two thousand. If he doesn't I shall go bankrupt.'

'Charlie!'

'It's true.'

'I'll speak to Gabriel,' said Lady Katherine quite loudly.

'No, no!' cried the Lampreys.

'Lord and Lady Wutherwood, m'lady,' said Baskett in the doorway.

III

Roberta knew that the Lampreys had not reckoned on Lady Wutherwood's arrival with her husband, and she had time to admire their almost instant recovery from this second and formidable shock. Charlot met her brother and sister-in-law halfway across the room. Her manner held a miraculous balance between the over-cordial and the too-casual. Her children and her husband supported her admirably. Lady Katherine for the moment, was too rattled by the Lampreys' news of impending disaster to make any disturbance. She sat quietly in her chair.

Roberta found herself shaking hands with an extremely old couple. The Marquis of Wutherwood and Rune was sixty years of age but these years sat heavily upon him and he looked like an old man. His narrow head, sunken between high shoulders, poked forward with an air that was at once mean and aggressive. His face was colourless. The bridge of his nose was so narrow that his eyes appeared to be impossibly close set. His mouth drooped querulously and the length of his chin, though prodigious, was singularly unexpressive of anything but obstinacy. His upper teeth projected over his under lip and hinted at a high and narrow palate. These teeth gave him an unpleasingly feminine appearance increased by his chilly old-maidish manner, which suggested that he lived in a state of perpetual offence. Roberta found herself wondering if he could possibly be as disagreeable as he looked.

His wife was about fifty years of age. She was dark, extremely sallow, and fat. There was a musty falseness about the dank hair which she wore over her ears in sibylline coils. She painted her face, but with such inattention to detail that Roberta was reminded of a cheap print in which the colours had slipped to one side, showing the original structure of the drawing underneath. She had curious eyes, very pale, with tiny pupils, and muddy whites. They were so abnormally sunken that they seemed to reflect no light and this gave them a veiled appearance which Roberta found disconcerting, and oddly repellent. Her face had once been round but like her make-up it had slipped and now hung in folds and pockets about her lips which were dragged down at the corners. Roberta saw that Lady Wutherwood had a trick of parting and closing her lips. It was a very slight movement but she did it continually with a faint click of sound. And in the corners of her lips there was a kind of whiteness that moved when they moved. 'Henry is right,' thought Roberta, 'she is disgusting.'

Lord Wutherwood greeted the Lampreys without much show of cordiality. When he saw Lady Katherine Lobe his attitude stiffened still further. He turned to his brother and in a muffled voice said: 'We're in a hurry, Charles.'

'Oh,' said Lord Charles. 'Are you? Oh – well – '

'Are you?' Charlot repeated. 'Not too much of a hurry, I hope, Gabriel. We never see anything of you.'

'You never come to Deepacres when we ask you, Imogen.'

'I *know*. We'd adore to come, especially the children, but you know it's so frightfully *expensive* to travel, even in England. You see we can't all get into one car – '

'The fare, third class return, is within the reach of most people.'

'*Miles* beyond us, I'm afraid,' said Charlot with a charming air of ruefulness. 'We're cutting down *everything*. We never *budge* from where we are.'

Lord Wutherwood turned to Henry.

'Enjoy your trip to the Côte d'Azur?' he asked. 'Saw your photograph in one of these papers. In my day we didn't strip ourselves naked and wallow in front of press photographers but I suppose you like that sort of thing.'

'Enormously, sir,' said Henry coldly.

There was a slight pause. Roberta felt uncomfortably that Charlot's plan should be amended and that they should leave the field to Lord Charles. She wondered if she herself should slip out of the room. Her thoughts must have appeared in her face for Henry caught her eye, smiled, and shook his head. The Wutherwoods were now seated side by side on the sofa. Baskett came in with the sherry.

'Ah, sherry,' said Lord Charles. Henry began to pour it out. Charlot made desperate efforts with her brother-in-law. Lady Katherine leant forward in her chair and addressed Lady Wutherwood.

'Well, Violet,' she said, 'I hear you have taken up conjuring.'

'You couldn't be more mistaken,' said Lady Wutherwood in a deep voice. She spoke with a very slight accent, slurring her words together. After each phrase she rearranged her mouth with those clicking movements and stealthily touched away the white discs at the corners. But in a little while they re-formed.

'Aunty Kit,' cried Frid, 'will you have some sherry? Aunt Violet?'

'No thank you, my dear,' said Lady Katherine. 'Yes,' said Lady Wutherwood.

'You'd better not, V.,' said Lord Wutherwood. 'You know what'll happen.'

Mike walked to the end of the sofa and stared fixedly at his aunt. Lord Charles turned to his brother with an air of cordiality. 'It's a sherry that I think you rather like, Gabriel, don't you?' he said, 'Corregio del Martez, '79.'

'If you can afford a sherry like that – ' began Lord Wutherwood. Henry hurriedly placed a glass at his elbow.

'Aunt Violet,' asked Mike suddenly, 'can you do the rope trick? I bet you can't. I bet you can't do that and I bet you can't saw a lady in half.'

'Don't be an idiot, Mike,' said Patch.

'Mikey,' said his mother, 'run and find Baskett, darling, and ask him to take care of Uncle Gabriel's chauffeur. I suppose he's there, isn't he, Gabriel?'

'He'll do very well in the car. Your aunt's maid is there, too. Your aunt insists on cartin' her about with us. I strongly object of course, but that makes no difference. She's a nasty type.'

Lady Wutherwood laughed rather madly. Her husband turned on her. 'You know what I mean, V.,' he said. 'Tinkerton's a bad lot. Put it bluntly, she's damn well debauched my chauffeur. It's been goin' on under your nose for years.'

Charlot evidently decided that it would be better not to have heard this embarrassing parenthesis. 'Of course they must come up,' she said cheerfully. 'Nanny will adore to see Tinkerton. Mikey, ask Baskett to bring Tinkerton and Giggle up to the servants' sitting-room and give them a drink of tea or something. Ask politely, won't you?'

'Okay,' said Mike. He hopped on one foot and turned to look at Lady Wutherwood.

'Isn't it pretty funny?' he asked. 'Your chauffeur's called Giggle and there's a man in the kitchen called Grumble. He's a – '

'Michael!' said Lord Charles, 'do as you're told at once.'

Mike went out, followed unostentatiously by Stephen who shut the door behind him. Stephen returned in a few moments.

'I wish you'd tell me, Violet,' said Lady Katherine, 'what it is you have taken up. One hears such extraordinary reports.'

'She's dabblin' in some damn-fool kind of occultism,' said Lord Wutherwood, turning pale with annoyance.

Roberta noticed that when he stopped speaking his upper teeth closed firmly on his under lip causing his whole mouth to settle down at the corners in an expression of maddening complacency.

'Gabriel,' said his wife, 'believes in what he sees. Nothing else. He thinks himself fortunate in that. He is not so fortunate as he supposes.'

'What the devil d'you mean?' demanded Lord Wutherwood. 'Don't look at me like that, V., I don't like it. These friends of yours are makin' a damned unpleasant woman of you. Of all the miserable footlin' crew! What d'you think you're doin' huntin' up a parcel of spooks? A lot of trickery. I've told you before, I've a damn good mind to speak to the police about the whole affair. If it wasn't for draggin' my name into it – '

'You had better be careful, Gabriel. It is not wise to sneer at the unseen.'

'The unseen what?' asked Lady Katherine who had caught this last phrase.

'The unseen forces.'

Lord Wutherwood made exasperated sounds and turned his back.

'What sort of forces?' persisted Lady Katherine against the combined mental opposition of the Lampreys.

'Do you seek,' asked Lady Wutherwood with a formidable air of contempt, 'to learn in a few words the wisdom of all the ages? A lifetime is too short to reach full understanding.'

'Of what?'

'Esoteric Lore.'

'What's that?'

Charlot suddenly made a bold dash into this strange conversation, and Roberta with something like terror saw that she had decided on the line she would take with her sister-in-law. Evidently it was to be a line of gentle banter. Charlot leant towards Lady Wutherwood and said gaily: 'I'm as bewildered as Aunty Kit, Violet. Is esoteric lore the same as – what? Witchcraft? Don't turn into a witch, darling.'

Lady Wutherwood stared at Charlot. 'It's a great mistake,' she said in her deep voice, 'to laugh at necromancy, Imogen. There are more things in Heaven and earth – '

'I suppose there are, Violet, but I don't want to meet them.'

'The Church,' said Lady Katherine in her loudest whisper, 'takes a firm stand in such matters. I imagine you know, Violet, that you are in danger of – '

The Lampreys all began to talk at once. They talked persistently, not raising their voices but overpowering their guests with a sort of gentle barrage. They seemed by tacit agreement to have split into two groups, Frid, Patch and their mother tackling Lord Wutherwood, while Henry and the twins concentrated on his wife. Lord Charles, nervously polishing his eyeglass, stood aside like a sort of inadequate referee. The scene now developed in accordance with the best traditions of polite drawing-room comedy. Roberta was irresistibly reminded of the play she had seen the previous night and, once possessed of this idea, it seemed to her that the Lampreys and their relations had begun to pitch their voices like actors and actresses and to use gestures that were a little larger than life. The scene was building towards some neat and effective climax. There was perhaps a superfluity of character parts and with Lady Katherine Lobe smiling and nodding in her corner the eccentric dowager was not lacking. Partly to dispel this idea and in the hope that she might be of some service to the cause, Roberta moved to Lady Katherine who, true to family form, instantly began to confide in her, saying that she had heard most disquieting news of Violet and asking

Roberta if she thought the Lampreys would rather she went away as poor Charlie must be given a free hand with Gabriel. All this was fortunately uttered in such a muffled aside that Roberta could hear no more than half of it. Lady Katherine was too insistent, however, for Roberta to divide her own attention and she had no idea of what went forward between the Lampreys and the Wutherwoods until she heard Frid say: 'No, Uncle Gabriel, I shall be bitterly humiliated if you don't ask us to do one for you.' Roberta saw that Lord Wutherwood looked slightly less disagreeable. Frid was presenting herself as a lovely and attentive niece.

'I'm so glad you agree with me,' whispered Lady Katherine. 'There is no doubt at all, in my mind, of our duty to these poor things.' Roberta did not know if she spoke of the Lampreys, of ailing children, or of Jewish refugees, in all of whom she seemed to be passionately interested. Frid had refilled her uncle's glass. Lady Wutherwood was droning interminably to Henry and the twins who appeared to be enraptured with the recital. Charlot suddenly broke up this comparatively peaceful picture by making the much discussed announcement.

'Children,' she said gaily, 'Frid's been telling Uncle Gabriel about your charades. Do you think you could do a very quick rhyming charade now, for Aunt Violet and Aunt Kit and Uncle Gabriel. Don't take ages deciding what to do, just do the first thing that comes into your heads. We'll give you a word. Out you go.'

'Come on, Robin,' said Henry.

Robin, full of misgivings, followed the Lampreys into the hall.

CHAPTER 5

Mike Puts the Pot On

'This is a mistake,' said Henry gloomily as soon as he had shut the door. 'Obviously Uncle G.'s in a foul temper and we won't improve it by cutting capers in front of him. I must say he's a loathsome old man.'

'Well, let's compromise,' said Frid. 'We won't do one about bums. Let's do one about witchcraft. Uncle G. will like that because he'll think it's making nonsense of Aunt V. and Aunt V. will be interested if we do it well enough.'

'She's quite m-mad, you know, poor thing,' said Stephen. 'D-don't you consider she's mad, Colin?'

'Stark ravers,' said Colin. 'Where's Mike?'

'Talking to Giggle about toy trains, I think. He's better out of this.'

'Let's get going,' said Patch. 'Mummy said we were to hurry.'

The door opened and Charlot looked out. 'It's to rhyme with "pale",' she said loudly and then lowering her voice she hissed: 'It's "nail". Don't do either of the other things. Too risky.' The door shut and Charlot called from the other side: 'Hurry up!'

Frid made a helpless gesture. 'Well, there you are,' she said. 'No bums and no witches and the word is "nail". Evidently Mummy wants us to get it right at the first stab. What shall we do?'

'Bite our nails?' suggested Patch.

'Put a nail in Uncle G.'s coffin,' said Henry viciously.

'Nailing our colours to the mast?'

'I know,' said Frid. 'We'll do Jael and Sisera.'

'What did they d-do?' asked Stephen.

'Something with a nail. What was it, Robin?'

'Didn't Jael hammer a nail through Sisera's head?'

'That's right,' said Colin. 'Well, we can be clever and do wail and hail and Jael all at once. A compound charade.'

The Lampreys threw open the door of their enormous hall cupboard and began to dress themselves up.

'I'll be Jael,' said Frid, 'and Henry can be Sisera and the twins guards and Robin a faithful slave.'

'What am I?' demanded Patch, putting on Lord Wutherwood's bowler.

'Another faithful slave. Wait a moment.'

Frid ran down the passage towards the kitchen. Roberta could hear her shouting: 'A skewer, Baskett, a skewer! We're doing a charade. Quick!'

'Did Jael make love to Sisera,' asked Colin, 'before he slew her?'

'Jael's the female,' said Stephen.

'Oh. Give me that ghastly scarf, will you. Is it Uncle G.'s?'

'Yes. I want it for a loin cloth.'

'I'm going to be a Circassian slave,' said Patch.

'This is most frightfully bogus,' said Henry, taking two yachting caps out of the wardrobe. 'I can't tell you how much I object to cavorting in front of these repellent people. You could use yachting caps as breastplates, Robin. There's some string.'

'Thank you. Aren't you going to dress up, Henry?'

Henry hung a pair of field glasses round his neck. 'I shall play it modern,' he muttered. 'Colonel Sisera Blimp.' He drew a pair of fur-lined motoring gloves over his hands.

Frid came back with a long silver-plated skewer.

'Be careful how you muck about round my head with that thing,' said Henry.

'I want a hammer.'

'Use your boot. Let's get it over.'

'In you go, Robin and Patch. Take that rug and hold it like a tent. You, too, twins. Say how beautiful I am,' ordered Frid, 'and wonder if the day has been Sisera's.'

Robin, Patch and the twins entered the drawing-room unnoticed. Their audience was sitting with its back to the door.

'We've begun,' said Patch loudly. 'I wonder how the battle went. Dost thou know if the day is Sisera's?'

'Nay,' said Stephen. 'Dost thou?'

'Nay,' said Colin.

'And thou?' continued Patch, irritably, to Robin.

'Nay, I wot not,' said Robin and she added hurriedly: 'how beautiful Jael is!'

'She is like the new-blown moon,' agreed Patch.

'Lo,' said Colin, 'here she comes.'

'How beautiful she is!' said Stephen.

Frid made an entrance. She had removed her stockings and shoes and had hitched her dress up with scarves. She carried the skewer in her sash and a shoe in her hand. She shut the door and leant against it in a dramatic manner.

'That's my scarf,' said Lord Wutherwood. He turned his back on the charade and began talking in a low querulous voice to his brother.

'I am a-weary with watching,' said Frid. 'Praise to Allah the day is ours. Ho, slaves!'

Patch and Robin threw themselves on their faces. The twins saluted.

'Lie down, O Jael,' said Colin abruptly.

Frid crawled into the tent. 'I am a-weary unto death,' she repeated.

'Here comes S-S-sis-sis – ' began Stephen.

'Hist!' shouted Patch, coming to his rescue. 'I hear footsteps. Stand to!'

'Stand!' said the twins.

The door opened and Henry came in. He wore a solar topee and his gauntlet driving gloves. He had turned up his trousers to resemble shorts. He focused his field glasses on the audience and said: 'An arid desert, by Gad!'

' 'Tis Sisera,' said Frid. 'Lure him hither, slaves.'

Roberta and Patch made winning gestures. Henry watched them through his field glasses. When they drew nearer he seized Roberta by the arm. 'A damn' fine girl, by Gad,' he said.

'Come hither, O Sisera,' invited Roberta uneasily. 'Come to yonder tent.'

Henry was led to the tent. Frid writhed on the carpet and extended her arms. 'Do I behold the valient Sisera?' she asked. 'All hail, O Captain.'

Henry was dragged down to the floor. A rather confused scene took place in the course of which Frid gave him a few lines from Titania's speech to Bottom and he began to snore.

'Vengeance is mine,' observed Frid. 'Quick, the nail.' She drew the skewer from her sash and hammered it into the carpet behind Henry's head. Henry yelled, gurgled, and lay still.

'Wail,' muttered Frid. The twins, Patch and Roberta wailed loudly.

'That's all,' said Frid. 'Were we right? It was a compound charade.'

Charlot and Lady Katherine clapped their hands. Lord Wutherwood glanced at them with annoyance and resumed his conversation. Lady Wutherwood stared out of the window with lack-lustre eyes.

'And now tidy up the mess,' Charlot ordered, 'I want to show Aunt Violet and Aunt Kit how we fitted into 26. Where's Mike?'

'We'll find him, Mummy,' said Frid. 'Come on, chaps. That's that.'

II

When they returned to the hall Roberta saw that the Lampreys were in a family rage. Henry and Frid were white and the twins and Patch scarlet with fury. Roberta wondered if these reactions were the natural consequences of their own complexions, if fair people were always more choleric than dark ones. Henry, she saw, was the angriest. He walked off down the passage calling 'Michael!' in a voice that brought Mike running. 'Your mama is asking for you,' said Henry.

'I've lost the pot,' said Mike. Henry turned on his heel and came back into the hall. He picked up rugs and hats and slung them indiscriminately into the cupboard.

'That was a howling success, wasn't it?' said Frid. 'Did either of them so much as glance at us, do you happen to know?'

'They've got the manners of hogs,' said Patch violently. 'Uncle Gabriel,' muttered Stephen slowly, 'is without doubt an old – '

'Shut up,' said Colin.

'Well, isn't he?'

'I hope Mummy's pleased,' said Henry. 'She's seen us make as big fools of ourselves as can reasonably be expected in one afternoon.'

'It's not Mummy's fault,' murmured Colin uncomfortably.

Mike came in looking scared. 'I can't find the pot I've got to give Uncle Gabriel,' he said. His brothers and sisters paid no attention, Roberta hunted helplessly round the littered hall. Mike, looking anxious, wandered into the drawing-room.

'Shut that d-door,' said Stephen.

Patch hurled Lord Wutherwood's bowler to the far end of the hall.

'Don't be a fool, Patch,' said Henry. Colin picked the bowler up and pretended to be sick into it. The others watched him moodily.

'This has been great fun for Robin,' said Henry. 'We're sorry our relations are so bloody rude, Robin.'

'What *does* it matter,' said Roberta.

Henry stared at her. 'You're quite right,' he said, 'it doesn't matter. But if any of you think that noisome old treasure-trove in there is going to hand us two thousand pounds, you're due for a disappointment. Daddy could go bankrupt six times over before his charming brother would help him.'

'You th-think we're for it then?' asked Stephen.

'I do.'

'We'll wiggle out,' said Frid. 'We always have.'

'Wolf, wolf,' said Henry.

'Why? I don't see it.'

'Let's get out of this,' suggested Patch. 'Mummy's going to take the aunts into 26, isn't she?'

'Let's go into the dining-room,' said Frid.

Colin reminded them of Mike and the Chinese vase and wondered vaguely if they ought to look for it. Stephen said Lord Wutherwood could be depended upon to take the vase and go away without offering them any assistance. Frid and Henry said they thought the gesture with the vase should be attempted.

'Was it wrapped up?' asked Roberta suddenly.

'Yes. Mummy bought a smart box for it,' said Patch.

'Then I know where it is. It's in her bedroom.'

'There let it lie, say I,' said Stephen

'But if Charlot wants it?'

'Robin,' said Frid, 'be a darling and go into the drawing-room. Hiss to Mummy where the pot is and then if she wants it she can send Mike.'

'All right,' agreed Roberta, and returned nervously to the drawing-room. She managed to give Charlot the message.

'Where's Mike?' murmured Charlot.

'Didn't he come in here?'

'Yes, but he's wandered away.'

'Shall I find him?'

'No, never mind.'

As Roberta made for the door she heard Charlot say brightly: 'Come along, Violet, come along, Aunt Kit, we'll leave the boys to talk business.' Roberta hurried through into the dining-room where she found the Lampreys lying close together on the floor with their heads to the wall.

'Lock the door,' they whispered.

Roberta locked the door. Henry moved slightly and invited her with a gesture to lie between Frid and himself.

'What's this in aid of?' asked Roberta.

'Ssh! Listen! Get closer.'

Roberta now saw that this part of the wall consisted of a boarded-up door which evidently had at one time opened into the drawing-room. The Lampreys were listening at the crack. The voices of Lord Charles and his brother could be clearly heard above the comfortable sounds made by the drawing-room fire.

'I'd better not,' breathed Roberta diffidently.

'It's all right,' said Frid in her ear. 'Daddy wouldn't mind. Ssh!'

' – so you see,' said Lord Charles's voice, 'it's been a series of misfortunes rather than any one disaster. The jewellery and *objets-d'art* idea seemed a capital one. I really couldn't foresee that poor Stein would shoot himself, you know. Now could I?'

'You go and tie yourself up with some miserable adventurer – '

'No, no, he wasn't that, Gabriel, really.'

'Why the devil didn't you make some inquiries?'

'Well, I – I did make a good many. The truth is – '

'The truth is,' said Lord Wutherwood's voice edgily, 'you drifted into this business as you have drifted into every conceivable sort of blunder for the last twenty years.'

There was silence for a moment, and then Lord Charles's voice: 'Very well, Gabriel. I'll take that. It's quite useless in my predicament to offer excuses. I readily confess that the sort of explanation I have to make would seem ridiculous to you.'

'And to anyone else. I may as well tell you at the outset that I can't do anything about it. I've helped you twice before and I might as well have thrown the money into the sea.'

'We were extremely grateful – '

'Is it too much to suggest that you might have shown it by pullin' yourselves together? I told you then that you should recognize the fact that you were a man with a small income and a large family and should cut your coat accordingly. It's preposterous, the way you live. Butlers, maids, cars, bringin' gels out, doin' the season, trips here, gamblin' there. Good God, you ought to be livin' like a – like a clerk or something! Why haven't you got some post for yourself where you earned a wage? What are those three boys doin'?'

'They've tried extremely hard to get jobs.'

'Nonsense. They could have gone into shops since they're not qualified for any professions. I said when they were at school that they ought to face the facts and work for professions!'

'We couldn't afford the University.'

'You could afford half a dozen white elephants. You could afford to traipse about the world in luxury liners, you could afford to take that place in the Highlands, entertain, and God knows what.'

'My dear Gabriel! The amount of entertaining we do!'

'You dribble money away. Why don't those gels run the house? Plenty of gels one knows are doin' that sort of thing. Domestic.'

'Frid's going on the stage.'

'Yah!' said Lord Wutherwood. 'Was that display she treated us to just now a sample? Showin' her legs and droopin' about in other people's scarves like a dyin' duck in a thunderstorm!'

Roberta felt Frid go rigid with hatred. Stephen and Colin thrust their fists into their mouths. Patch snorted and was savagely nudged by Henry.

' – I may tell you, Charles, that I'm plaguily hard pressed myself. Deepacres nearly kills me keepin' it up. I'm taxed up to the gullet. Looks as if I'll have to put down the London house. You don't know the calls there are on me in – well, in my position. When I remember what it'll end in I sometimes wonder why the devil I take the trouble.'

'What do you mean, Gabriel?'

'I've no boy of my own.'

'No.'

'And to be frank with you I don't imagine Deepacres is likely to survive the treatment of my heirs.'

'You mean Henry.'

'Oh, you'll outlive me, no doubt,' said Lord Wutherwood.

'Then you mean me?'

'Put it baldly, I mean the pair of you.'

There was a long pause. Roberta heard the fire in the next room settle down in the grate. She heard the breathing of the young Lampreys and the flurried ticking of a carriage-clock on the dining-room mantelpiece. When Lord Charles at last broke the silence, Roberta felt her companions stir a little as though something for which they had waited was about to appear. Lord Charles's voice had changed. It was at once gentler and more decisive.

'I think,' he said, 'that I can promise you neither Henry nor I will do much harm to Deepacres. We might possibly care to let other people share its amenities occasionally. That's all.'

'What do you mean?'

'I was thinking of your regard for Deepacres and wondering if after all it amounts to very much. As you say, one day it will be Henry's. Yet you are content to let him go down with the rest of us.'

'If he's got any guts he'll make his way.'

'I hope he will. I almost believe I am glad to go bankrupt without your aid, Gabriel. I've had to ask you for money. No doubt you would say I've come begging for money. You choose to refuse me. But please don't plead poverty. You could perfectly well afford to help me but you are a miserly fellow and you choose not to do so. It is not a matter of principle with you, I could respect that, it is just plain reluctance to give away money. I hoped that your vanity and snobbishness, for you're a hell of a snob, would turn the balance. I was wrong. You will go away bathed in the vapours of conscious rectitude. I doubt if you have ever in your life been guilty of a foolish generous action. Everything you have said about us is true; we *have* dribbled money away. But we've given something with it. Imogen and the children have got gaiety and warmth of heart and charm; overrated qualities perhaps, but they are generous qualities.

Indeed there is nothing ungenerous about my undisciplined children. They give something to almost everybody they meet. Perhaps they cheat a little and trade a little on their charm but I don't think that matters nearly so much as being tight-lipped monsters of behaviourism. They are full of what I dare to call loving-kindness, Gabriel, and that's a commodity I don't expect you to understand or applaud.'

'Oh Daddy!' whispered Frid.

'That's a damned impertinent stand to take,' said Lord Wutherwood. 'It's as much as to say that people with a conscience about money are bound to be bores.'

'Nothing of the sort, I – '

'You're as good as puttin' a premium on dishonesty. It's the way people talk these days. "Charm!" Plenty of scamps have got charm; wouldn't be scamps if they hadn't, I dare say. Where's this lovin'-kindness you talk about when it comes to lettin' down your creditors?'

'Touché, I'm afraid,' muttered Henry.

'If I hadn't thought of that,' said Lord Charles, 'nothing would have induced me to ask for your help.'

'You won't get it.'

'Then, as I fancy the Americans say, it is just too bad about my creditors. I rather think the poor devils have banked on you, Gabriel.'

'Insufferable impertinence!' shouted Lord Wutherwood, and Roberta heard the angry sibilants whistle through his teeth. 'Skulking behind my name, by God! Using my name as a screen for your dishonesty.'

'I didn't say so.'

'You as good as said so,' shouted Lord Wutherwood. 'By God, this settles it.'

The scene which had hitherto maintained the established atmosphere of drawing-room comedy, now blossomed agreeably into the more robust type of drama. The brothers set about abusing each other in good round terms and with each intemperate sally their phrases became more deeply coloured with the tincture of Victorian rodomontade. Incredible references to wills, entails, and family escutcheons were freely exchanged. Lord Charles was the first to falter and his brother's peroration rang out clearly.

'I refuse to discuss the matter any further. You can drag yourself and your fool of a wife and your precious brood through the bankruptcy court. If Deepacres wasn't entailed I'd see that you never got a penny of Lamprey money. As it is – '

'As it is you will no doubt re-write as much of your will as is not covered by the entail.' 'I shall do so, certainly.'

'You're a delightful fellow, Gabriel! I wish to God I'd left you alone.'

'You appear even to make a failure of the noble art of sponging.'

This, as Roberta and the Lampreys afterwards agreed, was the climax. Lord Charles and his brother in unison began to speak and in a moment to shout. It was impossible to understand anything but the fact that they had both lost their tempers. This lasted for perhaps fifteen seconds and stopped so abruptly that Roberta thought of a radio knob turned off in the midst of a lively dialogue. So complete was the ensuing silence that she heard a far door open and footsteps cross the drawing-room carpet.

Mike's voice sounded clearly: 'Uncle Gabriel, this is a little present from all of us with our love.'

Roberta and the four Lampreys sat on the dining-room floor and gaped at each other. Next door all was silence. Lord Charles had merely said: 'Michael, put that parcel down, will you, and come back later.'

The brothers had moved away and their following remarks were inaudible. Then Lord Wutherwood had marched out of the room, not neglecting to slam the door. Lord Charles had said: 'Run away, Mike, old man,' and Mike had hopped audibly to the door. Everything was quiet. Lord Charles, only a few inches away, must be standing motionless. Roberta wondered if he still looked after his brother, if he was white like Frid and Henry, or scarlet like Patch and the twins. She wished with all her heart that he would make some movement and pictured him staring with an air of blank wretchedness at the door his brother had slammed. The silence was unendurable. It was broken at last by a step in the passage outside. The dining-room door-handle rattled and Henry walked across and turned the key. The door opened and Mike stood on the threshold. He looked doubtfully at his brothers and sisters. 'I say, is anything up?' he asked.

'Not much,' said Henry.

'Well, any way, I bet something's up,' Mike persisted. 'I bet Uncle G.'s in a stink about something. He looks absolutely fed up and he and Daddy have been yelling blue murder. I say, do you know Giggle's fixed up my Hornby train? He's absolutely wizard with trains. I bet he could – '

'Mike,' said Henry. 'Did Mummy tell you to give the pot to Uncle Gabriel?'

'What? Oh. Well, no. You see Giggle and I were trying my Hornby in the passage and it goes absolutely whizzer now because – '

'The pot,' said Stephen.

'What? Well, I saw it through Mummy's door so I just – '

A distant voice yelled 'Violet!'

'Who's that?' asked Frid.

'It's Uncle G.,' explained Mike. 'He's in the lift. Giggle had his coat off because he says – '

'I'd better go to Mummy,' said Frid. 'She may be in difficulties with the aunts. Come on, Patch.' They went out.

'What *is* the matter with Uncle G.?' asked Mike with casual insistence.

Stephen looked at him. 'If you must know,' he said violently, 'Uncle Gabriel is – '

'Never mind that,' said Colin. 'Come on out of this, Step. We need air.'

'I think we had better go and talk to Father,' said Henry. 'It's beastly to leave him alone in there. Come on you two.'

The three boys went out together. Roberta was left in the dining-room with Mike.

'I suppose you're not interested in Hornby trains,' said Mike with an unconvincing air of casualness.

'I'd like to see yours,' said Roberta.

'We *could* play with it now, of course. It's in the passage in 26. That's if you'd like it.'

'Aren't there rather a lot of people about?' hedged Roberta lamely. 'I mean, aunts and people.'

'Well, of course I *could* bring it here. I'm allowed. Shall I, Robin? Shall I bring my Hornby in here?'

'Yes, do.'

Mike ran to the door but there he hesitated. He looked rather a solemn pale little boy. 'I say,' he said, 'as a matter of fact I think Uncle Gabriel's pretty ghastly.'

'Do you?' said Roberta helplessly.

A tall figure in chauffeur's uniform appeared in the passage behind Mike.

'Oh, hallo, Giggle,' cried Mike.

'Beg pardon, Miss,' said Giggle. 'Beg pardon, Master Michael, but I've got to go. There's that coupling – I've got it fixed. His lordship's in a hurry, so if you – '

'I'll come with you, Giggle,' said Mike warmly.

They disappeared together. Roberta heard Mike's eager voice die away. 'Violet!' yelled the distant voice again. She heard the groan of the lift. Roberta waited.

The tick of the carriage-clock came up again. In a distant part of the flat a door banged. The lift groaned once more. Outside, far beneath the windows and reaching away for miles and miles, surged the ocean of sound which is the voice of London. People were talking, now, in the room next door: a low murmur of voices.

Roberta felt lonely and irresolute and, for the moment, isolated from the calamity that had befallen her friends. She felt that wherever she went she would be hideously in their way. Perhaps if she played trains with Mike it would be a help. Mike was taking a long time. Roberta took a cigarette from a box on the sideboard and hunted about the room for matches. At last she found some. She lit her cigarette and leant over the window-sill. She became aware of a new sound. It came up through her conscious thoughts, gaining definition and edge. It was a thin blade of sound, sharp and insistent. It grew louder. It was inside the building, an intermittent horridly shrill noise that came closer. A hand closed round Roberta's heart. Someone was screaming.

CHAPTER 6

Catastrophe

When Roberta realized that this intolerable sound was on the landing, close at hand, part of the flat itself, she was filled with a strange irresolution. Someone was screaming in the Lampreys' flat and there didn't seem to be anything for Roberta to do about it. She was unable to feel the correct impulses and run helpfully towards the source of these unpleasing noises. No doubt the Lampreys were doing that. Roberta, with a leaping heart, could only stand and wonder at her behaviour. While she still hung off on this queer point of social procedure, someone pounded down the passage. Without conscious volition Roberta followed. She was just in time to see Baskett's coat-tails whisk round the corner. As she passed the drawing-room Henry ran through the hall from the landing. The screaming stopped suddenly like a train whistle.

'Frightfulness!' said Henry as he passed Roberta.

'Robin, for God's sake, get the kids out of it, will you? I'm for the telephone.'

Abruptly filled with initiative, Roberta ran through the hall to the landing.

All the other Lampreys were there on the landing with Baskett, Nanny and Lady Wutherwood. They were gathered round the lift. Patch and Mike were on the outskirts of this little crowd. Charlot held Lady Wutherwood by the arms. Roberta knew now that it was Lady Wutherwood who had screamed. Lord Charles and one of the twins seemed to be inside the lift. Frid, sheet-white, stood just behind them with the other twin. When Lord Charles and the boys turned, Roberta saw that their faces were as white as Frid's. They looked like people in a nightmare. From within the lift came a curious sound, as if somebody was gargling. It persisted. The Lampreys seemed to listen attentively to this noise. Nobody spoke for a moment and then Roberta heard Lord Charles whispering 'No! No! *No!*'

'Hallo,' said Mike, seeing her. 'What's happening to Uncle Gabriel?'

Patch took his hand. 'Come along, Mike,' she said. 'We'll go into the dining-room.'

So Roberta did not have to give Henry's message.

'Come on, Mike,' repeated Patch in a strange voice and dragged at Mike's hand.

They moved away. Roberta was about to follow them when the group at the lift broke up. Roberta saw inside the lift. Lord Wutherwood was sitting in there. A ray of light from the roof of the lift-well had caught the side of his head. For the fraction of a second she had an impression that in his left eye he wore a glass with a wide dark ribbon that clung to the contours of his face. Then she saw that the thing she had mistaken for a glass was well out in front of his eye. Lord Charles moved aside and the interior of the lift became lighter. Roberta's whole being was flooded with an intolerable nausea. She heard her own voice whisper hurriedly, *'But it can't – it can't –it's disgusting'* She could not drag her gaze off the figure in the lift. She felt as though her entire body strained away from the frozen pivot of her sight. His mouth and his right eye were wide open and inside his mouth the sound of gargling grew louder, and still Roberta could not move.

'Better out of that, m'lady,' said Nanny's trembling voice. 'Folks will be ringing for the lift. If Mr Baskett and one of the twins got the top of the ironing trestle – '

Charlot said: 'Yes. Will you, Baskett? And you, Colin, help him.'

The nearest twin went away with Baskett. Nanny followed them.

'Come away for a moment, Violet,' said Charlot. 'Violet, *come away.*' Lady Wutherwood opened her mouth. 'No!' said charlot. She propelled Lady Wutherwood forward into the hall and saw Roberta.

'Robin, get some brandy. Top shelf in the pantry.'

Robin had not been in the pantry. On the way she saw a maid's face looking palely out of a distant door. She found the pantry. Her brain worked frantically to push down, thrust out of mind, the picture of the figure in the lift. It must be repudiated, displaced, covered up. She must do things. How did one know which of these bottles was brandy? Cognac meant brandy. She took it with a glass to the drawing-room. Henry stood over the desk-telephone. 'At once. Couldn't be more urgent. Yes, to the head. Through his eye. I said his eye.' He put the receiver down. 'Dr Kantripp's coming, Mummy.'

'Good,' said Charlot. Roberta had given her a tumbler half-full of brandy. The edge of the tumbler chattered like a castanet against Lady Wutherwood's teeth. Henry, with an expression of disgust, glanced at his aunt.

'Better have some yourself,' he said to his mother. She shook her head. Henry added quickly: 'And I rang up the police.'

'Good.'

Feet stumbled on the landing beyond the hall.

'They're moving him,' said Charlot.

'I'd better go, then.'

Henry went out.

'Can I do anything?' asked Roberta. She had spoken to nobody since Mike left her alone in the dining-room. Her voice sounded oddly in her ears.

'What?' Charlot saw her. 'Oh, Robin, ask the maids to get plenty of boiling water. Doctors are so fond of boiling water, aren't they? And Robin, I don't know where the servants went, Tinkerton and Giggle, I mean. Could you find them and tell them there's been an accident. And the lift. Somebody may want the lift. The doctor will. Did we shut the door?'

'I'll see.'

'Thank you so much.'

Roberta hurried away and found time confusedly to marvel at Charlot's command of her nerves and of the situation. The Lampreys, she thought hurriedly, do rise to situations. She delivered the message to the maids. Now she must return to the landing. The lift was still open. Roberta stood stock-still with her hands on the doors, drilling her thoughts, telling them that he was gone, that she must look inside the lift. And, with a great effort, she lifted her head and looked. A little above the place where Lord Wutherwood had sat was a bright steel boss in the lift wall. In the centre of the boss was a small hollow which seemed to be stained. As she stared at it the stain grew longer. She heard a tap, a tiny dab of sound. She looked at the leather top of the seat. In the dent made by Lord Wutherwood she saw a little black pool where his blood had dropped from the stain on the wall. Back to the pantry, running as fast as she could go. A yellow duster. Then the lift again. It had looked so small a pool but it spread into her cloth and smeared over the leather. Now the wall. She heard a bell ringing. That would be someone who wanted the lift. Back on the landing, she slammed the doors and the lift at once sank beneath her fingers. Henry came out from 26 and looked at the cloth in her hands. He seemed like a figure in a dream and spoke like one.

'Clever, Robin,' said Henry. 'But it won't do much good, you know. You can't wipe away murder.'

Roberta had pushed that word out of her thought. She said: 'It's not that – I mean I wasn't trying to do that. Only people will be using the lift. It looked so frightful.' Henry took the cloth from her.

'There's a fire in the dining-room,' he said.

Roberta remembered her errands. 'Have you seen Tinkerton and Giggle?'

'I don't think they're in the flat. Why?'

'They must be in the car. Charlot wants them told.'

'I'll go,' Henry offered.

'No, please. If you'll do – that.'

'All right,' said Henry and went away with the cloth. Roberta was running downstairs. Four landings with blank walls and steel numbers. Long windows. Heavy carpet under her feet. The lift passed her, bearing an immobile man in an overcoat and a bowler hat, carrying a bag in his hand. Now the entrance hall with the porter who looked bewildered and perturbed and stared at Roberta. She remembered his name.

'Oh, Stamford, have you seen Lord Wutherwood's chauffeur?'

'Yes, Miss. He's in his lordship's car. My Gawd, Miss, what's gone wrong?'

'Someone has been taken ill.'

'The screaming, Miss. It was something frightful.'

'I know. A fit of hysterics. We're sorry about the lift. There's been an accident.'

Better, she thought, to say something about it. The doctor might have said something. She walked quickly through the entrance into the street. The sun had set on London and there was an evening coolness in the air. The sensation of dream receded a little. There was the car, a large grand car with Giggle sitting at the wheel and a woman in a drab hat beside him. They did not notice Roberta and she had to tap on the window, making them jump. Giggle got out and came round to her, touching his cap.

'Giggle,' Roberta began, wishing he had another name, 'there's been an accident.'

He looked at her, maddeningly stolid.

'An accident, Miss?'

'Yes, to Lord Wutherwood. He's hurt himself. Lady Charles thinks you had better come up.'

'Yes, Miss. Will Miss Tinkerton be needed, Miss?'

Roberta didn't know. She said: 'I think perhaps you should both come. Lady Wutherwood may want Tinkerton.'

They followed her into the hall. The lift was down again. Stamford opened the doors. Conquering a sudden and violent reluctance, Roberta went in. She saw that the two servants were preparing to walk up. English servants, she thought, and said: 'Will you both come up in the lift, please?'

They got in and Giggle pressed the button. Tinkerton was a small woman with black eyes and a guarded expression. They won't speak until I do, thought Roberta.

'The doctor has come,' she said. 'It's an upset, isn't it?'

They both said: 'Yes, Miss,' and Tinkerton added in a mumbling voice, 'Is her ladyship much hurt, Miss?'

'It's not her ladyship,' said Roberta, 'it's his lordship.' She remembered insanely that someone once said you had to use 'Your Majesty' in every phrase of a letter written to the king. Your Majesty, your lordship, his lordship, her ladyship.

'His lordship, Miss?'

'Yes. He has hurt his head. I don't really know what happened.'

'No, Miss.'

The lift reached the top landing. Roberta felt as if she was followed by two embarrassingly large dogs. She asked them to wait and left them standing woodenly on the landing.

Now she was back in the flat and didn't know where to go. Perhaps Patch and Mike were still in the dining-room. She stood in the hall and listened. There was a murmur of voices in the drawing-room. Baskett came along the passage carrying a tray with a decanter and glasses. Extraordinary sight, thought Roberta. Can they possibly have settled down for another glass of sherry? Baskett dated from the New Zealand days, he was an old friend of Roberta's and she did not feel shy with him.

'Baskett, who's in the drawing-room?'

'The family, Miss, with the exception of his lordship. His lordship is with the doctor, Miss.'

'And Lady Wutherwood?'

'I understand her ladyship is lying down, Miss.'

Baskett lingered for a moment looking down in a kindly and human manner at Roberta.

'The family will be glad to have you with them, Miss Robin,' he said.

'Have you heard how – how he is?'

'He seemed to be unconscious, Miss when we carried him into his lordship's dressing-room. But alive. I haven't heard any further report.'

'No. Baskett?'

'Yes, Miss?'

'What was the matter with – his eye?'

The network of thread-like veins across Baskett's cheek-bones started out against his bleached skin. The glasses on the tray jingled.

'I shouldn't worry about it, Miss. You'll only upset yourself.'

He opened the drawing-room door and stood aside for her to go in.

II

The Lampreys were nice to Roberta. She kept saying to herself, they *are* nice to think about me. Henry gave her a glass of sherry and Charlot said what a help she had been. They were all very quiet and seemed to listen attentively for something to happen. Charlot had just left Lady Wutherwood who was lying on her bed. She was no longer hysterical and had asked for Tinkerton. Roberta took Tinkerton to the door of the room and then rejoined the others. Nanny came in and in the usual way dragooned Mike off to bed. Charlot asked Patch to go with Nanny and Mike.

'But, Mummy – ' Patch began, 'it's hours before my bedtime. Can't I – '

'Please be with Mike, Patch.'

'All right.'

'What *is* the time?' asked Frid.

'Quarter to eight,' said Nanny from the door. 'Come along, Michael and Patricia.'

'Can it be no more than an hour since they came!' said Charlot.

'Aunt Kit got here earlier,' said Colin.

'*Aunt Kit!*' Charlot looked from one to another of her children. 'For pity's sake, what has become of Aunt Kit?'

'Has anybody seen her?' asked Frid.

Nobody, it appeared, had seen Lady Katherine since the brothers were left alone in the dining-room and Charlot took the aunts to her bedroom.

'We stayed there for about ten minutes, I suppose,' said Charlot, 'and then she said she wished to "disappear". She knows the flat quite well so I didn't lead the way or anything. Stephen – go and see if you can find her.'

Stephen went away but returned to say that unless Aunt Kit was in with the doctor and Lord Charles she was not in the flat.

'Well,' said Henry, 'she told you, Mummy, that she wished to disappear and she has.'

'But – '

'Darling,' said Frid jerkily, 'we can't be worried about Aunt Kit. Honestly.'

'At least,' said Stephen, 'she has behaved with d-decent reticence. Did you ever hear anything more disgraceful than Aunt V.?'

'Poor thing,' said Charlot.

'I simply can't feel sorry for her,' said Henry.

'I can only feel sick,' said Stephen. 'I feel very sick indeed. Does any one else?'

'Shut up,' said Colin automatically.

'Here's Daddy,' said Frid.

Lord Charles came in at the far door. He walked slowly across the room to his family. Charlot made a quick contained movement with her hands. Her husband stood before her.

'Well, darling?' she asked.

'Immy,' said Lord Charles, 'he's not dead. He's alive still.'

'Will he live?'

'It doesn't seem possible.'

'Charlie . . . if he dies?'

'It seems that if Gabriel dies he will have been murdered.'

There was a dead silence and then Henry said in a strange voice: 'Isn't there a book called "It Can't Happen Here"?' Stephen said: 'Of c-course he's murdered. Of course he'll die. With that thing through his b-brain, why didn't he die at once?'

'Shut up,' said Colin.

Lord Charles sat on the arm of his wife's chair and put his hand on her shoulder, it was the first time Roberta had ever seen him do this. 'Where's Patch?' he asked.

'I sent her away with Mike and Nanny. She . . . didn't see, but I thought – '

'Yes. She and Mike will know of course but it might be as well, Imogen, if you told them. The rest of you had better hear the whole story now. Unless Robin – ?'

Roberta said, 'If it's private of course – '

'Private! My dear child, it will be front-page news in every paper by tomorrow.'

'So it will!' Frid ejaculated. 'I say, we ought to tell Nigel Bathgate. It'd be a lovely scoop for him, wouldn't it?'

'I must say, Frid,' said Henry, 'I think that a particularly mad suggestion of yours.'

'I don't see why. As Daddy says, it will be in all the papers anyway so why not give Nigel a break? I dare say he'd fight off all the other pressmen for us. Shall I ring him up, Mummy?'

'Not now, Frid. And yet I don't know. Nigel might be a sort of protection, Charlie.'

'I really do *not* consider,' said Lord Charles with emphasis, 'that one rings up young journalists, however charming, and tells them that one's relations have been murderously assaulted! You none of you seem to realize – ' He broke off and looked at Roberta who was still hovering doubtfully. 'Robin, my dear, we have no secrets for you. I'm only so sorry that you should have been plunged into this nightmare. Stay by all means, if you will.'

'Don't go away, Robin,' said Henry.

'No, don't go,' said the others. So Roberta stayed.

Lord Charles beat gently on his wife's shoulder with his thin hand. Without looking up at him she leant towards him.

'I'm glad it's Dr Kantripp,' she said. 'He knows us so well. It would have been much worse if he had been a stranger.'

'It would have made no difference.'

'None?' asked Charlot on an indrawn breath.

'Very little, at any rate.'

'What will happen?' she asked.

'A man from the police station is here. At the moment he is telephoning Scotland Yard. There's another man in there with Gabriel.'

There was a short silence broken by Charlot.

'Well,' she said, 'none of us tried to kill him, of course, so I suppose we simply tell the truth.'

Nobody answered her.

'Don't we?' Charlot persisted.

'We'll tell the truth,' said Lord Charles, 'certainly.' He looked at his children. 'I want you to listen carefully. Your uncle was alone in the lift for some time before he and Aunt Violet were taken down. It seems that he was sitting in the lift with his hat pulled forward and his head bent. Your aunt only discovered that he was hurt after the lift had gone some way down. You all must have heard the return. Now each of you may have to account for your movements after your – after he got into the lift. Try to remember exactly what you did and where you were. If – '

He broke off abruptly. The doctor had come into the room.

Dr Kantripp was stocky, and dark, with a pleasingly ugly face. He looked profoundly unhappy.

'They're coming,' he said, 'immediately.'

'Good,' said Lord Charles.

'Dr Kantripp,' said Charlot, 'will he live?'

'He may – survive for a little, Lady Charles.'

'Will he be able to speak?'

'I think it most unlikely.'

'Pray God he does!'

He looked sharply at her and it would have been impossible to say whether he felt doubt or relief at her exclamation.

'We shall have a second opinion, of course,' he said. 'I've telephoned Sir Matthew Cairnstock. He's a brain man. I've sent for a nurse.'

'Yes. Will you look at Violet – my sister-in-law? She's in my room.'

'Yes, certainly.'

'I'll come if you want me. She asked to be alone with the maid.'

'I see.' Dr Kantripp hesitated and then said: 'They'll want to talk to the servants, you know.'

'Why the servants, particularly?' asked Lord Charles quickly.

'Well – the instrument. You see it looks as if it came from their part of the world. The kitchen.'

Frid spoke abruptly on a hard shrill note. 'It was a skewer, wasn't it?'

'Yes.'

'Then it wasn't in the kitchen. It was left on the hall table.'

'Dinner is served, m'lady,' said Baskett from the door.

III

Roberta would never have believed that dinner with the Lampreys could be a complete nightmare. It seemed incredible that they should be there, sitting in silence round the long table, solemnly helping themselves to dishes that repelled them. Charlot left the room twice, the first time to take another look at Lady Wutherwood, the second time to see the nurse and to ask if there was anything she needed for her patient. The specialist arrived at the same time as the men from Scotland Yard. Lord Charles went out to meet them but returned in a few minutes to say Dr Kantripp was still there and that he, with one of the police, had gone into the room where Lord Wutherwood lay. Only two of the police were in the flat now. They were plain-clothes men, Lord Charles said, and seemed to be very inoffensive fellows. The others had gone but he did not know for how long. Roberta wondered if the Lampreys shared her feeling that the flat no longer belonged to them. When they had chopped their savouries into small pieces and pushed them about their plates for a minute or two, Charlot said suddenly: 'This is too much. Let's go into the drawing-room.'

Before they could move, however, Baskett came in and murmured to Lord Charles.

'Yes, of course,' said Lord Charles. 'It had better be in here.' He looked at his wife. 'They want to see us all in turn. I suggest they use the dining-room and we go to the drawing-room. In the meantime they want me, Immy. There's a change in Gabriel's condition and the doctors think I should be there.'

'Of course, Charlie. Shall I tell Violet?'

'Will you? Bring her to the room. You don't mind bringing her in?'

'Of course not,' said Charlot, 'if – if she'll come.'

'Do you think – ?'

'I'll see. Come along, children.'

Lord Charles moved quickly to the door and held it open. For as long as Roberta had known the Lampreys he had made the same movement each night after dinner, always reaching the door before his sons and holding it open with a little bow to his wife as she passed him. Tonight they looked into each other's faces for a moment and then Roberta and Frid followed Charlot to the drawing-room. They left the door open and Roberta saw Lord Charles walk by on his way to his brother. That one glance gave her a vivid, an indelible impression of him. The light from the hall shone on his head making a halo of his thin hair and bright-rimmed silhouette of his face. He wore that familiar air of punctiliousness. The placidity, and the detachment to which she was accustomed still appeared in that mild profile, but, she afterwards thought she had seen a glint of something else, a kind of sharpness so foreign to her idea of Lord Charles that she attributed the impression to a trick of lighting or of her overstimulated imagination. The hall door slammed. Roberta was left with the others to sit in silence and to wait.

CHAPTER 7

Death of a Peer

Inspector Fox sat in a corner of the dressing-room, his note-book on his knee, his pencil held in a large, clean hand. He was perfectly still and quite unobtrusive but his presence made itself felt. The two doctors and the nurse were much aware of him and from time to time glanced towards the corner of the room where he sat waiting. A bedside lamp cast a strong light on the patient and a reflected glow on the faces that bent over him. The only sound in the room, a disgusting sound, was made by the patient. On a table close to Fox was a bag. It contained, among a good deal of curious paraphernalia, a silver-plated skewer, carefully packed.

At thirty-five minutes past eight by Fox's watch there was a slight disturbance. The doctors moved, the nurse's uniform crackled. The taller of the doctors glanced over his shoulder into the corner of the room.

'It's coming, I think. Better send for Lord Charles.' He pressed the hanging bell-push. The nurse went to the door and in a moment spoke in a low voice to someone outside. Fox left his chair and moved a little nearer the bed.

The patient's left eye was hidden by a dressing. The right eye was open and stared straight up at the ceiling. From somewhere inside him mingled with the hollow sound of his breathing came a curious noise. His complicated mechanism of speech was trying unsuccessfully to function. The bedclothes were disturbed and very slowly one of his hands crept out. The nurse made a movement which was checked by Fox.

'Excuse me,' said Fox, 'I'd be obliged if you'd let his lordship – '

'Yes, yes,' said the tall doctor. 'Let him be, nurse.'

The hand crept on laboriously out of shadow into light. The finger-tips, clinging to the surface of the neck, crawling with infinite pains, seemed to have a separate life of their own. The single eye no longer stared at the ceiling but turned anxiously in its deep socket as though questing for some attentive face.

'Is he trying to show us something, Sir Matthew?' asked Fox.

'No, no. Quite impossible. The movement has no meaning. He doesn't know – '

'I'd be obliged if you'd ask him, just the same.'

The doctor gave the slightest possible shrug, leant forward, slid his hands under the sheet, and spoke distinctly.

'Do you want to tell us something?'

The eyelid flickered.

'Do you want to tell us how you were hurt?'

The door opened. Lord Charles Lamprey came into the half-light. He stood motionless at the foot of the bed and watched his brother's hand move, lagging inch by inch, up the sharp angle of his jaw.

'There's no significance in this,' said the doctor.

'I'd like to ask him, though,' said Fox, 'if it's all the same to you, Sir Matthew.'

The doctor moved aside. Fox bent forward and stared at Lord Wutherwood.

A deep frown had drawn the eyebrows together. Some sort of sound came from the open mouth. 'You want to show us something, my lord, don't you?' said Fox. The fingers crawled across the cheek and upwards. 'Your eyes? You want to show us your eyes?' The one eye closed slowly, and opened again, and a voice oddly definite, almost articulate, made a short sound.

'Is he going?' asked Lord Charles clearly.

'I think so,' said the doctor. 'Is Lady Wutherwood – ?'

'She is very much distressed. She feels that she cannot face the ordeal.'

'She realizes,' said Dr Kantripp who had not spoken before, 'that there is probably very little time?'

'Yes. My wife says she made it quite clear.'

The doctors turned again to the bed and seemed by this movement to dismiss Lady Wutherwood. The patient's hand slipped away from his face. His gaze seemed to be fixed on the shadows at the foot of his bed.

'Perhaps,' said Fox, 'if he could see you, my lord, he might make a greater effort to speak.'

'He can see me.'

Fox reached out a massive arm and tilted the lamp. The figure at the foot of the bed was thrown into strong relief. Lord Charles blinked in the sudden glare but did not move.

'Will you speak to him, my lord?'

'Gabriel, do you know me?'

'Will you ask him who attacked him, my lord?'

'It is horrible – now – when he – '

'He might manage to answer you,' said Fox.

'Gabriel, do you know who hurt you?'

The frown deepened and the one eye and mouth opened so widely that Lord Wutherwood's face looked like a mask in a nightmare. There was a sharp violence of sound and then silence. Fox turned away tactfully and the nurse's hands went out to the hem of the sheet.

II

'I am very sorry, my lord,' said Fox, 'to have to trouble you at such a time.'

'That can't be helped.'

'That is so, my lord. Under the circumstances we've got to make one or two inquiries.'

'One or two!' said Lord Charles unevenly. 'Do sit down, won't you? I'm afraid I don't know your name.'

'Fox, my lord. Inspector Fox.'

'Oh, yes. Do sit down.'

'Thank you, my lord.'

Fox sat down and with an air of composure drew out his spectacle case. Lord Charles took a chair near the fire and held out his hands to the blaze. They were unsteady and with an impatient movement he drew them back and thrust them into his pockets. He turned to Fox and found the inspector regarding him blandly through steel-rimmed glasses.

'Before I trouble you with any questions, my lord,' said Fox, 'I think it would be advisable for me to ring up my superior officer and report this occurrence. If I may use the telephone, my lord.'

'There is one on that desk. But of course you'd rather be alone.'

'No, thank you, my lord. This will be very convenient. If you will excuse me.'

He moved to the desk, dialled a number, and almost immediately spoke in a very subdued voice into the receiver. 'Fox here, Mr Alleyn's room.' He waited, looking thoughtfully at the base of the telephone. 'Mr Alleyn? Fox, speaking from Flats 25–26 Pleasaunce Court Mansions, Cadogan Square. Residence of Lord Charles Lamprey. The case reported at seven thirty-five is a fatality. Circumstances point that way, sir. Well, I was going to suggest it, sir, if it's convenient. Yes, sir.' Here there was a longish pause during which Fox looked remarkably bland. 'That's so, Mr Alleyn,' he said finally. 'Thank you, sir.'

He hung up the receiver and returned to his chair.

'Chief Detective-Inspector Alleyn, my lord,' said Fox, 'will take over the case. He will be here in half an hour. In the meantime he has instructed me to carry on. So if I may trouble you, my lord.' He took out his note-book and adjusted his glasses. Lord Charles shivered, hunched up a shoulder, put his glass in his eye and waited.

'I have here,' said Fox, 'the statement taken by the officer who was called in from the local station. I'd just like to check that over, my lord, if I may.'

'Yes. It's my own statement, I imagine, but check it by all means if you will.'

'Yes. Thank you. Times. I understand Lord Wutherwood arrived here shortly after six and left at approximately seven fifteen?'

'About then. I heard seven strike some little time before he left.'

'Yes, my lord. Your butler gets a little closer than that. He noticed it was seven fifteen before his lordship rang for his man.'

'I see.'

'His lordship was alone in the lift for some minutes before any one went out to the landing,' read Fox.

'Yes.'

'Thank you, my lord. After he had been there for some minutes he was joined by her ladyship; Lady Wutherwood, that is, and by Lady Charles Lamprey and by Mr Lamprey. Which Mr Lamprey would that be, my lord?'

'Let me think. You must forgive me but my thoughts are intolerably confused.'

Fox waited politely.

'My brother,' said Lord Charles at last, 'left me in the drawing-room. Soon after that the boys, I mean my three sons, joined me there. Then I think my wife opened the door and asked if one of the boys would take my brother and sister-in-law down in the lift. They never take themselves down. One of the boys went out. That will be the one you mean?'

'Yes. That is so, my lord.'

'I don't know which it was.'

'You don't remember?'

'Not that exactly. It was one of the twins. I didn't notice which. Shall I ask them?'

'Not just yet, thank you, my lord. Do I understand you to say that the two young gentlemen are so much alike that you couldn't say which of them left the room?'

'Oh, I should have been able to tell you if I had looked at all closely but you see I didn't. I just saw one of the twins had gone. I – was thinking of something else.'

'The other two remained in the drawing-room with you? Mr Henry Lamprey and the other twin?'

'Yes.'

'Yes, my lord. Thank you. Then you will have noticed the remaining twin if I may put it that way?'

'No. No, I didn't. He didn't speak. I didn't look at the boys. I was sitting by the fire. Henry, my eldest son, said something, but otherwise none of us spoke. They'll tell you themselves which it was.'

'Yes, my lord, so they will. It would be correct to say that while the lift went down you remained in the drawing-room with Mr Lamprey and his brother until when, my lord?'

'Until – ' Lord Charles took out his glass and put it in his waistcoat pocket. It was an automatic gesture. Without the glass the myopic look in his weak eye was extremely noticeable. His lips trembled slightly. He paused and began afresh. 'Until I heard there was – until I heard my sister-in-law scream.'

'And did you realize, my lord – ?'

'I realized nothing,' interrupted Lord Charles swiftly. 'How could I? I know now, of course, that they had gone down in the lift and that she had made that – that terrible discovery, and that it was while the lift returned that she screamed. But at the time I was quite in the dark. I simply became aware of the sound.'

'Thank you,' said Fox again, and wrote in his note-book. He looked over the top of his spectacles at Lord Charles.

'And then, my lord? What would you say happened next?'

'What happened next was that I went out to the landing followed by the two boys. My wife and my girls – my daughters – came out of 26 at the same time. I think my youngest boy, Michael, appeared from somewhere but he wasn't there for long. The lift was returning and was almost up to our landing.'

'Up to the landing,' repeated Fox to his notes. 'And who was in the lift, my lord?'

'Surely that's clear enough,' said Lord Charles. 'I thought you understood that my brother and his wife and my son were in the lift.'

'Yes, my lord, that is how I understand the case at present. I'm afraid this will seem very annoying to you but you see we usually take statements separately for purposes of comparison.'

'I'm sorry, Mr Fox. Of course you do. I'm afraid I'm – '

'Very natural, my lord, that you should be, I'm sure. Then I take it that Lady Wutherwood must have begun to scream while the lift was near the bottom of the shaft?'

Lord Charles twisted his mouth wryly and said yes.

'And continued as it returned to your landing?'

'Yes.'

'Yes. Would you mind telling me what happened when the lift stopped at the top landing?'

'We were bewildered. We couldn't think what had happened, why she was – was making such an appalling scene. She – she – I should explain that she is rather highly-strung. A little hysterical, perhaps. The lift stopped and Henry opened the doors. She rushed out, almost fell out, into my wife's arms. My son, the twin – I – it's too stupid that

I can't tell you which it was, came out without speaking, or if he did speak I didn't hear him. You see, I was looking in the lift.'

'That must have been a great shock to you, my lord,' said Fox simply.

'Yes. A great shock.'

'I saw my brother,' said Lord Charles loudly and rapidly. 'He was sitting at the end of the seat. The injury – it was there – I saw it – I – I didn't understand then, that they – my sister-in-law and my son – had gone down in the lift without at first realizing there was anything the matter.'

'When *did* you realize this, my lord?'

'As soon as my wife had calmed her down a little she began to speak about it. She was very wild and incoherent, but I made out as much as that.'

'You did not question your son, my lord? Whichever son it was,' enquired Fox, as if the confusion of one's children's identities was the most natural thing in the world.

'No. There doesn't seem to have been any time to talk to anybody.'

'And of course if you had questioned him you would have known which he was?'

'Yes,' rejoined Lord Charles evenly, 'of course.'

'Did any of the others talk to him, my lord?'

'I really don't know. How should I? If I had heard that, I would – ' He stopped short. 'I really can't tell you more than that.'

'I understand, my lord. I must thank you for your courtesy and apologize again for causing you so much pain. There are only one or two other points. Did you touch your brother?'

'No!' said Lord Charles violently. 'No! No! They carried him out and took him to my room. That is all.'

'And you did not see him again until you came into his room while I was there?'

'I took Dr Kantripp to the room and waited with him. The children's old nurse was there. She helped the doctor until the trained nurse arrived.'

'I take it that Dr Kantripp – ' Fox paused for a moment – 'the doctor did everything that was necessary? I mean, my lord, that the injury was unattended until he came?'

Lord Charles made an effort to speak, failed to do so, and nodded his head. At last he managed to say: 'We thought it better not to – not to try to – we didn't know whether it might prove fatal to – '

'To remove anything? Quite so.'

'Is that all?'

'I shan't trouble you much further, my lord, but I should like to ask if you know whether his lordship had any enemies.'

'Enemies! That's an extravagant sort of way to put it.'

'It's the way we generally put it, my lord. I dare say it does sound rather exaggerated but you see the motive for this sort of crime is usually something a bit stronger than dislike.'

To this bland rejoinder Lord Charles found nothing to say.

'Of course,' Fox continued, 'the term enemies is used rather broadly, my lord. I might put it another way and ask if you know of anyone who had good reason to wish for Lord Wutherwood's death.'

Lord Charles answered this question instantly with a little spurt of words that sounded oddly mechanical.

'If you mean, do I know of anyone who would benefit by his death,' he said, 'I suppose you may say that his heirs will do so. I am his heir.'

'Well, yes, my lord. I know Lord Wutherwood had no son.'

'Do you, by God!' said Lord Charles. The exclamation was completely out of key with the level courtesy of his earlier rejoinder but Fox took it in his stride.

'I have heard that is the case,' he said. 'I understand that two of his lordship's servants were here. It's not very nice,' continued Fox with an air of one who apologizes for a slight error in taste, 'to have to think of people in this light, but – '

'Murder,' said Lord Charles, 'is not very nice either. You are quite right, Mr Fox. My brother's chauffeur and my sister-in-law's maid were both there.'

'Might I trouble you for their names, my lord?'

'Tinkerton and Giggle.'

'Giggle, my lord?'

'Yes. That's the chauffeur.'

'Quite an unusual name,' said Fox, placidly busy with his notes. 'Have they been long with his lordship?'

'I believe that Tinkerton was with my sister-in-law before she married and that's twenty-five years ago. Giggle began at Deepacres as an odd boy and under-chauffeur. His father was coachman to my father.'

'Family servants,' murmured Fox, placing them. 'And of course your own servants would be in the flat?'

'Yes. There's Baskett, the butler; and the cook and two maids. They may not all have been in. I'll find out.'

He stretched his hand out to the bell.

'In a minute, thank you, my lord. These are all the servants you employ?'

'Yes.'

'I thought you spoke of a nurse, my lord.'

'Oh – you mean Nanny,' said Lord Charles who now seemed to have himself very well in hand. 'Yes, of course there's Nanny. We don't think of her as one of the servants.'

'No, my lord?'

'No. She's the real head of affairs, you see.'

'Oh, yes!' said Fox politely. 'I would be much obliged if you would send for the butler now.'

Baskett came in with his usual ineffable butler's walk, executed with the arms held straight down, the hands lightly closed and turned out with the palms downwards. It was the deliberate relaxed pose of a man whose deportment is an important factor in his profession. Baskett did it superbly.

'Oh, Baskett,' said Lord Charles, 'Inspector Fox would like to ask you about the people who were in the servants' quarters this evening. Were all the maids in?'

'Ethel was out, my lord. Mrs James and Blackmore were in.' He glanced at Fox. 'That is the cook and the parlour-maid, sir,' he explained.

'Any visitors in your quarters?' asked Fox.

'Yes, sir. Lord Wutherwood's chauffeur and Lady Wutherwood's maid. The chauffeur was in the staff sitting-room, sir, for some time, and then went into No. 26 to help Master Michael with his trains. Miss Tinkerton was with Mrs Burnaby in her room.'

'Mrs Burnaby?'

'That's Nanny,' explained Lord Charles.

'Thank you, my lord. And that is the entire household at the time of the occurrence?'

'I think so,' said Lord Charles. 'Was there any one else in your part of the world, Baskett?'

Baskett looked anxiously at his employer and hesitated.

'You will of course tell us,' said Lord Charles, 'if you know of any one else in the flat.'

'Very good, my lord. There was another person, sir, in the kitchen.'

Fox paused, pencil in hand. 'Who was that?'

'Good God!' ejaculated Lord Charles, 'I'd entirely forgotten him.'

'Forgotten whom, my lord?'

'What's the miserable creature's name, Baskett?'

'Grumball, my lord.'

Fox said sharply: 'You mean Giggle. I've got him.'

'No, sir. This person's name is Grumball.'

Fox looked scandalized. 'Who is he, then?' he asked. Baskett was silent.

'He's the man in possession,' said Lord Charles.

'A bailiff, my lord?'

'A bum-bailiff, Mr Fox.'

'Thank you, my lord,' said Fox tranquilly. 'I'll see the rest of the staff, now, if it's agreeable.'

III

'Would it be one of these society affairs, sir?' asked Detective-Sergeant Bailey, staring with lack-lustre eyes through the police-car window.

'What society affairs, Bailey?' murmured Chief Detective-Inspector Alleyn.

'Well you know, sir. Cocktails, bottle-parties, flats and so forth.'

'One of the messy sort,' said Detective-Sergeant Thompson moving his photographic impedimenta a little farther under the seat.

'That's right,' agreed Bailey.

'I've no idea,' said Alleyn, 'in what sort of country we shall find ourselves.'

'The flat belongs to deceased's brother, doesn't it, sir?'

'Yes. Lord Charles Lamprey.'

The police-surgeon spoke for the first time. 'I fancy I've heard something about Lamprey,' he said. 'Can't remember what it was.'

'Wasn't he mixed up in that Stein suicide?' said Bailey.

Alleyn glanced at him. 'He was, yes. Stein left him with the baby.'

'The baby, sir?'

'Figuratively, Bailey. Lord Charles appeared to have developed an amazing flair for signing himself into every conceivable sort of responsibility. He turned out to be Stein's partner, you remember.'

'Did he go bust?' asked the doctor.

'I don't think so, Curtis. Must have felt the draught a bit, one would imagine.'

'Was the deceased a wealthy man, sir?' asked Bailey. 'This Lord Wutherwood, I mean.'

'Oh, pretty well, you know,' said Alleyn vaguely. 'There's a monstrous place in Kent, I think. Not that that tells one anything. May have been hanging on by the skin of his teeth.'

'It sounds an unpleasant business,' said Dr Curtis. 'Through the eye, didn't you say?'

'Yes. Beastly, isn't it? Fox was very guarded when he rang up. I recognized his suspect-listening manner.'

'Large family of Lampreys?' asked Dr Curtis.

'Masses of young, I fancy. Damn! We're in for a nasty run, no doubt. Why the devil do these people have to get themselves messed up in a case like this?'

'Another instance,' said Dr Curtis dryly, 'of the aristocracy mixing with the commonalty. They've tried trade and they've tried big business. Why not a spot of homicide? Sorry!' he added uncomfortably. 'Silly statement. Very unprofessional. The peer was probably pinked by a –what? A servant? A lunatic? Somebody with an axe to grind? Here we are in Sloane Street. Cadogan Gardens, isn't it?'

'Pleasaunce Court. Do you know the doctor, Curtis? His name's Kantripp.'

'I do, as it happens. He was in my first year at Thomas's. Nice fellow. Awkward business for him if, as one supposes, he's the family doctor.'

'It may not be awkward. Let's hope it's a simple matter. Some nice homicidal maniac wandering about the top storey of Pleasaunce Court Mansions and going all haywire at the sight of an elderly peer in a lift. Let's hope there are no axes to grind. Here's the turning. How anybody can get a kick out of homicide is to me one of the major puzzles of psychology.'

'Was there never a time,' asked Curtis, 'when you read murder cases in your newspaper with avidity?'

'Oh, yes. Yes.'

'And do they always bore you, nowadays?'

Alleyn grinned. 'No,' he said. 'I'm not bored by my job. One gets desperately sick of routine at times but it would be an affectation to pretend one was bored. People interest me and homicide cases are so terrifically concerned with people. Each locked up inside his mental bomb-proof shelter, and then, suddenly, the holocaust. Most murders are really very squalid affairs, of course, but there's always the element that pressmen call the human angle. All the same, Curtis, it's a beastly sort of stimulus. One would have to be very case-hardened to feel nothing but technical interest. O Lord, here we go! There's a gaggle of PCs coming along in the car behind. Fox said we might need some spare parts.'

The car pulled up. With that unmistakable air of being about their business, the four men got out and walked up the steps. A knives-to-grind, returning from a profitable day in Chelsea paused at Pleasaunce Court corner and addressed himself to a newsboy.

'Wot's up in vere?' asked the knives-to-grind.

'Wot's up in where?'

'In vere. In vem Mensions.'

The newsboy looked. 'Coo! P'lice.'

'P'lice!' said the knives-to-grind contemptuously. 'I believe you! 'Ere! Know 'oo that is? That's 'Endsome Ell-een.'

'Crippy, your right, mate! Fency me missing 'm! I've doubled me sales on 'Endsome Ell-een many an evenin'. Coo, there's 'is cemera-bloke. That's a cemera all right in that box. And 'tover bloke'll be 'is finger-print expert.'

'It's a cise for the Yawd,' said the knives-to-grind.

'Ar. Murder,' agreed the newsboy.

'Not necessairilly.'

'Garn! Wot's the cemera for if it's not murder? Taking photers of the lift-man? *Not necessairilly!* 'Ere, wite on! I'll git orf a Stendard on the old bloke in the 'all.'

The newsboy ran up the steps crying in a respectful manner. 'Stendard, sir, Stendard?' The knives-to-grind thoughtfully salvaged a cigarette butt from the kerb and put it in his waistcoat pocket. A second car drew up and four constables got out and entered the flats.

The newsboy reappeared and with an unconvincing show of nonchalance returned to his post.

'Well,' asked his friend, ''ow abaht it?'

'Been a neccident.'

'What sorta eccident?'

'Old bloke 'ad 'is eye jabbed aht in the lift.'

'Garn!'

'Yeah,' said the newsboy, assuming a slightly hard-boiled transatlantic manner. 'And it's just too bad abaht 'im. 'E's a gorner.'

'Dead?'

'Stiff.'

'Cor!'

'*Eccident!*' said the newsboy with ineffable scorn.

'*Eccident!* Oh yeah?'

'Wiv cops and cemeras floating in by dozins,' agreed his friend. 'Oh, yeah? Not 'alf. I *don't* fink.'

And taking up the shafts of his grindstone he trundled down Pleasaunce Court, pausing at the corner to raise the mournful cry of his trade.

'Knives to grind? Knives to grind?'

His voice floated up in the evening air. Alleyn heard it as he rang the Lampreys' doorbell.

'Any old knives to grind?'

CHAPTER 8

Alleyn Meets the Lampreys

Fox had lavished the most delicate attention on the skewer. It was tied down to a strip of cardboard and lay in a long box. Alleyn held the box under the lamp. The plated ring at the broad end of the skewer caught the light and glinted. The blade did not glint. It had had time to dry a little.

'Disgusting,' said Alleyn. He laid down the box. 'Yours, Bailey. The blade had obviously been lifted by the point.'

'That's me,' said Dr Kantripp. 'I thought it better to avoid the ring as much as possible, though of course in drawing it out – '

'Of course,' said Dr Curtis.

'Well, you'd better try the ring and top of the shaft, Bailey,' said Alleyn.

'It's a whale of a great skewer,' said Dr Curtis.

'Yes. An old one. People use them nowadays for paper-knives.'

'They got this one from the kitchen,' said Fox.

'Did they? We'd better take a look at the body, if you please, Dr Kantripp.'

They moved to the bed. Fox tilted the lamp. Dr Kantripp drew back the sheet.

'Nothing's been done,' he said. 'I thought, under the circumstances – '

'Yes, of course. His wife hasn't seen him like this?'

'No. She wouldn't come. Just as well perhaps.'

'Yes,' agreed Alleyn staring at the gargoyle's head on the sheet. 'Just as well.'

'No. He's not very pretty,' muttered Dr Curtis absently. He bent down. Fox moved the lamp.

'It seemed a bit queer to me his lasting so long, doctor,' said Fox.

'The head's a queer thing,' observed Dr Curtis. 'There have been cases of survival – What was the angle, Kantripp?'

'Slightly upward. But it may have shifted.'

'Yes.'

'You say, Fox,' said Alleyn, 'that he tried to speak?'

'Well, sir, not to say speak. He made noises.'

'It wasn't likely, I thought, that he could say anything,' said Dr Kantripp, 'but Mr Fox thought there was just a chance. As Curtis says, queer things happen with injuries to the brain. There have been cases – '

'I know. What are those marks beside the eyes? Hypostases?'

The two doctors exchanged glances.

'I didn't think so,' said Dr Kantripp diffidently.

'Bruises, more likely,' said Dr Curtis. 'You don't get hypostases there. Not with the way he's lying.'

'They said, Fox, that he sat on the right-hand end of the seat?'

'Yes, sir.'

'Have a look at the left temple, would you, Curtis?'

Dr Curtis began to take away the dressing over the left eye.

'You're quite right, Alleyn,' said Dr Kantripp. 'There's a cut on the temple under the bandage. I was going to show you. Yes, there it is.'

With a swift and delicate gesture Alleyn placed his long left hand across the staring right eye and the left socket. The heel of his hand was against the right side of the face, thumb downwards.

'There's a sort of fancy steel fretwork affair in the wall of the lift,' said Fox. 'With knobs on. There's a bit of a smear on one of the knobs. It looks as if it had been wiped.'

'Does it, indeed?' Alleyn murmured and swiftly drew away his hand. 'We'll get him out of here,' he added.

'I've left orders for the mortuary van.'

'Yes. Thank you, Curtis. You'll do the post-mortem tomorrow?'

'Yes.'

'I think before I see the family we'll take a look at the lift. You can get to work in here, Bailey. Try those bruises for prints. You'd better go all over the face. It's a faint hope but you'd better have a shot at it. Then the skewer. Then come along to the lift. And, Thompson, you get some shots of the head, will you?'

'Very good, Mr Alleyn.'

Alleyn did not move away from the bed. He stared at the face on the pillow and the single eye in the face seemed, in return, to glare sightlessly at him. Alleyn stooped and touched the jaw and neck.

'No rigor yet?'

'Just beginning. Why?'

'We may have to perform an unpleasant experiment. Is the nurse still here?'

'Yes,' said Dr Kantripp.

'When Bailey and Thompson have finished, get her to tidy him up. He's a nightmare as he is. Come on, Fox.'

II

Fox had caused the mechanism of the lift to be switched off, had sealed the doors and had posted a uniformed constable on the landing. The lift was dark inside and, waiting there at the Lampreys' landing, it wore an air of expectancy.

'Window at the top of the door,' said Alleyn.

'That's right, sir.'

'Didn't you say that he sat in here, yelling for his wife? With the doors shut?'

'So the butler said.'

'He might have been whisked down below.'

'Perhaps he kept his thumb on the stop button, Mr Alleyn.'

'Perhaps he did.' Alleyn switched on the light. 'Now, where was he?'

'From all accounts he was sitting in the right-hand corner with his head leaning against that steel grid affair and his bowler hat tilted over his face. Of course the lift's been used since then. The doctor, for one, came up in it. As soon as our chaps came in they attended to that. Still, it's a pity.'

'It is.' Alleyn peered at the steel framework of the wall. 'There's the smear you talked about on that bulge or knob or what-you-will.'

'Very fancy design, isn't it, sir?'

'Very, B'rer Fox. Grapes, you see, mixed up with decorative lumps. Modern applied art. How tall was he?'

'Six foot and a half an inch,' said Fox immediately.

'Good. You're six foot, aren't you? Just sit at the other end, Foxkin. Yes. Yes, I fancy that if you sat there and I caught you a snorter on the right side of your head, your left temple would miss that corresponding knob by half an inch or so. However, that's altogether too vague. It looks as if we'll have to get him in here to try. I see these knobs have got slight depressions in the surface. Look at our particular one. Somebody, as you capably observed, has wiped it. And the seat, as well. Not very proficiently. Bailey will have to deal with this. Hallo!'

Alleyn stooped and flashed his torch under the seat. 'I suppose you've already spotted those, you old devil,' he observed.

'Yes, sir. I thought I'd leave them for you.'

'What delicacy! What tact!' Alleyn reached under the seat and drew out a pair of heavy driving-gloves with long gauntlets. He and Fox squatted on the floor and examined them.

'Bloody,' said Fox.

'Blood, or something that looks like it. Between the middle and the third fingers of the left hand, and on the inner surface of those fingers. And a little on the palm. Can you see any on the right-hand glove? Yes. Again, a little on the palm. Bless my soul, Fox, we must take care of these. Give them to Bailey, like a good chap, and then tell me the whole story as far as you've got.'

Fox went into 26. The constable cleared his throat. Alleyn gazed at the lift well. The door into 25 opened and a good-looking pale young man peered out on to the landing.

'Oh, hallo,' he said politely. 'I'm sorry to bother you. You're Mr Alleyn, I expect.'

'Yes,' said Alleyn.

'Yes. I'm so sorry to make a nuisance of myself, but I thought I'd just ask if it was likely to be a very long time before you began to pitch into us. I'm Henry Lamprey.'

'How do you do,' said Alleyn politely. 'We'll be as quick as we can. Not long now.'

'Oh, good. It's just that my mama is rather exhausted, poor thing, and I think she ought to go to bed. That is, of course, if my Aunt

Violet can be moved off the bed or even out of the room which I must say seems to be doubtful . . . What is the right technique, do you know, with widows of murdered men who are also one's near relations?'

'Is Lady Charles with Lady Wutherwood at the moment?' asked Alleyn. Henry came out on the landing and shut the door. He stood in the shadow of the lift.

'Yes,' he said. 'My mama is in there and so is Tinkerton who is my Aunt Violet's maid. It appears that my Aunt Violet is in a sort of coma or trance and really doesn't notice who goes or comes. But you won't want to be bothered with all that. I was only going to suggest that if you could see my mother first and then Aunt Violet it would give us a chance to bundle mama off to bed.'

'I'll see what can be done about it. I'm afraid in this sort of business – '

'Oh, I know,' agreed Henry. 'The rest of us are all quite prepared for the dawn to rise on our lies and evasions.'

'I hope not,' said Alleyn.

'Actually we are a truthful family, only the things that happen to us are so peculiar that nobody ever believes in them. Still, I expect you've got a sort of winnowing ear for people's testimonies and will know in a flash if we try any hanky-panky.'

'I expect so,' agreed Alleyn gravely. From the shadow of the lift Henry seemed to look solemnly at him.

'Yes,' he said. 'I'm afraid I expect so too. My father suggested that you ought to be offered a drink and some sandwiches but the rest of us knew you wouldn't break bread with suspected persons. Or is that only in books? Anyway, sir, if you would like us to send something out here or if you would like to join us for a drink, we do hope you will.'

'That's very kind of you,' said Alleyn, 'but we don't on duty.'

'Or if there's anything at all that we can do.'

'I don't think there's anything at the moment. Oh, as you're here, I may as well ask you. Who is the owner of those gloves?'

'What gloves?' Henry's voice sounded blank.

'A pair of heavy driving-gloves with stiff gauntlets.'

'Lined with rather disgusting fur?'

'Fur-lined, yes.'

'Sound like mine,' said Henry. 'Where are they?'

'I'll return them to you. My colleague took them into the flat.'

'Where did you find them?'

'In the lift,' said Alleyn.

'But I wasn't in the lift.'

'No?'

'No. I expect – ' Henry stopped short.

'Yes?'

'Nothing. I can't imagine how they got there. You needn't return them, sir. I don't really think I want them any more.'

'I don't think you would,' agreed Alleyn, 'if you saw them.'

Henry's face shone like ivory on that dimly lit landing. His eyes were like black coals under the cold whiteness of his forehead.

'What do you mean?' he asked.

'They are stained.'

'Stained? With what?'

'It looks like blood.'

Henry turned on his heel and went blindly into the flat. Fox returned with Bailey.

'I want you to go all over the inside of the lift, Bailey,' said Alleyn. 'Try the stops and the door-knobs – everything. Get Thompson to take a close-up shot of the seat and wall.'

'Very good, sir.'

'And Fox, we'll go over your notes and then I think I'd better see the family.'

III

The twins stood side by side on the hearthrug. The lamplight glinted on their blond heads. They wore grey flannel suits and dark-green pullovers that their mother had knitted for them. Their hands were in their pockets, their heads were tilted slightly to one side. Their faces were screwed into an expression of apologetic attentiveness. From her stool by the fire Roberta watched them and felt a cold pang of alarm. For behind the twins Roberta saw, not the coal fire of a London grate, but the sweetly aromatic logs that burnt in the drawing-room at Deepacres in New Zealand. And with the sharpest emphasis of memory she heard each twin confess that he had taken out the forbidden big car, and had driven it through a water-race into a bank. She saw herself sitting mum, knowing all the time that it was Stephen who had taken the car while Colin was indoors. She heard herself asking Colin privately why he had made this quixotic gesture and she again heard his answer. 'It's a kind of arrangement we have!' 'Always?' she had asked him, and Colin, rumpling up his fair hair, had answered, 'Oh, no. Only when there's a really major row.' 'A twinny sort of arrangement,' Roberta had said, and Colin had agreed. 'Yes, that's the idea. As between twins.' So insistent was this memory that the past was clearer for a moment than the present and she was unaware of the voices in the drawing-room. Her mind seemed to change gear and she found herself thinking of the Lampreys as strangers. 'I don't know what they are like,' thought Roberta in her cold panic. 'I have no knowledge of their reality. I have fitted their words and actions into my own idea of them but my idea may be quite wrong.' And she began to wonder confusedly if anybody had a complete secret reality or if each layer of thought merely represented the level of someone else's idea of the thinker. 'This won't do,' thought Roberta. 'Stop!' Her mind changed gear again and Lord Charles's voice came back, familiar, gentle, a voice she knew and loved.

'Now listen to me,' Lord Charles was saying. 'There is going to be no more of this. One of you went down in the lift with Violet and with him. Which was it?'

'I d-did,' said Stephen.

'Shut up,' said Colin. 'I did.'

'Do you realize,' said Henry, 'that one of you is making things look just about as murky as may be for the other?'

'If you imagine,' said Lord Charles, 'that the police are to be checked by a childish trick of this sort, you are – ' he added hurriedly: 'you simply couldn't be more mistaken.'

'What about finger-prints?' said Frid.

'I didn't touch anything,' said Colin.

'I kept my hands in my p-pocket,' said Stephen.

'Whichever it was, must have worked the lift,' Frid pointed out.

'The lift's been used twice since then,' said Stephen.

'Twice, at least,' said Colin. 'There won't be any finger-prints worth talking about.'

'At any moment now,' Henry said, 'Alleyn will come in and begin to ask questions. As soon as he sees what you are up to he'll talk to you separately. If you think you've one sickly misbegotten hope of taking him in, you're bigger bloody fools than anybody outside a bughouse.'

'Mummy'll be back in a minute,' said Frid. 'Don't let's have this going on when she comes in.'

Lord Charles said: 'Stephen, did you commit this crime?'

'No, father, I didn't.'

'Colin?'

'No, father, honestly.'

'On your most solemn word of honour, both of you.'

'No, father,' repeated the twins. And Stephen added: 'We're not sorry he's dead, of course, but it's a filthy way to k-kill anybody.'

'Lousy,' agreed Colin cheerfully.

'I know very well that it seems grossly stupid and fantastic to ask you,' said Lord Charles. 'Of course you are quite incapable of it. What I – I implore you to believe is that it is the last word in dangerous lunacy for an innocent man to lie to the police.'

'That's what I keep t-telling Colin,' said Stephen.

'Then why don't you take your own advice?' asked Colin. 'Don't be a fool. I went down in the lift, father, and Stephen stayed in the drawing-room.'

'Which is a complete and sweltering lie,' added Stephen.

'So there you are,' said Frid. 'Come off it, twins. It's jolly clever, we all admit it's jolly clever, but this is a serious affair. You can't pit your puny wits against the master brain of Handsome Alleyn. You know, chaps, if it wasn't for the fact that Uncle G. was murdered, it'd be rather a big moment for me having Handsome Alleyn in the flat. I've nursed an illicit passion for that man ever since the Gospell murder. Is he really the answer to the maiden's prayer, Henry?'

'Do stop being crisp and modish, Frid,' begged Henry irritably. 'You know that, like all the rest of us, you're nearly dead with terror.'

'No, I'm not, honestly. I may wake up in the night bathed in a cold sweat but at the moment I'm sort of stimulated. Only I wish one of the twins would stop being mad.'

'I wish to God you'd all stop being mad,' said Lord Charles with sudden violence. 'I feel as if I were looking at you and listening to you for the first time. Someone in this flat killed my brother.'

There was an awkward silence broken by Frid.

'But, Daddy,' said Frid, 'you didn't like Uncle G. Now, did you?'

'Be quiet, Frid,' ordered Henry. 'You don't think any of the family did it, do you, father?'

'Good God, of course I don't!'

'Well, who does everybody think did it?' asked Frid brightly.

'Tinkerton,' said Colin.

'Or Giggle,' said Stephen.

'You only say Tinkerton or Giggle because you don't know them as well as Baskett and the maids,' Henry pointed out.

'And Nanny,' added Frid.

'If I'd been Uncle G.'s or Aunt V.'s servant,' said Colin, 'I'd have murdered both of them long ago. I must say I'm rather glad it's going to be Alleyn. If we've got to be grilled it may as well, be by a gent. But then I'm a snob, of course.'

'I th-think it'll be rather uncomfortable,' said Stephen. 'I'd rather it was the old-fashioned sort that says: " 'Ere, 'ere, 'ere, wot's all this?" '

'Which shows how ignorant you are,' said Frid. 'No detective speaks like that. But I *do* think, Daddy, that Henry ought to ring up Nigel Bathgate. You know how he raves about Mr Alleyn. He's his Watson and glories in it.'

'Why should I ring him up?' Henry demanded. 'Ring him up yourself.'

'Well, I will presently. I think it's only kind.'

'What's Alleyn like?' asked Colin.

'Oh, very nice,' said Henry. 'Sort of old-world without any Blimpishness. Rather frighteningly polite and quiet.'

'Hell!' said Stephen.

The drawing-room door opened and Patch came in wearing pyjamas and a dressing-gown. Her hair had been lugged off her forehead by Nanny with such ferocious emphasis that her eyebrows were slightly raised. Two hard plaits hung between her shoulders. Her round face shone and she smelt of bath powder. To Roberta she was a mere enlargement of herself at twelve and still very much of the nursery.

'Mike's asleep,' said Patch, 'and I've never been wider awake in my life. Please Daddy, don't send me back. My teeth keep chattering.'

'Oh, Patch, darling!' said Lord Charles helplessly. 'I'm so sorry. Come up to the fire.'

'You can't face the police like that, Patch,' said Frid. 'You're too fat for negligée appearances.'

'I don't care. I'm going to sit by darling Roberta and get warm. Daddy, are the police here now?'

'Yes.'

'Where's Mummy?'

'With Aunt Violet.'

'Was Uncle G. murdered? Nanny's being so maddening. She won't talk about it.'

'Yes, he was,' said Frid impatiently. 'It's no good trying to fob Patch off with a vague story, Daddy. Uncle G.'s been dotted one, Patch, and he's dead.'

'Who dotted him one?' asked Patch, rubbing her hands slowly over her knees.

'It must have been someone – ' Lord Charles waved his hand – 'some lunatic who wandered up here. A wandering lunatic. Obviously. Don't think about it, Patch. The police will find out about it.'

'Golly, how thrilling,' said Patch. She had squatted down by Roberta who could feel her quivering like a puppy. 'Daddy,' she said, 'I've thought of something.'

'What is it?' asked her father wearily.

'You'll be able to get rid of the bum.'

'Be quiet, Patch,' said Henry. 'You're not to talk about the bum.'

'Why not?'

'Because I tell you.'

Patch looked impertinently at Henry. 'Okay, Rune,' she said.

'What!' cried Roberta.

'It's quite right,' said Patch. 'Henry's to be called the Earl of Rune now. Isn't he, Daddy?'

'Good God!' said Henry slowly, 'so I am.'

'Yes,' said Patch with a certain complacency, 'you are. And I, for instance, am now the Lady Patricia Lamprey. Aren't I, Daddy?'

'Shut up, Patch,' said Colin.

'Yes, yes,' said Lord Charles hurriedly. 'Never mind about it now, Patch.'

'And Daddy,' Patch persisted stubbornly, 'you're now – '

The drawing-room door opened. Alleyn stood on the threshold with Fox behind him.

'May I come in, Lord Wutherwood?' asked Alleyn.

IV

Afterwards, when Roberta had time to review the events of that incredible day, she remembered that until Alleyn appeared, an image of a fictitious detective had hung about at the back of all her thoughts; an image of a man coldly attentive with coarse hands and a large soapy-shining face. Alleyn was so little like this image that for a moment she thought he must be some visitor, fantastically *de trop*, who had dropped in to see the Lampreys. The sight of Fox disabused her of this idea. There was no mistake about Fox.

The new Lord Wutherwood put his glass in his waistcoat pocket and, with his usual air of punctilious courtesy, hurried forward. He shook hands, bending his elbow sharply and holding his hand out at right-angles to his forearm, a modish, diplomatic handshake.

'Do come in,' he said. 'We have left you very much to yourselves out there but I hoped if there was anything we could do you would let us know.'

'There was nothing, thank you so much,' said Alleyn, 'until now. I felt I should go over the information Fox had already got before I bothered all of you. But now – '

'Yes, yes, of course. My wife and my small son are not here at the moment but this is the rest of the family . . . My eldest son you have already met. My daughter . . . '

The introductions were solemnly performed. Alleyn bowed to each of the Lampreys. Roberta on her footstool was so much in shadow that Lord Charles forgot her, but Alleyn's dark eyes turned gravely to the small figure.

'I beg your pardon, Robin, my dear,' said Lord Charles. 'Miss Grey is a New Zealand friend of ours, Mr Alleyn.'

'How do you do,' said Roberta.

'New Zealand?' said Alleyn.

'Yes. I only got here yesterday,' said Roberta and wondered why he looked so gently at her before he turned to Lord Charles.

'This is a dreadful thing, Alleyn,' Lord Charles was saying. 'We are quite bewildered and – and of course rather shaken. I hope you will forgive us if we are not very intelligent about remembering everything.'

'We know that it must have been a very grave shock,' agreed Alleyn. 'I shall try to be as quick as possible but I'm afraid that at the best it will be a long and unavoidably distressing business.'

'What happens?' asked Henry.

'First of all I want to get a coherent account of the events that preceded the moment when Lord and Lady Wutherwood entered the lift. I think I should tell you that Fox has seen the commissionaire downstairs. He was on duty in the hall all the afternoon and although he does not work the lift he can account for everybody who used it after Lord and Lady Wutherwood arrived. He also states very positively that no strangers used it earlier in the afternoon. There is of course the outside stairway, the iron fire-escape. To get into this flat by its aid you must pass through the kitchen. Your cook is prepared to make a definite statement that during the afternoon nobody came in by that entrance. Of course the commissionaire and the cook may be mistaken but on the face of it, it appears that no strangers have been up here since lunch.'

'I see.'

'We shall, of course, make much more exhaustive inquiries on this point. But you will see that under the circumstances – '

'It m-must have been someone in the flat,' said Stephen loudly.

'Yes,' said Alleyn, 'it looks like that. I only stress this point to make it clear to you that we must have a very accurate picture of everybody's movements.'

The Lampreys all murmured 'yes'. Alleyn placed his hands palm down on the arms of his chair and looked round the circle of faces. Patch, huddled in her woollen dressing-gown, still sat by Roberta. The twins, long-legged and blond, were collapsed as usual on the sofa, Henry sat in a deep chair, his hands driven into his trouser pockets, his shoulders hunched, his head dipped a little to one side. Henry, thought Roberta, looks like a watchful bird. Lord Charles sat elegantly on a thin chair and swung his glass like a pendulum above his crossed knees. Frid still leant against the mantelpiece in an attitude that was faintly histrionic.

'Before all this business starts,' Alleyn began, 'there is just one thing I would like to say. It is not very much use my pretending to avoid the implications in this case. It is scarcely possible that it can be a case of suicide or of accident. The word that must be in all your minds is one that, unfortunately, calls up all sorts of extravagant images. Detective fiction has made so much of homicide investigations that I'm afraid to most people they suggest official misunderstandings, dozens of innocent persons in jeopardy, red herrings by the barrow load, and surprise arrests. Actually, of course, the investigation in a case of homicide is a dull-enough business and it is extremely seldom that any innocent person is in the smallest degree likely to suffer anything but the inconvenience of routine.'

He was sitting with his back to the hall door. His face was strongly lit and the attention of the Lampreys was fixed upon it. Roberta, watching them, wondered if his assurances brought them any sense of relief. The quiet voice went on, clearly and without emphasis.

'– so, if I may, I would just like to ask you all to remember that, apart from the distress and sorrow that are the consequences of this crime, innocent people have nothing to fear beyond an exacting and wearisome series of questions. Presently I shall ask to see each of you separately. At the moment I think we shall get along a little quicker if we discuss things together. If Lady Wutherwood and – ' Alleyn hesitated, confronted by the embarrassment of twin titles.

'And Lady Wutherwood. Trap for young players,' said Frid in a sprightly manner.

'Frid!' said her father.

'Well, it is, Daddy. Aunt V. is the dowager now, isn't she? Violet, Lady Wutherwood. Or is she? Mr Alleyn wants both the ladies Wutherwood, I expect.'

'Please,' said Alleyn.

'I'll go and ask. I don't somehow think you'll have much luck, Mr Alleyn. My mother will come, of course. I'd better get Nanny while I'm at it. What about Aunt Kit, Daddy?'

Fox who had seated himself discreetly in the background glanced up in surprise and Alleyn said: 'Is there someone else?'

'I can't *imagine*,' said Lord Charles with an air of vexation, 'why nobody can remember Aunt Kit.'

'Well, she just popped off,' said Frid. 'We do remember her from time to time. Mummy said about an hour ago, "For pity's sake, what's become of Aunt Kit?" Shall I ring her up?'

'It's my aunt, Alleyn,' explained Lord Charles apologetically. 'Lady Katherine Lobe. She was here this afternoon but I'm afraid this terrible business put her out of our minds. She was with my wife just before it happened. I suppose she must have slipped away without realizing – I quite forgot to say anything about her. I'm so sorry. Shall we ring her up?'

'I think it might be as well,' said Alleyn. 'Her name is Lady Katherine Lobe, did you say?'

'Yes. Why?'

'The commissionaire saw her leave a few minutes before the accident was discovered.'

'Well,' said Lord Charles, 'I call it very odd to go off like that without a word. I hope to Heaven that nothing was the matter with her. We'd better ring her up. Frid, darling, will you?'

'Am I to tell her to come trundling in from Hammersmith?'

'I'll send the car,' said Lord Charles. 'Tell her I'll send the car, Frid, and then you'd better ring up Mayling. Mayling's my chauffeur, Alleyn. He wasn't here this afternoon, so I imagine – '

'That will do admirably.'

Frid knelt on a chair beside the desk and dialled a number.

'Aunt Kit,' said Henry, 'is almost quite deaf and not very bright. Shall I go and fetch my mama?'

'If you please.'

'And Aunt V.' Frid reminded Henry. She began talking into the telephone.

'Tell her about it gently, Frid,' said Lord Charles.

'She'll go into a flat spin anyway,' said Patch gloomily.

Henry went out into the hall. Colin said to nobody in particular: 'Isn't it rather a shame to summon Aunt Kit? I know maiden aunts are fashionable as murderesses but Mr Alleyn told us not to go by the detective novels. And honestly – Aunt Kit!'

'Even as a witness,' said Stephen, 'she'll be quite hopeless. She n-never knows what's going on under her own n-nose even.'

'Shut up,' hissed Frid. 'I can't hear. What did you say? What? But – oh well, thank you so much. Would you just say Miss Lamprey rang up. She knows our number. No, I'm afraid we don't but I expect it's quite all right really. Don't worry, Gibson. Goodnight.'

Frid replaced the receiver and gazed blankly at her father.

'It's a bit funny,' she said. 'Aunt Kit said she'd be in to dinner and there's someone coming to see her by appointment and, well, she's not telephoned or anything but she's simply not turned up.'

CHAPTER 9

Two, Two, the Lily-White Boys

Alleyn had been confronted with the Lampreys for only some twenty minutes but already he had begun to feel a little as though they were handfuls of wet sand which, as fast as he grasped them, were dragged through his fingers by the action of some mysterious undertow. He sent Fox off to find out, if possible from the commissionaire, when Lady Katherine Lobe had left the flat and what direction she had taken. Privately he instructed Fox to set the machinery of the department at work. Hospitals would be rung up, street accidents reported. And in the end, thought Alleyn, Lady Katherine would arrive home at half past eleven after an impulsive visit to the cinema. In the meantime he concentrated on the Lampreys still in hand.

Henry came back, bringing his mother and his old nurse. Again there were vague polite introductions for which Lady Charles did not wait. She advanced with a swift graciousness which Alleyn at once recognized as the fruit of an excellent social technique. They shook hands. Alleyn saw the small New Zealander give her hostess a startled glance and he wondered if Lady Charles Lamprey was usually so pale. But she greeted him with a perfection of manner that sketched with subtlety relief at his arrival, deference to his ability, and a delicate suggestion that they spoke the same language.

'Please forgive me,' she said, 'for keeping you waiting. My sister-in-law – ' she made a rueful grimace – 'too terribly upset. Henry says you want to see her.'

'I'm so sorry,' said Alleyn. 'I'm afraid I do.'

'At the moment she simply *can't* come. I mean I can't *move* her. Her maid may manage her better. She's going to try.'

'She must come, Immy,' said Lord Charles.

'Charlie darling, if you *saw* her. I mean *honestly.*'

'We'll carry on as we are for the present,' said Alleyn quickly. 'Has Dr Kantripp seen Lady Wutherwood?'

'Yes. He's given her something and the nurse is going to stay here tonight. Dr Kantripp guessed that you would ask to speak to her and said he would look in again later and see if she was up to it. Of course she's had the most appalling and overwhelming shock.'

'Of course.'

'She's not English,' said Lord Charles uncomfortably. Frid and Henry exchanged glances and grinned.

'Well,' said Alleyn hurriedly. 'To begin with – '

'Do sit down, everybody,' said Charlot. 'Nanny came too in case she was wanted.'

They sat down.

As he waited for a moment, collecting his thoughts and the attention of his audience, Alleyn received a sudden and extremely vivid impression of a united family.

Whatever their qualities of elusiveness, vagueness or apparent flippancy might be, he felt sure these qualities would never be used by the Lampreys against each other. They would always present a united if slightly ridiculous front. Until Lady Charles came in he had thought the children markedly resembled their father. He now saw that they bore in their faces and mannerisms confusing and subtle traces of both their parents. It was odd to see the complete separateness of Roberta Grey. Alleyn's attention had been arrested by Roberta, by her small compact figure, her pale face with its pointed chin and dark eyes set so very wide apart, by a certain air of grave watchfulness, by the Quakerish tidiness of her black dress and white collar. She had only arrived yesterday from New Zealand and yet she looked as though she had often sat on that Moroccan stool with her back set against the wall and her hands folded in her lap. And during the few seconds in which these impressions passed through his mind, Alleyn wondered if the Lampreys would close their ranks, and if in that case Roberta Grey would fall in with them. He had taken notes of Fox's enquiries. He now opened his book laid it on the arm of his chair. He began to speak.

'As far as we have gone,' he said, 'this is what seems to have happened. Lord Charles Lamprey and Lord Wutherwood were together in this room up to about ten minutes past seven. Lord Wutherwood decided to leave and went out of the room. He first rang the bell in the hall. Your butler, Baskett, answered it. Lord Wutherwood ordered his car. Baskett helped Lord Wutherwood into his coat and so on. I understand you didn't go out with your brother, sir?'

'No,' said Lord Charles. 'No. We said goodbye in here.'

'Yes. Baskett then opened the hall door. Lord Wutherwood went out to the lift. Baskett says that he was told not to wait and so returned to the servants' sitting-room. These notes, you will see, account for the movements, or some of the movements, of five persons during the few minutes after Lord Wutherwood left this room. Now, as Baskett left the hall and returned to the servants' sitting-room, he heard Lord Wutherwood call loudly for Lady Wutherwood. I should like to know next, if you please, how many of you also heard this call. Lady Charles – please forgive me if I still call you Lady Charles – '

'It will be much less muddling if you do, Mr Alleyn.'

'It will, won't it? Did you hear this call?'

'Oh, yes. Gabriel, my brother-in-law always shouted like that for people.'

'Where were you, please?'

'In my bedroom.'

Alleyn glanced at his note-book.

'I've made a very rough sketch-plan of both flats,' he said. 'Your room is the second from the lift end of No. 26?'

'Yes.'

'Were you alone?'

'When he shouted? No. My sister-in-law and – good heavens, Charlie, for pity's sake – '

'Yes, Immy, I know. Aunt Kit hasn't got home yet.'

'Not got *home?* But honestly, darling, it's too queer of Aunt Kit. We don't even know when she left. Why did she vanish like that, do you suppose?'

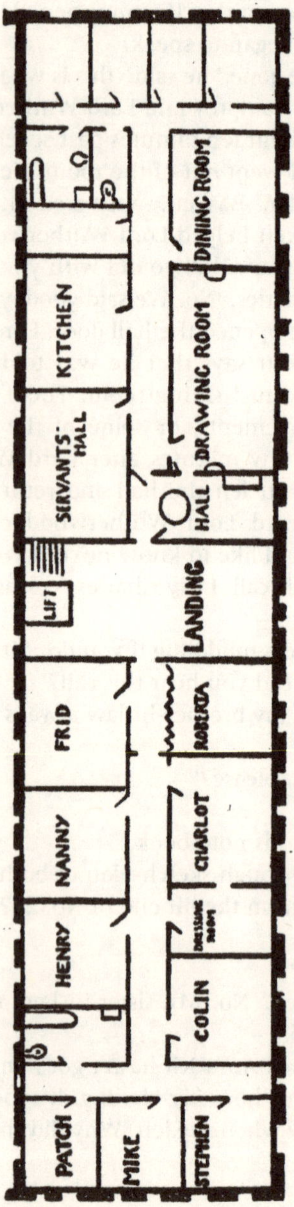
DINING ROOM
KITCHEN
DRAWING ROOM
SERVANTS' HALL
HALL
LIFT
LANDING
FRID
ROBERTA
CHARLOT
NANNY
HENRY
DRESSING ROOM
COLIN
PATCH
MIKE
STEPHEN

'I expect she just slipped away,' said Henry.

'She probably thought she'd said goodbye,' said Frid, 'you know how absent-minded she is.'

'I expect she *did* say goodbye, Mummy,' said Patch, 'and you didn't hear her. She talks in a whisper, Mr Alleyn.'

'What nonsense!' exclaimed Lady Charles. 'Of course I would know she was saying goodbye. For one thing she'd kiss me.'

'You might have thought she was just being effusive,' said Frid.

'She's always kissing people,' agreed Patch.

'Well, she didn't suddenly kiss me in the bedroom out of a clear sky,' said Lady Charles positively. 'Don't be absurd, Patch.'

'Lady Katherine was in your bedroom with Lady Wutherwood, then,' Alleyn interposed adroitly, 'when you heard the first call?'

'Yes, she was, and perfectly normal. She didn't hear Gabriel, of course, because she's deaf, but Violet did. Violet is my sister-in-law, Lady Wutherwood, you know.'

'Yes. What did they do?'

'Violet said she'd better not keep Gabriel waiting. She said she would like to go into the bathroom, so I told her about the one at the end of the passage.'

Lady Charles, who was sitting next to Alleyn leant over and looked at his note-book. 'Is this your plan?' she said.

'Let me see.'

'Immy, my dear!' protested her husband.

'Well, Charlie, I'm not going to read any of Mr Alleyn's notes and he'd snatch it away from me if there was anything secret in the drawing. There, it's as clear as daylight. That's the bathroom, Mr Alleyn. I told her where it was and off she went. And then Aunt Kit began to whisper – you know how that generation does – only even more so, because, as Patch says, she whispers anyway. So she went off to the other place which I see you've also got marked very neatly, and now I think of it that's the last I saw her.'

'It's as clear as glass,' Frid interrupted. 'She probably whispered: "I'll *have* to go. Bless you, my dear," and you thought she said: "Lavatory. I'll just disappear." '

'Anyone would think it was I who was deaf instead of Aunt Kit! She didn't say anything of the sort. She went down the passage in that direction.'

'Well, perhaps she's locked in,' suggested Frid. 'It happened to her once before, Mr Alleyn, on a railway station, and nobody heard her whispering.'

'Good Heavens, I wonder – '

'No, m'lady,' said Nanny firmly and unexpectedly.

'Oh. Are you certain, Nanny?'

With a scarlet face and a formidable frown Nanny said that she was certain.

'Then *that's* no good,' said Lady Charles. 'And then, Mr Alleyn, I waited for Violet. She was rather a long time and I remember that my brother-in-law shouted again for her. The two girls, Frid and Patch, came in, and then at last *she* came back and she reminded me that she and Gabriel didn't like working the lift themselves, so I came along here leaving her on the landing, and asked one of the boys to take her down.'

It seemed to Alleyn that as Lady Charles reached this point a curious stillness fell upon the room. He looked up quickly. The Lampreys had returned to their former postures. Lord Charles again swung his eyeglass, Henry's hands were again driven into his trouser pockets, and again the twins stared at the fire while Patch, her chin on her knees, squatted on the floor by Roberta Grey. And Miss Grey still sat erect on her stool. Alleyn was reminded of the childish game of Steps in which, whenever the 'he' had his back turned, the players creep nearer, only to freeze into immobility whenever he turns round and faces them. Alleyn felt sure that some signal had passed between the Lampreys, a signal that, by the fraction of a second, he himself had missed. At this hated and familiar sign of guardedness his own attention sharpened.

'Ah, yes,' he said. 'We may as well clear up this point as we come to it.' He looked at the twins. 'Mr Fox tells me that Lord Charles didn't notice which of you went down in the lift. Which was it?'

'I did,' said the twins.

So complete a silence fell upon the room that Alleyn heard a voice in the street below call for a taxi. The fire settled down in the grate with a little sigh and, as clearly as if, instead of sitting stone-still in their chairs, the Lampreys had made a swift concerted movement, Alleyn heard them close their ranks.

'Hallo,' he said amiably, 'a difference of opinion! Or did you both go down in the lift.'

'I went down, sir,' said the twins. Lord Charles, very white in the face, put his eyeglass away.

'My dear Alleyn,' he said, 'I must warn you that these two idiots have got some ridiculous idea of stonewalling us over this point. I have told them that it is extremely foolish and very wrong. I hope you will convince them of this.'

'I hope so, too,' said Alleyn. Out of the tail of his eye he saw Lady Charles's thin hands close on each other. He turned to her. 'Perhaps, Lady Charles, you will be able to clear this point up for us,' he said. 'Can you tell us who took Lord and Lady Wutherwood down in the lift?'

'No. I'm sorry. I didn't notice. One of the twins came out to the landing as soon as I asked for someone to work the lift.' She looked at the twins with a painful nakedness of devotion, made as if to speak to them, and was silent.

Alleyn waited. Fox returned and went silently to his chair. Nanny cleared her throat.

'Did anyone else,' asked Alleyn, 'notice which twin remained here and which went down in the lift?'

The twins looked at the fire. Frid made a sudden impatient movement. Henry lit a cigarette.

'No?' said Alleyn. 'Then we'll go on.'

There was a sort of stealthy shifting of positions. For the first time they all looked directly at him and he knew that they had expected him to pounce on this queer behaviour of the twins and were profoundly disconcerted by his refusal to do so. He went on steadily.

'When Lady Charles came and asked for someone to work the lift, Lady Frid and Lady Patricia were in their mother's bedroom, and their brothers were here in the drawing-room?'

'Yes,' said Henry.

'Where had you been before that?'

'In the dining-room.'

'All of you?'

'Yes. All of us. All the children and Roberta. Miss Grey.'

'While your father and Lord Wutherwood were talking in here?'

'Yes.'

'When did you leave the dining-room?'

'When the girls went out. The twins and I came in here.'

'And you, Miss Grey?'

'I stayed in the dining-room with Mike – with Michael.'

'And Michael,' said Alleyn, 'is of course now in bed?'

'He is,' said Nanny.

'Were you all in the dining-room when Lord Wutherwood called out?'

'Yes,' said Henry. 'He shouted "Violet!" twice. We were in the dining-room.'

'At what stage did Michael appear in the dining-room?'

Henry leant forward and pulled an ash-tray towards him. 'Not long before Uncle Gabriel called out. He'd been messing about with his trains in 26.'

'Right. *That's* perfectly clear. We've got to the moment when Lady Wutherwood and her escort went into the lift. Did you go out on the landing, Lady Charles?'

'I stood in the hall door and called out goodbye.'

'Yes? And then?'

'I turned back to come in here. I'd just gone to that table over there to get myself a cigarette when I heard – ' She only stopped for a second, 'when I heard my sister-in-law screaming. We all went out on the landing.'

'I'll go on,' said Henry. 'We went out to the landing. The lift came up. Aunt Violet was still screaming. Then whichever twin it was opened the lift doors and she sort of half fell out. Then we saw him.'

'Yes. Now, to go back a little way. This call Lord Wutherwood gave. Did it strike none of you as at all odd that he should sit in the lift and shout for Lady Wutherwood?'

'Not in the least,' said Frid. 'It was entirely in character. I can't tell you – '

'My brother,' interrupted Lord Charles hurriedly, 'was like that. I mean he did rather sit still and shout for people.'

'I see. You wouldn't say, on thinking it over, that there was any particular urgency in his voice?'

'I see what you mean, sir,' said Henry. 'I'm sure there was nothing wrong when he shouted. I'll swear nothing happened until after that.'

'But wait a moment.' Lady Charles leant forward and the light from a table lamp caught her face at an exacting angle. Shadows appeared beneath her eyes, her cheek-bones, shadows prolonged the small folds at the corners of her mouth and traced out the muscles of her neck. By that trick of lighting a prefiguration of age fell across her. Her voice sharpened. 'Wait a moment, all of you. Is it certain that he wasn't calling out in alarm? How do we know? How do we know that he hadn't seen something – someone?'

Alleyn saw Lord Charles look sharply at her.

'We don't *know*, of course,' he said slowly.

'Would any of you say there was an unusual quality in his voice?' asked Alleyn. For a moment nobody answered and then Henry said impatiently: 'He only sounded irritable.'

Frid said: 'Aunt V. had kept him waiting.'

Alleyn looked at Roberta. 'Lord Wutherwood was a comparative stranger to you, Miss Grey?'

'Yes.'

'Would you say that there was any particular ring of urgency or alarm in his voice?'

'I only thought that he sounded impatient,' said Roberta.

Alleyn waited for a moment and then with a freshening of his voice he said: 'Well now, to sum up. Each time Lord Wutherwood shouted, the younger members of the party were in the dining-room, Lady Charles was in her bedroom and Lord Charles was in here. Lady Wutherwood and Lady Katherine Lobe were with Lady Charles at the time of the first call. At the time of the second call they had gone severally to the bathroom and the other room at the far end of flat 26.'

'Neat as a new pin,' said Frid, and lit a cigarette.

'It doesn't take us very far, however,' said Alleyn. 'It merely leaves us with the presumption that at these times Lord Wutherwood was still uninjured.' He turned sharply in his chair, re-crossed his long legs and looked thoughtfully at the twins. The twins continued to stare at the fire while, under their clear skins, their faces rapidly turned a dull red. 'Yes,' said Alleyn. 'We arrive at a difficulty. The next step, as you will understand, is to find out the condition of Lord Wutherwood when Lady

Wutherwood and one or the other of these two gentlemen entered the lift. As both of these gentlemen agree that only one of them went down in the lift and as each of them protests that he was that one, it would appear that neither of their statements can be particularly valuable. At the moment I don't propose to argue this point. I propose, when she can see me, to ask for Lady Wutherwood's impressions of what happened when she entered the lift, and to find out from her exactly when the two uninjured occupants of the lift first realized what had happened. In the meantime, if I may, I should like to see Lord Wutherwood's chauffeur.' Alleyn glanced at his notes. 'Can his name be Giggle?'

'Yes, yes,' said Lady Charles drearily. 'The servants in both our families always have names like that. One of you boys go and find Giggle, will you?'

Alleyn watched the twin on the left-hand end of the sofa hitch himself up and walk away. 'That's the one that stammers,' thought Alleyn. 'He's got a mole behind his left ear.'

'Thank you, Stephen,' murmured his mother. The other twin stared uneasily at her, met Alleyn's glance and looked quickly away.

Alleyn asked Lady Charles when Dr Kantripp was expected to come back. She said that he had told her he had two visits to make and would call in to see Lady Wutherwood on his return. An image of Lady Wutherwood began to take hold of Alleyn's imagination and while he waited for Stephen Lamprey to fetch the chauffeur, he made a picture of her. She would be lying on Lady Charles's bed in the second room on the left in flat 26, the room next to that other where her husband waited for the police mortuary van. What was she like, this woman whose screams had risen with the returning lift, who had stumbled through the doors into Lady Charles's arms, who was (he remembered Lord Charles's profound uneasiness), not English? What lay at the back of her apparently severe prostration? Grief? Shock? Fear? Why did the Lampreys, incredibly garrulous on all other topics, close down on the subject of their aunt? It was not his habit to speculate on the characters of people whom he was about to interview, and he checked himself. Time enough for him to form an idea of Lady Wutherwood when he met her.

The far door opened. Stephen Lamprey came in followed by a tall man in a dark-grey chauffeur's uniform.

'This is G-Giggle,' said Stephen.

II

Evidently Giggle was nervous. He stood to attention and kept closing and unclosing his mechanic's hands. He sweated lightly and was inclined to show the white of his eyes. He had a large palish face and bleached eyebrows that met in a thicket over his snub nose. He eyed Alleyn with an air half-mulish, half-apprehensive, but gave his answers crisply enough, thinking for a moment, and then speaking without hesitation. Alleyn began by asking him if he knew what had happened to Lord Wutherwood. With an uneasy look at Lord Charles, Giggle said Mr Baskett had told him his lordship had met with a fatal accident.

'We are afraid,' said Alleyn, 'that it was not an accident.'

'No, sir?'

'No. It looks very much as though there has been foul play. You will understand that the police want to know the whereabouts of everyone in the flat from the time Lord Wutherwood was last seen, uninjured and apparently unthreatened, until the moment when the injury was discovered.'

He stopped and Giggle said doubtfully: 'Yes, sir.'

'All right. Now, did you hear his lordship call out after he went out on the lift landing?'

'Yes, sir.'

'Where were you?'

'In the passage, sir, in the flat. I'd been helping Master Michael with his train, sir.'

'Was Master Michael with you?'

'No, sir.'

'Do you know where he was?'

Giggle shifted his weight from one foot to the other. 'Well, sir, we was in the passage outside her ladyship's room and Master Michael saw a parcel in her ladyship's room and said something about giving it to his lordship. I mean his late lordship, sir.'

'Did Master Michael get this parcel?'

'Yes, sir.'

'And went away with it?'

'Yes, sir.'

Lord Charles cleared his throat and uttered a small deprecating sound. Alleyn turned to him.

'I'm so sorry, Alleyn. I quite forgot to tell you. Not that I imagine it can have the smallest bearing on anything. Michael had planned to give my brother a little present and actually came in here with it just before my brother went out.'

'I see, sir. There was no parcel in the lift.'

'No.' Lord Charles touched his moustache. 'No. Actually he didn't – he must have forgotten to take it.'

'Then it's still here?'

'I suppose so. I – '

'There it is,' said Frid. She went to the far end of the room and returned with a square brown-paper parcel. 'Do you want to see it, Mr Alleyn? Routine and all that.'

'Yes, please.' Alleyn took the parcel in his long hands. 'So he didn't open it?' he said.

'Well – well, no,' said Lord Charles. 'Actually I was talking to my brother and told Michael to put the parcel down. I didn't want to be interrupted.'

'I see, sir.' Alleyn turned the parcel over in his hand.

'Please, Mr Alleyn!' said Lady Charles suddenly, 'It's rather precious and terribly breakable.'

'I'm so sorry. I didn't realize. May I ask what it is?'

'A piece of Chinese pottery. As old as the hills and perfectly hideous, I think.'

'Good Heavens!' Alleyn put the parcel delicately on the table. 'Am I in a muddle,' he asked, 'or was Lord Wutherwood a collector? I seem to remember a loan exhibition – '

'That's right,' said Frid. 'There's a Ming or Ho or something gallery at Deepacres. All horses and smug goddesses, you know.'

'Well, Giggle,' said Alleyn, 'Master Michael got this parcel and went away with it. What did you do?'

'I waited for a while, sir, and then I heard his lordship call for her ladyship so I came along to this flat and got my coat and cap, sir, from the staff sitting-room and I looked in at the door to say I was going. Then I went downstairs, sir. Master Michael came as far as the landing.'

'I see. In coming across to this flat you used the landing?'

'Yes, sir.'

'Where was Lord Wutherwood?'

'His lordship was in the lift, sir.'
'Were the doors shut?'
'Yes, sir. I think they were.'
'Did he speak to you?'
'He told me to go down to the car, sir.'
'So you fetched your coat and hat, spoke to Master Michael, and returned to the landing?'
'Yes, sir.'
'Did you hear his lordship call a second time?'
'I can't say I remember, sir. I don't think so, sir.'
'Were the lift doors still shut when you returned?'
'I can't say, sir. I hurried downstairs, sir, without looking at the lift.'
'Yes, I see. What did you do then?'
'I went straight to the car, sir.'
'Meet anybody?'
'Beg pardon, sir? Yes, I did pass the commissionaire, sir.'
'Speak to him?'
Giggle turned a deep crimson. 'I just mentioned his lordship seemed to be in a bit of a hurry, sir.'
'How long were you in the car?'
'I couldn't rightly say, sir. Not long before Miss Tinkerton came down. She's her ladyship's maid, sir. She came downstairs and sat with me.'
'And then?'
Giggle looked towards Roberta. 'The young lady came and fetched us, sir.'
'You did, Miss Grey?'
'Yes.'
'We thought they might be wanted,' said Henry.
'Oh, yes. Thank you, Giggle, that'll do for the moment. I may want to see you later.'
'Thank you, sir.'
Giggle went away. Alleyn looked round that circle of politely attentive faces. 'That carries us to the time when Lord Wutherwood first called out, and, rather patchily, a little way beyond it. There's one small point we may as well clear up. I should like to know who wiped away the marks on the lift wall?'

'What marks?' asked Lord Charles while Roberta's heart sank into a chasm. 'I didn't notice any marks.'

'I did,' said Roberta, in a much louder voice than she intended, 'I wiped them off.'

'Why did you do this, Miss Grey?'

'I don't quite know.' Why had she wiped away the marks? 'I think it was because they looked so beastly. And I thought if other people used the lift – The lift was still working.'

'I see.' He was smiling at her. 'Just tidying up?'

'Yes.'

'You shouldn't, you know,' said Alleyn, dismissing it. 'Well,' he said, 'I don't think any purpose can be served by keeping you all together. I'm so sorry, Lady Charles, but I'm afraid I ought to see your small son.' Alleyn looked deprecatingly at Nanny, 'I know it's all against nursery law,' he said.

'The boy's worn out already,' said Nanny, 'sir.'

'Oh, Nanny, he isn't,' said Patch.

'That will do, Patricia.'

'Well, anyway – '

'It'll be a very nasty shock for him, m'lady,' said Nanny. 'Waking him up in the middle of the night and telling him his uncle's been done away with.'

'I'll explain, Nanny,' said Lady Charles.

'You needn't bother, Mummy,' said Patch. 'When I came out Mike was looking in the playbox for that magnifying glass you gave him. We guessed it was a murder and he thought he'd like to do some private detection.'

'*Honestly!*' said Frid, and burst out laughing.

'Look here, Nanny,' said Alleyn. 'Suppose you take me along to the nursery and stand by. If you think I'm exciting him you can order me out.'

Nanny pulled down the corners of her mouth, 'It's for his mother to say, sir,' she said.

'I think I'll just explain to Mike,' said Lady Charles, 'and bring him here to see you, Mr Alleyn.'

Alleyn stood up. The movement had the effect of calling them all to attention. Lady Charles rose and the men with her. She faced Alleyn. There was a brief silence.

Alleyn said: 'I think, if you don't mind, I'll go with Nanny. Of course if they think it would be advisable, his parents may be present while I speak to him.' Some shade of inflection in his voice seemed to catch the attention of the parents. Lady Charles said: 'Yes, I think I'd rather – ' hesitated and glanced at her husband.

'I'm sure Mr Alleyn will be very considerate with Mike,' he said, and behind the somewhat stylized courtesy which he was beginning to recognize as a characteristic of Lord Charles, Alleyn thought he heard a note of warning. Perhaps Lady Charles heard it too for she said quickly: 'Yes, of course. I expect Mike will be *too* thrilled. Nanny, will you wake him and explain?'

Alleyn went to the door and opened it. 'I don't expect we shall be very long,' he said.

Henry laughed unpleasantly. Frid said: 'When you've met Mike, Mr Alleyn, you'll realize that no one on earth could prime him with any story.'

'Don't be an ass, Frid,' said Colin.

'What you may not realize,' said Henry suddenly, 'is that Mike is a most accomplished little liar. He'll think he's telling the truth but if an agreeably dramatic invention occurs to him he'll use it.'

'How old is Michael?' Alleyn asked Lady Charles.

'Eleven.'

'Eleven? A splendid age. Do you know that in the police courts we regard small boys between the ages of ten and fifteen as ideal witnesses. They almost top the list.'

'Really?' said Henry. 'And what type of witness do the experts put at the bottom of the list?'

'Oh,' said Alleyn with his politely deprecating air, 'young people, you know. Young people of both sexes between the ages of sixteen and twenty-six.'

'Why?' asked the twins and Henry and Frid simultaneously.

'The textbooks say that they are generally rather unobservant,' Alleyn murmured. 'Too much absorbed in themselves and their own reactions. May we go, Nanny?'

Without a word Nanny led the way into the hall. Alleyn followed her and shut the door but not before he heard Frid say: 'And that, my dears, takes us off with a screech of laughter and a couple of loud thumps.'

CHAPTER 10

Statement from a Small Boy

Mike was fast asleep and therefore looked his best. The treachery of sleep is seen in the circumstances of its adding years to the middle-aged and taking them away from children. Mike's cheeks were filmy with roses, his lips were parted freshly and his lashes made endearing smudges under his delicate eyelids. His mouse-coloured hair was tousled and still moist from his bath. Near to his face one hand, touchingly defenceless, lay relaxed across the handle of a Woolworth magnifying glass. He looked about seven years old and alarmingly innocent. Nanny, scowling hideously, smoothed the bedclothes and laid a gnarled finger against Mike's cheek. Mike made a babyish sound and curled down closer in his bed.

'Damn' shame to wake him,' Alleyn said under his breath.

'Needs must, I suppose,' said Nanny, unexpectedly gracious. 'Michael.'

'Yes, Nanny?' said Mike and opened his eyes.

'Here's a gentleman to see you.'

'Gosh! Not a doctor!'

'No,' said Nanny grimly, 'a detective.'

Mike lay perfectly still and stared at Alleyn. Alleyn sat on the edge of the bed.

'I'm sorry to rouse you up,' he said civilly, 'but you know what these cases are. One must follow the trail while it's fresh.'

Mike swallowed and then, with admirable nonchalance said: 'I know.'

'I wonder if you'd mind going over one or two points with me.'

'Okay,' breathed Mike. He uttered a luxurious sigh.

'Then it *is* murder,' he said.

'Well, it looks a bit like it!'

'Golly!' said Mike, 'what a whizzer!' He appeared to think deeply for a moment and then said: 'I say, sir, have you got a clue?'

'At the moment,' said Alleyn, 'I am completely baffled.'

'Jiminy cricket!'

'I know.'

'Well, it wouldn't be any of us, of course.'

'Of course not,' said Nanny. 'It was some good-for-nothing out in the street. One of these Nazzys. The police will soon have them locked up.'

'An outside job,' said Mike deeply.

'That's what we're working on at the moment,' agreed Alleyn. 'But there are one or two points.' He looked at Mike's parted lips and brilliant eyes and thought: 'I must keep this unreal and how the devil I'm to do it's a problem. No element of danger but plenty of fictitious excitement.' He said, 'As a matter of fact it's quite possible that the bird has flown to a hide-out miles and miles away from here. We just want to check one or two points and I think you can help us. You were in the flat this afternoon, weren't you?'

'Yes. I was having a bit of a go with my Hornby train. Giggle helped me. He's absolutely wizard with trains. Being a motor expert helps, of course.'

'Yes, of course. Where do you do it? Not much room in here, is there?'

Mike shrugged his shoulders. 'Hopeless,' he said. 'We used the passage. And then, just when he'd got the coupling mended and everything, Giggle had to go.'

'So I suppose you simply carried on without him?'

'As a matter of fac', I didn't. Ackshully, Robin was going to play with me. You see I had to give Uncle G. the parcel.' Mike looked out the corners of his eyes at Nanny, 'I say,' he said, 'it's pretty funny to think of, isn't it? I mean, where *is* dead?'

'Heaven,' said Nanny firmly. 'Your Uncle Gabriel's as happy as the day's long. Well content, he is, you may depend upon it.'

'Well, Henry said this afternoon that Uncle G. could go to hell for all he cared.'

'Nonsense. You didn't hear Henry properly.'

'Where was the parcel?' asked Alleyn.

'In Mummy's room. Just by the screen inside the door. I couldn't find it when Robin said Mummy wanted me to give it to Uncle G.'

'When was that?' asked Alleyn, taking out his cigarette-case.

'Oh, before. After they'd done their charade. The others were horribly waxy because Uncle G. didn't look at the charade. Stephen said he was an old – '

'That'll do, Michael.'

'Well, Nanny, he did. I heard him when I was looking for the parcel.'

'Did you give the parcel up as a bad job?' asked Alleyn.

Mike shrugged again. It was a gesture that turned him momentarily into a miniature of his mother. 'Sort of,' he admitted. 'I went back to Giggle and the Hornby and then I saw the parcel. We were by the door.'

'Was anyone in the bedroom?'

'Mummy and Aunt V. and Aunt Kit had come in. They were gassing away behind the screen.'

'So what did you do?'

'Oh, I just scooped it up and took it to Uncle G. in the drawing-room. Uncle G. looked as waxy as hell.'

'Michael!'

'Well, sorry, Nanny, but he did. He didn't say anything. Not thank you or anything like that. He just goggled at me and Daddy told me to put it down and bunk. So I bunked. Patch said they had the manners of hogs and I think they had too. Not Daddy, of course.'

'Don't speak like that, Michael,' said Nanny. 'It's silly and rude. Mr Alleyn doesn't want to hear – '

'I *say*.' Mike sat up abruptly. 'You're not *Handsome Alleyn*, are you?'

Alleyn's face turned a brilliant red. 'You've been reading the lower type of newspapers, young Lamprey.'

'I say, you are! Gosh! I read all about the Gospell murder in "The True Detective!" A person in my form at school knew a person whose father is a friend of – gosh, of yours. He bucked about it for weeks. He won't buck much longer, ha-ha. I say, sir, I'm sorry I mentioned that name. You know – H.A.'

'That's all right.'

'I suppose you think it's a pretty feeble sort of nickname to have. At school,' said Mike lowering his voice, 'some people call me Potty. Potty Lamprey.'

'One lives down these things.'

'I know. Ackshully, I suppose you wouldn't remember a person called N. Bathgate. He's a reporter.'

'Nigel Bathgate? I know him very well indeed.'

Mick achieved an admirable expression of detachment. 'So,' he said off-handedly, 'as a matter of fac' do we. He told me he called you Hand – you know – as a sort of joke. In the paper. To make you waxy.'

'He did.' Mike giggled and gave Alleyn a sidelong glance.

'I suppose there's not much hope nowadays,' he said, 'for anybody to get into detection. I suppose you have to be rather super at everything.'

'Are you thinking of it?'

'As a matter of fac' I am, rather. But I suppose I'm too much of a fool to be any use.'

'It's largely a matter of training. What sort of memory have you got?'

'He's the most forgetful boy *I* ever had the training of,' said Nanny. Mike gave Alleyn a man-to-mannish look.

'Let's see how you shape,' Alleyn suggested. 'Have a stab at telling me as closely as you can remember just exactly what happened, let's say from the time you picked up the parcel and onwards. Go along inch by inch and tell me exactly what you saw and heard and smelt for the next fifteen minutes. That's the sort of stuff you have to do at this game.'

Alleyn opened his note-book. 'We'll say you're an expert witness and I'm taking your statement. Off you go. You picked up the parcel? With which hand?'

'With my left hand because I had a Hornby signal in my right.'

'Good. Go on.'

'Everything?'

'Everything.'

'Well, I stepped over the rails. Giggle was fitting two curved bits together. I said I wouldn't be a jiffy and he said all right, Master

Mike. And I walked down the passage past the curtains of Robin's room. Robin's room is generally a sort of hall in 26 but Mummy had the curtains put there to make a room and a passage. Is this the right way, sir?'

'Yes.'

'The curtains were shut. They're a kind of blue woolly stuff. The door at the end of the passage was shut. I opened it and went on to the landing.'

'Did you shut the door?'

'I don't think so,' said Mike simply. 'I hardly ever do. No, I didn't because I heard Giggle winding up the engine of the Hornby and I looked back at him.'

'Good. Then?'

'Well, I crossed the landing.'

'Was the lift up?'

'Yes, it was. You can see the light through the glass in the tops of the doors. There wasn't anybody on the landing or outside the lift. Not standing up, anyway. So I went into the hall of No. 25 and I don't suppose I shut the door. I'm afraid I'll be a bit feeble if you say I've got to describe the hall because there were all the things the others had for their charade. They'd just sort of bished them into the cupboard and they were bulging out and there were coats lying on the table and – ' Mike stopped and screwed up his eyes.

'What is it?'

'Well, sir, I'm just sort of trying to *see*.'

'That's right,' said Alleyn quietly. 'You know your brain is really rather like a camera. It takes a photograph of everything you see, only very often you never develop the photograph. Try to develop the photograph your brain took of the hall.'

Nanny said: 'The boy's getting flushed.'

'I'm not,' said Mike without opening his eyes. '*Honestly*, Nanny. Well, in my photograph the light is sort of coming through the window in front of me. Into my eyes. So everything has got its shadow coming my way. There's a thing of flowers on the round table and a bowler. I think it was Uncle G.'s bowler. And I saw Henry's gloves. And a scarf and some race-glasses and one of those hats people wear in hot places. Wait a bit, sir. There's something else. It's sort of on the edge of the picture. Not quite developed, like you said.'

'Yes?'

'I'll get it in a jiffy, all right. It's a shining kind of thing. Not 'zackly big but long and bright.'

Nanny uttered a brusque exclamation and made an anxious gesture with her hands as though she fended something away from herself and from Mike.

'Wait a bit,' Mike repeated impatiently. 'Don't tell me. Long and thin and bright.'

He opened his eyes and stared triumphantly at Alleyn, 'I've got it,' he said. 'It was on the edge of the table. One of those long pointed things they keep in the sideboard drawer. A skewer. That's what it was, sir. A skewer.'

II

Mike paused and regarded Alleyn with some complacency. Nobody stirred. The nursery clock ticked loudly on the mantelpiece. A little gust of wind shook the window panes. Down below in Pleasaunce Court a sequence of cars changed gears and accelerated. A paper-seller yelled something indistinguishable and somebody shouted 'Taxi!' Nanny's roughened hands, working together stealthily against her apron, made a faint susurration.

'They used it in their charade,' said Mike. 'I heard Frid yelling out for it?'

'The charade?' Alleyn echoed. 'Well, never mind. Go on.'

'About the skewer? Well, there's one thing – ' Mike stopped. His face lost its look of eagerness and, as small boys' faces can, became extremely blank.

'What's up?' asked Alleyn.

'I was only wondering. Is the skewer a clue?'

'Anything might be a clue,' said Alleyn carefully.

'I know. Only – '

'Yes?'

Mike asked in a small voice: 'What *happened* to Uncle G.?'

Alleyn took his time over this. 'He was hurt,' he said. 'Somebody went for him. It's all over now. Nothing of the sort can possibly happen again.'

Mike said: 'What was wrong with his eye?'

'It was hurt. People's eyes bleed rather easily, you know. Are you a boxer?'

'A bit. I was only wondering – '

'Yes?'

'About the skewer. You see I sort of remembered. After I tried to give the parcel to Uncle G. I went to the dining-room and after I went to the dining-room I went back with Giggle to the landing because Giggle was going away and we went through the hall and I said goodbye to Giggle because he's rather a friend of mine, and I saw him go downstairs and I leant on the table and – well, I was only just mentioning it because I happened to remember – well, anyway, the skewer wasn't on the table then.'

'Michael,' said Nanny loudly, 'don't make things up.'

'It *wasn't*. I put my hands where it would have been.'

There was another silence. Mike sat up and clasped his arms round his knees. 'Shall I go back?' he asked. 'Back to where I took the parcel to Uncle G.?'

'Yes,' said Alleyn, 'go back.'

'Well, that's everything I can remember about the first time in the hall. I went through the hall into the drawing-room. Daddy and him were by the fire. So I gave him the parcel. Well, I mean I didn't give it to him because of what Daddy told me. I mean it was a bit awkward.'

'What was awkward?'

'Uncle G. being in such a stink about something. Gosh, he was in a stink.'

'You mean he was upset?'

'Absolutely livid. Gosh, you should have seen his face! Jiminy cricket!'

'Don't exaggerate,' said Nanny. 'You're letting your fancy run away with you.'

'I am *not*,' cried Mike indignantly. 'He wants me to tell him ezackly all I can remember and I am telling him. You are silly, Nanny.'

'That will do, Michael.'

'Well, anyway – '

'Never mind,' Alleyn interrupted. 'Have you any idea why your uncle was angry?'

Nanny said: 'I don't think Michael ought to answer these questions without his parents' say that he may.'

'O *Nanny*!' cried Mike in accents of extreme provocation. 'You are!'

'Then we shall ask them to come in,' said Alleyn. 'Bailey.' A figure stepped out of the shadows on the other side of the scrap-covered screen by Mike's bed. 'Will you give my compliments to his lordship and ask him if he would mind coming to the nursery?'

'Very good, sir.'

'Is he another detective?' asked Mike when Bailey had gone.

'He's a finger-print expert.'

Mike suddenly gave a galvanic leap ending in a luxurious writhe among the blankets, 'I suppose he's brought his insnufferlater,' he said.

'All his kit,' agreed Alleyn gravely. 'What happened when you left the drawing-room?'

'Well, I went to the dining-room and talked to Robin. The others had gone out. And then Giggle came along and said he had to go because Uncle G. was yelling in the lift. So I went to the landing with Giggle and he went downstairs. When he'd gone Uncle G. yelled out for Aunt V. So I bunked into 26. Gosh, he did sound livid. Absolutely waxy. I bet I know why.'

'Are you sure he called out after Giggle had gone?'

'Yes, of course I am. Certain sure.'

'Did you see anybody else?'

'What? Let's see. Oh, yes. I saw Tinkerton in the hall.

I sort of just spotted her out of the tail of my eye. She was tidying up the wardrobe, I think.'

'Nobody else?'

'No.' Mike thrashed his legs about. 'Well, anyway,' he said, 'I'll jolly well tell you why – '

'You wait for your father, Michael,' said Nanny. Somewhat childishly, Mike thrust his fingers in his ears and, fixing a defiant gaze on his nurse, he shouted: it was because Mr Grumball and all the other – '

'Michael,' said Nanny in a really terrible voice. 'Do you hear what I tell you? Be quiet.' She reached out and pulled Mike's hands away from his ears. 'Be quiet,' she repeated.

Mike flew into a Lamprey rage of some violence. His cheeks flamed and his eyes blazed. He roared out a confused sequence of orders. Nanny was to leave him alone. Must he remind her that he was no longer under her complete authority? Did she realize his age? Why did she continue to treat him like a child? 'Like a silly damned kid,' roared poor Mike and, pausing to take breath, glared about him and encountered the cold gaze of his father. Lord Charles had come round the corner of the screen.

'Mike,' he said, 'may I ask you why you are making an ass of yourself?'

'Over-excited, m'lord,' said Nanny. 'I knew how it would be.'

Mike opened his mouth, found nothing to say, and beat on the counterpane with closed fists.

Alleyn, who had risen, said: 'You're not shaping too well at the moment, you know. You won't make anything of a policeman if you can't keep your temper.'

Mike stared at Alleyn. Tears welled into his large eyes. He hauled the bedclothes over his head and turned his face to the wall.

'Oh, damn!' said Alleyn softly.

'What *is* all this?' asked Lord Charles rather peevishly. Alleyn looked significantly at the crest of mouse-coloured hair which was all that could be seen of Mike, and turned down his thumb.

'I've blundered,' he said.

'Come outside,' said Lord Charles.

In the nursery passage, Alleyn closed the door and said: 'I'm afraid Michael is upset because your nurse quelled the remarkably steady flow of his narrative. He told me that in your interview with him, Lord Wutherwood had been annoyed about something. Nanny very properly suggested that you should be present. Michael, who is an enthusiastic maker of statements, resented her taking a hand.'

'Did he – ?'

'Yes, I'm afraid he did deliver himself of one rather curious phrase. I'm so sorry he's upset. If I may I should like to try and mend matters a little. If I could just say goodnight to him?' Alleyn looked at Lord Charles and added dryly: 'I hope you will come with me, sir.'

'The horse having apparently bolted,' said Lord Charles. 'I shall be glad to assist at the ceremony of closing the stable door.'

They returned to the nursery. Nanny had tidied up the bed. Mike lay with the sheet clutched to the lower part of his face. His eyes were tightly shut and his cheeks stained with tears.

'Sorry to wake you up again,' said Alleyn. 'I just wanted to ask if you would very kindly lend me that lens of yours. I could do with it.'

Without opening his eyes, Mike scuffled under the pillow and produced his Woolworth magnifying glass. He thrust it up. Alleyn took it. Mike was shaken by a sob and retreated farther under the sheet.

'It's a jolly good glass,' said a muffled voice.

'I can see that. Thank you so much. Goodnight, Lord Michael.'

The sheet was thrown back and Mike's eyes opened accusingly upon his father.

'*Daddy*!' he said. 'It's not going to be *that*!'

'Well,' said Lord Charles, 'well, yes. I'm afraid – well, yes, Mike, it is.'

'Good Lord, that puts the absolute lid on it! Good Lord, that's absolutely frightful! Good Lord,' repeated Mike on a note of tragedy, 'it's a damn' sight worse than Potty!'

III

Mr Fox had remained in the drawing-room with the Lampreys and Roberta Grey. Alleyn, on his return with Lord Charles, found Fox sitting in a tranquil attitude on a small chair, with the family grouped round him rather in the manner of an informal conversation piece. Fox had the air of a successful raconteur, the Lampreys that of an absorbed audience. Frid, in particular, was discovered sitting on the floor in an attitude of such rapt attention that Alleyn was immediately reminded of a piece of information gleaned earlier in the evening: Frid attended dramatic classes. On his superior's entrance, Fox rose to his feet. Frid turned upon Alleyn a gaze of embarrassing brilliance and said: 'Oh, but you *can't interrupt* him. He's telling us all about *you*.' Alleyn looked in astonishment at Fox who coughed slightly and made no remark. Alleyn turned to Lady Charles.

'Has Dr Kantripp come back?' he asked her.

'Yes. He's seeing my sister-in-law now. The nurse says she's a good deal better. So that's splendid, isn't it?'

'Splendid. We can't go very much further without Lady Wutherwood. I think, as you have kindly suggested, Lady Charles, the best plan will be for us to use the dining-room for a sort of office. I shall ask the police-constable on duty on the landing to come in here. Fox and I shall go to the dining-room and as soon as we have sorted out our notes I shall ask you to come in separately.'

Fox went out into the hall. 'What's the time?' asked Henry suddenly.

Alleyn looked at his watch. 'It's twenty past ten.'

'Good God!' Lord Charles ejaculated, 'I would have said it was long past midnight.'

'I think we ought to ring up Aunt Kit again, Charlie,' murmured Lady Charles.

'I think we ought to ring up Nigel Bathgate,' said Frid.

'Bathgate!' cried Alleyn, jerked to attention by this recurrence of his friend's name. 'Bathgate? But why?'

'He's a friend of yours, isn't he, Mr Alleyn? So he is of ours. As he's a pressman I thought it would be nice,' said Frid, 'to let him in at the death.'

'Frid, darling!' her mother expostulated.

'Well, Mummy darling, it *is* just that. Shall I ring Nigel up, Mr Alleyn?'

Alleyn stared at her. 'It's not a matter for us to decide, you know,' he said at last. 'He might serve to keep his fellow scavengers at bay. I may say that you will be creating a precedent if – if you actually invite a pressman to your house when – ' His voice petered out. He drove his fingers through his hair.

'Yes, I know,' said Lady Charles with an air of sympathy. 'We no doubt seem a very unbalanced family, poor Mr Alleyn, but you will find that there is generally a sort of method in our madness. After all, as Frid points out, it *would* be a help to Nigel Bathgate who works desperately hard at his odious job, and as *you* point out, it may save us from masses of avid red-faced reporters asking us difficult questions about Gabriel and poor Violet. Ring him up, Frid.'

Frid went to the telephone and a uniformed constable came in from the hall and stood inside the door. With the mental sensations usually associated with the gesture of throwing up one's hands and casting one's eyes towards Heaven, Alleyn joined Fox in the hall. He drew Fox on to the landing and shut the door behind them.

'And what the hell,' he asked, 'have you been telling that collection of certifiable grotesques about me?'

'About you, Mr Alleyn? Me?'

'Yes, you. Sitting there, with them clustered round your great fat knees as if it was a bedtime story. Who do you think you are? Oie-Luk-Oie the dream god, or what?'

'Well, sir,' said Fox placidly, 'they asked me such awkward questions about this case that one way and the other I was quite glad to switch off on to some of the old ones. I said nothing but what was to your credit. They think you're wonderful.'

'Like hell they do!' muttered Alleyn. 'Where's that doctor?'

'In with the dowager. I strolled along the passage but I couldn't pick anything up. She seems to be shedding tears.'

'I wish to high Heaven he'd give her a corpse-reviver and let her loose on us. I'll go along and wait for him. I've told that PC to note down anything they said.'

'I hope he'll keep his wits about him,' said Fox. 'He'll need 'em.'

'He's rather a bright young man,' said Alleyn. 'I think he'll be all right. I'll tell you one thing about the Lampreys, B'rer Fox. They're only mad nor'-nor'-west and then not so that you'd notice. They can tell a hawk from a handsaw, I promise you, or from a silver-plated meat skewer, if it comes to that. Get along to the dining-room. I'll catch the doctor as he comes out and I'll join you later.'

But as Alleyn crossed the landing he heard a muffled thump somewhere beneath him. He moved to the stairhead and looked down. Somebody was mounting the stairs, slowly, laboriously. He heard this person cross the landing of the flat beneath. He caught sight of a pancake-like hat, a pair of drooping shoulders, an uneven skirt. This new arrival assisted herself upstairs with her umbrella. That was the origin of the thumping sound. He heard breathing and another faint sibilant noise. She appeared to be whispering to herself. A sentence of Henry's came into Alleyn's memory. He coughed.

The toiling figure, now quite close, paid no attention. Alleyn coughed stertorously but to no effect. He moved so that his shadow fell across the stairs. The pancake hat tilted backwards revealing a few strands of grey hair and a flushed elderly face wearing an expression of exhausted enquiry.

'Oh,' she whispered, 'I didn't see – The lift doesn't seem to – Oh, I beg your pardon. I thought for a moment you were one of my nephews.'

Alleyn, remembering her name and praying no Lampreys would hear him and come out, said loudly: 'I'm so sorry if I startled you, Lady Katherine.'

'Not a bit. But I'm afraid I don't quite – I've got such a very bad memory.'

'We haven't met before,' shouted Alleyn. 'I wonder if I might have a word with you.' He saw that she hadn't heard him and in desperation groped for one of his official cards. Feeling ridiculous, he offered it to her. Lady Katherine peered at it, uttered a little cry of alarm and gazed at Alleyn with an expression of horror.

'Not the police!' she wailed. 'It hasn't come to that? Not already!'

IV

Alleyn wondered distractedly if there was anywhere at all in the flat where he could yell in privacy into the ear of this lady. He decided that the best place would be in the disconnected lift with the doors shut. By a series of inviting gestures he managed to lure her in. She sank on to the narrow seat. He had rime to reflect that Bailey and Thompson had finished their investigation of the lift. He leant against the doors and contemplated his witness. She was a little like a sheep, and a rapid association of ideas led him instantly to the White Queen. He bent towards her and she blinked apprehensively.

'I didn't realize,' he said loudly, 'that you knew this had happened.'

'What?'

'You know all about the accident?'

'About what?'

'This tragedy,' shouted Alleyn.

'Yes, indeed. Too distressing. My poor nephew.'

'I'm afraid it has proved to be serious.'

'He told me all about it this afternoon.'

'What!' Alleyn ejaculated.

'All about it, poor fellow.'

'Who did, Lady Katherine? Who told you?'

She shook her head at him. 'Very sad,' she said.

'Lady Katherine, *who told you what?*'

'Why, my nephew, Lord Charles Lamprey, to be sure. Who else? I do hope – ' She peered again at his card. 'I do hope, Mr Alleyn, that the police will not be too severe. I'm sure he regrets it very deeply.'

Alleyn swallowed noisily. 'Lady Katherine, what did he tell you?'

'About Gabriel and himself. My nephew Wutherwood and my nephew Charles. I was so terrified that it would come to this.'

'To what?'

'Even now,' said Lady Katherine, 'after this has happened I still hope that Gabriel may soften.'

Across Alleyn's thoughts ran a horrible phrase. 'Gabriel shall grow hard and Gabriel shall grow soft.' He pulled himself together, reassorted Lady Katherine's series of remarks and thought he began to see daylight.

'Of course,' he said, 'you left before – I mean when you left, Lord Wutherwood was still living.'

'What did you say?'

'I'm afraid,' roared Alleyn, changing his course again, 'I have bad news for you.'

'Very bad news,' agreed Lady Katherine with one of those half-knowledgeable phrases by which the deaf bewilder us. 'Very bad indeed.'

Alleyn threw all delicacy overboard. He placed his face on a level with Lady Katherine's and shouted, 'He's dead.'

Lady Katherine turned very pale and clasped her hands together. 'No, no!' she whispered. 'You didn't say – dead? Did you? I don't hear very well and I thought – Please tell me. It wasn't that?'

'I'm afraid so.'

'But – Oh, how terrible. And such a grave sin if – did he lay hands upon himself? Oh, poor Charlie. Poor Immy! And poor children!'

'Good God!' cried Alleyn. 'Not Lord Charles! *Lord Wutherwood. Lord Wutherwood is dead.*'

He saw the colour return in patches to her large soft cheeks.

'Gabriel?' she said quite loudly. 'Gabriel is dead?'

Alleyn nodded violently. For perhaps thirty seconds she said nothing and then on a sort of sigh she whispered astoundingly: 'Then I needn't have taken all this trouble.'

CHAPTER 11

Conversation Piece

Roberta had thought that when the two Scotland Yard officials went to the dining-room they would all be able to relax a little, and talk to each other in a normal fashion. It seemed to Roberta that, since the appearance of Alleyn and Fox, neither herself nor the Lampreys had been real persons. She was conscious, perhaps for the first time in her life, of making a deliberate and strenuous refusal to examine her own thoughts. Near the surface of her mind there waited, with the ominous insistence of images in a nightmare, a sequence of ideas and conjectures. And as, even during the experience of a nightmare, the dreamer may sometimes fight down his own images, so Roberta fought down the rising terrors of her thoughts, thrust them into the background, covered them with other thoughts less menacing to the love that six years ago she had so queerly dedicated to each one of the Lampreys. It seemed to her that the Lampreys themselves had completely withdrawn from her and that, without having had an opportunity to consult in private, they had nevertheless come to some understanding among themselves. She had hoped that when at last she was alone with them they would draw her towards them and, by an exhibition of the devastating frankness that so many of their friends mistook for a sign of flattering confidence, would let her join the common front they were to present to the police. But it appeared that they were not to be alone. Alleyn and Fox left a large policeman behind them and, more than anything else that had happened during that incredible evening, the sight of this stolid figure with scrubbed face and shining buttons, standing inside the drawing-room door, sent an icy thrill of panic through Roberta. Apparently the Lampreys were not so affected. Obeying a murmur from his mother, Colin offered the constable an armchair and asked him if he would like to move nearer to the fire at the opposite end of the room. With a glance at the man's note-book, Colin turned on a table lamp at his elbow. At this astonishing anticipation of his activities the constable turned a deep crimson, put away his note-book and hurriedly took it out again. Colin begged him to take the chair and in some confusion he finally sat down.

Colin rejoined his family at the other end of the room.

'*Eh bien,*' said Frid, '*maintenant, nous parlerons comme si le monsieur n'etait pas là.*'

'Frid!' cried her mother. '*Attention!*' Frid peered down the length of the room and, raising her voice, said to the constable: 'I do hope you won't mind us trying to talk in French. You see, we have got one or two things to discuss and as they are sort of rather private it will be less embarrassing for all of us, won't it? I mean, you won't feel that we are too odiously rude, will you?'

The policeman rose, cleared his throat and said: 'No, Miss,' and as though he ardently desired a ruling on the point, cast an anguished look at the door. After a moment's hesitation he again took the armchair offered by Colin, and now all the Lampreys could see of him was the top of his head which was red.

'*That's* all right, then, Mummy,' said Frid. '*Alors. A propos les jumeaux –* '

Roberta's heart sank. Charlot and Lord Charles, she knew, spoke French with some fluency. Frid had been to a finishing school in Paris. Henry and the twins had attended the university at Grenoble and had spent most of their holidays with friends on the Côte d'Azur. Even Patch and Mike, in the New Zealand days, had made life hideous for a sweating Frenchwoman who had followed the Lampreys to England and was still sporadically employed during the holidays. Roberta, on the contrary, had merely taken French at school and knew from bitter experience that when the Lampreys spoke in that language their conversation resembled a continuous rattle of fricatives and plosives, maddeningly leavened with occasional words that Roberta could understand. They were at it now. Lord Charles seemed to expostulate, Henry to argue. The twins were comparatively silent and looked mulish. Once, in answer to a prolonged harangue from Frid, Colin said: '*Laissez-vous donc tranquilles*, Frid. In fact, shut up.'

Henry said: 'This is fun for Robin, I must say.'

'Darling Robin,' said Charlot, 'you don't mind, do you?'

'Of course I don't. And I *have* followed a bit.'

'*Taisez-vous donc!*' commanded Frid dramatically. '*Ecoutez!*'

'What's the matter?' asked Henry testily.

'Listen, all of you.'

From a distant part of the flat came the sound of a deep voice.

'It's Mr Alleyn,' said Frid. 'What's he yelling like that for?'

'Perhaps he's flown into a black rage,' suggested Patch.

'Perhaps he's arresting Nanny or someone,' said Stephen.

'I must say I don't see why he should roar at her, even if he is. And anyway,' added Frid, 'he doesn't sound like that. He sounds as if he's yelling to someone downstairs.'

'Or to someone deaf,' Stephen amended.

'Good Heavens,' cried Charlot, 'can it be Aunt Kit?'

'Really, Immy!' said Lord Charles, 'why on earth should Aunt Kit come back here at this hour?'

'Everything is so odd that I don't consider the return of Aunt Kit at midnight would be at all surprising.'

'It isn't midnight,' said Patch.

'Mr Alleyn is growing fainter,' observed Colin. 'He must be going downstairs and roaring as he goes.'

'Perhaps,' suggested Patch, 'he's sitting in the lift and shouting to find out *si nous avons parlé vrai, au sujet de mon oncle.*'

'Patch, darling!' lamented Charlot, 'your *accent*. Honestly!'

'Well, I suppose we can't go and find out,' said Frid with a glance at the back of the constable's head.

'Good God!' ejaculated Lord Charles. 'It *is* Aunt Kit.'

And through the door into the drawing-room came Lady Katherine Lobe.

'Immy *darling*,' she whispered, as she embraced Charlot. 'So *terrible* but in a way such a dispensation. His ways are indeed mysterious and no doubt He has chosen this instrument. Charlie, my dear!'

'Aunt Kit, where have you been?'

'To Hampstead. By tube and bus. I should have returned sooner but most unfortunately I caught the wrong bus and then again

Mr Nathan took such a long time. And all for nothing as it turns out. Though even now with the death duties – '

'Whom did you go to see at Hampstead?'

'A Mr Isadore Z. Nathan, Charlie. I thought I should find him in his shop but of course when I left here it was after closing hours. But I found his private address in the telephone book and luckily he was at home. Such an amazing house, Immy. Enormous pictures and a great deal of velvet. But Mr Nathan was charming.'

'You *can't* mean Uncle Izzy from the pop-shop round the corner!' Frid ejaculated.

'What, darling?'

'Not the pawnbroker in Admiral Street, Aunt Kit?'

'Yes. You see, Charlie, I had often thought of doing it for my lame ducks, because it *did* seem rather extravagant and useless to pay all those large premiums when I am not well off, but as they were family things and almost the only family things that I had, I always imagined that mama would not have approved, so I didn't. But this was *quite* different because you *are* the family and it gave me the very greatest pleasure, darling. I *couldn't* be more pleased. Now, perhaps, you will feel you would like to redeem them, though, for the time being – '

'Aunt Kit,' said Lord Charles hastily, 'you're not talking about the Indian pearls?'

'What, dear?'

'Not Great-Aunt Caroline's pearls?'

'It's such luck that I always wear them.' Lady Katherine fumbled in her reticule and produced a slip of paper over which she enclosed Lord Charles's nerveless fingers.

'There, Charlie, my dear. And I'm *so* glad. I'm sure Mr Nathan is perfectly all right. He took a very long time examining them and you see I knew their value because of the insurance and I drove quite a shrewd bargain with him. I asked him to make the cheque out to you because – '

Charlot, rather belatedly, interrupted Lady Katherine with a loud patter of French. Lady Katherine peered towards the far end of the room, uttered a whispered ejaculation, and sank into the nearest chair. Lord Charles stared through his glass at the cheque, seemed to try to speak to his aunt, made a small helpless gesture and turned to his wife.

'Darling Aunt Kit,' began Charlot and stopped short. *'C'est trop* – '
She stopped again, 'I simply cannot go on *yelling* French,' said
Charlot. She glanced at the top of the policeman's head, went to the
desk near Roberta, drew out a sheet of paper, and took up her pen.

'Surely,' said Lady Katherine, 'he can't *dream* of thinking any of
you – ' She turned with an air of tragedy to her nephew. 'It's too
impossible,' she whispered. 'He seemed to be a gentleman.'

'Give her this,' said Charlot. Into Roberta's hand she thrust a
sheet of paper on which she had written in block capitals: 'Darling,
did you tell him we asked Gabriel for two thousand?'

In obedience to signals from the rest of the family, Roberta
displayed this communication before handing it to Lady Katherine
who instantly began to fumble for her glasses. These secured and
slung across her nose, she read Charlot's message, her lips forming
the words, her hands trembling. She laid the paper on her knees
and, looking piteously from one to the other of the Lampreys, she
whispered: 'I didn't tell him how much.'

Frid groaned. There was a short silence. Roberta watched Lady
Katherine's hand, swollen a little with arthritis and still trembling
very much, grope in her bag for a handkerchief. Suddenly Henry
walked over to his aunt and stooped to kiss her.

'Dear Aunt Kit,' said Henry gently. 'You are so kind.'

It was perhaps at this moment that Roberta first realized that she
was in love with Henry.

II

It is not easy to thank a deaf person for a large sum of money when
every word of thanks may compromise the speaker in the ears of an
attentive policeman. The Lampreys pulled themselves together and
made a pretty good job of it. Lady Katherine seemed to have some
difficulty in hearing French though she whispered away at it herself
with great fluency. The conversation was therefore conducted along
bi-lingual lines, the Lampreys' less dangerous remarks being made
in English, though Roberta thought there seemed to be very little
point in disguising the deplorable state of Lord Charles's finances if
Lady Katherine had already told Alleyn about the object of the

interview with her brother, and if Inspector Fox knew about Mr Grumball.

After a few minutes there was a tap on the far door which the constable opened. Fox's voice was heard in a brief mumble and in a moment he came in.

'Mr Alleyn, my lord,' said Fox, 'would be obliged if Lady Patricia could come to the dining-room for a few minutes.'

'Off you go, Patch,' said her mother. Her voice had lost nothing of its crispness, but, as Patch passed her, she took her hand and gave her a smile that to Roberta seemed like a brief flash of desperate anxiety. Patch went out.

'It's rather like French Revolutionary films,' said Frid. 'You know. The ones where the little group of aristocrats gets thinner and thinner.'

'For God's sake, Frid,' said Henry, 'hold your tongue.'

'Manners, love,' said Frid in Cockney.

The door opened again and Dr Kantripp came in. Roberta wondered if this endless night was to be punctuated by visits from Dr Kantripp. Each time he came in it was with the same hurried air of concern. Each time he shook hands with Charlot and with Lord Charles.

'Well,' he said, 'she'll do all right, Lady Charles. She's better. Had a sleep and less agitated. Still rather upset, of course. Inclined to be – ' He made an expressive gesture.

'Mad?' asked Frid. 'Stark ravers, would you say?'

'My dear girl, not that of course, but rather unsettled and unlike her usual self, no doubt.'

'My poor Dr Kantripp,' said Charlot, 'you don't know her usual self.'

'She's pretty grim even when at her jolliest, poor Violet,' said Lord Charles gloomily.

'Has there ever been any trouble?' asked Dr Kantripp delicately. 'Up aloft, you know? Hysteria and so forth?'

'We've always considered her a little odd,' said Lord Charles.

'A *little*, Daddy,' said Frid. 'My dears, let's face it, she's ga-ga. You know she is, Daddy. What about that nursing home she used to whizz off to?'

'An occasional *crise-de-nerfs*,' Lord Charles muttered.

'She's seen an alienist?'

'Yes, yes, I think so. Not for some time, though. She became a Christian Scientist about five years ago and I dare say my brother hoped that would help. But it didn't last very long and lately she's been tremendously taken up with some kind of occultism.'

'Black magic,' said Frid. 'She's a witch.'

'Dear me!' said Dr Kantripp mildly. 'Well,' he added, 'I've suggested that she should see her own doctor.'

'What did she say to that,' asked Charlot.

'She didn't say anything.' Dr Kantripp glanced at the constable. 'She doesn't say very much.'

'I know,' agreed Charlot. 'She just stares. It's rather alarming.'

'Do you know if she's in the habit of taking anything? Ah – aspirin? Anything to make her sleep?'

'I don't know,' said Charlot sharply. 'Why?'

'Oh, I merely thought that if there was anything already prescribed she might as well go on with the same dosage.'

'Tinkerton would know.'

'She doesn't know of anything.'

'Dr Kantripp,' Charlot began, 'what are you – ' She was interrupted with some violence by Stephen.

'*What's that!*' he demanded loudly. '*Listen!*'

There was a distant rumbling. A doorbell rang.

Baskett's step sounded in the passage and in a moment he came in.

'If Mr Fox might speak to you, my lord?'

'Yes, Baskett, of course.' Lord Charles hurried out. The door shut, but not before Roberta heard a sort of muffled rattle from the direction of the landing.

'That was the l-lift,' said Stephen. 'I thought the police had d-disconnected it.'

'They had,' said Henry.

'I think I know what it is,' said Dr Kantripp. 'Don't worry, Lady Charles. The police are attending to things, you know, and we have been expecting the – ah – the – '

'They're taking him away?'

'Yes.'

'I see. Does my sister-in-law know?'

'I asked the nurse to explain. Lady Wutherwood is so very – I didn't suggest that she should be present. Only distress her. If you'll excuse me I think I'd better have a word with Alleyn.'

He went out, meeting Patch in the doorway.

'I say,' said Patch, 'there are more men going into 26. They're using the lift.'

'Shut that door,' said Colin.

But even with the door shut they could hear unmistakable and heavy sounds of Uncle G.'s departure. Even the Lampreys had nothing to say and sat in an uncomfortable hush, listening and yet not appearing to listen. With a clank and a heavy mechanical sigh, Uncle G. went down again in the lift.

Henry moved to a window of the drawing-room, pulled aside the curtains and looked down into the street. The others watched him uneasily and in a moment the twins joined him. Unwillingly, Roberta read in their faces the stages of Uncle G.'s progress. Henry opened his window more widely. Down in Pleasaunce Court, doors were shut.

An engine started, a motor horn sounded. Henry dropped the curtain and turned back into the room.

'I suppose,' he said, 'I shall not be promoted to first suspect if I merely observe, thank God for that.'

'Patch,' said Charlot, 'has Mr Alleyn finished with you?'

'Yes, Mummy.'

'Then go to bed, darling. I'll come and say goodnight if I can. But don't stay awake for me. Run along.'

Patch wandered to the door where she turned. 'He hardly asked me anything,' she said. 'Only what we were all doing in the dining-room when – '

'*Pas pour le jeune homme,*' said Frid warningly.

Patch made a rapid grimace at the constable's chair and opened the door.

'Here, wait a minute,' cried Frid in alarm. But she was too late: Patch had gone.

'Look here,' said Frid to the constable, 'can I go after her? I want to ask her something.'

'I'm afraid you can't Miss. I can ask the young lady to come back, if it's any use,' offered the constable, who had risen to his feet.

'I don't think it is,' said Frid gloomily, 'her French isn't up to it.' She wandered in a desultory manner round the room.

Lord Charles came in from the hall and went to the fireplace. He leant his arms on the mantelpiece and his head on his arms.

'Well, old man?' said Charlot.

'Well, Immy,' he said without changing his position, 'they've taken him away. You didn't know him when he was a young man, did you?'

'No.'

'No. When we were boys we were good friends. It seems a queer thing for him to go away like this.'

'Yes,' said Charlot, 'I expect it does.' He went and sat beside her.

'Well,' said Henry, 'what happens now?'

'Examination of witnesses continues, I trust,' said Frid. 'Who do you say he'll ask for next? I'm longing for my turn.'

'Frid, my dear,' said her father, 'don't.'

'Don't what, Daddy?'

'Don't be quite so whatever it is you are being. We're all rather tired. Immy, ought I to ask if I may see Violet?'

'I don't think so, darling. Dr Kantripp says she seems to be much quieter and more sensible. No doubt she'll – '

The drawing-room door opened slowly. The young constable scrambled to his feet, followed, one after another, by the Lampreys. Framed in the doorway, supported on one hand by a uniformed nurse and on the other by her maid, stood the dowager Lady Wutherwood.

Roberta had been given a good many frights that evening and perhaps her resistance to shock had been weakened. There is no doubt that the appearance of Lady Wutherwood in the drawing-room doorway struck terror to Roberta's heart. It was as if some malicious stage-manager had planned this entrance along the best traditions of Victorian melodrama. By some chance of lighting, the colour of the green-painted door jamb was reflected in Lady Wutherwood's face. Her chin was lowered and her cavernously set eyes were in shadow while her mouth, which was wet but which still retained a trace of rouge, caught the light and glittered. The coils of dyed hair had become loosened and hung forward. Perhaps she had thrust Tinkerton aside, for her dress was ill-fastened and much in disarray. She seemed to have no bones. Even her hands showed no clear highlights on fingers and wrists, but hung puffily among the folds of her dress. Propped up by the nurse and maid, her posture was so odd that it suggested to Roberta a horrid notion. She thought

Lady Wutherwood looked for all the world as though she dangled by the neck like some ill-managed puppet. Her lips moved and so still was the room that Roberta heard that clicking sound as Lady Wutherwood arranged her mouth for speaking. But when she did speak it was in an unremarkable voice, a voice that held no overtones of tragedy or horror.

'Charles,' said Lady Wutherwood, 'I've come to see the police.'

'Yes, Violet. I'll tell them.'

'I've come to see them because there is something they must understand. They have taken away Gabriel's body. It must come back to me, to my house. The funeral will be from my house and nowhere else. I want to tell them that. Gabriel must come back.'

III

Charlot hurried to her sister-in-law's side and Roberta heard her speak in the voice she had used in the old days when one of the children was hurt or distressed. It was a tranquil voice but Lady Wutherwood seemed scarcely aware of it. The nurse professionally soothing said: 'Now, come along. We'll just sit and wait while they bring the doctor.'

'Not in there,' said Lady Wutherwood. 'I won't go into that room.'

'Now, now, dear.'

'Where is the detective? I must see the people in authority.' Lady Wutherwood's head turned with a rolling movement and from the shadowed caverns of her eyes she seemed to look at Charlot. 'Go away,' she said loudly.

Lord Charles turned to the constable. 'Will you tell Mr Alleyn?'

He said: 'Yes, my lord, certainly,' and looked at Lady Wutherwood who, with her escort, completely blocked the doorway.

'There's a chair in the passage, nurse,' said Charlot.

Tinkerton said: 'Come along now, m'lady,' in a thin voice but with an air of authority. Her mistress leant towards her and with a clumsy lurch turned and went into the passage, still supported by the two women. Charlot shut the door and eyeing her family spread out her hands and shrugged her shoulders.

'What,' she began, 'do you suppose – '

But Frid interrupted her. Frid, standing in the centre of the room, urgent, and for once unconsciously dramatic, harangued her family in a sort of impassioned whisper.

'Look here,' she said, 'he's out of the way. What are we going to do? What has Patch said we did in the dining-room?'

'Obviously,' said Henry, 'she told the truth.'

'She may have lied like a book.'

'Shall I whizz out and ask her?' Stephen suggested.

'My dear,' said Charlot, 'the place is solid with policemen. You'd be arrested.'

'Well,' said Frid impatiently, 'what shall we say? Quick. Before he comes back.'

'You will tell Alleyn the truth, Frid,' said Lord Charles.

'But, Daddy – '

'You will tell him the truth.' He looked at Lady Katherine. 'After all,' he added, 'nothing matters much now, after what has been already told.'

'But – all right, Daddy,' said Frid. 'The truth it is. I don't know what everybody else thinks, but to me it's pretty obvious who did it.'

The others stared at her. Frid gestured towards the door.

'Oh, *no*,' said her father.

'Daddy, but of *course*. She's mad. She's stark ravers. You know how they hated each other. And Mummy, you said that you left her alone when you came here to ask one of the boys to work the lift. She must have done it then. Who else?'

'Charlie, do you think – ?'

Lord Charles stared at his wife. 'Who else, Immy?' he said. 'Who else?'

'I think Frid's right,' said Stephen.

'Then,' said Henry, 'for God's sake come off your racket, you and Colin, and tell us who went down in the lift with them.'

Colin said: 'I went down in the lift.'

'Don't be a bloody fool,' said Stephen. 'If Aunt V. did it, what do you want to muck in for? You're mad.'

'You're both mad,' said Henry. 'If Aunt V. did it – '

'If Violet killed Gabriel,' said Charlot suddenly, 'it is not our business to do anything but clear ourselves.'

'Immy, my dear – '

'If it's you, Charlie, or one of my children, against Violet, then I'm against Violet. I believe Frid's right. If Violet killed Gabriel she's mad. She's been shut up before, she'll be shut up again. Does that matter so much? Does it matter so much, even if she didn't do it?'

'Immy!'

'A mad woman, and what's more, a horrible woman. You know you think she's horrible, Charlie. And if she wasn't demented before, she is now. She'll have to be shut up anyway. When I see Mr Alleyn I shall make it perfectly clear that Violet had the opportunity. And if he asks what the relationship has been between them I shall tell him. Why not. Why, in God's name, shouldn't I? You yourself say we should speak the truth. What is it but the truth that Violet and Gabriel have hated each other for years? We all know they have. Let us say so. What about that woman you told me Gabriel installed – '

'Immy – '

'I know, you've never told the children. Tell them now. Tell them.'

'It's all right, Mama,' said Henry, 'we know all about Uncle G.'s bits of nonsense.'

'Mummy's right,' said Frid. 'For God's sake let's stick to it. Aunt V. won't be hanged. It's odds on she did it. Then let them know as much as we know. The twins have put themselves in a pretty bad light with their Sydney Carton stuff. Let's get them out of it. If it's a twin or Aunt V., personally I prefer the twin. If she jabbed Uncle G. in the eye with a meat skewer – '

'I know,' said Henry, 'but if she didn't?'

'If she didn't, she only gets shut up. Which is what she ought to be anyway.'

'What,' asked Henry, 'does Robin think?'

But Robin, jerked abruptly into the picture, her thoughts racing down strange corridors, could only say with desperate emphasis that she knew none of them had done it, that she would do anything to save them from suspicion. And then, catching her breath over the implication of this avowal, she stopped short and looked with something like horror into Henry's eyes.

'It's no good, Robin,' said Henry, 'you've got your views. So have I. I've only just realized it. But I've got them.'

'What do you mean, Henry?' demanded Charlot, clenching her hands, 'we've only got a few seconds. That man will be back.'

'We can still talk in French,' said Frid.

'It's not the same. We don't understand each other in the same way.'

'We don't understand each other now,' said Henry.

'I don't know what you mean,' cried Charlot.

'I mean that I don't think Aunt V. killed Uncle G.'

'Why, why, why?'

'Because she's asked for his body.'

'She's mad,' said Frid.

'Mad or sane, and in my opinion she's not as mad as all that, I don't believe she'd want his company if she'd dug a skewer into his brain and murdered him.'

Nobody answered Henry. The silence was broken by Lady Katherine Lobe. Lady Katherine had turned her deaf inquisitive face to each of the Lampreys as they spoke. She now rose and going to her nephew laid her hand upon his arm.

'Charlie, my dear,' she said, 'what has happened to Violet? She looks like a lost soul. Charlie, what has Violet done?'

But before Lord Charles could answer his aunt the door opened and the constable returned.

CHAPTER 12

According to the Widow

Alleyn sat at the head of the dining-room table with Fox on his right hand and Dr Curtis on his left. Lady Wutherwood sat at the far end, with Tinkerton and the nurse standing behind her chair like a couple of eccentric parlour-maids. In the background, and just inside the door, stood a constable, looking queerly at home without his helmet. A little closer to the table and gravely attentive, Dr Kantripp looked on at this odd interview. At their first meeting Dr Kantripp had warned Alleyn that Lady Wutherwood was greatly shaken. 'I suppose she is,' Alleyn had said. 'One expects that, but you mean something else, don't you?' And Kantripp, looking guarded, muttered about hysteria, possible momentary derangement, extreme and morbid depression. In other words, a bit dotty.' Alleyn grunted. 'Curtis had better have a look at her, if you don't mind.' He left the doctors together and afterwards accepted Dr Curtis's view that Kantripp was walking like Agag but that it might be as well to wait a bit before they attempted an interview with Lady Wutherwood. 'She's got a nasty eye,' Curtis said. 'I couldn't get her to utter. Can't say anything on a mere look at the woman but she don't seem too bright. Kantripp's their family doctor but he's never seen *her* before. He seems to have got wind of a dubious history. Private home. Periods of depression. I should go slow.'

So Alleyn went slow, finished his examination of the flat and the servants, had his general interview with the family and his separate interviews with Mike and Patch. Patch, under pressure and with evidence of the liveliest reluctance, had informed him that while her father and uncle talked together in the drawing-room, she and her brothers and sister, together with Roberta, had lain down on the dining-room floor. It had been a kind of game, she said. 'Game be damned,' Alleyn had said after Patch left them. 'Look at that corner of the room. It's out of the regular beat and the carpet retains its pristine pile. That's where they lay. There's a smudge of brown boot polish off the toes of one of those blasted twin's shoes. Come over here.' He knelt by the sealed door. 'Yes, and there's a bit of red close to the crack. I can hear a murmuring of voices. Have a listen, Br'er Fox.'

Fox lay on the carpet and advanced his brick-coloured face towards the crack.

'By gum,' he said, 'they're talking French. It's the twin that doesn't stammer. Can you beat that? *"Taisez-vous donc."* That's French.'

'So it is,' said Alleyn. 'Leave them to it, just now, Br'er Fox. Yes, there's no doubt about it they had their ears to that sealed-up door there. Listening. Have you seen the bum, Fox?'

'Yes, Mr Alleyn. It's a matter of forty-one pounds. Lane and Eagle, house decorators of Beauchamp Place, put him in. Carpet, and a couple of armchairs. His name is Grimball not Grumball. They wouldn't know. I wouldn't be surprised if this Giggle is really called Higgins or something. They're like that – funny.'

'If they continue funny through this case,' Alleyn rejoined, 'it'll be a *tour de force*. Let them crack jokes at the coroner and see how he likes it.'

'Grimball says they're a very nice family.'

'So they may be. Damn' good company and as clever as a cage full of monkeys. They'll diddle us if we don't look out, Br'er Fox. The Lady Friede's as hard as they come. They've taken a line and they're going to stick to it. Look at those blasted twins. The noble lords Stephen and Colin, doing a Syracuse and Ephesus comedy turn. How the devil are we to find out which of them went down in the lift?'

'The widow?' Fox suggested.

'Don't you believe it. If they weren't very certain of themselves they wouldn't have taken the risk. I'll bet you their aunt will say she didn't know which twin it was. Equally I'll bet you their mother knows, and has taken her cue from her lily-white boys. Of course she knows. Can a mother's tender care muddle up the kids she bear, bad luck to them.'

'I never heard anything like it,' said Fox warmly. 'Trying to work off this twin stuff on the investigating officers. It's unheard of. You can't *have* that sort of nonsense.'

'And what are you going to do about it?'

'It's disgraceful. Come to think of it, it's a kind of contempt.'

'It's no good getting cross, Foxkin. Let us but once lose our tempers with the Lampreys and we're done. Yes? Come in. Open the door, Gibson.'

The red-headed constable, who had tapped on the door, was admitted by his mate.

'Why have you left your post?' snapped Fox.

'What is it, Martin?' asked Alleyn.

'I beg your pardon, sir, but I thought I'd better come. The dowager Lady Wutherwood's in the passage and wants to see you. So I thought I'd better come.'

'And as soon as you turned your back,' said Fox angrily, 'they got together and agreed on the tale they'd tell.'

'They've already done that, sir.'

'*What!*'

'While you were there?' asked Alleyn.

'Yes, sir. They spoke in French, sir. I've got it down in shorthand. They speak quite good French, with the exception of Lady Patricia. I thought that, before proceeding, you'd like to see what they said.'

'Here!' said Fox. 'Do you understand French?'

'Yes, Mr Fox. I lived at Concarneau until I was fifteen. I didn't know, Mr Alleyn, what the ruling was about listening-in under those circumstances. I don't remember anything in the regulations as to whether it could be put in as evidence. Seeing they didn't know.'

'We'll look it up,' said Alleyn dryly.

'Yes, sir. Will you see the dowager Lady Wutherwood, sir?'

'Give me your notes,' said Alleyn, 'and three minutes to look at them. Then bring her along. Wait a second. Did they say anything of importance?'

'They argued a good deal, sir. Principally about the two younger gentlemen. The twins. His lordship and Lady Friede wanted them to come clean. Her ladyship seemed to be frightened and rather in favour of nobody knowing which twin went down in the lift. Lord Henry was non-committal. They spoke principally about the motive against themselves, sir. I gather that Lord Charles – Lord Wutherwood – '

'Stick to Lord Charles,' said Fox irritably. 'The whole thing's lousy with lords and ladies. I beg your pardon, Mr Alleyn.'

'Not a bit, Brer Fox. Well, Martin?'

'It seems he's in debt for about two thousand, sir. Pressing, I mean. He asked Lord Wutherwood to lend him two thousand and he refused.'

'Yes, I see.' Alleyn had been looking at the notes. 'Well done, Martin. Now, go and tell Lady Wutherwood that I shall be very pleased and grateful and all the rest of it, if she'll be good enough to come in here. Then return to your shorthand. What's your impression of Lady Wutherwood?'

'Well, sir, she looks very peculiar to me. Either she's out of her mind, sir, or else she'd like everybody to think she was. That's how she struck me, sir.'

'Indeed? Well, off you go, Martin.'

The red-headed constable went out and Fox stared at Alleyn. 'We get some unexpected chaps in the force these days,' he said. 'In your time, sir, you were a bit of a rarity. Now they go round spitting foreign tongues all over the place. Did you know he spoke French?'

'I did, as it happened, Br'er Fox.'

'I must get him to try some on me,' said Fox with his air of simplicity. 'I don't get on as fast as I'd like.'

'You're getting on very nicely. Here she comes. Or rather, I fancy, here they come. I think I hear the voices of the medical gents.'

The door opened and the curious procession came in.

II

And now Alleyn faced the woman whom he had previously begun to think of as his principal witness. It was his practice to discourage in himself any imaginative speculation, but on seeing her he could not escape the feeling that with the belated appearance of Lady Wutherwood the case had darkened. She was, he thought, such a particularly odd-looking woman. She sat very still at the foot of the table and stared at him with remarkable fixedness. The presence of

Dr Kantripp and of the nurse and the maid lent an air of preposterous consequence to the scene. Lady Wutherwood might almost have been holding some sort of audience.

There was no doubt that she was antagonistic, but she had asked to see Alleyn and he decided that he would wait for her to open the conversation. And so it fell out that Lady Wutherwood and Alleyn, for perhaps half a minute, contemplated each other in silence across the long table.

At last she spoke. Her deep voice was unemphatic, her enunciation so level as to suggest that English was not her native tongue.

'When,' asked Lady Wutherwood, 'will my husband's body be given to me? They have taken him away. He must return.'

'If you wish it,' said Alleyn, 'certainly.'

'I do wish it. When?'

'Tomorrow night, perhaps?' Alleyn looked at Curtis who nodded. 'Tomorrow night, Lady Wutherwood.'

'What are they going to do with him?'

Curtis and Kantripp made deprecatory noises. The nurse put her hand on Lady Wutherwood's shoulder. Tinkerton, the maid, clucked thinly.

'Under the circumstances,' said Alleyn, 'there will be an examination.'

'What will they do to him?'

Dr Kantripp went to her and took her hand. 'Now, now,' he said, 'you must not distress yourself by thinking about these things.' He might have been a hundred miles away for all the notice she paid him. She did not withdraw her hand but he moved away, quickly and awkwardly.

'Will they do dreadful things to him?' she asked.

'The surgeon will examine the injury,' Alleyn said. She was silent for a moment and then on the same level note: 'Before he returns,' she said, 'tell them to cover his face.'

Curtis murmured something inaudible. Alleyn said: 'That will be done.'

'Tell them to cover it with something heavy and thick. Close down his eyes. The eyes of the dead can see where the eyes of the living are blind. That is established, else how could they find their way, as they sometimes do, into strange houses?'

Mr Fox wrote in his note-book, the nurse looked significantly towards Dr Kantripp. Tinkerton, over her mistress's shoulder, executed a little series of nods and grimaces and shakes of the head. Alleyn and Lady Wutherwood stared into each other's faces.

'That is all,' said Lady Wutherwood. 'But for one thing. It must be understood that I will not be touched or persecuted or followed. I warn you that there is a great peril in wait for anybody who intercepts me. I have a friend who guards me well. A very powerful friend. That is all.'

'Not quite,' said Alleyn. 'Lady Wutherwood, if you had not asked for this interview I should have done so. You see, the circumstances of your husband's death have obliged me to make very close inquiries.'

Without changing her posture or the fixed blankness of her gaze, she said: 'You had better be careful. You are in danger.'

'I,' murmured Alleyn. 'How should I be in danger?'

'My husband died because he offended against one greater than himself. I have not been told by whose agency he died. But I know the force that killed him.'

'What force is that?'

The corners of the shifting mouth moved up. Small wrinkles appeared about her eyes. Her face became a mask of an unlovely Comedy. She did not answer Alleyn's question.

'I must tell you,' he said, 'that if you know of anything that would explain even the smallest detail in the sequence of events that led to his death, you should let the police know what it is. On the other hand we cannot compel you to give information. You may think it advisable to send for your solicitor who, if he considers that you are likely to prejudice yourself by answering any question, will advise you not to do so.'

'I know very well,' said Lady Wutherwood, 'by what means I may be brought to betray myself into a confession of things I have not done and words I have never uttered. But I remember Marguerite Loundman of Begweiler, and Anna Ruffa of Douzy. As for a solicitor, I have no need or desire for such protection. I am well protected. I am in no danger.'

'In that case,' said Alleyn equitably, 'you will not object, perhaps, to answering one or two questions.'

She did not reply. He waited for a moment and had time to notice the scandalized expression of Mr Fox, and the alert and speculative glances of the two doctors.

'Lady Wutherwood,' said Alleyn, 'who took you down in the lift?'

She answered at once: it seemed to be one of his nephews.'

'Seemed?'

Lady Wutherwood laughed. 'Yes,' she said, 'seemed.'

'I don't understand that,' said Alleyn. 'Lady Charles Lamprey asked for one of her sons to take you down in the lift, didn't she?'

Lady Wutherwood nodded.

'And one of them came out of the flat and, in fact, entered the lift and took you down? You saw him come out? And you stood close beside him in the lift? It was one of the twins, wasn't it?'

'I thought so, then.'

'You thought so, then,' Alleyn repeated and was silent for a moment. Lady Wutherwood laughed again and her laughter, Alleyn thought, was for all the world like the cackle of one of the witches in a traditional rendering of *Macbeth*. This idea startled him and he went back in his mind over the string of inconsequent statements to which she had treated them. He was visited by an extremely odd notion.

'Lady Wutherwood,' he began, 'do you think it is possible that somebody impersonated one of the twin brothers?'

She gave him an extraordinary look and with a movement that startled them all by its abruptness and shocking irrelevancy, wrapped her arms across her breast and hugged herself. Then with a sidelong glance, horridly knowing, she nodded again very slightly.

'Was there any recognizable mark?' asked Alleyn.

Her right hand crept up to her neck and round to the back of it. She moved her head slightly and, catching sight of the nurse, hurriedly withdrew her hand and laid one of her fingers across her lips. And through Alleyn's thoughts ran the memory of three lines:

> 'You seem to understand me
> By each at once her choppy finger laying
> Upon her skinny lips.'

'Only,' thought Alleyn, 'Lady Wutherwood's finger is not choppy nor are her lips skinny. Damnation, what the devil is all this!'

And aloud he said: 'He stood with his back towards you in the lift?'

'Yes.'

'And you noticed the mark on the back of his neck?'

'I saw it.'

'Just there?' asked Alleyn, pointing to the startled Fox.

'Just there. It was a sign. Ssh! He does that sometimes.'

'The Little Master?' asked Alleyn.

'Ssh! Yes. Yes.'

'Do you think it happened before you were there? The attack on your husband, I mean.'

'He sat huddled in the corner, not speaking. I knew he was angry. He called for me in an angry voice. He had no right to treat me as he did. He should have been more careful. I warned him of his peril.'

'Did you speak to him when you entered the lift?'

'Why should I speak to him?' This was unanswerable. Alleyn pressed his questions, however, and gathered that Lady Wutherwood had scarcely glanced at her husband who was sitting in the corner of the lift with his hat over his eyes. With an unexpected turn for mimicry she slumped down in her own chair and sunk her chin on her chest. 'Like that,' she said, looking slyly at them from under her brows. 'He sat like that. I thought he was asleep.' Alleyn asked her when she first noticed that something was amiss. She said that when the lift was halfway down she turned to rouse him. She spoke to him and finally, thinking he was asleep, put her hand on his shoulder. He fell forward. When she had reached this point in her narrative she began to speak with great rapidity. Her words clattered together and her voice became shrill. Dr Kantripp gave the nurse a warning signal and they moved nearer to Lady Wutherwood.

'And there he was,' she gabbled, 'with a ring in his eye and a red ribbon on his face. He was yawning. His mouth was wide, *wide* open. To see him like that! Wasn't it wonderful, Tinkerton? Tinkerton, when I saw him, I knew it was all true and I opened my mouth like Gabriel and I screamed and screamed – '

'She's off,' said Dr Curtis gloomily, and rose to his feet. Lady Wutherwood's voice soared in the indecent crescendo of hysteria. Fox began methodically to shut the windows. Dr Kantripp issued crisp orders to Tinkerton who showed signs of following the example of her mistress, and was thrust out of the room by the nurse. The nurse suddenly became a dominant figure, bending in an authoritative manner over her patient. Alleyn went to the sideboard, dipped a handkerchief in a jug of water, and looked on with distaste while Dr Kantripp slapped it across and across the screaming face. The screams were broken by gasps and the disgusting sound of gnashing teeth. Kantripp who had his fingers on her wrist said loudly: 'You'll have to bring me that jug of water, nurse, if you please.'

Alleyn fetched the water. Curtis said: 'Unfortunate for the carpet,' and pulled a grimace. The nurse said in a firm, brightly genteel voice: 'Now, Lady Wutherwood, I'm afraid we must pour this *all* over you. *Isn't* that a shame?' Lady Wutherwood scarcely seemed to be aware of this impending disaster yet her paroxysms began to abate and in a few minutes she was led away by Dr Kantripp and the nurse.

III

'Open the window again, Br'er Fox, if you please,' said Alleyn. 'Let's get some air into the room. That was a singularly distasteful scene.'

'I suppose you know what you were both talking about?' said Dr Curtis, 'but I'm damned if I did.'

'What's your opinion of her, Curtis? No sign of epilepsy, was there?'

'None that I could see. Plain hysteria. That doesn't say there's nothing wrong mentally, of course.'

'No. What about it? Think she's ga-ga?'

'Ah,' said Dr Curtis, 'you're wondering if she's the answer to the detective's prayer for a nice homicidal lunatic.'

'Well,' said Alleyn, 'what about it? Is she?'

Dr Curtis pulled down his upper lip. 'Well, my dear chap, you know how tricky it is. She seemed to speak very wildly, of course, although I must say you appeared to take an intelligent hand in the conversation.'

'What was she getting at, Mr Alleyn?' asked Fox. 'All that stuff about having a powerful protector and it *seemed* to be one of the twins. You don't seriously suggest anybody impersonated one of those young fellows?'

'I don't, Fox, but she does.'

'Then she *must* be dotty. What was the big idea, anyway?'

'It's so damned preposterous that I hardly dare to think I'm on the right track. However, I'll tell you what I imagine was the burden of her song.'

Dr Kantripp returned. 'The nurse and the maid are getting her to bed,' he said. 'The maid will come along as soon as she can.'

'Right. Sit down, Dr Kantripp, and tell us what you know of this lady's history.'

'Very little,' said Dr Kantripp instantly. 'I never saw her until tonight. As far as I can gather from Lady Charles and the others, there's a history of eccentricity. You'd better ask them about that.'

'Yes, of course,' agreed Alleyn with his air of polite apology, 'but I thought that first of all I would just ask you. I suppose they didn't happen to mention whether the lady was interested in black magic?'

'Now, how the devil,' asked Dr Kantripp, 'did you get hold of that?'

'I was just going to explain. You heard her saying something about Marguerite Loundman of Gebweiler and Anna Ruffa of Douzy?'

'I've got them down in these notes,' said Fox, 'though I didn't know how to spell them.'

'Well, unless my extremely unreliable memory is letting me down, those two were a brace of medieval witches.'

'Oh, Lor',' said Fox disgustedly.

'Go on,' said Curtis.

'Taking them in conjunction with her suggestions that she had a powerful protector, that her husband had been punished, that she had warned him of his peril, that she recognized her lift conductor by a mark on his neck, that this was a sign from her Little Master, together with all the rest of her mumbo-jumbo, I came to the preposterous conclusion that Lady Wutherwood thinks her husband was destroyed by a demon.'

'Oh, no, really!' cried Dr Curtis. 'It's a little too much.'

'Have you ever come across a book called *Compendium Maleficorum?*'

'I have not. Why?'

'I don't mind betting Lady Wutherwood's got a copy.'

'You think she's been mucking about with some sort of occultism and gone so far that she actually has hallucinations or illusions.'

'Is it so very unusual among women of her age, restless by temperament, to become hag-ridden by the bogus-occult?'

'You come across some funny things,' said Fox, 'in these fortune-telling cases. I suppose you might say this is only going a step further.'

'That's it, Br'er Fox. If it's genuine.'

'You surely don't believe – ' began Dr Kantripp.

'Of course not. I mean, if Lady Wutherwood's apparent condition is genuine, she's just another gullible woman with a taste for the occult. But is her condition genuine?' Alleyn looked at Dr Kantripp. 'What do you say?'

'I should like to see more of her and hear more of her history before venturing on an opinion,' said Dr Kantripp uneasily.

'And also,' murmured Alleyn, 'you would like, I fancy, to consult with the family.'

'My dear Alleyn!'

'I'm not trying to be offensive. Please don't think that. But as well as being the Lampreys' family doctor you are, aren't you, personally rather attached to them?'

'I think everybody who gets involved with the Lampreys ends by falling for them,' said Dr Kantripp. 'They've got something. Charm, I suppose. You'll fall for it yourself if you see much of them.'

'Shall I?' asked Alleyn vaguely. 'That conjures up a lamentable picture, doesn't it? The investigating officer who fell to doting on his suspects. Now, look here. You are two eminent medical gents. I should be extremely grateful for your opinion on the lady who has just made such a very dramatic exit. Without prejudice and all that – which way would you bet? Was the lady shamming or was she not? Come now, it won't be used against you. Give me a snap judgement, do.'

'Well,' said Dr Curtis, 'on sight I – it's completely unorthodox to say so, of course – but on sight and signs I incline to think she was not shamming. There was no change in her eye. The characteristic look persisted. And when you turned away there were no sharp glances to see how you were taking it. If she was shamming it was a well-sustained effort.'

'I thought so,' said Alleyn. 'There was no "see how mad I am" stuff. And there was, didn't you think, that uncanny thread of logic that one finds in the mentally unsound? But of course she may be as eccentric as a rabbit on skates and not come within the meaning of the act. "It is quite impossible," as Mr Taylor says, "to define the term insanity with any precision." '

'In this case,' said Kantripp, 'you needn't try. It doesn't arise.'

'If,' said Fox in his stolid way, 'she'd killed her husband?'

'Yes,' agreed Alleyn, 'if she had done that.'

Dr Kantripp put his hands in his trouser pockets, took them out again, and walked restlessly round the room.

'If she had done that,' Alleyn repeated, 'the question of her sanity or degree of insanity would be of the very first importance.'

'Yes, yes, that's obvious. As a matter of fact I understand that she has paid visits to some sort of nursing home. You can find out where and what it is, no doubt. Frid seemed to suggest there had been a bit of mental trouble at some time but – see here, Alleyn, do you suspect her of murder? Have you any reason to suppose there's a motive?'

'No more reason, perhaps, than I have for suspecting motive with the Lampreys.'

'But, damn it all,' Dr Kantripp burst out, 'you can't possibly think any one of those delightful lunatics is capable – to my mind it's absolutely grotesque to imagine for one moment – I mean, look at them.'

'Look at the field if it comes to that,' said Alleyn. 'The Lampreys, Lady Katherine Lobe. Lady Wutherwood – '

'And the servants.'

'And the servants. The nurse, the butler, the cook, and the housemaids belonging to this flat; and the chauffeur and lady's maid belonging to the Wutherwoods. Oh, *and* a bailiff's man at present in possession here.'

'Good Lord!'

'Yes. I expect when Messrs Lane and Eagle learn in the morning's paper that Lord Charles has come in for the peerage, they will slacken the pressure. But in the meantime there is Mr Grumball, the bum-bailiff, to be added to the list of possibles. A fanciful speculation might suggest that Mr Grumball fell for the Lamprey charm and, moved by remorse and distaste for his job, altruistically decided to murder Lord Wutherwood; or, if you like, that Mr Grumball dispatched Lord Wutherwood as an indirect but certain method of collecting the debt.'

'I'd believe that,' said Dr Kantripp rather defiantly, 'before I'd believe one of the Lampreys did it.'

'How would you describe the Lampreys?' asked Alleyn abruptly.

'You've met them.'

'I know. But to someone who hadn't met them. Suppose you had to find a string of appropriate adjectives for the Lampreys, what would they be? Charming, of course. What else?'

'What the devil does it matter how I describe them?'

'I should like to hear, however.'

'Good Lord! Well, amusing, and ah – well ah – '

'Upright?' suggested Alleyn. 'Business-like? Scrupulous? Reliable? Any of those jump to the mind?'

'They're kind,' said Dr Kantripp turning rather red. 'They're extremely good-natured. They wouldn't hurt a fly.'

'Never do anybody any sort of injury?'

'Never, wittingly, I'm sure.'

'Scrupulous over money matters?'

'Very generous. Look here, Alleyn, I know what you're driving at but it's no good. They may be in a hole. They may be a bit vague about accounts and expenses and what-not. I don't say they're not. Since we're being so amazingly unprofessional, I don't mind confessing I wish they did tidy up their bills a bit more regularly. The whole thing is that while they've got money they blue it and when they haven't they can't haul in their sails. But it's only because they're vague. It never occurs to them that other people don't live in the same way. They don't really think that money is of any importance. They would never in this world do anything desperate to get money. They couldn't. It's the way they are bred, I suppose.'

'Oh, no,' said Alleyn. 'I don't agree with that. Business-consciences aren't entirely bounded by the little fences of class, are they? However, that is beside the point.'

'Well, look here,' said Dr Kantripp hastily, 'I really must run along. Curtis has got my address if you should want me. I asked Lady Wutherwood about her own doctor and she said she hadn't one. Hadn't had a consultation for three years. I've got *his* man, if it's relevant. Cairnstock, the brain man we called in, you know, has left a report. He couldn't wait to see you, but Mr Fox was here.'

'Yes, Fox got the report.'

'Right. Well, goodbye, Alleyn.' Dr Kantripp offered his hand. 'I – ah – I hope you will find – ah – '

'Somebody,' suggested Alleyn with a faint twinkle, 'that nobody is at all fond of?'

'Oh well, dammit, it's a nasty business, isn't it?' said Dr Kantripp who presented the agreeable paradox of a man in a tearing hurry, unable to take his departure when there was nothing to stop him. 'She'll do all right. Lady W., I mean. I've given her a sedative and so on.' He went to the door and executed a little shuffle. 'Ah – Curtis will tell you we noticed – ah – a slight condition of the – ah – the eyes.'

'Pin-point pupils?' asked Alleyn.

'Oh, you saw that, did you? Well – ah – Goodbye. Goodbye, Fox. Goodbye.'

'Very awkward for him,' said Alleyn, after the door had shut.

CHAPTER 13

The Sanity of Lady Wutherwood

'It'll take that Abigail some time to stow away her mistress for the night,' said Alleyn. 'Before she comes back, let's go over what we've got. Check me as I go, Br'er Fox. We've got, in a half-baked sort of way, the positions of the Lampreys and Co., according to themselves, from the time their charade came to an end until the time they carried him, dying and unconscious, out of the lift. We now know which of the twins took him down in the lift?'

'Do we?' asked Dr Curtis.

'Oh, yes, rather. I'll come to that in a bit. We know the Lampreys are in deep water and we gather they had hopes of extracting two thousand pounds from the victim. We know they used the skewer in their charade, that it was lying on the hall table just before Lord Wutherwood left the drawing-room, and that it had disappeared a few minutes later. Young Michael is our authority here, and he's very positive about it. So it looks as though our homicide was somebody who was in the hall at a moment after Lord W. went to the lift and before Michael returned to the hall from the dining-room. According to evidence; during this brief interlude the Ladies Friede and Patricia went from the dining-room to Lady Charles's bedroom in flat 26, and therefore passed through the hall. The Ladies Wutherwood and Katherine Lobe went from the bedroom to their respective lavatories and did *not* pass through the hall. Lady Katherine afterwards stole out to visit a pawnbroker. She tells me she didn't enter this flat. Lord Charles remained in the drawing-room where he was later joined by his sons who did not pass through the hall; Giggle, the chauffeur, went from the passage in 26 to the servants' hall in this flat, thence to the dining-room where he collected Michael, who saw him go downstairs. The fact that Lord Wutherwood was heard to call out again in a normal manner, after this, is a good mark for Giggle but will have to be checked. As for the servants, you've found, haven't you, Fox, that the butler, Baskett, was in the servants' sitting-room with the exception of a trip to the hall where he put Lord W. into his coat and gave him his scarf and bowler. From this trip to the hall, he returned directly to the sitting-room. One maid was out, the other was in the kitchen with the cook and the sinister Mr Grumball. Nanny, a redoubtable dragon, was in the room with Lady Wutherwood's maid, Miss Tinkerton. Presumably Tinkerton left to get her bonnet and tippet from the servants' hall and subsequently went downstairs. But Tinkerton's movements are vague, as she has been too much in waiting on her mistress for us to question her. That will be attended to in a moment. Now then. All this is hellishly involved, but one infuriating fact emerges. According to their several accounts of themselves it would have been possible for any one of them to have slipped into the hall, grabbed the skewer, and subsequently have visited the lift. If one of the Lampreys did this, the others will no doubt lie like flatfish to save his or her mutton. The girls will swear they did not separate. So will the boys. But Lord Charles and Lady Charles *were* alone for some of the time. So, by the way, was that quiet little New Zealander, who I must say has visited her Motherland in time for a pretty holiday. All right. At the moment we can't wipe anybody off the slate with the exception of the cook, the maid, and the bum. As a lively coda to all this rigmarole, follows the suggestion that Lady W. did not love her lord, and although she screamed industriously all the way up in the lift, was not altogether astonished that he should die of a meat skewer in his eye. And, by that same token, Curtis, wouldn't you expect him to die a bit sooner? That thing must have made a filthy mess of his brain, surely?'

'Just now,' said Dr Curtis, 'you quoted Taylor. Do you remember the American Crowbar Case?'

'Phineas P. Gage?'

'The same. Do you remember that an iron rod forty-three inches long and one and a quarter inches in diameter, with a tapering point and weighing thirteen and a quarter pounds, passed completely through Phineas's head?'

' "There was much haemorrhage," ' Alleyn chanted drearily, ' "and escape of brain matter." '

'He eventually recovered all his faculties of body and mind – '

' " – with the loss of the injured eye." I knew you'd flatten me with Phineas P. And what of Mr J. Collyer Adam (Public Prosecutor, Madras) and his case of the man with the knife in his forehead?'

'Well,' said Dr Curtis with a grin, 'with those examples before you, what d'you mean by asking why he didn't die sooner? For all we know, until I've had a peep inside, he might have survived to tell you 'oo done it and saved us all a night's work.'

'He's got a swinging great crack on the temple,' Alleyn observed.

'Yes. I was going to ask you how you account for it.'

'The smudge, inefficiently removed off the chromium steel boss in the lift-wall, accounts for it. So, I fancy, do the bruises on the right temple and round the eyes, and the cut on the left temple, as well as a dent in the side of Lord W.'s bowler and the bloodstains on a pair of driving gloves we found in the lift. Henry Lamprey's gloves, they are, as he very airily admitted. Michael saw them in the hall, so no doubt they were taken at the same time as the knife. I get a picture of a great buffet on the side of the head. Then I see a picture of a left hand laid thumb downwards across the eyes, with the heel of the hand against the right temple. The head is pressed hard against the wall. While the left hand is still in position and the subject unconscious, the point of the skewer, held in the right hand and guided through the fingers of the left, completes a singularly nasty piece of work.'

'A bit conjectural, isn't it?'

'Before they took the body away, Fox and I made an experiment. We stopped the lift at the uninhabited flat below this one and reconstructed the scene. Luckily rigor was not far advanced. The body fitted the marks exactly. The dent in the bowler tallies with a bit of chromium steel fancy-work above the stain. Thompson's taken some shots of it. The results should be illuminating and calculated to give a tender jury-man convulsions. And here, I fancy, comes Miss Tinkerton.'

II

Tinkerton was a thin ambling sort of woman of about fifty. The only expression observable in her face was one of faint disapproval. She was colourless, not only in complexion, or merely because she gave no impression of character; but all over and in detail. Her eyes, her lashes, her lips, her voice, and her movements, were all without colour. It was as if she existed in a state of having recently uttered the phrase 'not quite nice', and forgotten its inspiration, while her mouth idiotically maintained the form given by the sentiment. She was dressed with great neatness in clothes that, a long time ago, might have belonged to someone else but had since absorbed nonentity. She wore pince-nez and a hair net. When Alleyn invited her to sit down, she edged round a chair and, with an air of suspicion, cautiously lowered her rump. She fixed her eyes on the edge of the table.

'Well, Tinkerton,' said Alleyn, 'I hope her ladyship has settled down more comfortably.'

'Yes, sir.'

'Is she asleep, do you know?'

'Yes, sir.'

'Then she won't need you again, we hope. I've asked you to come in here because we want you, if you will, to give us as detailed account as you can of your movements from the time you came here this afternoon, until the discovery of Lord Wutherwood's injury. We are asking everybody who was in the flat to account as far as possible for their movements. Can you remember yours, do you think?'

'Yes, sir.'

'Right. You arrived with Lord and Lady Wutherwood in their car. We'll start there.'

But it was a thin account they got from Tinkerton. She did not seem actually to resent the interview, but she maintained a question-and-answer attitude, replying in the most meagre phrases, never responding to Alleyn's invitation for a running narrative. It seemed that she spent most of the visit with Nanny in her sitting-room, from which she emerged at some vague moment and went to the servants' hall in flat 25. By dint of patient and dogged questions, Alleyn discovered that on leaving Nanny's room she found Giggle and Michael playing trains in the passage, and the rest of the Lamprey children in the hall of flat 25, dressing themselves for their charade. Tinkerton waited modestly on the landing until they went into the drawing-room and then slipped across into the passage and the servants' hall where she met Baskett with whom she enjoyed conversation and a glass of sherry. She also called on cook. She could give no idea of the time occupied by these visits. On being pressed for further information, she said she had washed her hands in flat 25. From this ambiguous employment she went down the passage towards the hall, meaning to return to Nanny in flat 26. However, she saw Baskett in the hall, putting Lord Wutherwood into his coat. She immediately went into the servants' sitting-room, heard Lord Wutherwood yell for his wife, collected her handbag, and hurried to the landing in time to see Giggle go downstairs. Alleyn got her to repeat this. 'I want to be very clear about it. You were in the passage. You looked into the hall where you caught a glimpse of Lord Wutherwood and Baskett. You went into the servants' sitting-room, which was close at hand, picked up your bag, went out again, walked along the passage, through the hall, and on to the landing. Did you meet any one?'

'No,' she said. She answered nothing immediately but met each question with an air of obstinate disapproval.

'You simply saw Giggle's back as he made for the stairs. Anyone else?'

'Master Michael was going into the other flat.'

'Where was Lord Wutherwood when you reached the landing?'

'In the lift.'

'Sitting down?'

'Yes, sir.'

'Sure?'

'Yes, sir.'

'All right. Will you go on, please?'

Tinkerton primmed her lips.

'What did you do after that?' asked Alleyn patiently.

Tinkerton said huffily that she followed Giggle downstairs. She remembered hearing Lord Wutherwood yell a second time. When he did that she was already some way downstairs. She joined Giggle in the car and remained there with him until the young lady came to fetch them. This came out inch by reluctant inch.

Alleyn made very careful notes, taking her over the stages of her movements several times. She seemed to be perfectly sure of her own accuracy and repeated monotonously that she had seen nobody but Giggle and Michael, as she went along the passage, through the hall, across the landing and downstairs.

'Please think very carefully,' Alleyn repeated. 'You saw nobody else? You are absolutely positive?'

'Yes, sir.'

'All right,' said Alleyn cheerfully. 'And now, what did you talk about all the afternoon?' At this sudden change of tone and of tactics, Tinkerton's air of disapproval deepened. 'I really couldn't say, sir,' she said thinly.

'You mean you don't remember?'

'I don't recollect.'

'But you must remember *something*, Tinkerton. You had a long chat with Lady Charles Lamprey's nurse didn't you? It must have been a long chat, you know, because when you came out Giggle and Master Michael were playing trains and they didn't do that until some time after your arrival. What did you and Nanny (Mrs Burnaby, isn't she?) discuss together?'

Tinkerton primmed her lips again and said several things were mentioned.

'Well, let us hear some of them.'

Tinkerton said: 'The young ladies and gentlemen came up.'

'Of course,' said Alleyn amiably, 'you would discuss the family. Naturally.'

'They came up,' Tinkerton repeated guardedly.

'In what connection?'

'Mrs Burnaby brought them up,' said Tinkerton, as if Nanny had suffered from a surfeit of Lampreys and had taken an emetic for it. 'Miss Friede's theatricals. I should,' added Tinkerton, 'have said Lady Friede. Pardon.'

'I suppose you are all very interested in her theatricals?'

A slightly acid tinge crept over Tinkerton's face as she agreed that they were.

'And in all the family's doings, I expect. Did Lord and Lady Wutherwood often pay visits to this flat?'

Not very often, it seemed. Alleyn began to feel as if Tinkerton was a bad cork and himself an inefficient cork-screw, drawing out unimportant fragments, while large lumps of testimony fell into the wine and were lost.

'So this visit was quite an event,' he suggested. 'Have you been in the London house for long?'

'No.'

'For how long?'

'We have not been there.'

'You mean you arrived in London today.' She didn't answer. 'Is that what you mean? Where did you come from?'

'From Deepacres.'

'From Deepacres? That's in Kent, isn't it? Did you come straight to this flat?'

'Yes, sir.'

'Had his lordship ever done that before, do you know?'

'I don't recollect.'

'When were you to return to Deepacres?'

'Her ladyship remarked to his lordship on the way up, that she would like to stay in town for a few days.'

'What did he say to that?'

'His lordship did not wish to remain in town. His lordship wished to return tomorrow.'

'What decision did they come to?' asked Alleyn. Was it imagination, or had he got a slightly firm grip on the cork?

'His lordship,' said Tinkerton, 'remarked that he had been dragged up to London and wouldn't stay away longer than one night.'

'Then,' said Alleyn, 'they had come to London solely on account of this visit to the flat?'

'I believe so, sir.'

'Where were you to spend the night?'

'In his lordship's town residence,' said Tinkerton genteelly. '14 Brummell Street, Park Lane.'

'At such short notice?'

'A skeleton staff is kept there,' said Tinkerton. 'Of course,' she added.

'Do you know why this visit was undertaken?'

'His lordship received a telegram yesterday.'

'From Lord Charles Lamprey?'

'I believe so.'

'Have you any idea why Lord Charles wanted to see his brother?'

Tinkerton's expression of disapproval became still deeper. Alleyn thought he saw a glint of complacency behind it. Perhaps, after all, Miss Tinkerton was not altogether proof against the delights of gossip.

'Her ladyship,' she said, 'mentioned that it was a business visit. H'm.'

'And do you know the nature of the business?'

'It came up,' said Tinkerton, 'on the drive during conversation between his lordship and her ladyship.'

'Yes?'

'I sat with Mr Giggle in front and did not catch the remarks, beyond a word here and there.'

'Still, you gathered – '

'I did not listen,' said Tinkerton, 'of course.'

'Of course not.'

'But his lordship raised his voice once or twice and said he would not do something that his brother wished him to do.'

'What was that, do you know?'

'It was money-matters.' Something very like a sneer appeared on Tinkerton's lips.

'What sort of money-matters?'

'The usual thing. Wanting his lordship to pay out.'

He could get no more from her than that. She showed no particular reluctance to answering his questions and no particular interest in them. He began to wonder if she had any warmth of feeling or any sense of partizanship in her make-up. As an experiment, he led the conversation towards Lady Wutherwood, and found that Tinkerton had been in her service for fifteen years. Her ladyship she said mincingly, was always very kind. Alleyn remembered those lack-lustre eyes and that sagging mouth and wondered wherein the kindness lay. He asked Tinkerton if she had noticed any change in her mistress. Tinkerton said dully that her ladyship was always the same, very kind. 'And generous?' Alleyn ventured. Yes, it seemed her ladyship was generous and considerate. Pressing a little more persistently Alleyn asked if she had noticed no mental instability in Lady Wutherwood. Tinkerton instantly became an oyster and to his next questions either answered no, or did not answer at all. She did not think Lady Wutherwood's behaviour was so very peculiar. She could not say whether Lady Wutherwood was interested in the occult. Lady Wutherwood did not take any medicine or drug of any sort. Lady Wutherwood's relations with her husband were not in any way unusual. She couldn't say what sort of nursing-home it was that Lady Wutherwood went to. She did not notice anything very odd in Lady Wutherwood's manner a few minutes ago. Her ladyship was upset, said Tinkerton of her own accord, and people often spoke wildly when they were upset. It was only natural.

'Was that why you made signs to the nurse over her ladyship's shoulder?' asked Alleyn.

'Her ladyship is suffering from shock,' said Tinkerton in a burst of comparative candour. 'I understand her ladyship. I knew she ought not to be upset by questions. I knew she ought to be in bed.'

It was the same thing when they came to the late Lord Wutherwood. He was, said Tinkerton, a very quiet gentleman. She wouldn't describe him as mean nor would she describe him as generous. She couldn't say whether he had understood his wife. By using the strictest economy of words Tinkerton managed to convey the impression that Alleyn was making an exhibition of himself and, if that was really her opinion, he was inclined to agree with her. He ran out of questions and sat looking at this infuriating woman. Suddenly he rose to his feet and, walking round the table, stood over her. Unlike most tall men Alleyn had the trick of swift movement. Tinkerton stiffened uneasily on the edge of her chair.

'You know, of course, that Lord Wutherwood was murdered?'

She actually turned rather pale.

'You know that?' Alleyn repeated.

'Everybody is saying so, sir.'

'Who is everybody. You have been with Lady Wutherwood ever since it happened. Does she say her husband was murdered?'

'The nurse said so.'

'Did the nurse tell you how he died?'

'Yes, sir.'

'What did she tell you? Describe it, exactly, if you please.'

Tinkerton moistened her lips. 'The nurse said he was injured with a knife.'

'What sort of knife?'

'I mean a skewer.'

'How was it done?'

'The nurse said he had been stabbed through his eye.'

'Who did it?' Tinkerton gaped at him. 'You heard me, I think,' said Alleyn. 'Who murdered Lord Wutherwood?'

'I don't know. I don't know anything about it.'

'You know he must have been killed by someone in this flat.'

'The nurse said so.'

'It was so. Very well, then. You understand that if you can prove it was impossible for you to have stabbed Lord Wutherwood through his eye into his brain, you had better do so.'

'But I said – I said I was downstairs when he was still calling her ladyship. I said so.'

'How am I to know that is true?'

'Mr Giggle will have heard. He knew I was behind him. Ask Mr Giggle.'

'I have asked him. He doesn't remember hearing Lord Wutherwood call a second time.'

'But he did call a second time, sir. I tell you I heard him, sir. Mr Giggle must have been too far down to have heard. I was behind Mr Giggle.'

'And you say you met nobody and saw nobody as you passed along the passage, through the hall, and across the landing?'

'Only Mr Giggle, sir, and he didn't notice me. I just caught sight of his back as he went down and Master Michael's back as he went into the other flat. Before God, sir, it's true.'

'You are voluble enough,' said Alleyn, 'when it comes to your own safety.'

'It's true,' Tinkerton repeated shrilly. 'I've said nothing that wasn't true.'

'You've been with Lady Wutherwood fifteen years yet you don't know the name of the nursing-home she went to nor why she went. You don't know whether she is interested in the supernatural or whether she isn't. You say she never takes any medicine or drug. Do you still insist that all three statements are truthful?'

'I won't talk about my lady. My lady hasn't done anything wrong. She's frightened and ill and shocked. It's not my place to answer questions about her.'

Her hands worked dryly together against the fabric of her skirt. Alleyn watched her for a moment and then turned aside.

'All right,' he said. 'We'll leave it at that. Before you go I want you to mark on this plan, your exact position when Master Michael went into the other flat and when you saw Lord Wutherwood sitting in the lift.'

'I don't know that I remember exactly.'

'Try.'

He put his sketch-plan on the table with a pencil.

Tinkerton took the pencil in her left hand and, after consideration, made two faint dots on the plan.

'Your statement will be written out in longhand,' said Alleyn, 'and you will be asked to sign it. That's all for the moment. Thank you. Goodnight.'

III

'You were remarkably crisp with the woman,' said Curtis. 'I've never heard you less amiable. What was wrong?'

'She's a liar,' said Alleyn.

'Because she wouldn't talk about her mistress? Wasn't that rather commendable?'

'Not because of that. She told a string of lies. Have a look at the statement later on and you'll spot them.'

'You flatter me, I'm afraid. Why was she lying, do you suppose?'

'Not because she murdered Master,' grunted Alleyn. 'It's a right-handed job if ever there was one.'

'She may be ambidexterous.'

'I don't think so. She opened and closed the door, marked the plan, and took out her handkerchief, with the left hand. She used the left hand every time she ministered to Lady Wutherwood. She's not our pigeon unless she's an accessory to the blasted fact. What do you think, Fox?'

'I should say she's got a snug job with her ladyship,' said Fox, glancing up from his notes and over the top of his glasses.

'Well, I must be off,' said Curtis. 'See about this PM. Fox rang up the coroner. I'll start first thing in the morning. Cairnstock has an operation tomorrow and said he'd come and have a look later on. Don't expect we'll find anything of interest to you. I'll ring you up about midday. Goodnight.'

He went out. Fox closed his note-book and removed his spectacles. Somewhere in the flat a clock struck eleven.

'Well, Br'er Fox,' said Alleyn. 'So it goes on. We'd better see another Lamprey. What's your fancy? Suppose we follow Master Henry's suggestion and talk to his mother.'

'Very good,' said Fox.

'We'd better let Lady Katherine go home. We can't keep them all boxed up in here indefinitely, I suppose.' He looked at the constable. 'My compliments to Lady Charles Lamprey, Gibson, and I'd be grateful if she could spare me a few minutes. And say that we shall not trouble Lady Katherine Lobe any further tonight. You won't call them Lady Lamprey and Lady Lobe, will you? And warn the man on duty in the entrance that Lady Katherine is to be allowed out. She lives at Hammersmith, Fox. We'll have to keep an eye on her, I suppose.'

'She's not exactly the cut of a murderess, is she?' Fox remarked.

'You wouldn't say so. You wouldn't say she was the cut of a fairy, either, but apparently she vanishes.'

'How d'you make that out, Mr Alleyn?'

'According to herself, she met Michael on the landing just as he was going into the other flat. Tinkerton saw Michael but didn't see Lady Katherine.'

'Perhaps the young gentleman made two trips, Mr Alleyn.'

'The young gentleman is our prize witness up to date, Fox. He tells the truth. As far as one can judge the family talent for embroidery has given him a miss. He's a good boy, is young Michael. No. Either Tinkerton added another lie to her bag or else – '

Gibson, the constable, opened the door and stood aside. Lady Charles Lamprey came in.

'Here I am, Mr Alleyn,' she said, 'but I hope you don't expect any intelligent answers because I promise you that you won't get them from me. If you told me that Aunt Kit was steeped in Gabriel's blood I should only say: "Fancy. So it's Aunt Kit after all. How too naughty of her." '

He pulled out the armchair at the foot of the table and she sank down on it, taking the weight of her body on her wrists as elderly people do.

'Of course you must be deadly tired,' Alleyn said. 'Do you know, that is the one thing that seems to happen to all people alike when a case of this sort crops up? Everyone feels mentally and physically exhausted. It's a sort of carry over from shock, I suppose.'

'It's very unpleasant whatever it is. Would you be an angel and see if there are cigarettes on the sideboard?'

The box was empty. 'Would you like to ring for some,' Alleyn asked, 'or would these be any use?' He opened his case and put it on the table in front of her with an ashtray and matches. 'They are your sort, I think.'

'So they are. That *is* kind. But I must see that there are some here, because if we are going to be any time at all I shall smoke all these and then what will you do?'

'Please smoke them. I'm not allowed cigarettes on duty.'

He watched her light the cigarette and inhale deeply. Her hands were not quite steady.

'Now I'm ready for anything,' she said.

'It won't be a solemn affair. I just want to check over your own movements, which seem to be very plain sailing and then I'll ask you to tell me anything you can think of that may help us to sort things out a little.'

'I expect I'm much more likely to muddle them up, but I'll try to keep my head.'

'According to my notes,' said Alleyn, looking dubiously at them, 'you went to your room with Lady Wutherwood and Lady Katherine Lobe and remained there until you heard Lord Wutherwood call for the second time. Then, followed by Lady Wutherwood, you went to the drawing-room.'

'Yes. She didn't come into the drawing-room, you know. I hurried on ahead of her.'

'To ask for someone to take them down in the lift?'

'Yes,' she said steadily, 'that's it.'

'Did you see anybody else on your way to the drawing-room?'

'I think Mike was in the passage. Nobody else.'

'And Lord Wutherwood was in the lift?'

'I suppose he was. I didn't look. He sounded cross so I rather skidded past, do you know?'

'I see. And then you asked for someone to work the lift and Mr Stephen Lamprey went out and worked it.'

IV

Alleyn felt, rather than heard, her draw in her breath. She said lightly: 'No, that's not quite right. You remember that we don't know which twin went out.'

'I think I know,' said Alleyn. 'I'm not trying to trap you into an admission. We'll leave it that a twin went out and you followed, as far as the hall, to say goodbye. Lady Wutherwood got into the lift and you returned to the drawing-room. That's all right?'

'About me – yes.'

'I'll ask you to sign it later, if you will. What I hope you will do now, is give us some sort of sidelight on Lord Wutherwood himself. I'm afraid many of my questions will sound impertinent. Perhaps the most offensive part of police investigation is the ferreting. We have to ferret, you know, like anything.'

'Ferret away,' said Lady Charles.

'Well, can you think of anybody who would want to kill Lord Wutherwood?'

'That's not ferreting, it's more like bombing. I can't think of anybody who, in their right minds, would actually and literally want to kill Gabriel. I expect lots of people have, as one says, *felt* like killing him. He was a frightfully irritating fellow, poor dear. Not a fragment of charm and so drearily *un-gay*, do you know? I mean, it does help if people are *gay*, doesn't it? I set *enormous* store on gaiety. But of course one doesn't kill people simply because they are not exactly one's own cup of tea and I suppose he had his grey little pleasures. He was passionately interested in plumbing and drainage, I understand, and carried out all sorts of experiments at Deepacres where one pulls chains when one would expect to turn taps and the other way round. So, what with his drains and his Chinese pots, I dare say he had quite a giddy time. And with Violet wrapped up in her black magic, you may say they both had hobbies.'

'I thought I smelt black magic in Lady Wutherwood's conversation.'
'She didn't start off about it to you!'
'Well, there were some rather cryptic allusions to unseen forces.'
'Oh, *no*. Really, Violet is *too* odd.'
'Lady Charles,' said Alleyn, 'do you think she's at all – ?'
'Dotty?'
'Well – '
'You needn't be apologetic, Mr Alleyn. Violet popped into the drawing-room on her way to see you and if she kept up the form she showed then, I'm surprised that you didn't whisk a strait-jacket out of your black bag. Was she very queer?'

'I thought her so, certainly. I wondered if it could all be put down to shock.'

Lady Charles said nothing but solemnly shook her head.

'No?' murmured Alleyn. 'You don't think so?'

'No. I'm afraid I can't honestly say I do.'

'Has there ever been any serious trouble?'

'Well, of course, we don't see very much of them. My husband rather lost touch with Gabriel when we were in New Zealand but we did hear from Aunt Kit and people, that she had gone away to a private nursing-home in Devonshire. It had been recommended by old Lady Lorrimer, whose husband, as everybody knows, has been under lock and key for a hundred years. We heard that Violet's trouble comes in sort of bursts, do you know? Cycles.'

'Is there anything of that sort in the family history?'

'Of that one hasn't the faintest idea. Violet is a Hungarian, or a Yugo-Slav. One or the other. Her name isn't Violet at all. It's something beginning with "Gla", like Gladys, but ending too ridiculously. So Gabriel called her Violet. I think her maiden name was Zadody, but I'm not sure. She was nobody that anyone knew, even in Hungaria or Yugo-Slavia, which was quite another country, of course, in Gabriel's wild-oatish youth. Gabriel said he had found her at the Embassy. I'm afraid Charlie used to say it was at a cabaret of that name or something slightly worse. You must remember her when you were a gay young man at parties. Or perhaps you are too young. He had her presented, of course, and everything. She was rather spectacular in those days, and looked like a Gibson Girl who didn't wash very often. Of course you *were* too young, but I remember them both very well. I believe that even then there were *crises-de-nerfs.*'

'That must have been rather difficult for Lord Wutherwood?'

'Yes, *miserable* for him. Luckily there were no children. Luckily for us too, I suppose, as things have turned out, although I must say I don't think it's the pleasantest way of becoming the head of the family.'

Her cigarette had gone out and she lit another. Alleyn felt quite certain that there was more than a touch of bravura in this rapid flow of narrative. It was a little too bright, the inconsequence was over-stressed, the rhythm somewhere at fault. He thought that he was being shown a perilous imitation of the normal Lady Charles Lamprey by a Lady Charles Lamprey who was by no means normal. Once or twice he heard the faintest suggestion of a stutter and that reminded him of Stephen, who, he felt sure, was overwhelmingly present in his mother's thoughts. Extreme maternal devotion had never seemed to Alleyn to be a sentimental or a pretty attachment, but rather a passionate concentration which, when its object was threatened, developed a painful intensity. Maternal anxiety, he thought, was the emotion that human beings most consistently misrepresent, degrading its passion into tenderness, its agony with pathos. He was too familiar with the look that appears in frightened maternal eyes to miss recognizing it in Lady Charles's, and though he was perfectly prepared to make use of her terror, he did not enjoy the knowledge that he had stimulated it. He heard her voice go rattling on and knew that she was trying to force an impression on him. 'She wants me,' he thought, 'to believe that her sister-in-law is insane.'

' – and I'm so terrified,' she was saying, 'that this really will throw her completely off her balance although to be quite honest, we all thought she was very alarming when she arrived this afternoon.'

'In what way?'

'Well, quite often she didn't answer when you spoke to her and then when she did speak it was all about this wretched supernatural nonsense, unseen forces, and all the rest of it. The oddest part about it was – '

'Yes?' asked Alleyn, as she hesitated.

'Perhaps I shouldn't tell you this.'

'We shall be grateful if you will tell us anything that occurs to you. I think,' Alleyn added with emphasis, 'that I can promise you we shall not lose our sense of proportion.'

She glanced at Fox who was placidly contemplating his notes.

'I'm sure you won't,' she said. 'It's only that I'm afraid of losing mine. It's just that it seems so strange, now, to remember what Violet said to me.'

'What was that?'

'It was when we were in my bedroom. Gabriel had been rather acid about Violet's black magic, or whatever it is, and apparently she rather hated him sort of sneering at her. She sat on my bed and stared at the opposite wall until really I could have shaken her, she looked so gloomy and odd, and then suddenly, she said in a very bogus voice (only somehow it wasn't *quite* bogus, do you know): "Gabriel is in jeopardy." It was so melodramatic that it made one feel quite shy. She went on again, very fast, about somebody who foretold the future and had said that Gabriel's sands were running out at a great rate. I supposed she must go in for a little fortune-telling or something, as a kind of relaxation from witchcraft. It all sounds too silly and second-rate but she herself was so wildly incoherent that I honestly *did* think she had gone completely dotty.'

Lady Charles paused and looked up at Alleyn. He had not returned to his chair but stood with his hands in the pockets of his jacket, listening. Perhaps she read in his face something that she had not expected to see there – a hint of compassion or of regret. Her whole attitude changed. She broke into a storm of words.

'Why do you look like that?' Lady Charles cried out. 'You ought to be an effigy of a man. Don't look as if you were sorry for somebody. I – ' She stopped as abruptly as she had begun, beat twice with her closed hands on the wooden arms of her chair, and then leant towards him. 'I'm so sorry,' she said. 'I'm afraid you are quite right about people's nerves. Mr Alleyn, it's no use for me to beat about the bush, with you looking on at my antics. I'm not a clever or a deliberate woman. My tongue moves faster than my brain and already I am in a fair way to making a fool of myself. I think perhaps I shall do better if I'm terribly frank.'

'I think so, too,' Alleyn said.

'Yes. I'm sure you have guessed my view of this awful business. Everything that I have told you is quite true. I do exaggerate sometimes, I know, but not over important things, and I haven't exaggerated or over-stressed anything that I have told you about Violet

Wutherwood. I think she is quite mad. And I believe she killed her husband.'

The point of Fox's pencil broke with a sharp snap. He looked resignedly at it and took another from his pocket.

'You will think,' said Lady Charles, 'that I am working for my husband and my children. I know Aunt Kit told you we were practically sunk and had asked Gabriel for money. I know that will look like a pretty strong motive. I know the twins have behaved idiotically. I don't even expect you to believe me when I tell you that it's always been their way, when one of them is in trouble, for both to stand the racket. I realize that all these things must make you a bit wary of anything I say and I can't expect you to be very impressed when I tell you I know, as surely as I breathe, that none of my children could, under circumstances a thousand times worse than ours, hurt any living creature. But if they were not my children, if I'd only been a looker-on, like Robin Grey, only less interested, less of a partizan than Robin, I would still be certain that Gabriel was killed by his wife.'

'It's a perfectly tenable theory,' said Alleyn, 'at present. Can you give me anything more than her condition and her conversation in the bedroom? Motive?'

'They have been at daggers drawn for years. Once or twice they have separated. Not legally. Gabriel would never have considered a divorce, I'm sure. He wouldn't like the idea of displaying his failure, he would never admit that anything he did was a mistake. And I don't suppose Violet has ever been normal enough to think of getting rid of him. She seemed to have merely settled down to hating him. And even if she had ever thought of it I don't suppose she'd altogether fancy the idea. I mean there are certain amenities – Deepacres and the London house and all the rest of it. She *could* have divorced him, of course. He had a series of rather squalid little affairs that everybody knew about and nobody mentioned. They'd loathed each other for years, in a dreary sort of way, but this afternoon there was something quite different. I mean Violet seemed to be actively venomous. It was as if *she* had poured all her dislikes of other people or things into one enormous hatred of Gabriel. That's how it was, exactly.'

'I see. When do you think she could have done it?'

'I've been thinking it out. You see, she left Aunt Kit and me in the bedroom round about the first time Gabriel yelled for her. She didn't come back until after the second time he yelled, and then we both went along to the landing and I went into the drawing-room. There was no one else on the landing or in the hall.'

'Did she seem very odd at that time?'

'I can't *tell* you how strange and ominous. I put out my hand to bring her along the passage, but she drew away as though I'd hit her and followed behind me. I was almost alarmed. I scuttled away as quickly as I could to get out of her reach. But she muttered along after me. It was like having a doubtful dog at one's heels. At any moment I expected her to growl and snap.'

There was a pause. Alleyn had turned aside and moved to one of the windows. Fox looked up in surprise.

'*Mr Alleyn*,' said Lady Charles, 'what are you doing? You – you're not *laughing*?'

Alleyn turned round. His face was scarlet. He stood before her, his hands stretched out. 'Lady Charles,' he said, 'I fully deserve that you should report me and have me turned out of the force. I've done the unforgivable thing – there's no excuse for me but I do apologize with all my heart.'

'I don't want you to be turned out of any force. But why did you laugh?'

'It – I'm afraid the explanation will only add to the offence. I – you see – '

'It was at me,' said Lady Charles with conviction. The strain had gone from her voice. 'People do laugh at me. But what did I say? Mr Alleyn, I insist on knowing what it was.'

'It was nothing. There are some people who can't hold back a nervous laugh when they hear of somebody's death. Heaven knows, a detective officer isn't one of them, but I'm afraid that if I hear anything very sinister and dramatic related with great *empressment*, it sometimes has that effect on me. It was the way you described Lady Wutherwood as she followed you, muttering. I – it's no use. I'm abject.'

'I suppose you're not a relation of ours by any chance,' said Lady Charles thoughtfully.

'I don't think so.'

'You never know. All the Lampreys laugh at disastrous pieces of news so I thought you might be. We must go into it some time. I'm a distant Lamprey myself, you know. Nothing hygienically sinister. What was your mother's maiden name?'

'Blandish,' said Alleyn helplessly.

'I must ask Charlie. Blandish. But in the meantime hadn't we better go back to poor Violet?'

'By all means.'

'Not that there's very much more to say. Except that she might have done it *instead* of going to the lavatory or *while* I was in the drawing-room, although she would have to be pretty nippy to manage it then.'

'Yes.'

'Is that all?'

'One other question. Can you give the name of the doctor Lady Wutherwood saw before she went to the nursing-home?'

'Good Heavens, no! It was years ago.'

'Or the nursing-home?'

'It was in Devonshire. Could it have been on Dartmoor or am I thinking of something else?'

'How did you get on, Mama?' asked Frid in French.

'Not so badly,' answered her mother in the same tongue.
'I have made him laugh, at least.'

'Laugh!' Lord Charles ejaculated. *'Mon Dieu, what at?'*

'I had to work for it,' said Charlot wearily. *'He thinks I'm a sort of elderly enfant terrible. He thinks he made the most formidable gaffe in laughing at me. He apologized quite charmingly.'*

'I hope you didn't overdo it, Immy.'

'Not I, darling. He hasn't the faintest inkling of what I was up to. Don't worry. Soyez tranquil.'

'Soyez tranquil,' wrote PC Martin faithfully, on the last page of his notebook, and with a sigh, took a fresh one from the pocket of his tunic.

'Blast that woman!' said Alleyn in the dining-room. 'She was determined to break me up, and damn her, so she did. I hope she thinks she got away with it.'

'You apologized very nicely, Mr Alleyn,' said Fox. 'I expect she does.'

'We'll have the twins, Gibson,' said Alleyn.

CHAPTER 14

Perjury By Roberta

'You see,' said Alleyn, looking carefully at the twins, 'you are not absolutely identical. In almost everybody the distance between the outer corner of the left-hand eye and the left-hand corner of the mouth, is not precisely the same as the distance between the outer corner of the right-hand eye and the right-hand corner of the mouth. A line drawn through both eyes and prolonged is hardly ever parallel with a line drawn along the lips and prolonged. You get an open-angle and close-angled side to every face. That's why the reflection in a looking-glass of somebody you know very well, always seems distorted and queer. In both of your faces, the close angle is on the left. But in Lord Stephen the angle is the least fraction more emphatic.'

'Is this the B-b-Bettillion system?' asked Stephen. 'P-portrait parlé?'

'A version of it,' said Alleyn. 'Bertillion paid great attention to ears. He divided the ear into twelve major sections and noticed a great many subdivisions. Yours are not quite identical with your brother's. And then, of course, there's that mole on the back of your neck. Lady Wutherwood noticed it in the lift.' He turned to Colin. 'So you see you really would be rather foolish if you persisted in saying you went down in the lift. It would be a false statement and the law is not every amiable about false statements.'

'Bad luck, Col.,' said Stephen with a shaky laugh. 'You're sunk.'

'I think you're trying to bamboozle us, Mr Alleyn,' Colin said. 'You've got a fifty-fifty chance, after all. I don't believe Aunt V.

would have noticed a carbuncle, much less a mole, on anybody's neck. She's too dotty. I stick to my statement. I can tell exactly what happened.'

'I'm sure you can,' said Alleyn politely. 'But do you know, I don't think we want to hear it. You both had plenty of time to put your heads together before the police arrived. I'm sure the stories would tally to a hair's breadth, but I don't think we'll trouble you for yours. I don't ask you for a statement. I don't think we need bother you any longer. Goodnight.'

'It's a trap,' said Colin slowly. 'I'm not going. You'll damn well take my statement, whether you like it or not.'

'We're not allowed to set traps, I promise you. I should be setting a trap if I pretended not to know which of you worked the lift and so encouraged you to carry on with your comedy of errors.'

'Do p-pipe down, Colin,' said Stephen rapidly. 'It's no go. I didn't want you to do it. Mr Alleyn, you're quite right. I didn't kill Uncle G. but, on my word of honour, I t-took him down in the lift and Colin stayed in the drawing-room. Don't commit any more p-perjury, Col., for God's sake just to b-buzz off.'

The twins, white to the lips, stared at each other. It so chanced that each of them reflected the other's pose to the very slant of their narrow heads. The impression made by identical twins is always startling to strangers. It is accompanied by a sensation of shifted focus. It seems to us that the physical resemblance must be an outward sign of mental unity. It is easy to believe that twins are aware of each other's thoughts, difficult to imagine them in dissonance. And Alleyn wondered if these twins were in agreement when Colin suddenly said: 'Let me stay here while you talk to Stephen, please. I'm sorry I was objectionable. I'd like to stay.'

Alleyn did not answer and Colin added: 'I won't butt in. I'd just be here, that's all.'

'He knows everything about it,' Stephen said. 'I t-told him.'

'If he first tells us what he did while you were in the lift,' said Alleyn, 'he may stay.'

'Please do, Col.,' said Stephen. 'You'll only make me look every kind of bloody skunk if you d-don't.'

'All right,' said Colin slowly. 'I'll explain.'

'That's excellent,' said Alleyn. 'Suppose you both sit down.'

They sat on opposite sides of the table, facing each other.

'I'd better explain first of all,' Colin began, 'that it's not a new sort of stunt, our joining with the same story. It's a kind of arrangement we've always had. When we were kids we fixed it up between us. I dare say it sounds pretty feeble-minded and sort of "I did it, sir! said little Eric," but it doesn't strike us like that. It's just an arrangement. Not over everything but when there's a really major row brewing. It doesn't mean that I think Stephen bumped off Uncle G. I know he didn't. He told me he didn't. So I know.'

Colin said this with an air of stolid assurance. Stephen looked at him dully. 'Well, I didn't,' he said.

'I know. I was only explaining.'

'Later on,' said Alleyn, 'we'll look for something that sounds a little more like police-court evidence. In the meantime, what did you do?'

'Me?' asked Colin. 'Oh, I just stayed in the drawing-room with Henry and my father.'

'What did you talk about?'

'I didn't. I looked at a *Punch*.'

'What did they talk about?'

'Henry said: "Have they gone?" and my father said "Yes," and Henry said "Three rousing cheers." I don't think anybody said anything else until Aunt V. started yelling, and then Henry said: "Is that a fire-engine or do they ring bells?" and my father said: "It's a woman," and Henry said: "How revolting," and my father said: "It's coming from the lift," and Henry said: "Then it must be Aunt V. and she's coming back." It had got a good deal nearer by then. I think Henry said: "How revolting" again and then my father said: "Something has happened," and went out of the room. Henry said: "She's gone completely crackers, it seems. Come on." So he went out. My mother and Frid and, I think, Patch, were on the landing and the lift was up. Stephen opened the doors and came out. He held the doors back. Aunt V. came screeching out. The rest of it's rather a muddle and I dare say you've heard it already.'

'I should like to know when your brother decided to take up the option on your agreement.'

'I didn't want – ' Stephen began.

'Shut up,' said Colin. 'While they were all fussing round and ringing up doctors and policemen Stephen said: "I'm going to be sick," so I went with him and he was. And then we went to my room and he told me all about it. And I said that if anything cropped up like you, and so on, the arrangement would be good. Stephen said he didn't want me to crash in on the party but I did, of course, as you know. That's all.'

'Thank you,' said Alleyn. Colin lit a cigarette.

'I suppose I say what happened in the lift,' said Stephen.

'If you will,' Alleyn agreed. 'From the time Lady Charles came to the drawing-room.'

Stephen played a little tattoo with his fingers on the table. His movements as well as his speech, Alleyn noticed, were much more staccato than his twin's. Colin had spoken with a deliberation so marked as to seem studied. He had looked placidly at Alleyn through his light eyelashes. Stephen spoke in spurts, his stutter became increasingly marked, he kept glancing at Alleyn and away again. Fox's notes seemed to disturb him.

'My mother,' Stephen said, 'asked for someone t-to work the lift. So I went out.'

'To the lift?'

'Yes.'

'Who was in the lift?'

'He was. Sitting there.'

'With the doors shut?'

'Yes.'

'Who opened them?'

'I did. Aunt V. was sort of hovering about on the landing. When I opened the d-doors she tacked over and floated in.'

'And then? Did you follow at once?'

'Well, I stopped long enough to wink at my mother and then I got in and s-simply t-took the lift down – '

'Just a moment. What were Lord and Lady Wutherwood's positions in the lift?'

'He was sitting in the corner. His hat was on and his scarf pulled up and his c-coat collar turned up. I – th-thought he was asleep.'

'Asleep? But a minute or so before, he had shouted at the top of his voice.'

'Well, asleep or sulking. As a matter of fact, I rather thought he was s-sulking.'

'Why should he do that?'

'He was a sulky sort of man. Aunt V. had kept him waiting.'

'Did you notice his hat?'

'It was a poisonous hat.'

'Anything in particular about it?'

'Only that it looked as if it belonged to a bum. As a matter of fact I couldn't see him very well. Aunt V. – Violet stood b-between us and the light wasn't on.'

'Was she facing him?'

'N-no. Facing the doors.'

'Right. And then?'

'Well, I p-pushed the button and we went down.'

'What happened next?'

'When we'd got about half-way d-down she started screaming. I hadn't looked at either of those two. I just heard the scream and jumped like hell and sort of automatically shoved down the stop button. So we stopped. We were nearly down. Just below the first floor.'

'Yes?'

'Well, of course, I turned round. I didn't see Uncle G. She was between us, with her b-back to me, yelling in a disgusting sort of way. It was b-beastly. As sudden as a train whistle. I've always hated t-train whistles. She moved away a bit and I l-looked and s-saw him.'

'What did you see?'

'You know what it was.?

'Not exactly. I should like an exact description.'

Stephen moistened his lips and passed his fingers across his face. 'Well,' he said, 'he was sitting there. I remember now that there was a dent in his hat. She had hold of him and she sort of sh-shook him and he s-sort of t-tipped forward. His head was between his knees and his hat fell off. Then she pulled him up. And then I s-saw.'

'What did you see? I'm sorry,' said Alleyn, 'but it really is important and Lady Wutherwood's description was not very clear. I want a clear picture.'

'I wish,' said Stephen violently, 'that I hadn't got one. I c-can't – Col., tell him I c-can't – it was t-too beastly.'

'Do you know,' said Alleyn. 'I think there's something in the theory that it's a mistake to bury a very bad experience. The Ancient

Mariner's idea was a sound one. In describing something unpleasant you get rid of part of its unpleasantness.'

'*Unp-pleasant!* My God, the skewer was jutting out of his eye and blood running down his face into his mouth. He made noises like an animal.'

'Was there any other injury to his face?' Alleyn asked.

Stephen hid his own face in his hands. His voice was muffled. 'Yes. The side of his head. Something. I saw that when – I saw it!' His fingers moved to his own temple. 'There.'

'Yes. What did you do?'

'I had my hand near the thing – the switchboard – you k-know. I must have p-pushed the top b-button. I don't think I did it on purpose. I d-don't know. We went up. She was screaming. When I opened the d-doors she sort of fell out. That's all.' Stephen gripped the edge of the table and for the first time looked steadily at Alleyn. 'I'm sorry I'm not clearer,' he said. 'I don't know why I'm like this. I've been all right t-till now. I even sort of wondered why I *was* so all right.'

'Shock,' said Alleyn, 'seems to have a period of incubation with some people. Now, as you went down in the lift you faced the switchboard?'

'Yes.'

'All the time?'

'Yes.'

'Did you hear any sort of movement behind you?'

'I d-don't remember hearing anything at all. It's not long, is it?'

'It's precisely thirty seconds to the bottom,' said Alleyn. 'You didn't go all the way. Did you hear any sort of thud?'

'If I did, I don't remember it.'

'All right. To go back a little. While your father interviewed Lord Wutherwood, you were all in here, lying on the carpet in that corner.'

Stephen and Colin exchanged a glance. Colin silently framed the word 'Patch' with his lips.

'No,' said Alleyn. 'Lady Patricia only told us you lay on the floor. She said it was a kind of game. We noticed it took place in that corner where a door has been boarded up. There's a trace of lipstick on the carpet close to the crack under the door and a bit of boot polish further out. It's difficult to avoid the presumption that your game involved listening to the conversation next door.'

'I say,' said Stephen suddenly, 'do you speak French? Yes, I suppose you do. Yes, of course you do.'

'Shut up,' said Colin.

'I haven't been lying on the carpet,' said Alleyn. 'And Mr Fox only stayed there long enough to catch a phrase, spoken I think, by you. *"Taisez-vous donc!"* '

'He's always saying it,' Stephen muttered gloomily. 'In English or in French.'

'And a fat lot of notice you take,' Colin pointed out. 'If you'd only – '

'We won't go into that,' said Alleyn. 'Now, when this unusual game was ended, and after your brother Michael had come in, you two, with your elder brother went into the drawing-room, while your sisters went into flat 26. Did you go together and directly into the drawing-room?'

There was a moment's silence before Colin answered. 'Yes. We all went out together. The girls went first.'

'Henry just had a little snoop d-down the passage.'

'In which direction?'

'Towards the hall. He was only a second or two. He came into the d-drawing-room just after we did.'

'And did you all stay in the drawing-room until Lady Charles came?'

'Yes,' said the twins together.

'I see. That pretty well covers the ground. One more question and I think I may put it to both of you. You'll understand that we wouldn't ask it unless we felt that it was entirely relevant. What impression did you get of Lady Wutherwood during the afternoon?'

'Mad,' said the twins together.

'In the strict sense of the word?'

'Yes,' said Colin. 'We all thought so. Mad.'

'I see,' said Alleyn again. 'That's all, I think. Thank you.'

II

When the twins reappeared in the drawing-room Roberta thought they had a slightly attenuated and shivery air, rather as if they had been efficiently purged by Nanny. They looked coldly at the rest of their family, walked to the sofa and collapsed on it.

'Well,' said Colin after a long silence, 'I see no reason why we should not announce in anything but plain English the fact that the gaffe is blown, the cat out of the bag, and the balloon burst.'

'What do you mean?' cried Charlot. 'You didn't – ?'

'No Mama, we didn't tell him because he already knew,' said Stephen. 'I was the l-liftman. I did it with my little button.'

'I told you so,' Frid observed. 'I told you that you'd never get away with it.'

Stephen looked icily at her. 'Is it possible,' he said, 'that any sister of mine can utter that detestable, that imbecilic phrase? Yes, Frid dear, you told us so.'

'But, Stephen,' said Charlot in a voice so unlike her own that Roberta wondered for a second who had spoken. 'Stephen, he doesn't think – you – *Stephen?*'

'It's all right, Mum,' said Colin, 'I don't see how he could.'

'Of course not,' said Lord Charles loudly. 'My dear girl, you're so upset and tired you don't know what you're saying. The police are not fools, Immy. You've nothing to upset yourself about. Go to bed, my dear.' And he added without great conviction, an ancient phrase of comfort. 'Things will seem better in the morning,' said Lord Charles.

'How can they?' asked Charlot.

'My darling heart, of course they will. We're in for a very disagreeable time no doubt. Somebody has killed Gabriel, and although it's all perfectly beastly, we naturally hope that the police will find his murderer. It's a horrible business, God knows, but there's no need for us to go adding to its horror by imagining all sorts of fantastic developments.' He touched his moustache. 'My dear,' he said, 'to suppose that the boys are in any sort of danger is quite monstrous, it is to insult them, Immy. Innocent people are in no kind of danger in these cases.'

Frid looked towards the far end of the room, where the constable's red head showed over the back of his chair. 'Do you agree to all that?' she said loudly. The constable, slightly startled, got to his feet.

'I beg your pardon, Miss?'

'It would be grand,' Frid said, 'if we knew your name.'

'Martin, Miss.'

'Oh. Well, Mr Martin, I asked if you would say innocent people are as safe as houses, no matter how fishy things may look?'

'Yes, Miss,' said the constable.

'My good ass,' said Henry, glaring at Frid, 'who looks fishy?'

'Henry, don't speak like that to Frid.'

'I'm sorry, Mama, but *honestly!* Frid is.'

'I'm *not,*' said Frid. 'We all look fishy. Don't we?' she demanded of the constable, 'don't we look as fishy as Billingsgate?'

'I couldn't say, Miss,' said the constable uneasily, and Roberta suddenly felt extremely sorry for him.

'That will do, Frid,' said Lord Charles. Roberta had not imagined his voice could carry so sharp an edge. Frid crossed the room stagily and sat on the arm of her mother's chair.

There was a tap at the door and the constable, with an air of profound relief, answered it. The usual muttered colloquy followed, but it was punctuated by a loud interruption outside. 'It's perfectly all right,' said a cheerful voice in the hall. 'Mr Alleyn knows all about it and Lady Lamprey expects me. If you don't believe me, toddle along and ask.'

'It's Nigel!' cried the Lampreys and Frid shouted: 'Nigel! Come in, my angel! We're all locked up but Mr Alleyn said you could come.'

'*Hallo,* my dear!' answered the voice. 'I know. I'll be there in a jiffy. They're just asking – oh, thanks. Tell him I'll come and see him later on, will you? Where are we? Thanks.'

The constable admitted a robust young man who, to Roberta's colonial eyes, instantly recalled the fashionable illustrated papers, so compactly did his clothes fit him, and so efficiently barbered and finished did he seem, with his hair drilled back from his reddish face, his brushed-up moustaches, and his air of social efficiency. He came in with a lunging movement, smoothing the back of his head and grinning engagingly, and rather anxiously, at the Lampreys.

'Nigel, my dear,' cried Charlot, 'we're so *delighted* to see you. Did you think it *too* queer of Frid to ring up? Everyone else did.'

'I thought it marvellous of Frid,' said Nigel Bathgate. 'Hallo, Charles, I'm terribly sorry about whatever it all is.'

'Damnable, isn't it,' said Lord Charles gently. 'Sit down. Have a drink.'

'Robin,' said Henry, 'you haven't met Nigel, have you? Mr Bathgate, Miss Grey.'

Roberta while she shook hands, had time to be pleased because Henry did not seem to forget she was there. As soon as Henry remembered Roberta, so did all the other Lampreys. 'Poor Robin,' said Charlot, 'she's just this *second* arrived from the remotest antipodes to be hurled into a family homicide. Do get your drink quickly, Nigel, and listen to our frightful story. We're so dreadfully worried, but we thought that if we were having a *cause célèbre* you might as well get in first.'

'And perhaps stave off the pressmen,' added Frid. 'You will, won't you, Nigel? It really is a scoop for you.'

'But *what* is?' asked Nigel Bathgate. 'I only got your message ten minutes ago and of course I came round at once. Why are Alleyn and his merry men all over the place? What's occurred?'

The Lampreys embarked on a simultaneous narrative. Roberta was greatly impressed by the adroit manner in which Nigel Bathgate managed to disentangle cold facts from a welter of Lampresian embroideries. His round red face grew more and more solemn as the story unfolded. He looked in dismay from one to another of the Lampreys and finally, with a significant grimace, jerked his head in the direction of the constable.

'Oh, we've given up bothering about him,' said Frid. 'At first we talked French but really there's nothing left to conceal. Aunt Kit told Mr Alleyn about the financial crisis and Daddy had to come clean about the bum.'

'What!'

'My dear Nigel,' said Lord Charles, 'there's a man in possession. Could anything look worse?'

'And as for the twins,' said Frid, 'your boy-friend turned them inside out and hung them up to dry.'

'And I m-may t-tell you, Frid,' said Stephen, 'that he knows just what we did in the dining-room. You would wipe your painted mouth on the carpet, wouldn't you?'

'Good Lord!' Henry ejaculated, and he threw two cushions down in front of the sealed door. 'Why the devil didn't we think of that before?'

'Oh,' said Stephen, 'he says he didn't bother to listen. I suppose we all give ourselves away t-too freely for it to be necessary.'

'But what *is* all this?' demanded Lord Charles. 'What did you do in the dining-room?'

Rather self-consciously his children told him.

'Not very pretty,' said Lord Charles. 'What can he think of you?'

There was a short silence. 'Not much, I dare say,' said Henry at last.

'You had better – ' Lord Charles made a small despairing gesture and turned away. Frid spoke rapidly in French. Roberta thought she said that they had not been asked to give an account of the interview.

'But no doubt,' said Colin, 'anything that we haven't told him has been madly divulged by Aunt V. So why be guarded?'

'But,' Nigel interrupted firmly, 'where is your Aunt Violet? Where is Lady Wutherwood?'

'Asleep in my bed,' said Charlot, 'with a nurse on one side of it and her maid, who is determined not to leave her, on the other. So where Charlie and I are to spend the night is a secret. We don't know. We've also got to bed down somewhere a chauffeur called Giggle, in addition to Mr Grumball.'

'Yes, but look here, this is really serious,' Nigel began.

'Well, of course it is, Nigel. We know it's serious. We're all shaken to our foundations,' said Frid. 'That's partly why we asked you to come.'

'Yes, but you don't *sound* – ' Nigel began and then caught sight of Charlot's face. 'Oh, my dear,' he said, 'I'm so terribly sorry. But you needn't worry. Alleyn – '

'Nigel,' said Charlot, 'what's he like? You've so often talked about your friend and we've always thought it would be such fun to meet him. Little did we know how it would come about. Here I've been, sitting in my own dining-room, trying to sort of *see* into him, do you know? I thought I'd got the interview going just my way. And now, when I think it over, I'm not so sure.'

'My dear Imogen,' said Nigel, 'I know you're a genius for diplomacy but honestly, with Alleyn, if I were you, I wouldn't.'

'He laughed at me,' said Charlot defensively.

'Are you certain, Mummy,' said Frid, 'that it wasn't sinister laughter? "Heh-heh-heh!"'

'It wasn't in the least sinister. He giggled.'

'I wish he'd send for me,' Frid muttered.

'I suppose you think,' Henry began, 'that you're going to have a fat dramatic scene, ending in Alleyn throwing up the case because you're *trop troublante*. My dear girl, your histrionic antics – '

'I shan't go in for any histrionic antics, darling. I shall just be very still and dignified and rather pale and very lovely.'

'Well, if Alleyn isn't sick, he's got a stronger stomach than I have.'

Frid laughed musically. The constable answered a tap on the door.

'This is my entrance cue,' said Frid. 'What do you bet?'

'It may be your father or Henry,' said Charlot.

'Inspector Alleyn,' said the constable, 'would be glad if Miss Grey would speak to him.'

Roberta followed a second constable down the passage to the dining-room door. Her heart thudded disturbingly. She felt that she wanted to yawn. Her mouth was dry and she wondered if, when she spoke, her voice would be cracked. The constable opened the dining-room door, went in, and said: 'Miss Grey, sir.'

Roberta, feeling her lack of inches, walked into the dining-room.

Alleyn and Fox had risen. The constable pulled out a chair at the end of the table. Through a thick mental haze, Roberta became aware of Alleyn's deep and pleasant voice. 'I'm so sorry to worry you, Miss Grey. It's such bad luck that you should find yourself landed in such a disagreeable affair. Do sit down.'

'Thank you,' said Roberta in a small voice.

'You only arrived yesterday, didn't you?'

'Yes.'

'From New Zealand. That's a long journey. What part of New Zealand do you come from?'

'The South Island. South Canterbury.'

'Then you know the McKenzie Country?'

The scent of sun-baked tussock, of wind from the tops of snow-mountains, and the memory of an intense blue, visited Roberta's transplanted heart. 'Have you been there?' she asked.

'I was there four years ago.'

'In the McKenzie Country? Tekapo? Pukaki?'

'The sound of the names makes the places vivid again.' He spoke for a little while of his visit and, like all colonials, Roberta rose to the bait. Her nervousness faded and soon she found herself describing the New Zealand Deepacres, how it stood at the foot of Little Mount Silver, how English trees grew into the fringes of native bush, and how English birdsong, there, was pierced by the colder and deeper notes of bell-birds and mok-e-moks.

'That was Lord Charles's station?'

'Oh yes. Not ours. We only lived in a small house in a small town. But you see I was so much at Deepacres.'

'It must have been rather a wrench for them leaving such a place.'

'Not really,' said Roberta. 'It was only a New Zealand adventure for them. A kind of interlude. They belong here.'

'Did Lord Charles like farming?'

Roberta had never even thought of Lord Charles as being a farmer. He had merely been at Deepacres. She found it difficult to answer the question. Had he enjoyed himself in New Zealand? It was impossible to say, and she replied confusedly that they had all seemed quite happy, but of course they were glad to be home again.

'They are a very united family?'

Roberta could see no harm in speaking of the Lampreys' attachment to each other, and she quite lost her apprehensions in the development of this favourite theme. It was easy to relate how kind the Lampreys had been to her; how, although they argued incessantly, they were happiest when they were together, how she believed they would always come to each other's aid.

'We had an example of that,' Alleyn agreed, 'in the present stand made by the twins.'

Roberta caught her breath and looked at him. His eyes with their turned-down corners, seemed to express only sympathetic amusement, as though he invited her to laugh a little with him at the twins.

'But they have always been like that,' cried Roberta. 'Even at Deepacres when Colin took the big car – ' and she was off again, all her anecdotes of the Lampreys tending to show their devotion to each other. Alleyn listened as though everything Roberta said amused and interested him, and she had ridden her hobby-horse down a long road before she stopped suddenly, feeling herself blush with embarrassment.

'I'm sorry,' she stammered, 'I'm talking too much.'

'Indeed you're not. You're giving me a delightful picture. But I suppose we must get down to hard facts. I just want to check your own movements. You were in here from the time Lord Charles had his interview with his brother, right up to the discovery of the accident. That right?'

'Yes.' Roberta had sorted this out carefully and gave him a clear account of her talk with Michael and her final move to the landing.

'That's grand,' said Alleyn. 'Crisp and plain. There are two points I want to check very carefully. The times when Lord Wutherwood shouted. You tell me that when he first called you were all in here.'

'Yes. Including Mike. He had just come in. But the others went out a second or two after he called out.'

'And the second time?'

'Mike went away with Giggle. A very short time after that Lord Wutherwood called out the second time.'

'You're quite certain?'

'Yes, quite. Because it was so quiet in the room when they had gone. I remember that, after he had called again, I heard the sound of the lift. Then I heard someone call out in the street below and the voices next door in the drawing-room. It's all very clear. I heard the lift again just as I took a cigarette out of that box. After that, I remember I walked about hunting for matches. I'd just lit my cigarette and was leaning out over the window-sill looking at London when I heard her – Lady Wutherwood. It was awful, that screaming.'

'I want you to go through that again if you will.'

Roberta went through it again and, greatly to her astonishment, again. Alleyn read over his notes to her and she agreed that they were correct and signed them. He was silent for a moment and then returned to the subject of the family.

'Do you find them much changed now you have seen them again?' he asked.

'Not really. At first they seemed rather fashionable and grown-up but that was only for a little while. They are just the same.'

'They haven't grown-up as far as their pockets are concerned,' Alleyn said lightly. But Roberta was ready for this and said that the Lampreys didn't worry about money, that it meant nothing to them.

With a sensation of peril she carried her theme a little further. They would never, she said, do anything desperate to get money.

'But if they are faced with bankruptcy?'

'Something always happens to save them. They know they will fall on their feet. They *seem* desperately worried but inside themselves they continually forget to be worried.' And seeing that he listened attentively to her, she went on quickly: 'Even now this has happened they are not remembering all the time to be alarmed. They know they are all right.'

'All of them?'

Roberta said truthfully: 'Perhaps not . . . Charlot – Lady Charles. She is frightened because Colin pretended he was in the lift and she wonders if that may make you think Stephen is hiding something. But I am sure, inside herself, she knows it will be all right.' Roberta was silent and perhaps she smiled a little to herself for Alleyn said: 'Of what are you thinking, Miss Grey?'

'I was thinking that they are like children. You can see them remembering to be solemn about all that has happened and then for a time they are quite frightened. But in a minute or two one of them will think of something amusing to say and will say it.'

'Does Lord Charles do this?'

A cold sensation of panic visited Roberta. Was it, after all, Lord Charles whom they suspected? And again it seemed to her that it was impossible to guess at Lord Charles's thoughts. He was always politely remote, a background to his family. She discovered that she had no understanding of his reaction to his brother's murder. She said that of course it was more of a tragedy for him. Lord Wutherwood had been his only brother. She regretted this immediately, anticipating Alleyn's next question.

'Were they much attached to each other?'

'They didn't meet very often,' Roberta said and knew that she had blundered. Alleyn did not press this point but asked her what she had thought of Lord Wutherwood. She said quickly that she had seen him for the first time that afternoon.

'May we have your first impression?' Alleyn asked. But Roberta was nervous now and racked her brains for generalities. Lord Wutherwood, she said, was not very noticeable. He was rather quiet and colourless. There had been so many people, she hadn't paid any particular attention – She broke off, disturbed by Alleyn's gently incredulous glance.

'But it seems to me,' he said, 'that you are a good observer.'

'Only of people who interest me.'

'And Lord Wutherwood did not interest you?' Roberta did not speak, remembering that she had watched both the Wutherwoods with an interest inspired by the object of their visit. A vivid picture of that complaisant yet huffy face rose before her imagination. She saw again the buck teeth, the eyes set too close to the thin nose, the look of speculative disapproval. She couldn't quite force herself to deny this picture. Alleyn waited for a moment and then as she remained stubbornly silent he said: 'And what about Lady Wutherwood?'

'You couldn't *not* notice her,' Roberta said quickly. 'She was so very odd.'

'In what way?'

'But you've seen her.'

'Since her husband was murdered, remember.'

'There's not all that difference,' said Roberta bluntly.

Alleyn looked steadily at her. Under cover of the table Roberta clasped her hands together. What next?

Alleyn said: 'Did you join the reconnaissance party, Miss Grey?'

'The – ? I don't understand.'

'Perhaps reconnaissance is not quite the word. Did you listen with the others to the conversation next door?'

It hadn't seemed such an awful thing to do at the time, Roberta told herself wildly. The Lampreys had assured her that Lord Charles wouldn't mind. In a way it had been rather fun. Why, oh why, should it show so shabbily, now that this man asked her about it! Lying on the floor with her ears to the door! Spying! Her cheeks were burning coals. She would not unclasp her hands. She would sit there, burning before him, not lowering her gaze.

'Yes,' said Roberta clearly, 'I did.'

'Will you tell me what you heard?'

'No. I'd rather not do that.'

'We'll have to see if any of the servants were about,' said Alleyn thoughtfully. A hot blast of fury and shame prevented Roberta from understanding that he was not deliberately insulting her, deliberately suggesting that she had behaved like an untrustworthy housemaid. And she could say nothing to justify herself. She heard her own voice stammering out words that meant nothing. In a nightmare of shame she looked at her own indignity. 'It wasn't like that – we were together – we weren't doing it like that – it was because we were anxious to know – ' The unfamiliar voice whined shamefully on until out of the fog of her own discomfiture she saw Alleyn looking at her with astonishment, and she was able to be silent.

'Here, I say, hi!' said Alleyn. 'What's all this about?' Roberta, on the verge of tears, stared at the opposite wall. She felt rather than saw him get up and come round the table towards her. Now he stood above her. In her misery she noticed that he smelt pleasantly. Something like a new book in a good binding, said her brain which seemed to be thinking frantically in several directions. She would not, *she would not* cry in front of these men.

'I'm so sorry,' the deep voice was saying. 'I see. Look here, Miss Grey, I wasn't hurling insults at you. Really. I mean it would have been perfectly outrageous if I had suggested – ' He broke off. His air of helplessness steadied Roberta. She looked up at him. His face was twisted into a singular grimace. His left eyebrow had climbed half-way up his forehead. His mouth was screwed to one side as if a twinge of toothache bothered him. 'Oh damn!' he said.

'It's all right,' said Roberta, 'but you made it sound so *low*. I suppose it was really.'

'We're all low at times,' said Alleyn comfortably. 'I can see why you wanted to hear the interview. A good deal depended on it. Lord Charles asked his brother to get him out of his financial box, didn't he?'

Desperate speculations as to the amount of information he had already collected joggled about in Roberta's brain. If he knew positively the gist of the interview she would do harm in denying Lord Charles's appeal. If he didn't know he might yet find out. And what had Lady Katherine told him?

She said: 'I may have listened at door cracks but at least I can hold my tongue about what I heard.' And even that sounded bad. If Alleyn had been mistaken, of course she would have said so. 'He knows,' she thought desperately. 'He knows.'

'You will understand,' Alleyn said, 'that from our point of view this discussion between the brothers is important. You see we know why Lord Wutherwood came here. We know what it was hoped would be the result of the interview. I think you would all have been only too ready to tell us if Lord Wutherwood had agreed to help his brother.'

What would Henry and Lord Charles tell him? They had spoken about it in French. She had caught enough of the conversation to realize this. What had the twins told him? Had they agreed to lie about it? Why not? Why not, since Uncle G. was dead and could not give them away? But Alleyn could not have asked the twins about the interview or they would have said so on their return. So it was up to her. The word perjury was caught up in her thoughts with a dim notion of punishment. But she could do them no harm. Only herself, because she lied to the police in the execution of their duty. That wasn't right. Lying statement. False statement. She must speak now. *Now.* With conviction. She seemed to hover for eternity on the edge of utterance and when her voice did come it was without any conscious order from her brain.

'But,' said Roberta's voice, 'didn't they tell you? Lord Wutherwood promised to help his brother.'

'Do you speak French, Miss Grey?' asked Alleyn.

'No,' said Roberta.

Back in the drawing-room Roberta returned to her fireside seat. The Lampreys watched her with guarded inquisitiveness.

'Well, Robin,' said Henry, 'I trust your little spot of inquisition passed off quietly.'

'Oh yes,' said Roberta. 'Mr Alleyn just wanted to know where I was and all that.' And nerving herself, she said: 'You know, my dears, I've been thinking you must be very glad he was so generous after all. It'll be nice to remember that, won't it?'

There was a dead silence. Roberta looked into Lord Charles's eyes and then into Henry's. 'Won't it?' she repeated.

'Yes,' said Henry after a long pause. 'It'll be nice to remember that.'

CHAPTER 15

Entrance of Mr Bathgate

'Courageous little liar,' said Alleyn, 'isn't she?'

'I suppose so,' said Fox.

'Of course she is, Br'er Fox. Do you imagine if it was true they wouldn't have been out with the whole story as soon as we mentioned the interview? They've shied away like hell whenever we got near it. She's a good plucked 'un is the little New Zealander. She can't understand French and unless they managed to slip her a message she's decided to lie like hell and take the consequences. If Martin isn't careful she'll manage to warn Master Henry and his father. Let's see what the bilingual Martin has to say in his notes. Yes. Here we are. Have a look.'

Fox eyed the notes. 'I'd have to get it out in longhand,' he said. 'May I trouble you to translate, Mr Alleyn?'

'You may, Foxkin. They seemed to have discussed the twins' proposition and got no further. Here Lady Charles cut in and said: "It's very necessary that we should come to some decision about Gabriel and the money." That devilish girl seems to have chipped in with a remark to the effect that what we didn't know wouldn't hurt us.'

'Lady Friede, sir?'

'The same. Master Henry said that only their father knew what had happened at the interview. I catch the warning note here, Foxkin. He was instructing his brothers and sisters to forget they had overheard the interview. It's evident that Lord Charles didn't know they had listened.'

'What did his lordship say?'

'His lordship is cryptic. He doesn't say much. Here's a stray observation. *"Par rapport à Tante Kit."* Oh! He says: considering what Aunt Kit has probably told us, we're not likely to suppose they were out of the financial wood. Very true. Lady Charles asks what Gabriel said at the interview and Lord Charles replies that he thinks it will be better if his family can truthfully say it doesn't know. I imagine an awkward silence among members of the carpet party. By this time, no doubt, the twins will have told their parents about the carpet party and that we have spotted it. That's all they seemed to have said about the interview between the brothers. You'd better have another go at the servants, Br'er Fox.'

'I don't think the butler would give anything away, sir. He's a quiet old chap and seems to like the family. If that parlour-maid overheard anything, she might be persuaded to speak up.'

'Go and have a word with her. Use your charm. And in the meantime, Fox, I'll deal with Master Henry.'

So Fox went off to the kitchen and the constable fetched Henry. Alleyn came straight to the point with Henry, asking him whether his uncle had promised to lend his father a sum of money. Henry instantly said that he had.

'So the financial crisis was over?'

'Yes.'

'Why did none of you tell me of this before?'

'Why should we?' asked Henry coolly. 'It didn't arise.'

'The question of the guilt or innocence of every single one of you arises,' said Alleyn. 'As you no doubt realize, Lady Katherine has told us of your financial difficulties. Lord Charles has told us that there is a baliff in the flat. People do not murder a man who is on the point of rescuing them from bankruptcy.'

'Well,' said Henry, 'we didn't murder Uncle G.'

'Who, in your opinion, did murder him?'

'I've no opinion about it.'

'You don't share your mother's conviction of Lady Wutherwood's homicidal insanity?'

'Does my mother feel convinced about that?'

'She told me so.' Henry said nothing. 'In plain words,' said Alleyn, 'do you think Lady Wutherwood is insane and killed her husband?'

'I don't see how one can possibly know,' said Henry slowly. 'I think she's mad.'

'That's an honest speech,' said Alleyn unexpectedly. Henry looked up quickly. 'I think she's mad, too,' Alleyn said, 'but like you I don't know if she killed her husband. I wonder if we hesitate for the same reason. It seems strange to me that a woman who murdered her husband should demand his body.'

'I know,' said Henry quickly, 'but if she's mad – ?'

'There's always that, of course. But to me it doesn't quite fit. Nor to you, I think?'

'To me,' said Henry impatiently, 'nothing fits. The whole thing's a nightmare. I know none of us did it and that's all I do know. I can't think either of their servants are murderers. Giggle's been with them since he was a kid. He's a mild stupid man and plays with trains with Mike. Tinkerton is objectionable on the general grounds that she's got a face like a dead flounder and smells of haircombings. Perhaps *she* killed him.'

'We'd get on a good deal faster, of course,' Alleyn murmured, 'if everybody spoke the flat truth.'

'Really? Don't you think we're telling the truth?'

'Hardly any of you except your brother Michael. Of course we have to be polite and make sympathetic gullible noises but when all's said and done it's little but a hollow mockery. You'll give yourselves away in time, and that's the best we can hope for.'

'Do you often talk like this to your suspects? It seems very un-Yardlike to me,' said Henry lightly.

'We vary our tune a bit. Why didn't you go straight to the drawing-room with your brothers?'

Henry jumped, seemed to pull himself together, and said: 'I didn't at first see what you meant. Hustling tactics, I perceive. I went to the hall door to see if they'd gone.'

'Anybody in the hall?' Henry shook his head. 'Or the landing?'

'No.'

'Or the passage?'

'No.'

'How long were you about it?'

'Not long enough to find a meat skewer and kill my uncle.'

'Where was the meat skewer?'

'*I* don't know,' said Henry. 'We had it in our charade. I suppose it was either in – '

'Yes?'

'It must have been in the hall with all the other stuff.'

'You were going to say in the drawing-room or in the hall?'

'Was I?' said Henry.

'Well,' said Alleyn amiably, 'I'm only asking. Were you?'

'Yes, but I stopped because I realized it couldn't have been in the drawing-room. If anyone had taken it from there we would have seen them.'

'I see by my notes,' said Alleyn, 'that Lord Charles was alone in the drawing-room for some time.'

'Then,' said Henry stolidly, 'he would have seen anybody who came in and took the skewer.'

'Did you happen to look at the hall table on this visit?'

'Yes, I did. I looked to see if his hat and coat were gone. Of course they were. He was in the lift, I suppose, by then.'

Alleyn clasped his hands together on the table and seemed to contemplate them. Then he raised his head and looked at Henry. 'Can you remember anything on the table?'

'I remember very well that there was nothing on it but a vase of flowers.'

'Nothing? You are positive?'

'Quite. I remember the look of the table very clearly. It reflected the light from the window. Someone must have given the vase a knock because there was some water lying on the table. It's rather a favourite of my father's and I remember thinking that the water ought to be mopped up. I gave it a wipe with my handkerchief, but it wasn't very successful. I didn't do anything more about it. I was afraid that Aunt V. might come out of cover and I'd had a bellyful of Aunt V. I went into the drawing-room. But there was nothing on the table.'

'Would you swear to that? I mean, take a legal oath?'

'Yes,' said Henry, 'I would.'

'What did you talk about when you went into the drawing-room?'

For the first time during the interview Henry seemed to be disconcerted. His eyes were blank. He repeated: 'talk about?' on a note that held an overtone of helplessness.

'Yes. What did you say to your father and your brothers or they to you?'

'I don't remember. I – oh, yes, I asked if the Gabriels had gone.'

'Anything else?'

'No. I don't think anybody said anything.'

'And yet,' said Alleyn, 'you must have all been feeling most elated.'

'We – yes. Yes, of course we were.'

'Everything all right again. Lord Wutherwood had promised to see you out of the wood. Crisis averted.'

'Yes. Oh, rather. It was wonderful,' said Henry.

'And yet you all sat there saying nothing except to ask if the benefactor was out of the way. Your younger sister tells me that she and Lady Friede, who went into flat 26 at this stage of the proceedings, also had nothing to say. A curious reaction.'

'Perhaps our hearts,' said Henry recovering his poise, 'were too full for words.'

'Perhaps they were,' said Alleyn. 'I think that's all. Thank you so much.'

Looking rather startled, Henry got up and moved to the door. Here he paused and after a moment's hesitation returned to Alleyn.

'We didn't do it, sir,' he said. 'Honestly. None of us. We are not at all a homicidal family.'

'I'm glad of that,' said Alleyn tranquilly.

Henry stared at him and then shrugged his shoulders. 'Not an impressive effort on my part, I see,' he said.

'Have you been honest with us?'

Henry didn't answer. His face was quite colourless. 'Well, goodnight,' he said and, on some obscure impulse, held out his hand.

II

Fox had not returned. Alleyn looked at his watch. Almost midnight. They'd done not so badly in four hours. He added another column to a tabulated record of everybody's movements from the time of Lord Wutherwood's first yell up to the return of the lift. PC Gibson, at the door, coughed.

'All right,' said Alleyn without looking up. 'We'll get going again in a moment. Been following the statements?'

'Yes, sir.'

'And what do you think about it?' asked Alleyn, scowling at his notes.

'Well, sir, I seem to think there's a good deal in the old lady myself.'

'Yes, Gibson, and so will everybody else. But why, why, why does she want the body? Can you tell me that, Gibson?'

'Because she's mad, sir?' Gibson ventured.

'It won't cover everything. She screamed the roof off when the injury was discovered. She wouldn't go and see him when he was dying. If she killed him why, mad or sane, should she want to take him home? The funeral could have been arranged to leave from the house with all the trappings and the suits of woe, if that's what she's after. It may be, and yet – and yet – it doesn't seem to me like the inconsistency of a *homicidal* lunatic, but Lord knows I'm no alienist. I don't think I've got the dowager right, somehow, and that's a fact. All right, Gibson. My compliments to his lordship and I'd be glad if he'd see me. The others may go to bed, of course.'

'Yes, sir. Martin asked me to mention, sir, that Mr Bathgate has arrived and is with the family. He's been asking if he could see you.'

'So they did ring him up,' Alleyn muttered. 'Incredible! I'd better see him now, Gibson, before you give the message to Lord Charles.'

'Very good, sir.'

Nigel lost no time in making his appearance. Alleyn heard him hurrying along the passage and in a moment he burst into the dining-room.

'Look here, Alleyn,' Nigel cried, 'I've got to talk to you.'

'Talk away,' said Alleyn, 'but not at the top of your voice, and not, if you've any mercy, at great length. I'm on duty.'

'I can't help it if – ' Nigel broke off and looked at Gibson. 'It's – I'd like to see you alone.'

Alleyn nodded good-humouredly at Gibson who went out.

'Now, what is it?' Alleyn asked. 'Have you come to tell me I mustn't speak to your friends as if there's been a murder in their flat?'

'I've come to tell you it's utterly out of the question that any of them should be implicated. I've come to save them, if possible, from opening their mouths and putting their feet in them. See here, Alleyn, I've known the Lampreys all my life. Known them well. They're as mad as mayflies but there's not a vicious impulse in the make-up of a single one of them. Oh hell, I'm not going about this in the right way! I got such a damned jolt when they told me what was up that I'm all anyhow. Let me explain the Lampreys.'

'Two of their friends have already explained them this evening,' said Alleyn. 'Their descriptions tallied fairly well. Boiled down to a few unsympathetic adjectives they came to this: "Charming. Irresponsible. Unscrupulous about money. Good-natured. Lazy. Amusing. Enormously popular." Do you agree?'

'Nobody knows better than you,' said Nigel, 'that people can *not* be boiled down into a few adjectives.'

'I entirely agree. So what do you suggest we do about it?'

'If I could make you understand the Lampreys! God knows what they've been saying to you! I can see that in spite of the shock it's given them, they're beginning to look at this business as a sort of macabre parlour game with themselves on one side and you on the other. They're hopeless. They'll try to diddle you merely to see if they can get away with it. Can you understand that?'

'No,' Alleyn said. 'If they're making false statements for the sheer fun of the thing, I've completely misjudged them.'

'But, Alleyn – '

'See here, Bathgate, you'd much better stay out of this. We had the same difficulty when we first met. The Frantock case is almost seven years old now, isn't it? Do you remember how hot you were about our work over that case? Because the people involved were friends of yours? It's the same thing over again. My dear old Bathgate, it's only being friends with a policeman when you're not also friends with his suspects.'

'Then,' said Nigel turning very pale, 'do you suspect one of them?'

'They were in the flat, together with some eight other persons of whom three are also possible murderers. We've only been four hours on the damned case and haven't had much of a chance to thin out names. I tell you quite honestly we've only got the faintest glimmering so far.'

'I'd risk everything I've got in the world on the Lampreys being out of it.'

'Would you? Then you've nothing to worry about.'

'I know. But I'm so deadly afraid of what they may take it into their heads to say. They're such lunatics.'

'So far, beyond a few superficial flourishes, they haven't behaved like lunatics. They've behaved with an air of irresponsibility, but considering that they're working under police supervision they've managed to keep their misrepresentations pretty consistent. They've displayed a surprising virtuosity. They're nobody's fools.'

'Alleyn,' said Nigel, 'will you let me stand by? I'm not pretending I'm any good at this sort of thing. "Oh God, your only Watson" is my cry. But I – I would like to – to sort of look out for the Lampreys.'

'I don't think I advise you to do it. I tell you we don't know – '

'And I tell you I'm prepared to risk it. I'm only asking to do what I've so often done before. I'll cover the case for my paper. They've actually given me *carte blanche* for that. Did you ever hear of such a thing? Frid said it was a nice scoop for me. And so, of course, it is,' added Nigel honestly. 'Better me than one of the others, after all.'

'You may stay if you think it advisable, of course. But suppose that as things fall out we find ourselves being drawn to – '

'I know what you're going to say and I'm convinced it's entirely out of the question.'

'Then you're in?'

'I'm in.'

'All right,' said Alleyn. 'Gibson!' The door opened. 'I'm ready for Lord Charles, if he can come.'

III

Alleyn had grown accustomed to Lord Charles's walk. It recalled vividly a year out of his own past. From 1919 to 1920 Alleyn's youthful and speculative gaze had followed tail-coated figures hurrying with discretion through the labyrinths of diplomatic corridors. These figures had moved with the very gait of Lord Charles Lamprey and Alleyn wondered if at any time he had been among them. He came into the dining-room with this well-remembered air, taking out his eyeglass as he moved to the table. There was a kind of amateurish gravity about him, linked to an expression of guarded courtesy. He was one of those blond men at whose age it is difficult to guess. Somewhere, Alleyn thought, between forty-five and fifty.

'You will be glad to hear, sir,' said Alleyn, 'that we have nearly finished for tonight.'

'Oh yes,' said Lord Charles. 'Splendid. Hallo, Nigel. Still with us? That's good.'

'He's asked for an unofficial watching-brief,' Alleyn explained. 'Subject, of course, to your approval.'

'Do you mind, Charles?' asked Nigel. 'As you know, I'm Alleyn's Watson. Of course, you'll tell me if you'd rather I made myself scarce.'

'No, no,' said Lord Charles, 'do stay. It was our suggestion. I'm afraid, Alleyn, that by this time you must have decided that we are a fantastically unconventional family.'

The old story, thought Alleyn. It seemed to him that the Lampreys showed great industry in underlining their eccentricity.

He said: 'I think it was a very sensible suggestion, sir. Bathgate is remarkably well equipped as a liaison officer between the press, yourselves, and the police.' This remark met with a silence. Nigel fidgeted and Lord Charles looked blank. Alleyn said: 'As far as your own movements are concerned we've got a complete statement. You didn't leave the drawing-room from the time Lord Wutherwood arrived until the lift returned after the injury was inflicted?'

'No. I was there all the time.'

'Yes. Well, now, I think I must ask you for some account of your conversation with Lord Wutherwood after the others left you alone together.'

Lord Charles rested his right arm on the table, letting his hand hang from the wrist. His left hand was thrust into his trouser pocket. He looked a little as though he sat for a modish portrait. 'Well, Alleyn,' he began, 'from what my Aunt Kit tells me and from what I have already told you and Mr Fox, I expect you will have guessed why my brother called today. I was in a desperate financial case and I appealed to my brother for help. This was the subject of our conversation. My appalling children tell me they overheard us. No doubt they have given you a highly coloured account.'

'I should like to have your own account, sir.'

'Would you? Well, I told Gabriel how things were and he – ah – he read me a pretty stiff lecture. I fully deserved it. I don't know how it is but I have never been able to manage very well. I think I may plead that I've had extraordinarily bad luck. A little while ago things seemed to be most promising. I ventured into business with a very able partner but unfortunately, poor fellow, he became mentally deranged and – ah – was foolish enough to shoot himself.'

'Sir David Stein?'

'Yes, it was,' said Lord Charles opening his eyes very wide. 'Did you know him?'

'I remember the case, sir.'

'Oh. Ah yes, I suppose you would. Very sad and for me, quite disastrous.'

'You explained all this to Lord Wutherwood?'

'Oh, yes. And of course he scolded away about it. Indeed, we quite blazed at each other. It's always been like that. Gabriel would give me hell and we would both get rather angry with each other and then, poor old boy, he would come to the rescue.'

'Did he come to the rescue this time?'

'He didn't write a cheque there and then,' said Lord Charles. 'That was not his way, you know. I expect he wanted me to have a night to think over my wigging and feel properly ashamed of myself.'

'Did he promise to do so?' There was a fraction of a pause.

'Yes,' said Lord Charles.

Alleyn's pencil whispered across his note-book. He turned a page, flattened it, and looked up. Neither Lord Charles nor Nigel had stirred but now Nigel cleared his throat and took out a cigarette-case.

'He promised,' said Alleyn, 'quite definitely in so many words, to pay up your debts?'

'Not exactly in so many words. He muttered that he supposed he would have to see me through as usual, that – ah – that I would hear from him.'

'Yes. Lord Charles, your children, as you evidently have heard, lay in the corner there and listened to the conversation. Suppose I told you they had not heard this promise of your brother's, what would you say?'

'I shouldn't be in the least surprised. They could not possibly have heard it. Gabriel had walked to the far end of the room and I had followed him. I only just heard it myself. He – ah – he mumbled it out as if he was half ashamed.'

'Then suppose, alternatively, that I tell you they state they did hear him promise to help you, would you say that they were not speaking the truth.'

'Somebody once told me,' said Lord Charles, 'that detective officers were not allowed to set traps for their witnesses.'

'They are not allowed to hold out veiled promises and expose them to implied threats,' said Alleyn. 'It is not quite the same thing, sir. I'm sure you know that you may leave any question unanswered if you think it advisable to do so.'

'I can only repeat,' said Lord Charles breathlessly, 'that he promised to help me and that I think it unlikely that they could have heard him.'

'Yes,' said Alleyn, writing.

Nigel leant across the table offering his cigarettes to Lord Charles. Lord Charles had not changed his modish attitude. He looked perfectly at his ease, perfectly aware of his surroundings, and yet he did not notice Nigel's gesture. There was something odd in this unexpected revelation of his detachment. Nigel touched his sleeve with the cigarette-case. He started, moved his arm sharply and, with a murmured apology, took a cigarette.

'I really don't think there's very much else,' said Alleyn. 'There's a small point about the arrival of your three older sons after Lord Wutherwood left. In what order did they come into the drawing-room?'

'The twins came in first. Henry appeared a moment or two later.'

'How long, should you say, sir? A minute? Two minutes?'

'I shouldn't think longer than two minutes. I don't think anyone had spoken before he came in.'

'You didn't at once tell them that Lord Wutherwood had promised to see you out of the wood?'

'I didn't, no. I was still rather chastened, you see, by my scolding.'

'Oh, yes,' said Alleyn politely. 'Of course. That really is all, I think, sir. I'm so sorry but I'm afraid I shall have to litter a few men about the flat for a little while still.'

'Surely we may go out tomorrow?'

'Of course. You won't, any of you, want to leave London?'

'No.'

'The inquest will probably be on Monday. I wonder, sir, if you can give me the name of Lord Wutherwood's solicitors.'

'Rattisbon. They've been our family lawyers for generations. I must ring up old Rattisbon, I suppose.'

'Then that really is everything.' Alleyn stood up. 'We shall ask you to sign a transcript of your statement tomorrow if you will. I must thank you very much indeed, sir, for so patiently enduring all this police procedure.'

Lord Charles did not rise. He looked up with an air of hesitancy. 'As a matter of fact,' he said, 'there's one other thing that rather bothers us, Alleyn. Tinkerton, my sister-in-law's maid, you know, came into the dining-room just now in a great state. It seems that my sister-in-law, whom I may say we all thought was safely asleep in my wife's bed, has now woken up and is in a really appalling frame of mind. She says she must have something or other from their house in Brummell Street and that Tinkerton and only Tinkerton can find it. Some patent medicine or another, it seems to be. Well now, your men are allowing no one to leave the flat. I explained all that to Tinkerton and she went off to return saying Violet was out of bed trying to dress herself and proving too big a handful for the nurse. The nurse, for her part, says she won't tackle the job single-handed. We've rung up for a second nurse but now Tinkerton, although she's perfectly willing to carry on with the nurses, has obviously taken fright. It's all a frightful bore, and Imogen and I are both at our wits' end. I won't pretend we wouldn't be most relieved to see the last of poor Violet, but we also feel that if you allowed her to go she ought to have somebody who is not a servant or a strange nurse to be with her in that mausoleum of a house. Imogen says she will go but that I will not have. She's completely fagged out and where she is to sleep if Violet stays here for the rest of the night I simply don't know. I – really the whole thing is getting a little more than we can reasonably be expected to endure. I wonder if you could possibly help us?'

'I think so,' Alleyn said. 'We can arrange for Lady Wutherwood to go to her own house. We shall have to send someone along to be on duty there, but that can easily be done. I can spare a man from here.'

'I'm extraordinarily relieved.'

'About somebody else going – who do you suggest?'

'Well – ' Lord Charles passed his hand over the back of his head. 'Well, Robin Grey – Roberta Grey, you know – has very nicely offered to go.'

'Rather a youthful guardian,' said Alleyn with a lift of his eyebrow.

'Ah – yes. Yes, but she's a most resourceful and composed little person and says she doesn't mind. My wife suggests that Nanny might go to keep her company. I mean she will be perfectly all right. Two trained nurses and Tinkerton, who for all her fright insists that she can carry on as usual and says Violet will be quite quiet when she has had this medicine of hers. You see Frid, my eldest girl, may be a bit shaken, and of course Patch – Patricia – is too young. And we feel it ought to be a woman – I mean just for the look of things. You see, the nurse says that without someone besides Tinkerton she feels she can't take the responsibility until the second nurse comes. So we thought that if Robin – I mean, of course, with your approval.'

Alleyn remembered a steadfast face, heart-shaped and colourless, with wide-set eyes of grey. His own phrase 'a courageous little liar' recurred to him. But it was no business of his who the Lampreys sent to keep up the look of things in Brummell Street. Better perhaps that it should be the small New Zealander who surely did not come into this tragi-comedy except in the dim role of confidante and wholehearted admirer of the family. With a remote feeling of uneasiness Alleyn agreed that Miss Grey and Nanny Burnaby should go in a taxi to Brummell Street; that Lady Wutherwood, Tinkerton, and the nurses, should be driven there by Giggle with Gibson as police escort. Lord Charles hurried away to organize these manoeuvres. Nigel, with a dubious look at Alleyn, murmured something about returning in a minute or two and slipped out after Lord Charles. Alleyn, left alone, walked restlessly about the dining-room. When Fox returned Alleyn instantly thrust the notes of Lord Charles's statement at him.

'Look at that,' he said, 'or rather don't. I'll tell you. He said that when they got to the far end of the drawing-room his brother promised in a mumble to help him. He said that none of his precious brood could have heard it. He was in a fix. He didn't know what they'd told me. I tripped him, Br'er Fox.'

'Nicely,' said Fox, thumbing over the notes.

'Yes, but damn him, it still might be true. *They* may have lied but he may have spoken the truth. I'll swear he didn't, though.'

'I know he didn't,' said Fox.

'Do you, by George?'

'Yes, sir. I've been talking to the parlour-maid.'

'With parlour-maids,' said Alleyn, 'you stand supreme. What did she say?'

'She was in the pantry at the time,' said Fox, hauling out his spectacles and note-book. 'The pantry door was open and she heard most of what was said between the brothers. I got her to own up that she slid out into the passage after a bit and had a good earful. I asked her why none of the other servants heard what she says she heard and her answer was that they all hung together with the family. She's under notice and doesn't mind what she says. Rather a vindictive type of girl with very shapely limbs.'

'That's nice,' said Alleyn. 'Go on. What's her name?'

'Blackmore's the name. Cora. She says that the two gentlemen got very hot with each other and there was a lot of talk about the deceased cutting his brother out of everything that he could. Blackmore says he went on something terrible. Called his present lordship everything from a sponger to a blackguard, and fetched up by saying he'd see him in the gutter before he'd give him another penny piece. Then she says his present lordship lost his temper and things got very noisy until the boy – Master Michael – went into the drawing-room with a parcel. When Blackmore saw Master Michael she made out that she was doing something to the soda-water machine in the passage. He went in and they pulled up and said no more to each other. The deceased came away almost at once. As he got to the door he said, speaking very quiet and venomous according to Blackmore: "That's final. If there's any more whining for help I'll take legal measures to rid myself of the lot of you." Now sir,' said Fox looking over the top of his spectacles, 'Blackmore was playing round behind the soda-water machine which is close to the wall. She *says* she heard his present lordship say, very distinctly: "I wish that there was some measure, legal or illegal, by which I could get rid of *you!*"'

'Crikey!' said Alleyn.

'That's what I thought,' said Fox.

CHAPTER 16

Night Thickens

It was in a sort of trance that Roberta offered to spend the rest of an endless night in an unknown house with the apparently insane widow of a murdered peer. Lord Charles had displayed an incisiveness that surprised Roberta. When Charlot said she would go to Brummell Street he had said: 'I absolutely forbid it, Immy,' and rather to Roberta's surprise Charlot had at once given in. Frid offered to go, but not with any great show of enthusiasm, and Charlot looked dubious. So Roberta, wondering if she spoke out of turn or if at last here was something she could do for the Lampreys, made her offer. With the exception of Henry they all seemed to be gently relieved. Roberta knew that the Lampreys, persuaded perhaps by dim ideas of pioneering hardihood, were inclined to think of all colonials as less sheltered and more inured to nervous strain, than their English contemporaries. They were charmingly grateful and asked if she was sure she wouldn't mind.

'You won't see a sign of Aunt V.,' said Frid, and Charlot added: 'And you really ought to see the house, Robin. I can't *tell* you what it is like. All Victorian gloom and glaring stuffed animals. *Too* perfect.'

'I don't see why Robin should go,' said Henry.

'Robin says she doesn't mind,' Frid pointed out. 'And if Nanny goes she'll feel as safe as a crown jewel. Isn't Robin sweet, Mummy?'

'She's very kind indeed,' said Charlot. 'Honestly, Robin darling, are you *sure?*'

'I'm quite sure if you think I'll do.'

'It's just for *somebody* to be there with the nurses. If Violet should by any chance make some sort of scene you can ring us up. But I'm sure she won't. She needn't even know you are there.'

And so it was arranged. PC Martin, no longer in his armchair, stared fixedly at a portrait of a Victorian Lamprey. Lord Charles went off for his interview with Alleyn. Frid did her face, the twins looked gloomily at old *Punches*, Charlot, having refused to go to bed until the interviews were over, put her feet up and closed her eyes.

'Every moment,' said Henry, 'this room grows more like a dental waiting-parlour. Here is a particularly old *Tatler*, Robin. Will you look at it and complete the picture?'

'Thank you, Henry. What are you reading?'

'The Bard. I am reading *Macbeth*. He has a number of very meaty things to say about murder.'

'Do you like the Bard?'

'I suppose I must, as quite often I find myself reading him.'

'On this occasion,' Stephen said, 'I call it bad form t-to read *Macbeth*.'

' "Night thickens," ' said Frid in a professionally deep voice.

' "And the crow makes wing to the rooky wood:
  Good things of day begin to droop and drowse,
  While nights black agents to their prey do rouse." '

'You *would*,' said Colin bitterly.

Roberta turned over the pages of the *Tatler*, unsolaced by studio portraits of ladies looking faintly nauseated and by snapshots of the same or closely similar ladies, looking either partially concussed or madly hilarious. She would have liked to put down the *Tatler* but was prevented from doing so by the circumstances of finding, whenever she looked up, that Henry's eye was upon her. Strange thoughts visited Roberta. She supposed that many of the ladies in the *Tatler* were personally known to Henry. Perhaps the mysterious Mary was one of them. Perhaps she was long-limbed, with that smooth expensive look so far beyond the reach of a small whey-faced colonial. So why, thought Roberta, with murder in the house and nobody being anything but vaguely kind, and with smooth ladies everywhere for Henry, should she be feeling happy? And before she could stop herself she had pictured the smooth ladies gliding away from Henry because he was mixed up in murder while she, Roberta Grey, dawned upon him in her full worth. With these and similar fancies her mind was so busily occupied that she did not notice the passing of the minutes and when Lord Charles and Nigel Bathgate returned, she thought that Alleyn must have kept them a very short time in the dining-room. She roused herself to notice that Lord Charles looked remarkably blank and Mr Bathgate remarkably uneasy.

'Immy, darling,' said Lord Charles, 'why haven't you gone to bed?'

'If anyone else tells me to go to bed,' said Charlot, 'knowing full well that my bed is occupied by a mad woman, I shall instantly ask Mr Martin to arrest them.'

'Well, it won't be occupied much longer. Alleyn says she may go home and that Robin and Nanny may go with her. He's sending a policeman too, so you'll be quite safe, Robin, my dear. The rest of us are – ' Lord Charles fumbled for his glass, 'are free to go to bed.'

'Except me,' said Frid. 'Mr Alleyn will want to see me. He's evidently saved me up for the last.'

'He didn't say anything about you.'

'Wait and see,' said Frid, touching her hair.

Fox came in.

'Excuse me, my lady,' Fox said, 'Mr Alleyn has asked me to thank you and his lordship and the other ladies and gentlemen for their patience and courtesy and to say he will not trouble you any further tonight.'

'Make a good exit out of that, if you can,' said Henry unkindly to Frid.

II

Could it possibly, Robin wondered confusedly, be no longer than forty hours ago that she packed this little suitcase in her cabin? Time, she thought, meant nothing at all when strange things were happening. It was incredible that she had slept only one night in England. The bottom of the suitcase was littered with small objects for which she had not been able to find a place; the final menu card of the ship, with signatures that had already become quite meaningless, snapshots of deck sports, a piece of ship's notepaper. They belonged to a remote experience but for a fraction of a second Roberta longed for the secure isolation of her cabin and thought of how in the night, sometimes, she would listen contentedly to the sound of the ship's progress through the lonely ocean. She packed the suitcase, trying to keep her head about the things she would need and wondering how long she would have to stay with the Lampreys' mad aunt in Brummell Street. There were sounds of activity next door in Charlot's room and presently Roberta heard the door open. A dragging clumsy footstep sounded in the passage and the nurse's voice, professionally soothing: 'Now, we shall *soon* be home and tucked up in our own bed. Come along, dear. That's the way.' Then that deep grating voice: 'Leave me alone. Where's Tinkerton?' And Tinkerton: 'Here, m'lady. Come along, m'lady. We're going home.' Roberta heard them pass and go out to the landing. She had fastened down the lid of her suitcase but was still sitting on the floor when the curtains of her improvised room rattled and, turning quickly, she saw Henry.

He wore a greatcoat and scarf and in his hands he held a small heap of clothes.

'Oh, Robin,' Henry said, 'I'm coming to Brummell Street. Do you mind?'

'Henry! I don't mind at all. I'm terribly glad.'

'Then that's all right. I asked Alleyn. He seems to think it's in order. I'll just pack these things and then we'll get a taxi and go. Mama has rung up Brummell Street and told the servants. Tinkerton has told Aunt V.'

'What did she say?'

'I don't think she was particularly ravished at the thought. Patch is having a nightmare and Nanny isn't coming.'

'I see.'

Henry looked gravely at Roberta and then smiled. There was a quality in Henry's smile that had always touched Roberta and endeared him to her. He made a comic family grimace, winked, and laid his finger against his nose. Roberta made the same grimace and Henry withdrew. With an illogical singing in her heart she put on her own overcoat and hat and took her suitcase out into the passage to wait for Henry. This time last night they had been dancing together.

It was not very pleasant crossing the landing where a policeman stood on guard by the dark lift but Henry lightened the situation by saying: 'We're not fleeing from justice, officer.'

'That's quite all right, sir,' answered policeman. 'The Chief Inspector told us all about you.'

'Goodnight,' said Henry, piloting Roberta down the stairs.

'Goodnight, sir,' said the policeman and his voice rang hollow in the lift well.

Roberta remembered her last trip down the stairs when she went to fetch Giggle and Tinkerton and how like a nightmare it had seemed. Now the stairs seemed a way of escape. It was glorious to reach the ground floor and see the lights of traffic through the glass doors. It was splendid when the doors were opened to breathe the night air of London. Henry took her elbow and they moved forward into a blinding whiteness that flashed and was gone. A young man came up to Henry and with a queer air of hardened deference said: 'Lord Rune? I wonder if you would mind – '

'I'm afraid I would, do you know,' said Henry. 'Taxi!'

A cruising taxi drew up at once but before they could get in there was another flash and this time Roberta saw the camera.

Henry bundled her in and slammed the doors, keeping his face turned from the window. 'Damn!' he said. 'I'd forgotten about Nigel's low friends.' And he yelled the address through to the driver.

'Lord Rune,' said Roberta's thoughts. 'Henry is Lord Rune. The Earl of Rune. Pressmen lie in wait for him with cameras. Everything is very odd.'

She was awakened by Henry giving her a little pat on the back. 'Aren't you the clever one?' he said.

'Am I?' asked Roberta. 'How?'

'Tipping us the wink what you'd told Alleyn.'

'Do you think that policeman noticed?'

'Not he. You know I didn't exactly enjoy lying to Alleyn.'

'I hated it. And, Henry, I don't think he believes it – about your Uncle G. promising the money.'

' 'More do I. Oh well, we could but try.' He put his arm round Roberta. 'Brave old Robin Grey,' said Henry. 'Going into the witch's den. What have we done to deserve you?'

'Nothing,' said Robin with spirit. 'Without the word of a lie you're a hopeless crew.'

'Do you remember a conversation we had years ago on the slope of Little Mount Silver?'

'Yes.'

'So do I. And here I am still without a job. I dare say it would have been a good thing if Uncle G. had lived to chortle at our bankruptcy. It would take a major disaster to cure us. Perhaps when the war comes it will do the trick. Kill, as they say, or cure.'

'I expect you'll manage to slope through a war in the same old way. But don't you call this a major disaster?'

'I suppose so. But you know, Robin, somehow or another although I feel very bothered and frightened, I don't inside myself, think that any of us are bound for the dock.'

'Oh *don't*. How *can* you gossip away about it!'

'It's not really affectation. I ought to be in a panic but I'm not. Not really.'

The taxi carried them into Hyde Park Corner. Roberta looked through the window and saw the four heroic horses snorting soundlessly against a night sky, grandiloquently unaware of the less florid postures of some bronze artillerymen down below.

'We shan't be long now,' said Henry. 'I can't tell you how frightful this house is. Uncle G.'s idea of the amenities was a mixture of elephantine ornament and incredible hardship. The servants are not allowed to use electricity once the gentry are in bed so they creep about by candlelight. It's true, I promise you. The house was done up by my grandfather on the occasion of his marriage and since then has merely amassed a continuous stream of hideous *objets d'art.*'

'I read somewhere that Victorian things are fashionable again.'

'So they are, but with a difference. And, anyway, I think it's a stupid fashion. Sometimes,' said Henry, 'I wonder if there is such a thing as beauty.'

'Isn't it supposed to exist in the eye of the beholder?'

'I won't take that. There are eyes and eyes. Fashion addles any true conception of beauty. There's something inherently vulgar in fashion.'

'And yet,' said Roberta, 'if Frid dressed herself up like a belle of 1929 you wouldn't much care to be seen with her.'

'She'd only be putting her fashion back eleven years.'

'Well, what do you want? Nudism? Or bags tied round the middle?'

'You are unanswerable,' said Henry. 'All the same – ' and he expounded his ideas on fashion, giving Roberta cause to marvel at his detachment.

The taxi bucketed along Park Lane and presently turned into a decorous sidestreet where the noise of London was muffled and the rows of great uniform houses seemed fast asleep.

'Here we are,' Henry said. 'I *think* I've enough to pay the taxi. How much is it? Ah yes, I can just do it *with* the tip. So that's all hotsy-totsy. Come on.'

As Henry rang the front doorbell, Roberta heard a clock chime and strike a single great note.

'One o'clock,' she said. 'Where is it striking?'

'I expect it was Big Ben. You hear him all over the place at night-time.'

'I've only heard him on the air before.'

'You're in London now.'

'I know. I keep saying so to myself.'

'It's a damn shame you should be landed in our particular soup. Here comes somebody.'

The great door swung inwards. With the feeling that an ominous fairy-tale was unfolding, Roberta saw a very old woman dressed in black satin and carrying a lighted candle in a silver candlestick. She stood against a dim background of stuffed bears, marble groups, gigantic pictures and a wide staircase that ascended into blackness. Henry said: 'Good morning Moffatt,' to this woman, and added, 'I expect Tinkerton has explained that Miss Grey and I have come to stay with her ladyship.' The woman answered: 'Yes, Mr Henry. Yes, my lord.' And like all the portresses of elfland she added: 'You are expected.'

They followed her, crossing a deep carpet and ascending the stairs. They climbed two flights up to a muffled landing. The air was both cold and stuffy. Moffatt whispered an apology for her candle. A detective had arrived and insisted that the light should not be turned off at the switchboard, but at least they could keep his poor lordship's rule and not go using the lights before, as Moffatt said with relish, he was scarcely cold. Great shadows marched and stooped across unseen walls as Moffatt walked ahead with her candle. There was no sound but the stealthy whisper of her satin hem. Sometimes, as she held the candle before her she was a black figure with a golden rim but sometimes she turned to light them, and then her shadow sprang up beyond her. They came at last to a doorway which Moffatt opened. With a murmured apology she went in before them. Roberta, pausing on the threshold, saw a dim reflection of Moffatt in a dark looking-glass. Branched candlesticks stood on an immense dressing-table. Moffatt lit the candles and looked at Roberta who, on this hint, entered her new bedroom. Henry followed.

'If there is anything you require, Miss?' suggested Moffatt. 'Perhaps I may unpack for you? We only keep two maids when the family is not in residence and they are both in bed.'

Roberta said that she would unpack for herself and Moffatt and the candle and Henry went away.

The bedroom had a very high ceiling with a central plaster ornament. The walls were covered with a heavily patterned paper and hung at intervals with thick curtains. Enormous pieces of furniture stood about the room, perpetuating some Victorian cabinetmaker's illegitimate passion for mahogany and low relief. But the bed was a distinguished four-poster with fine carvings, a faded French canopy, and brocaded curtains where gold threads shone among rose-coloured flowers. The carpet was deep and covered with vegetable conceits. Upon the walls Roberta found four steel engravings and one colour print of a child with a kitten. There was a great charm in this print, so artlessly did the beribboned child simper over the blue bow of the kitten. Beside her bed Roberta found a Bible, a novel by Marie Corelli, and a tin of thick dry biscuits. She unpacked her suitcase and, too timid to hunt down back passages for a bathroom, washed in cold water provided by a garlanded ewer. There was a tap at the door. Henry came in wearing his dressing-gown.

'Are you all right?' he asked.

'Yes.'

'Isn't it frightful? I'm over the way so if you want anything you've only to cross the passage. There's nobody else on this side. Aunt V. is across the landing in a terrible suite. Goodnight, Robin.'

'Goodnight, Henry.'

'You interrupted me,' said Henry. 'I was going to add, "my darling".'

He winked solemnly and went out.

III

A wind got up during the small hours. It hunted desolately about London, its course deflected by sleeping buildings. It moaned about Pleasaunce Court Mansions, shaking the skylight of the lift well. The policeman on duty there stared upwards and wished the black rattling panes would turn grey for the dawn. It blew the curtains of Patch's windows across her face, giving her another nightmare and causing her to make horrid noises in her throat. The rest of the family, hearing Patch, turned fretfully in their beds and listened for the thud of Nanny's feet as she stumped down the passage. Gathering strength in the open places of Hyde Park, the wind howled across Park Lane and whistled up Brummell Street so that the old chimney-cowls in No. 24 swung round with a groan and Roberta heard a voice in the chimney moaning 'Rune – Rune Rune.' Out at Hammersmith the wind ruffled the black waters of the Thames and the blameless dreams of Lady Katherine Lobe. Indeed the only actor in the Pleasaunce Court case who was not disturbed by that night wind was the late Lord Wutherwood who lay in a morgue awaiting his tryst with Dr Curtis.

'Wind getting up,' said Fox in the chief inspector's room at Scotland Yard. 'Shouldn't be surprised if we had rain before dawn.' He pulled a completed sheet and two carbons from his typewriter, added them tidily to the stacked papers on his desk, and took out his pipe.

'What's the time?' asked Alleyn.

'Five-and-thirty past two, sir.'

'We've about finished, haven't we, Fox?'

'I think so, sir. I've just got out the typescript of your report.'

Alleyn crumpled a sheet of paper and threw it at Nigel Bathgate who was asleep in an office chair. 'Wake up, Bathgate. The end's in view.'

'What? Hallo, are we going home? Is that the report? May I see it?' asked Nigel.

'If you like. Give him a carbon, Fox. We'll all have a brood over the beastly thing.' And for twenty minutes they read and smoked in silence broken by the rustle of papers and occasional gusts that shook the window frames.

'That covers it, I think,' said Alleyn at last. He looked at Nigel who with the nervous half-irritated concentration of a pressman was still reading the report.

'Yes,' said Fox heavily, 'as far as the family goes it's all pretty plain sailing. Their truthful statements seem to hang together and so, if you can put it that way, do their untruthful statements.'

Nigel looked up. 'Are you so positive,' he said, 'that some of their statements are not true?'

'Certainly,' Alleyn said. 'The story of Wutherwood promising to pay up is without doubt a tarradiddle. Roberta Grey tipped the wink to Lord Charles and Master Henry. Martin, the constable on duty, heard her do it. She said: "You must feel glad he was so generous, after all. It'll be nice to remember that." You'll find it in the report. I said she was a courageous little liar, didn't I?'

'Is it the only lie she handed us?' asked Fox deeply.

'I'm sure it is. She made a brave shot at it but she had her ears laid back for the effort. I should say she was by habit an unusually truthful little party. I'll stake my pension she hadn't the remotest notion of the significance of her one really startling bit of information. She was absolutely sure of herself, too. Repeated it twice, and signed a statement to the same effect.'

'Here, wait a bit,' Nigel ejaculated and hastily turned back the pages of his report.

'If she's right,' said Fox, 'it plays Bobs-a-dying with the whole blooming case.'

'It may make it a good deal simpler. Is that commissionaire fellow all right, Fox? Dependable?'

'I should say so. He noticed the eccentric old Lady Katherine Lobe – all right. She *walked* down but he didn't miss her. And he didn't miss that chap Giggle nor Miss Tinkerton either. Passed the time of day with them as they went out. And, by the way, you'll notice he confirms Tinkerton's story that she got downstairs, just after Giggle.'

'Miserable female,' Alleyn muttered. 'There's a liar if you like! Still, the commissionaire seems sound enough.'

'Rather an observant sort of chap, I should say,' Fox agreed. 'They have a knack of noticing people at that job.'

'And he says the lift was not used between the time the Wutherwoods went up and what I feel sure Bathgate's paper will call the fatal trip?'

'That's right. He says he can't be mistaken. He always has a look to see who comes down or goes up because it's his job to keep that "In and Out" affair up to date. After the Wutherwoods went up to the flat the lift didn't return. He says the people on the first floor never use it. The second floor's away on a holiday and the third is unlet. The lift is really only used by the Lampreys just now.'

'Ah, well,' said Alleyn. 'It's a line of country. We'll have to follow it up.'

'What is?' Nigel demanded. 'What are you talking about?' He pored over the report for a minute and then said: 'Here! Are you thinking of those two servants? Giggle and Tinkerton?'

'Have you read that report carefully?'

'Yes, I have. I know what you mean. Young Michael says Wutherwood yelled out for his wife after Giggle went downstairs. Suppose that was a blind? Suppose Giggle came back and did the job?'

'Passing Tinkerton on his way up and probably running into Lady Charles as she came out of the lift? Remember Lady Charles came out of 26 and went to the drawing-room in the other flat.'

'Then whoever the murderer was, he took the risk of meeting her.'

'The murderer,' said Alleyn, 'took great risks but I'm inclined to think that was not one of them.'

'For God's sake, Alleyn, what do you mean by that?'

'I told you it would be better if you kept out of it. I can't discuss the case fully with you. It wouldn't be fair to any of us. If we find ourselves drawn away from the Lampreys you'd burst to tell them so. If we find ourselves drawn towards one of them – what then? Your position would be intolerable. Better keep out.'

'No,' said Nigel. 'I'll stick. What about this Tinkerton who's a liar?'

'She's almost the only member of the crowd of whom I am certain. She didn't kill Wutherwood. It's actually a physical impossibility.'

'Then,' said Nigel, 'in my mind there's only one answer. It must be the dowager. Homicidal lunacy. She must have taken the skewer when Imogen went into the dining-room to ask for a twin to work the lift.'

'The skewer had gone by then. *Vide* Michael.'

'Well, if he's right, she took it before that and did the trick while she was supposed to be in the lavatory.'

'Yes,' said Alleyn, 'that's arguable. But see what Roberta Grey says.'

'Oh, damn Roberta Grey. What do you mean, Roberta Grey?'

'If you want to see things as a whole,' said Alleyn, 'get it down as a sort of table. Take Lord Wutherwood's movements from the time he left the drawing-room until the lift returned, not forgetting the two yells he gave for his wife. Then look at the statements and correlate all the other people's moves with his. You'll find that after Wutherwood called the second time the landing was deserted until Lady Charles went from 26 to the drawing-room. During that period, according to the statements, Lord Charles and his three elder sons were in the drawing-room, Lady Charles and her daughters in her bedroom, Lady Wutherwood and Lady Katherine in the two lavatories, Giggle on his way downstairs, Tinkerton following him, Baskett in the servants' hall, Roberta Grey in the dining-room, Michael in flat 26, and Nanny in her bedroom. The other servants and the bum were in the kitchen, and during that same period Lady Katherine Lobe went downstairs and into the street.'

'And that's the crucial time?'

'It's unlikely that he yelled for his wife in what they all agree was his normal voice, after he'd got a skewer in his brain.'

'Lady Katherine told me that she slipped away after Lady Charles crossed the landing. That means that she herself was on the landing and making for the stairs. She looked at the lift but could see nobody inside. With those doors you can't see anybody who is sitting down. Wutherwood must have been in the lift then but his murderer, unless he sat beside his victim, was not there. Nor, of course, was he on the landing. A moment later Stephen Lamprey came out to work the lift.'

Nigel dabbed his finger on the carbon copy.

'And when Stephen went out on the landing his aunt was there – alone.'

'That is what he gave in his statement,' said Alleyn without emphasis.

'Have you any reason to doubt his statement?'

'At the moment, none.'

'Very well, then. She had been alone on the landing.'

'I thought your argument was that she did it before that, in which case why did she stay on the landing?'

'I'm only showing that she had opportunities.'

'All right.'

'Alleyn,' said Nigel, 'please tell me. Do you think she did it?'

'There you go, you see,' said Alleyn wearily. 'Stick to your pressmanship, my boy. Go away and write a front-page story and let me see it before you hand it over to your evening screecher. Come on. We'll go home to our unfortunate wives and Fox to his blameless pallet.'

They parted on the Embankment, Nigel hailed a taxi. Fox, his head bent sideways, his hand to his bowler and his overcoat flapping about his formidable legs, tacked off into the wind, making for his lodgings in Victoria. Alleyn crossed the Embankment and leaning on the parapet looked down into the black shadows of Westminster Pier. The river slapped against wet stones and Alleyn felt a thin touch of spray on his face. He stood for so long that a constable on night duty paused and finally marched down upon his superior, flashing his torch into Alleyn's face.

'It's all right,' said Alleyn. 'I'm not yet tired of life.'

'I beg pardon, sir, I'm sure. Mr Alleyn isn't it? Didn't recognize you for a minute. It's a thick night.'

'It's a beastly night,' agreed Alleyn, 'and we're at the worst part of it.'

'Yes, sir. That's right, sir.'

'Dull job, night duty, isn't it?'

'Chronic, sir. Nothing much to do as a general rule except walk and think.'

'I know.'

Gratified by this encouragement, the constable said: 'Yes, sir. I always reckon that if there's any chap or female on this beat, hanging off and on, wondering whether they'll make a hole in the river or not, it's between two and four of the morning they'll go overboard if they're ever going. The river patrols say the same thing.'

'Yes,' said Alleyn. 'So do doctors and nurses. It's the hour of low vitality.' He did not move away and the constable still further encouraged, continued the conversation.

'Have you ever read a play called *Macbeth*, sir?' he asked.

'Yes,' said Alleyn, turning his head to look at the man.

'I wonder if it'd be the same thing, sir. The one I have in mind is by this Shakespeare.'

'I think it'll be the same.'

'Well, sir, I saw that piece once at the Old Vic. On duty there, sir, I was. It's a funny kind of a show. Not the type of entertainment that appeals to me as a general rule. Morbid. But it kind of caught my fancy and afterwards I got hold of a copy of the words and read them. There's one or two bits I seem to be reminded of when I'm on night duty. I don't know why, I'm sure, because the play is a countrified affair. Blasted heaths and woods and so on.'

'And witches,' said Alleyn.

'That's so, sir. Very peculiar. Fanciful. All the same there's one or two bits that stick in my mind. Something about "night thickens" and it goes on about birds flying into trees, and "good things of day begin to droop and drouse" – and – er – '

' "While night's black agents to their prey do rouse." '

'Ah. It's the same, then. Gives you a sort of sensation, doesn't it, sir?'

'Yes.'

'And there's another remark that took my fancy. This chap Macbeth asks his wife, "What is the night," meaning what's the time and she says "Almost at odds with morning, which is which." It's the kind of way it's put. They were a very nasty couple. Bad type. Superstitious, like most crooks. She was the worst of the two, in my opinion. Tried to fix the job so's it'd look as if the servants had done it. Do you recollect that, sir?'

'Yes,' said Alleyn slowly, 'yes.'

'Mind,' said the constable warming a little, 'I reckon if he hadn't lost his nerve they'd have got away with it. No finger-printing in those days, you see. And you know how it'd be, sir. You don't expect people of their class to commit murder.'

'No.'

'No, you don't. And with the weapons lying there beside these grooms or whatever they were, and so on, well the first thing anybody would have said was: "Here's your birds." Not that there seemed to be anything like what you'd call an inquiry.'

'Not precisely,' said Alleyn.

'No, sir. No,' continued the constable, turning his back to the wind, 'if Macbeth hadn't got jumpy and mucked things up I reckon they'd have got away with it. They seemed to be well-liked people in the district. Some kind of royalty. Aristocratic like. Well, nobody suspects people of that class. That's my point.'

Alleyn pulled his hat on more firmly and turned up the collar of his coat.

'Well,' he said, 'I'll go off duty."

'Yes, sir. I beg pardon, sir. Don't know what came over me speaking so freely, sir.'

'That's all right,' said Alleyn. 'You've put a number of ideas in my head. Goodnight to you.'

CHAPTER 17

Mr Fox Finds an Effigy

The north wind that had come up during the night brought clouds. Before dawn these broke into teeming rain. At nine o'clock Roberta and Henry breakfasted in a room heavy with Victorian appointments. The windows were blind with rain and the room so dark that Henry turned on the lights.

'I don't suppose that's ever been done before except in a pea-soup fog,' he said cheerfully. 'How did you sleep, Robin?'

'Not so badly,' said Roberta, 'but for the wind in the chimney. It would drone out your name.'

'My name?' said Henry quickly. 'I've never heard the north wind make a noise like "Henry".'

'Your new name.'

'Oh,' said Henry, 'that. Yes, it is rather flatulent, isn't it?'

'Have you heard how Lady Wutherwood is this morning?'

'I met Tinkerton on the landing. She says Aunt V. slept like a log. "Very peaceful," Tinkerton said, as if Aunt V. was a corpse.'

'Don't.'

'I suppose it's real,' said Henry returning with eggs and bacon from the side table. 'I suppose somebody did kill Uncle G. last night. This morning it scarcely seems credible. What shall we do all day, Robin? Do you imagine that if we go out our footsteps will be dogged by a plainclothes detective? It might be fun to see if we could shake him off. I've always thought how easy it must be to lose a follower. Shall we try, or is it too wet?'

'There's a policeman down in the hall.'

'How inexpressibly deadly for him,' said Henry. 'I think the hall is possibly the worst part of this house. When we were small the direst threat Nanny had for us was that we should be sent to live in Brummell Street. Even now I slink past that stuffed bear, half expecting him to reach out and paw me to his bosom.'

'It's such a large house,' said Roberta, 'even the bear looks smallish. Has it been your family's house for long?'

'It dates from a Lamprey who did some very fishy bit of hankypanky for Good Queen Anne or one of her ministers. A pretty hot bit of work, one would think, to be rewarded with such a monstrous tip. She made him a Marquis into the bargain. The house must have been rather a fine affair in those days. It took my grandfather to ruin it. Uncle G. and Aunt V. merely added a few layers of gloom to the general chaos.'

'I suppose it's your father's house now.'

Henry paused in the act of raising his cup. 'Golly,' he said, 'I wonder if it is. One could make rather a lovely house of it, you know.' And into Henry's face came a speculative expression which Roberta, with a sinking heart, recognized as the look of a Lamprey about to spend a lot of money.

'There'll be terrific death duties,' she cried in panic.

'Oh, yes,' said Henry, grandly dismissing them.

They finished their breakfast in silence. An extremely old manservant, who Roberta thought must be Mrs Moffatt's husband, came in to say Henry was wanted on the telephone.

'I'll answer it in the library,' said Henry, and to Roberta: 'It'll be the family. Come on.'

In a dimly forbidding library Roberta listened to Henry on the telephone: 'Good morning, good morning,' said Henry brightly. 'Anybody arrested yet or are you all at liberty? . . . Oh, good . . . Yes, thank you, Mama . . . No, but Tinkerton says she's all right . . . ' He ambled on in a discursive manner and Roberta's attention strayed but was presently caught again by Henry ejaculating: *'Baskett!* Why on earth? . . . Good Lord, how preposterous.' He said rapidly to Roberta: 'That vast person Fox has been closeted with Baskett and Nanny for an hour and they're wondering if he thinks Baskett – All right, Mama . . . no, I thought of showing Robin the house and then we might pay you a visit . . . tonight. Oh. Oh, I see . . . Yes, if you think we ought to . . . Yes, I know its monstrous but it might be made rather pleasant don't you think?' Henry lowered his voice. 'I say, Mum,' he said guardedly, 'will it be Aunt V.'s or ours? Oh. Oh, well, goodbye, darling.'

He hung up the receiver. 'I'm afraid we'll have to stay tonight, Robin,' he said, 'they're bringing him here, you see.'

'I see.'

'And mama rather thinks we get this house. Let's have a look at it.'

II

At eleven o'clock Alleyn got the surgeon's report on the post-mortem. It was accompanied by a note from Dr Curtis. The skewer, he said, had been introduced into the left orbit and had penetrated the fissure at the back of the eye and had entered the blood vessels at the base of the brain. 'That's all the coroner or his jury need to know,' wrote Dr Curtis, 'but I suppose I shall have to give them a solemn mumbo-jumbo as usual. They don't think they've got their money's worth without it. For your information, this expert must have groped a bit before finding the gap and played his weapon about as much as he could after it got through into the brain. Nasty mess. No doubt about it being a right-handed job. I shall say that the wound on the left temple was caused by its coming into sharp contact with the chromium steel boss on the lift wall and that he was probably unconscious when the stuff with the skewer was done, and that death was caused by injury to the brain. Hope you get him (or her). Yours, S. C.'

Alleyn brooded over the report, put it aside, and rang up Mr Rattisbon, the Lamprey's family solicitor. Mr Rattisbon was an old acquaintance of Alleyn's. He said that he was just leaving to wait upon the new Lord Wutherwood but would call on Alleyn in an hour's time. He sounded extremely bothered and fussily remote. Alleyn was heartily thankful that the Lampreys had not sent for Mr Rattisbon last night. If anyone could keep their tongues from uttering indiscretions it was surely he. 'I shall get very little out of him,' Alleyn thought. 'He'll be as acid as a lime and as dry as a biscuit. He will look after the Lampreys.' And with a sigh he turned back to his report. Presently Fox came in, beaming mildly, with his white scarf folded neatly under his wet mackintosh and his umbrella and hat in his hand.

'Hallo, Br'er Fox. Enjoy your game of Happy Families this morning?'

'I got on quite nicely, thank you, Mr Alleyn. I looked in at the house in Brummell Street. I didn't see Mr Henry Lamprey – Lord Rune, rather – or Miss Grey, but I understand they passed a quiet night. Her ladyship's quieted down a lot too, so the nurse told me. She thinks one nurse will be enough tonight. I saw that chap Giggle, the chauffeur, and passed the time of day with him. He didn't seem to like it.'

'Your method of "passing the time of day", is sometimes a bit ominous, Foxkin. What did you say to Giggle?'

'I thought I'd have a shot at shaking his story about when he went downstairs. He got very nervous, of course, when I hammered away at it, but he stuck to it that he went down just after Lord Wutherwood called out the first time.'

'It's the truth,' said Alleyn. 'Young Michael saw him go. You won't shake that story, Br'er Fox.'

'So I found, sir. I left the chap in a great taking on, however, and went along to Pleasaunce Court. They all seem to be much the same. Quite enjoyed signing their statements. I don't fancy they slept a great deal, but they were as bright as ever and uncommonly friendly.'

'A fig for their friendliness,' muttered Alleyn.

'Lady Friede seemed very put out that you didn't interview her last night,' Fox continued as he opened the door and shook his dripping umbrella into the corridor.

Alleyn grunted.

'You appear to have made quite an impression, sir.'

'Shut that door, and put your gamp away and come here, damn you.'

Fox obeyed these instructions with an air of innocence. He sat down and took out his official note-book. Alleyn reflected that his affection for Fox must be impregnable since it survived the ordeal of watching him moisten his forefinger on his lower lip whenever he turned a page, a habit that in any other associate would have filled Alleyn with a desire to be rid of him.

'Yes,' said Fox, finding his place. 'Yes. Baskett. Well, now, Mr Alleyn, I've been able to get very little out of him beyond what we already knew. He helped his late lordship into his coat and went back to the servants' hall. He states positively that he didn't meet Miss Tinkerton on the way. Says he didn't see her at all. But if her story's correct that she saw Baskett and his lordship from the passage and fetched her things from the servants' hall, then they must have met in one place or another. He seems a straightforward old chap, too.'

'And she doesn't seem a straightforward middle-aged girl. No, by gum, Fox, she doesn't. But she's not our pigeon, you know.'

'I reckon she was up to something, however, and I fancy I've found what it is.'

'Have you now! This is what we keep you for, Foxkin.'

'Is that so?' said Fox with his slow smile. 'Well, Mr Alleyn, I thought I'd better finish in the flat and let them get it straight again. Following your suggestion I had a look round the hall. Now, as you know, the hall was in a mess. The young people had had these charades and hadn't done much to clear up beyond slinging things into the cupboard. Now the cupboard was open. The cupboard door is flush with the hall floor. All right. *On* the floor, half in and half out, was one of those thin transparent mackintoshes that ladies go in for nowadays. All right. *Inside* the cupboard and *on* the mackintosh I found a couple of prints. Female shoes, with what they call cuban heels, pointing inwards and to the left. Now one heel has gone through the stuff and the other has made a deep dent. Very nice prints, the surface being a bit tacky and taking a good impression. Now, sir, which of those ladies wore cuban-heeled shoes?'

'Tinkerton, for one,' said Alleyn. 'What about the parlourmaid?'

'No. I checked up on Cora. She wears narrow round heels. I've brought away the mackintosh, Mr Alleyn, and with your approval I'll take a chance and try to lay my hands on Miss Tinkerton's shoes.'

'Better ask Master Henry or Miss Grey to do it for you,' said Alleyn dryly. 'They'll be only too pleased if they think we're sniffing round after the servants.'

'Should you say they were dependable?'

'She is. But I don't give it as a serious suggestion, Br'er Fox. What do you think Tinkerton may have been up to?'

'I was going to ask you for an opinion.'

'Having one of your own up your sleeve, you old dog. Well, Fox, the cupboard is in the hall between the hall and the drawing-room. Isn't it at least possible that the lady in the cupboard was listening to the conversation in the drawing-room?'

'Ah,' said Fox. 'When?'

'There's only one possible time if it was yesterday afternoon.'

'*Which* it was,' said Fox. 'Baskett says the cupboard was all spick and span before the charade. We're lucky it wasn't tidied up later on. He was going to put things straight when the accident happened and after that our chaps told him not to. So it must have been during the conversation between the brothers. I got the old nurse talking. She won't say anything against the family but she's got her knife into Miss Tinkerton. You know what these old girls are like, sir? Mrs Burnaby kept sort of hinting at things, suggesting Miss Tinkerton's a very inquisitive sort of woman and very much in with her ladyship and against his late lordship. I reckon Miss T. and Mrs B. had a row at some time or other and Mrs Burnaby doesn't forget it. I reckon they're kind of bosom enemies if you know what I mean.'

'I do. Not very reliable evidence.'

'No, but there may be something in it all the same. She couldn't say a good word for Miss Tinkerton but there was nothing you could get your teeth into. At one time it was Miss Tinkerton carrying on with the menservants – that Giggle, as Mrs B. called him, in particular.'

'Good Lord!'

'Yes. At another time it was Miss Tinkerton repeating gossip about Miss Friede, as Mrs Burnaby calls her.'

'What sort of gossip?'

'Oh, saying the stage was a funny life for a young lady. Nothing definite. She kept saying "those two".'

'Who did she mean?'

'That's what I asked her, and she gave a bit of a laugh and said: Never mind, but they were hand-in-glove against his late lordship and there was more in it than met the eye. Seemed as if she meant Tinkerton and her ladyship. Later on she said her ladyship would be properly in the soup if it wasn't for Miss T. *I* don't know,' said Fox.

'Search me what she was driving at half the time, but I've got it all down and you can see it, sir, for what it's worth. Based on imagination from start to finish, as like as not, but it did seem to suggest that Miss Tinkerton's a bit of a sly one. And taking the prints in the cupboard into consideration, if they *are* hers, I wondered if she was sort of keeping watch – well, for somebody else. Naming no names, as Mrs B. would say.'

'On the other hand,' Alleyn said, 'she may have been merely snooping for the love of the sport, like your friend Cora.'

'That's so. You know, sir, I sometimes wonder how people would react if they heard everything their servants said about them.'

'I should think the Lampreys would laugh till they were sick,' said Alleyn. 'I remember one afternoon when my brother George and I were conceited youths we took a couple of deck chairs and our books to a spot which happened to be under the window of the servants' hall. The window was open and we heard a series of very spirited imitations of ourselves and our parents. The boot-boy was particularly gifted. George was conducting a not very reputable affair-of-the-heart of which even I knew nothing. But the boot-boy had it all pat.' Alleyn broke into one of his rare laughs. 'It was damn good for us,' he said.

'Would you say they were usually correct, though. If this old nurse lets on that Miss Tinkerton and the chap Giggle are carrying on a bit, or that Miss T. is in some sort of cahoots with her mistress or that Miss T.'s got her knife into the Lampreys, is she more likely to be lying or talking turkey?'

'If she's got her knife into Miss T.,' said Alleyn, 'it's a fifty-fifty chance. I should say Nanny Burnaby was a bit of a tartar. Inclined to be illogically jealous and touchy but a very faithful old dragon with the family. I bet you didn't get her to say anything about them.'

'Lor' no. They were a bunch of cherubs.'

'Yes, I dare say. I wonder if it'd be a good idea to see Giggle again. If he's Tinkerton's boy-friend (and it's a grim thought), he may possibly throw a new ray of light on that unlovely figure. We'll see him, Fox. Ring up the Brummell Street house and get him to come here. And I tell you what, Foxkin,' said Alleyn gloomily, 'it looks very much as if we'll have to go into that Kent visit. It'll be one of those little jaunts that sound such fun in the detective books and are such a crashing bore in reality. Do you read detective novels, Br'er Fox?'

'No,' said Fox. And perhaps with some idea of softening this shortest of all rejoinders he added: 'It's not for the want of trying. Seeing the average person's knowledge of the department is based on these tales I thought I'd have a go at them. I don't say they're not very smart. Something happening on every page to make you think different from what you thought the one before, and the routine got over in the gaps between the chapters. In two of the ones I tried, the investigating officers let the case run for a couple of more murders and listened in to the fourth attempt in order to hear the murderer tell the victim how the first three were done. Then they walked in and copped him just before the cosh. Well, you don't do that sort of thing in the department. There'd be questions asked. I don't say it's not clever but it's fanciful.'

'A little, perhaps.'

'The truth is,' said Fox gravely, 'homicidal cases are not what people would like them to be. How often do we get a murder with a row of suspects, each with motive and opportunity?'

'Not often, thank the Lord, but it has happened.'

'Well, yes. But motives aren't all of equal weight. You don't have much trouble in getting at the prime motive.'

'No.'

'No. Mostly there's one suspect and our problem is to nail the job on him.'

'What about this case?'

'Well, sir. I'll give you there's two motives. First, money. In which case either one of the family or one of the servants did the job. Second, insane hatred. In which case it's her ladyship we're after. That's on the face of it, never mind what we've found out since we came in on the job. Something else may crop up but if so I'll be surprised if it doesn't fit in with one or other motive. Do you know if he's left anything to the servants, sir?'

'I'll try and get it out of Mr Rattisbon. I don't suppose he'll object to telling me. None of them gives a tuppenny damn about the servants. Except perhaps Lady Wutherwood. She'd find Tinkerton hard to replace.'

'Maybe,' said Fox, 'she won't be wanting a maid.'

III

Mr Rattisbon came mumbling in with his chin poked forward and his leather case under his arm. He was a family solicitor who reeked of his trade. A story was told of him that on emerging from his chambers one summer evening he was accosted by a famous film producer who walked half-way along the Strand with Mr Rattisbon, imploring him to play the part of a family solicitor in his new picture. Mr Rattisbon's refusals were so gloriously in character that each tittupping pernickety refusal stung the producer into making a fresh financial assault, until, so the story said, Mr Rattisbon threatened him shrilly with the Municipal Corporation Act of 1882 and looked about him for a constable.

When he saw Alleyn he hurried across the room, shook hands, snatched his claw away, looked sharply from Alleyn to Fox, and finally took a chair. He then formed his mouth into a tight circle and vibrated the tip of his tongue rather as if he had taken a sip of scalding liquid.

'We are very grateful to you for coming, sir,' said Alleyn.

'Not at all, not at all,' gabbled Mr Rattisbon. 'Shocking affair. Dreadful.'

'Appalling.'

Mr Rattisbon repeated the word with great emphasis: 'A-PALL-ing' and waited for Alleyn to make the first move. Alleyn decided that his only hope lay in direct attack. He said: 'I expect you know why we have asked to see you, sir.'

'Frankly,' said Mr Rattisbon, 'no.'

'For the usual reason, I'm afraid. We hope you will tell us something about the late Lord Wutherwood's estate.' Mr Rattisbon's tongue vibrated rapidly in preparation for utterance and Alleyn hurried on. 'We realize, of course, that you are in a – how shall I put it – a confidential position: a position that might become delicate if we began to press in certain definite directions. But in what we still trustfully call the interests of justice – '

'In those interests, Chief Inspector,' Mr Rattisbon cut in neatly, 'I have a duty to my client.'

'Of course, sir.'

'I have, as you know, this morning had an interview with the present Lord Wutherwood. I may tell you that at the inquest I shall watch proceedings on his behalf. I think I may, with propriety, add that my client is naturally most anxious to give the police every assistance that lies in his power. He desires above all things that his brother's assailant shall be brought to justice. You will appreciate, however, that as regards any information prejudicial to my client (should such information exist which I by no means suggest) my own attitude is – most clearly defined.'

Alleyn had expected nothing better and he said: 'And as Lady Wutherwood's solicitor – ?'

'The present Lady Wutherwood?'

'The dowager Lady Wutherwood, sir.'

'M-a-a-ah,' said Rattisbon with a formidable and sheep-like cry. 'I am not the dowager Lady Wutherwood's solicitor, Chief Inspector.'

'No, sir?'

'No. I understand that she has in the past consulted solicitors. I have this information from a reliable source. I think I may tell you that I understand her solicitors to be Messrs Hungerford, Hungerford and Butterworth.'

'Thank you,' said Alleyn, making a note of it. 'Then, sir, our position is not so delicate as I supposed.' He paused, wishing heartily that Mr Rattisbon's conversational style was less infectious. 'Perhaps,' he said, 'you won't mind telling me how Lord Wutherwood's widow is affected by his will.'

'I anticipated this question. I may say I have considered it closely and – in short, Chief Inspector, I have decided that there are certain details of the will with which I may acquaint you.' With his entire person Mr Rattisbon effected a kind of burrowing movement which, in a less emaciated person, would have suggested he was settling down to a square meal. 'The dowager Lady Wutherwood,' he said rapidly, 'by her marriage settlement becomes possessed of a very considerable fortune. Apart from this actual fortune she inherits a life interest in the Dower House of Deepacres St Jude, Deepacres, Kent, and a Manor House near Bognor Regis.'

'She will be a very wealthy woman, then?'

'Very wealthy?' repeated Mr Rattisbon as if the expression was altogether too loose and unprofessional. 'Ah – you may say she will be possessed by a very considerable, I may say a very handsome inheritance. Yes.'

'Yes.' Alleyn knew very well that it was no good trying any approach to the Lamprey side of the picture. Better, he thought, to make what he could of Mr Rattisbon's 'unprejudiced' information. He said: 'I believe I may be quite frank about Lady Wutherwood. Her behaviour since the catastrophe has been, to put it mildly, eccentric. From what I've been able to learn from the others, one cannot put her eccentricity down to shock. It's an old story. You'll understand, sir, that in the course of routine we are concerned with the relationship between Lord Wutherwood and his wife. Now, do you feel inclined to tell me anything about it?'

Mr Rattisbon executed several small snatching gestures which resulted in the appearance of a pair of pince-nez. These he waved at Alleyn. 'Under less extraordinary circumstances – ' he began, and Alleyn listened to an exposition of Mr Rattisbon's professional reticence under less extraordinary circumstances. Gradually, however, small flakes of information were wafted through the dry wind of his discourse. It appeared that Mr Rattisbon knew a good deal about Lady Wutherwood. Alleyn learnt that she was the daughter of a Hungarian minor official and a Russian cabaret artiste, that her maiden name was Glapeera Zadody. He learnt that, from the beginning, the marriage had been disastrous and that at one time Lord Wutherwood had seriously considered the advantages of divorce. Mr Rattisbon had been consulted. The question of insanity had been discussed. All this, though it was something was not much, and Alleyn perceived that Mr Rattisbon hovered on the brink of more daring disclosures. At last, after a series of sheep-like cries and strange grimaces Mr Rattisbon told his secret.

'It occurs to me,' he said, for all the world as if he was some stray Dickensian character embarking on a tale within a tale: 'It occurs to me that a certain incident, which, though I dismissed it as childish when I was made aware of it, should be brought to your attention. No longer than February last, the late Lord Wutherwood called upon me at my rooms. He appeared to be in an unusual state of agitation. I may say that I was quite startled by his manner which I can only describe as furtive and uneasy. It was some time before I got from him the object of his visit, but at last it appeared that he wished to know if he could take legal measures to protect himself from menaces to his person threatened by his wife. I pressed him for closer information and he gave it to me. I may say that his story seemed to me ridiculous and, if it pointed to anything, merely furnished us with additional proof of his wife's mental condition.'

Mr Rattisbon cleared his thoat, darted an uncomfortable glance at Alleyn, waved his pince-nez and gabbled rapidly: 'He informed me of a discovery. He had found in a drawer of Lady Wutherwood's dressing-table – maa – a – ah – evidence, or so he assured me, of an attempt upon her part to – ah – to – ah perform upon him by some supernatural agency.'

Alleyn uttered a stifled ejaculation.

'You may well say so,' said Mr Rattisbon. 'Fantastic! I questioned him rather closely, but he would give me no sort of evidence to support his story though he hinted at definite and concrete proof. He became quite hysterical and was unutterly unlike himself. I – really I found myself at a loss how to deal with him. I pointed out that anything in the nature of legal protection was out of the question. He actually replied that the laws against witchcraft should not have been repealed. I suggested an alienist. He raised the extraordinary objection that if Lady Wutherwood were placed in confinement she would still find some means of harming him. I should add that while he was obviously in a state little removed from terror, he also professed to ridicule the idea of danger. His manner was extraordinary and illogical. He contradicted himself repeatedly and became more and more agitated. I could do little to reassure him. He displayed irritation and hostility. When he finally left me he turned in the doorway and – and – ah – '

Mr Rattisbon vibrated his tongue and sucked in his breath. 'Lord Wutherwood,' he said, made this final statement. He said: "You mark my words. If somebody doesn't do something to stop her she'll get me yet!" '

'Oh, hell!' said Alleyn.

'Well, now,' said Mr Rattisbon after a long silence, 'you may dismiss this incident, Chief Inspector, as absurd and irrelevant. I assure you that I deliberated at some length whether I should acquaint you with it.'

'I'm very glad you decided to tell me about it. What did he do with this concrete proof of her activities, whatever it may have been?'

'He locked it away in some hiding-place of his own. It appeared that for some superstitious reason which I don't pretend to understand, he was unwilling to destroy it, though he refused to tell me what it was.'

'Did he ever discuss the affair with his wife, do you know? Tax her with it?'

'Never. I asked the same question. Never.'

'No. No, I suppose he wouldn't. Well, it's a strange story.'

'Is it a significant story?'

'It fits into the pattern, I think.'

'Ah,' said Mr Rattisbon who knew Alleyn. 'The pattern. Your pet theory, Chief Inspector.'

'Yes, sir, my pet theory. I hope you may provide me with another lozenge in the pattern. Did he leave any large sums to his servants?'

'He made the customary bequests of a man in his position. One hundred pounds to each servant who had been in his employment for five years or more. In the cases of old family servants the legacies were in some cases considerable.'

'What about the two servants who were with them yesterday? William Giggle and Grace Tinkerton.'

'William Stanley Giggle,' said Mr Rattisbon, 'is the son of Lord Wutherwood's late coachman and the grandson of his father's coachman. He receives a more substantial inheritance in the form of an invested sum that should produce three hundred pounds per annum together with a small freehold property – a cottage and some three acres of land on the outskirts of the village of Deepacres.'

'Is this a recent bequest?'

'No, no. Lord Wutherwood has made several wills and many alterations but this bequest appears in the earliest of them. I understand that it was done at the request of Lord Wutherwood's father.'

'And Tinkerton?'

'Is that Lady Wutherwood's personal maid?'

'Yes.'

'Nothing.'

Alleyn grimaced and dropped his pencil on the desk before him.

'Isn't it strange under the circumstances that Lady Wutherwood receives so much?'

'She would have received a great deal less,' said Mr Rattisbon, 'if the late Lord Wutherwood had lived until noon today.' And with some appearance of relishing the effect of this statement he added: 'I was to wait upon the late Lord Wutherwood this morning with the purpose of obtaining his signature to a will. By that will Lady Wutherwood received the minimum upon which the law insists and not one penny piece more.'

IV

Giggle's arrival coincided with Mr Rattisbon's departure. He was brought in by Mr Fox. The stolid indifference of the previous night had deserted him. He was very pale and seemed to make no attempt to conceal his obvious alarm. Evidently, thought Alleyn, his morning's interview with Fox had shaken him. He stood to attention, turning his chauffeur's cap round in his hands, and staring with signs of the liveliest distrust at Mr Fox.

'Now then, Giggle,' Alleyn said, 'there's no need to worry, you know, if you've given us a straightforward account of yourself.'

'I have so, sir. I've told the truth, sir, so help me. I wasn't there, sir, honest I wasn't. Master Michael will bear me out, sir. He saw me go downstairs, and they say they heard his lordship sing out after I'd gone, sir.'

'All right. We only want the facts, you know. If you've given us the facts you've nothing to worry about.'

'If I might ask, sir, has Master Michael spoken for me?'

'Yes, he has. He says he saw you go down.'

Giggle wiped his hand across his mouth. 'Thank God! I beg your pardon, sir, but young gentlemen of his age don't always notice much, and I've been that worried.'

'We've asked you to come here this morning,' Alleyn said, 'to see if you can give us any further information.'

'I will if I can, sir, but I don't know a thing. I've got nothing to do with it. I never wished his lordship dead. His lordship always treated me fair enough.'

'Even to the extent of leaving you a nice little property, I understand.'

Giggle burst into a clumsy tirade of self-defence. It was not his doing, he cried, that his lordship had favoured him. 'It was along of what my dad did for his lordship's father. I never asked for anything nor never expected it. You can't pin anything on me. It's always the same. If it's gentry and working men in trouble the police go for the working men every time. My Gawd, can't you understand – ' Alleyn let him talk himself to a standstill. At last he was silent and stood there sweating freely and showing the whites of his eyes like a startled horse.

'Now you've got that off your chest,' said Alleyn, 'perhaps you'll listen to one or two questions. Sit down.'

'I'd as soon stand.'

'All right. You tell us you went downstairs to the car, and that the first thing you knew about the tragedy was when Miss Grey came for you. Very well. Now, as you went downstairs did the lift overtake you and go to the bottom?'

'No, sir.'

'It didn't come down at all while you were on the stairs?'

Giggle seemed to shy all over. 'What's this about the lift? It was up top. I never seen it after I went down.'

'That's all I wanted you to tell me,' said Alleyn.

'Oh cripes!' said Giggle under his breath.

'Another point. How did his lordship get on with his servants?'

'Good enough,' said Giggle cautiously.

'Really?'

'I'm not going to get myself trapped – '

'Don't talk silly,' said Inspector Fox austerely. 'What's the matter with you? The Chief Inspector asked you a plain question. Why can't you answer it? You're making yourself look awkward, that's what you're doing.'

'Come along, now, Giggle,' said Alleyn. 'Pipe up, there's a good fellow.'

'Well, sir, I'm sorry, but I'm all anyhow. His lordship got on good enough with his staff in a manner of speaking. There was some thought he was a bit on the near side and there was some didn't like his sarcastic ways but I never minded. He treated me fair.'

'Did some of the staff prefer her ladyship to his lordship?'

'They might of.'

'The maid for instance?'

'She might of.'

'Are you friendly with her maid?'

'We get on all right,' said Giggle eyeing Alleyn suspiciously.

'Any attachment between you?'

'What the hell's that got to do with this business?' roared Giggle. 'Who says there's anything?'

'Away you go again,' observed Alleyn wearily. 'Will you answer the question or won't you?'

'There's nothing between us, then. We might have been a bit friendly like. What's there in that? I don't say we're not friendly.'

'Would you say that Tinkerton took Lady Wutherwood's part against her husband? Sympathized with her?'

'She's very fond of her ladyship. She's been with her a long time.'

'Quite so. *Did* she sympathize with Lady Wutherwood when it came to any difference between them?'

'I suppose so.'

'Then there were differences between Lord and Lady Wutherwood?'

'Yes, sir,' said Giggle obviously relieved at this turn of the conversation.

'What did they quarrel about, do you know?'

'Her ladyship's got funny ideas. She takes up with funny people.'

'Do you think she's normal mentally?'

Giggle shuffled his feet and looked at his cap. His lips were trembling.

'Come on,' said Alleyn.

'It's pretty well known she's a bit funny. Grace Tinkerton doesn't like it said, but it's a fact. She was shut up for a time and she's never what you'd call the same as other people. I think most of us on the staff have that opinion.'

'Except Miss Tinkerton?'

'She knows,' said Giggle, 'but she won't let on. Loyal-like.'

'All right,' said Alleyn. 'That's everything, I think.'

Giggle wiped his face with a shaking hand. He seemed to hover on the edge of speech.

'What is it?' Alleyn asked.

'Gawd, sir, I'm that upset! It's got me down. Thinking about it.' He stopped again and then with a curious air of taking control of himself said rapidly, 'I beg pardon, sir, for forgetting myself. I got that rattled thinking about it when Mr Fox come at me again this morning – '

'That's all right,' said Alleyn, 'goodbye.'

Giggle gave him a terrified glance and went out.

V

A midday train took Alleyn, Fox and Nigel Bathgate into Kent. Nigel rang up Alleyn two minutes before he left for Victoria and climbed into the restaurant carriage two seconds after it had started moving. 'Ever faithful, ever sure,' he said and ordered drinks for the three of them.

'You won't get much out of this,' said Alleyn.

'You never know, do you? We sent a cameraman down there this morning. I hope to fix up some trimmings for the pictures.'

'Have you seen your friends this morning?'

'Yes.' Nigel looked doubtfully at Alleyn, seemed about to speak, but evidently changed his mind.

'Let's have lunch,' said Alleyn.

During the journey he was amiable but uncommunicative. After lunch Fox and Nigel went to sleep and did not wake until they reached Canterbury. Here they found the sun shining between ponderous clouds moving slowly to the south. They changed to a branch line, arriving at Deepacres Halt at three o'clock.

'Out we get,' said Alleyn. 'The local superintendent is supposed to have sent a car. It's three miles, I understand, to the chateau Wutherwood. There's our man.'

The superintendent himself waited for them on the platform and led the way out to a village road and the police car. He was evidently much stimulated by this visit from the Yard and showed great readiness to discuss Deepacres Park and the Lamprey family. As they drove away from the village he pointed to a pleasant cottage standing back from a side lane.

'That'll be Bill Giggle's property now,' he said.

'Nice for Bill Giggle,' said Alleyn.

'Very nice. Funny, the way's he come by it. Ancient history, it is. Bill Giggle's old man was coachman to his late lordship's father and saved his life. Runaway horse affair, it was. His old lordship promised Bill Giggle's dad the cottage for his work which was very courageous and smart, but in the end, it was horses did for his old lordship, just the same, for he was killed in the hunting field. Only lived a few minutes but in the hearing of them that were there he said he was sorry he'd never made that addition to his will, and asked his son – that's his late lordship – to make it good. Well, his new lordship, as he was then, didn't actually hand over the cottage, being a bit on the near side, but he sent for his lawyers and made his will and let it be known young Bill Giggle would get the place when he himself was dead and gone.'

'I see.'

'Yes, and they're going to take the railroad that way now, so it looks as if Bill Giggle's in for a nice thing, doesn't it?'

'Yes,' said Alleyn, 'it does.'

He was rather silent after that. They drove through country lanes past a mild sequence of open fields, smallholdings, spinneys, and a private golf course, to the gates of Deepacres Park. The house was hidden by trees and as they climbed a long winding avenue Fox began to look solemnly impressed.

'A show place, seemingly,' said Fox.

'Wait till you see the house,' said the superintendent. 'It's as fine a seat as you'll find in Kent after Leeds Castle. Not so big, but impressive, if you know what I mean.'

He was right. The great house stood on a terrace above a deer park. It was built at the time of John Evelyn and that industrious connoisseur of fine houses could have found no fault in it. Indeed he might have described it as a perfectly uniform structure, observable for its noble site and showing without like a diadem. The simile would have been well chosen, thought Alleyn, for in the late afternoon sunshine, the house glowed like a jewel against the velvet setting of its trees.

'Lummy!' said Nigel. 'I never knew it was as grand as all this. Good Lord, it's funny to think of the Lampreys coming home to this sort of roost.'

'I suppose Lord Charles was born here?' observed Alleyn.

'Oh, yes. Yes, I suppose so. Yes, of course he was. Rather terrific, isn't it?' And Nigel's fingers went to his tie.

'I've told the servants to expect you,' said the superintendent. 'They'll be in a fine taking-on over this, I'll be bound.'

But the butler and the housekeeper, when Alleyn saw them, seemed to be less agitated than bewildered. They were more concerned, it seemed, with the problem of their own responsibilities, and for the moment were made uneasy by the lack of them. They had heard of his lordship's death through the stop-press column of the newspaper. They had received no orders. Should they and a detachment of servants go up to London? Where was his lordship to be buried? Alleyn suggested they should ring up Brummell Street or the Pleasaunce Court flat. He produced a search-warrant and got to work. It would take weeks to go over the whole of Deepacres but he hoped to bring off a lucky dip. Lord Wutherwood's secretary, it appeared, was away on his holiday. Alleyn did not regret his absence. He asked to see the rooms Lord Wutherwood used most often and was shown a library and a sort of office. Fox went off to a dressing-room in a remote wing. Nigel sought out the housekeeper to get, so he said, the faithful retainer's angle on the story. Alleyn had brought a bunch of keys taken from Lord Wutherwood's body. One of them fitted the lock of a magnificent Jacobean cupboard in the library. It was full of bundles of letters and papers. With a sigh he settled down to them, pausing every now and then to glance through the tall windows at the formal and charming prospect outside.

He found little to help him in the Jacobean cupboard. There were gay begging letters from Lord Charles, acidly blue-pencilled by his brother: – 'Answered 10/5/38. Refused'. 'Answered 11/12/39. Final refusal'. But Lord Charles's letters still came in and there were further final refusals. The late Lord Wutherwood, Alleyn saw, had been a methodical man. But he had not always refused to help his brother. A letter from New Zealand was blue-pencilled 'Replied 3/4/33. £500', and a still-earlier appeal: '£500 forwarded B.N.Z'. These appeared to be the only occasions on which Lord Charles had not drawn a blank. There were letters from Lady Katherine Lobe in which the writer reminded her nephew of his obligations to the poor and placed her pet charities before him. These were emphatically pencilled 'No'. Among a bundle of ancient letters Alleyn came upon one from a Nedburn Nursing Home, Otterton, Devon. It reported

Lady Wutherwood's condition as being somewhat improved. He made a note of the address.

It was Fox who made the strange discovery. The sun had crept low on the library windows and the room had begun to be filled with a translucent dusk when a door at the far end opened and Fox, bulkily dark, materialized from the shadows of the hall beyond. Alleyn was down on the floor groping in the bottom shelf of the cupboard. He sat back on his heels and watched Fox advance slowly from dark into thick golden light. Fox looked a huge and portentous figure. He seemed to carry some small object on the palm of his hands. Without speaking Alleyn watched him. The carpet was deep and he advanced as silently as a robust ghost. It was not until he drew quite near that Alleyn could distinguish the object he held in his hands.

It was a small and very ugly doll.

Without a word Fox put it on the carpet. It was a pale misshapen figure, ill-modelled from some dirtily glossy substance of a livid colour. It was dressed, after a fashion, in a black coat and grey trousers. On the tip of its deformity of a head were stuck a few grey hairs. Black-headed pins formed the eyes, a couple of holes, the nostrils. A row of match ends projected horridly from beneath a monstrous upper lip. Alleyn advanced a long finger and pointed to the end of the figure where the feet should have been. They had dwindled away like the feet of the suffering Jews in Cruickshank's drawing for The Ingoldsby Legends.

'Melted,' said Fox loudly.

Alleyn's fingers travelled up to the breast of the doll. A long pin stuck out from its travesty of a waistcoat.

'Where was it?'

'In the back of his dressing-table drawer.'

'This is the thing he wouldn't show old Rattisbon. I wonder why.'

'Perhaps he was afraid he'd laugh.'

'Perhaps,' said Alleyn.

CHAPTER 18

Scene By Candlelight

There was no break that day in the clouds over London. From morning to night it rained inexorably. Whenever they went to the library window in Brummell Street, Roberta and Henry looked down on a pattern of bobbing umbrellas, on the glistening mackintosh of the Brummell Street policeman, on the roofs of wet cars and on the jets of water that spurted from under their wheels. When, after lunch, they went out into Brummell Street under a borrowed umbrella, the wind drove them sideways, and Henry tucked Roberta's hand under the crook of his elbow. In spite of everything that had happened, Roberta felt her heart warm to this adventure, to the Londoners hurrying intently through the rain, to the lamplit shop windows, to the scarlet buses that sailed above the traffic, to the sea of noises, and to Henry who piloted her through the rain. She was glad that Henry had no more than one and elevenpence in his pockets and that, instead of borrowing her proffered ten shillings and taking a taxi, he suggested they should go roundabout by bus and tube to Pleasaunce Court. Splendid, sang Roberta's heart, to mount the swaying bus and go cruising down Park Lane, splendid to plunge into the entrance of the tube station, to smell the unexpected sweetness of air that was driven through the world of underground, to sink far below the streets and catch a roaring subterranean train. Splendid, she thought, to sit opposite Henry in the tube and to see his face, murkily lit but smiling at her.

'Like London?' he asked, guessing at her thoughts, and she nodded back at him, feeling independent and adventurous. Best of all, it seemed to Roberta, was this sense of independence. Nobody in the crowded tubes knew she was Roberta Grey from New Zealand. She didn't matter to them or they to her and she warmed to them for their very indifference. It didn't even matter that she and Henry must be back at Brummell Street before Uncle G. came home in his coffin.

It was ridiculous to suppose that the Lampreys were in any sort of danger. For Roberta was twenty and abroad in London.

The behaviour of the Lampreys did nothing to subdue her mood. Charlot was resting and Lord Charles had gone to see his bank manager but the others, though rather black under the eyes, displayed flashes of their usual form. They all had tea in the dining-room including Mike, who wore an air of triumph. Frid absent-mindedly poured tea into all the cups before her and then strolled about the room smoking. Patch consumed oranges from a side table and the twins ate quantities of toast.

'I suppose you've heard,' said Colin, 'that Mr Grumball's gone.'

'And his name is Grimball,' added Stephen.

'He went,' explained Patch, 'because Daddy's all hotsytotsy now as regards money.'

'You don't suppose, do you,' said Henry, 'that Uncle G.'s hoarded gold becomes ours in the flash of an eye? There are death duties, my child.'

'What are death duties?'

None of the Lampreys seemed to know the answer to Patch's question. Even Henry, though vaguely depressing, was uninformed.

'Oh, well,' said Patch, 'there's always Aunt Kit's money from the pearls she popped. Perhaps that'll square the death duties.'

'Or pay for learned counsel to defend one of us,' said Frid.

'You *would* think of that, Frid,' said Henry.

'Well, let's face it, one of us may – '

'Pas pour le jeune homme,' said Colin.

'I know what that means,' said Mike. 'But you needn't worry. Chief Detective-Inspector Alleyn'll solve the mystery some time today, I should think. Robin, did you know Chief Detective-Inspector Alleyn happened to have rather an important talk with me last night?'

'Did he, Micky? That was fun, wasn't it?'

'Not bad. He happened to want to know one or two things and I happened to remember them. I must say he's an absolute whizzer. Well,' added Mike, 'I mean he's the kind of person another person knows bang off for a whizzer. You can kind of recognize it. I say, Robin, do you know he hadn't got his magernifying-glass with him and I happened to be able to lend him mine? I bet he finds some pretty hot clue with my magernifying-glass. Hoo!' said Mike kicking the leg of his chair, 'I bet old B-K's chops fall when I tell him about the magernifying-glass.'

'Who's old B-K?'

'A person,' said Mike. 'As a matter of fac' it's Benham-Kaye in my form at school. He's pretty high-hat. I bet he won't be so high-hat when I tell him – '

'Your conversation,' said Frid, 'is like a round or catch sung by one person only.'

'What did you tell Mr Alleyn, Mike?' asked Henry.

'Oh, about when the skewer was in the hall and when it wasn't and who I saw and when. He said I was a pretty good witness.

'Robin,' said Henry, 'it's half past five. I think we should return to duty.'

II

The return trip to Brummell Street was not quite so satisfactory. Henry, having borrowed a little money from Nanny, took a taxi. He was very silent and Roberta had time to think of the night that awaited them in the Brummell Street house. She had time to wonder where they would put Uncle G., and whether Aunt V., hitherto invisible, would appear for dinner. It seemed that Roberta and Henry were expected by Charlot to remain at Brummell Street and she began to wonder nervously if Henry would be bored by a long evening with her in that cadaverous library. Perhaps the aunt would be there too, and Roberta began to imagine how Aunt V. would sit and stare at Henry and herself and how, when bedtime came, they would climb the stairs and walk silently through the long passages. Perhaps they would have to pass the door of the room where Uncle G. lay in his coffin. Perhaps Aunt V. would madly insist on them looking at Uncle G. Roberta wished the rain would stop and that the clouds would roll away and let a little evening sun into Brummell Street. For the first time since she came to England she felt lonely. She decided that after dinner she would write to her own unknown middle-class aunt who, thought Roberta with an inward smile, must have been rather shaken by her evening paper. The evening papers were evidently full of Uncle G. At the street corners Roberta saw placards with: 'Death of a Peer' and 'Shocking Tragedy. Lord Wutherwood Killed'. She couldn't help wondering if inside these papers there were photographs of herself and Henry coming out of Pleasaunce Court Mansions. Perhaps underneath the photograph would be written: 'Lord Rune and a friend leaving the fatal flat last night'. Henry stopped the taxi at a street corner and bought a paper. 'This is Nigel's affair,' he said. 'Let's see what sort of gup he's handed out, shall we?' They read the paper in the taxi and sure enough there was the flashlight photograph with their faces, appropriately haggard, like white puddings with startled blackcurrant eyes. Roberta thought the letterpress quite indecently frightful but Henry said it might have been worse and that Nigel had spared them a lot. The taxi drew up at 24 Brummell Street. They left the paper behind and once more entered that heavy house. They were immediately aware of a sort of subdued activity. They smelt flowers and there, climbing the stairs, was a maid with a great wreath of lilies in her arms. Moffatt, the old manservant who had let them in, told them that part of the Deepacres staff were coming up to London by the morning train. 'But we've managed very well, my lord,' said Moffatt. 'Everything is prepared. The flowers are beautiful.'

'Which room?' Henry asked.

'The green drawing-room, my lord. On the second landing.'

'Upstairs?' said Henry dubiously.

'Her ladyship wished the green drawing-room, my lord.'

'Is her ladyship dining, Moffatt?'

'Not downstairs, my lord. In her room.'

'How is she, do you know?'

'I – I understand not very well, my lord. Miss Tinkerton tells me, not very well. If it's convenient, my lord, perhaps the nurse on duty may dine with you.'

'Oh, Lord, yes,' said Henry.

Tinkerton appeared in the shadows at the far end of the hall. Henry hailed her and asked after her mistress. She came nearer and with a glance at the stairs replied in a whisper that Lady Wutherwood was not well. Very restless and strange, she added, and as Henry said no more, glided away into the shadows.

'Very restless and strange,' Henry repeated gloomily. 'That's jolly.'

A clock in the rear of the hall struck six. At that moment, in Lady Wutherwood's bedroom at Deepacres, Alleyn looked up from a copy of the *Compendium Maleficorum*.

'Fox,' he said, 'how many men did we leave at Brummell Street?'

'One, sir. Campbell. The house is being watched.' And staring at his superior's face, Fox asked: 'What's wrong?'

Alleyn's long finger went out in that familiar gesture. 'Read that.'

Fox put on his glasses and bent over the *Compendium*. ' "The second book," ' he read, ' "dealing with the various kinds of witchcraft and certain other matters which should be known." '

'Go on.'

' "Chapter One. Of Soporific Spells. Argument." ' Fox read on in his best police court manner until Alleyn stopped him. 'Well,' said Fox, 'it seems to be very silly sort of stuff. It's marked in the margin so she evidently made something of it. I suppose it's given her ideas.'

'There are several more works on witchcraft down in the library. Some of them are very rare. Yes, I think it's given her ideas, Fox. I'm wondering if we've bumped our heads on the keystone of her behaviour. How soon can we get back?'

'To London? Not before 11.30, sir.'

'Damn. Fox, I've got a very rum notion, so rum that I'm half-ashamed of it. I believe I know why she wanted his body brought home.'

'Lor'!' said Fox. 'You don't think she would get up to any of these capers?'

'I wouldn't put it past her. I'm uneasy, Fox. Pricking of the thumbs or something. When are they delivering the goods? About ten, isn't it?'

'Yes, sir. The mortuary van – '

'Yes, I know. Let's get back to London.'

III

It was a few minutes after ten when they brought Uncle G. to Brummell Street. Henry and Roberta were in the library. The rain made a great drumming noise on the windows and the wind soughed in the chimney but they were at once aware of new sounds inside the house and Henry said: 'You stay here, Robin. I'll come back soon.'

He went out, shutting the door but not shutting away the heavy sounds of Uncle G.'s progress across the great hall and up the long stairway. Roberta sat on the hearthrug and held her hands to the fire. Her heart-beat was faster than the bump of feet on the stairs. In their morning's exploration Henry and Roberta had visited the green drawing-room. It was over the library and soon the ceiling gave back to her the sound of Uncle G.'s progress. The footsteps stopped for a little while and then lost their heaviness. Now the men were coming downstairs again, crossing the hall, leaving 24 Brummell Street for the kindlier storm-swept streets. She heard the great front door close. In a little while Henry came back. He carried a tray with a decanter and two glasses.

'I got them out of the dining-room,' he explained. 'We'll have a little drink, Robin. Yes, I know you don't, but tonight I prescribe it.'

The unaccustomed glow did drive away the cold sunken feeling of Roberta's inside. Henry threw more logs on the fire and for half an hour they sat before it talking of the old days in New Zealand.

'I am quite determined,' Henry said, 'that after this is all over I shall get a job. Yes, I know I've talked about it for six years.'

'And now,' said Robin tartly, 'when, for the first time it isn't a crying necessity – '

' – I make up my mind to do it. Yes. I shall continue in the territorials in my humble but exacting capacity. I shall sit for strange examinations and thus prepare myself for the obscure and unattractive performance known as doing one's bit. And when war comes,' said Henry in a melancholy manner, 'Henry Lamprey, Earl of Rune, will take his place among the flower of England's manhood guarding an entrance to some vulnerable public convenience.'

Roberta knew that Henry was trying to brighten this ominous night and although his jokes were not quite up to Lamprey standard she contrived to laugh at them. The clock struck eleven. They couldn't stay all night by the library fire. Some time those stairs must be climbed, those passages traversed. In an exhausted uncertain fashion Roberta longed for her bed. She ached for sleep yet was not sleepy. Her throat and mouth kept forming half-yawns and her head throbbed.

'How about it, Robin?' asked Henry presently. 'Bed?'

'I think so.'

Past the stuffed bear with his open mouth and extended paws. Past the cold marble persons at the foot of the stairs. Past the second landing where Aunt V. and her nurses and perhaps Tinkerton slept or watched behind closed doors. Then the long passage, lit now by electric lights.

'I asked them to put a fire in your room, Robin.' Heavenly of Henry to think of that. Better by far to undress by this cheerful fire. And when she crept out in her dressing-gown there was Henry in his dressing-gown, and they went to the bathroom together and Henry sat on the edge of the bath in a friendly manner while Roberta brushed her teeth. They returned together to their bedroom doors.

'Goodnight, Robin, darling. Sleep well.'

'Goodnight.'

The Kentish slow train was late. The police car had punctured a tyre half a mile from Deepacres Halt and they had missed their connection with the express. At every station the slow train halted, breathing long steamy sighs which were echoed by Alleyn.

'What's biting you, Inspector?' asked Nigel cheerfully.

'I don't know.'

'I've never seen you so jumpy.'

'That fellow Campbell was told to keep his wits about him, Fox?'

'Yes, Mr Alleyn.'

'Good God, we're stopping again!'

IV

Roberta's heart beat so thickly that she wondered if it alone had awakened her. She lay with her eyes opened upon blackness. She could not see so much as the form of the curtains that hung beside her head nor the shape of her hand held close to her eyes. For a moment she was confused. The memory of this room was gone from her. She had no sense of her position nor of her invisible surroundings but felt as though she had opened her eyes on nothingness. She dared not put out her hand lest the wall should not be there. Now she was wide awake. She remembered her room and knew that round the curtains on her left side she should be able to see the fire. She touched the curtain, so close, invisible, and it moved. Somewhere beyond her bed glowed a point of redness. The fire was almost dead; she had slept a long time. Outside it was still raining and the wind still moaned in the chimney but neither the wind nor the rain had awakened Roberta. She knew that someone had walked past her door. She began to reason with herself, telling her thumping heart that there was no cause for fear. Perhaps it was the man on guard in the house, making some cold round of inspection. Yet even while she sought in panic for comfort; she knew, so densely woven are the strands of thought, that the footstep in the passage was the secondary cause of her alarm and rushed her upwards into wakefulness. She lay still and waited, tingling, for full realization. Presently it came. Beneath her, beyond the mattress of her bed, the carpet on the floor, the floor itself, the ceiling below the floor; beyond all these, there was a sound that fretted the outer borders of her hearing. It had a kind of rhythm. It suggested some sort of harsh movement with which Roberta was familiar. At the moment when she recognized it, it ceased, and she was left with a picture of a hand and a saw. Then she remembered that underneath her bedroom was the green drawing-room.

Perhaps if the sound had not begun again Roberta would have lain still in her bed. There are degrees of terror and with the stealthy resumption of the sound she knew that she could not endure it alone. She snapped down the switch by her door but no light came and she supposed that it had been turned off at the main. She groped on her bedside table, found a box of matches and lit her candle. Now her room was there with her clothes lying across a chair. Her shadow reared up the wall and stretched half-way across the ceiling. She put on her dressing-gown and, taking her candle, went to her door and opened it. As she did this the sound stopped again.

Henry's door was wide open. Roberta crossed the passage and went into his room but before she looked at the bed she knew he would not be there. The clothes were turned back and there was no candle on his table. She found some comfort in being in Henry's room. It smelt faintly of the stuff he put on his hair. Roberta wrapped his eiderdown quilt round herself and sat on the bed. Henry had heard the noise and had gone to see about it. But at once she grew afraid for Henry and as the seconds went by this fear increased until it became intolerable. She went to the door and listened. The sound had stopped for some minutes and she heard only the rain, muffled here where there were no windows. She faced the passage and perceived a thinning of darkness at the far end, where the landing was and where the well of the house gaped up to the roof. As she peered down the passage this dimness changed stealthily to a faint moving glow. It must be Henry returning with his candle. Now she could see the landing with its gallery rail and stairhead. She caught a glint of light on a far wall and remembered that a looking-glass hung there. A glowing circle appeared on the landing floor. It widened and grew more clearly defined. Henry was coming upstairs. In a moment she would see him.

Framed by the black walls of the passage, a figure carrying a lighted candle moved from the stairs across the landing. It paused, and slowly turned. The light from the candle shone upwards into its face. It was Lady Wutherwood. Her head was slanted as if she listened intently, her eyes were turned upwards towards the next landing. She moved away, became a receding shape rimmed by a golden nimbus, and disappeared.

Roberta in the dark passage stood still. Henry's door, caught in a draught from his open window, banged shut, and her whole body leapt to the sound and was still again. At last the landing began to grow light once more. The manner of its lighting was so exactly as it had been before that her nerves expected Lady Wutherwood to come upstairs again like a ghost that punctually repeated its gestures. But of course it was Henry. He shielded his candle with his hand and seemed to look directly into Roberta's eyes. Forgetting she was invisible she wondered at his look which held nothing of the comfort she had expected. Then, realizing that he had not seen her, she went down the passage to meet him.

'Robin! Why have you come out! Go back.' He scarcely breathed the words.

'I can't. What's happening?'

'What have you seen?'

'I saw her. I think she went up to the next landing.'

'Go back to your room,' Henry said.

'Let me stay. Give me something to do.'

He seemed to hesitate. She touched his arm. 'Please, Henry.'

'What wakened you?'

'A noise in that room. Like sawing. Have you been there?'

Again Henry hesitated. 'It's locked,' he said.

'Where's the detective? Shouldn't you find him?'

'Come with me.'

So he was going to let her stay with him. She followed him across the landing. He paused at a door, bent down to listen. Then, very gingerly, he turned the handle and with his head motioned Roberta to come closer. She obeyed. Through the crack of the door came the sound of snoring, very deep and stertorous.

'Night nurse,' breathed Henry and closed the door.

'What are you going to do? Find the detective?'

'I'd like to find out for myself what she's up to.'

'No, Henry. If anything's wrong it would look so strange. Ssh!'

'What?'

'Look.'

A circle of light bobbed up the stairs and across the landing.

'Damn!' whispered Henry, 'he's coming.'

He walked swiftly to the stairhead. 'Hallo,' he said softly, 'who's that?'

'Just a minute, sir.'

The man came up quickly, flashing his torch on Henry. As he moved into the candlelight Roberta saw he wore a heavy overcoat and muffler and remembered that she herself was cold.

'What's wrong here, sir?' asked the man. 'Who's been interfering with these lights? I said they were to be left on.'

Henry told him quickly that he had been awakened by a sound from the green drawing-room, and that he had seen Lady Wutherwood walk across the landing with a candle in her hand. 'Miss Grey saw her too. Miss Grey came out soon after I did.'

'Where did she go, sir?'

'Upstairs.'

'You stay here, if you please, sir. Both of you. Don't move.'

He threw his torchlight on the upper stairs. They were half the width of the lower flight and steeper. The man ran lightly up and then disappeared. Roberta and Henry heard a door open and close, then another, and another. Then silence.

'Hell!' said Henry loudly, 'I'm going – ' Roberta snatched at his arm and he stopped short. Somewhere in the top floor of the house Lady Wutherwood screamed. Roberta knew at once it was she who screamed. It was the same note that had drilled through the silence of the lift-well. It persisted for some seconds, intolerable and imbecilic, and then a door slammed it away into the background. Other voices sounded on the top floor. Somebody had joined them on the landing. It was the night nurse with her veil askew.

'Where's she gone?' cried the night nurse. 'I don't accept the responsibility for this. Where's she gone?'

On the top floor the man in the overcoat was saying: 'Get back to your rooms, the lot of you. Move along now. Do what you're told.' And a voice, Tinkerton's. 'I'm going to my lady.' 'You're doing what you're told. Into your rooms, now, all of you. I'll see you later.' 'You can't lock me out.' 'I have locked you out. Stand aside, if *you* please.'

The man in the overcoat came downstairs.

'Where's my patient?' said the nurse. 'I must get to my patient.'

'You're too late,' said the man, and to Henry: 'You two come along with me, sir. I'm going to the telephone.'

They followed him to a small study on the second landing. He sat down to a desk and dialled Whitehall 1212. His fingers shook and his mouth looked stiff.

' – Campbell here on duty at 24 Brummell Street. Mr Alleyn, please. What's that? On his way? Right. There's been a fatality here. We'll want the divisional surgeon quick. Get him, will you, I'm single-handed.'

He replaced the receiver.

'Look here,' said Henry violently. 'What was she doing? You can't drag us around like a brace of dummies and tell us nothing. What's happened? What's this fatality?'

The man Campbell bit his fingers and stared at Henry.

'Who locked the door of the room where the body is?' he demanded.

'I didn't,' said Henry.

'But you knew it was locked, sir?'

'Of course I did. I heard a damned ghastly noise in the room and went down to investigate. What's happened upstairs?'

The man seemed to weigh something in his mind and come to a decision. 'Come and see,' he said.

They seemed to have forgotten Roberta but she followed them up the long stairs. On the next landing they picked up the nurse and went on to the top floor, a strange procession. The nurse and Campbell had a torch and Henry his candle. The top landing gave on to a narrow passage. The detective opened the first door. The Moffatts, two girls, and Tinkerton, fantastic in their night-clothes, were huddled round a candle.

'Here, you,' said Campbell, 'Mr Moffatt. Go down and fix up the lights. Someone's pulled out the main fuse. Find it and get it back. Or have you got a spare?'

'Yes, sir.'

'Well, fix it. Have you got a police whistle?'

'Yes, sir.'

'Go to the front door and blow it. When the constable comes, take him up to the door of the room where the body is and tell him I said he was to stay there. Detective-Sergeant Campbell. Then wait by the front door. Let in a doctor who will be here in a few minutes and send him upstairs to the top floor. Then wait for Chief Inspector Alleyn who's on his way from Victoria Station. Send him up too.'

He passed the next door and paused by a third. 'Your patient's in there, nurse. We'll take a look at her first. We'll have to see if there's a key on her. You come in with me, sir, and look out for yourself. She may give trouble.' He turned to Roberta. 'You slip in after us if you please, miss, take my torch and shut the door. If we've got to hold her I may trouble you to help. And you, nurse. Now then.'

He unlocked the door, glanced at Henry, and then opened it quickly. He went in, with Henry on his heels. The nurse followed, Roberta slipped in behind her and shut the door.

It was an unused servant's bedroom. For a moment Roberta thought Lady Wutherwood was not there but the light from the torches found her. She sat on the floor at the head of the stretcher bed. She turned her head and looked blindly into the light and though her retracted lips at first suggested a snarl it was evident by the noise she made that she was laughing. Her hair hung about her eyes, the white discs at the corners of the mouth glistened, she turned her head gently from side to side. Her throat was bare and in its pale thickness a pulse beat rapidly. She wore a dark gown over her nightdress and her hands moved among its folds.

'Now, my lady,' said Campbell, 'nobody's going to hurt you. Here's nurse come to take you back to bed.'

The nurse in a most unnatural voice said: 'Come along, dear. We can't stay in a nasty cold room, can we? Come along.' Lady Wutherwood shrank back against the wall. The nurse said: 'We'll just help you up, shall we?' and moved forward.

She was on her feet with a swiftness that suggested some violent wrench of pain. She pressed herself against the wall. Her hands were in the pockets of her gown, holding them together, crushed tight against herself.

'That's better,' said the nurse. Campbell moved closer to Lady Wutherwood and in answer to his signal Henry followed him.

'Now you come along with nurse, my lady,' said Campbell. 'We'll just take your arms. *Look out!*'

Henry's candle rolled on the floor and went out. The nurse and Roberta pointed their torches at the three struggling figures. Lady Wutherwood struck twice at Campbell with her right hand before he caught her arm. Henry had her left arm. The left hand was still rammed down in the pocket of her dressing-gown but she fought with the violence of an animal. Suddenly the room was flooded by a hard white light. Roberta threw her torch on the bed. 'Collar her low, Robin,' said Henry's voice. Roberta was on the floor. Her arms embraced a pair of soft legs, struggling inside the folds of robe and nightgown. 'Disgusting, *disgusting,*' said her thoughts but she held on. 'That's better,' Campbell said, and abruptly they were all quiet, blinking in the glare. The nurse still pointed the torch at them. She was talking. 'It's a case for a mental attendant. I should never have been asked to take the case,' gabbled the nurse, carefully pointing her torch. 'It's not a case for ordinary duty.' Lady Wutherwood's left hand, doubled inside her pocket, touched the top of Roberta's head.

The hand and arm were rigid, yet they moved with their owner's violent breathing. A new voice, harsh and broken, sounded and was silent.

'What's she say?' Campbell demanded. 'She said something. What was it?'

'German, I think,' said Henry.

'What's she got in her pocket? Here, nurse! Get rid of that torch.' The nurse looked at her hand. 'Oh. Silly of me,' she said, and put the torch down.

'Now,' said Campbell, 'put your hands in her pocket and see what she's got hold of. Carefully. It may be a knife.'

'Why a knife?' asked Henry.

Campbell didn't answer him. The nurse approached her patient and over Roberta's head gingerly slid her hand down Lady Wutherwood's arm into the pocket. Roberta, looking up, saw the nurse's face bleach out abruptly to the colour of parchment.

'What's the matter?' Campbell demanded.

'She's – she's – got – both her hands – in her pocket.'

Henry said violently: 'Don't be an ass, nurse. What d'you mean?'

The nurse backed away from Lady Wutherwood, pointing at the pocket and nodding her head.

'I've got her right hand,' said Campbell impatiently. 'What are you talking about?'

'There are two hands in her pocket,' said the nurse, and fainted.

CHAPTER 19

Severed Hand

The taxi pulled up at 24 Brummell Street, discharged its fares and skidded off into the rain.

'Quiet enough,' said Nigel. 'You've got a jitter-bug, Inspector.'

'There's a light on in the hall,' said Alleyn. 'What about the entrance here, Fox. Wasn't there a man outside?'

'The PC on this beat,' said Fox. 'He was told to stay outside and another chap was put on the beat.'

'Well, where is the PC?'

'Taking shelter, most likely,' said Fox. 'He'll hear about this.' Alleyn rang the bell of 24. Immediately they heard inside the click of a lock.

'Hallo,' said Alleyn. 'That's sudden.'

The door opened. Moffatt, very pale, with a rug clutched about him stared at them.

'Are you from Scotland Yard, sir?'

'Yes. Anything wrong?'

'Yes, sir. Something terrible's happened. I don't know what it is, but – ' Moffatt followed them up, leaving the door open behind him.

'Where is it?' Alleyn asked. 'We're all here. You'd better shut the door. Where's the man on duty?'

'Mr Campbell, sir? He's upstairs, sir, and there's a doctor there too, sir.'

'A doctor!' said Alleyn sharply.

'And there's a policeman outside the room where his lordship's lying. Something terrible – '

'We'll go up,' said Alleyn. 'How many floors?'

'Three, sir. And his lordship's lying on the next floor. Her ladyship, sir, has been screaming something frightful to hear and – '

Alleyn was half-way up the first flight. The others followed him, Moffatt bleating in the rear. The fourth floor landing was brightly lit. On the top stair Alleyn found a group of three. A uniformed nurse, white to the lips, was on the floor, propped against the stairhead. Above her stood Henry Lamprey and Roberta Grey. They, too, were deadly pale. As soon as she saw Alleyn the nurse said: 'I'm quite all right and ready for duty. I don't know what happened to me. It wasn't natural. I've never slept on duty before, never. If the doctor wants me – '

'Where is the doctor?'

'In the fourth room along that passage,' said Henry. 'Don't mistake it for the third room. My aunt is locked in there. Stark mad, with her husband's hand in her pocket.'

'They took it away,' said the nurse in a high voice.

Alleyn strode down the passage followed by Fox.

'Henry,' said Nigel, 'what in Heaven's name are you talking about?'

'Hallo, Nigel,' said Henry. 'Follow your boy-friends and find out.'

'But – '

'For God's sake,' said Henry, 'leave us alone.'

Nigel followed Alleyn and Fox.

II

In the fourth room along the passage Alleyn examined the body of William Giggle. He lay in his bed on his right side with the clothes drawn up to his mouth. There was a blood-stained dent on his left temple, a horse-shoe-shaped mark pointing downwards towards the cheek with the arched end near the brow. When Alleyn drew down the bedclothes he saw Giggle's throat. A razor lay on the sheet close to Giggle's head. Alleyn bent lower.

'Cooling,' he said.

'He's been dead at least two hours,' said Dr Curtis.

'Has he, by gum,' said Fox.

The bed was against the left-hand wall of the room. There was a space between the head of the bed and the back wall. Alleyn moved into it and made a gesture over the throat.

'Yes,' Curtis said, 'like that. You notice it begins low down on the right near the clavicle, and runs upwards almost to the left ear.'

'There's no blood on any of them, sir,' said Campbell. 'Not on her or any of them.'

Alleyn pointed to a slash in the collar of the pyjama jacket and Curtis nodded. 'I know. It was done under the bedclothes. Look at them. Yes,' as Alleyn stooped to peer at an object at his feet. 'She knocked him out with that boot. There's blood on the heel.'

'Put it away carefully, Campbell. Chalk the positions. We'll want Bailey and Thompson.'

'They're coming,' said Curtis.

'Good.' Alleyn took a counterpane from the end of the bed and covered the body with it. 'The same idea, you see,' he said, 'with a difference. She's learnt that an injury to the brain doesn't always mean instant death but she's stuck to the preliminary knockout. It works well. Two hours, you say?'

'Or more.'

'We wouldn't have saved him, Fox, if we had caught the express.'

'No, sir.'

'If only I'd seen that book a little earlier. What have you got in there, Campbell?'

Campbell had taken a rolled-up towel from the top of the dressing-table.

'It just doesn't make sense,' said Campbell. 'My Gawd, sir, we found it in her pocket with the key of the room downstairs. It's like one of these damn-fool stories.'

'The case of the severed hand?'

'How did you know, sir?'

'Her nephew told me. I'll see the thing later.'

'Mr Alleyn expected it,' said Fox quickly.

'I'm afraid it makes very good sense, Campbell,' said Alleyn. 'Where is Lady Wutherwood?'

'Next door,' said Curtis. 'I gave her an injection. Had to. She'd have hurt herself otherwise. She's quieter now. I've telephoned Kantripp.'

'And the others?'

'The servants are all in the room at the end of the passage,' said Campbell. 'Her personal maid, Tinkerton the name is, keeps asking to see her.'

'Let her stay where she is,' Alleyn moved to the door, turned, and looked at the bed.

'Well,' he said, 'I suppose if he'd been asked he'd have preferred this.'

'To what?' asked Nigel.

'To the quick drop, Mr Bathgate,' said Fox.

'Good God, was he the murderer?'

'Yes, yes,' said Alleyn impatiently. 'Come on.'

III

Alleyn sent Curtis to look at Lady Wutherwood, and Campbell to the servants' room where one of the maids could be heard enjoying a fit of hysterics. Henry, Roberta, and the nurse were still on the landing. The nurse again expressed her devotion to duty and was told she could report to the doctor. Henry and Roberta were sent upstairs.

'If you can find a room with a heater,' said Alleyn, 'I should use it. I'll see you in a few minutes.'

'I want to know – ' Henry began.

'Of course you do. Give me a little longer, will you?'

'Yes, sir.'

Alleyn and Fox went down to the green drawing-room followed by a completely silent Nigel. Alleyn sent the policeman on guard there up to Campbell. He unlocked the door with the key that had been found in Lady Wutherwood's dressing-gown pocket. The room was heavy with flowers. The sound of wind and rain was loudest here. Gilded chairs and china cupboards stood at intervals round the walls which were hung with green silk. Behind these sad folds the wainscoting uttered furtive little noises. A monstrous chandelier chimed dolefully as someone walked along the passage overhead. On three trestles in the middle of the room lay Lord Wutherwood's body in an open coffin. The face was covered and a sheaf of lilies quite hid the breast. Alleyn moved them away. For a moment they were all silent. Then Nigel took out his handkerchief.

'God,' said Nigel shakily, 'this is – it's a bit too much.'

'Hacked off at the wrist,' said Fox. 'Sawn off, isn't it?'

'Yes,' said Alleyn. 'If you're going to be sick, Bathgate, I implore you to go outside.'

'I'm all right.'

Alleyn slid his hand out of sight round the sharp outline of the body. After a moment he drew something out of the coffin. Nigel had turned away. He heard Fox's exclamation and then Alleyn's level voice: 'So the tool, you see, was to be buried with the crime.'

'It's come from the kitchen,' said Fox. 'They saw up stock bones with them.'

'Put it away, Fox. Bailey will have to see it. Thompson had better take a shot of the dismembered arm. In the meantime – '

Alleyn replaced the sheaf of lilies and stood for a moment looking at the shrouded figure.

'What sort of epitaph,' he said, 'can be written for the late Lord Wutherwood, killed by cupidity and mutilated in the interests of black magic? We'd better finish our job, Fox. We haven't got a warrant. She'll have to be taken away and charged later. You attend to that, will you? I'd better see that young man.'

IV

'Robin may stay and listen too, mayn't she?' asked Henry.

'Certainly. In a sense,' said Alleyn, 'Miss Grey is the heroine of this case.'

'I am?' asked Roberta. 'How can that be?'

'Your statement last night gave us the first inkling as to Giggle's activities. You remember that you told us how, when you were alone in the dining-room, you heard the lift. Do you mind repeating that story once more?'

'Of course not. I heard Lord Wutherwood call out the second time. Then I heard the lift go down. Then I took a cigarette. Then I heard the lift again. Coming up. Then I hunted for matches. I found the matches and leant out of the window, smoking and listening to London. Then I heard Lady Wutherwood scream. The screams got louder and louder as – ' Roberta stopped and stared at Alleyn. 'Now,

I see,' she said slowly. 'That's why you made me repeat it twice over. The lift noises didn't fit with the screams.'

'That's it,' said Alleyn. 'You see, according to all the other evidence, Lady Wutherwood began screaming while the lift was still going down and all the time it was coming up. But you heard the lift go down and come up with no disturbance. Then you leant out of the window and listened to London so you didn't hear the lift go down on the fatal trip. You only heard her scream as it returned.'

'So there was a trip down and up unaccounted for,' said Henry.

'Yes. But the commissionaire said positively that the lift only made one trip and that the fatal one, when your brother stopped it before it actually reached the ground floor but when it was within view of the hall. What of this other trip? The only explanation was that it didn't go all the way down. Now, when Miss Grey heard the lift, Michael and Giggle had just left her. They both say that Giggle went straight downstairs. Yet Giggle stated that the lift made no movement while he was going downstairs. He swore that it was at the top landing with Lord Wutherwood inside. It is at least true that Lord Wutherwood was inside. But we know it went down and we know Giggle must have seen it. The lift can be summoned from any floor at any time. The flat on that landing below yours is unoccupied. Our theory is, that Giggle, on leaving Michael, went down to that landing. Michael saw him go and went into flat 26. That gave Giggle his dubious alibi. He summoned the lift with Lord Wutherwood inside it. He entered the lift and inflicted the injuries. He was wearing your motoring gloves. He threw them under the seat, got out of the lift, and went on down to the ground level where the commissionaire spoke to him. He then walked through the front entrance and got into the car.'

'But why?' Henry said. 'Why did he kill him?'

'Because he knew he would come into £300 a year and a small property.'

'For so little!'

'Not so little to him. And I learnt today that the property has increased considerably in value. He would have been comfortably set up for life. But there was another driving factor which we shall come to in a minute or two.'

'One moment,' said Henry. 'Did Aunt V. know Giggle was the murderer?'

'We'll take her next. As your family pointed out with tireless emphasis, Lady Wutherwood is mentally unhinged. May I say in passing that the emphasis was just a little too pointed. They would have been wiser to have left us to form our own opinion. However, she is undoubtedly insane and – a point that you may have missed – she is almost certainly taking some form of drug; morphia, I should think. She has also become deeply interested in witchcraft and black magic. The interest, I think, is pathological. In the police service we see a good deal of the effect of superstition on credulous and highly-strung people. We learn of middle-aged men and women losing their money and their sanity in the squalid little parlours of fortune-tellers, spirit-mongers, and self-styled psychiatrists. Lady Wutherwood, I think, is an extreme example of this sort of thing. She has wooed the supernatural in the grand macabre manner and has paid for her enthusiasm with her wits.'

'She's always been a bit dotty,' said Henry.

'When Dr Curtis and Fox and I interviewed her, we were puzzled by her reference to a couple of obscure medieval witches. A little later she certainly suggested that her husband had been killed by some supernatural agent who had taken the form of your brother, Stephen.'

'Well!' said Henry. 'I must say I call that a bit thick. Why pick on poor old Step?'

'Simply because she saw him in the lift. Her behaviour at this interview was in every way extraordinary. She had, we were assured, screamed violently and persistently when she discovered the injury to her husband, yet one couldn't miss a kind of terrified exulting in her manner when she spoke of it. Lastly, and most importantly, she insisted that his body was to be sent to their London house. I'm no psychiatrist but it seemed to me that however insane she was, if she had murdered her husband she wouldn't desire, ardently, to spend a couple of nights in a half-deserted house with the dead body. *Unless,* and here's an important point, she had some motive connected with the body. Very stupidly, I could think of no motive and was therefore still doubtful if she was guilty of her husband's death, since Giggle's guilt was not certainly known. This afternoon at Deepacres Park I believed I had discovered the motive. In a copy of a medieval work on witchcraft we found a chapter dealing with the various kinds of soporific spells.'

'My God!' Henry whispered. ' "The Hand of Glory".'

'Yes. The hand cut from the wrist of a corpse, preferably a felon or a murdered man. It renders the possessor safe from discovery since – but you know your *Ingoldsby Legends*, I see.'

' "Sleep all who sleep
Wake all who wake
But be as the dead for the dead man's sake." '

'That's it. Lady Wutherwood determined to make the experiment. As soon as her copy of the *Compendium Maleficorum* opened itself at that chapter, as soon as I saw her pencilled marks in the margin, I guessed what was up. I ought to have guessed before.'

'I don't see how you could,' said Roberta.

'Lord, no,' said Henry. 'I call it quite remarkable to have got it when you did.'

'Do you?' said Alleyn. 'I'm afraid you're easily impressed. Well, there you are. She waited till the house was still and her night nurse was snoring. By the way, the night nurse's virtuous denials may have some foundation. I fancy she'd been treated to a morphia tablet in her cocoa. You will have noticed that her pupils were contracted.'

'We didn't,' said Henry. 'But how cunning of Aunt V.'

'Oh, Lady Wutherwood didn't do that,' said Alleyn, 'any more than she murdered Giggle.'

Neither Henry nor Roberta spoke. Alleyn looked from one to the other and then at Nigel who sat self-effacingly in a corner of the room. 'Haven't you told them?' asked Alleyn.

'I – I thought I had,' murmured Nigel.

'What *have* you told them?'

'I – that – well, that Lady Wutherwood – '

'I left you with Fox. If you still held this remarkable theory surely you made certain, before you communicated it, that it was his idea too?'

'No,' stammered Nigel. 'No. You said "she". How the devil – '

'You've seen the files. Who hid in the hall cupboard and listened to the quarrel between Lord Charles and his brother? Who lied about it and gave us a string of impossible moves? Who brought the lift back to the top landing after Giggle had done the job downstairs? You've seen Giggle's body. What sort of murderer could inflict that sort of injury from behind the head of a victim lying on his right side in a bed by the left-hand wall of a room?'

'I – well. I – '

'A left-handed murderer to be sure. Tinkerton, you great gump, Tinkerton, Tinkerton, Tinkerton.'

CHAPTER 20

Preparation for Poverty

Roberta was so deadly tired that she was not able to feel anything but a sort of dull astonishment and a sense of release. This was followed by the ironical reflection that once more the Lampreys, through no effort of their own, had got out of a scrape. They would not even have to face the distasteful ordeal of giving evidence against their uncle's widow. She looked at Henry and wondered if she only imagined there was an unfamiliar glint of purpose in his eye, or if in sober truth the horrors of the last thirty hours had developed some latent possibilities in his character. He seemed to be listening intently to Alleyn. Roberta forced herself to listen too.

' – all we had to work on,' the pleasant voice was saying. 'If she had done what she said she did, she would have met Baskett on his way from the hall or in the servants' sitting-room. She told us she met nobody. She didn't know, or had forgotten, that Baskett went down the passage while she was hiding in the hall cupboard. She heard Michael say goodbye to Giggle and remembered to fit that in with her story. But she told us that as she crossed the landing and followed Giggle downstairs she saw Lord Wutherwood sitting in the lift. You can't see anyone who sits in that lift. The doors were shut and the window in the outer door is too high. If Tinkerton was innocent, why did she tell those purposeless lies? Our theory is that Tinkerton, knowing that Lord Wutherwood meant to refuse his brother, left Nanny Burnaby in flat 26, got as far as the hall door, found the hall full of the charade party and, as she told us, hung back until they went into the drawing-room, then joined Baskett for a glass of sherry, saw cook in the kitchen and, leaving the kitchen ostensibly to wash her hands, went back to the hall and slipped into the open cupboard where she left impressions of her heels. She overheard the quarrel between your father and his brother. We have a detailed account of that quarrel from Miss Cora Blackburn.'

'Miserable little snooper,' said Henry. 'You can't open a door in that flat without finding Blackburn tiptoeing away on the other side.'

'A good many people overheard the interview,' Alleyn remarked.

'One up to you, sir,' said Henry.

'But Blackburn's account happened to be the only one we felt inclined to believe.'

'Robin,' said Henry, 'we have not distinguished ourselves, my darling. But why, Mr Alleyn, did you reject our united story (unhappily somewhat fanciful), in favour of a curious parlour-maid's (probably correct)!'

'Well,' Alleyn said, 'it's a long story but the constable on duty in the drawing-room speaks French. That's one reason.'

'Dear me! I must say we *have* made fools of ourselves.'

'To go on with Tinkerton. Tinkerton heard the quarrel and thought it a wonderful opportunity to secure Giggle, together with a nice fat legacy, and throw suspicion of guilt on somebody else. She and Giggle would no doubt keep their respective jobs with Lady Wutherwood. Your old Nanny told Fox there was something between them. Old Nannies are not always reliable witnesses but – '

'She's right about that,' said Henry. 'I remember now. There was some row about it between Uncle G. and Aunt V. He said Tinkerton was debauching Giggle. How Giggle could! Imagine it!'

'We won't,' said Alleyn. 'To continue. Michael left Giggle and took the parcel into the drawing-room. The coast was clear for Tinkerton. We think she may have crossed the landing and got Giggle to come out there. She probably told him then of the quarrel. I fancy Tinkerton, like Lady Macbeth, was the brains of the party, and I may add that a casual conversation with a Shakespearian PC first gave me this idea. Some time between Michael's departure to the drawing-room and Lady Charles's return from flat 26, the thing was concocted. Either a tentative plot was interrupted by Lord Wutherwood coming out and getting into the lift, or the whole thing took shape in Tinkerton's fertile brain after he was there. Here was their opportunity. He was alone and he had quarrelled violently with his brother who had audibly wished him dead. They made themselves scarce while Baskett put Lord Wutherwood into his coat. As soon as Baskett had gone, out they came. Giggle got his instructions. He was to go to the deserted landing below, summon the lift with Lord Wutherwood inside it, kill him, and go on downstairs. Tinkerton would recall the lift and as soon as she had touched the button, hurry down after Giggle and leaving all of you upstairs with a very healthy motive. All went according to plan, except that neither of them knew that injuries to the brain are not always instantly fatal. As soon as Lord Wutherwood entered the lift she gave Giggle the skewer and gloves, sent him along to get Michael as his witness, took to her old hidey-hole until Giggle had gone, and then returned to the landing. She would see the lift go down and stop at the lower landing. She would hear the doors open. Possibly she would hear another more ominous sound. She would hear the doors close again. That was her cue. She pressed the button and followed Giggle downstairs. The lift returned to the top floor and Tinkerton, having summoned it, passed it on her way down. The commissionaire saw them go out to the car, one after another, just as they said. If it seemed impossible for Giggle to have killed him then it must have seemed equally impossible for Tinkerton to do so since she was hard on Giggle's heels. Michael provided the upstairs alibi. The commissionaire provided the downstairs alibi. The pause on the second floor was sandwiched neatly between their two appearances.'

'They took frightful risks, sir.'

'They took one big risk. I think Giggle left the doors open while he attacked Lord Wutherwood. Tinkerton, in that case, would be quite safe, if she kept her thumb on the call button up above. That would prevent anybody summoning the lift to the ground floor and it would return to the top floor the moment Giggle left it and closed the doors behind him. The great risk was that somebody would come out on the landing and notice that the lift was not there, or catch it on its return, or even see it returning. In that case the job would have been up to Tinkerton. If somebody appeared as the lift was going down, she would have to keep her thumb on the button and no sooner did it stop than it would return, with Lord

Wutherwood angrily alive inside it. If somebody appeared during the few seconds after the attack but before the lift returned and before Tinkerton got away, she would have had to distract the newcomer's attention. Ask if she might fetch Lady Wutherwood. Faint, like Lady Macbeth. Slam the hall door on her own finger. Anything to draw attention away from the lift. That was their difficult moment, but it only lasted a few seconds and remember that Tinkerton knew pretty well what you were all doing. She wouldn't have been implicated but Giggle would. Giggle was the mug.'

'Why did she kill him?'

'Because he'd lost his nerve. This morning we questioned him about the lift and about his legacy. He went to pieces. He was a stupid fellow, ready enough to act quickly when the brains of the party shoved the weapon in his hand and egged him on, but wildly incapable of keeping his head afterwards, when the mental rot set in. No doubt he returned to Brummell Street in a state of terror and Tinkerton decided he was dangerous. She's a clever, a desperate and a courageous woman. Moreover she is in her mistress's confidence. I'll bet you anything you like that Tinkerton is the buyer of whatever drug Lady Wutherwood takes and that she gets a little commission on the side. As Lady Wutherwood's confidante, she undoubtedly knows a great deal about the witchcraft business. We shall only find Lady Wutherwood's prints on the – ' Alleyn checked himself – 'on the objects connected with this last crime, but I'll stake my life that Tinkerton visited the kitchen some time during the night and brought away an instrument which she laid ready to hand in the green drawing-room. You may be sure Tinkerton knew very well what her mistress meant to do during the small hours. You may be sure it was Tinkerton who suggested that Lady Wutherwood should test the power of the Hand of Glory and Tinkerton who slipped down the back stairs and pulled out the fuse plug. One can imagine the instructions that were poured into that demented ear. First she was to secure the hand, then take it up to the top landing and down the deserted passage to the end room. There she would find a sleeping man. Let her make any noise she could think of, drop his heavy boots on the floor, scream, shake the bed. No one would stir, said Tinkerton, for all would be under the soporific spell of the severed hand.'

'So poor old Aunt V. was the cat's paw.'

'Yes. Tinkerton may even have persuaded her that her Little Master required the death of the chauffeur. She may have told her where to find the razor. Her prints on the razor would be useful and her reaction when she found Giggle already murdered wouldn't matter. Let her make whatever noise she liked. Let her be found there, with the razor in her hand. I'm so sorry, Miss Grey, it's a beastly story but I think you'll feel better if you know exactly what happened, however unpleasant the recital.'

'Yes,' said Roberta. 'But I still don't quite see.'

'It may be Aunt V., after all,' said Henry. 'Egged on by Tinkerton.'

'No. Only a left-handed person could have done it. I shan't describe the nature of the injury.'

'I'd rather you did,' said Henry. 'Robin, dear, perhaps if you – '

'I'd rather know, too, Henry. It's beastly to wonder.'

'Well,' said Alleyn, 'the murderer stood behind the head of the bed and the angle and position of the injury precludes any possibility of it being a right-handed attack. That's all you need know, isn't it?'

'But why didn't she arrange it to look like a suicide?' asked Henry and Alleyn saw with astonishment that the passionate interest of the amateur had already replaced in Henry's mind the horror of the scene with Lady Wutherwood. Henry had not seen Giggle and so, though he lay upstairs with his throat slit, his injury had an academic interest and Henry was prepared to discuss it.

'Tinkerton was very careful that it should not look like a suicide,' Alleyn said. 'A theory of suicide might have led to the possibility of Giggle's complicity and that would have come altogether too close to Tinkerton. No. Tinkerton was desperate. With Giggle in a state of terror, blundering in his statements to the police, threatening perhaps to confess and be hanged, she had to revise her plans drastically and disastrously. We must now be led to plump for Lady Wutherwood as a homicidal maniac. The whole object of the first crime went west to cut her losses and Giggle's throat.'

'Won't it be very hard to prove all this, sir?'

'If Miss Grey hadn't heard the lift and if you both had slept through this night, we should have had little against her beyond the left-handed evidence and her earlier lies. As it is you heard Lady

Wutherwood downstairs and saw her come upstairs and go to the top landing on the errand that was to be thought murderous. But when Campbell followed her to the chauffeur's bedroom and found her there with the body, Giggle had been dead for over two hours. We've medical evidence for that. It was half past two then. The nurse will swear that at one o'clock Lady Wutherwood was in bed and had not stirred. The nurse had her cocoa in a Thermos flask. Tinkerton brought it to her at eleven o'clock. The previous night she drank it immediately. Tonight she was about to drink it, she had actually set out her cup and saucer before Tinkerton went away, when the storm reminded her that she had left a window open in the next room. She shut the window, decided to write a letter and forgot her cocoa. She did not drink it until two hours later. In the meantime Tinkerton had killed Giggle. The nurse drank her cocoa at two o'clock and immediately fell into a deep sleep.'

'How much did Aunt V. know?'

'She knew, at least, that she must keep still and pretend to be asleep for as long as the nurse was waking. She had been well instructed, it seems. She has made one statement. I'm afraid it will not be much use as evidence but it is illuminating. Dr Curtis tells me she has said over and over again: "Why were they not asleep? She said they would all sleep like the dead." And when he asks her: "Who said this?" she answers "Tinkerton"!'

II

'Well, that's over,' said Charlot raising her black hat until it perched on her grey curls and tipped over her nose, 'I must say that we do look a collection of old black scarecrows.'

'We always turn rather peculiar at funerals,' said Frid. 'I suppose it's because we all wear each other's clothes. Where did you get that hat, Mummy?'

'It's Nanny's. I haven't got a black. And these are Nanny's gloves. Aren't they frightful?'

'Really, it's rather as if we were dressed up for another charade,' said Stephen. 'Robin's the only girl among you who doesn't look p-peculiar.' And perhaps remembering that Roberta's black clothes were rather tragically her own, Stephen hurried on. 'Why didn't you all b-buy yourselves funeral garments, darling?'

'Much too expensive,' said Charlot. 'And that reminds me. You've all got to pay the greatest attention. I'm going to speak seriously to you.'

'Immy,' said Lord Charles suddenly, 'where is Aunt Kit?'

'For pity's sake, Charlie, don't tell me Aunt Kit is lost again.'

'No, Mummy,' said Patch. 'She's just "disappeared" into 26.'

'Well, you know what happened the last time she did that.'

'Talking about hats,' said Frid, 'did you ever see anything to equal hers?'

'We are not talking about hats,' said Charlot seriously. 'We are talking about money.'

'Oh gosh!' groaned Mike. He was lying on the hearthrug with sheets of expensive notepaper scattered about him. He was writing.

'About money,' Charlot repeated firmly. 'I do think, Charlie, darling, don't you, that we should make our plans at the very outset. Let's face it, we're poor people.' And catching sight of Roberta's astonished eyes, Charlot repeated: 'We're going to be very hard up for a long time.'

'Well,' said Colin, 'Step and I are going to get jobs.'

'And I shall be playing small but showy parts in no time,' added Frid.

'My poor babies,' Charlot exclaimed dramatically, 'you *are* so sweet. But in the *meantime* – ' She broke off. 'What *are* you doing, Mike?'

'Writing a letter,' said Mike, blushing.

'To whom, darling?'

'Chief Detective-Inspector Alleyn.'

'What about?' asked Colin.

'Oh, something. As a matter of fac' I just wanted to remind him about something. We were talking about jobs and I said I might rather like to be a detective.' He returned to his letter. Charlot shook her head fondly at him, lit a cigarette, and with an air of the greatest solemnity, took up her theme. 'In the meantime,' she said, 'there will be the most ghastly death duties and then we shall have Deepacres and Brummell Street and all the rest of it, hung round our necks like mile-stones.'

'Mill-stones, darling,' said Henry.

'You're wrong,' said Charlot. 'Hung round our necks like the upper and nether mile-stones is the full expression. You're thinking of the mills of God. Charlie, how much do you suppose we'll have when everything has been paid up?'

'Really, darling, I don't quite know. Old Rattisbon will tell us, of course.'

'Well, at a guess.'

'I really – well, I suppose it should be about thirty thousand.'

'Per annum?' asked Patch casually, 'or just the bare thirty thousand to last for ever?'

'My dear child; a year, of course.'

'And, of course,' said Charlot, 'at least half of that will go in taxes and then there will be people like Mr Grumball to pacify and those enormous places to run. What shall we have left?'

'Nothing,' said Colin deeply.

'So there you are, you see,' cried Charlot triumphantly. 'Nothing! I was thinking about it during the funeral and I clearly foresee that we must use our cunning and cut our capers according to our cloth. Now, this is my plan. We'll never manage to let Brummell Street, shall we?'

'Well – ' began Lord Charles.

'My dear, *look* at it! It's *monstrous*, Charlie. Still it's a house and it's quite large. My plan is that we get rid of this flat and live in it. Rent free. Until we decide whether we are to use Deepacres.'

'Mummy, we *can't*,' said Frid. 'It's too ghastly.'

'What?'

'The Brummell Street house.'

'Do you mean Giggle or the furniture, Frid?'

'Well, both. The furniture, really. I don't believe in ghosts though of course it would be rather awful if Giggle's blood – '

'That will do, Frid,' said Lord Charles.

'Drip, drip, drip.'

'Frid!'

'What does Frid mean?' asked Michael.

'Nothing,' said Frid. 'But, Mummy, 24 Brummell Street! *Honestly!*'

'My poor baby, I *know*. But attend to me. Let me finish. My cunning tells me that we can *improve* Brummell Street. Sell the most valuable of Aunt V.'s monsters – '

'Good heavens, Immy,' Lord Charles interrupted, 'what about V.?'

'I mean, haven't we got V. on our hands? I mean she's mad.'

'We must keep our heads about that,' said Charlot capably. 'Dr Kantripp will help. As soon as she has given her evidence – '

'But will she give evidence?' Henry asked. 'She'd cut a pretty queer figure in the witness-box talking about soporific spells.'

'Do let's keep to the point,' said his mother. 'We were in Brummell Street. Now, with what we save on rent we shall be able to make a few meagre alterations to the Brummell Street house. Paint the walls and change the curtains and get at least enough bathrooms for ordinary cleanliness. We could cover the worst of the chairs that we don't sell with something dirt cheap but amusing.'

'French chintz?' suggested Frid, taking fire.

'Yes. I mean, something that will simply tide us over our bad times. We'll consult a clever decorator. What I *do* want to *hammer* into your heads,' said Charlot, 'is that we are poor. Poor, poor, *poor.*'

Henry who had been watching Roberta, burst out laughing. Charlot gazed at him with an air of enquiry.

'What are you laughing at, Henry?'

'I was wondering if Robin could be persuaded to tell us her thoughts.'

Roberta became very pink. She had been reflecting on that agreeable attitude of mind which enabled the Lampreys, after a lifetime of pecuniary hazards, to feel the pinch of poverty upon the acquisition of an income of thirty thousand pounds. There they were, as solemn as owls, putting a brave face on penury and at the same time warming to the redecoration of 24 Brummell Street.

'Robin,' said Henry, 'I shall guess at your thoughts.'

'No, Henry, don't. But you can make another kind of guess. What family in fiction would you most resemble if you belonged to a different class?'

'The Macbeths?' asked Frid. 'No. Because, after all, Daddy and Mummy didn't murder Uncle G. and the sleeping groom.'

'I think I'm rather a Spartan mother,' said Charlot. 'Isn't there a Spartan family in a play? That's what we *shall* resemble in the future, I promise you.'

'I think Mummy's Congrevian,' said Stephen.

'Millament?' murmured Lord Charles.

'Robin means the *Comedy of Errors,*' said Patch, 'because of the twins.'

'Jemima Puddleduck,' said Mike and burst into one of his small boy fits of charming laughter. 'You're Jemima Puddleduck, Mummy, and you go pit-pat-paddle-pat, pit-pat-waddle-pat.'

'Mikey!' cried Charlot. Michael screwed up a piece of the expensive notepaper and threw it at her, 'Pit-pat-waddle-pat,' he shouted.

'I'm afraid I know which family Robin means,' said Henry. He took Roberta by the shoulders. 'The Micawbers.'

The others stared innocently at Robin and shook their heads.

'Poor old Robin,' said Frid. 'It's all been a bit too much for her.'

'It's been a bit too much for all of us,' said Charlot, 'which brings me to the rest of my story. It's got a little plan, Charlie, darling. I think it would be such a good idea if we all crept away somewhere for a little holiday before the trial comes off or war breaks out and nobody can go anywhere. I don't mean anywhere smart like Antibes or the Lido but some *un-smart* place, do you know? Somewhere where we could bathe and blow away the horrors and have a tiny bit of mild gambling at night. I think the Côte d'Azur somewhere would be best because it's not the season and so we shouldn't need many clothes.'

'Monte Carlo?' Frid suggested. 'It's very un-smart nowadays.'

'Yes, somewhere quite dull and cheap. After all,' said Charlot looking affectionately at her family, 'when you think of what we've been through you're bound to agree that we must have *some* fun.'

III

'Well, there's Uncle G. under the turf at last,' said Nigel. 'What do you suppose the Lampreys will do now?'

'They're your friends,' Alleyn grunted. 'God forbid that I should prophesy about them.'

'They'll be damned rich, won't they?'

'Pretty well.'

'I wonder if they'll turn comparatively careful about money. People do sometimes when they get a lot.'

'Sometimes.'

'Henry's been talking about a job.'
'Good Lord! Not the little New Zealander?'
'I think so.' Alleyn grimaced. 'I told you she was a courageous little party,' he said.

Death and the Dancing Footman

For Mivie and Greg with my love

Contents

PART ONE

1 Project 287
2 Assembly 303
3 Contact 320
4 Threat 337
5 Attempt 352
6 Flight 370
7 Booby Trap 389
8 Third Time Lucky 406

PART TWO

9 Alibi 425
10 Journey 446
11 Alleyn 466
12 Recapitulation 483
13 Examination 503
14 Interrogation 519
15 Document 536
16 Arrest 549
17 Departure 568

Cast of Characters

Jonathan Royal	*Of Highfold Manor, Cloudyfold, Dorset*
Caper	*His butler*
Aubrey Mandrake	*Born Stanley Footling, poetic dramatist*
Sandra Compline	*Of Penfelton Manor*
William Compline	*Her elder son*
Nicholas Compline	*Her younger son*
Chloris Wynne	*William's fiancée*
Dr Francis Hart	*A plastic surgeon*
Madame Elise Lisse	*A beauty specialist, of the Studio Lisse*
Lady Hersey Amblington	*Jonathan's distant cousin; beauty specialist, of the Salon Hersey*
Thomas	*A dancing footman*
Mrs Pouting	*Jonathan's housekeeper*
James Bewling	*An outside hand at Highfold*
Thomas Bewling	*His brother*
Roderick Alleyn	*Chief Detective-Inspector, CID, New Scotland Yard*
Agatha Troy Alleyn	*His wife*
Walter Copeland	*Rector of Winton St Giles*
Dinah Copeland	*His daughter*
Fox	*Detective-Inspector, CID, New Scotland Yard*
Detective-Sergeant Thompson	*A photographic expert*
Detective-Sergeant Bailey	*A fingerprint expert*
A Housemaid	
Superintendent Blandish	*Of the Great Chipping Constabulary*

Part One

CHAPTER 1

Project

On the afternoon of a Thursday early in 1940, Jonathan Royal sat in his library at Highfold Manor. Although daylight was almost gone, curtains were not yet drawn across the windows, and Jonathan Royal could see the ghosts of trees moving in agitation against torn clouds and a dim sequence of fading hills. The north wind, blowing strongly across an upland known as Cloudyfold, was only partly turned by Highfold woods. It soughed about the weathered corners of the old house, and fumbled in the chimneys. A branch, heavy with snow, tapped vaguely at one of the library windows. Jonathan Royal sat motionless beside his fire. Half of his chubby face and figure flickered in and out of shadow, and when a log fell in two and set up a brighter blaze, it showed that Jonathan was faintly smiling. Presently he stirred slightly and beat his plump hands lightly upon his knees, a discreetly ecstatic gesture. A door opened, admitting a flood of yellow light, not very brilliant, and a figure that paused with its hand on the door-knob.

'Hallo,' said Jonathan Royal. 'That you, Caper?'

'Yes, sir.'

'Lighting-up time?'

'Five o'clock, sir. It's a dark afternoon.'

'Ah,' said Jonathan, suddenly rubbing his hands together, 'that's the stuff to give the troops.'

'I beg your pardon, sir?'

'That's the stuff to give the troops, Caper. An expression borrowed from a former cataclysm. I did not intend you to take it literally. It's the stuff to give my particular little troop. You may draw the curtains.'

Caper adjusted Jonathan's patent blackout screens and drew the curtains. Jonathan stretched out a hand and switched on a table lamp at his elbow. Fire and lamplight were now reflected in the glass doors that protected his books, in the dark surfaces of his desk, in his leather saddle-back chairs, in his own spectacles, and in the dome of his bald pate. With a quick movement he brought his hands together on his belly and began to revolve his thumbs one over the other sleekly.

'Mr Mandrake rang up, sir, from Winton St Giles rectory. He will be here at 5.30.'

'Good,' said Jonathan.

'Will you take tea now, sir, or wait for Mr Mandrake?'

'Now. He'll have had it. Has the mail come?'

'Yes, sir. I was just – '

'Well, let's have it,' said Jonathan eagerly. 'Let's have it.'

When the butler had gone, Jonathan gave himself a little secret hug with his elbows, and, continuing to revolve his thumbs, broke into a thin falsetto, singing:

'Il était une bergère
Qui ron-ton-ton. Petit pat-a-plan.'

He moved his big head from side to side, in time with his tune and, owing to a trick of the firelight on his thick-lensed glasses, he seemed to have large white eyes that gleamed like those of the dead drummer in the *Ingoldsby Legends*. Caper returned with his letters. He snatched them up and turned them over with deft, pernickety movements, and at last uttered a little ejaculation. Five letters were set aside and the sixth opened and unfolded. He held it level with his nose, but almost at arm's length. It contained only six lines of writing, but they seemed to give Jonathan the greatest satisfaction. He tossed the letter gaily on the fire and took up the thin tenor of his song. Ten minutes later, when Caper brought in his tea, he was still singing, but he interrupted himself to say:

'Mr Nicholas Compline is definitely coming tomorrow. He may have the green visitors' room. Tell Mrs Pouting, will you?'

'Yes, sir. Excuse me, sir, but that makes eight guests for the weekend?'

'Yes. Yes, eight.' Jonathan ticked them off on his plump fingers. 'Mrs Compline. Mr Nicholas and Mr William Compline. Dr Francis Hart. Madame Lisse. Miss Wynne. Lady Hersey Amblington, and Mr Mandrake. Eight. Mr Mandrake tonight, the rest for dinner tomorrow. We'll have the Heidsiek '28 tomorrow, Caper, and the Courvoisier.'

'Very good, sir.'

'I am particularly anxious about the dinner tomorrow, Caper. Much depends upon it. There must be a warmth, a feeling of festivity, of anticipation, of – I go so far – of positive luxury. Large fires in the bedrooms. I've ordered flowers. Your department now. Always very satisfactory, don't think there's an implied criticism, but tomorrow' – he opened his arms wide – 'Whoosh! Something quite extra. Know what I mean? I've told Mrs Pouting. She's got everything going, I know. But your department – Ginger up that new feller and the maids. Follow me?'

'Certainly, sir.'

'Yes. The party' – Jonathan paused, hugged his sides with his elbows and uttered a thin cackle of laughter – 'the party may be a little sticky at first. I regard it as an experiment.'

'I hope everything will be quite satisfactory, sir.'

'Quite satisfactory,' Jonathan repeated. 'Yes. Sure of it. Is that a car? Have a look.'

Jonathan turned off his table lamp. Caper went to the windows and drew aside their heavy curtains. The sound of wind and sleet filled the room.

'It's difficult to say, sir, with the noise outside, but – yes, sir, there are the headlamps. I fancy it's coming up the inner drive, sir.'

'Mr Mandrake, no doubt. Show him in here, and you can take away these tea things. Too excited for 'em. Here he is.'

Caper closed the curtains and went out with the tea things. Jonathan switched on his lamp. He heard the new footman cross the hall and open the great front door.

'It's beginning,' thought Jonathan, hugging himself. 'This is the overture. We're off.'

II

Mr Aubrey Mandrake was a young poetic dramatist and his real name was Stanley Footling. He was in the habit of telling himself, for he was not without humour, that if it had been a little worse; if, for instance, it had been Albert Muggins, he would have clung to it, for there would have been a kind of distinction in such a name. Seeing it set out in the programme, under the titles of his 'Saxophone in Tarleton,' the public would have enclosed it in mental inverted commas. But they would not perform this delicate imaginary feat for a Stanley Footling. So he became Aubrey Mandrake, influenced in his choice by such names as Sebastian Melmoth, Aubrey Beardsley and Peter Warlock. In changing his name he had given himself a curious psychological setback, for in a short time he grew to identify himself so closely with his new names that the memory of the old ones became intolerable, and the barest suspicion that some new acquaintance had discovered his origin threw him into a state of acute uneasiness, made still more unendurable by the circumstance of his despising himself bitterly for this weakness. At first his works had chimed with his name, for he wrote of Sin and the Occult, but as his by no means inconsiderable talent developed, he found his subject in matters at once stranger and less colourful. He wrote, in lines of incalculable variety, of the passion of a pattern-cutter for a headless bust, of a saxophonist who could not perform to his full ability unless his instrument was decked out in tarleton frills, of a lavatory attendant who became a gentleman of the bed-chamber (this piece was performed only by the smaller experimental theatre clubs), and of a chartered accountant who turned out to be a reincarnation of Thäis. He was successful. The post-surrealists wrangled over him, the highest critics discovered in his verse a revitalizing influence on an effete language, and the Philistines were able to enjoy the fun. He was the possessor of a comfortable private income derived from his mother's boarding-house in Dulwich and the fruit of his father's ingenuity – a patent suspender clip. In appearance he was tall, dark, and suitably cadaverous; in manner, somewhat sardonic, in his mode of dressing, correct, for he had long since passed the stage when unusual cravats and strange shirts seemed to be a necessity for his æsthetic development. He was lame and extremely sensitive about the deformed foot which caused this disability. He wore a heavy boot on his left foot and always tried as far as possible to hide it under the chair on which he was sitting. His acquaintance with Jonathan Royal was some five years old. Late in the nineteen-thirties Jonathan had backed one of Mandrake's plays, and though it had not made a fortune for either of them it had unexpectedly paid its way and had established their liking for one another. Mandrake's latest play, 'Bad Blackout' (finished since the outbreak of war but, as far as the uninstructed could judge, and in spite of its title, not about the war), was soon to go into rehearsal with an untried company of young enthusiasts. He had spent two days at Winton St Giles rectory with his leading lady and her father, and Jonathan had asked him to come on to Highfold for the weekend.

His entrance into Jonathan's library was effective, for he had motored over Cloudyfold bareheaded with the driving-window open, and the north wind had tossed his hair into elf-locks. He usually did the tossing himself. He advanced upon Jonathan with his hand outstretched, and an air of gay hardihood.

'An incredible night,' he said. 'Harpies and warlocks abroad. Most stimulating.'

'I trust,' said Jonathan, shaking his hand and blinking up at him, 'that it hasn't stimulated your Muse. I cannot allow her to claim you this evening, Aubrey – '

'O God!' said Mandrake. He always made this ejaculation when invited to speak of his writing. It seemed to imply desperate æsthetic pangs.

' – because,' Jonathan continued, 'I intend to claim your full attention, my dear Aubrey. Our customary positions are reversed. For tonight, yes, and for tomorrow and the next day, I shall be the creator and you the audience.' Mandrake darted an apprehensive glance at his host.

'No, no, no,' Jonathan cried, steering him to the fireside, 'don't look so alarmed. I've written no painful middle-aged belles-lettres, nor do I contemplate my memoirs. Nothing of the sort.'

Mandrake sat opposite his host by the fire. Jonathan rubbed his hands together and suddenly hugged them between his knees. 'Nothing of the sort,' he repeated.

'You look very demure,' said Mandrake. 'What are you plotting?'

'Plotting! That's the word! My dear, I am up to my ears in conspiracy.' He leant forward and tapped Mandrake on the knee. 'Come now,' said Jonathan, 'tell me this. What do you think are my interests?'

Mandrake looked fixedly at him. 'Your *interests?*' he repeated.

'Yes. What sort of fellow do you think I am? It is not only women, you know, who are interested in the impressions they make on their friends. Or *is* there something unexpectedly feminine in my curiosity? Never mind. Indulge me so far. Come now.'

'You skip from one query to another. Your interests, I should hazard, lie between your books, your estate, and – well, I imagine you are interested in what journalists are pleased to call human contacts.'

'Good,' said Jonathan. 'Excellent. Human contacts. Go on.'

'As for the sort of fellow you may be,' Mandrake continued, 'upon my word, I don't know. From my point of view a very pleasant fellow. You understand things, the things that seem to me to be important. You have never asked me, for instance, why I don't write about real people. I regard that avoidance as conclusive.'

'Would you say, now, that I had a sense of the dramatic?'

'What is the dramatic? Is it merely a sense of theatre, or is it an appreciation of æsthetic climax in the extroverted sense?'

'I don't know what that means,' said Jonathan impatiently. 'And I'm dashed if I think you do.'

'Words,' said Mandrake. 'Words, words, words.' But he looked rather put out.

'Well, damnit, it doesn't matter two ha'po'th of pins. I maintain that I have a sense of drama in the ordinary un-classy sense. My sense of drama, whether you like it or not, attracts me to your own work. I don't say I understand it, but for me it's got *something*. It jerks me out of my ordinary reactions to ordinary theatrical experiences. So I like it.'

'That's as good a reason as most.'

'All right. But wait a bit. In me, my dear Aubrey, you see the unsatisfied and inarticulate artist. Temperament and no art. That's me. Or so I thought until I got my Idea. I've tried writing and I've tried painting. The results have on the whole been pitiable – at the best negligible. Music – out of the question. And all the time, here I was, an elderly fogey plagued with the desire to create. Most of all have I hankered after drama, and at first I thought my association with you, a delightful affair from my point of view, I assure you, would do the trick; I would taste, at second-hand as it were, the pleasures of creative art. But no, the itch persisted and I was in danger of becoming a disgruntled restless fellow, a nuisance to myself and a bore to other people.'

'Never that,' murmured Mandrake, lighting a cigarette.

'It would have been the next stage, I assure you. It threatened. And then, in what I cannot but consider an inspired moment, my dear Aubrey, I got My Idea.'

With a crisp movement Jonathan seized his glasses by their nose-piece and plucked them from his face. His eyes were black and extremely bright.

'My Idea,' he repeated. 'One Wednesday morning four weeks ago, as I was staring out of my window here and wondering how the devil I should spend the day, it suddenly came to me. It came to me that if I was a ninny with ink and paper, and brush and canvas, and all the rest of it, if I couldn't express so much as a how-d'ye-do with a stave of music, there was one medium that I had never tried.'

'And what could that wonderful medium be?'

'Flesh and blood!'

'What!'

'Flesh and blood!'

'You are *not*,' said Mandrake, 'I implore you to say you are *not* going in for social welfare.'

'Wait a bit. It came to me that human beings could, with a little judicious arrangement, be as carefully "composed" as the figures in a picture. One had only to restrict them a little, confine them within the decent boundaries of a suitable canvas, and they would make a pattern. It seemed to me that, given the limitations of an imposed stage, some of my acquaintances would at once begin to unfold an exciting drama; that, so restricted, their conversation would begin to follow as enthralling a design as that of a fugue. Of course the right, how shall I put it, the right ingredients must be selected, and this was where I came in. I would set my palette with human colours and the picture would paint itself. I would summon my characters to the theatre of my own house and the drama would unfold itself.'

'Pirandello,' Mandrake began, 'has become quite – '

'But this is *not* Pirandello,' Jonathan interrupted in a great hurry. 'No. In this instance we shall see, not six characters in search of an author, but an author who has deliberately summoned seven characters to do his work for him.'

'Then you mean to write, after all?'

'Not I. I merely select. As for writing,' said Jonathan, 'that's where you come in. I make you a present of what I cannot but feel is a golden opportunity.'

Mandrake stirred uneasily. 'I wish I knew what you were up to,' he said.

'My dear fellow, I'm telling you. Listen. A month ago I decided to make this experiment. I decided to invite seven suitably chosen characters for a winter weekend here at Highfold, and I spent a perfectly delightful morning compiling the list. My characters must, I decided, be, as far as possible, antagonistic to each other.'

'O God!'

'Not antagonistic each one to the other seven, but there must at least be some sort of emotional intellectual tension running like a connecting thread between them. Now a very little thought showed me that I had not far to seek. Here, in my own corner of Dorset, here in the village and county undercurrents, still running high in spite of the war, I found my seven characters. And since I must have an audience, and an intelligent audience, I invited an eighth guest – yourself.'

'If you expect me to break into a paean of enraptured gratitude – '

'Not just yet, perhaps. Patience. Now, in order to savour the full bouquet of the experiment you must be made happily familiar with the dramatis personæ. And to that end,' said Jonathan cosily, 'I propose that we ring for sherry.'

III

'I propose,' said Jonathan, filling his companion's glass, 'to abandon similes drawn from painting or music, and to stick to a figure that we can both appreciate. I shall introduce my characters in terms of dramatic art and, as far as I can guess, in the order of their appearance. You look a little anxious.'

'Then my looks,' Mandrake rejoined, 'do scant justice to my feelings. I feel terrified.'

Jonathan uttered his little cackle of laughter. 'Who can tell?' he said. 'You may have good cause. You shall judge of that when I have finished. The first characters to make their unconscious entrances on our stage are a mother and two sons. Mrs Sandra Compline, William Compline, and Nicholas Compline. The lady is a widow and lives at Penfelton, a charming house some four miles to the western side of Cloudyfold village. She is the grand dame of our cast. The Complines are an old Dorset family and have been neighbours of ours for many generations. Her husband was my own contemporary. A rackety, handsome fellow, he was, more popular perhaps with women than with men, but he had his own set in London and a very fast set I fancy it was. I don't know where he met his wife, but I'm afraid it was an ill-omened encounter for her, poor thing. She was a pretty creature and I suppose he fell in love with her looks. His attachment didn't last as long as her beauty, and that faded pretty fast under the sort of treatment she had to put up with. When they'd been married about eight years and had these two sons, a ghastly thing happened to Sandra Compline. She went to stay abroad somewhere and, I suppose with the idea of winning him back, she had something done to her face. It was more than twenty years ago, and I dare say these fellows weren't as good at their job as they are nowadays. Lord knows what the chap she consulted did with Sandra Compline's face. I've heard it said (you may imagine how people talked) that he bolstered it up with wax and that the wax slipped. Whatever happened, it was quite disastrous. Poor thing,' said Jonathan, shaking his head while the lamplight glinted on his glasses, 'she was a most distressing sight. Quite lop-sided, you know, and, worst of all, there was a sort of comical look. For a long time she wouldn't go out or receive anyone. He began to ask his own friends to Penfelton, and a very dubious lot they were. We saw nothing of the Complines in those days, but local gossip was terrific. She used to hunt, wearing a thick veil and going so recklessly that people said she wanted to kill herself. Ironically, though, it was her husband who came a cropper. Fell with his horse and broke his neck. What d'you think of that?'

'Eh?' said Mandrake, rather startled by this sudden demand. 'Why, my dear Jonathan, it's quite marvellous. Devastatingly Edwardian.

Gloriously county. Another instance of truth being much more theatrical than fiction, and a warning to all dramatists to avoid it.'

'Well, well,' said Jonathan. 'I dare say. Let's get on. Sandra was left with her two small sons, William and Nicholas. After a little she seemed to take heart of grace. She began to go about a bit; this house was the first she visited. The boys had their friends for the holidays, and all that, and life became more normal over at Penfelton. The elder boy, William, was a quiet sort of chap, rather plain on the whole, not a great deal to say for himself; grave, humdrum fellow. Well enough liked, but the type that – well, you can never remember whether he was or was not at a party. That sort of fellow, do you know?'

'Poor William,' said Mandrake unexpectedly.

'What? Oh yes, yes, but I haven't quite conveyed William to you. The truth is,' said Jonathan, rubbing his nose, 'that William's a bit of a teaser. He's devoted to his mother. I think he remembers her as she was before the tragedy. He was seven when she came back, and I've heard that although he was strangely self-possessed when he saw her, he was found by their old nurse in a sort of hysterical frenzy, remarkable in such a really rather commonplace small boy. He *is* quiet and humdrum certainly, but for all that there's something not quite – well, he's a little *odd*. He's usually rather silent, but when he does talk his statements are inclined to be unexpected. He seems to say more or less the first thing that comes into his head, and that's a sufficiently unusual trait, you'll agree.'

'Yes.'

'Yes. Odd. Nothing wrong really, of course, and he's done very well so far in this war. He's a good lad. But sometimes I wonder . . . However, you shall judge of William for yourself. I want you to do that.'

'You don't really like him, do you?' asked Mandrake suddenly.

Jonathan blinked. 'What can have put that notion into your head?' he said mildly. He darted a glance at Mandrake. 'You mustn't become *too* subtle, Aubrey. William is merely rather difficult to describe. That is all. But Nicholas!' Jonathan continued. 'Nicholas was his father over again. Damned good-looking young blade, with charm and gaiety, and dash, and all the rest of it. Complete egoist, bit of a showman, and born with an eye for a lovely lady. So they grew up and so they are today. William's thirty-two and Nick's twenty-nine. William (I stress this point) is concentrated upon his mother, morbidly so, I think, but that's by the way. Gives up his holidays for no better reason than she's going to be alone. Watches after her like an old Nanny. He's on leave just now, and of course rushed home to her. Nick's the opposite, plays her up for all she's worth, never lets her know when he's coming or what he's up to. Uses Penfelton like a hotel and his mother like the proprietress. You can guess which of these boys is the mother's favourite.'

'Nicholas,' said Mandrake. 'Of course, Nicholas.'

'Of course,' said Jonathan, and if he felt any disappointment he did not show it. 'She dotes on Nicholas and takes William for granted. She's spoilt Nicholas quite hopelessly from the day he was born. William went off to prep-school and Eton; Nick, if you please, was pronounced delicate, and led a series of tutors a fine dance until his mother decided he was old enough for the Grand Tour and sent him off with a bear-leader like some young regency lordling. If she could have cut William out of the entail I promise you she'd have done it. As it is she can do nothing. William comes in for the whole packet, and Nick, like the hero of Victorian romance, must fend for himself. This, I believe, his mother fiercely resents. When war came she moved heaven and earth to find a safe job for Nicholas, and took it in her stride when William's regiment went to the front. Nick has got some department job in Great Chipping. Looks very smart in uniform, and his duties seem to take him up to London pretty often. William, at the moment, as I have told you, is spending his leave with his mamma. The brothers haven't met for some time.'

'Do they get on well?'

'No. Remember the necessary element of antagonism, Aubrey. It appears, splendidly to the fore, in the Compline family. William is engaged to Nicholas's ex-fiancée.'

'Really? Well done, William.'

'I need scarcely tell you that the lady is the next of my characters, the ingenue, in fact. She will arrive with William and his mamma, who detests her.'

'Honestly, my dear Jonathan – '

'She is a Miss Chloris Wynne. One of the white-haired kind.'

'A platinum blonde?'

'The colour of a light Chablis, and done up in plaster-like sausages. She resembles the chorus of my youth. I'm told that nowadays the chorus looks like the county. I find her appearance startling and her conversation difficult, but I have watched her with interest and I have formed the opinion that she is a very neat example of the woman scorned.'

'Did Nicholas scorn her?'

'Nicholas wished to marry her, but being in the habit of eating his cake in enormous mouthfuls, and keeping it, he did not allow his engagement to Miss Chloris to cramp his style as an accomplished philanderer. He continued to philander with the fifth item in our cast of characters – Madame Lisse.'

'O God!'

'More in anger than in sorrow, if Sandra Compline is to be believed, Miss Chloris broke off her engagement to Nicholas. After an interval so short that one suspects she acted on the ricochet, she accepted William, who had previously courted her and been cut out by his brother. My private opinion is that when William returns to the front, Nicholas is quite capable of recapturing the lady, and, what's more, I think she and William both know it. Nicholas and William had quarrelled in the best tradition of rival brothers and, as I say, have not met since the second engagement. I need not tell you that Mrs Compline, William, and his betrothed, none of them knows I have invited Nicholas, nor does Nicholas know I have invited them. He knows, however, that Madame Lisse will be here. That, of course, is why he has accepted.'

'Go on,' said Mandrake, driving his fingers through his hair.

'Madame Lisse, the ambiguous and alluring woman of our cast, is an Austrian beauty specialist. I don't suppose Lisse is her real name. She was among the earliest of the refugees, obtained naturalization papers, and established a salon at Great Chipping. She had letters to the Jerninghams at Pen Cuckoo, and to one or two other people in the county. Diana Copeland at the rectory rather took her up. So, as you have gathered, did Nicholas Compline. She is markedly a dasher. Dark-auburn hair, magnolia complexion, and eyes – whew! Very quiet and composed, but undoubtedly a dasher. Everybody got rather excited about Madame Lisse . . . everybody, that is, with the exception of my distant cousin, Lady Hersey Amblington, who will arrive for dinner tomorrow evening.'

The spectacles glinted in Mandrake's direction, but he merely waved his hands.

'Hersey,' said Jonathan, 'as you may know, is also a beauty specialist. She took it up when her husband died and left her almost penniless. She did the thing thoroughly and, being a courageous and capable creature, made a success of it. The mysteries of what I believe is called "beauty culture" are as a sealed book to me, but I understand that all the best complexions and coiffures of Great Chipping and the surrounding districts were, until the arrival of Madame Lisse, Hersey's particular property. Madame Lisse immediately began to knock spots out of Hersey. Not, as Hersey explained, that she now has fewer customers, but that they are not quite so smart. The smart clientele has, with the exception of a faithful few, gone over to the enemy. Hersey considers that Madame used unscrupulous methods and always alludes to her as "The Pirate." You haven't met my distant cousin, Hersey?'

'No.'

'No. She has her own somewhat direct methods of warfare, and I understand that she called on Madame Lisse with the intention of giving her fits. I'm afraid Hersey came off rather the worse in this encounter. Hersey is an old friend of the Complines and, as you may imagine, was not at all delighted by Nicholas's attentions to her rival. So you see she is linked up in an extremely satisfactory manner to both sides. I have really been extraordinarily fortunate,' said Jonathan, rubbing his hands. 'Nothing could be neater. And Dr Hart fills out the cast to perfection. The "heavy," I think, is the professional term for his part.'

'Doctor –?'

'Hart. The seventh and last character. He, too, is of foreign extraction, though he became a naturalized Briton some time after the last war. I fancy he is a Viennese, though whether I deduce this conclusion subconsciously from his profession I cannot tell you.' Jonathan chuckled again and finished his sherry.

'What, in Heaven's name, is his profession?'

'My dear Aubrey,' said Jonathan, 'he is a plastic surgeon. A beauty specialist *par excellence*. The male of the species.'

IV

'It seems to me,' said Mandrake, 'that you have invited stark murder to your house. Frankly, I can imagine nothing more terrifying than the prospect of this weekend. What do you propose to do with them?'

'Let them enact their drama.'

'It will more probably resemble some disastrous vaudeville show.'

'With myself as compère. Quite possibly.'

'My dear Jonathan, you will have no performance. The actors will either sulk in their dressing-rooms or leave the theatre.'

'That is where we come in.'

'We! I assure you – '

'It is where I come in, then. May I, without exhibiting too much complacency, claim that if I have a talent it lies in the direction of hospitality?'

'Certainly. You are a wonderful host.'

'Thank you,' said Jonathan, beaming at his guest. 'It delights me to hear you say so. Now, in this party I have set myself, I freely admit, a stiff task.'

'I'm glad you realize it,' said Mandrake. 'The list of opponents is positively ghastly. I don't know if I have altogether followed you, but it appears that you hope to reconcile a rejected lover both to his successor and to his late love, a business woman to her detested rival, a ruined beauty to an exponent of the profession that made an effigy of her face, and a mother to a prospective daughter-in-law who has rejected her favourite son for his brother.'

'There is another permutation that you have not yet heard. Local gossip rings with rumours of some secret understanding between Dr Hart and Madame Lisse. It appears that Madame recommends Dr Hart's surgery to those of her clients who have passed the stage when Lisse creams and all the rest of it can improve their ageing faces.'

'A business arrangement?'

'Something more than that if Hersey, a prejudiced witness, certainly, is to be believed. Hersey's spies tell her that Dr Hart has been observed leaving Madame Lisse's flat at a most compromising hour; that he presented to an exciting degree the mien of a clandestine lover, his hat drawn over his brows, his cloak (he wears a cloak) pulled about his face. They say that he has been observed to scowl most formidably at the mention of Nicholas Compline.'

'Oh, no,' said Mandrake, 'it's really a little too much. I boggle at the cloak.'

'It's a Tyrolean cloak with a hood, a most useful garment. Rainproof. He has presented me with one. I wear it frequently. You shall see it tomorrow.'

'What's he like, this face-lifter?'

'A smoothish fellow. I find him amusing. He plays very good bridge.'

'We are *not* going to play bridge?'

'No. No, that, I feel, would be asking for trouble. We *are* going to play a round game, however.'

'O God!'

'You will enjoy it. A stimulating game. I hope that it will go far towards burying our little armoury of hatchets. Imagine what fun, Aubrey, if on Monday morning they all go gaily away, full of the milk of human kindness.'

'You're seeing yourself in the detestable rôle of uplifter. I've got it! This is not Pirandello, nor is it vaudeville. Far from it. But it *is*,' cried Mandrake with an air of intense disgust, 'it *is* "The Passing of the Third Floor Back." '

Jonathan rose and stood warming his hands at the fire. He was a small man, very upright, with a long trunk and short legs. Mandrake, staring at him, wondered if it was some trick of firelight that lent a faintly malicious tinge to Jonathan's smile; it was merely his thick-lensed glasses that gave him that air of uncanny blankness.

'Ah, well,' said Jonathan, 'A peacemaker. Why not? You would like to see your room, Aubrey. The blue room, as usual, of course. It is no longer raining. I propose to take a look at the night before going up to change. Will you accompany me?'

'Very well.'

They went out, crossing a wide hall, to the entrance. The wind had fallen, and as Jonathan opened his great outer doors the quiet of an upland county at dusk entered the house, and the smell of earth still only lightly covered with snow. They walked out on the wide platform in front of Highfold. Far beneath them, Cloudyfold village showed dimly through treetops, and beyond it the few scattered houses down in the Vale, four miles away. In the southern skies the stars were out, but northward above Cloudyfold Top there was a well of blackness. And as Jonathan and his guest turned towards the north they received the sensation of an icy hand laid on their faces.

'That's a deathly cold, sir,' said Mandrake.

'It's from the north,' said Jonathan, 'and still smells of snow. Splendid! Let's go in.'

CHAPTER 2

Assembly

On the following day Mandrake observed his host to be in a high state of excitement. In spite of his finicky mannerisms and his somewhat old-maidish pedantry, it would never have occurred to his worst enemy to call Jonathan effeminate. Nevertheless he had many small talents that are unusual in a man. He took a passionate interest in the appointments of his house. He arranged flowers to perfection, and on the arrival of three boxes from a florist in Great Chipping, darted at them like a delighted ant. Mandrake was sent to the Highfold glasshouses for tuberoses and gardenias. Jonathan, looking odd in one of his housekeeper's aprons, buried himself in the flower room. He intended, he said, to reproduce bouquets from the French prints in the boudoir. Mandrake, whose floral tastes ran austerely to dead flowers, limped off to the library and thought about his new play, which was to represent twelve aspects of one character, all speaking together.

The morning was still and extremely cold. During the night there had been another light fall of snow. The sky was leaden and the countryside seemed to wait ominously for some portent from the north. Jonathan remarked several times, and with extraordinary glee, that they were in for a severe storm. Fires were lit in all the guest rooms, and from the Highfold chimneys rose columns of smoke, lighter in tone than the clouds they seemed to support. Somewhere up on Cloudyfold a farmer was moving his sheep, and the drowsy sound of their slow progress seemed uncannily near. So dark was the sky that the passage of the hours was seen only in a stealthy alteration of shadows. Jonathan and Mandrake lunched by lamplight. Mandrake said that he felt the house to be alive with anticipation, but whether of a storm without or within he was unable to decide. 'It's a grisly day,' said Mandrake.

'I shall telephone Sandra Compline and suggest that she brings her party for tea,' said Jonathan. 'It will begin to snow again before six o'clock, I believe. What do you think of the house, Aubrey? How does it feel?'

'Expectant and luxurious.'

'Good. Excellent. You have finished? Let us make a little tour of the rooms, shall we? Dear me, it's a long time since I looked forward so much to a party.'

They made their tour. In the great drawing room, seldom used by Jonathan, cedar-wood fires blazed at each end. Mrs Pouting and two maids had put glazed French covers on the armchairs and the bergere sofas.

'Summertime uniforms,' said Jonathan, 'but they chime with the flowers and are gay. Admire my flowers, Aubrey. Don't they look pleasant against the linen-fold walls? Quite a tone-poem, I consider.'

'And when seven furious faces are added,' said Mandrake, 'the harmony will be complete.'

'You can't frighten me. The faces will be all smiles in less than no time, you may depend on it. And, after all, even if they are not to be reconciled, I shall not complain. My play will be less pretty but more exciting.'

'Aren't you afraid that they will simply refuse to stay under the same roof with each other?'

'They will at least stay tonight, and tomorrow, I hope, will be so inclement that the weather alone will turn the balance.'

'Your courage is amazing. Suppose they all sulk in separate rooms?'

'They won't. I won't let 'em. Confess now, Aubrey, aren't you a little amused, a little stimulated?'

Mandrake grinned. 'I feel all the more disagreeable sensations of first-night nerves, but – all right, I'll admit to a violent interest.'

Jonathan laughed delightedly and took his arm. 'You must see the bedrooms and the boudoir and the little smoking room. I've allowed myself some rather childish touches, but they may amuse you. Elementary symbolism. Character as expressed by vegetation. As the florists' advertisements would have it, I have said it with flowers.'

'Said what?'

'What I think of every one.'

They crossed the hall to the left of the front door and entered the room that Jonathan liked to call the boudoir, an Adams sitting room painted a light green and hung with French brocades whose pert garlands were repeated in noesgays which Jonathan had set in the window and upon a spinet and a writing-desk.

'Here,' said Jonathan, 'I hope the ladies will forgather to write, gossip and knit. Miss Chloris, I should explain, is a "Wren," not yet called up, but filling the interim with an endless succession of indomitable socks. My distant cousin, Hersey, is also a vigorous knitter. I feel sure poor Sandra is hard at work on some repellent comfort.'

'And Madame Lisse?'

'The picture of Madame in close co-operation with strands of khaki wool is one which could be envisaged only by a surrealist. No doubt you will find yourself able to encompass it. Come along.'

The boudoir opened into the small smoking room where Jonathan permitted a telephone and a radio set, but which, he explained, had in other respects remained unaltered since his father died. Here were leather chairs, a collection of sporting prints flanked by a collection of weapons and by fading groups of Jonathan and his Cambridge friends in the curious photographic postures of the nineties. Above the mantelpiece hung a trout rod complete with cast and fly.

'Sweet-scented tobacco plants, you see,' said Jonathan, 'in pots. A trifle obvious, but I couldn't resist them. Now the library.'

The library opened out of the smoking room. It had an air of being the most-used room in the house, and indeed it was here that Jonathan could generally be found among a company of books that bore witness to generations of rather freakish taste and to the money by which such taste could be gratified. Jonathan had added lavishly to the collection. His books ranged oddly from translations of Turkish and Persian verse to the works of the most inscrutable of the moderns, and text-books on criminology and police detection. He had a magpie taste in reading, but it was steadied by a constancy of devotion to the Elizabethans.

'Here,' he said, 'I was troubled by an embarrassment of riches. A Shakespearian nosegay seemed a little *vieux jeu*, but on the other hand it had the advantage of being easily recognized. I was tempted by Leigh Hunt's conceit of "saying all one feels and thinks in clever daffodils and pinks; in puns of tulips and in phrases, charming for their truth, of daisies." Unfortunately the glasshouses were not equal to Leigh Hunt in mid-winter, but here, you see, is the great Doctor's ensign of supreme command, the myrtle, and here, after all, is most of poor Ophelia's rather dreary little collection. The sombre note predominates. But upstairs I have let myself go again. A riot of snowdrops for Chloris (you take the allusion to William Stone's charming conceit?), tuberoses and even some orchids for Madame Lisse, and so on.'

'And for Mrs Compline?'

'A delightful arrangement of immortelles.'

'Aren't you rather cruel?'

'Dear me, I don't think so,' said Jonathan, with a curious glance at his guest. 'I hope you admire the really superb cactus on your windowsill, Aubrey. John Nash might pause before it, I believe, and begin to plan some wonderful arrangement of greys and elusive greens. And now I must telephone to Sandra Compline, and after that to Dr Hart. I am making the bold move of suggesting he drives Madame Lisse. Hersey has her own car. Will you excuse me?'

'One moment. What flowers have you put in your own room?'

'Honesty,' said Jonathan.

II

Mrs Compline, her son William, and his fiancée Chloris Wynne, arrived by car at four o'clock. Mandrake discovered himself to be in almost as high a state of excitement as his host. He was unable to decide whether Jonathan's party would prove to be disastrous, amusing, or merely a bore, but the anticipation, at least, was enthralling. He had formed a very precise mental picture of each of the guests. William Compline, he decided, would present the most interesting subject-matter. The exaggerated filial devotion hinted at by Jonathan, brought him into the sphere of Mandrake's literary interest. And, muttering 'Mother-fixation' to himself, he wondered if indeed he should find William the starting-point for a new dramatic poem. Poetically, Mrs Compline's disfigurement might best be conveyed by a terrible mask, seen in the background of William's spoken thought. 'Perhaps in the final scene,' thought Mandrake, 'I should let them turn into the semblance of animals. Or would that be a little banal?' For not the least of a modern poetic dramatist's problems lies in the distressing truth that where all is strange nothing escapes the imputation of banality. But in William Compline, with his dullish appearance, his devotion to his mother, his dubious triumph over his brother, Mandrake hoped to find matter for his art. He was actually picturing an opening scene in which William, standing between his mother and his fiancée, appeared against a sky composed of cubes of greenish light, when the drawing room door opened and Caper announced them.

They were, of course, less striking than the images that had grown so rapidly in Mandrake's imagination. He had seen Mrs Compline as a figure in a sombre robe, and here she was in Harris tweeds. He had envisaged a black cowl, and he saw a countrified hat with a trout fly in the band. But her face, less fantastic than his image, was perhaps more distressing. It looked as if its maker had given it two or three vicious tweaks. Her eyes, large and lack-lustre, retained something of their original beauty, her nose was short and straight, but the left corner of her mouth drooped and her left cheek fell into a sort of pocket, so that she looked as though she had hurriedly stowed a large mouthful into one side of her face. She had the exaggerated dolorous expression of a clown. As Jonathan had told him, there was a cruelly comic look. When Jonathan introduced them, Mandrake was illogically surprised at her composure. She had a cold, dry voice.

Miss Chloris Wynne was about twenty-three, and very, very pretty. Her light-gold hair was pulled back from her forehead and moulded into cusps so rigidly placed that they might have been made of any material rather than hair. Her eyes were wide apart and beautifully made-up, her mouth was large and scarlet and her skin flawless. She was rather tall and moved in leisurely fashion, looking gravely about her. She was followed by William Compline.

In William, Mandrake saw what he had hoped to see – the commonplace faintly touched by a hint of something that was disturbing. He was in uniform and looked perfectly tidy but not quite smart. He was fair, and should have been good-looking, but the lines of his features were blunted and missed distinction. He was like an unsuccessful drawing of a fine subject. There was an air of uneasiness about him, and he had not been long in the room before Mandrake saw that whenever he turned to look at his fiancée, which was very often, he first darted a glance at his mother, who never by any chance returned it. Mrs Compline talked easily and with the air of an old friend to Jonathan, who continually drew the others into their conversation. Jonathan was in grand form. 'A nice start,' thought Mandrake, 'with plenty in reserve.' And he turned to Miss Wynne with the uneasy feeling that she had said something directly to him.

'I didn't in the least understand it, of course,' Miss Wynne was saying, 'but it completely unnerved me, and that's always rather fun.'

'Ah,' thought Mandrake, 'one of my plays.'

'Of course,' Miss Wynne continued, 'I don't know if you were thinking when you wrote it, what I was thinking when I saw it, but if you were, I'm surprised you got past the Lord Chamberlain.'

'The Lord Chamberlain,' said Mandrake, 'is afraid of me, and for a similar reason. He doesn't know whether it's my dirty mind or his, so he says nothing.'

'Ah,' cried Jonathan, 'is Miss Wynne a devotee, Aubrey?'

'A devotee of what? asked Mrs Compline in her exhausted voice.

'Of Aubrey's plays. The Unicorn is to reopen with Aubrey's new play in March, Sandra, if all goes well. You must come to the first night. It's called "Bad Blackout" and is enormously exciting.'

'A war play?' asked Mrs Compline. It was a question that for some reason infuriated Mandrake, but he answered with alarming politeness that it was not a war play but an experiment in two-dimensional formulism. Mrs Compline looked at him blankly and turned to Jonathan.

'What does that mean?' asked William. He stared at Mandrake with an expression of offended incredulity. 'Two-dimensional? That means flat, doesn't it?'

Mandrake heard Miss Wynne give an impatient sigh, and guessed at a certain persistency in William.

'Does it mean that the characters will be sort of unphotographic?' she asked.

'Exactly.'

'Yes,' said William heavily, 'but *two-dimensional*. I don't quite see – '

Mandrake felt a terrible apprehension of boredom, but Jonathan cut in neatly with an amusing account of his own apprenticeship as an audience to modern drama, and William listened with his mouth not quite closed and an anxious expression in his eyes. When the others laughed at Jonathan's facetiæ, William looked baffled. Mandrake could see him forming with his lips the offending syllables 'two-dimensional.'

'I suppose,' he said suddenly, 'it's not what you say but the way you say it that you think matters. Do your plays have plots?'

'They have themes.'

'What's the difference?'

'My darling old Bill,' said Miss Wynne, 'you mustn't browbeat famous authors.'

William turned to her and his smile made him almost handsome. 'Mustn't you?' he said. 'But if you do a thing, you like talking about it. I like talking about the things I do. I mean the things I did before there was a war.'

It suddenly occurred to Mandrake that he did not know what William's occupation was. 'What do you do?' he asked.

'Well,' said William, astonishingly, 'I paint pictures.'

Mrs Compline marched firmly into the conversation. 'William,' she said, 'has Penfelton to look after in peace time. At present, of course, we have our old bailiff, who manages very well. My younger son, Nicholas, is a soldier. Have you heard, Jonathan, that he did *not* pass his medical for active service? It was a very bitter blow to him. At the moment he is stationed at Great Chipping, but he longs so much to be with his regiment in France. Of *course*,' she added. And Mandrake saw her glance at the built-up shoe on his club foot.

'But you're on leave from the front, aren't you?' he asked William.

'Oh, yes,' said William.

'My son Nicholas . . . ' Mrs Compline became quite animated as she spoke of Nicholas. She talked about him at great length, and Mandrake wondered if he only imagined there was a sort of defiance in her insistence on this awkward theme. He saw that Miss Wynne had turned pink and William crimson. Jonathan drew the spate of maternal eulogy upon himself. Mandrake asked Miss Wynne and William if they thought it was going to snow again, and all three walked over to the long windows to look at darkening hills and vale. Naked trees half-lost their form in that fading light and rose from the earth as if they were its breath, already frozen.

'Rather menacing,' said Mandrake, 'isn't it?'

'Menacing?' William repeated. 'It's very beautiful. All black and white and grey. I don't believe in seeing colour into things. One should paint them the first colour they seem when one looks at them. Yes, I suppose it is what you'd call menacing. Black and grey and white.'

'What is your medium?' Mandrake asked, and wondered why everybody looked uncomfortable when William spoke of his painting.

'*Very* thick oil paint,' said William gravely.

'Do you know Agatha Troy?'

'I know her pictures, of course.'

'She and her husband are staying with the Copelands at Winton St Giles, near Little Chipping. I came on from there. She's painting the rector.'

'Do you mean Roderick Alleyn?' asked Miss Wynne. 'Isn't he her husband? How exciting to be in a house-party with the handsome Inspector. What's he like?'

'Oh,' said Mandrake, 'quite agreeable.'

They had turned away from the windows, but a sound from outside drew them back again. Only the last turn of the drive as it came out of the Highfold woods could be seen from the drawing room windows.

'That's a car,' said William. 'It sounds like – ' he stopped short.

'Is any one else coming?' asked Miss Wynne sharply, and caught her breath.

She and William stared through the windows. A long and powerful-looking open car, painted white, was streaking up the last rise in the drive.

'But,' stammered William, very red in the face, 'that's – that's – '

'Ah!' said Jonathan from behind them. 'Didn't you know? A pleasant surprise for you. Nicholas is to be one of our party.'

III

Nicholas Compline was an extremely striking version of his brother. In figure, height, and colouring they were alike. Their features were not dissimilar, but the suggestion of fumbled drawing in William was absent in Nicholas. William was clean-shaven, but Nicholas wore a fine blond moustache. Nicholas had a presence. His uniform became him almost too well. He glittered a little. His breeches were superb. His face was not unlike a less dissipated version of the best-known portrait of Charles II, though the lines from nose to mouth were not so dominant, and the pouches under the eyes had only just begun to form.

His entrance into the drawing room at Highfold must have been a test of his assurance. Undoubtedly it was dramatic. He came in smiling, missed his brother and Miss Wynne, who were still in the window, shook hands with Jonathan, was introduced to Mandrake, and, on seeing his mother, looked surprised but greeted her charmingly. Jonathan, who had him by the elbow, turned him towards the window.

There was no difficult silence, because Jonathan talked briskly, but there was, to a degree, a feeling of tension. For a moment Mandrake wondered if Nicholas Compline would turn on his heel and walk out, but after checking, with Jonathan's hand still at his elbow, he merely stood stock-still and looked from William to Chloris Wynne. His face was as pale as his brother's was red, and there was a kind of startled sneer about his lips. It was Miss Wynne who saved the situation. She unclenched her hands and gave Nicholas a coster's salute, touching her forehead and spreading out her palm towards him. Mandrake guessed that this serio-comic gesture was foreign to her and applauded her courage.

'Oi,' said Miss Wynne.

'Oi, oi,' said Nicholas, and returned her salute. He looked at William and said in a flat voice: 'Quite a family party.'

His mother held out her hand to him. He moved swiftly towards her and sat on the arm of her chair. Mandrake saw adoration in her eyes and mentally rubbed his hands together.

'The Mother-fixation,' he thought, 'is *not* going to let me down.' And he began to warn himself against the influence of Eugene O'Neill. William and his Chloris remained in the window. Jonathan, after a bird-like glance at them, embarked on a comfortable three-cornered chat with Mrs Compline and Nicholas. Mandrake, sitting in the shadow, found himself free to watch the lovers, and again he gloated. At first William and Chloris stared out through the windows and spoke in undertones. She pointed to something outside, but Mandrake felt certain the gesture was a bluff and that they discussed hurriedly the arrival of Nicholas. Presently he observed a small incident that he thought curious and illuminating. It was a sort of dumb-show, an interplay of looks subdued to the exigencies of polite behaviour, a quarter of glances. William had turned from the window and was staring at his mother. She had been talking, with an air that almost approached gaiety, to Nicholas. She looked into his face and a smile, painful in its intensity, lifted the drooping corners of her mouth. Nicholas's laugh was louder than the conversation seemed to warrant, and Mandrake saw that he was looking over his mother's head full at Chloris Wynne. Mandrake read a certain insolence in this open-eyed direct stare of Nicholas. He turned to see how the lady took it, and found that she returned it with interest. They looked steadfastly and inimically into each other's eyes. Nicholas laughed again, and William, as if warned by this sound, turned from his sombre contemplation of his mother and stared first at Nicholas and then at Miss Wynne. Neither of them paid the smallest attention to him, but Mandrake thought that Nicholas was very well aware of his brother. He thought Nicholas, in some way that was clearly perceived by the other two, was deliberately baiting William. Jonathan's voice broke across this little pantomime.

' – a long time,' Jonathan was saying, 'since I treated myself to one of my own parties, and I don't mind confessing that I look forward enormously to this one.'

Miss Wynne joined the group round the fire and William followed her.

'Is this the party?' she asked, 'or are we only the beginning?'

'The most important beginning, Miss Chloris, without which the end would be nothing.'

'Who else have you got, Jonathan?' asked Nicholas, with his eyes still on Miss Wynne.

'Well, now, I don't know that I shall tell you, Nick. Or shall I? It's always rather fun, don't you think,' Jonathan said, turning his glance towards Mrs Compline, 'to let people meet without giving them any preconceived ideas about each other? However, you know one of my guests so well that it doesn't matter if I anticipate her arrival. Hersey Amblington.'

'Old Hersey's coming, is she,' said Nicholas, and he looked a little disconcerted.

'Don't be too ruthless with your adjectives, Nick,' said Jonathan mildly. 'Hersey is ten years my junior.'

'You're ageless, Jonathan.'

'Charming of you, but I'm afraid people only begin to compliment one on one's youth when it is gone. But Hersey, to me, really does seem scarcely any older than she was in the days when I danced with her. She still dances, I believe.'

'It will be nice to see Hersey,' said Mrs Compline.

'I don't think I know a Hersey, do I?' This was the first time Chloris had spoken directly to Mrs Compline. She was answered by Nicholas.

'She's a flame of Jonathan's,' Nicholas said. 'Lady Hersey Amblington.'

'She's my third cousin,' said Jonathan sedately. 'We are all rather attached to her.'

'Oh,' said Nicholas, always to Chloris. 'She's a divine creature. I adore her.'

Chloris began to talk to William.

Mandrake thought that if anybody tried to bury any hatchets in the Compline armoury it would not be William. He decided that William was neither as vague nor as amiable as he seemed. Conversation went along briskly under Jonathan's leadership, with Mandrake himself as an able second, but it had a sort of substratum that was faintly antagonistic. When inevitably, it turned to the war, William, with deceptive simplicity, related a story about an incident on patrol when a private soldier uttered some comic blasphemy on the subject of cushy jobs on the home front. Mrs Compline immediately told Jonathan how few hours sleep Nicholas managed to get, and how hard he was worked. Nicholas himself spoke of pulling strings in order to get a transfer to active service. He had, he said, seen an important personage. 'Unfortunately, though, I struck a bad moment. The gentleman was very liverish. I understand,' said Nicholas, with one of his bright stares at Chloris, 'that he has been crossed in love.'

'No reason, surely,' said Chloris, 'why he shouldn't behave himself with comparative strangers.'

Nicholas gave her the shadow of an ironical bow.

Jonathan began an account of his own activities as chairman of the local evacuation committee, and made such a droll affair of it that with every phrase his listeners' guardedness seemed to relax. Mandrake, who had a certain astringent humour of his own, followed with a description of a member of the chorus who found himself in an ultra-modern play. Tea was announced and was carried through on the same cheerful note of comedy. 'Good Lord,' Mandrake thought, 'if he should bring it off after all!' He caught Jonathan's eye and detected a glint of triumph.

After tea Jonathan proposed a brisk walk, and Mandrake, knowing his host shared his own loathing for this sort of exercise, grinned to himself. Jonathan was not going to risk another session in the drawing room. With any luck there would be more arrivals while they were out, and the new set of encounters would take place in the propitious atmosphere of sherry and cocktails. When they assembled in the hall Jonathan appeared in a sage-green Tyrolese cape. He looked a quaint enough figure, but Chloris Wynne, who had evidently decided to like her host, cried out in admiration, and Mandrake, who had decided to like Chloris Wynne, echoed her. At the last moment Jonathan remembered an important telephone message, and asked Mandrake to see the walking-party off. He flung his cape over Nicholas's shoulder. It hung from his shoulder-straps in heavy folds, and turned him into a Ruritanian figure.

'Magnificent, Nick,' said Jonathan, and Mandrake saw that Mrs Compline and Chloris agreed with him. The cloak neatly emphasized the touch of bravura that seemed an essential ingredient of Nicholas's character. They went out of doors into the cold twilight of late afternoon.

IV

'But,' said Dr Hart in German, 'it is an intolerable position for me – for *me*, do you understand.'

'Don't be ridiculous,' said Madame Lisse in English. 'And please, Francis, do not speak in German. It is a habit of which you should break yourself.'

'Why should I not speak in German? I am a naturalized Austrian. Everybody knows that I am a naturalized Austrian and that I detest and abhor the Nazi régime with which we – *we* British – are in conflict.'

'Nevertheless, the language is unpopular.'

'Very well, very well, I now speak English. In plain English I tell you that if you continue your affair with this Captain Nicholas Compline I shall take the strongest possible steps to – '

'To do what? You are driving too fast.'

'To put an end to it.'

'How will you do that?' asked Madame Lisse, settling down into her furs with an air of secret enjoyment.

'By taking you up to London next week.'

'With what object? Here is Winton. I beg that you do not drive so fast.'

'On our return,' said Dr Hart, shifting his foot to the brake, 'we shall announce our marriage. It will have taken place quietly in London.'

'Are you demented? Have we not discussed it already a thousand times? You know very well that it would injure your practice. A woman hideous with wrinkles comes to me. I see that I can do nothing, cannot even pretend to do anything. I suggest plastic surgery. She asks me if I can recommend a surgeon. I mention two or three, of whom you are one. I give instances of your success, you are here in Great Chipping, the others are abroad or in London. She goes to you. But can I say to my client with the same air of detached assurance: "Certainly. Go to my husband. He is marvellous!" And can you, my friend, whose cry has been the utter uselessness of massage, the robbery of foolish women by beauty specialists, the fatuity of creams and lotions; can you produce as your wife Elise Lisse of the Studio Lisse, beauty specialist *par excellence?* The good Lady Hersey

Amblington would have something to say to that. I promise you, and by no means to our advantage.'

'Then give up your business.'

'And halve my income, in effect *our* income? And, besides, I enjoy my work. It has amused me to win my little victories over the good Lady Hersey. The Studio Lisse is a growing concern, my friend, and I propose to remain at the head of it.'

Dr Hart accelerated again as his car mounted the steep road that climbed from the Vale of Pen Cuckoo up to Cloudyfold.

'Do you see the roofs of the large house up in those trees?' he asked suddenly.

'That is Pen Cuckoo. It is shut up at present. What of it?'

'And you know why it is shut up? I shall remind you. Two years ago it housed a homicidal lunatic, and her relatives have not returned since her trial.'

Madame Lisse turned to look at her escort. She saw a sharp profile, a heavy chin, light-grey eyes, and a complexion of extreme though healthy pallor.

'Well,' she murmured. 'Again, what of it?'

'You have heard of the case, of course. She is said to have murdered her rival in love. They were both somewhere between forty-five and fifty-five. The dangerous age in both sexes. I am myself fifty-two years of age.'

'What conclusions am I supposed to draw?' asked Madame Lisse tranquilly.

'You are to suppose,' Dr Hart rejoined, 'that persons of a certain age can go to extremes when the safety of their – shall I call it lovelife? – is in jeopardy.'

'But, my dear Francis, this is superb. Am I to believe that you will lie in ambush for Nicholas Compline? What weapon shall you choose? Does he wear his sword? I believe that it is not extremely sharp, but one supposes that he could defend himself.'

'Are you in love with him?'

'If I answer no, you will not believe me. If I answer yes, you will lose your temper.'

'Nevertheless,' said Doctor Hart calmly, 'I should like an answer.'

'Nicholas will be at Highfold. You may observe us and find out.'

There followed a long silence. The road turned sharply and came out on the height known as Cloudyfold. For a short distance it followed the snow-covered ridge of the hills. On their right, Madame Lisse and Dr Hart looked down on the frozen woods of Pen Cuckoo; on cold lanes, on slow columns of chimney-smoke, and, more distantly, towards a long dark mass that was the town of Great Chipping. On their left the powdered hills fell away smoothly into the Vale of Cloudyfold. Under clouds that hung like a pall from horizon to horizon the scattered cottages of Dorset stone looked almost black, while their roofs glistened with a stealthy reflected light. A single flake of snow appeared on the windscreen and slid downwards.

'Very well,' said Dr Hart loudly, 'I shall see.'

Madame Lisse drew a gloved hand from under the rug and with one finger touched Dr Hart lightly behind his ear. 'I am really devoted to you,' she said.

He pulled her hand down, brushing the glove aside with his lips.

'You know my temperament,' he said. 'It is a mistake to play the fool with me.'

'Suppose I am only playing the fool with Nicholas Compline?'

'Well,' he said again, 'I shall see.'

V

Through the office window of the Salon Cyclamen Hersey Amblington watched two of her clients walk off down the street with small steps and certain pert movements of their sterns. They paused outside the hated windows of the Studio Lisse, hesitated for a moment, and then disappeared through the entrance.

'Going to buy Lisse Foundation Cream,' thought Hersey. 'So that's why they wouldn't have a facial.' She turned back into her office and was met by the familiar drone of driers, by the familiar smells of hot hair, setting lotion, and the sachets used in permanent waving, and by the familiar high-pitched indiscretions of clients in conversation with assistants.

' – long after the milk. I look like death warmed up and what I feel is nobody's business.'

' – much better after a facial, Moddam. Aye always think a facial is marvellous, what it does for you.'

' – can't remember his name so of course I shall never see them again.'

'Common woman,' thought Hersey. 'All my clients are common women. Damn that Lisse. Blasted pirate.'

She looked at her watch. Four o'clock. She'd make a tour of the cubicles and then leave the place to her second-in-command. 'If it wasn't for my snob-value,' she thought grimly, 'I'd be living on the Pirate's overflow.' She peered into the looking-glass over her desk and automatically touched her circlet of curls. 'Greyer and greyer,' said Hersey, 'but I'll be shot if I dye them,' and she scowled dispassionately at her face. 'Too wholesome by half, my girl, and a fat lot of good "Hersey's Skin Food" is to your middle-aged charms. Oh, well.'

She made her tour through the cubicles. With her assistants she had little professional cross-talk dialogues, calculated to persuade her clients that the improvement in their appearance was phenomenal. With the clients themselves she sympathized, soothed and encouraged. She refused an invitation to dinner from the facial, and listened to a complaint from a permanent wave. When she returned to the office she found her second-in-command at the telephone.

'Would Madam care to make another appointment? No? Very good.'

'Who's that?' asked Hersey wearily.

'Mrs Ainsley's maid to say she wouldn't be coming for her weekly facial tomorrow. The girls say they've seen her coming out of the Studio Lisse.'

'May she grow a beard,' muttered Hersey, and grinned at her second-in-command. 'To hell with her, anyway. How's the appointment book?'

'Oh, we're full enough. Booked up for three days. But they're not as smart as they used to be.'

'Who cares! I'm going now, Jane. If you should want me tomorrow, I'll be at my cousin Jonathan Royal's, Highfold, you know.'

'Yes. Lady Hersey. It looked as if the Lisse was going away for the weekend. I saw her come out of the shop about half an hour ago and get into Dr Hart's car. I wonder if there's anything in those stories. She had quite a big suitcase.'

'I wish she'd had a pantechnicon,' said Hersey. 'I'm sick of the sound of the wretched woman's name. She may live in sin all over Dorset as long as she doesn't include Highfold in the tour.'

The second-in-command laughed. *'That's* not very likely, Lady Hersey, is it?'

'No, thank the Lord. Goodbye, Jane.'

CHAPTER 3

Contact

'Not very propitious weather for looking at a bathing pool,' said Mandrake, 'but I insist on showing it to you.'

He had sent the guests off at a round pace to go through Highfold woods, where the rides were heavy with sodden leaves, down to Jonathan's model farm, and back up a steep lane to the north side of the house, where he limped out to meet them. Here they came on a wide terrace. Beneath them, at the foot of a flight of paved steps flanked by bay trees, was a large concrete swimming pool set in smooth lawns and overlooked by a charming eighteenth-century pavilion, now trimmed, like a Christmas card, with snow. The floor of the pool had been painted a vivid blue, but now the water was wrinkled, and in the twilight of late afternoon reflected only a broken pattern of repellent steely greys flecked by dead leaves. Mandrake explained that the pavilion had once been an aviary, but that Jonathan had done it up in keeping with its empire style, and that when summer came he meant to hold *fêtes galantes* down there by his new swimming pool. It would look very Rex Whistlerish, Mandrake said, and would have just the right air of formalized gaiety.

'At the moment,' said Chloris, 'it has an air of formalized desolation, but I see what you mean.'

'Wouldn't you like to come for a nice bracing plunge with me, Chloris, before breakfast tomorrow?' asked Nicholas. 'Do say yes.'

'No, thank you,' said Chloris.

'It would have been awkward for you,' said William, 'if Chloris *had* said yes.' It was the first remark William had addressed directly to his brother.

'Not at all,' rejoined Nicholas, and he made his stiff little bow to Chloris.

'I'll bet ten pounds,' William said to nobody in particular, 'that nothing on earth would have got him into that water before or after breakfast.'

'Would you?' asked Nicholas. 'I take you. You've lost.'

Mrs Compline instantly protested. She reminded Nicholas of the state of his heart. William grinned derisively, and Nicholas, staring at Chloris, repeated that the bet was on. The absurd conversation began to take an unpleasant edge. Mandrake felt an icy touch on his cheek and drew attention to a desultory scatter of snowflakes.

'If that was our brisk walk,' said Chloris, 'I consider we've had it. Let's go in.'

'Is it a bet?' Nicholas asked his brother.

'Oh, yes,' said William. 'You may have to break the ice, but it's a bet.

To the accompaniment of a lively torrent of disapprobation from Mrs Compline they walked towards the house. Mandrake's interest in William mounted with each turn of the situation. William was as full of surprises as a lucky-bag. His sudden proposal of this ridiculous wager was as unexpected as the attitude which he now adopted. He looked hang-dog and frightened. He hung back and said something to his mother, who set that tragically distorted mouth and did not answer. William gave her a look strangely compounded of malice and nervousness, and strode after Chloris who was walking with Mandrake. Nicholas had joined them, and Mandrake felt sure that Chloris was very much aware of him. When William suddenly took her arm she started and seemed to draw back. They returned to the accompaniment of an irritating rattle of conversation from Nicholas.

As soon as they came out on the platform before the house, they found that someone else had arrived. Nicholas's car had been driven away, and in its place stood a very smart three-seater from which servants were taking very smart suitcases.

'That's not Hersey Amblington's car,' said Mrs Compline.

'No,' said Nicholas. And he added loudly: 'Look here; what's Jonathan up to?'

'What do you mean, darling?' asked his mother quickly.

'Nothing,' said Nicholas. 'But I think I recognize the car.' He hung back as the others went into the house, and waited for Mandrake. He still wore Jonathan's cape over his uniform, and it occurred to Mandrake that since Nicholas allowed himself this irregularity he must be very well aware of its effectiveness. He put his hand on Mandrake's arm. The others went into the house.

'I say,' he said. '*Is* Jonathan up to anything?'

'How do you mean?' asked Mandrake, wondering what the devil Jonathan would wish him to reply.

'Well, it seems to me this is a queerly assorted house-party.'

'Is it? I'm a complete stranger to all the other guests, you know.'

'When did you get here?'

'Last night.'

'Well, hasn't Jonathan said anything? About the other guests, I mean?'

'He was very pleased with his party,' said Mandrake, carefully. 'He's longing for it to be an enormous success.'

'Is he, by God!' said Nicholas. He turned on his heel and walked into the house.

Mrs Compline and Chloris went up to their rooms; the three men left their overcoats in a downstairs cloakroom, where they noticed the twin of Jonathan's cape. When they came back into the hall they could hear voices in the library. As if by common consent they all paused. There were three voices – Jonathan's, a masculine voice that held a foreign suggestion in its level inflections, and a deep contralto.

'I thought as much,' said Nicholas, and laughed unpleasantly.

'What's up?' William asked Mandrake.

'Nothing, so far as I know.'

'Come on,' said Nicholas. 'What are we waiting for? Let's go in.'

He led the way into the library.

Jonathan and his new arrivals stood before a roaring fire. The man had his back turned to the door, but the woman was facing it with an air of placid anticipation. Her face was strongly lit by a wall lamp, and Mandrake's immediate reaction to it was a sort of astonishment that Jonathan could have forgotten to say how spectacular she was. In Mandrake's world women were either sophisticated and sleek or hideous and erratic. 'Artificiality,' he was in the habit of saying, 'is a fundamental in all women with whom one falls in love, and to so exquisite an extreme has artifice been carried that it sometimes apes nature with considerable success.' This subtlety of grooming appeared in Madame Lisse. Her hair was straight and from a central parting was drawn back and gathered into a knot at the nape of her neck. It lay close to her head like a black satin cap with blue highlights. Her face was an oval, beautifully pale, her lashes needed no cosmetic to darken them, her mouth alone proclaimed her art, for it was sharply painted a dark red. Her dress was extremely simple, but in it her body seemed to be gloved rather than clothed. She was not very young, not as young as Chloris Wynne, not perhaps as pretty as Chloris Wynne either, but she had to the last degree the quality that Mandrake, though he knew very little French, spoke of and even thought of as *soignée*. And, in her own vein, she was exceedingly beautiful.

'Madame Lisse,' Jonathan was saying, 'you know Nicholas, don't you? May I introduce his brother, and Mr Aubrey Mandrake? Hart, do you know – ?' Jonathan's introductions faded gently away.

Dr Hart's bow was extremely formal. He was a pale dark man with a compact paunch and firm white hands. He was clad in the defiant tweeds of a firmly naturalized ex-Central European. Mandrake gathered from his manner that either he had not met Nicholas Compline and didn't wish to do so, or else that he had met him and had taken a firm resolve never to do so again. Nicholas, for his part, acknowledged the introduction by looking at a point some distance beyond Dr Hart's left ear, and by uttering the words 'How do you do?' as if they were a malediction. Madame Lisse's greeting to Nicholas was coloured by that particular blend of composure and awareness with which Austrian women make Englishmen feel dangerous and delighted. With something of the same air, but without a certain delicate underlining, she held out her hand to William and to Mandrake. Mandrake remembered that Nicholas had known Madame Lisse was coming to the party, and saw him take up a proprietory position beside her. 'He's going to brazen it out,' thought Mandrake. 'He's going to show us the sort of dog he is with the ladies, by heaven.'

Mandrake was right. Nicholas, with a sort of defiant showmanship, devoted himself to Madame Lisse. He stood beside her in an attitude reminiscent of a Victorian military fashion-plate, one leg straight and one flexed. Occasionally he placed one hand on the back of her chair, while the other went to his blond moustache. Whenever Dr Hart glared at them, which he did repeatedly, Nicholas bent towards Madame Lisse and uttered a loud and unconvincing laugh calculated, Mandrake supposed, to show Dr Hart how vastly Nicholas and Madame Lisse entertained each other. Madame was the sort of woman whose natural habitat was the centre of a group of men and, with the utmost tranquillity, she dominated the conversation and even, in spite of Nicholas, contrived to instil into it an air of genuine gaiety. In this she was ably supported by Jonathan and by Mandrake himself. Even William, who watched his brother pretty closely, responded in his own odd fashion to Madame's charm. He asked her abruptly if anybody had ever painted her portrait. On learning that this had never been done, he started to mutter to himself, and Nicholas looked irritated. Madame Lisse began to talk to Mandrake about his plays, Jonathan chimed in, and once again the situation was saved. It was upon a conversation piece, with Madame Lisse very much in the centre of vision, that Mrs Compline and Chloris made their entrances. Mandrake thought that Mrs Compline could not be aware of the affair between Nicholas and Madame Lisse, so composedly did she acknowledge the introduction. But, if this was the case, what reason had Chloris given for the broken engagement with Nicholas? 'Is it not impossible that everybody but his mother should be aware of *l'affaire Lisse?*' Mandrake speculated. 'Perhaps she sees him as a sort of irresistible young god, choosing where he will, and, without resentment, accepts Madame as a votaress.' There was no doubt about Chloris's reaction. Mandrake saw her stiffen and go very still when Jonathan pronounced Madame Lisse's name. For perhaps a full second neither of the women spoke, and then, for all the world as if they responded to some inaudible cue, Chloris and Madame Lisse were extremely gracious to each other. 'So they're going to take *that* line,' thought Mandrake, and wondered if Jonathan shared his feelings of relief. He felt less comfortable when he saw Mrs Compline's reaction to Dr Hart. She murmured the conventional greeting, looked casually and then fixedly into his face, and turned so deadly white that for a moment Mandrake actually wondered if she would faint. But she did not faint. She turned away and sat in a chair farthest removed from the light. Caper brought in sherry and champagne cocktails.

II

The cocktails, though they did not perform miracles, helped considerably. Dr Hart in particular became more sociable. He continued to avoid Nicholas, but attached himself to Chloris Wynne and to William. Jonathan talked to Mrs Compline; Mandrake and Nicholas to Madame Lisse. Nicholas still kept up his irritating performances, now, apparently, for the benefit of Chloris. Whenever Madame Lisse spoke he bent towards her, and whether her remark was grave or gay, he broke out into an exhibition of merriment calculated, Mandrake felt certain, to arouse in Chloris the pangs proper to the woman scorned. If she suffered this discomfort she gave no more evidence of her distress than might be discovered in an occasional thoughtful glance at Nicholas, and it seemed to Mandrake that if she reacted at all to the performance it was pleasurably. She listened attentively to Dr Hart, who became voluble and bland. Chloris had asked if anyone had heard the latest wireless news. Hart instantly embarked on a description of his own reaction to radio. 'I cannot endure it. It touches some nerve. It creates a most disagreeable – an unendurable *frisson*. I read my papers and that is enough. I am informed. I assure you that I have twice changed my flat because of the intolerable persecution of neighbouring radios. Strange, is it not? There must be some psychological explanation.'

'Jonathan shares your dislike,' said Mandrake. 'He has been persuaded to install a wireless next door in the smoking room, but I don't believe he ever listens to it.'

'My respect for my host grows with everything I hear of him,' said Dr Hart. He became expansive, enlarged upon his love of nature, and spoke of holidays in the Austrian Tyrol.

'When it was still Austria,' said Dr Hart. 'Have you ever visited Kaprun, Miss Wynne? How charming it was at Kaprun in those days! From there one could drive up the Gross Glockner, one could climb into the mountains above that pleasant wein-stube in the ravine, and on Sunday mornings one went to Zelleum-Zee. Music in the central square. The cafés! and the shops where one might secure the best shoes in the world.'

'And the best cloaks,' said Chloris with a smile.

'Hein? Ah, you have seen the cloak I have presented to our host.'

'Nicholas,' said Chloris, 'wore it when we went for a walk just now.'

Dr Hart's eyelids, which in their colour and texture a little resembled those of a lizard, half closed over his rather prominent eyes. 'Indeed,' he said.

'I hope,' said Jonathan, 'that you visited my swimming pool on your walk.'

'Nicholas is going to bathe in it tomorrow,' said William, 'or hand over ten pounds to me.'

'Nonsense, William,' said his mother. 'I won't have it. Jonathan, please forbid these stupid boys to go on with this nonsense.' Her voice, coming out of the dark corner where she sat, sounded unexpectedly loud. Dr Hart turned his head and peered into the shadow. When Chloris said something to him it appeared for a moment that he had not heard her. If, however, he had been startled by Mrs Compline's voice, he quickly recovered himself. Mandrake thought that he finished his cocktail rather rapidly, and noticed that when he accepted another it was with an unsteady hand.

'That's odd,' thought Mandrake. 'He's the more upset of the two, it appears, and yet they've never met before. Unless – but no! That would be too much. I'm letting the possibilities of the situation run away with me.'

'Lady Hersey Amblington, sir,' said Caper in the doorway.

Mandrake's first impression of Hersey Amblington was characteristic of the sort of man his talents had led him to become. As Stanley Footling of Dulwich, he would have been a little in awe of Hersey. As Aubrey Mandrake of the Unicorn Theatre, he told himself she was distressingly wholesome. Hersey's face, in spite of its delicate make-up, wore an out-of-doors look, and she did not pluck her dark brows, those two straight bars that guarded her blue eyes. She wore Harris tweed and looked, thought Mandrake, as though she would be tiresome about dogs. A hearty woman, he decided, and he did not wonder that Madame Lisse had lured away Hersey's smartest clients.

Jonathan hurried forward to greet his cousin. They kissed. Mandrake felt certain that Jonathan delayed the embrace long enough to whisper a warning in Lady Hersey's ear. He saw the tweed shoulders stiffen. With large, beautifully shaped hands, she put Jonathan away from her and looked into his face. Mandrake, who was nearer to them than the rest of the party, distinctly heard her say: 'Jo, what are you up to?' and caught Jonathan's reply: 'Come and see.' He took her by the elbow and led her towards the group by the fire.

'You know Madame Lisse, Hersey, don't you?'

'Yes,' said Hersey, after a short pause. 'How do you do?'

'And Dr Hart?'

'How do you do? Sandra, darling, how nice to see you,' said Hersey, turning her back on Dr Hart and Madame Lisse, and kissing Mrs Compline. Her face was hidden from Mandrake, but he saw that her ears and the back of her neck were scarlet.

'You haven't kissed me, Hersey,' said Nicholas.

'I don't intend to. How many weeks have you been stationed in Great Chipping, and never a glimpse have I had of you? William, my dear, I didn't know you had actually reached home again. How well you look.'

'I feel quite well, thank you, Hersey,' said William gravely. 'You've met Chloris, haven't you?'

'Not yet, but I'm delighted to do so, and to congratulate you both,' said Hersey, shaking hands with Chloris.

'And Mr Aubrey Mandrake,' said Jonathan, bringing Hersey a drink.

'How do you do? Jonathan told me I should meet you. I've got a subject for you.'

'O God,' thought Mandrake, 'she's going to be funny about my plays.'

'It's about a false hairdresser who strangles his rival with three feet of dyed hair,' Hersey continued. 'He's a male hairdresser, you know, and he wears a helmet made of tin waving clamps and no clothes at all. Perhaps it would be better as a ballet.'

Mandrake laughed politely. 'A beguiling theme,' he said.

'I'm glad you like it. It's not properly worked out yet, but of course his mother had long hair, and when he was an infant he saw his father lugging her about the room by her pigtail, and it gave him convulsions, because he hated his father and was in love with his mother, and so he grew up into a hairdresser and worked off his complexes on his customers. And I must say,' Hersey added, 'I wish I could follow his example.'

'Do you dislike your clients, Lady Hersey?' asked Madame Lisse. 'I do not find in myself any antipathy to my clients. Many of them have become my good friends.'

'You must be able to form friendships very quickly,' said Hersey sweetly.

'Of course,' Madame Lisse continued, 'it depends very much upon the class of one's clientele.'

'And possibly,' Hersey returned, 'upon one's own class, don't you think?' And then, as if ashamed of herself, she turned again to Mrs Compline.

'I suppose,' said William's voice close to Mandrake, 'that Hersey was making a joke about her subject, wasn't she?'

'Yes,' Mandrake said hurriedly, for he was startled, 'yes, of course.'

'Well, but it *might* be a good idea, mightn't it? I mean, people do write about those things. There's that long play – I saw it in London about four years ago – where the brother and sister find out about their mother and all that. Some people thought that play was a bit thick, but I didn't think so. I thought there was a lot of reality in it. I don't see why plays should say what people feel in the same way as pictures ought to. Not what they do. What they do in their thoughts.'

'That is my own contention,' said Mandrake, who was beginning to feel more than a little curious about William's pictures. William gave a rather vapid laugh, and rubbed his hands together. 'There you are, you see,' he said. He looked round the circle of Jonathan's guests, and lowered his voice. 'Jonathan has played a trick on all of us,' he said unexpectedly. Mandrake did not answer, and William went on: 'Perhaps you planned it together.'

'No, no. This party is entirely Jonathan's.'

'I'll bet it is. Jonathan is doing in the ordinary way what he does in his thoughts. If you wrote a play of him what would it be like?'

'I really don't know,' said Mandrake hurriedly.

'Don't you? If I painted his picture I should make him egg-shaped, with quite a merry smile, and a scorpion round his head. And then, you know, for eyes he would have the sort of windows you can't see through. Clouded glass.'

In Mandrake's circles this sort of thing was more or less a commonplace. 'You are a surrealist, then?' he murmured.

'Have you ever noticed,' William continued placidly, 'that Jonathan's eyes are quite blank. Impenetrable,' he added, and a phrase from *Alice through the Looking Glass* jigged Mandrake's thoughts.

'It's his thick glasses,' he said.

'Oh,' said William, 'is that it? Has he told you about us? Nicholas and Chloris and me? And, of course, Madame Lisse?' To Mandrake's intense relief William did not pause for an answer. 'I expect he has,' he said. 'He likes talking about people, and of course he would want somebody for an audience. I'm quite glad to meet Madame Lisse, and I must say it doesn't surprise me about her and Nicholas. I should like to make a picture of her. Wait a moment. I'm just going to get another drink. My third,' added William, with the air of chalking up a score.

Mandrake had had one drink and was of the opinion that Jonathan's champagne cocktails were generously laced with brandy. He wondered if in this circumstance lay the explanation of William's astonishing candour. The rest of the party had already responded to the drinks, and the general conversation was now fluent and noisy. William returned, carrying his glass with extreme care.

'Of course,' he said, 'you will understand that Chloris and I haven't seen Nicholas since we got engaged. I went to the front the day after it was announced, and Nicholas has been conducting the war in Great Chipping ever since. But if Jonathan thinks his party is going to make any difference . . . ' William broke off and drank a third of his cocktail. 'What was I saying?' he asked.

'Any difference,' Mandrake prompted.

'Oh, yes. If Jonathan, *or* Nicholas for that matter, imagine I'm going to lose my temper, they are wrong.'

'But surely if Jonathan has any ulterior motive,' Mandrake ventured, 'it is entirely pacific. A reconciliation . . .'

'Oh, no,' said William, '*that* wouldn't be at all amusing.' He looked sideways at Mandrake. 'Besides,' he said, 'Jonathan doesn't like me much, you know.'

This chimed so precisely with Mandrake's earlier impression that he gave William a started glance. 'Doesn't he?' he asked helplessly.

'No. He wanted me to marry a niece of his. She was a poor relation, and he was very fond of her. We were sort of engaged but I didn't really like her so very much, I found, so I sort of sloped off. He doesn't forget things, you know.' William smiled vaguely. 'She died,' he said. 'She went rather queer in the head, I think. It was very sad, really.'

Mandrake found nothing to say and William returned to his theme. 'But I shan't do anything to Nicholas,' he said. 'Let him cool his ardour in the swimming pool. After all, I've won, you know. Haven't I?'

'He *is* tight,' thought Mandrake, and he said with imbecile cheerfulness: 'I hope so.'

William finished his drink. 'So do I,' he said thoughtfully. He looked across to the fireplace where Nicholas, standing by Madame Lisse's chair, stared at Chloris Wynne.

'But he always *will* try,' said William, 'to eat his cake and keep it.'

III

Madame Lisse fastened three of Jonathan's orchids in the bosom of her wine-coloured dress, and contemplated herself in the looking-glass. She saw a Renaissance picture smoothly painted on a fine panel. Black, magnolia, and mulberry surfaces, all were sleek and richly glowing. Behind this magnificence, in shadow, was reflected the door of her room, and while she still stared at her image this door opened slowly.

'What is it, Francis?' asked Madame Lisse without turning her head.

Dr Hart closed the door, and in a moment his figure stood behind hers in the long glass.

'It was unwise to come in,' she said, speaking very quietly. 'That woman has the room next to yours, and Mrs Compline is on the other side of this one. Why have you not changed? You will be late.'

'I must speak to you. I cannot remain in this house, Elise. I must find some excuse to leave immediately.'

She turned and looked fixedly at him.

'What is it now, Francis? Surely you cannot be disturbed *à cause de* Nicholas Compline. I assure you . . . '

'It is not solely on his account. Although . . . '

'What, then?'

'His mother's!'

'His *mother's!*' she repeated blankly. "That unfortunate woman? Have you ever seen a more disastrous face? What do you mean? I wondered if perhaps Mr Royal had thought that by inviting her he might do you a service.'

'A service,' Dr Hart repeated. '*A service. Gott im Himmel!*'

'Could you not do something?'

'What you have seen,' said Dr Hart, 'I did.'

'*You!* Francis, she was not – '

'It was in my early days. In Vienna. It was the Schmitt-Lipmann treatment – paraffin wax. We have long ago abandoned it, but at that time it was widely practised. In this case – as you see – '

'But her name. Surely you remembered her name?'

'She did not give her own name. Very often they do not. She called herself Mrs Nicholas, after her accursed son, I suppose. Afterwards, of course, she made a great scene. I attempted adjustments, but in those days I was less experienced, the practice of plastic surgery was in its infancy. I could do nothing. When I came to England my greatest dread was that I might one day encounter this Mrs Nicholas.' Dr Hart uttered a sort of laugh. 'I believe my first suspicions of that young man arose from the associations connected with his name.'

'Obviously she did not recognize you.'

'How do you know?'

'Her manner was perfectly calm. How long ago was this affair?'

'About twenty-five years.'

'And you were young Doktor Franz Hartz, of Vienna? Did you not wear a beard and moustache then? Yes. And you were slim in those days. Of course she did not recognize you.'

'Franz Hartz and Francis Hart; it is not such a difference. They all know I am a naturalized Austrian, and a plastic surgeon. I cannot face it. I shall speak, now, to Royal. I shall say I must return urgently to a case – '

'And by this behaviour invite her suspicion. Nonsense, my friend. You will remain and make yourself charming to Mrs Compline and, if she now suspects, she will say to herself: "I was mistaken. He could never have faced me." Come now,' said Madame Lisse, drawing his face down to hers, 'you will keep your head, Francis, and perhaps tomorrow, who knows, you will have played your part so admirably, that we shall change places.'

'What do you mean?'

Madame Lisse laughed softly. 'I may be jealous of Mrs Compline,' she said. 'No, no, you are disarranging my hair. Go and change and forget your anxiety.'

Dr Hart moved to the door and paused. 'Elise,' he said, 'suppose this was planned.'

'What do you mean?'

'Suppose Jonathan Royal knew. Suppose he deliberately brought about this encounter.'

'What next! Why in the world should he do such a thing?'

'There is something mischievous about him.'

'Nonsense,' she said. 'Go and change.'

IV

'Hersey. I want to speak to you.'

From inside the voluminous folds of the dress she was hauling over her head Hersey said: 'Sandra, darling, come in. I'm longing for a gossip with you. Wait a jiffy. Sit down.' She tugged at the dress and her head, firmly tied up in a strong net, came out at the top. For a moment she stood and stared at her friend. That face, so painfully suggestive of an image in some distorting mirror, was the colour of parchment. The lips held their enforced travesty of a smile, but they trembled and the large eyes were blurred by tears.

'Sandra, my dear, what is it?' cried Hersey.

'I can't stay here. I want you to help me. I've got to get away from this house.'

'Sandra! But why?' Hersey knelt by Mrs Compline. 'You're not thinking of the gossip about Nick and The Pirate? blast her eyes.'

'What gossip? I don't know what you mean? What about Nicholas?'

'It doesn't matter. Nothing. Tell me what's happened.' Hersey took Mrs Compline's hands between her own, and, feeling them writhe together in her grasp, was visited by an idea that the distress which Mrs Compline's face was incapable of expressing had flowed into these struggling hands. 'What's happened?' Hersey repeated.

'Hersey, that man, Jonathan's new friend. I can't meet him again.'

'Aubrey Mandrake?'

'No, no. The other.'

'Dr Hart?'

'I can't meet him.'

'But why?'

'Don't look at me. I know it's foolish of me, Hersey, but I can't tell you if you look at me. Please go on dressing and let me tell you.'

Hersey returned to the dressing-table, and presently Mrs Compline began to speak. The thin, exhausted voice, now well controlled, lent no colour to the story of despoiled beauty. It trailed dispassionately through her husband's infidelities, her own despair, her journey to Vienna, and her return. And Hersey, while she listened, absently made up her own face, took off her net, and arranged her hair. When it was over she turned towards Mrs Compline, but came no nearer to her.

'But can you be sure?' she said.

'It was his voice. When I heard of him first, practising in Great Chipping, I wondered. I said so to Deacon, my maid. She was with me that time in Vienna.'

'It was over twenty years ago, Sandra. And his name – '

'He must have changed it when he became naturalized.'

'Does he look at all as he did then?'

'No. He has changed very much.'

'Then – '

'I am not positive, but I am almost positive. I can't face it, Hersey, can I?'

'I think you can,' said Hersey, 'and I think you will.'

V

Jonathan stood in front of a blazing fire in the drawing room. Brocaded curtains hung motionless before the windows, the room glowed with reflected light and, but for the cheerful hiss and crackle of burning logs, was silent. The night outside was silent too, but every now and then Jonathan heard a momentary sighing as if the very person of the North Wind explored the outer walls of Highfold. Presently one of the shutters knocked softly at its frame and then the brocaded curtains stirred a little, and Jonathan looked up expectantly. A door at the far end of the room opened and Hersey Amblington came in.

'Hersey, how magnificent! You have dressed to please me, I believe. I have a passion for dull green and furs. Charming of you, my dear.'

'You won't think me so charming when you hear what I've got to say,' Hersey rejoined. 'I've got a bone to pick with you, Jo.'

'What an alarming phrase that is,' said Jonathan. 'Will you have a drink?'

'No, thank you. Sandra Compline has been threatening to go home.'

'Indeed? That's vexing. I hope you dissuaded her?'

'Yes. I did.'

'Splendid. I'm so grateful. It would have quite spoiled my party.'

'I told her not to give you the satisfaction of knowing you had scored.'

'Now, that really *is* unfair,' cried Jonathan.

'No, it's not. Look here, did you know about Sandra and your whey-faced boy-friend?'

'Mandrake?'

'Now, Jo, none of that nonsense. Sandra confides in her maid, and she tells me the maid is bosom friends with your Mrs Pouting. You've listened to servants' gossip, Jo. You've heard that Sandra thought this Hart man might be the Dr Hartz who made that appalling mess of her face.'

'I only wondered. It would be an intriguing coincidence.'

'I'm ashamed of you, and I'm furious with you on my own account. Forcing me to be civil to that blasted German.'

'Is she a German?'

'Whatever she is, she's a dirty fighter. I've heard on excellent authority she's started a rumour that my Magnolia Food Base grows beards. But never mind about that. I can look after myself.'

'Darling Hersey! If only you had allowed me to perform that delightful office!'

'It's the cruel trick you've played on Sandra that horrifies me. You've always been the same, Jo. You've a passion for intrigue, wedded to an unholy curiosity. You lay your plans, and when they work out and people are hurt or angry, nobody is more sorry or surprised than you. It's a sort of blind patch in your character.'

'Was that why you refused me, Hersey, all those years ago?'

Hersey caught her breath, and for a moment was silent.

'Not that I agree with you, you know,' said Jonathan. 'One of my objectives is a lavish burial of hatchets. I hope great things of this weekend.'

'Do you expect the Compline brothers to become reconciled because you have given Nicholas an opportunity to do his barnyard strut before Chloris Wynne? Do you suppose Hart, who is obviously in love with The Pirate, will welcome the same performance with her, or that The Pirate and I will wander up and down your house with our arms round each other's waists, or that Sandra Compline will invite Hart to have another cut at her face? You're not a fool, Jo.'

'I *had* hoped for your co-operation,' said Jonathan wistfully.

'*Mine!*'

'Well, darling, to a certain extent I've had it. You made a marvellous recovery from your own encounter with Madame Lisse, and you tell me you've persuaded Sandra to stay.'

'Only because I felt it was better for her to face it.'

'Don't you think it may be better for all of us to face our secret bogey-men? Hersey, I've collected a group of people each one of whom is in a great or small degree hag-ridden by a fear. Even Aubrey Mandrake has his little bogey-man.'

'The poetic dramatist? What have you nosed out from his past?'

'Do you really want to know?'

'No,' said Hersey, turning pink.

'You are sitting beside him at dinner. Say, in these exact words, that you understand he has given up footling, and see what sort of response you get.'

'Why should I use this loathsome phrase to Mr Mandrake?'

'Why, simply because, although you won't admit it, darling, you have your share of the family failing – curiosity.'

'I *don't* admit it. And I won't do it.'

Jonathan chuckled. 'It is an amusing notion. I shall make the same suggestion to Nicholas. I believe it would appeal to him. To return to our cast of characters. Each of them, Sandra Compline to an extreme degree, has pushed his or her fear into a cupboard. Chloris is afraid of her old attraction to Nicholas, William is afraid of Nicholas's fascination for Chloris and for his mother, Hart is afraid of Nicholas's fascination for Madame Lisse, Sandra is afraid of a terrible incident in her past, Madame Lisse, though I must say she does not reveal her fear, is perhaps a little afraid of both Hart and Nicholas. You, my dearest, fear the future. If Nicholas has a fear it is that he may lose prestige, and that is a terrible fear.'

'And you, Jo?'

'I am the compère. Part of my business is to unlock the cupboards and show the fears to be less terrible in the light of day.'

'And you have no bogey-man of your own?'

'Oh, yes, I have,' said Jonathan, and the light gleamed on his spectacles. 'His name is Boredom.'

'And therein am I answered,' said Hersey.

CHAPTER 4

Threat

While he was dressing, Mandrake had wondered how Jonathan would place his party at dinner. He actually tried to work out, on several sheets of Highfold notepaper, a plan that would keep apart the most bitterly antagonistic of the guests. He found the task beyond him. The warring elements could be separated, but any such arrangement seemed only to emphasize friendships that were in themselves infuriating to one or another of the guests. It did not enter his head that Jonathan, with reckless bravado, would choose the most aggravating and provocative arrangement possible. But this was what he did. The long dining-table had been replaced by a round one. Madame Lisse sat between Jonathan and Nicholas, Chloris between Nicholas and William. Sandra Compline was on Jonathan's right, and had Dr Hart for her other partner. Hersey Amblington was next to Dr Hart, and Mandrake himself, the odd man, sat between Hersey and William. From the moment when they found their places it was obvious to Mandrake that the success of the dinner-party was most endangered by Mrs Compline and Dr Hart. These two had been the last to arrive, Mrs Compline appearing after Caper had announced dinner. Both were extremely pale and, when they found their place-cards, seemed to flinch all over: 'Like agitated horses,' thought Mandrake. When they were all seated, Dr Hart darted a strange glance across the table at Madame Lisse. She looked steadily at him for a moment. Jonathan was talking to Mrs Compline; Dr Hart, with an obvious effort, turned to Hersey Amblington. Nicholas, who had the air of a professional diner-out, embarked upon a series of phrases directed equally, Mandrake thought, at Madame Lisse and Chloris Wynne. They were empty little phrases, but Nicholas delivered them with many inclinations of his head, this way and that, with archly masculine glances, punctual shouts of laughter, and frequent movements of his hand to his blond moustache. 'In the nineties,' Mandrake thought, 'Nicholas would have been known as a masher. There is no modern word to describe his gallantries.' They were successful gallantries, however, for both Chloris and Madame Lisse began to look alert and sleek. William preserved a mulish silence, and Dr Hart, while he spoke to Hersey, glanced from time to time at Madame Lisse.

Evidently Jonathan had chosen a round table with the object of keeping the conversation general, and in this project he was successful. However angry Hersey may have been with her cousin, she must have decided to pull her weight in the rôle of hostess for which he had obviously cast her. Mandrake, Madame Lisse, and Nicholas all did their share, and presently there appeared a kind of gaiety at the table. 'It's merely going to turn into a party that is precariously successful in the teeth of extraordinary obstacles,' Mandrake told himself. 'We have made a fuss about nothing.' But this opinion was checked when he saw Dr Hart stare at Nicholas, when on turning to William he found him engaged in what appeared to be some whispered expostulation with Chloris, and when, turning away in discomfort, he saw Mrs Compline with shaking hands hide an infinitesimal helping under her knife and fork. He emptied his glass and gave his attention to Hersey Amblington, who seemed to be talking about him to Jonathan.

'Mr Mandrake sniffs at my suggestion,' Hersey was saying. 'Don't you, Mr Mandrake?'

'Do I?' Mandrake rejoined uneasily. 'What suggestion, Lady Hersey?'

'There! He hasn't even heard me, Jo. Why, the suggestion I made before dinner for a surrealist play.'

Before Mandrake could find an answer Nicholas Compline suddenly struck into the conversation.

'You mustn't be flippant with Mr Mandrake, Hersey,' he said. 'He's looking very austere. I'm sure he's long ago given up footling.'

Mandrake experienced the sensation of a violent descent in some abandoned lift. His inside seemed to turn over, and the tips of his fingers went cold. 'God!' he thought. 'They know. In a moment they will speak playfully of Dulwich.' And he sat with his fork held in suspended animation, halfway to his mouth. 'This atrocious woman,' he thought, 'this atrocious woman. This loathsome, grinning young man.' He turned to Hersey and found her staring at him with an expression that he interpreted as knowing. Mandrake shied away and, looking wildly round the table, encountered the thick-lensed glasses of his host. Jonathan's lips were pursed, and in the faint creases at the corners of his mouth Mandrake read complacency and amusement. 'So that's it,' thought Mandrake furiously. 'He knows and he's told them. It's the sort of thing that would delight him. My vulnerable spot. He's having a tweak at it, and he and his cousin and his bloody friend will laugh delicately and tell each other they were very naughty with poor Mr Stanley Footling.' But Jonathan was speaking to him, gently carrying forward the theme of Hersey's suggestion for a play.

'I have noticed, Aubrey, that the layman is always eager to provide the artist with ideas. Do you imagine, Hersey darling, that Aubrey is a sort of aesthetic scavenger?'

'But mine was such a *good* idea.'

'You must excuse her, Aubrey. No sense of proportion, I'm afraid, poor woman.'

'Mr Mandrake *does* excuse me,' said Hersey, and her smile held such a warmth of friendliness that it dispelled Mandrake's panic. 'I was mistaken,' he thought. 'Another false alarm. Why must I be so absurdly sensitive? Other people have changed their names without experiencing these terrors.' The relief was so great that for a time he was lost in it, and heard only the gradual quieting of his own heartbeats. But presently he became aware of a lull in the general conversation. They had reached dessert. Jonathan's voice alone was heard, and Mandrake thought that he must have been speaking for some little time.

II

'No one person,' Jonathan was saying, 'is the same individual to more than one other person. That is to say, the reality of individuals is not absolute. Each individual has as many exterior realities as the number of encounters he makes.'

'Ah,' said Dr Hart, 'this is a pet theory of my own. The actual "he" is known to nobody.'

'Does the actual "he" even exist?' Jonathan returned. 'May it not be argued that "he" has no intrinsic reality since different selves arise out of a conglomeration of selves to meet different events?'

'I don't see what you mean,' said William, with his air of worried bafflement.

'Nor do I, William,' said Hersey. 'One knows how people will react to certain events, Jo. We say: "Oh, so-and-so is no go when it comes to such-and-such a situation." '

'My contention is that this is exactly what we do not know.'

'But, Mr Royal,' cried Chloris, 'we *do* know. We know, for instance, that some people will refuse to listen to gossip.'

'We know,' said Nicholas, 'that one man will keep his head in a crisis where another will go jitterbug. This war – '

'Oh, don't let's talk about this war,' said Chloris.

'There are some men in my company – ' William began, but Jonathan raised his hand and William stopped short.

'Well, I concede,' said Jonathan, 'that the same "he" may make so many appearances that we may gamble on his turning up under certain circumstances, but I contend that it *is* a gamble and that though under these familiar circumstances we may agree on the probability of certain reactions, we should quarrel about theoretical behaviour under some unforeseen, hitherto un-experienced circumstances.'

'For example?' asked Madame Lisse.

'Parachute invasion – ' began William, but his mother said quickly: 'No, William, not the war.' It was the first time since dinner that Mandrake had heard her speak without being addressed.

'I agree,' said Jonathan. 'Let us not draw our examples from the war. Let us suppose that – what shall I say – '

'That the Archangel Gabriel popped down the chimney,' suggested Hersey, 'and blasted his trumpet in your ear.'

'Or that Jonathan told us,' said Nicholas, 'that this was a Borgia party and the champagne was lethal and we had but twelve minutes to live.'

'*Not* the Barrie touch, I implore you,' said Mandrake, rallying a little.

'Or,' said Jonathan, peering into the shadows beyond the candle-lit table, 'that my new footman, who is not present at the moment, suddenly developed homicidal mania and was possessed of a lethal weapon. Let us, at any rate, suppose ourselves shut up with some great and impending menace.' He paused, and for a moment complete silence fell upon the company.

The new footman returned. He and Caper moved round the table again. 'So he's keeping the champagne going,' thought Mandrake, 'in case the women won't have brandy or liqueurs. Caper's being very judicious. Nobody's tight, unless it's William or Hart. I'm not sure of them. Everybody else is nicely, thank you.'

'Well,' said Jonathan, 'under some such disastrous circumstance, how does each of you believe I would behave? Come now, I assure you I shan't cavil at the strictest censure. Sandra, what do you think I would do?'

Mrs Compline raised her disfigured face. 'What you would do?' she repeated. 'I think you would talk, Jonathan.' And for the first time that evening there was a burst of spontaneous laughter. Jonathan uttered his high-pitched giggle.

'*Touché*,' he said. 'And you, Madame Lisse?'

'I believe that for perhaps the first time in your life you would lose your temper, Mr Royal.'

'Nick?'

'I don't know. I think – '

'Come on, now, Nick. You can't insult me. Fill Mr Compline's glass, Caper. Now, Nick?'

'I think you might be rather flattened out.'

'I don't agree,' said Chloris quickly. 'I think he'd take us all in hand and tell us what to do.'

'William?'

'What? Oh, ring up the police, I suppose,' said William, and he added in a vague mumble only heard by Mandrake: 'Or you might go mad, of course.'

'I believe he would enjoy himself,' said Mandrake quickly.

'I agree,' said Hersey, to Mandrake's surprise.

'And Dr Hart?'

'In a measure, I too agree. I think that you would be enormously interested in the behaviour of your guests.'

'You see?' said Jonathan in high glee. 'Am I not right? So many Jonathan Royals. Now shall we go further. Shall we agree to discuss our impressions of each other, and to keep our tempers as we do so? Come now.'

'How clever of Jonathan,' thought Mandrake, sipping his brandy. 'Nothing interests people so much as the discussion of their own characters. His invitation may be dangerous, but at least it will make them talk.' And talk they did. Mrs Compline believed that Nicholas would suffer from extreme sensibility, but would show courage and resource. Nicholas, prompted, as Mandrake considered, by a subconscious memory of protective motherhood, thought his mother would console and shelter. William, while agreeing with Nicholas about their mother, hinted that Nicholas himself would shift his responsibilities. Chloris Wynne, rather defiantly, supported William. She suggested that William himself would show up very well in a crisis, and her glance at Nicholas and at Mrs Compline seemed to say that they would resent his qualities. Mandrake, nursing his brandy-glass, presently felt his brain clear, miraculously. He would speak to these people in rhythmic, perfectly chosen phrases, and what he said would be of enormous importance. He heard his own voice telling them that Nicholas, in the event of a crisis, would treat them to a display of pyrotechnics, and that two women would applaud him and one man deride. 'But the third woman,' said Mandrake solemnly, as he stared at Madame Lisse, 'must remain a shadowed figure. I shall write a play about her. Dear me, I am afraid I must be a little drunk.' He looked anxiously round, only to discover that nobody had been listening to him, and he suddenly realized that he had made his marvellous speech in a whisper. This discovery sobered him. He decided to take no more of Jonathan's brandy.

III

Jonathan did not keep the men long in the dining room, and Mandrake, who had taken stock of himself and had decided that he would do very well if he was careful, considered that his host had judged the drinks nicely as far as he and the Complines were concerned, but that in the case of Dr Hart, Jonathan had been over-generous. Dr Hart was extremely pale, there were dents in his nostrils and a smile on his lips. He was silent and fixed his gaze, which seemed a little out of focus, on Nicholas Compline. Nicholas was noisily cheerful. He moved his chair up to William's, and subjected his brother to a kind of banter that made Mandrake shudder and cause William to become silent and gloomy. Jonathan caught Mandrake's eye and suggested that they should move to the drawing room.

'By all means,' said Nicholas. 'Here's old Bill as silent as the grave, Jonathan, longing for his love. And Dr Hart not much better, though whether it's from the same cause or not we mustn't ask.'

'You are right,' said Dr Hart thickly. 'It would not be amusing to ask such a question.'

'Come along, come along,' said Jonathan quickly, and opened the door. Mandrake hurriedly joined him, and William followed. At the door Mandrake turned and looked back. Nicholas was still in his chair. His hands rested on the table, he leant back and smiled at Dr Hart, who had risen and was leaning heavily forward. Mandrake was irresistibly reminded of an Edwardian problem picture. It was a subject for the Hon. John Collier. There was the array of glasses, each with its highlight and reflection, there was the gloss of mahogany, of boiled shirt-fronts, of brass buttons. There was Dr Hart's face, so violently expressive of some conjectural emotion, and Nicholas's, flushed, and wearing a sneer that dated perfectly with the Hon. John's period: all this unctuously lit by the candles on Jonathan's table. "The title,' thought Mandrake, 'would be "The Insult." '

'Come along, Nick,' said Jonathan, and when it appeared that Nicholas had not heard him, he murmured in an undertone: 'You and William go on, Aubrey. We'll follow.'

So Mandrake and William did not hear what Nicholas and Dr Hart had to say to each other.

IV

Mandrake had suspected that if Jonathan failed it would be from too passionate attention to detail. He feared that Jonathan's party would die of over-planning. Having an intense dislike of parlour-games, he thought gloomily of sharpened pencils and pads of paper neatly set out by the new footman. In this he misjudged his host. Jonathan introduced his game with a tolerable air of spontaneity. He related an anecdote of another party at which the game of Charter had been played. Jonathan had found himself with a collection of six letters and one blank. When the next letter was called it chimed perfectly with his six, but the resulting word was one of such gross impropriety that even Jonathan hesitated to use it. A duchess of formidable rigidity had been present. 'I encountered her eye. The glare of a basilisk, I assure you. I could not venture. But the amusing point of the story,' said Jonathan, 'is that I am persuaded her own letters had fallen in the same order. We played for threepenny points, and she loathes losing her money. I hinted at my own dilemma, and saw an answering glint. She was in an agony.'

'But what is the game?' asked Mandrake, knowing that somebody was meant to ask this question.

'My dear Aubrey, have you never played Charter? It is entirely *vieux jeu* nowadays, but I still confess to a passion for it.'

'It's simply a crossword game,' said Hersey. 'You are each given the empty crossword form and the letters are called one by one from a pack of cards. The players put each letter, as it is read out, into a square of the diagram. This goes on until the form is full. The longest list of complete words wins.'

'You score by the length of the words,' said Chloris. 'Seven-letter words get fifteen points, three-letter words two points, and so on. You may not make any alterations, of course.'

'It sounds entertaining,' said Mandrake with a sinking heart.

'Shall we?' asked Jonathan, peering at his guests. 'What does everybody think? Shall we?'

His guests, prompted by champagne and brandy to desire, vaguely, success rather than disaster, cried out that they were all for the game, and the party moved to the smoking room. Here, Jonathan, with a convincing display of uncertainty, hunted in a drawer where Mandrake had seen him secrete the printed block of diagrams and the requisite number of pencils. Soon they were sitting in a semicircle round the fire with their pencils poised and with expressions of indignant bewilderment on their faces. Jonathan turned up the first card:

'X,' he said, 'X for Xerxes.'

'Oh, *can't* we have another,' cried Madame Lisse, 'there aren't any– Oh, no, wait a moment. I see.'

'K for King.'

Mandrake, finding himself rather apt at the game, began to enjoy it. With the last letter he completed his long word, 'extract,' and with an air of false modesty handed his Charter to Chloris Wynne, his next-door neighbour, to mark. He himself took William's Charter, and was embarrassed to find it in a state of the strangest confusion. William had either failed to understand the game, or else had got left so far behind that he could not catch up with the letters. Many of the spaces were blank, and in the left-hand corner William had made a singular little drawing of a strutting rooster, with a face that certainly bore a strong resemblance to his brother Nicholas.

'Anyway,' said William, looking complacently at Mandrake, 'the drawing is quite nice. Don't you think so?'

Mandrake was saved from making a reply by Nicholas, who at that moment uttered a sharp ejaculation.

'What's up, Nick?' asked Jonathan.

Nicholas had turned quite pale. In his left hand he held two of the Charter forms. He separated them and crushed one into a wad in his right hand.

'Have I made a mistake?' asked Dr Hart softly.

'You've given me two forms,' said Nicholas.

'Stupid of me. I must have torn them off the block at the same time.'

'They have both been used.'

'No doubt I forgot to remove an old form, and tore them off together.'

Nicholas looked at him. 'No doubt,' he said.

'You can see which is the correct form by my long word. It is "threats." '

'I have not missed it,' said Nicholas, and turned to speak to Madame Lisse.

V

Mandrake went to his room at midnight. Before switching on his light he pulled aside the curtains and partly opened the window. He saw that at last the snow had come. Fleets of small ghosts drove steeply forward from darkness into the region beyond the windowpanes, where they became visible in the firelight. Some of them, meeting the panes, slid down their surface and lost their strangeness in the cessation of their flight. Though the room was perfectly silent, this swift enlargement of oncoming snowflakes beyond the windows suggested to Mandrake a vast nocturnal whispering. He suddenly remembered the blackout and closed the window. He let fall the curtain, switched on the light, and turned to stir his fire. He was accustomed to later hours and felt disinclined for sleep. His thoughts were busy with memories of the evening. He was filled with a nagging curiosity about the second Charter form, which had caused Nicholas Compline to turn pale and to look so strangely at Dr Hart. He could see Nicholas's hand thrusting the crumpled form down between the seat and the arm of his chair. 'Perhaps it is still there,' Mandrake thought. 'Without a doubt it is still there. Why should it have upset him so much? I shall never go to sleep. It is useless to undress and get into bed.' And the prospect of the books Jonathan had chosen so carefully for his bedside filled him with dismay. At last he changed into pyjamas and dressing-gown, visited the adjoining bathroom, and noticed that there was no light under the door from the bathroom into William's bedroom at the farther side. 'So William is not astir.' He returned to his room, opened the door into the passage, and was met by the indifferent quiet of a sleeping house. Mandrake left his own door open and stole along the passage as far as the stairhead. In the wall above the stairs was a niche from which a great brass Buddha, indestructible memorial to Jonathan's Anglo-Indian grandfather, leered peacefully at Mandrake. He paused here, thinking. 'A few steps down to the landing, then the lower flight to the hall. The smoking room door is almost opposite the foot of the stairs.' Nicholas had sat in the fourth chair from the end. Why should he not go down and satisfy himself about the crumpled form? If by any chance someone was in the smoking room he could get himself a book from the library next door and return. There was no shame in looking at a discarded paper from a round game.

He limped softly to the head of the stairs. Here, in the diffused light, he found a switch and turned it on. A wall-lamp halfway down the first flight came to life. Mandrake descended the stairs. The walls sighed to his footfall, and near the bottom one of the steps creaked so loudly that he started and then stood rigid, his heart beating hard against his ribs. 'This is how burglars and illicit lovers feel,' thought Mandrake, 'but why on earth should I?' Yet he stole cat-footed across the hall, pushed open the smoking room door with his fingertips and waited long in the dark before he groped for the light-switch and snapped it down.

There stood the nine armchairs in a semicircle before a dying fire. They had an air of being in dumb conclave, and their irregular positions were strangely eloquent of their late occupants. There was Nicholas Compline's chair, drawn close to Madame Lisse's and turned away contemptuously from Dr Hart's saddle back. Mandrake actually fetched a book from a sporting collection in a revolving case before he moved to Nicholas's chair, before his fingers explored the crack between the arm and the seat. The paper was crushed into a tight wad. He smoothed it out on the arm of the chair and read the five words that had been firmly pencilled in the diagram.

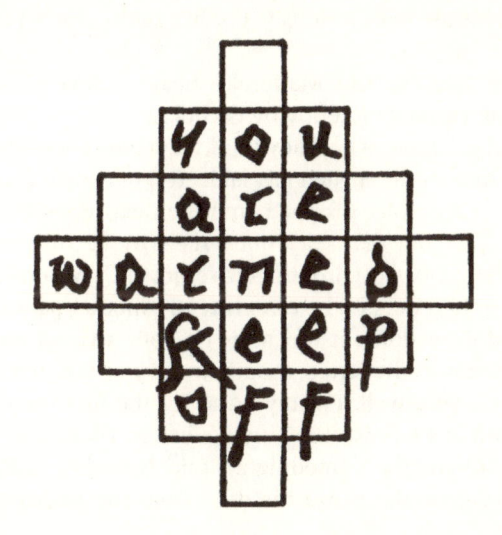

YOU ARE WARNED KEEP OFF

The fire settled down with a small clink of dead embers, and Mandrake, smiling incredulously, stared at the scrap of paper in his hand. It crossed his mind that perhaps he was the victim of an elaborate joke, that Jonathan had primed his guests, had invented their antipathies, and now waited maliciously for Mandrake himself to come to him, agog with this latest find. 'But that won't wash,' he thought. 'Jonathan could not have guessed I would return to find the paper. Nicholas *did* change colour when he saw it. I must presume that Hart *did* write this message and hand it to Nicholas with the other. He must have been crazy with fury to allow himself such a ridiculous gesture. Can he suppose that Nicholas will be frightened off the lady? No, it's too absurd.'

But, as if in answer to his speculations, Mandrake heard a voice speaking behind him: 'I tell you, Jonathan, he means trouble. I'd better get out.'

For a moment Mandrake stood like a stone, imagining that Jonathan and Nicholas had entered the smoking-room behind his back. Then he turned, and found the room still empty, and realized that Nicholas had spoken from beyond the door into the library, and for the first time noticed that this door was not quite shut. He was still speaking, his voice raised hysterically.

'It will be better if I clear out now. A pretty sort of party it'll be! The fellow's insane with jealously. For her sake – don't you see – for her sake – '

The voice paused, and Mandrake heard a low murmur from Jonathan, interrupted violently by Nicholas.

'I don't give a damn what they think.' Evidently Jonathan persisted, because in a moment Nicholas said: 'Yes, of course I see that, but I can say . . . ' His voice dropped, and the next few sentences were half-lost. '. . . it's not that . . . I don't see why . . . urgent call from headquarters . . . Good Lord, of course not! . . . Miserable fat little squirt. I've cut him out and he can't take it.' Another pause, and then: '*I* don't mind if *you* don't. It was more on your account than . . . But I've told you about the letter, Jonathan . . . not the first. . . Well, if you think . . . Very well, I'll stay.' And for the first time Mandrake caught Jonathan's words: 'I'm sure it's better, Nick. Can't turn tail, you know. Goodnight.' 'Goodnight,' said Nicholas, none too graciously, and Mandrake heard the door from the library to the hall open and close. Then from the next room came Jonathan's reedy tenor:

*'Il était une bergère
Qui ron-ton-ton, petit pat-a-plan.'*

Mandrake stuck out his chin, crossed the smoking room, and entered the library by the communicating door.

'Jonathan,' he said, 'I've been eavesdropping.'

VI

Jonathan was sitting in a chair before the fire. His short legs were drawn up, knees to chin, and he hugged his shins like some plump and exultant kobold. He turned his spectacles towards Mandrake, and, by that familiar trick of light, the thick lenses obscured his eyes and glinted like two moons.

'I've been eavesdropping,' Mandrake repeated.

'My dear Aubrey, come in, come in. Eavesdropping? Nonsense. You heard our friend Nicholas? Good! I was coming to your room to relate the whole story. A diverting complication.'

'I only heard a little of what he said. I'd come down to the smoking room.' He saw Jonathan's spectacles turned on the book he still held in his hand. 'Not really to fetch a book,' said Mandrake.

'No? One would seek a book in the library, one supposes. But I am glad my choice for your room was not ill-judged.'

'I wanted to see this.'

Like a small boy in disgrace, Mandrake extended his right hand and opened it, disclosing the crumpled form.

'Ah,' said Jonathan.

'You have seen it?'

'Nick told me about it. I wondered if anyone else would share my own curiosity. May I have it? Ah – Thank you. Sit down, Aubrey.' Mandrake sat down, tortured by the suspicion that Jonathan was laughing at him.

'You see,' said Mandrake, 'that I am badly inoculated with your virus. I simply could not go to bed without knowing what was on that form.'

'Nor I, I assure you. I was about to look for it myself. As perhaps you heard, Nick is in a great tig. It seems that before coming here he had had letters from Hart warning him off the lady. According to Nick, Hart is quite mad for love of her and consumed by an agonizing jealousy.'

'Poor swine,' said Mandrake.

'What? Oh, yes. Very strange and uncomfortable. I must confess that I believe Nick is right. Did you notice the little scene after dinner?'

'You may remember that you gave me to understand very definitely that my cue was to withdraw rapidly.'

'So I did. Well, there wasn't much in it. He merely glared at Nick across the table, and said something in German which neither of us understood.'

'You'll be telling me next he's a fifth columnist,' said Mandrake.

'Not at all. He gives himself away much too readily. But I fancy he has frightened Nick. I have observed, my dear Aubrey, that of the two Complines, William catches your attention more than Nicholas. I have known them all their lives, and I suggest that you turn your eyes on Nicholas. Nicholas is rapidly becoming the – not perhaps the *jeune premier* – but the central character of our drama. In Nicholas we see the vain man, frightened. The male flirt who finds an agreeable stimulant in another man's jealousy, and suddenly realizes that he has roused the very devil in his rival. Would you believe it, Nicholas wanted to leave tonight? He advanced all sorts of social and gallant reasons, consideration for me, for the lady, for the success of the party; but the truth is Nick had a jitterbug and wanted to make off.'

'How did you prevent him?'

'I?' Jonathan pursed his lips. 'I have usually been able to manage Nicholas. I let him see I understood his real motive. He was afraid I would make a pleasing little anecdote of his flight. His vanity won. He will remain.'

'But what does he think Hart will do?'

'He used the word "murderous." '

There was a long silence. At last Mandrake said: 'Jonathan, I think you should have let Nicholas Compline go.'

'But why?'

'Because I agree with him. I have watched Hart tonight. He did look murderous.'

'Gorgeous!' Jonathan exclaimed, and hugged his hands between his knees.

'Honestly, I think he means trouble. He's at the end of his tether.'

'You don't think he'll go for Nick with a dinner-knife?'

'I don't think he's responsible for his behaviour.'

'He was a little tipsy, you know.'

'So was Compline. While the champagne and brandy worked he rather enjoyed baiting Hart. Now, evidently, he's not so sure. Nor am I.'

'You disappoint me, Aubrey. Our aesthetic experiment is working beautifully and your only response – '

'Oh, I'm absorbingly interested. If *you* don't mind – after all, it's your house.'

'Exactly. And my responsibility. I assembled the cast, and, my dear fellow, I offered you a seat in the stalls. The play is going too well for me to stop it at the close of the first act. It falls very prettily on Nick's exit, and I fancy the last thing we hear before the curtain blots out the scene is a sharp click.'

'What?'

'Nicholas Compline turning the key in his bedroom door.'

'I hope to God you're right,' said Mandrake.

CHAPTER 5

Attempt

The next morning Mandrake woke at the rattle of curtain rings to find his room penetrated by an unearthly light, and knew that Highfold was under snow. A heavy fall, the maid said. There were patches of clear sky, but the local prophets said they'd have another storm before evening. She rekindled his fire and left him to stare at his tea-tray and to remember that, not so many years ago, Mr Stanley Footling, in the attic-room of his mother's boarding-house in Dulwich, had enjoyed none of these amenities. Stanley Footling always showed a tendency to return at the hour of waking, and this morning Mandrake asked himself for the hundredth time why he could not admit his metamorphosis with an honest gaiety; why he should suffer the miseries of unconfessed snobbery. He could find no answer, and, tired of his thoughts, decided to rise early.

When he went downstairs he found William Compline alone at the breakfast-table.

'Hallo,' said William. 'Good morning. Jolly day for Nick's bath, isn't it?'

'What!'

'Nick's bath in the pool. Have you forgotten the bet?'

'I should think *he* had.'

'I shall remind him.'

'Well,' said Mandrake, 'personally I should pay a good deal more than ten pounds to get out of it.'

'Yes, but you're not my brother Nicholas. He'll do it.'

'But,' said Mandrake uncomfortably, 'hasn't he got something wrong with his heart? I mean – '

'It won't hurt him. The pool's not frozen. I've been to look. He can't swim, you know, so he'll just have to pop in at the shallow end and duck.' William gave a little crow of laughter.

'I'd call it off, if I were you.'

'Yes,' said William, 'but you're not me. I'll remind him of it, all right.'

And on this slightly ominous note they continued with their breakfast in silence. Hersey Amblington and Chloris Wynne came in together, followed by Jonathan, who appeared to be in the best of spirits.

'We shall have a little sunshine, I believe,' said Jonathan. 'It may not last long, so doubtless the hardier members of the party will choose to make the most of it.'

'I don't propose to build a snowman, Jonathan, if that's what you're driving at,' said Hersey.

'Don't you, Hersey?' said William. 'I rather thought I might. After Nick's bath, you know. Have you heard about Nick's bath?'

'Your mother told me. You're not going to hold him to it, William?'

'He needn't if he doesn't want to.'

'Bill,' said Chloris, *don't* remind him of it. Your mother – '

'She won't get up for ages,' said William, 'and I don't suppose there'll be any need to remind Nick. After all, it *was* a bet.'

'I think you're behaving rather badly,' said Chloris uncertainly. William stared at her.

'Are you afraid he'll get a little cold in his nose?' he asked, and added: 'I was up to my waist in snow and slush in France not so long ago.'

'I know, darling, but – '

'Here *is* Nick,' said William placidly. His brother came in and paused at the door.

'Good morning,' said William. 'We were just talking about the bet. They all seem to think I ought to let you off.'

'Not at all,' said Nicholas. 'You've lost your tenner.'

'*There!*' said William. 'I said you'd do it. You mustn't get that lovely uniform wet, Nick. Jonathan will lend you a bathing suit, I expect. Or you could borrow my uniform. It's been up to – ' Mandrake, Chloris, Hersey, and Jonathan all began to speak at once, and

William, smiling gently, fetched himself another cup of coffee. Nicholas turned away to the sideboard. Mandrake had half-expected Jonathan to interfere, but he merely remarked on the hardihood of the modern young man and drew a somewhat tiresome analogy from the exploits of ancient Greeks. Nicholas suddenly developed a sort of gaiety that set Mandrake's teeth on edge, so falsely did it ring.

'Shall you come and watch me, Chloris?' asked Nicholas, seating himself beside her.

'I don't approve of your doing it.'

'Oh, Chloris! Are you angry with me? I can't bear it. Tell me you're not angry with me. I'm doing it all for your sake. I must have an audience. Won't you be my audience?'

'Don't be a fool,' said Chloris. 'But, damn it,' thought Mandrake, 'she's preening herself, all the same.' Dr Hart arrived, and was very formal with his greetings. He looked ghastly and breakfasted on black coffee and toast. Nicholas threw him a glance curiously compounded of malice and nervousness, and began to talk still more loudly to Chloris Wynne of his bet with William. Hersey, who had evidently got sick of Nicholas, suddenly said she thought it was time to cut the cackle and get to the 'osses.

'But everybody isn't here,' said William. 'Madame Lisse isn't here.'

'Divine creature!' exclaimed Nicholas affectedly, and showed the whites of his eyes at Dr Hart. 'She's in bed.'

'How do you know?' asked William, against the combined mental opposition of the rest of the party.

'I've investigated. I looked in to say good morning on my way down.'

Dr Hart put down his cup with a clatter and walked quickly out of the room

'You are a damned fool, Nick,' said Hersey softly.

'It's starting to snow again,' said William. 'You'd better hurry up with your bath.'

II

Mandrake thought that no wager had ever fallen as inauspiciously as this one. Even Jonathan seemed uneasy, and when they drifted into the library made a half-hearted attempt to dissuade

Nicholas. Lady Hersey said flatly that she thought the whole affair extremely boring and silly. Chloris Wynne at first attempted an air of jolly house-party waggishness, but a little later Mandrake overheard her urging William to call off the bet. Mrs Compline somehow got wind of the project and sent down a message forbidding it, but this was followed by a message from Madame Lisse saying that she would watch from her bedroom window. Mandrake tried to get up a party to play badminton in the barn, but nobody really listened to him. An atmosphere of bathos hung over them like a pall, and through it William remained complacent and Nicholas embarrassingly flamboyant.

Finally it was resolved by the Complines that Nicholas should go down to the pavilion, change there into a bathing suit, and, as William put it, go off at the shallow end. William was to watch the performance, and Nicholas, rather offensively, insisted upon a second witness. Neither Hersey nor Chloris seemed able to make up her mind whether she would go down to the pool. Jonathan had gone out, saying something about Dr Hart. It appeared that Mandrake would be obliged to witness Nicholas's ridiculous antics, and, muttering to himself, he followed him into the hall.

The rest of the party had disappeared. Nicholas stood brushing up his moustache and eyeing Mandrake with an air half-mischievous, half-defiant. 'Well,' he said, 'this is a pretty damn-fool sort of caper, isn't it?'

'To be frank,' said Mandrake, 'I think it is. It's snowing like hell again. Don't you rather feel the bet's fallen flat?'

'I'll be damned if I let Bill take that tenner off me. Are you coming?'

'I'll go up and get my coat,' said Mandrake unwillingly.

'Take one out of the cloakroom here. I'm going to. The Tyrolese cape.'

'Jonathan's?'

'Or Hart's!' Nicholas grinned. 'Hart's mantle may as well fall across my shoulders, what? I'll go down now and change in that bloody pavilion. You follow. Bill's running down from the west door when he's given me time to undress.'

Nicholas went into the cloakroom and reappeared wearing one Tyrolese cape and carrying another. 'Here you are,' he said, throwing it at Mandrake. 'Don't be long.'

He pulled the hood of his cape over his head and went out through the front doors. For a moment Mandrake saw him, a fantastic figure caught in a flurry of snow. Then Nicholas lowered his head to the wind and ran out of sight.

Mandrake's club foot prevented him from running. It was some distance from the front of the house to the pool, and he remembered that the west door opened directly on a path that led to the terrace above the pool. He decided that, like William, he would go down that way. He would go at once, before William started. He loathed people to check their steps to his painful limp. Imitating Nicholas, he pulled the hood of the second cape over his head and made his way along a side passage to the west door, and as he opened it heard somebody call after him from the house. He ignored the call and, filled with disgust at the whole situation, slammed the door behind him and limped out into the storm.

The north wind drove against him, flattening the cloak against his right side and billowing it out on his left. He felt snow on his eyelids and lips and pulled the hood farther over his brows so that he could see only the ground before him. As he limped forward, snow squeaked under his steps. It closed over his sound foot above the rim of his shoe. The path was still defined, and he followed it to the edge of the terrace. Below him lay the pool and the pavilion. The water was a black hole in a white field, but the pavilion resembled a lighthearted decoration, so well did the snow become it. Mandrake was tempted to watch from the terrace, but the wind was so violent there that he changed his mind and crept awkwardly down the long flight of steps, thinking to himself that it would be just like this party if he slipped and broke his good leg. At last he reached the rounded embankment that curved sharply above the pool, hiding the surface of the water from anybody who did not climb its steps. Mandrake reached the top of this bank with difficulty and descended the far side to the paved kerb, now covered in snow. He glanced at the pavilion and saw Nicholas wave from one of the windows. Mandrake walked to the deep end of the pool, where there was a diving platform, and stood huddled in his cloak watching fleets of snow die on the black surface of the water. He looked back towards the terrace steps, but the embankment hid the bottom flight. There was nobody on the top flight. Perhaps, after all, none of the others would come. 'Damn!' said Mandrake. 'Damn Nicholas, damn William, and damn Jonathan for his filthy party. I've never been so bored or cold or angry in my life before.' He staggered a little against a sudden gust of wind and snow.

The next moment something drove hard against his shoulders. He took a gigantic stride forward into nothingness and was torn from head to foot with the appalling shock of icy water.

III

The fabric of the cape was in his eyes and mouth and clamped about his arms and legs. The cold cut him with terrible knives of pain. As he sank he thought: "This is disgusting. This is really bad. A terrible thing has happened to me.' Water rushed in at his nose and ears. His heavy boot pulled at his leg. His arms fought the cape, and after a timeless interval it rose above his head, free of his face, and he saw a green prison about him. Then with frozen limbs he struggled and fought, and at last, feeling the bottom of the pool, struck at it with his feet and rose into the folds of the cape. His lungs were bursting, his body dying of cold. His hands wrenched at the fastening about his throat and broke it, his arms fought off the nightmare cape, and after an age of suffocating despair he reached the surface. He drew a retching gasp and swallowed air. For a moment he felt and saw snow, and heard, quite close by, a voice. As he sank again, something slapped the water above his head. 'But I can swim a little,' he thought, as wheels clashed and whirred behind his brain, and he made frog-like gestures with his arms and legs. Immediately the fingers of his right hand touched something smooth that slipped away from them. He made a more determined effort and, after three violent strokes, again reached the surface. As he gasped and opened his eyes, he was confronted by a scarlet face, beaked, on the end of a long scarlet neck. He flung his arms round this neck, fell backwards and was half-suffocated with another in-drawn jet of water. Then he found himself lying on the pond, choking into the face of a monstrous bird. Again he heard voices, but they sounded unreal and very far away.

'Are you all right? Kick. Kick out. You're coming this way.'

'But that is *my* cloak.'

'Kick, Aubrey, kick.'

He kicked, and, after an aeon of time, floated into the view of five faces, upside down with their mouths open. His head struck against hardness.

'The rail. There's a rail here. Get hold of it.'

'You're all right now. Here!'

He was drawn up. His arms scraped against stone. He was lying on the edge of the pool clasping an inflated india-rubber bird to his bosom. He was turned so that his face hung over the edge of the pond. His jaws had developed an independent life of their own, and his teeth chattered like castanets. His skin, too, leapt and jerked over the surface of his frozen muscles. When he tried to speak he made strange ugly noises. Acrid water trickled from his nostrils over his lips and chin.

'How the devil did it happen?' somebody – William – was asking.

'The edge is horribly slippery,' said Chloris Wynne. 'I nearly fell in myself.'

'I didn't fall,' Mandrake mouthed out with great difficulty. 'I was pushed.' Nicholas Compline burst into a shout of laughter and Mandrake wondered dimly if he could make a quick grab at his ankle and overturn him into the pool. It was borne in on Mandrake that Nicholas was wearing bathing drawers under his cape.

'Did he fall or was he pushed?' shouted Nicholas.

'Shut up, Nicholas.' That was Chloris Wynne.

'My dear fellow,' Jonathan made a series of little dabs at Mandrake, 'you must come up at once. My coat. Take my coat. Ah, yours too, William, that's better. Help him up, now. A hot toddy and a blazing fire, eh, Hart? There never was anything more unfortunate. Come now.'

Mandrake was suddenly torn by a violent retching. 'Disgusting,' he thought. *'Disgusting!'*

'That will be better,' said a voice. Dr Hart's! 'We should get him up quickly. Can you walk, Mr Mandrake?'

'Yes.'

'Your arm across my shoulders. So, come now.'

'I'll just get into my clothes,' said Nicholas.

'Perhaps, Mr Compline, as you are in bathing dress, you will be good enough to retrieve my cape.'

'Sorry, I can't swim.'

'We'll fish it out somehow,' said Chloris. 'Take Mr Mandrake in.'

Jonathan, William, and Dr Hart took him back. Over the embankment, up the terrace steps, through a mess of footprints left by the others. The heavy boot on his club foot dragged and hit against snow and sodden turf. Halfway up he was sick again. Jonathan ran ahead and, when at last they reached the house, could be heard shouting out orders to the servants. 'Hot-water bottles. All you can find. His bath – quickly. Brandy, Caper. The fire in his room. What are you doing, all of you! God bless my soul, Mrs Pouting, here's Mr Mandrake, half-drowned.'

If only his teeth would stop chattering he would enjoy being in bed, watching flames mount in the fireplace, feeling the toddy set up a little system of warmth inside him. The hot bath had thawed his body, the hot bottles lay snug against his legs. Jonathan again held the glass to his lips.

'What happened?' asked Mandrake.

'After you fell, you mean? Nick looked out from the window of his dressing-room. He saw you and ran out. He can't swim, you know, but he snatched up the inflated pelican – there are several in the pavilion – and threw it into the pond. By that time I fancy William and Hart were there. They arrived before Miss Wynne and myself. It appears that William had stripped off his overcoat and was going after you when you seized the improvised lifebuoy. When we arrived your arms were wreathed about its neck and you were fighting your way to the side. My dear Aubrey, I can't tell you how distressed I am. Another sip, now, do.'

'Jonathan, somebody came behind me and thrust me forward.'

'But my dear fellow – '

'I tell you they did. I can still feel the impact of their hands. I did *not* slip. Good God, Jonathan, I'm not romancing! I tell you I was deliberately thrown into that water.'

'Nicholas saw nobody,' said Jonathan uncomfortably. He primmed his lips and gave a little cough.

'When did he look out?' Mandrake said. 'I know he saw me when I first got there. But afterwards?'

'Well – the first thing he saw was your cape – Dr Hart's cape, unhappily – on the surface of the water.'

'Exactly. Whoever pushed me in, had by that time hidden himself. He had only to dodge over the embankment and duck down.'

'But we should have seen him,' said Jonathan.

'Hart and William Compline were already there when you arrived?'

'Yes, but – '

'Did they go down together to the pond?'

'I – no, I think not. Hart left by the front door and came by the other path, past the pavilion. William came by the west door.'

'Which of them arrived first? Thank God I've stopped chattering.'

'I don't know. I persuaded Hart to go out. I managed to calm him down after that *most* unfortunate passage with Nicholas at breakfast. I suggested he should go out for a – for a sort of breather, do you know – and I supposed he followed the path to the pavilion, and was arrested by Nicholas's shouts for help. I myself heard Nicholas as I went to the west door. I overtook Miss Wynne who was already on the terrace. When I reached the edge of the terrace, Hart and the two Complines were all by the pond. My dear Aubrey, I shall tire you if I go on at this rate. Finish your drink and try to go to sleep.'

'I don't in the least want to go to sleep, Jonathan. Somebody has just tried to drown me, and I do not find the experience conducive to slumber.'

'No?' murmured Jonathan unhappily.

'No. And don't, I implore you, look as though I was mentally unhinged.'

'Well, you *have* had a shock. You may even have a slight fever. I don't want to alarm you – '

'If you try to fob me off, I shall certainly run a frightful temperature. At the moment I assure you I am perfectly normal, and I tell you, Jonathan, somebody tried to drown me in your loathsome pond. I confess I should like to know who it was.'

'A thoughtless piece of foolery, perhaps,' mumbled Jonathan. Mandrake suddenly pointed a trembling finger at the mound in the bedclothes made by his left foot.

'Does any one but a moron play that sort of prank on a cripple?' he asked savagely.

'Oh, my dear fellow, I know, but – '

'Madame Lisse!' Mandrake cried. 'She was to watch from her window. She must have seen.'

'You can't see that end of the pool from her window,' said Jonathan quickly. it's hidden by the yew trees on the terrace.'

'How do you know?'

'I do know. Yesterday, when I did her flowers, I noticed. I assure you.'

Mandrake looked at him. 'Then whoever did it,' he said, 'must have also known that she could not see him. Or else – '

There was a tap on the door.

'Come in,' cried Jonathan in a loud voice. 'Come in.'

IV

It was Nicholas Compline. 'Look here,' he said. 'I hope you don't mind my butting in. I had to see Jonathan. Are you all right?'

'Thanks to you,' said Mandrake, 'I believe I am.'

'Look here; I'm damn sorry I laughed.'

'It was infuriating, but I can't quarrel with you. As we say in the provinces, you quite literally gave me the bird. Not the first time I have been so honoured, but certainly the first time I have welcomed it with both arms.'

'Jonathan,' said Nicholas, 'you realize the significance of this business?'

'The significance, Nick?'

'It was done deliberately.'

'Just what I've been trying to tell Jonathan, Compline. My God, I was literally hurled into that water. I'm sorry to dwell on a tiresome subject, but somebody tried to drown me.'

'No, they didn't.'

'What!'

'They tried to drown *me*.'

'Here!' shouted Mandrake, 'what the hell d'you mean!'

'Jonathan,' said Nicholas, 'we'd better tell him about me and Hart.'

'Oh, that,' said Mandrake. 'I know all about that.'

'May I ask how?'

'Need we go into it?'

'My dear Nick,' began Jonathan in a great hurry, 'Mandrake noticed all was not well between you. The scene at the dinner-table. The game of Charter. He asked if I – if I – '

'Well, never mind,' Nicholas interrupted impatiently. 'You know he's been threatening me? All right. Now, let me tell you that as I went down to the pond I glanced up at the front of the house. You know the window on the first floor above the front door?'

'Yes,' said Jonathan.

'All right. He was watching me through that window.'

'But my dear Nick – '

'He was watching me. He saw me go down wearing that cape. He didn't see Mandrake go down wearing the other cape, because Mandrake went out at the west door. Don't interrupt me, Jonathan, this is serious. When Mandrake was shoved overboard, he was standing up to his hocks in snow on the kerb of the pool, with that embankment hiding his legs from anybody that came up from behind. You had the hood pulled over your head, I suppose, Mandrake?'

'Yes.'

'Yes. Well, it was Hart shoved you overboard, and Hart thought he was doing me in, by God!'

'But, Nick, we must keep our heads and not rush impetuously into conclusions . . .'

'See here,' said Nicholas, always to Mandrake. 'Had anybody in this party reason to wish you any harm?'

'I'd never met one of them in my life before. Except Jonathan, of course.'

'And I can assure you, my dear Aubrey, that I entertain only the kindest – '

'Of course.'

'Well, then?' said Nicholas.

'I believe you're right,' cried Mandrake.

The door opened and Dr Hart came in.

Nicholas, who had been sitting on the edge of the bed, sprang up and walked out of the room. Jonathan uttered a series of little consolatory noises, and moved to the window. Hart went to the bed and laid his fingers on Mandrake's wrist.

'You are better,' he said. "That is right. It will be well to remain in bed today, perhaps. There has been a little shock.' He looked placidly at Mandrake and repeated: 'Just a little shock.'

'Yes,' said Mandrake.

Hart turned to Jonathan. 'If I might speak to you, Mr Royal.'

'To me?' Jonathan gave a little start. 'Yes, of course. Here?'

'I was about to suggest – somewhere else. But, perhaps– I remember, Mr Mandrake, that as we brought you to the house, you declared repeatedly that you had been deliberately pushed into this swimming pool.'

Mandrake looked at that large pale face, surely more pale than ever since its owner began to speak, and thought: 'This may be the face of a potential murderer.' Aloud, he said: 'I am quite convinced of it.'

'Then perhaps it would be well to set your mind at ease on this matter. No attempt was made wittingly upon you, Mr Mandrake.'

'How do you know?'

'It was a case of mistaken identity.'

'Good God!' said Jonathan with violence.

Dr Hart tapped the palm of one hand with the fingers of the other. 'The person who made this attack,' he said, 'believed that he was making it upon me.'

V

Mandrake's first reaction to this announcement was a hysterical impulse to burst out laughing. He looked at Jonathan, who stood with his back to the light, and wondered if he only imagined that an expression of mingled relief and astonishment had appeared for a moment on his host's face. Then he heard his voice, pedantic and high-pitched as usual.

'But, my dear Hart,' Jonathan said, 'what can have put such a strange notion into your head?'

'The fact that there is, among your guests, a man who wishes most ardently for my death.'

'Surely not,' said Jonathan, making a little purse of his lips.

'Surely, yes. I had not intended to go so far. I merely wished to reassure Mr Mandrake. Perhaps if we withdrew . . . ?'

'For pity's sake,' Mandrake ejaculated, 'don't withdraw. I'm all right. I want to get this straight. After all,' he added peevishly, 'it *was* me in the pond.'

'True,' said Jonathan.

'And I think I should tell you, Doctor Hart, that as I came down the steps, Compline saw me through the pavilion window and waved. He must have recognized me.'

'It was snowing very heavily. Your face, no doubt, was in shadow, hidden by the hood of my cape.'

'I hope you got your cape,' said Jonathan anxiously.

'Thank you, yes. There must be a considerable amount of weed in your pond. It is to me quite evident, Mandrake, that Compline mistook you for myself. He came out of the pavilion and ran up quickly behind you, giving you a sharp thrust on the shoulder-blades.'

'It *was* a sharp thrust on the shoulder-blades. But you forget that there is one thing about me that is quite distinctive.' Mandrake spoke rapidly, with an air of jeering at himself. 'I am lame. I wear a heavy boot. I use a stick. You can't mistake a man with a club foot, Doctor Hart.'

'Your foot was hidden. One does not walk evenly in snow, and I assure you that while I, as a medical man, would not make such a mistake, Compline, glancing out through heavy sheets of falling snow, might easily do so.'

'I don't agree with you. And didn't Compline see you looking from an upper window as he went to the pond? He could hardly imagine you would spirit yourself down there as quickly as that.'

'Why not? I could have done so. A matter of a few moments. In actual fact I did go down a few minutes later. Mr Royal saw me leave.'

'Is it altogether wise to stress that point, do you think?'

'I do not understand you, Mr Mandrake.'

Jonathan began to talk very quickly, stuttering a little, and making sharp gestures with both hands.

'And, my dear Hart, even if, as you suggest, any one could mistake Mandrake for yourself; even supposing, and I cannot suppose it, that any one could entertain the idea of thrusting you into that water, surely, *surely* it would be preposterous to suggest that it was with any – any – ah – murderous intent. Can you not swim, my dear Doctor?'

'Yes, but – '

'Very well, then. I myself cannot help thinking that Mandrake is mistaken, that a sudden gust of wind caught him . . . '

'No, Jonathan.'

'Or that at the worst it was a stupid and dangerous practical joke.'

'A *joke!*' shouted Dr Hart. 'A *joke.*'

Mandrake suppressed a nervous giggle. Hart stared sombrely at him, and then turned to Jonathan. 'And yet I do not know,' he said heavily. 'Perhaps with an Englishman it is possible. Perhaps he did not mean to kill me. Perhaps he wished to make me a foolish figure, shivering, dripping stagnant water, my teeth chattering– yes, I can accept that possibility. He recognized the Tyrolese cape and thought – '

'Wait a moment,' Mandrake interrupted, 'before we go any further I must put you right about the cape. It is impossible that Nicholas should have thought you were inside your own Tyrolese cape.'

'And why?'

'Because he himself gave it to me to wear to the pond.'

Dr Hart was silent. He looked from Mandrake to Jonathan, and those little dents appeared in his nostrils. 'You are protecting him,' he said.

'I assure you I am speaking the truth.'

'There is one explanation that seems to have occurred to nobody.' Jonathan raised his hand to his spectacles and adjusted them slightly. 'I myself wear a Tyrolese cape, your own gift, my dear Hart, and a delightful one. Is it not at least possible that somebody may have thought it would be amusing to watch me flounder in my own ornamental pool?'

'But who the hell?' Mandrake objected.

'It might be argued,' said Jonathan, smiling modestly, 'almost every member of my house-party.'

VI

When they had left him alone, Mandrake surrendered himself to a curious state of being, engendered by exhaustion, brandy, speculation, and drowsiness. His thoughts floated in a kind of hinterland between sleep and wakefulness. At times they were sharply defined, at times nebulous and disconnected, but always they circled about the events leading to his plunge into the swimming pool. At last he dozed off into a fitful sleep from which he was roused, as it seemed, by a single, clear inspiration. 'I must see William Compline,' he heard himself say. 'I must see William Compline.' He was staring at the ridge of snow that had begun to mount from the sill up the windowpane when his door moved slightly, and Chloris Wynne's beautifully groomed head appeared in the opening.

'Come in.'

'I thought you might be asleep. I called to inquire.'

'The report is favourable. Sit down and have a cigarette. I haven't the remotest idea of the time.'

'Nearly lunch-time.'

'Really. What are you all doing?'

'I've known house-parties go with a greater swing. Nicholas is sulking by the radio in the smoking room. Lady Hersey and Mr Royal seem to be having a quarrel next door, in the library, and when I tried the boudoir on the other side of the smoking room I ran into Dr Hart and Madame Lisse both quite green in the face, and obviously at the peak of an argument. My ex-future mother-in-law has developed a bad cold, and I have had a snorter of a row with William.'

'Here!' said Mandrake. 'What *is* all this?'

'I ticked him off for harping on about the bet with Nicholas, and then he said some pretty offensive things about Nicholas and me, and I said he was insane, and he huffed and broke off our engagement. I don't know why I tell you all this, unless it's to get in first with the news bulletin.'

'It's all very exciting, of course, but I consider the human interest really centres about me.'

'Because you fell in the pool?'

'Because I was pushed in.'

'That's what we're quarrelling about, actually. So many people seem to think it was all a mistake.'

'The fact remains, I was pushed in.'

'Oh, they've dropped saying it was an *accident*. But each of the men seems to think you were mistaken for him.'

'Does William think that?'

'No. William confines himself to saying he wishes it had been Nicholas. He's made Nicholas pay him the ten pounds.'

'I suppose,' said Mandrake, *'you* didn't push me in?'

'No, honestly, I didn't. When I got to the top of the steps William and Nicholas and Dr Hart were all down by the pool screaming instructions to you. I got a frightful shock. I thought you were Mr Royal drowning in his own baroque waters.'

'Why?'

'I don't know. Oh, because of the cloak, I suppose. It was floating about like a large water-lily leaf, and I said to myself: "Crikey, that's Jonathan Royal." '

Mandrake sat up in bed and bent his most austere gaze upon Miss Wynne. 'How did you feel,' he asked, 'when you knew it was I?'

'Well, when Mr Royal came up behind me, I knew it was thee, if that's the right grammar. And then I saw you clinging to that bathing-bird, and your hair was over your face like seaweed, and your tie was round at the back of your neck, and so on, and' – her voice quivered slightly – 'and I was terribly sorry,' she said.

'No doubt I was a ludicrous figure. Look here, from what you tell me it seems that you were the last to arrive.'

'No, Mr Royal came after me. He'd been round at the front of the house, I think. He overtook me on the steps.'

'Will you tell me something? Please try to remember. Did you notice the footprints on the terrace and the steps?'

'I *say,'* said Miss Wynne, 'are we going to do a bit of 'teckery? Footprints in the snow!'

'Do leave off being gay and inconsequent, I implore you, and try to remember the footprints. There would be mine, of course.'

'Yes. I noticed yours. I mean I – '

'You saw the marks of my club foot. You needn't be so delicate about it.'

'You needn't be so insufferably on the defensive,' said Chloris with spirit, and immediately added: 'Oh, gosh, I'm so sorry. At least let there not be a quarrel up here by your bed of sickness. Yes, I saw your footprints, and I think I saw – no, I can't remember, except that there were others. William's, of course.'

'Any coming back to the house?'

'No, I'm sure not. But – '

'Yes?'

'Well, you're wondering, aren't you, if somebody could have gone down and shoved you overboard and then come back up the steps and then sort of pretended they were going down for the first time? I'd thought of that. You see, as I went down I stepped in your footprints because it was easier going. Anybody else might have done that. It was snowing so hard nobody would have noticed the steps within the steps.'

'Hart came by a different path from the front of the house, William came down the terrace steps, then you, then Jonathan. I don't think William would have had time unless he came hard on my heels. I'd only just got there when it happened. Nicholas didn't do it, because he gave me the cloak and therefore couldn't have mistaken me for any one else. I believe Nicholas is right. I believe Hart did it. He saw Nicholas, wearing his cloak, go by the front way, and followed him. Then he skulked round the corner of the pavilion, saw a figure in a cloak standing on the kerb, darted out through the snow and did his abominable stuff. Then he darted back and reappeared, all surprise and consternation, when he heard Nicholas yell. By that time William was coming down the steps, no doubt, and you, followed by Jonathan, were leaving the house. Hart's our man.'

'Yes, but *why?*'

'My dear girl – '

'All right, all right. Because of Madame Lisse. We only met last night and you talk as if I were a congenital idiot.'

'There's nothing like attempted murder to bring people together.'

'Nicholas is a fool.'

'You ought to know. I thought you still seemed to get a flutter out of him.'

'Now *that,*' said Chloris warmly, 'I do consider an absolutely insufferable remark.'

'It's insufferable because it happens to be true. Nicholas Compline is the sort of person that all females get self-conscious about, and all males instinctively wish to award a kick in the pants.'

'Barnyard jealousy.'

'You know,' said Mandrake, 'you've got more penetration than I first gave you credit for. All the same,' he said, after a long pause, 'there's one little thing that doesn't quite fit in with my theory. It doesn't exactly contradict it, but it doesn't fit in.'

'Well, don't mumble about it. Or aren't you going to tell me?'

'When they brought me back up those unspeakable steps, I was sick.'

'You don't have to tell me that. I was looking after you.'

'I'm damned if I know how I came to notice them, but I did notice them. At the top of the terrace, leading out from the house, coming round from the front door and stopping short at the edge of the terrace. You didn't see them when you went down. Neither did I. Which proves – '

'Do you mind,' Chloris interrupted, 'breaking the thread of your narrative just for a second? Surrealism may be marvellous in poetic drama, but it's not so good in simple conversation. What didn't we see going down that you saw coming back, sick and all as you were?'

'A row of footprints in the snow coming out from the house as far as the top of the terrace, and turning back again.'

'Oh.'

'They were small footprints.'

CHAPTER 6

Flight

The afternoon was remarkable for an increasing heaviness in the snowfall, the state of Mandrake's feelings, and the behaviour of William Compline. Snow mounted from the windowsill in a tapering shroud, light diminished stealthily in Mandrake's bedroom, while he felt too relaxed and too idle to stretch out his hand to the bedside lamp. Yet though his body was fatigued, his brain was active and concerned itself briskly with the problem of his immersion and with speculations on the subject of Chloris Wynne's strange relations with the Compline brothers. He was convinced that she was not in love with William, but less sure that she did not still hanker after Nicholas. Mandrake wondered testily how a young woman who did not try the eyes and was by no means a ninny, could possibly degrade her intelligence by falling for the brummagen charms of Nicholas Compline, 'A popinjay,' he muttered, 'a stock figure of dubious gallantry.' And he pronounced the noise usually associated with the word 'Pshaw.' He had arrived at this point when he received a visit from William and Lady Hersey.

'We hear you're better,' Hersey said. 'Everybody's being quite frightful downstairs, and William and I thought we'd like a little first-hand information, so we've come to call. They're all saying you think somebody tried to drown you. William's afraid you might suspect him, so I've brought him up to come clean.'

'Do you suspect me?' asked William anxiously. 'Because I didn't, you know.'

'I don't in the least suspect you. Why should I? We've had no difference of opinion.'

'Well, they seem to think I might have mistaken you for Nicholas.'

'Who suspects this?'

'My mama, principally. Because I stuck to the bet, you see. So I thought I'd like to explain that when I got there you were already in the pool.'

'Was Hart there?'

'No. No, he turned up a minute or so later.'

'Did you notice the footprints on the terrace steps?'

'Yes, rather,' said William unexpectedly. 'There were your footsteps. I noticed them because one was bigger than the other.'

'William!' Hersey murmured.

'Well, Hersey, he'd know about that, wouldn't he? And then, you know, Chloris and Jonathan arrived.'

'Perhaps you'd like my alibi, Mr Mandrake,' said Hersey. 'It's not an alibi at all, I'm afraid. I sat in the smoking room and listened to the wireless. The first intimation I had about your adventure was provided by Jonathan, who came in shouting for restoratives. I *could* tell you about the wireless programme, I think.'

Hersey went to the window and looked out. When she spoke again her voice fell oddly on the silence of the room. 'It's snowing like mad,' she said. 'Has it struck either of you that in all probability, whether we like it or not, we are shut up together in this house with no chance of escape?'

'Dr Hart wanted to go after lunch,' William said. 'I heard him say so to Jonathan. But Jonathan said they've had word that you can't get over Cloudyfold, and, anyway, there's a drift inside the front gates. Jonathan seemed pleased about that.'

'He would be.' Hersey turned and rested her hands behind her on the sill. Her figure appeared almost black against the hurried silence of the storm beyond the window. 'Mr Mandrake,' she said, 'you know my cousin quite well, don't you?'

'I've known him for five years.'

'But that doesn't say you know him well,' she said quickly. 'You arrived before all of us. He was up to something, wasn't he? No, that's not a fair question. You needn't answer. I know he was up to something. But, whatever his scheme was, it didn't involve *you* unless – yes, William, that must be it, of course. Mr Mandrake was to be the audience.'

'I don't like performing for Jonathan,' William said. 'I never have.'

'Nor do I, and, what's more, I won't. The Pirate can register fatal woman in heaps all over the house, but she won't get a rise out of me.'

'I suppose I *have* performed, Hersey. Chloris and I broke off our engagement before lunch.'

'I thought something had happened. Why?'

William hunched his shoulders and drove his hands into his trousers pockets. 'She ticked me off about the bet,' he said, 'and I ticked her off about Nicholas, so what have you?'

'Well, William my dear, I'm sorry, but, honestly, *is* she quite your cup of tea?' Hersey confronted Mandrake. 'What do you think?' she demanded abruptly. He was not very much taken aback. For some reason that he had never been able to understand, Mandrake was a man in whom his fellow-creatures confided. He was by no means obviously sympathetic and he seldom asked for confidences, but, perhaps, because of these very omissions, they came his way. Sometimes he wondered if his lameness had something to do with it. People were inclined to regard a lame man as an isolated being, set apart by his disability, as a priest is set apart by his profession. He usually enjoyed hearing strange confessions, and was surprised, therefore, at discovering in himself a reluctance to receive William's explanations of his quarrel with Chloris Wynne. He was profoundly glad that the engagement was broken, and quite determined to make no suggestions about mending it.

'You must remember,' he said, 'that we met for the first time last night.'

Hersey fixed him with a bright blue eye. 'How guarded!' she said. 'William, I believe Mr Mandrake has – '

'Since we are being so frank,' Mandrake interrupted in a great hurry, 'I should like to know whether you believe somebody pushed me into that loathsome pond, and if so, who.'

'Nick says it was Hart,' said Hersey. 'He's gone and thrown his mother into a fever by telling her Hart has tried to drown him. He's behaving like a peevish child.'

'Mightn't you have been blown in?' William asked vaguely.

'Does a gust of wind hit you so hard on the shoulder-blades that you can feel the bruises afterwards? Damn it, I *know*. They're my shoulder-blades.'

'So they are,' Hersey agreed, 'and I for one think it was Dr Hart. After all, we know he was gibbering with rage at Nicholas, and it seems he saw Nicholas go down wearing a cape. I don't suppose he meant to drown him. He simply couldn't resist the temptation. I rather sympathize. Nicholas has bounded like a tennis ball, I consider, from the time he got here.'

'But Hart must have known Nick couldn't swim,' said William. 'He kept explaining that was why he wouldn't go in at the deep end.'

'True. Well, perhaps he meant to drown him.'

'What does Madame Lisse say about it?' Mandrake asked.

'The Pirate?' Hersey helped herself to a cigarette. 'My dear Mr Mandrake, she doesn't say anything about it. She dressed herself up in what I happen to know is a Chanel model at fifty guineas, and came down for lunch looking like an orchid at a church bazaar. Nicholas and William and Dr Hart curvet and goggle whenever they look at her.'

'Well, you know, Hersey, she is rather exciting,' said William.

'Does Jonathan goggle?'

'No,' said Hersey. 'He looks at her as he looks at all the rest of us – speculatively, from behind those damned glasses.'

'I've always wanted,' William observed, 'to see a really good specimen of the *femme fatale*.' Hersey snorted, and then said immediately: 'Oh, I grant you her looks. She's got a marvellous skin, thick and close. You can't beat 'em.'

'And then there's her figure, of course.'

'Yes, William, yes. I suppose you and your girl didn't by any chance quarrel over The Pirate?'

'Oh, no. Chloris isn't jealous. Not of me, at any rate. It is I,' said William, 'who am jealous. Of course you know, don't you, that Chloris broke her engagement to Nick because of Madame Lisse?'

'Is Madame at all in love with your brother, do you suppose?' Mandrake asked.

'I don't know,' said William, 'but I think Chloris is.'

'Rot!' said Hersey. Mandrake suddenly felt abysmally depressed. William walked to the fireplace and stood with his back to them and his head bent. He stirred the fire rather violently with his heel, and through the splutter and rattle of coals they heard his voice.

'. . . I think I'm glad. It's always been the same . . . *You* know, Hersey. Second best. For a little while I diddled myself into thinking I'd cut him out. I thought I'd show them. My mother knew. At first she was furious, but pretty soon she saw it was me that was the mug as usual. My mother thinks it's all as it should be, Nick having strings of lovely ladies falling for him – *le roi s'amuse* sort of idea. By God!' said William with sudden violence, 'it's not much fun having a brother like Nick. By God, I wish Hart *had* shoved him in the pond.'

'William, don't.'

'Why not? Why shouldn't I say for once what I think of my lovely little brother? D'you suppose I'd blame Hart, if he was after Nicholas? Not I. If I'd thought of it myself, be damned if I wouldn't have done it.'

'Stop!' Hersey cried out. 'Stop! Something appalling is happening to all of us. We're saying things we'll regret for the rest of our lives.'

'We're merely speaking the truth.'

'It's the sort that shouldn't be spoken. It's a beastly lopsided exaggerated truth. We're behaving like a collection of neurotic freaks.' Hersey moved to the window. 'Look at the snow,' she said, 'it's heavier than ever. There's a load on the trees, they're beginning to droop their branches. It's creeping up the sides of the house, and up the windowpanes. Soon you'll hardly be able to see out of your window, Mr Mandrake. What are we going to do, shut up in the house together, hating each other? What are we going to do?'

II

At half-past four that afternoon, Nicholas Compline suddenly announced in a high voice that he must get back to his headquarters at Great Chipping. He sought out Jonathan and with small regard for plausibility informed him that he had received an urgent summons by telephone.

'Strange!' said Jonathan, smiling. 'Caper tells me that the telephone is out of commission. The lines are down.'

'The order came through some time ago.'

'I'm afraid you can't go, Nick. There's a six-foot drift in Deep Bottom at the end of the drive, and it'll be worse up on Cloudyfold.'

'I can walk over Cloudyfold to Chipping and get a car there.'

'Twelve miles!'

'I can't help that,' said Nicholas loudly.

'You'll never do it, Nick. It'll be dark in an hour. I can't allow you to try. It's a soft fall. Perhaps tomorrow, if there's a frost during the night – '

'I'm going, Jonathan. You used to have a pair of Canadian snowshoes, usen't you? May I borrow them? Do you know where they are?'

'I gave them away years ago,' said Jonathan blandly.

'Well, I'm going.'

Jonathan hurried up to Mandrake's room with this piece of news. Mandrake had dressed and was sitting by his fire. He still felt extremely shaky and bemused, and stared owlishly at Jonathan, who plunged straight into his story.

'He's quite determined, Aubrey. Perhaps I had better remember that after all I didn't give away the snowshoes. And yet, even with snowshoes, he will certainly lose his way in the dark, or smother in a drift. Isn't it too tiresome?' Jonathan seemed to be more genuinely upset by this turn of events than by anything else that had happened since his party assembled. 'It will ruin everything,' he muttered, and when Mandrake asked him if he meant that the death of Nicholas Compline from exposure would ruin everything, he replied testily: 'No, no, his *departure*. The central figure! The whole action centres round him. I couldn't be more disappointed.'

'Honestly, Jonathan, I begin to think you are suffering from some terrible form of insanity. The *idèe fixe*. People may drown in your ornamental waters or perish in your snowdrifts, and all you can think of is your hell-inspired party.' Jonathan hastened to protest, but in a moment or two he was looking wistfully out of the window and declaring that surely even Nicholas could not be so great a fool as to attempt the walk over Cloudyfold in such a storm. As if in answer to this speech there came a tap on the door, and Nicholas himself walked in. He wore his heavy khaki waterproof and carried his cap. He was rather white about the mouth.

'I'm off, Jonathan,' he said.

'Nick, my dear fellow – I implore – '

'Orders is orders. There's a war on. Will you let me leave my luggage. I'll collect the car as soon as possible.'

'Do I understand,' said Mandrake, 'that you are walking over Cloudyfold?'

'Needs must.'

'Nick, have you considered your mother?'

'I'm not telling my mother I'm going. She's resting. I'll leave a note for her. Goodbye, Mandrake. I'm sorry you had the rôle of my stand-in forced upon you. If it's any satisfaction you may be quite certain that in a very short space of time I shall be just as wet and possibly a good deal colder than you were.'

'If you persist, I shall come as far as Deep Bottom with you,' said Jonathan wretchedly. 'We'll have some of the men with shovels, and so on.'

'Please don't bother, Jonathan. Your men can hardly shovel a path all the way over Cloudyfold.'

'Now listen to me,' said Jonathan. 'I've talked to my bailiff, who came in just now, and he tells me that what you propose is out of the question. I told him you were determined and he's sending two of our men – '

'I'm sorry, Jonathan. I've made up my mind. I'm off. Don't come down. Goodbye.'

But before Nicholas got to the door, it burst open and William, scarlet in the face, strode in and confronted his brother.

'What the hell's this nonsense I hear about your going?' he demanded.

'I don't know what you've heard, but I'm going. I've got orders to report at – '

'Orders my foot! You've got the wind up and you're doing a bolt. You're so damn' frightened, you'd rather die in a snowdrift than face the music here. You're not going.'

'Unusual solicitude!' Nicholas said, and the lines from his nostrils to the corners of his mouth deepened.

'Don't imagine I care what happens to you,' said William, and his voice broke into a higher key. He used the clumsy, vehement gestures of a man who, unaccustomed to violence of speech or action, suddenly finds himself consumed with rage. He presented a painful and embarrassing spectacle. 'You could drown yourself and welcome, if it weren't for Mother. D'you want to kill her? You'll stay here and behave yourself, my bloody little Lothario.'

'Oh, shut up, you fool,' said Nicholas, and made for the door. 'No you don't!' William said, and lurched forward. His brother's elbow caught him a jolt in the chest, and the next moment Nicholas had gone.

'William!' said Jonathan sharply. 'Stay where you are.'

'If anything happens to him, who do you suppose she'll blame for it? For the rest of her life his damned dead sneer will tell her that but for me – *He's not going.*'

'You can't stop him, you know,' said Mandrake.

'*Can't* I! Jonathan, please stand aside.'

'Just a moment, William.' Jonathan's voice had taken an unaccustomed edge. He stood, an unheroic but somehow rather menacing figure, with his plump fingers on the door-knob and his back against the door. 'I cannot have you fighting with your brother up and down my house. He is determined to go and you can't stop him. I am following him to the first drift in the drive. I am quite convinced that he will not get through it, and I do not propose to let him come to any grief. I shall take a couple of men with me. If you can behave yourself you had better accompany us.' Jonathan touched his spectacles delicately with his left hand. 'Depend upon it,' he said, 'your brother will not leave Highfold tonight.'

III

Mandrake's bedroom windows overlooked the last sweep of the drive as it passed the west wing of Highfold and turned into the wide sweep in front of the house. Through the white-leopard mottling on his windowpane he saw Nicholas Compline, head down, trudge heavily through the snow and out of sight. A few moments later, Jonathan and William appeared, followed at some distance by two men carrying long-handled shovels. 'Nicholas must have delayed a little, after he left here,' Mandrake thought. 'Why? To say goodbye to Madame Lisse? Or to Chloris?' And at the thought of a final interview between Nicholas and Chloris Wynne he experienced an unaccustomed and detestable sensation, as if his heart sank with horrid speed into some unfathomable limbo. He looked after the trudging figures until they passed beyond the range of his window, and then suddenly decided that he could no longer endure his own company but would go downstairs in search of Chloris Wynne.

'The difference,' Jonathan observed, 'between a walk in an ordinary storm and a walk in a snowstorm is the difference between unpleasant noise and even more unpleasant silence. One can hear nothing but the squeak of snow under one's feet. I'm glad you decided to come, William.'

'It's not for love of dear little Nicholas, I promise you,' William muttered.

'Well, well, well,' said Jonathan equitably.

They plodded on, walking in Nicholas's steps. Presently Highfold wood enclosed them in a strange twilight where shadow was made negative by reflected whiteness, and where the stems of trees seemed comfortless and forgotten in their naked blackness. Here there was less snow and they mended their pace, following the drive on its twisting course downhill. At first they passed between tall banks and heard the multiple voices of tiny runnels of water, then they came out into open spaces where the snow lay thick over Jonathan's park. It stretched away before their eyes in curves of unbroken pallor and William muttered: 'White, grey, and black. I don't think I could paint it.' When they entered the lower wood, still going downhill, they saw Nicholas, not far ahead, and Jonathan called to him a shrill 'Hallo!' that set up an echo among the frozen trees. Nicholas turned and stood motionless, waiting for them to overtake him. With that air of self-consciousness inseparable from such approaches, they made their way towards him, the two farmhands still some distance behind.

'My dear Nick,' Jonathan panted, 'you should have waited a little. I told you I'd see you as far as the first obstacle. See here, I've brought two of the men. They know more about the state of affairs than I do. My head shepherd and his brother. You remember James and Thomas Bewling?'

'Yes, of course,' said Nicholas. 'Sorry you've both been dragged out on my account.'

'If there is a way through Deep Bottom,' said Jonathan, 'the Bewlings will find it for you. Eh, Thomas?'

The older of the two men touched his cap and moved nearer. 'I do believe, sir,' he said, 'that without us goes at it hammer and tongs with these yurr shovels for an hour or so, they bain't *no* way over Deep Bottom.'

'There, you see, Nick. And in an hour or so it'll be dark.'

'At least I can try,' said Nicholas stiffly.

Jonathan looked helplessly at William, who was watching his brother through half-closed eyes. 'Well,' said Jonathan on a sudden spurt of temper, 'it's beginning to snow quite abominably hard. Shall we go on?'

'Look here,' William said, 'you go back, Jonathan. I don't see why you should be in this. Nor you two Bewlings. Give me your shovel, Thomas.'

'I've said I'll go along, and I'm perfectly ready to do so,' said Nicholas sulkily.

'Oh damn!' said Jonathan. 'Come on.'

As they moved off downhill, the snow began to fall even more heavily.

Deep Bottom was at the foot of a considerable slope beyond the wood, and was really a miniature ravine extending for some two miles inside Jonathan's demesnes. It was crossed by the avenue, which dipped and rose sharply to flatten out on the far side with a level stretch of some two hundred yards ending at the entrance gates. As they approached it, the north wind, from which they had hitherto been protected, drove full in their faces with a flurry of snow. Thomas Bewling began a long roaring explanation: 'She comes down yurr proper blustracious like, sir. What with being druv by the wind and what with being piled up be the natural forces of gravitation, like, she slips and she slides in this yurr bottom till she's so thick as you'd be surprised to see. Look thurr, sir. You'd tell me there was nothing but a little tiddly bit of a slant down'ill, but contrariwise. She's deceptive. She's-a-laying out so smooth and sleek enough to trap you into trying 'er, but she's deep enough and soft enough to smother the lot on us. You won't get round her and you won't make t'other side, Mr Nicholas, as well you ought to know, being bred to these parts.'

Nicholas looked from one to another of the four faces, and without a word turned and walked on. Half a dozen strides brought him up to his knees in snow. He uttered a curious inarticulate cry and plunged forward. The next second he was floundering in a drift, spreadeagled and half-buried.

'And over he goes,' William observed mildly. 'Come on.'

He and the two Bewlings brought Nicholas out of his predicament. He had fallen face first into the drift, and presented a ridiculous figure. His fine moustache was clotted with snow, his cap was askew, and his nose was running.

'Quite the little snowman,' said William. 'Ups-a-daisy.'

Nicholas wiped his face with his gloved hands. It was blotched with cold. His lips seemed stiff, and he rubbed them before he spoke.

'Very well,' Nicholas whispered at last. 'I give up. I'll come back. But, by God, I tell you both I'd have been safer crossing Cloudyfold in the dark than spending another night at Highfold.'

IV

'Francis,' said Madame Lisse, 'we may not be alone together again this evening. I cannot endure this ridiculous and uncomfortable state of affairs any longer. Why do Nicholas and William Compline and the Wynne girl all avoid you? Why, when I speak of Mr Mandrake's accident, do they look at their feet and mumble of other things? Where have they all gone? I have sat by this fire enduring the conversation of Mrs Compline and the compliments of our host until I am ready to scream, but even that ordeal was preferable to suffering your extraordinary gloom. Where is Nicholas Compline?'

Dr Hart stood inside the boudoir door, which he had closed behind him. In his face was reflected the twilight of the snowbound world outside. This strange half-light revealed a slight tic in his upper lip, a tic that suggested an independent life in one of the small muscles of his face. It was as if a moth fluttered under his skin. He raised his hand and pressed a finger on his lip, and over the top of his hand he looked at Madame Lisse.

'Why do you not answer me? Where is Nicholas?'

'Gone.'

'Gone? Where?'

Without shifting his gaze from her face, Hart made a movement with his head as much as to say: 'Out there.' Madame Lisse stirred uneasily. 'Don't look at me like that,' she said. 'Come here, Francis.'

He came and stood before her with his hands clasped over his waistcoat and his head inclined forward attentively. There was nothing in his pose to suggest anger, but she moved back in her chair almost as if she was afraid he would strike her.

'Ever since we came here,' said Hart, 'he has taken pains to insult me by his attentions to you. Your heads together, secret jokes, and then a glance at me to make sure I have not missed it. Last night after dinner he deliberately baited me. Well, now he is gone, and immediately I enter the room you, *you* ask for him.'

'Must there be another of these scenes? Can you not understand that Nicholas is simply a type? It is as natural to him to pay these little attentions as it is for him to draw breath.'

'And as natural for you to receive them? Well, you will not receive them again, perhaps.'

'What do you mean?'

'Look out there. It has been snowing all day. In a little while it will be dark and your friend will be on those hills we crossed yesterday. Do not try to seem unconcerned. Your lips are shaking.'

'Why has he gone?'

'He is afraid.'

'Francis,' cried Madame Lisse, 'what have you done? Have you threatened him? I see that you have, and that they all know. This is why they are avoiding us. You fool, Francis. When these people go away from here they will lunch and dine on this story. You will be a figure of fun, and what woman will choose to have a pantaloon with a violent temper to operate on her face? And my name, *mine*, will be linked with yours. The Amblington woman will see to it that I look as ridiculous as you.'

'Do you love this Compline?'

'I have grown very tired of telling you. I do not.'

'And I am tired of hearing your lies. His behaviour is an admission.'

'What has he done? What are you trying to suggest?'

'He mistook Mandrake for me. He tried to drown me.'

'What nonsense is this! I have heard the account of the accident. Nicholas saw Mr Mandrake through the pavilion window and recognized him. Nicholas told me that he recognized Mandrake and that Mandrake himself realizes that he was recognized.'

'Then you have seen Compline. When did you see him?'

'Soon after the affair at the swimming pool.'

'You did not appear until nearly lunch-time. He came to your room. You had forbidden me, and you received him. Is that true? Is it?'

'Cannot you see – ' Madame Lisse began, but he silenced her with a vehement gesture and, stooping until his face was close to hers, began to arraign her in a sort of falsetto whisper. She leant away from him, pressing her shoulders and head into the back of her chair. The movement suggested distaste rather than fear, and all the time that he was speaking her eyes looked over his shoulder from the door to the windows. Once she raised her hand as if to silence him, but he seized her wrist and held it, and she said nothing.

'. . . you said I should see for myself, and, *Lieber Gott*, have I not seen? I have seen enough, and I tell you this. He was wise to go when he did. Another night and day of his insolence would have broken my endurance. It is well for him that he has gone.'

He was staring into her face and saw her eyes widen. He still had her by the wrist, but with her free hand she pointed to the window. He turned and looked out.

He was in time to see Jonathan Royal and William Compline trudge past laboriously in the snow. And three yards behind them, sullen and bedraggled, trailed Nicholas Compline.

V

Hersey Amblington, Mrs Compline, Chloris Wynne, and Aubrey Mandrake were in the library. They knew that Dr Hart and Madame Lisse were in the boudoir, separated from them by the small smoking room. They knew, too, that Jonathan and William had gone with Nicholas on the first stage of his preposterous journey. Hersey was anxious to have a private talk with Sandra Compline, Mandrake was anxious to have a private talk with Chloris Wynne; but neither

Mandrake nor Hersey could summon up the initiative to make a move. A pall of inertia hung over them all, and they spoke, with an embarrassing lack of conviction, about Nicholas's summons to his headquarters in Great Chipping. Mrs Compline was in obvious distress, and Hersey kept assuring her that if the road was unsafe Jonathan would bring Nicholas back. 'Jonathan shouldn't have let him go, Hersey. It was very naughty of him. I'm extremely displeased with William for letting Nicholas go. He should never have allowed it.'

'William did his best to dissuade him,' said Mandrake dryly.

'He should have come and told me, Mr Mandrake. He should have used his authority. He is the elder of my sons.' She turned to Hersey. 'It's always been the same. I've always said that Nicholas should have been the elder.'

'I don't agree,' said Chloris quickly.

'No,' Mrs Compline said, 'I did not suppose you would,' and Mandrake, who had thought that Mrs Compline's face could express nothing but its own distortion, felt a thrill of alarm when he saw her look at Chloris.

'I speak without prejudice,' said Chloris, and two spots of colour started up in her cheeks. 'William and I have broken off our engagement.'

For a moment there was silence, and Mandrake saw that Mrs Compline had forgotten his existence. She continued to stare at Chloris, and a shadow of a smile, painful and acrid, tugged at her distorted mouth. 'I am afraid you are too late,' she said.

'I don't understand.'

'My son Nicholas – '

'This has nothing whatever to do with Nicholas.'

'Hersey,' Mrs Compline said, 'I am terribly worried about Nicholas. Surely Jonathan will bring him back. How long have they been gone?'

'*It has nothing whatever to do with Nicholas,*' Chloris said loudly.

Mrs Compline stood up. 'Hersey, I simply cannot sit here any longer. I'm going to see if they're coming.'

'You can't, Sandra. It's snowing harder than ever. There's no need to worry, they're all together.'

'I'm going out on the drive. I haven't stirred from the house all day. I'm stifled.'

Hersey threw up her hands and said: 'All right. I'll come with you. I'll get our coats. Wait for me, darling.'

'I'll wait in the hall. Thank you, Hersey.'

When they had gone, Mandrake said to Chloris: 'For God's sake, let's go next door and listen to the news. After this party, the war will come as a mild and pleasurable change.'

They moved into the smoking room. Mrs Compline crossed the hall and entered the drawing room, where she stood peering through the windows for her son Nicholas. Hersey Amblington went upstairs. First she got her own raincoat, and then she went to Mrs Compline's room to fetch hers. She opened the wardrobe doors and stretched out her hand to a heavy tweed coat. For a moment she stood stock-still, her fingers touching the shoulders of the coat.

It was soaking wet.

And through her head ran the echo of Sandra Compline's voice: 'I haven't stirred from the house all day.'

VI

In the days that followed that weekend Mandrake was to trace interminably the sequence of events that in retrospect seemed to point so unmistakably towards the terrible conclusion. He was to decide that not the least extraordinary of these events had been his own attitude towards Chloris Wynne. Chloris was not Mandrake's type. If, in the midst of threats, mysteries, and mounting terrors, he had to embark upon some form of dalliance, it should surely have been with Madame Lisse. Madame was the sort of woman to whom Aubrey Mandrake almost automatically paid attention. She was dark, sophisticated, and – his own expression – immeasurably *soignée*. She was exactly Aubrey Mandrake's cup of tea. Chloris was not. Aubrey Mandrake was invariably bored by pert blondes. But – and here lay the reason for his curious behaviour – Stanley Footling adored them. At the sight of Chloris's shining, honey-coloured loops of hair and impertinent blue eyes, the old Footling was roused in Mandrake. Bloomsbury died in him and Dulwich stirred ingenuously. He was only too well aware that in himself was being enacted a threadbare theme, a kind of burlesque, hopelessly out of date, on Jekyll and

Hyde. It had happened before but never with such violence, and he told himself that there must be something extra special in Chloris so to rouse the offending Footling that Mandrake scarcely resented the experience.

He followed her into the smoking room and tuned in the wireless to the war news, which in those almost forgotten days largely consisted of a series of French assurances that there was nothing to report. Chloris and Mandrake listened for a little while, and then he switched off the radio, leant forward and kissed her.

'Ah!' said Chloris. 'The indoor sport idea, I see.'

'Are you in love with Nicholas Compline?'

'I might say: "What the hell's that got to do with you?" '

'Abstract curiosity.'

'With rather un-abstract accompaniments.'

'When I first saw you I thought you were a little nitwit.'

Chloris knelt on the hearthrug and poked the fire. 'So I am,' she said, 'when it comes to your sort of language. I'm quite smartish, but I'm not at all clever. I put up a bluff, but you'd despise me no end if you knew me better.'

She smiled at him. He felt his mouth go dry, and with a sensation of blank panic he heard his own voice, distorted by embarrassment, utter the terrible phrase.

'My real name,' said Mandrake, 'is Stanley Footling.'

'Oh, my dear, I'm so sorry,' said Chloris. He knew that for a moment, when she recovered from her astonishment, she had nearly laughed.

'Stanley Footling,' he repeated, separating the detestable syllables as if each was an offence against decency.

'Sickening for you. But, after all, you've changed it, haven't you?'

'I've never told any one else. In a squalid sort of way it's a compliment.'

'Thank you. But lots of people must know, all the same.'

'No. All my friendships occurred after I changed it. I got a hideous fright last night at dinner.'

Chloris looked up quickly. 'Why, I remember! I noticed. You went all sort of haywire for a moment. It was something Nicholas said, something about – '

'My having given up footling.'

'Oh Lord!' said Chloris.

'Go on – laugh. It's screamingly funny, isn't it?'

'Well it *is* rather funny,' Chloris agreed. 'But it's easily seen that you don't get much of a laugh out of it. I can't quite understand why. There are plenty of names just as funny as Footling.'

'I'll tell you why. I can't brazen it out because it's got no background. If we were the Footlings of Fifeshire, or even the Footlings of Furniture Polish, I might stomach it. I'm a miserable snob. Even as I speak to you I'm horrified to hear how I give myself away by the very content of what I'm saying. I'm committing the only really unforgivable offence. I'm being embarrassing.'

'It seems to me you've merely gone Edwardian. You're all out of focus. You say you're a snob. All right. So are we all in our degree, they say.'

'But don't you see it's the *degree* I'm so ashamed of. Intellectual snob I may be; but I don't care if I am. But to develop a really bad social inferiority complex – it's so degrading.'

'It seems a bit silly, certainly. And, anyway, I don't see, accepting your snobbery, what you've got to worry about. If it's smartness you're after, isn't it smart to be obscure nowadays? Look at the prize-fighters. Everybody's bosoms with them.'

'That's from *your* point of view. *De haut en bas.* I want to be the *haut*, not the *bas*,' Mandrake mumbled.

'Well, intellectually you are.' Chloris shifted her position and faced him squarely, looking up, her pale hair taking a richness from the fire, 'I say,' she said, 'Mr Royal knows all about it, doesn't he? About your name?'

'No. *Why?*'

'Well, I thought last night . . . I mean after Nicholas dropped that brick, I sort of felt there was something funny and I noticed that he and Lady Hersey and Mr Royal looked at each other.'

'By God, he put them up to it! I wondered at the time. By God, if he did that, I'll pay him for it!'

'For the love of Heaven, why did I go and say that! I thought you and I were going to remain moderately normal. Nobody else is. Do snap out of being all Freudian over Footling. Who cares if you're called Footling? And, anyway, I must say I think "Aubrey Mandrake" is a bit thick. Let's talk about something else.'

The invitation was not immediately accepted, and in the silence that followed they heard Hersey Amblington come downstairs into the hall and call Mrs Compline:

'Sandra! Where are you? Sandra!' They heard an answering voice, and in a moment or two the front doors slammed.

Mandrake limped about the room inwardly cursing Jonathan Royal, Chloris Wynne, and himself. Most of all, himself. Why had he given himself away to this girl who did not even trouble to simulate sympathy, who did not find even so much as a pleasing tang of irony in his absurd story, who felt merely a vague and passing interest, a faint insensitive amusement? He realized abruptly that it was because she made so little of it that he wanted to tell her. An attitude of sympathetic understanding would have aggravated his own morbid speculations. She had made little of his ridiculous obsession, and for the first time in his life, quite suddenly, he saw it was a needless emotional extravaganza.

'You're perfectly right, of course,' he said. 'Let's talk about something else.'

'You needn't think I'll shrink from you on account of your name and I won't tell any one else.'

'Not even Nicholas Compline?'

'Certainly not Nicholas Compline. At the moment I never want to see a Compline again. You needn't think you're the only one to feel sick at yourself. What about me and the Complines? Getting engaged to William on the rebound from Nicholas.'

'And continuing to fall for Nicholas's line of stuff?'

'Yes. All right! I'll admit it. Up to an hour ago I knew Nicholas was faithless, horrid-idle, a philanderer, a he-flirt – all those things, and not many brains into the bargain. But, as you say, I fell for his line of stuff. Why? I don't know. Haven't you ever fallen for a little bit of stuff? Of course you have. But when *we* do it, you hold up your hands and marvel.'

Through Mandrake's mind floated the thought that not so long ago he had considered himself in much the same light as regards Chloris. He began to feel ashamed of himself.

'What *does* attract one to somebody like Nicholas?' Chloris continued. 'I don't know. He's got "It", as they say. Something in his physical make-up. And yet I've often gone all prickly and irritated over his physical tricks. He does silly things with his hands and he's got a tiresome laugh. His idea of what's funny is too drearily all on one subject. He's a bit of a cat, too, and bone from the eyes up if you try to talk about anything that's not quite in his language. And yet one more or less went through one's paces for him; played up to his barn door antics. Why?'

'Until an hour ago, you said.'

'Yes. I met him in the hall when he was going. He was in a blue funk. That tore it. I suppose the barn-door hero loses his grip when he loses his nerve. Anyway, I'm cured of Nicholas.'

'Good.'

'You know, I'm quite certain that Dr Hart *did* think you were Nicholas and shoved you in the pond. I think Nicholas was right about that. We ought to be making no end of a hullabaloo, staying in the same house with a would-be murderer, and all we do is let down our back hair and talk about our own complexes. I suppose it'll be like that in the air raids.'

'Nicholas was making a hullabaloo, anyway.'

'Yes. I'm afraid he's a complete coward. If he'd brazened it out and stayed, I dare say I shouldn't have been cured, but he scuttled away and that wrecked it. I wonder if The Lisse feels the same.'

'Poor Nicholas,' said Mandrake. 'But I'm glad he didn't stay.'

'What's that?'

Chloris scrambled to her feet. She and Mandrake stood stock-still gaping at each other. The hall was noisy with voices, Mrs Compline scolding, Jonathan explaining, Hersey Amblington asking questions. It went on for some seconds, and then Mandrake limped to the door and threw it open.

Outside in the hall was a group of five – Jonathan, Mrs Compline, Hersey, William, and, standing apart, bedraggled, patched with snow, white-faced and furtive, Nicholas. Mandrake turned and stared at Chloris.

'So now, what?' he asked.

CHAPTER 7

Booby Trap

With the return of Nicholas the house-party entered upon a new phase. From then onwards little attempt was made by anybody to pretend there was nothing wrong with Jonathan Royal's weekend. Jonathan himself, after a half-hearted effort to treat the episode as a mere inconvenient delay, fluttered his hands, surveyed the apprehensive faces of his guests, and watched them break away into small groups. Nicholas muttered something about a bath and change, and followed his mother upstairs. Dr Hart and Madame Lisse, who had come out of the boudoir on the arrival of the outdoors party, returned to it. Mandrake and Chloris returned to the smoking room. The others trailed upstairs to change.

Darkness came with no abatement of the storm. A belated pilot of the Coastal Command, who had flown off his map, battled over Cloudyfold through the driving misery of snow, and for a fraction of time passed through the smoke from Jonathan's chimneys. Peering down, he discerned the vague shapes of roofs, and pictured the warmth and joviality of some cheerful weekend party. Just about cocktail time, he thought, and was gone over the rim of Cloudyfold.

It was cocktail time down in Highfold. Jonathan ordered the drinks to be served in the drawing room. Mandrake joined him there. He was filled with a strange lassitude, the carryover, he supposed, from half-drowning. His thoughts clouded and cleared alternately. He was glad of the cocktail Jonathan brought him.

'After all,' Jonathan said as they waited, 'we've got to meet at dinner, so we may as well assemble here. What am I to do with them, Aubrey?'

'If you can prevent them from gettting at each other's throats, you will have worked wonders. Jonathan, I insist on your telling me. Who do you suppose tried to drown me, and who do you suppose they thought I was?'

'It's an interesting point. I must confess, Aubrey, that I am now persuaded that an attack *was* made.'

'Thank you. If you had felt – '

'I know, I know. I agree that you could not have been mistaken. I also agree that whoever made the attempt believed it to be made upon someone other than yourself. Now let us, perfectly cold-bloodedly, examine the possibilities. You wore a cloak, and for this reason might have been taken for Nicholas, for Hart, or for myself. If you were mistaken for Nicholas then we must suppose that the assailant was Hart, who resents his attentions to Madame Lisse, and who had threatened him; or William, who resents his attentions to Miss Chloris; or possibly Miss Chloris herself, whose feelings for Nicholas – '

'Don't be preposterous!'

'Eh? Ah, well, I don't press it. If you were mistaken for Hart, then, as far as motive goes, the assailant might have been Nick himself – '

'Nicholas knew Hart was indoors. He saw him looking out of the bedroom window.'

'He might have supposed Hart had hurried down by the shorter route.'

'But I swear Nicholas recognized me through the pavilion window, and, over and above all that, he knew I had the cloak.'

'I agree that Nicholas is unlikely. I am examining motive only. Who else had motive, supposing you were thought to be Hart?'

'Madame Lisse?'

'There we cannot tell. What are their relations? Could Madame have risen from her bed and picked her way down to the pavilion without being seen by anybody? And why, after all should she do so? She, at least, could not have known any one was going down, singly or otherwise.'

'She might have seen me from her window.'

'In which case she would have realized that you were yourself, and not Hart. No, I think we may dismiss Madame as a suspect. There remains Sandra Compline.'

'Good God, why Mrs Compline?'

Jonathan blinked and uttered an apologetic titter. 'A little point which I could not expect you to appreciate. My housekeeper, the excellent Pouting, is a sworn crony of Sandra's maid. It seems that when Hart first arrived in our part of the world, this maid, who was with Sandra at the time of the catastrophe in Vienna, thought she recognized him. She said nothing to her mistress, but she confided her news to Pouting. And I, in my turn, did a little gleaning. The Viennese surgeon was a Doktor Franz Hartz, I learnt, and I knew that Hart, when he changed his nationality, also changed his name. The temptation was too great for me, Aubrey. I brought them together.'

'It was a poisonous thing to do.'

'You think so? Perhaps you are right. I am quite ashamed of myself,' said Jonathan, touching his spectacles.

'There's one thing I'd rather like to hear from you, Jonathan. How did you find out my name was Stanley Footling?' Mandrake watched his host and saw him give a little inward start.

'My dear fellow!' Jonathan murmured.

'It's only a point of curiosity. I should be amused to know.'

A pink flush mounted from Jonathan's chin up into his bald pate. 'I really forget. It was so long ago. In the early days of our delightful association. Somebody connected with your theatre. I quite forget.'

'Ah yes,' said Mandrake. 'And is Lady Hersey in the joke?'

'No. No, I assure you. Word of honour.'

'What about Nicholas Compline? He knows. You've told him.'

'Well, I – I – really, Aubrey – I – '

'You put him up to saying what he did at dinner.'

'But without any intention of hurting you, Aubrey. I had no idea your secret – '

'You asked me the other night what sort of man I considered you to be. I didn't know then, and I'm damned if I know now.'

The light flickered on Jonathan's spectacles. 'In a sense,' he said, 'you might call me an unqualified practitioner.'

'Of what?'

'The fashionable pursuit, my dear Aubrey. Psychology.'

II

Madame Lisse dressed early that evening, and got rid of the maid Mrs Pouting had sent to help her. She sat by her fire listening intently. She heard a delicate sound as if someone tapped with his fingernails at the door. She turned her head quickly but did not rise. The door opened and Nicholas Compline came in.

'Nicholas! Are you certain – '

'Quite certain. He's in his bath. I listened outside the door.'

He stooped swiftly and kissed her. 'I had to see you,' he said.

'What has happened? He's furious.'

'You needn't tell me that. I suppose you realize that he tried to kill me this morning. They won't listen to me. Elise, I can't put up with this any longer. Why can't we – '

'You know very well. I cannot risk it. A scandal would ruin me. He would make scenes. God knows what he would not do. You should have gone away.'

'Damn it, I did my best! Did you want me to do myself in? I tell you I *couldn't* get away. I assure you I don't enjoy the prospect of another attack.'

'Quiet! Are you mad, to make such a noise? What is the matter with you? You've had too much to drink.'

'I came in half-dead with cold,' he said. 'Do you suppose he'll have another go at me? Pleasant, isn't it, waiting?'

She looked at him attentively.

'I cannot believe he would go to such lengths, and yet one can find no other explanation. You must be careful, Nicholas. Devote yourself again to the Wynne child. You deliberately baited Francis by your behaviour. I warned you. You should have refused the invitation; it was madness to come here.'

'I wanted to see you. God, Elise, you seem to forget that I love you.'

'I do not forget. But we must be careful.'

'Careful! Listen here. For the last time, will you make a clean break? We could meet in London. You could write and – '

'I have told you, Nicholas. It is impossible. How could I continue my work? And when this war ends, my friend, what then? How should we live?'

'I could find something – ' He broke off and looked fixedly at her. 'You're very mercenary, Elise, aren't you?'

'All my life I have had to fight. I have known the sort of poverty that you have never dreamed of. I will not endure such poverty again, no, nor anything approaching it. Why can you not be content? I love you. I give you a great deal, do I not?'

He stooped down to her, and behind them on the far wall their fire-shadows joined and moved only with the movement of the fire itself. From this embrace Nicholas was the first to draw back. His shadow started from hers, and in the silence of the room his whisper sounded vehemently:

'*What's that?*'

'*What do you mean?*'

'*Ssh!*'

He stepped back quickly towards a screen near her bed. It was the serio-comic movement of a surprised lover in some Restoration play, and it made a foolish figure of Nicholas. Madame Lisse looked at him, and in response to his gesture moved to the door, where she stood listening, her eyes on Nicholas. After a moment she motioned him to stand farther aside, and with a shamefaced look he slipped behind the screen. The door was opened and closed again, and her voice recalled him.

'There is nobody.'

'I swear I heard somebody at that door,' Nicholas whispered.

'There is nobody there. You had better go.'

He crossed to the door and paused, staring at her, half hang-dog, half-glowering. Nicholas did not cut a brave figure at that moment, but Madame Lisse joined her hands behind his neck and drew his face down to hers. There was an urgency, a certain rich possessiveness in her gesture.

'Be careful,' she whispered. 'Do go, now.'

'At least *you* believe he means trouble. *You* know it's he that's at the back of this.'

'Yes.'

'I feel as if he's behind every damn door in the place. It's a filthy feeling.'

'You must go.'

He looked full in her face, and a moment later slipped through the door and was gone.

Madame Lisse seemed to hesitate for a moment and then she too went to the door. She opened it a very little and looked through the crack after Nicholas. Suddenly she flung the door wide open and screamed. Immediately afterwards came the sound of a thud, a thud so heavy that she felt its vibration and heard a little glass tree on her mantlepiece set up a faint tinkling. And a second later she heard the shocking sound of a man screaming. It was Nicholas.

III

Mandrake and Jonathan heard the thud. The drawing room chandelier set up a little chime, and immediately afterwards, muffled and far away, came the sound of a falsetto scream. With no more preface than a startled exclamation, Jonathan ran from the room. Mandrake, swinging his heavy boot, followed at a painful shamble. As he toiled up the stairs, the quick thump of his heart reminded him of his nocturnal prowl. He reached the guest-wing passage and saw, halfway down it, the assembled house-party, some in dressing-gowns, some in evening clothes. They were gathered in Nicholas's doorway; William, Chloris, Dr Hart, Madame Lisse, and Hersey Amblington. From inside the room came the sound of Mrs Compline's voice, agitated and emphatic, punctuated by little ejaculations from Jonathan, and violent interjections from Nicholas himself. As he came to the doorway, Mandrake was dimly aware of some difference in the appearance of the passage. Without pausing to analyse this sensation he joined the group in the doorway. William, who was scarlet in the face, grabbed his arm. 'By gum!' said William, 'it's true after all. Somebody's after Nick, and, by gum, they've nearly got him.'

'Bill, *don't!*' cried Chloris, and Hersey said fiercely: 'Shut up, William.'

'No, but isn't it extraordinary, Mandrake? He didn't want to come back, you know. He said . . .'

'What's happened?'

'Look.'

William stepped aside and Mandrake saw into the room.

Nicholas sat in an armchair nursing his left arm. He was deadly pale, and kept turning his head to look first at Jonathan and then at his mother who knelt beside him. Between this group and the door, lying on its back on the carpet and leering blandly at the ceiling, was an obese brass figure, and when Mandrake saw it he knew what it was he had missed from the passage. It was the Buddha that had watched him from its niche when he stole downstairs in the night.

' . . . it all seemed to happen at once,' Nicholas was saying shakily. 'I went to push open the door – it wasn't quite shut – and it felt as if someone were resisting me on the other side. I gave it a harder shove and it opened so quickly that I sort of jumped back. I suppose that saved me, because at the same time I felt a hell of a great thud on my arm, and Elise screamed.'

From down the passage, Madame Lisse said: 'I saw something fall from the door and I screamed out to him.'

'A booby trap,' said William. 'It was a booby trap, Mandrake. Balanced on the top of the door. We used to do it with buckets of water when we were kids. It *would* have killed him, you know. Only, of course, its dead weight dragged on the door, and when it overbalanced the door shot open. That's what made him jump back.'

'His arm's broken,' said Mrs Compline. 'Darling, your arm's broken.'

'I don't think so. It was a glancing blow. It's damn' sore, but, by God, it might have been my head. Well, Jonathan, what have you to say? Was I right to try and clear out?' Nicholas raised his uninjured arm and pointed to the crowded doorway. 'One of them's saying to himself: "Third time lucky." Do you realize that, Jonathan?'

Jonathan said something that sounded like 'God forbid.' Mrs Compline began again:

'Let me look at your arm, darling. Nicky, my dear, let me see it.'

'I can't move it. Look out, Mother, that hurts.'

'Perhaps you would like me . . . ' Dr Hart came through the door and advanced upon Nicholas.

'No, thank you, Hart,' said Nicholas. 'You've done enough. Keep off.'

Dr Hart stopped short, and then, as though growing slowly conscious of the silence that had fallen upon his fellow-guests, he turned and looked from one face to another. When he spoke it was so softly that only a certain increase in foreign inflexions in the level stressing of his words, gave any hint of his agitaton.

'This has become too much,' he said. 'Is it not enough that I should be insulted, that Mr Compline should insult me, I say, from the time that I arrived in this house? Is that not enough to bear without this last, this fantastic accusation? I know well what you have been saying against me. You have whispered among yourselves that it was I who attacked Mr Mandrake thinking he was Compline, I who goaded by open enmity as well as by secret antagonism, have plotted to injure, to murder Compline. I tell you now that I am not guilty of these outrages. If, as Compline suggests, anything further is attempted against him, it will not be by my agency. That I am his enemy I do not deny, but I tell him now that somewhere amongst us he has another and a more deadly enemy. Let him remember this.' He glanced at Nicholas's injured arm. Nicholas made a quick movement. 'I do not think your arm is fractured,' said Dr Hart. 'You had better let someone look at it. If the skin is broken it will need a dressing, and perhaps a sling. Mrs Compline will be able to attend to it, I think.' He walked out of the room.

Mrs Compline drew back the sleeve of Nicholas's dressing-gown. His forearm was swollen and discoloured. A sort of blind gash ran laterally across its upper surface. He turned his hand from side to side, wincing at the pain. 'Well,' said William, 'it seems he's right about that, Nick. It can't be broken.'

'It's bloody sore, Bill,' said Nicholas, and Mandrake was astounded to see an almost friendly glance pass between these extraordinary brothers.

William came forward and stooped down, looking at the arm. 'We could do with a first-aid kit,' he said, and Jonathan bustled away muttering that Mrs Pouting was fully equipped.

'It's Hart all right,' said William. He turned to contemplate Madame Lisse, who still waited with Chloris and Mandrake in the passage. 'Yes,' William repeated with an air of thoughtfulness, 'it's Hart. I think he's probably mad, you know.'

'William,' said his mother, 'what are you saying? You have been keeping something from me, both of you. *What do you know about this man?*'

'It doesn't matter, Mother,' said Nicholas impatiently.

'It does matter. I *will* know. What have you found out about him?'

'Sandra,' cried Hersey Amblington, 'don't. It's not that. Don't, Sandra.'

'Nicky, my dear! You know! You've guessed.' Mrs Compline's eyes seemed to Mandrake to be living fires in her dead face. She, like Nicholas, looked at Madame Lisse. 'I *see,*' she said. 'You know too. You've told my son. Then it is true.'

'I don't know what you're talking about, Mother,' said Nicholas querulously.

'Nor I,' said Madame Lisse, and her voice was shriller than Mandrake could have imagined it. 'This is ridiculous. I have said nothing.'

'Hersey,' said Mrs Compline, 'do you see what has happened?' She put her arms round Nicholas's neck and her hand, with agonized possessiveness, caressed his shoulder. 'Nicky has found out and threatened to expose him. He has tried to kill Nicholas.'

'Look here,' William demanded, 'what *is* all this?'

'It's a complete and miserable muddle,' said Hersey sharply, 'and it's certainly not for publication. Mr Mandrake, do you mind . . . ?'

Mandrake muttered: 'Of course,' turned away, and shut the door, leaving himself, Chloris Wynne, and Madame Lisse alone in the passage.

'This woman is evidently insane,' said Madame Lisse. 'What mystery is this she is making? What am I supposed to have told Nicholas Compline?'

Mandrake, conscious of a violent and illogical distaste for Madame Lisse, said loudly: 'Mrs Compline thinks you have told her son that Dr Hart is the surgeon who operated on her face.'

He heard Chloris catch her breath, and whisper: 'No, no, it's impossible. It's too fantastic.' He heard his own voice trying to explain that Jonathan was responsible. He was conscious in himself of a sort of affinity with Mrs Compline, an affinity born of disfigurement. He wanted to explain to Chloris that there was nothing in the world as bad as a hideous deformity. Through this confusion of emotions and thought he was aware of Madame Lisse watching him very closely, of the closed door at his back, of the murmur of Mrs Compline's voice beyond it in Nicholas's room where, Mandrake supposed, her sons listened to the story of Dr Franz Hartz of Vienna. The truth is, Mandrake was suffering from a crisis of nerves. His experience of the morning, his confession to Chloris, the sense of impending disaster that like some grotesque in a dream, half-comic, half-menacing, seemed to advance upon Nicholas; all these circumstances had scraped at his nerves and wrought upon his imagination. When Jonathan came hurrying along the passage with a first-aid outfit in his hands, Mandrake saw him as a shifty fellow, as cold-blooded as a carp. When Madame Lisse began to protest that she knew nothing of Dr Hart's past, that Mrs Compline was insane, that she herself could endure no longer to be shut up at Highfold, Mandrake was conscious only of a sort of wonder that this cool woman should suddenly become agitated. He felt Chloris take him by the elbow and heard her say: 'Let's go downstairs.' He was steadied by her touch, and eager to obey it. Before they moved away, the door opened and William came stumbling out, followed by Jonathan.

'Wait a bit, Bill,' Jonathan cried. *'Wait* a bit.'

'The bloody swine,' William said. 'Oh, God, the bloody swine.' He went blindly past them and they heard him run downstairs. Jonathan remained in the doorway. Beyond him, Mandrake saw Hersey Amblington with her arms about Mrs Compline, who was sobbing. Nicholas, very pale, stood, looking on.

'It's *most* unfortunate,' Jonathan said. He shut the door delicately. 'Poor Sandra has convinced William that there has been a conspiracy against her. That Hart has made a story of the catastrophe for Madame Lisse, that – oh, you're there, Madame. Forgive me; I hadn't noticed. It's all *too* distressing, Aubrey. Now William's in a frightful tantrum and won't listen to reason. Nicholas assures us he knew nothing of the past but he might as well speak to the wind. We're in the very devil of a mess. It's snowing harder than ever, and what in heaven's name am I to do?'

A loud and ominous booming sound welled up through the house. Caper, finding no one to whom he could announce dinner, had fallen upon an enormous gong and beaten it. Jonathan uttered a mad little giggle.

'Well,' he said, 'shall we dine?'

IV

The memory of that night's dinner party was to be a strange one for Mandrake. It was to have the intermittent vividness and the unreality of a dream. Certain incidents he would never forget, others were lost the next day. At times his faculty of observation seemed abnormally acute and he observed exactly, inflexions of voices, precise choice of words, details of posture. At other times he was lost in a sensation of anxiety, an intolerable anticipation of calamity, and at these moments he was blind and deaf to his surroundings.

Only six of the party appeared for dinner. Madame Lisse, Mrs Compline, and Dr Hart had all excused themselves. Dr Hart was understood to be in the boudoir where he had gone after his speech in his own defence, and where, apparently at Jonathan's suggestion, he was to remain during his waking hours, for the rest of his stay at Highfold. Mandrake wondered when Jonathan had told the servants. The party at dinner was therefore composed of the less antagonistic elements. Even William's and Chloris's broken engagement seemed a minor dissonance, quite overshadowed by the growing uneasiness of the guests. Nicholas, Mandrake decided, was now in a state of barely suppressed nerves. His injured arm was not in a sling but evidently gave him a good deal of pain, and he made a clumsy business of cutting up his food, finally allowing Hersey Amblington to help him. He had come down with Hersey, and something in their manner suggested that this arrangement was not accidental. 'And really,' Mandrake thought, 'it would be better not to leave Nicholas alone. Nothing can happen to him if somebody is always at his side.' Mandrake was now positive that it was Hart who had made the attacks upon Nicholas and himself, and he found that the others shared this view and discussed it openly. His clearest recollection of the dinner party was to be of a moment when William, who had been silent until now, leant forward, his hands gripping the edge of the table, and said: 'What's the law about attempted murder?' Jonathan glanced nervously at the servants, and Mandrake saw Hersey Amblington nudge William. 'Oh, damn,' William muttered, and was silent again. As soon as they were alone, he returned to the attack. He was extraordinarily inarticulate and blundered about from one accusation to another, returning always to the ruin of his mother's beauty. 'The man who did that would do anything,' seemed to be the burden of his song. 'The Œdipus complex with a vengeance,' thought Mandrake, but he was still too bemused and shaken to crystallize his attention upon William, and listened through a haze of weary lassitude. It was useless for Nicholas to say that he had never heard the name of his mother's plastic surgeon. 'Hart must have thought you knew,' William said. 'He thought that Mother had told you.'

'Rot, Bill,' said Nicholas. 'You're barking up the wrong tree. *It's because of Elise Lisse.* The fellow's off his head with jealousy.'

'I'm older than you,' William roared out with startling irrelevancy. 'I remember what she was like. She was beautiful. I remember the day she came back. We went to the station to meet her. She had a veil on, a thick veil. And when I kissed her she didn't lift it up and I felt her face through the veil and it was stiff.'

'Don't, Bill,' Hersey said.

'You heard what she said – what Mother herself said. She said up there in your room: "Nicky's found out. He's afraid Nicky will expose him." God, *I'll* expose him. He's gone to earth, has he! I'm damn' well going to lug him out and – '

'William!' Jonathan's voice exploded sharply, and Mandrake roused himself to listen. 'William, you will be good enough to pull yourself together. Whether you choose to do your mother an appalling wrong by reviving for public discussion a tragedy that is twenty years old, is your affair. I do not attempt to advise you. But this is my house and I am very much your senior. I must ask you to attend to me.'

He paused, but William said nothing, and after a moment Jonathan cleared his throat and touched his spectacles. Mandrake thought dimly: 'Good heavens, he's going to make another of his speeches.'

'Until this evening,' Jonathan said, 'I refused to believe that among my guests there could be one – ah – individual who had planned, who still plans, a murderous assault upon a fellow-guest. I argued that the castastrophe at the swimming pool was the result of a mischievous, rather than a malicious attack. I even imagined that it was possible poor Aubrey had been mistaken for myself.' Here Jonathan blinked behind his spectacles and the trace of a smirk appeared on his lips. He smoothed it away with his plump hand and went on very gravely. "This second attempt upon Nicholas has convinced me. If that idol, which I may say I have always rather disliked, had fallen, as without a shadow of doubt it was intended to fall, upon his head, it would have killed him. There is no doubt at all, my dear Nick, it would have killed you.'

'Thank you, Jonathan,' said Nicholas with a kind of sneer, 'I think I realize that.'

'Well, now, you know,' Jonathan continued, 'this sort of thing is pretty bad. It's preposterous. It's like some damn' pinchbeck storybook.'

'Jo,' Hersey Amblington interjected suddenly, 'you really can't keep us all waiting while you grizzle about the aesthetic poverty of your own show. We're all agreed it's a rotten show, but at least it has the makings of a tragedy. What are you getting at? Do you think Dr Hart's out for Nick's blood?'

'I am forced to come to that conclusion,' said Jonathan primly. 'Who else are we to suspect? Not one of ourselves, surely. I am not breaking confidence, I hope, Nick, when I say that Hart has threatened you, and threatened you repeatedly.'

'We've heard all about that,' Hersey grunted.

'Ah – yes. So I supposed. Well, now, I am a devotee of crime fiction. I have even dabbled in quite solemn works on the detection of crime. I don't pretend to the smallest degree of proficiency, but I *have* ventured to carry out a little investigation. Nicholas tells me that ten minutes before he so nearly became the victim of that atrocious booby trap, he left his room and – ah – visited that of Madame Lisse.'

'Oh Lord!' Hersey muttered, and Mandrake thought he heard Chloris utter a small contemptuous sound.

'This was, of course, a reckless and foolish proceeding,' said Jonathan. 'However, it has this merit – it frees Madame Lisse from any imputation of guilt. Because Nick, when he left his room, opened and shut the door with impunity, and was talking to Madame Lisse until he returned to sustain the injury to his arm. Nick tells me he heard the clock on the landing strike the half-hour as he walked down the passage to Madame's room. I had glanced at the drawing-room clock not more than a minute before the crash, and it was twenty to eight. The two clocks are exactly synchronized. As the trap could not have been set until after Nick left his room, that gives us ten minutes for our field of inquiry. Now, at the time of the accident, Aubrey and I were both in the drawing-room. I found him there when I came down, and actually heard him go downstairs some little time before that. I am therefore able to provide Aubrey with an alibi, and I hope he will vouch for me. Now, can any of you do as much for each other?'

'I can for Sandra,' said Hersey, 'and I imagine she can for me. I was in her room talking to her when Nick yelled, and I'm sure I'd been there longer than ten minutes. I remember quite well that when I passed Nick's door it was half open and the light on. I saw him beyond the door in his room, and called out something.'

'I remember that,' said Nicholas. 'I left the room a very short time afterwards.'

'So there was no Buddha on the top of the door *then*,' said Jonathan. 'I am persuaded that apart from Nick having gone out in safety, proving that the trap was laid later than this, we might rest assured that if the room light was on the trap had not been set. One would be almost certain to see the dark shape on the top of the door if the light was on. I have found out, by dint of cautious inquiries, that there were no servants upstairs at that time. It appears that those members of my staff who were not with Caper in the dining room were listening to the wireless in the servants' hall. Now, you see, I have done quite well, haven't I, with my amateur detection? Let me see. We have found alibis for Sandra, Hersey, Madame Lisse, Aubrey, and, I hope, myself. What do you think, Aubrey?'

'Eh? Oh, I think it was more than ten minutes before the thud that you came downstairs,' Mandrake said.

'Well, now, Miss Chloris,' said Jonathan, with a little bend in her direction, 'what about you?'

'When it happened I was in my room. I'd had a bath and was dressing. I don't think I can prove I didn't go out of my room before that. But I didn't leave it after I went upstairs except to go into the bathroom next door. When I heard the crash and Nicholas cried out, I put on my dressing-gown and ran into the passage.'

Mandrake was roused by a sharp sensation of panic. 'What does that thing weigh?' he asked. 'The Buddha thing?'

'It's heavy,' said Jonathan. 'It's solid brass. About twenty pounds, I should say.'

'Do you think Miss Wynne could raise an object weighing twenty pounds above her head, and balance it on the top of a door?'

'Nobody's going to worry about whether she could or couldn't,' said Nicholas impatiently. 'She didn't.'

'Quite so,' said Mandrake.

'Well,' said Chloris mildly, 'that's true enough.'

'Nobody's asked me for my alibi,' said William. 'I think it's rather feeble, all this, because, I mean, we know that Hart did it.'

'But the point is – ' Jonathan began.

'I was in the smoking room,' said William ruthlessly, 'listening to the wireless. I suddenly realized I was a bit late and started to go upstairs. I was just about up when Nick let out that screech. I heard you come down, Jonathan, about ten minutes earlier. You spoke to Caper in the hall about drinks at dinner, and I heard you. But that proves nothing, of course. Oh, wait a bit, though. I could tell you what the news was. There's been a reconnaissance flight over . . . '

'Oh, what the hell's it matter?' said Nicholas. 'What's the good of talking like little detective fans? I'm sorry to be rude, but while you're all trying to bail each other out, our charming beauty specialist is probably thinking up a new death-trap on the third-time-lucky principle.'

'But to try anything else, when he knows perfectly well we suspect him!' Hersey exclaimed. 'It'd be the action of a madman.'

'He is a madman,' said Nicholas.

'I say,' said William. 'Has anybody done anything about that Buddha? I mean, it's probably smothered in his fingerprints. If we're going to give him in charge . . . '

'But are we going to give him in charge?' asked Hersey uneasily.

'I will,' said William. 'If Nick doesn't, I will.'

'I don't think you can. It's not your business.'

'Why not?' William demanded.

Jonathan cut in hurriedly, asking William if he proposed to make his mother's tragedy front-page publicity. The conversation became fantastic. William showed a tendency to shout and Nicholas to sulk. Chloris turned upon Mandrake a face so eloquent of misery and alarm that he instantly took her hand and found more reality in the touch of her fingers, moving restlessly in his grasp, than in anything else that was happening. Jonathan began to explain that he had locked the Buddha away in his room. He reminded them of the nature of the trap. When Nicholas returned to his room he found the door not quite closed. The room was in darkness as he had left it. He pushed at the door with his left hand. The door resisted him and then gave way suddenly. At the same instant his arm was struck and Madame Lisse screamed. He cried out and stumbled into the room.

Nicholas irritably confirmed this description, and cut in to say he had seen Dr Hart go into the bathroom adjoining his room and had heard him turn on the taps. 'Of course he simply dodged out when he knew I had gone. He was spying on me, I suppose, through the crack of the door. His room's only about fourteen feet away from mine on the opposite side of the passage.'

Mandrake, nervously tightening his grip on Chloris's hand, thought with a sort of unreal precision of the guest wing. Mrs Compline in the front corner room, then Madame Lisse, a cupboard, and Mandrake himself, all in a row, with a bathroom; then William, and then Hart in the corner room at the back, and another bathroom round the corner. Hersey Amblington in the converted nursery beyond. On the other side of the passage, overlooking the central court round which the old Jacobean house was built, were Nicholas's room, opposite William's, and then a bathroom, and an unoccupied room. Nicholas's was diagonally opposed to Hart's. Hart could easily have spied on Nicholas, and Mandrake pictured him turning on the bath taps and then perhaps opening the door to return to his room for something and seeing Nicholas stealing down the passage towards Madame Lisse's door. He pictured Hart as the traditional figure of the suspicious lover, his compact paunch curving above the girdle of his dressing-gown. 'He clutched a sponge-bag to his breast and his eye was glued to the crevice,' Mandrake decided. Perhaps he saw Nicholas tap discreetly at Madame Lisse's door, or scratch with his fingernail. Perhaps Nicholas slipped in without ceremony. 'And then, what?' Mandrake wondered. A quick sprint down the passage to the niche? A lopsided shuffle back to Nicholas's room? Did Dr Hart carry the Buddha under the folds of his dressing-gown? Did he turn on the light in Nicholas's room and climb on the chair? Was his somewhat remarkable face distorted with fury as he performed these curious exercises? No. Try as he might, Mandrake could not picture Hart and the Buddha without investing the whole affair with an improper air of *opéra bouffe*.

He was roused from his reverie by Chloris withdrawing her hand, and by William saying in a loud voice: 'You know, this is exactly like a thriller, except for one thing.'

'What do you mean, William?' asked Jonathan crossly.

'In a thriller,' William explained, 'there's always a corpse and he can't give evidence. But here,' and he pointed his finger at his brother, 'you might say we have the corpse with us. That's the difference.'

'Let us go to the library,' said Jonathan.

CHAPTER 8

Third Time Lucky

Hersey Amblington and Chloris did not stay long with the party in the library. They went upstairs to visit, severally, Mrs Compline and Madame Lisse. Jonathan had suggested this move to Hersey.

'I'll go and see how Sandra's getting on, with the greatest of pleasure,' Hersey said. 'I was going to do so in any case. But I must say, Jo, I don't think The Pirate will welcome my solicitude. What's supposed to be the matter with her?'

'A sick headache,' said Jonathan. 'The migraine.'

'Well, the sight of me won't improve it. Damn the woman; what business has *she* to throw a migraine?'

'Naturally,' Nicholas said, 'she's upset.'

'Why? Because she's afraid her face-lifting friend will make another pass at you? Or because she's all shocked and horrified that we should suspect him? Which?'

Nicholas looked furious but made no rejoinder.

'Would I be any use?' asked Chloris. 'I don't mind casting an eye at her.'

'Good girl,' said Hersey. 'Come on.' And they went upstairs together.

Hersey found Mrs Compline sitting by her fire, still wearing the dress into which she had changed for dinner.

'I ought to have come down, Hersey. It's *too* cowardly and difficult for me to hide like this. But I couldn't face it. Now that they all know! Imagine how they would avoid looking at me. I thought I had become hardened to it. For twenty years I've drilled myself, and now, when this happens, I am as raw as I was on the day I first let Nicholas look at me. Hersey, if you had seen him that day! He was only a tiny boy, but he – I thought he would never come to me again. He looked at me as though I were a stranger. It took so long to get him back.'

'And William?' Hersey asked abruptly

'William? Oh, he was older, of course, and not so sensitive. He seemed very shocked for a moment, and then he began to talk as if nothing had happened. I've never understood William. Nicky was just a baby, of course. He asked me what had happened to my pretty face. William never spoke of it. And after a while Nicky forgot I had ever had a pretty face.'

'And William, it seems, never forgot.'

'He was older.'

'I think he's more sensitive.'

'You don't understand Nicky. I see it all so plainly. He has got to know this Madame Lisse, and of course she has thrown herself at his head. Women have always done that with Nicky. I've seen it over and over again.'

'He doesn't exactly discourage them, Sandra.'

'He *is* naughty, I know,' admitted Mrs Compline, dotingly. 'He always tells me all about them. We have such laughs together sometimes. Evidently there was something between Madame Lisse and – that man. And then when she met Nicholas, of course, she lost her heart to him. I've been thinking it out. That man must have recognized me. His own handiwork! Twenty years haven't changed it much. I suppose he was horrified and rushed to her with the story. She, hoping to establish a deeper bond between herself and Nicky, told him all about it.'

'Now, Sandra, Nicholas himself denies this.'

'Of course he does, darling,' said Mrs Compline rapidly. 'That's what I've been trying to explain – you don't understand him. He wanted to spare me. It was for *my* sake he threatened this man. It's because of what Hartz did to *me*. But to spare me he let it be thought that it was some ridiculous affair over this woman.'

'That seems very far-fetched to me,' said Hersey bluntly.

A dull flush mounted in Mrs Compline's face. 'Why,' she said, 'the woman is on her knees to him already. He has no cause to trouble himself about this Madame Lisse. It's Dr Hart who's troubling himself.'

'But why?'

'Because he has found out that Nicholas knows his real identity and is afraid of exposure. Hersey, I've made William promise that he won't leave Nicholas. I want you to do something for me. I want you to send them both up here. I'm terrified for Nicky.'

'But if, as you seem to think, Hart's afraid of exposure, there wouldn't be any point in his attacking Nick. He'd have to polish off the lot of us. We all know now.'

But Hersey was up against an inflexible determination, and she saw that Sandra Compline would accept no explanation that did not show Nicholas in an heroic light. Nicholas must be upheld as the pink of courtesy, the wooed but never the wooer, the son who placed his mother above all women – a cross between Hollywood ace and a filial Galahad. She argued no more, but tried to convince Mrs Compline that however dangerously Hart might have threatened Nicholas he would attempt no more assaults since he now realized that they all suspected him. She left, promising to send the two sons to their mother, and returned to the library.

II

Chloris found Madame Lisse extremely difficult. For one thing, she made not the smallest effort to conceal her boredom when, after tapping at the door, Chloris came into her room. It was impossible to escape the inference that she had suspected someone else. When she saw Chloris, in some subtle way she sagged. 'As if,' thought Chloris, 'she unhooked her mental stays.' She was in bed, most decoratively. There was a general impression of masses of tawny lace, from which Madame Lisse emerged in pallor and smoothness. 'She *is* lovely,' thought Chloris, 'but I believe she's bad-tempered.' Aloud she said: 'I just looked in to see if there was anything I could do for you.'

'How kind,' said Madame Lisse in an exhausted voice. 'There is nothing, thank you.'

'Have you got aspirin and everything?'

'I cannot take aspirin, unfortunately.'

'Then I can't be of any use?'

Madame pressed the tips of her wonderfully manicured fingers against her shaded eyelids. 'Too kind,' she said. 'No, thank you. It will pass. In time, it will pass. It is an affliction of the nerves, you understand.'

'Beastly for you. I'm afraid,' said Chloris after a pause, 'your nerves had a bit of a jolt. We're all feeling rather temperamental at the moment.'

'Where is – what is everybody doing?' Madame Lisse asked with a certain freshening of her voice.

'Well, Lady Hersey's talking to Mrs Compline, who's pretty poorly too, it seems. Mr Royal and Aubrey Mandrake are in the library, and William and Nicholas are next door in the smoking room, holding a sort of family council or something. Dr Hart's in the boudoir, I believe.' Chloris hesitated, wondering if it were possible for her to establish some sort of understanding with this woman who made her feel so gauche and so uncertain of herself. It seemed to her that if any one member of the house-party fully comprehended the preposterous situation, that person must be Madame Lisse. Indeed she might be regarded as a sort of liaison officer between Nicholas and Dr Hart. 'Surely, *surely,*' Chloris thought, 'she must know for certain if Hart is after Nicholas, and if so, why. Is she lying there, sleeking herself on being a successful *femme fatale?* I believe she really is in a funk.' And, taking a deep breath, Chloris thought: 'I'll ask her.' With a sensation of panic she heard her own voice:

'Madame Lisse, please forgive me for asking you, but, honestly, things are so desperate with all of us eyeing each other and nobody really knowing what they're talking about, it would be a ghastly sort of relief to know the worst, so I thought I'd just ask you.'

'You thought you would just ask me what, Miss Wynne?'

'It sounds so bogus when you say it out loud.'

'I can hardly be expected to understand you unless you say it out loud.'

'Well, then. Is Dr Hart trying to kill Nicholas Compline?' Madame Lisse did not answer immediately, and for a second or two the room was quite silent. Chloris felt the palms of her hands go damp, and a sensation of panic mounted her brain. She thought: "This is frightful. My nerve must be going.' And then suddenly: 'I wish Aubrey was here.'

When Madame Lisse spoke her voice was clear and very cold: 'I know nothing whatever about it.'

'But – '

'Nothing, do you hear me? Nothing.'

And with a gesture whose violence shocked Chloris, she gripped the lace at her bosom. 'How dare you look at me like that,' cried Madame Lisse. 'Leave me alone. Go out of this room. I know nothing, I tell you. Nothing. Nothing. Nothing.'

III

Jonathan struck his plump hands together and uttered a little wail of despair. 'It's all very well to sit there and tell me something must be done, but what can I *do?* We've no proof. Nicholas had better go to bed and lock his door. I shall tell Nicholas to go to bed and lock his door.'

'I'm not worrying so much about Nicholas,' said Mandrake. 'He'll look after himself. I've no opinion at all of Nicholas. He hasn't got the nerve of a louse. It's William I'm thinking about. William's dangerous, Jonathan. He's out for blood. I don't think Hart'll get Nicholas, but, by God, I believe unless you do something about it, William will get Hart.'

'But why, why, why!'

'Jonathan, you pride yourself on your astuteness, don't you? Can't you understand what's happened to William? Didn't you see his face when they were up there in Nicholas's room? When their mother had told them that Hart was responsible for her disfigurement? Why, you yourself told me that when he was a child the disfigurement made an indelible impression on him. You have always recognized the intensity of his absorption in his mother. You've seen how readily he's adopted her extraordinary explanation of Hart's attacks on Nicholas. You've seen how he's abandoned all his private rows with Nicholas and come out strong in his defence. Can't you see that psychologically he's all of a piece. I tell you, the pent-up repressions of a lifetime have come out for an airing. William's dangerous.'

'Freudian mumbo-jumbo,' said Jonathan uneasily.

'It may be, but I don't think you can risk ignoring the possibilities.'

'What am I to do?' Jonathan repeated angrily. 'Lock up the Complines? Lock up Hart? Come, my dear Aubrey!'

'I think that at least you should have it out with Hart. Tell him flatly that we all think he's the author of these attacks. See what sort of a defence he can make. Then tackle William. You shut him up pretty successfully a little while ago, but there he is in the next room with Nicholas, who's no doubt busily engaged in churning it all up again.'

'You've suddenly become wonderfully purposeful, Aubrey. At dinner I thought you seemed half in a trance.'

'The look in William's eye has effectually roused me.'

'And the touch of Miss Wynne's hand, perhaps?' Joanthan tittered.

'Perhaps. Are you going to tackle Hart?'

'What an odious expression that is: "Tackle." Very well, but you must come with me.'

'As you please,' said Mandrake. They moved towards the door. It opened and Chloris came in. 'What's the matter?' Mandrake ejaculated.

'Nothing. At least, I've been talking to Madame Lisse. I suddenly felt I couldn't stand it. So I asked her, flat out, if she knew what Dr Hart was up to. She turned all venomous and sort of spat at me. I've got a jitterbug. This house gets more and more noiseless every hour. Out there the snow's piling up thicker and thicker. I'm sorry,' said Chloris, turning to Jonathan, 'but it's suffocating isn't it, to be shut up with something that threatens and doesn't quite come off? It's as if something's fumbling about the passages setting silly, dangerous booby traps, something mad and dangerous. Do you know, I keep wishing there'd be an air raid. That's pretty feeble-minded, isn't it?'

'Here,' said Mandrake, 'you sit down by the fire. What the devil do you mean by talking jitterbugs? We look towards you for a spot of brave young mem-sahib. Do your stuff, woman.'

'I'm all right,' said Chloris. 'I'm sorry. I'm all right. Where were you off to, you two?'

Mandrake explained while Jonathan fussed round Chloris, glad, so Mandrake fancied, of an excuse to postpone the interview with Dr Hart. He threw a quantity of logs on the fire, hurried away to the dining room, and returned with the decanter of port. He insisted on

Chloris taking a glass, helped himself, and, as an afterthought, Mandrake. Hersey came in and reported her interview with Mrs Compline. She uttered a phrase that Mandrake had began to dread. 'I looked out through the west door. It's snowing harder than ever.' Jonathan showed an inclination to settle down to a chat, but Mandrake said firmly that they might now leave Hersey and Chloris together. He waited for Jonathan, who gulped down his port, sighed, and got slowly to his feet. In the smoking room next door the drone of William's and Nicholas's conversation rose to some slight and amicable climax, ending in a light laugh from Nicholas. Perhaps, after all, thought Mandrake, he is making William see sense. Better not to disturb them. And he led the reluctant Jonathan by way of the hall, into the green boudoir.

When he saw Dr Hart the fancy crossed Mandrake's mind that Highfold was full of solitary figures crouched over fires. The door had opened silently, and for a moment Hart was not aware of his visitors. He sat on the edge of an armchair, leaning forward, his arms resting upon his thighs, his hands dangling together between his knees. His head, a little sunken and inclined forward, was in shadow, but the firelight found those hands whose whiteness, firm full flesh and square fingertips, were expressive of their profession. 'They've got a look of prestige,' thought Mandrake, and he repeated to himself, 'professional hands.'

Jonathan shut the door, and the hands closed like traps as Dr Hart turned and sprang to his feet.

'Oh – er – hallo, Hart,' began Jonathan, unpromisingly. 'We – ah – we thought perhaps we might have a little conference.'

Hart did not answer, but he turned his head and stared at Mandrake. 'I've asked Aubrey to come with me,' said Jonathan quickly, 'because, you see, he's one of the – the victims, and because, as a complete stranger to all of you' – ("A complete stranger to Chloris?" thought Mandrake) – 'we can't possibly suspect him of any complicity.'

'Complicity?' Hart said, still staring at Mandrake. 'No. No, I suppose you are right.'

'Now,' said Jonathan more firmly and with a certain briskness. 'Let us sit down, shall we, and discuss this affair sensibly?'

'I have said all that I have to say. I made no attack upon Mr Mandrake, and I made no attack upon Nicholas Compline. That I am at enmity with Compline I admit. He has insulted me, and I do not care for insults. If it were possible I should refuse to stay in the same house with him. It is not possible, but I can at least refuse to meet him. I do so. I take advantage of your offer to remain here or in my room until I am able to leave.'

'Now, my dear Hart, this really won't do.' Jonathan drew up two chairs to the fire and, obeying a movement of his hand, Mandrake sat in one while Jonathan himself took the other. Hart remained standing, his hands clasped behind his back.

'It won't do, you know,' Jonathan repeated. 'This last affair, this balancing of a Buddha, this preposterous and malicious trap, could have been planned and executed with one object only, the object of doing a fatal injury to Nicholas Compline. I have made tolerably exhaustive inquiries, and I find that, motive apart, it is extremely improbable that any of my guests, excepting yourself, had an opportunity to set the second trap for Nicholas Compline. I tell you this at the outset, Dr Hart, because I feel certain that if you can advance some proof of your – your innocence, you will now wish to do so.' Jonathan struck the arms of his chair lightly with the palms of his hands. Mandrake thought: 'He's not doing so badly, after all.' He looked at Jonathan because he found himself unable to look at Dr Hart, and, on a flash of irrelevant thinking, he remembered that a barrister had once told him that if the members of a returning jury studiously averted their eyes from the prisoner, you could depend upon it that their verdict would be 'Guilty.'

'I do not know when this trap is supposed to have been set,' said Dr Hart.

'Can you tell us what you were doing during the fifteen or twenty minutes before Nicholas Compline cried out?'

Dr Hart lifted his chin, drew down his brows, and glared at the ceiling. 'He's rather like Mussolini,' thought Mandrake, stealing a glance at him.

'When Compline returned with you and with his brother,' said Hart, 'I was in this room. I went to that door and saw you in the hall. I then returned and continued a conversation with Madame Lisse, who left the room some time before I did. I remained here until it was time to dress. I went upstairs at quarter-past seven, and immediately entered my room. Perhaps it was ten minutes later that I entered my bathroom next to my bedroom. I bathed and returned directly to my room. I had almost completed my dressing when I heard Compline scream like a woman. I heard voices in the passage. I put on my dinner-jacket and went out into the passage, where I found all of you grouped about the doorway to his room.'

'Yes,' said Jonathan. 'Quite so. And between the time of your leaving this room and the discovery of the injury to Nicholas Compline, did you see any other member of the party or any of the servants?'

'No.'

'Dr Hart, do you agree that before you came here you wrote certain letters – I'm afraid I must call them threatening letters – to Nicholas Compline?'

'I cannot submit to these intolerable questions,' said Hart breathlessly. 'You have my assurance that I have made no attack.'

'If you won't answer me, you may find yourself questioned by a person of greater authority. You oblige me to press you still further. Do you know where Nicholas Compline was when the trap was set for him?'

Hart's upper lip twitched as that moth fluttered under the skin. Twice he made as if to speak. At the third effort he uttered some sort of noise – a kind of moan. Mandrake felt actually embarrassed, but Jonathan cocked his head like a bird, and it seemed to Mandrake that he was beginning to enjoy himself again. 'Well, Dr Hart?' he murmured.

'I do not know where he was. I saw nobody.'

'He tells us that he was talking to Madame Lisse, in her room. What did you say?'

Hart had again uttered that inarticulate sound. He wetted his lips and after a moment said loudly: 'I did not know where he was.'

Jonathan's fingers had been at his waistcoat pocket. He now withdrew them and with an abrupt movement held out a square of paper. Mandrake saw that it was the Charter form which he had found on the previous night in Nicholas's chair. He had time to think: 'It seems more like a week ago,' as he read again the words that had seemed so preposterous: 'You are warned. Keep off.'

'Well, Dr Hart,' said Jonathan, 'have you seen this paper before?'

'Never,' Hart cried out shrilly. 'Never!'

'Are you sure? Take it in your hand and examine it.'

'I will not touch it. This is a trap. Of what do you accuse me?'

Jonathan, still holding the paper, crossed to a writing-desk in the window. Mandrake and Hart watched him peer into a drawer and finally take out a sheet of notepaper. He turned towards Hart. In his right hand he held the Charter form, in his left the sheet of notepaper.

'This is your acceptance of my invitation for the weekend,' said Jonathan. 'After the Charter form came into my hands,' he smiled at Mandrake, 'I bethought me of this note. I compared them and I came to an interesting conclusion. Your letters are characteristically formed, my dear Doctor. You use a script, and it retains its Continental character. The leg of the German "K" is usually prolonged. Here we have a "K" in "kind invitation." I am looking at the note. Turning to the Charter form we find that the letters are in script, and the "K" of "keep" has a leg that is prolonged through the square beneath it. Now, you sat next to Nicholas on his right hand. You passed your forms to him for scoring. Instead of receiving one form from you, he received two – the legitimate Charter, which curiously enough contained the word "threats," and this somewhat childish but, in the circumstances, quite significant warning, which you tell us you have never seen before. Now, you know, that simply won't do.'

'I did not write it. It – I must have torn two sheets off together. They were stuck together at the top. Someone else had written on the bottom form.'

'Ridiculous!' said Jonathan very sharply. He thrust the two papers into his pocket and moved away. When he spoke again, it was with a return to his usual air of pedantry. 'No, really, Dr Hart, that will *not* do. I myself gave out the forms. Nobody could have foretold to whom I would hand this particular block. You are not suggesting, I hope, that a member of the party, by some sleight-of-hand trick, took your block of forms out of your fingers, wrote on the lower form, and returned it without attracting your attention?'

'I suggest nothing. I know nothing about it. I did not write it. Perhaps Compline himself wrote it in order to discredit me. He is capable of anything – of anything. *Ach Gott!*' cried Dr Hart, 'I can endure this no longer. I must ask you to leave me. I must insist that you leave me alone.' He clasped his hands together and raised them to his eyes. 'I am most unhappy,' he said, 'I am in great trouble. You do not understand, you are not of my race. I tell you that these accusations mean nothing to me – nothing. I am torn by the most terrible of all emotions and I cannot fight against it. I am near breaking-point. I entreat you to leave me alone.'

'Very well,' said Jonathan, and rather to Mandrake's surprise he walked to the door. 'But I warn you,' he said, 'if anything should happen to Nicholas Compline, you, and only you, will immediately fall under the gravest suspicion. I firmly believe you tried to kill Nicholas. If there is one more threat, one more suspicious move upon your part, Dr Hart, I shall take it upon myself to place you under arrest.' He made a quick, deft movement, and the next moment Mandrake saw that in his right hand Jonathan held a very small pistol. 'A few moments ago,' said Jonathan, 'I removed this little weapon from my desk. I am armed, Dr Hart, and I shall see to it that Nicholas Compline also is armed. I wish you goodnight.'

IV

Mandrake did not follow Jonathan from the room. Something had happened to him. He had succumbed to an irresistible feeling of pity for Dr Hart. He had not ceased to believe that Hart was responsible for the attacks on Nicholas; on the contrary, he was more than ever convinced that he was their author. But something in Hart's attitude, in his air of isolation, in the very feebleness of his efforts to defend himself, had touched Mandrake's sympathetic nerve. He saw Hart as a man who had been driven hopelessly off his normal course by the wind of an overwhelming jealousy. The old phrase 'Madly in love' occurred to him, and he thought Hart was indeed the victim of an insane passion. He found in himself a burning anxiety to prevent any further attack, not so much for Nicholas Compline's sake as for Hart's. It would be terrible, he thought, if Hart were to kill Nicholas and then by this dreadful consummation of his passion be brought to his right mind, to a full realization of the futility of what he had done. He felt that he must try to find something to say to this plump figure of tragedy, something that might reach out to him and rouse him as some actual sound will penetrate and dispel a nightmare. Hart had turned away when Jonathan had shut the door, and had flung himself into a chair by the fire and covered his face with his hands. After a moment's hesitation Mandrake crossed to him and touched him lightly on the shoulder. He started, looked up, and said: 'I thought you had gone.'

'I shall go in a moment. I have stayed because I want to wake you.'

'To wake me? How often have I repeated to myself that most futile of all phrases, "If only it were a dream." If only I could be certain, *certain*. Then it would not be so bad.'

Mandrake thought: 'He *is* going to talk to me.' He took the chair opposite to Dr Hart and lit a cigarette. 'If only you could be certain?' he repeated.

'That it is all lies, that he is her lover, that she has betrayed me. But when she denies I cannot help half-believing her. I wish so much to believe. And then I see a look of boredom in her eyes, a look of weariness, of contempt. And with that comes the memory of the glances I have surprised between them, and although I know that with each denial, each scene, I injure myself still further, immediately I begin to make new scenes, demand fresh denials. I am caught in the toils of hell. I am so weary of it, yet I cannot be done with it.'

'Why did you come here?'

'To prove to myself, one way or the other. To know the worst. She told me he was to be here and said quite lightly: "Watch us and find out. It is nothing." And then when I saw him with all the airs of proprietorship, of complacent ownership, *laughing* at me! Do you know what should have been done in my country, if any one insulted me as this man has insulted me? We should have met and it would have been decided once and for all. I should have killed Nicholas Compline.'

'In England,' said Mandrake, 'we find it difficult to believe that in other countries duelling is still regarded as a satisfactory means of settling a difference. A successful duellist would be regarded as a murderer.'

'In any case,' said Hart, 'he would not consent. He is a poltroon as well as a popinjay.'

Mandrake thought: 'Such glorious words!' Aloud he said. 'He has some cause to be nervous, don't you think?'

'Yet in spite of his terror,' Hart continued, beating his clenched hands against his forehead, 'in spite of his terror, he goes to her room. He waits until he hears me in the bathroom and then he goes to her. This morning he was in her room. I trapped her into admitting it. And now, a few minutes after she leaves me, after she has seen my agony, she keeps another assignation.'

'But, you know, in this country, we are not conventional. I mean, we wander about into each other's rooms. I mean, Chloris Wynne and Lady Hersey, for example, both came and saw me. One thinks nothing of it. The modern Englishwoman – '

'In these matters she is not an Englishwoman, and I, Mr Mandrake, am not an Englishman. We are naturalized, but we do not change our ideas of what is *convenable*. For what reason should she admit him, for what innocent reason? No, it is useless to torture myself any further. She has betrayed me.'

'Look here, it's none of my business, but if you are so certain, why not make a clean break? Why take a course that must lead to disaster? Let them go their ways. Things can never be as they were. Why ruin your career' – Mandrake stammered over his series of conventional phrases – 'and jeopardize your own life over Nicholas Compline? Is he worth it? And, after all, is she worth it? Let her go. You could never be happy with her now. Even if she married you – '

'*Married* me!' cried Hart. '*Married me!* She has been my wife for five years.'

V

Mandrake stayed with Hart for a time, hearing a story in which the themes of Madame Lisse's business instinct, her husband's enslavement, and Nicholas Compline's perfidy, were strangely interwoven. Madame, it seemed, had decided that their respective professions, though allied, were in a public sense incompatible. 'She felt that as my wife she could not recommend me to her clients. I have always expressed considerable scepticism about the efficacy of face massage and creams. I have even published a short treatise on the subject. She said that to announce our marriage would be to embarrass my prestige with my *clientele.*' His voice went on and on in a breathless hurry. He seemed unable to stop. Always he returned to Nicholas Compline, and with each return he rekindled his own fury against Nicholas. The sudden outpouring of a long-suppressed emotion is supposed to bring relief, but Dr Hart did not appear to take comfort from his self-revelation. He looked wretchedly ill and his nervous distress mounted with his recital. 'He really is *not* responsible,' Mandrake thought. 'I've done no good at all. I'd better clear out.' He could think of no suitable speech with which to end the conversation. Ridiculous phrases occurred to him ('Now, you *won't* kill Nicholas, *will* you?') and he wished with all his heart that he could rid himself of the notion that in some way Dr Hart was making an appeal to him. He pulled himself to his feet. Dr Hart, his finger pressed against that twitching lip of his, looked up desolately. At that moment, beyond the communicating door into the smoking room, Nicholas Compline uttered a laugh loud enough to reach the ears of Dr Hart and Mandrake. Hart sprang to his feet, and for a moment Mandrake thought that he would actually make a blackguard rush into the smoking room and go for his tormentor. Mandrake grabbed at his arm. They heard Nicholas's voice say 'All right,' so clearly that he must have crossed the room. There was a discordant burst of static and distorted music from the wireless just inside the door. Hart cried out for all the world as if he had been struck, tore himself away from Mandrake, and flung open the door into the smoking room.

'*Gott im Himmel,*' he screamed out, 'must I be tortured by that devilish, that intolerable noise? *Turn it off. I insist that you turn it off!*'

Nicholas appeared in the doorway. 'You go to hell,' he said pleasantly. 'If I choose to listen to the wireless I'll bloody well listen to it.' He slammed the door in Hart's face. Mandrake stumbled between Hart and the door. With a string of expletives that rather astonished himself he shouted out instructions to Nicholas to switch off the radio, which was now roaring 'Roll Out the Barrel.' It stopped abruptly, and William was heard to say: 'Pipe down, for God's sake.' Nicholas said: 'Oh, *all* right. Go to bed, Bill,' and Mandrake and Hart stared at each other for some seconds without speaking.

'Dr Hart,' said Mandrake at last, 'if you cannot give me your assurance that you will either go to your own room or remain in this one, I shall – I shall lock you in.'

Hart sank back into his chair. 'I shall do nothing,' he said. 'What can I do?' and to Mandrake's unbounded dismay he uttered a loud sob and buried his face in his hands.

'Oh *God!*' thought Mandrake, 'this is too much.' He tried to form soothing phrases, but was dismayed by their inadequacy, and finally ran out of words. For a moment he watched Dr Hart, who was now fetching his breath in shuddering gasps and beating his hands on the arms of his chair. Mandrake remembered Jonathan's treatment for Chloris. He went to the dining room, found a decanter of whisky, poured out a stiff nip, and returned with it to the boudoir.

'Try this,' he said. Hart motioned to him to leave it beside him. Seeing he could do no more, he prepared to leave. As an afterthought he turned at the door. 'May I give you one word of advice,' he said. 'Keep clear of both the Complines.' And he limped away to the library.

Here he found Jonathan with Hersey Amblington and Chloris. It seemed quite natural to Mandrake to go at once to Chloris and sit on the arm of her chair, it seemed enchantingly natural that she should look up at him with pleasure.

'Well,' she said, 'any good?'

'None. He's in an awful state. What about the brothers Compline? We could hear snatches of their cross-talk act in there.'

'Lady Hersey's been in to see them.'

'And I may say,' said Hersey, 'that I got a surprise. Nick's pulled himself together, it seems, and is doing his best to let a little sense into poor old William.'

'He has also been doing his best to drive Dr Hart into an ecstasy of hatred by not quite tuning in at full volume to a particularly distressing rendering of "The Beer Barrel Polka,"' said Mandrake, and described the incident. 'Possibly this was an essential step in the soothing of William.'

'It must have happened after I left,' said Hersey.

'I wonder you didn't hear us yelling at each other from here.'

'This room is practically sound-proof,' said Jonathan.

'It must be. How is Nicholas getting on with William, Lady Hersey?'

'He's not made a great deal of headway, but at least he's trying. They're supposed to go and see their mother, but they don't seem to be very keen on the idea. They said they particularly want to be left to themselves. What do we do now, Mr Mandrake?'

'It's nearly ten o'clock,' said Mandrake. 'I'm damned if I know what we do. What do you think, Jonathan?'

Jonathan waved his hands and said nothing.

'Well,' Mandrake said, 'I suppose we see Nicholas to his room when he wants to go to bed. Do we lock William in *his* room or what?'

'I think we shut up Dr Hart,' said Hersey. 'Then William can't get at Dr Hart and Dr Hart can't get at Nicholas. Or am I confused?'

'They may not fancy being locked up,' Chloris pointed out. 'Honestly, it's *too* difficult.'

'Jo,' said Hersey suddenly, 'do you remember the conversation at dinner last night? When we said what we thought everybody would do in a crisis? It seems we were all wrong about each other. We agreed that you, for instance, would talk. You've not uttered a word since you came into this rom. Somebody said Mr Mandrake would be the impractical member of the party, and here he is showing the most superb efficiency. Chloris – I hope you don't mind me calling you Chloris – suggested that Bill would turn up trumps, while his mother was all for Nicholas. Hopelessly incorrect! It looks as if you were right, Jo. We know nothing about each other.'

'Jonathan was eloquent in the boudoir,' said Mandrake listlessly.

They made disjointed conversation until Nicholas, wearing a dubious expression, came out of the smoking room. He grimaced at the others and shut the door.

'How goes it?' Hersey asked. 'Thumbs up?'

Nicholas, with exaggerated emphasis, mimed: 'Thumbs down.'

'It's all right,' said Jonathan impatiently. 'He can't hear.'

'He's still pretty bloody-minded,' said Nicholas, throwing himself into a chair. 'He's left off threatening to beat up the doctor, thank God, but he's gone into a huddle over the fire and does *not* exactly manifest the party spirit. You know how he used to go as a kid, Hersey. All thunderous.'

'Black Bill?' said Hersey. 'I remember. Couldn't you do anything?'

'I've been kicked out,' said Nicholas with a sheepish grin. 'Hart's gone to bed, I fancy. We heard him snap off the light. So perhaps Bill might work his black dog off on the wireless.'

'This is a shocking state of affairs,' cried Jonathan. 'I suppose we'd better leave him to himself, um?'

'Well, he's not so hot when he's like this. He'll get over it. I think I've persuaded him to keep away from Hart.'

'You *think!*'

'I tell you Hart's gone upstairs. Possibly,' said Nicholas showing the whites of his eyes, 'he's thought up a really foolproof way of bumping me off.'

'My dear Nick, we shall go up with you. I cannot believe, when he knows what we suspect, and I may say in the face of the little speech I made him, that he will attempt – But, of course,' added Jonathan in a fluster, 'we must take every precaution. Your door, now – '

'Make no mistake,' said Nicholas grimly. 'I shall lock my door.'

There was a short pause broken by Hersey. 'I simply can't believe it,' she said abruptly. 'It's so preposterous it just isn't true. All of us sitting round like a house-party in a play, waiting for frightfulness. And that booby trap! A brass Buddha! No, it's *too* much. Tomorrow Dr Hart will apologize to all of us and say he's sorry his sense of fun carried him too far, and he'll explain that in the Austrian Tyrol they all half-kill each other out of sheer *joie de vivre*, and we'll say we're sorry we didn't take it in the spirit in which it was meant.'

'A murderous spirit,' Jonathan muttered. 'No, no, Hersey. We've got to face it. The attack on Nicholas was deliberately planned to injure him.'

'Well, what are we going to *do?*'

'At least we could hear the war news,' said Mandrake. 'It might work as a sort of counter-irritant.'

'We'd better not disturb William,' said Jonathan quickly.

'I dare say he'll turn it on in a minute,' Nicholas said wearily. 'He's keen on the news. Shall I ask him?'

'No, no,' said Jonathan. 'Leave him alone. It's not quite time yet. Would you like a drink, my dear Nick?'

'To be quite frank, Jonathan, I'd adore a very, very large drink.'

'You shall have it. Would you ring? The bell's beside you. No, you needn't trouble. I hear them coming.'

A jingle of glasses sounded in the hall and the new footman came in with a tray. For the few seconds that he was in the room Chloris and Hersey made a brave effort at conversation. When he had gone Jonathan poured out the drinks. 'What about William?' he asked. 'Shall we – ? Will you ask him?'

Nicholas opened the study door and stuck his head round it. 'Coming in for a drink, Bill? No? All right, old thing, but would you mind switching on the wireless? It's just about time for the news and we'd like to hear it. Thanks.'

They all waited awkwardly. Nicholas glanced over his shoulder and winked. The study wireless came to life.

'Hands, Knees, and Boomps-a-daisy,' sang the wireless robustly.

'Oh, God!' said Mandrake automatically, but he felt an illogical sense of relief.

'Can you stick it for a minute or two?' asked Nicholas. 'It's almost news time. I'll leave the door open.'

'Hands, Knees, and Boomps-a-daisy.'

'I think,' said Jonathan, at the third repetition of the chorus, 'that I'll just make certain Dr Hart is *not* in the boudoir.' He got up. At the same moment the dance band ended triumphantly: 'Turn to your partner and bow-wow-wow.'

'Here's the news,' said Hersey.

Jonathan, after listening to the opening announcement, went out into the hall. The others heard the recital of a laconic French bulletin and a statement that heavy snow was falling in the Maginot Line sector. The announcer's voice went on and on, but Mandrake found himself unable to listen to it. He was visited by a feeling of nervous depression, a sort of miserable impatience. 'I can't sit here much longer,' he thought. Presently Jonathan returned and in answer to their glances nodded his head. 'No light in there,' he said. He poured himself out a second drink. 'He's feeling the strain, too,' thought Mandrake.

'I wish old Bill'd come in,' said Nicholas suddenly.

'He's better left alone,' said Jonathan.

'Shall I take him in a drink?' Hersey suggested. 'He can but throw it in my face. I *will*. Pour him out a whisky, Jo.'

Jonathan hesitated. She swept him aside, poured out a good three fingers of whisky, splashed in the soda, and marched off with it into the smoking room.

'It is learned in London tonight,' said the announcer, 'that Mr Cedric Hepbody, the well-known authority on Polish folk-music, is a prisoner in Warsaw. At the end of this bulletin you will hear a short recorded talk made by Mr Hepbody last year on the subject of folk-music in its relation and reaction to primitive behaviourism. And now . . .'

Hersey was standing in the doorway. Mandrake saw her first, and an icy sensation of panic closed like a hand about his heart. The red-leather screen at her back threw her figure into bold relief. The others turned their heads, saw her, and, as if on a common impulse, rose at once to their feet. They watched her lips moving in her sheet-white face. She mouthed at them and turned back into the smoking room. The announcer's voice was cut off into silence.

'Jo,' Hersey said. 'Jo, come here.'

Jonathan's fingers pulled at his lips. He did not move.

'Jo.'

Jonathan crossed the library and went into the smoking room. There was another long silence. Nobody moved or spoke. At last Hersey came round the screen.

'Mr Mandrake,' she said, 'will you go in to Jonathan?'

Without a word Mandrake went into the smoking room. The heavy door with its rows of book-shelves shut behind him.

It was then that Nicholas cried out: 'My God, what's happened?'

Hersey went to him and took his hands in hers. 'Nick,' she said, 'he's killed William.'

Part Two

CHAPTER 9

Alibi

William was sitting in a low chair beside the wireless. He was bent double. His face was between his knees and his hands were close to his shoes. His posture suggested an exaggerated scrutiny of the carpet. If Mandrake had walked in casually he might have thought at first glance that William was staring at some small object that lay between his feet. The cleft in the back of his head looked like some ugly mistake, preposterous rather than ghastly, the kind of thing one could not believe. Mandrake had taken in this much before he looked at Jonathan, who stood with his back against the door into the boudoir. He was wiping his hands on his handkerchief. Mandrake heard a tiny spat of sound. A little red star appeared on the toe of William's left shoe.

'Aubrey, look at this.'

'Is he – ? Are you sure – ?'

'Good God, *look* at him!'

Mandrake had no wish to look at William, but he limped over to the chair. Has any one measured the flight of thought? In a timeless flash it can embrace a hundred images, and compass a multitude of ideas. In the second that passed before Mandrake stooped over William Compline he was visited by a confused spiral of impressions and memories. He thought of William's oddities, of how he himself had never seen any of William's paintings, of how William's mouth might now be open and full of spilling blood. He thought in a deeper layer of consciousness of Chloris, who must have been kissed by William, of Dr Hart's hands, of phrases in detective novels, of the fact that he might have to give his own name if he was called as a witness. The name of Roderick Alleyn was woven in his thoughts, and over all of them rested an image of deep snow. He knelt by William and touched his right hand. It moved a little, flaccidly, under the pressure of his fingers, and that shocked him deeply. Something hit the back of his own hand, and he saw a little red star like the one on William's shoe. He wiped it off with a violent movement. He stooped lower and looked up into William's face, and that was terrible because the eyes as well as the mouth were wide open. Then Mandrake rose to his feet and looked at the back of William's head and felt abominably sick. He drew away with an involuntary sideways lurch, and his club foot struck against something on the floor. It lay in shadow, and he had to stoop again to see it. It was a flatfish, spatulate object that narrowed to a short handle. He heard Jonathan's voice babbling behind him:

'It hung on the wall there, you know. I showed it to you. It came from New Zealand. I told you. It's called a mere.* I told you. It's made of stone.'

'I remember,' said Mandrake.

When he turned to speak to Jonathan he found that Nicholas had come into the room.

'Nick,' said Jonathan, 'my dear Nick.'

'He's not dead,' Nicholas said. 'He can't be dead.'

He thrust Jonathan from him and went to his brother. He put his hands on William's head and made as if to raise it.

'Don't,' said Mandrake. 'I wouldn't. Not yet.'

'You must be mad. Why haven't you tried – ? Leaving him! You must be mad.' He raised William's head, saw his face, and uttered a deep retching sound. The head sagged forward again, loosely, as he released it. He began to repeat William's name. 'Bill, Bill, Bill,' and walked distractedly about the room, making strange uneloquent gestures.

'What are we to do?' asked Jonathan, and Mandrake repeated to himself: 'What are we to do?'

Aloud he said: 'We can't do anything. We ought to get the police. A doctor. We can't do anything.'

---

* Pronounced 'merry'

'Where's Hart?' Nicholas demanded suddenly. *'Where is he?'*

He stumbled to the door beyond William, fumbled with the key and flung it open. The green boudoir was in darkness and the fire there had sunk to a dead glow.

'By God, yes, where is he?' cried Mandrake.

Nicholas turned to the door into the hall, and on a common impulse Mandrake and Jonathan intercepted him. 'Clear out of my way,' shouted Nicholas.

'Wait a minute, for Heaven's sake, Compline,' said Mandrake. *'Wait a minute!'*

'We're up against a madman. He may be lying in wait for you. Think, man.'

He had Nicholas by the arm and he felt him slacken. He thought he saw something of the old nervousness come into his eyes.

'Aubrey's right, Nick,' Jonathan was gabbling. 'We've got to keep our heads, my dear fellow. We've got to lay a plan of campaign. We can't rush blindly at our fences. No, no. There's – there's your mother to think of, Nick. Your mother must be told, you know.'

Nicholas wrenched himself free from Mandrake, turned away to the fireplace and flung himself into a chair: 'For Christ's sake, leave me alone,' he said. Mandrake and Jonathan left him alone and whispered together.

'Look here,' Mandrake said, 'I suggest we lock up this room and go next door where we can talk. Are those two women all right in there? Better not leave them. We'll go back into the library, then.' He turned to Nicholas. 'I'm terribly sorry, Compline, but I don't think we ought to – to make any changes here, just yet. Jonathan, are there keys in all these doors? Yes, I see.'

The door into the boudoir was locked. He withdrew the key, locked the door into the hall, and gave both keys to Jonathan. As he crossed the room to open the library door he felt a slight prick in the sole of his normal foot, and in one layer of his conscious thoughts, cursed his shoemaker. They shepherded Nicholas back into the library. Mandrake found that behind its rows of dummy books the door into the library also had a lock.

They found Hersey and Chloris sitting together by the fire. Mandrake saw that Chloris had been crying. 'I'm out of this,' he thought. 'I can't try to help.' And, unrecognized by himself, a pang of jealousy shook him, jealousy of William, who, by getting himself murdered, had won tears from Chloris.

Mandrake, for the first time, noticed that Jonathan was as white as a ghost. He kept opening and closing his lips, his fingers went continually to his glasses, and he repeatedly gave a dry, nervous cough. 'I dare say I look pretty ghastly myself,' thought Mandrake. Jonathan, for all his agitation, had assumed a certain air of authority. He sat down by Hersey and took her hand.

'Now, my dears,' he began, and though his voice shook his phrases held their old touch of pedantry, 'I know you will be very sensible and brave. This is a most dreadful calamity, and I feel that I am myself, in a measure, responsible for it. That is an appalling burden to carry upon one's conscience, but at the moment I dare not let myself consider it. There is an immediate problem, and we must deal with it as best we may. There is no doubt at all, I am afraid, that it is Dr Hart who has killed William, and in my mind there is no doubt that he is insane. First of all, then, I want you both to promise me that you will not separate, and also that when we leave you alone together you will lock this door after us and not unlock it until one of us returns.'

'But he's not going for either of us,' said Hersey. 'He's got nothing against us, surely.'

'What had he against William?'

'William had quite a lot against *him*,' said Hersey.

'It must have been the radio,' Mandrake said to Nicholas. 'He nearly went for you when you turned it on.'

Nicholas said: 'I told him to go to hell and locked the door in his face.' He leant his arms on the mantelpiece and beat his skull with his fists.

'You *locked* the door?' Mandrake repeated.

'He looked like barging in. I was sick of it all. Going for me. Screaming out his orders to me! I wanted to shut him up.'

'I remember now. I heard you lock it. He must have gone out into the hall and then into the smoking room through the hall door.'

'I suppose so,' said Nicholas, and drove his fingers through his hair.

'Look here,' Mandrake said slowly, 'this makes a difference.'

'If it does,' Jonathan interrupted him, 'we can hear what it is later, Aubrey. Nick, my dear chap, I think you must see your mother. And we,' he looked at Mandrake, 'must find Hart.' They made a plan of action. The men were to search the house together, leaving the two women in the library with the doors locked on the inside. Nicholas said that his service automatic was in his room. They decided to go upstairs at once and get it. 'Bill had his,' Nicholas said, and Jonathan said they would take it for Mandrake.

Hersey offered to go with Nicholas to his mother, and Chloris insisted that she would be all right left by herself in the library. 'She's a good, gallant girl,' thought Mandrake, 'and I'm in love with her.' He gave her shoulder a pat and thought how out of character his behaviour was.

'Come on,' said Hersey.

The library door shut behind them and they heard Chloris turn the key in the lock. The hall was quiet, a dim, hollow place with a dying fire and shadows like the mouths of caverns. Bleached walls faded like smoke up into darkness; curtains, half-seen, hung rigidly in the entrance. Pieces of furniture stood about with a deadly air of expectancy.

Jonathan's hand reached out and a great chandelier flooded the hall with light. The party of four moved to the stairs. Mandrake saw Jonathan take out his pistol. He led the way upstairs and switched on the wall lamps. Hersey and Nicholas followed him, and Mandrake, lifting his club foot more quickly than he was wont to do, brought up the rear. The nail in his right shoe still pricked him, and he was dimly irritated by this slight discomfort. Up the first flight to the halfway landing where the stairs divided into two narrower flights, of which they took the one that turned to their left. Up to the top landing, where the grandfather clock ticked loudly. Here they paused. Hersey took Nicholas's arm. He squared his shoulders and, with a gesture that for all its nervousness was a sort of parody of his old swagger, brushed up his moustache and went off with her to his mother's room. Mandrake and Jonathan turned to the right and walked softly down the passage.

They found Nicholas's automatic where he had told them to look for it, in a drawer of his dressing-table. William's, Nicholas had said, was in his room, beside a rucksack containing his painting materials.

'His room's next door to Hart's,' whispered Jonathan. 'If he's there, he'll hear us go in. What shall we do?'

'We can't leave stray automatics lying about, Jonathan. Not with a homicidal lunatic at large.'

'Come on, then.'

William's room was opposite his brother's. Mandrake stood on guard in the passage while Jonathan, looking extraordinarily furtive, opened the door by inches and crept in. There was no light under Hart's door. Was he there behind it, listening, waiting? Mandrake stared at it, half-expecting it to open. Jonathan came back carrying a second automatic. He led the way into Mandrake's room.

'If he's in there, he's in the dark,' said Mandrake.

'Quiet! You take this, Aubrey. Nicholas should have had his,' whispered Jonathan. 'He should have come here first.'

'Are they loaded? I couldn't know less about them.'

Jonathan examined the two automatics. 'I think so. I myself . . . ' his voice faded away and Mandrake only caught odd words: ' . . . last resort . . . most undesirable . . . ' He looked anxiously at Mandrake. 'The safety catches are on, I think, but be careful, Aubrey. We must not fire, of course, unless something really desperate happens. Let him see we are armed. Wait one moment.'

'What is it?'

A curious smile twisted Jonathan's lips. 'It occurs to me,' he whispered, 'that we are at great pains to defend ourselves, Nicholas, and three of the ladies. We have quite overlooked the fourth.'

'But – do you think? Good Heavens, Jonathan – '

'We can do nothing there. It is an abstract point. Are you ready? Let us go, then.'

Outside Hart's door they paused. William's automatic sagged heavily in the pocket of Mandrake's dinner-jacket. Nicholas's automatic was in his right hand. His heart thumped uncomfortably, and he thought: 'This is *not* my sort of stuff. I'm hating this.'

The latch clicked as Jonathan turned the handle. 'If it's locked,' thought Mandrake, 'do we break it in or what?'

It was not locked. Jonathan pushed the door open quietly, slipped through, and switched on the light. The room was orderly and rather stuffy. Dr Hart's trousers were hung over the back of a chair, his underclothes were folded across the seat, his shoes neatly disposed upon the floor. These details caught Mandrake's eye before he saw the bed, which contained Dr Hart himself.

II

Apparently he was fast asleep. He lay on his back, his mouth was open, his face patched with red, and his eyes not quite shut. The whites just showed under the lashes, and that gave him so ghastly a look that for a fraction of a second Mandrake's nerves leapt to a conclusion that was at once dispelled by the sound of stertorous breathing.

Jonathan shut the door. He and Mandrake eyed each other and then, upon a common impulse, approached closer to the sleeping beauty-doctor. Mandrake was conscious of a great reluctance to waken Hart, a profound abhorrence of the scene that must follow the awakening. His imagination called up a picture of terrified expostulations or, still worse, of a complete breakdown and confession. He found himself unable to look at Hart, his glance wandered from Jonathan's pistol to the bedside table, where it was arrested by a small chemist's jar half-full of a white crystalline powder, and by a used tumbler, stained with white sediment. 'Veronal?' wondered Mandrake, who had once used it himself. 'If it is I didn't know it made you look so repellent. He must have taken a big dose.'

How big a dose Dr Hart had taken only appeared when Jonathan tried to wake him.

Under other circumstances Jonathan would have cut a comic figure. First, keeping his own pistol pointed at the sleeping doctor, he called his name. There was no response, and Jonathan repeated his effort, raising his voice, finally to a cracked falsetto. 'Hart, Dr Hart! Wake up!'

Hart stirred, uttered an uncouth sound, and began to snore again. With an incoherent exclamation, Jonathan pocketed his pistol and advanced upon the bed.

'Look out,' said Mandrake, 'he may be foxing.'

'Nonsense!' said Jonathan crisply. He shook Hart by the shoulder. 'Never heard of such a thing,' said Jonathan furiously. 'Dr Hart! Wake up.'

'A-a-ah? *Was haben Sie* . . . ' The prominent eyes opened and stared into Jonathan's. The voice tailed away, the eyes became bored and closed again. There followed a slightly ridiculous scene, Jonathan scolding and shaking Hart, Hart mumbling and sagging off into a doze. Finally Jonathan, his face pink with vexation, dipped a towel in the water jug and slapped the doctor's cheeks with it. This did the trick. Hart shuddered and shook his head. When he spoke again his voice was normal.

'Well,' said Dr Hart, 'what in Heaven's name is all this? What now? May I not sleep, even! What now?'

He turned his head and saw Mandrake. 'What are you doing with that thing in your hand?' he demanded. 'Do not point it at me. It's a firearm. What has happened?' Mandrake fidgeted uneasily with the automatic, and curled the toes of his right foot in an attempt to avoid that pestilent shoe nail. Hart rubbed the back of his hand across his mouth and shook his head vigorously.

Jonathan said: 'We are armed because we have come to speak with a murderer.'

Hart uttered a sound of exasperation. 'Mr Royal,' he said, 'how often am I to explain that I know nothing about it? Am I to be awakened at intervals during the night to tell you that I was in my bath?'

'What, again!' Mandrake ejaculated.

'Again? *Again!*' shouted Hart. 'I do not know what you mean by again. I was in my bath at the time it was done. I know nothing. I did not sleep all last night. For weeks I have been suffering from insomnia, and tonight I have taken a soporific. If I do not sleep I shall go mad. Leave me alone.'

'There is the body of a murdered man downstairs, Doctor Hart,' said Mandrake. 'I think you must stay awake a little longer to answer for it.'

Hart sat up in bed. His pyjama jacket was unbuttoned, and the smooth whiteness of his torso made a singularly disagreeable impression on Mandrake. Hart was fully awake now, on his guard, and sharply attentive.

'Murdered?' he repeated, and to Mandrake's astonishment he smiled. 'I see. So he has done it after all. I did not think he would go so far.'

What the devil are you talking about?' Jonathan demanded.

'He is killed, you say? Then I am speaking of his brother. I guessed that the brother set that trap. A booby trap you call it, do you not? He betrayed himself when he reminded them of the tricks they played in their childhood. It was obvious the lady still loved her first choice. He was attractive to women.' He paused and rubbed his lips again. Jonathan and Mandrake found nothing to say. 'How was it done?' asked Hart.

Jonathan suddenly began to stutter. Mandrake saw that he was beside himself with rage. He cut in loudly before Jonathan had uttered a coherent phrase:

'Wait a moment, Jonathan.' Mandrake limped nearer to the bed. 'He was killed,' he said, 'by a blow on the head from a stone club that hung with other weapons on the wall of the smoking room. He was bending over the wireless. His murderer must have crept up behind him. No, Jonathan, wait a minute, please. A short while before he was killed, Doctor Hart, we were all in the library, and we heard him turn on the radio. You will remember that the smoking room is between the library and the green sitting room, the room that you were in, alone. You will remember that it communicates with both these rooms and with the hall. With the exception of Mr Royal, who did not enter either of the other two rooms, none of us left the library after we heard the wireless until Lady Hersey went in and found him there – murdered.'

The uneven patches of red in Hart's cheeks were blotted out by a uniform and extreme pallor.

'This is infamous,' he whispered. 'You suggest that I – *I* killed him.' With a movement of his hand Mandrake checked a further outburst from Jonathan.

'I could not,' said Hart. 'The door was locked.'

'How do you know?'

'After you had gone, I tried it. He had turned that intolerable thing on again. I could not endure it. I admit – I admit I tried it. When I found it locked I – I controlled myself. I decided to leave that room of torture. I came up here and to bed. The door was locked, I tell you.'

'The door from the hall into the smoking room was not locked.'

'I did not do it. There must be some proof. It is the brother. The brother hated him as much as I. It is a pathological case. I am a medical man. I have seen it. He had stolen the mother's love and the girl still adored him.'

'Doctor Hart,' said Mandrake, 'it is not Nicholas Compline who is dead. It is his brother, William.'

In the silence that followed, Mandrake heard a door, some distance down the passage, open and close. He heard voices, a footfall, somebody coughing.

'*William,*' repeated Hart, and his hands moved across his chest, fumbling with his pyjama coat. '*William* Compline? It cannot be William. It *cannot.*'

III

They did not have a great deal of trouble with Dr Hart after that. He seemed at first to be completely bewildered and (the word leapt unbidden into Mandrake's thoughts) disgusted. Mandrake found himself quite unable to make up his mind whether Hart was bluffing, whether his air of confusion, his refusal to take alarm, and his obstinate denials were false or genuine. He seemed at once to be less panic-stricken and more hopeless than he was when he believed, or feigned to believe that the victim was Nicholas. He also seemed to be profoundly astonished. After a few minutes, however, he roused himself and appeared to consider his own position. He gave them quite a clear account of his movements from the time Mandrake left him alone in the green boudoir, until he fell asleep. He said that he had taken some minutes to recover from his breakdown in Mandrake's presence. He was fully roused by tentative noises from the wireless, not loud but furtive. He found these sounds as intolerable to his raw nerves as the defiant blasts that preceded them. They must have affected Hart, Mandrake thought, in much the same way as he himself was affected by stealthy groping in chocolate boxes at the play. The intermittent noises continued, snatches of German and French, scraps of music, muffled bursts of static. Hart imagined Nicholas Compline turning the dial-control and grinning to himself. At last the maddened doctor had rushed to the communicating door and found it locked. He had not, he seemed to suggest, meant to do more than expostulate with Nicholas, turn off the wireless at the wall switch and leave the room. However, the locked door checked him. He merely shouted a final curse at Nicholas and after a minute or two decided to fly from torment. He switched off the lights in the boudoir and went upstairs. As he crossed the hall to the foot of the stairs he passed the new footman with his tray of glasses. He said the man saw him come out of the boudoir and that he was about halfway up the first flight when the man returned from the smoking room and moved about the hall. He was still in the hall, locking up, when Hart reached the halfway landing and turned off to the left-hand flight. 'He will tell you,' said Hart, 'that I did not enter the smoking room.'

'You could very easily have finished your work in the smoking room before the man came,' Jonathan said icily. 'You could have returned to the boudoir and come out when you heard the man crossing the hall.'

Mandrake, by a really supreme effort of self-control, held his tongue. He wanted with all his soul to cry out: 'No! Don't you *see*, don't you *see* . . . ?' He knew Jonathan was wrong, off the track altogether. He was amazed at Jonathan's blindness. Yet because he felt certain that somewhere, beyond his own reach, lay the answer to Hart's statement, he said nothing. Better, he thought, to wait until he had that answer.

'His skull is fractured, you say?' Hart's voice, more composed than it had been since their last interview, roused Mandrake to listen. 'Very well, then. You must lock up the room. The weapon must not be touched. It may have the assassin's fingerprints. The door into the hall must be examined by the police. A medical practitioner must be found. Naturally I cannot act in the matter. My own position . . . '

'You!' Jonathan ejaculated. 'Great merciful heavens, sir. . . . '

Again Mandrake interrupted. 'Doctor Hart,' he said, 'suppose the rest of the party agreed, would you be prepared, in the presence of witnesses, to look at the body of William Compline?'

'Certainly,' said Hart promptly. 'If you wish, I will do so, though it can serve no purpose. In view of your preposterous accusations I will not prejudice myself by making an examination, but I am perfectly ready to look. But, I repeat, you must immediately procure a medical man and communicate with the police.'

'Have you forgotten that we're isolated?' And repeating the phrase which he had learned to dread, Mandrake added: 'It's snowing harder than ever.'

'This is most awkward,' said Hart primly.

Jonathan burst incontinently into a tirade of abuse. Mandrake had never, until that day, seen him put out of countenance, and it was a strange and disagreeable experience to hear his voice grow shrill and his speech incoherent. His face scarlet, his small mouth pouted and trembled, and behind those blind glasses of his Mandrake caught distorted glimpses of congested eyeballs. Without a trace of his usual precision he poured out a stream of accusations. 'In my house,' he kept repeating, 'in my house.' He ordered Hart to admit his guilt, he predicted what would happen to him. In the same breath he reminded him of Mrs Compline's ruined beauty, of his threats to Nicholas and of Mandrake's immersion. His outburst had the curious effect of steadying Hart. It was as though that house could hold only one hysterical middle-aged man at a time. Finally, Jonathan flung himself into a chair, took out his handkerchief, saw a dark stain upon it, and with singular violence hurled it from him. He looked at Mandrake and perhaps he read astonishment and distaste in Mandrake's face, for when he spoke again it was with something of his old manner.

'You must forgive me, Aubrey. I'm exceedingly upset. Known that boy all his life. His mother's one of my oldest friends. I beg of you, Aubrey, to tell me what we should do.'

Mandrake said: 'I think, if Dr Hart consents, we should leave him and lock the door after us.'

'If I did not consent,' said Hart, 'you would still do so. One thing I shall ask of you. Will you arrange that someone, Lady Hersey perhaps, explains my present dilemma to my wife. If you permit, I should like to speak to her.'

'His wife? *His wife!*'

'Yes, yes, Jonathan,' said Mandrake. 'Madame Lisse is Madame Hart. We can't go into it now. Do you agree to these suggestions?'

Jonathan waved his hands and, taking this as an assent, Mandrake went to the bedside table and picked up the chemist's jar. 'I'll take charge of this, I think,' he said. 'Is it veronal?'

'I most strongly object, Mr Mandrake.'

'I thought you would. Coming, Jonathan?'

He dropped the jar into his pocket and led the way to the door. He stood aside allowing Jonathan to go out before him. He removed the key from inside the door. The last thing he saw before closing the door was Dr Hart, his hands on his chest, staring after him. Then he stepped back over the threshold, pulled to the door, and locked it.

'Jonathan,' he said, 'somewhere or another we've gone incredibly wrong. Let's find Nicholas. We've got to talk.'

IV

Nicholas, wearing an expression that reminded Mandrake of a nervous colt, stood at the end of the passage outside his mother's door. He hurried to meet them.

'Well,' he whispered, 'for God's sake, what's happened? What's wrong?'

'At the moment, nothing,' said Mandrake.

'But I heard Jonathan shouting. Hart's in his room, then? Why have you left him?'

'He's locked up. Come downstairs, Compline. We've got to talk.'

'I'm deadly tired,' said Nicholas suddenly. And indeed he looked exhausted. 'It was pretty ghastly, telling my mamma, you know.'

'How is she?' asked Jonathan, taking Nicholas's arm. They moved towards the stairs.

'Hersey's with her. She's all to blazes, to be quite frank. She's got it into her heard that it all hangs on – you know. What he did to her face. She thinks it's because of what Bill said about it. I couldn't do anything much. Of course she's – God, it sounds a rotten thing to say, but you know how things are – she's – in a sort of way – glad it's not me. That makes me feel pretty foul, as you may imagine. I'd better tell Hersey it's safe for her to come out when she wants to.'

He put his head in at his mother's door and gave this message. They went downstairs to the library. Chloris was sitting very upright in her chair with her hands pressed together in her lap.

'All right?' Mandrake asked.

'Me? Yes; all right. It's nice to see you again. What's happened?'

Jonathan gave Chloris and Nicholas an account of the interview. It was an accurate narrative until he came to Hart's story. Then his indignation seemed to get the better of him, and abandoning Hart's statement altogether, Jonathan talked excitedly of preposterous evasions, trumped-up alibis, and intolerable hardihood. Seeing that Chloris and Nicholas grew more and more anxious and bewildered, Mandrake waited until Jonathan had exhausted his store of phrases and then cut in with an explicit account of Hart's movements according to himself.

'A monstrous conglomeration of lies!' Jonathan fumed.

'I don't think we can altogether dismiss them, Jonathan. I take it that we none of us doubt his guilt, but I'm afraid it's not going to be easy to get over that business of his meeting the footman – supposing, of course, that the man confirms Hart's story. There must *be* an explanation, of course, but – '

'My good Aubrey,' cried Jonathan, 'of course there's an explanation. When he encountered Thomas – that's the fellow's name, Thomas – it was all over. That's your explanation.'

'Yes, but it isn't, you know. Because it was after Thomas came in with the drinks that we heard William turn up the wireless.'

There was a rather stony silence, broken by Jonathan. 'Then he came downstairs and slipped into the smoking room.'

'But he says Thomas stayed in the hall.'

'*He says, he says.* The answer is that he waited in the shadows on the stairs until Thomas left the hall.'

'Do you remember,' Mandrake asked the other two, 'the sequence of events? You, Compline, came out of the smoking room, leaving your brother – where?'

'He was over by the fire, I think. He wouldn't talk much, but I remembered he did say he was damned if Hart was going to stop him getting the news. It wasn't quite time for it. I'd heard Hart switch off the light in the boudoir and I said he'd evidently gone, so it'd be all right. I didn't want to hear the damn news myself and I'd told you I'd pipe down, so I came away.'

'Exactly. As I remember, you came in and shut the door. Later, when you opened it and called out to him about the news, could you see him?'

'No. The screen hid him. But he grunted something and I heard him cross the room.'

'Right. And a moment later he turned on the wireless.'

'I maintain,' said Jonathan, 'that it was Hart we heard in there. Hart had murdered him, and when he heard Nick ask for the news he turned it on and got out of the room.'

'By that time Hart, according to himself, had met Thomas coming with the tray, had got some way up the stairs and had seen Thomas re-enter the hall. It was only a matter of a minute or two after Thomas left that Lady Hersey went into the smoking room. Does that give Hart time to return and do – what he did?'

'It was longer than that,' said Jonathan; 'the news had run for some minutes before Hersey went in.'

'But . . . ' Chloris made a sudden movement.

'Yes?' asked Mandrake.

'I suppose it's no good, but a wireless does take a little time to warm up. Could Dr Hart have switched it on, after – after he'd – after it was over, and then hurried out of the room so that it would sound like Bill tuning in? Do you see what I mean?'

'By heaven!' Nicholas said, 'I believe she's got it.'

'No,' said Mandrake slowly. 'No, I'm afraid not. The wireless was still warm. It was only a few minutes since it had been switched off. Even when they're cold they don't take longer than fifteen to twenty seconds, I fancy. For that idea to work, Hart would have had to switch it on before Thomas came in with the drinks, and we didn't hear a thing until after Thomas left. And, what's more, it gives a still smaller margin of time for the actual crime. It would have to be done after you, Compline, left your brother, and before Thomas appeared with the glasses. Remember he had to leave the boudoir by the door into the hall, enter the smoking-room by *its* door into the hall, seize his weapon, steal up – I'm sorry, but we've got to think of these things, haven't we? – do what he did, turn on the radio, return to the boudoir and come out of it again in time for Thomas to see him.'

'It takes much longer to describe these things than to do them,' said Jonathan.

'No,' said Chloris, 'I think Aubrey's right, Mr Royal. It doesn't seem to fit.'

'My dear child, you can't possibly tell.'

'What do you think, Nicholas?' This was the first time Chloris had spoken to Nicholas. He shook his head and pressed the palms of his hands against his eyes.

'I'm sorry,' he said, 'but I'm no good. Just about all in.'

Mandrake suppressed a feeling of irritation. He found Nicholas in sorrow as difficult to stomach as Nicholas in good form. He realized that his impatience was unkind and his feeling of incredulity unjust. Nicholas *was* upset. He was white and distraught, and it would have been strange if he had not been so affected. Mandrake realized with dismay that his own annoyance arose not from Nicholas's behaviour but from the compassionate glance that Chloris had given him. 'Good heavens,' Mandrake thought, 'I'm a pretty sort of fellow!' And to make amends to his conscience he joined Chloris and Jonathan in urging Nicholas to go to bed. Hersey Amblington came in.

'Your mother's a little calmer, Nick,' she said. 'But I'm afraid she's not likely to sleep. Jonathan, are there any aspirins in this house? I haven't got any.'

'I – I really don't know. I never use them. I can ask the servants. Unless any of you – '

Nobody had any aspirins. Mandrake remembered Dr Hart's veronal and groped in his pocket.

'There's this,' he said. 'Hart had taken as much or more than was good for him and I removed it. It's got the correct dosage on the label. It's a veronal preparation, I think, and is evidently a proprietary sample of sorts. The kind of thing they send out to doctors. Would it do?'

'It couldn't hurt, could it? She could try a small dose. I'll see, anyway.'

Hersey went away and returned in a few minutes to say that she had given Mrs Compline half the amount prescribed. Nicholas offered to go up to his mother, but Hersey said she thought it better not to disturb her.

'She locked her door after me,' Hersey said. 'She's quite safe and I hope she'll soon be asleep.'

Hersey asked for an account of the interview with Hart, and Mandrake gave it to her. She listened in silence to the story of Thomas and the encounter in the hall.

'What about The Pirate?' she asked suddenly. 'Is she enjoying her beauty sleep under a good dollop of her own skin food, or does she know what's happened?'

'If you mean Madame Lisse,' said Nicholas, with a return to his old air of sulkiness, 'I've told her. She's frightfully upset.'

'That's just too bad,' said Hersey.

'She's Hart's wife,' said Mandrake drearily. 'Haven't we told you?'

'What?'

'Don't ask me why it was a secret. Something to do with face-lifting. It's all too fantastically involved. Perhaps you knew, Compline?'

'I didn't know, I don't believe it,' said Nicholas dully, and nothing, Mandrake thought, could have shown more clearly the shock of William's death than the amazing apathy with which this news was received. They discussed it half-heartedly and soon returned to the old theme.

'What I can't understand,' said Chloris, 'is *why* he did it. I know Bill had talked wildly about exposing him, but after all *we* knew about the Vienna business too. He couldn't hope to frighten us into silence.'

'I think he's mad,' said Nicholas. 'I think it was simply that last outburst of anger at the wireless that sent him off at the deep end. I think he probably went into the room with the idea of screaming out at Bill as he had already screamed at me. And I think he had a sort of hysterical crisis and grabbed the nearest weapon and – ' He caught his breath in a sort of sob, and for the first time Mandrake felt genuinely sorry for him. 'That's what I think,' said Nicholas, 'and you can imagine what it feels like. I'd deliberately goaded him with the wireless. You heard me, Mandrake.' He looked from one to another of his listeners. 'How could I know? I suppose it was a silly thing to do, a rotten thing to do, if you like, but he'd been pretty foul with his threats and his booby traps. It was me he was after, wasn't it? How could I know he'd take it out on old Bill? How could I know!'

'Don't, Nick,' said Hersey. 'You couldn't know.'

Mandrake said: 'You needn't blame youself. You've got it wrong. Don't you see, all of you? He came in at the hall door. William was sitting with his back to the door, bending over the radio. All Hart could see from there was the back of his tunic and the nape of his neck. A few minutes before, he had heard you, Compline, tell him face to face that you were going to use the radio if you wanted to. A few seconds later both Hart and I heard you say: "Oh, *all* right. Go to bed, Bill." There, when he entered the room, was a man in uniform bending over the controls. The only light in the room was over by the fireplace. Don't you understand, all of you? When he struck at William Compline he thought he was attacking his brother.'

V

'Aubrey, my dear fellow,' said Jonathan, 'I believe you are right. I am sure you are right. It is quite masterly. An admirable piece of reasoning.'

'It doesn't get us over the hurdle, though,' said Mandrake. 'He's been too clever for us. You'll have to talk to that man, Jonathan. If he saw Hart go upstairs and remained in the hall for any length of time afterwards, Hart's got an alibi that we're going to have a devilish job to break. What's the time?'

'Five past eleven,' said Chloris.

'They won't be in bed yet, will they? You'd better send for him, Jo,' said Hersey.

Jonathan fidgeted and made little doubtful sounds. 'My dear Jo, you'll have to tell the servants some time.'

'I'll go and speak to them in the servants' hall.'

'I wouldn't,' said Hersey. 'I'd ring and speak to them here. I think we ought to be together when you talk to Thomas. After all,' said Hersey, 'I suppose if we can't break Dr Hart's alibi, we're all under suspicion.'

'My dear girl, that's utterly preposterous. Please remember we were all together in this room when William produced the war news on the wireless. Or, which I think more likely, when Hart produced it.'

'No,' Mandrake said. 'We've tried that. It won't work. Jonathan, you went into the hall after the news began. Was Thomas there then?'

'No,' shouted Jonathan angrily, 'of course he wasn't. The hall was empty and there was no light in the boudoir. I crossed the hall and went into the downstairs cloakroom. When I returned it was still empty.'

'Then perhaps his story about Thomas . . . '

'For heaven's sake,' cried Hersey, 'let's ask Thomas.'

After a good deal of demurring, Jonathan finally rang the bell. Caper answered it, and accepted the news of sudden death and homicide with an aplomb which Mandrake had imagined to be at the command only of family servants in somewhat dated comedies. Caper said 'Indeed, sir?' some five or six times with nicely varied inflexions. He then went in search of Thomas, who presently appeared wearing the air of one who has crammed himself hastily into his coat. He was a pale young man with damp waves in his hair. Evidently he had been primed by Caper, for he was not quite able to conceal a certain air of avidity. He answered Jonathan's questions promptly and sensibly. Yes, he had met Dr Hart in the hall as he brought up the tray. Dr Hart came out of the boudoir as Thomas walked up the passage and into the rear of the hall. He was quite positive it was the boudoir. He noticed that the lights were out. He noticed light coming from under the door into the smoking room. Before Thomas entered the library, Dr Hart had reached the stairs and had turned on the wall switch belonging to the stair lamps. When Thomas came out of the library, Dr Hart had reached the visitors' room flight. Thomas stayed in the hall. He locked the front doors, made up the fire and tidied the tables. In answer to a question from Mandrake he said that he heard music from the radio in the smoking room.

'What sort of music?' asked Mandrake.

'Beg pardon, sir?'

'Did you recognize the music?'

' "Boomps-a-daisy", sir,' said Thomas unhappily.

'Well, go on, go on,' said Jonathan. 'You went away then, I suppose.'

'No, sir.'

'What the devil did you do with yourself, hanging about the hall?' demanded Jonathan, who was beginning to look extremely uneasy.

'Well, sir, excuse me, sir, I – I . . . '

'You *what!*'

'I went through the movements, sir. "Hands, knees", in time to the music, sir. I don't know why, I'm sure, sir. It just came over me. Only for a minute like, because the music only lasted a very short time, sir, and then it was turned off.'

'Cavorting about the hall like a buck-rabbit!' said Jonathan.

'I'm sure I'm very sorry, sir.'

For a moment Jonathan seemed to be extraordinarily put out by this confession of animal spirits on the part of Thomas, but suddenly he made one of his quick pounces and cried out triumphantly: 'Aha! So you were dancing, Thomas, were you? An abrupt attack *of joie de vivre?* And why not? Why not? You were intent upon it, I dare say. Turning this way and that, eh? I suppose it would take you right across the hall. I'm not familiar with the dance, I must confess, but I imagine it's pretty lively, what?'

'Yes, sir. Rather lively, sir.'

'Rather lively,' repeated Jonathan. 'Quite so. You'd be so taken up with it, I dare say, that you wouldn't notice if somebody came into the hall, um?'

'Beg pardon, sir, but nobody came into the hall, sir. The music stopped and the news started and I went back to the servants' sitting room, sir, but nobody came into the hall while I was there.'

'But, my good Thomas, I – I put it to you. I put it to you, that while you were clapping your hands and slapping your knees and all the rest of it, it would have been perfectly easy for someone to cross the hall unnoticed. Come now!'

'Look here, Thomas,' said Mandrake. 'Let's put it this way. Somebody *did* come downstairs while you were in the hall. This person came downstairs and went into the smoking room. Don't you remember?'

'I'm very sorry, sir, to contradict you,' said Thomas, turning a deep plum colour, 'but I assure you they didn't. They couldn't of. I was close by the smoking room door, sir, and facing the stairs. What I mean to say, I just 'eard, heard, the tune, sir, and I'm sure I don't know why, I did a couple of hands, knees, and boomps; well, for the fun of it, like.'

'Thomas,' Mandrake said, 'suppose you were in a court of law and were asked to swear on the Bible that nobody was in the hall from the time you came out of the library until the time you went back to your own quarters? What about it?'

'I'd swear, sir.'

'There's nothing to be gained by going on with this, Aubrey,' said Jonathan. 'Thank you, Thomas.'

'Thank you, sir,' said Thomas, and retired.

'There's only one explanation,' said Nicholas. 'He must have come back after that chap went back to his quarters.'

'All the way downstairs and across the hall?' said Mandrake. 'I suppose it's possible. In that case he avoided running into Jonathan, and did the whole thing while that short news bulletin was being read. It was all over and he'd bolted when Lady Hersey went into the smoking room and turned off the radio. It's a close call.'

He bent down and slipped a finger inside his shoe. 'Damn!' he said. 'Does any one mind if I take off my shoe? I've got a nail sticking into my foot.'

He took off the shoe and noticed how they all glanced at his sound foot and away again quickly. He groped inside the shoe. 'There it is,' he muttered; 'a damn' great spike of a thing.'

'But there's something in the sole of your shoe,' said Chloris. 'Look.'

Mandrake turned the shoe over. 'It's a drawing pin,' he said.

'There's *some* explanation,' said Nicholas with a real note of despair in his voice. 'He's upstairs there, lying in his bed, by God, and laughing at us. Somehow or other he worked it. During the news. It must have been then. Somehow or other. When I think about it I'm sure it was Bill who worked the wireless. I know you'll say it was easy for anybody to grunt and cross the room, but somehow, I can't explain why, I believe it was Bill – it sort of *felt* like Bill.'

'Ssh!' said Hersey suddenly. 'Listen!'

They stared at her. Her hand was raised and her head tilted. Into a profound silence that fell upon them came a wide, vague drumming. The shutters of the library windows creaked. As they listened, the room was filled with that enveloping outside noise.

'It's beginning to rain,' said Jonathan.

CHAPTER 10

Journey

They had exhausted themselves arguing about the gap in Hart's story. They had said the same things over and over again. They longed to go to bed, and yet were held prisoner in their chairs by a dreadful lassitude. They kept telling Nicholas to go to bed, and he kept saying that he would go. They spoke in low voices to a vague background of drumming rain. Mandrake felt as if it was William himself who kept them there, William who, behind locked doors, now suffered the indignities of death. He could not help but think of that figure in the chair. Suppose, with those stealthy changes, William's body was to move? Suppose they were to hear, above the murmur of rain, a dull thud in the room next door? Nicholas, too, must have been visited by some such thoughts, for he said: 'I can't bear to think of him – can't we – can't we?' And Mandrake had to explain again that they must not move William.

'Do you think,' he asked Jonathan, 'that with this rain the roads will be passable in the morning? What about the telephone? Is there any chance that the lines will be fixed up?'

There was a telephone in the library, and from time to time they had tried it, knowing each time that it was useless. 'If the roads are anything like passable,' Mandrake said, 'I'll drive into Chipping in the morning.'

'You?' said Nicholas.

'Why not? My club foot doesn't prevent me from driving a car, you know,' said Mandrake. This was one of the speeches, born of his deformity, which he sometimes blurted out and always regretted.

'I didn't mean that,' said Nicholas. 'I'm sorry.'

'Why shouldn't I go?' asked Mandrake, looking from one to another. 'Even if we can't break Hart's alibi, I suppose none of you will suspect me. After all, I *was* shoved in the pond.'

'I keep forgetting that complication,' said Jonathan.

'I don't,' Mandrake rejoined warmly.

'We ought none of us to forget it,' said Chloris. 'It's the beginning of the whole thing. If *only* you'd gone on looking out of the pavilion window, Nicholas.'

'I know. But I was half-undressed and hellish cold. I just saw it was Mandrake and answered his wave. If only I had looked out again!'

'I've not the least doubt about what you'd have seen,' Mandrake rejoined. 'You'd have seen that infamous little man come up in a flurry of snow from behind the pavilion, and you'd have seen him launch a sort of flying tackle at my back.'

'I've made a complete hash of everything,' Nicholas burst out. 'You're all being very nice about it, I know, but the facts stare you in the eye, don't they? I know what you're thinking. You're thinking that if I hadn't baited Hart this would never have happened. Well, let him get on with it, by God. He's messed it up three times, hasn't he? Let him have another pot at me. I shan't duck.'

'Nick,' said Hersey, 'don't show off, my dear. Are we never to register dislike of anyone for fear they go off and murder our near relations? Don't be an ass, my dear old thing. Since we are being candid, let's put it this way. Dr Hart was crossed in love and he couldn't take it. You did the crossing. I don't say I approve of your tactics, and, as I dare say you've noticed, I don't admire your choice. But, for pity's sake, don't go all broken-with-remorse on us. You've got your mother to think of.'

'If anybody other than Hart is to blame,' said Jonathan, 'very clearly it is I.'

'Now, Jo,' said Hersey roundly, 'none of that from you. You've been a very silly little man, trying to rearrange people's lives for them. This is what you get for it, and no doubt it'll be a lesson to you. But it's no good putting on that face about it. We must be practical. We've got a man whom we all believe to be a murderer, locked up in his room, and as we don't seem to be very good at bringing it home to him the best thing we can do is to accept Mr Mandrake's offer and to hope that in the morning he will be able to reach a telephone and find us a policeman.'

'Hersey, my dear,' said Jonathan with a little bob in her direction, 'you are perfectly right. Nick and I must bow to your ruling. If Aubrey can and will go, why then go he shall.'

'I thought,' said Mandrake, 'that I'd try to reach the rectory at Winton St Giles. You see, there's rather a super sort of policeman staying there, and as I know him . . . '

'Roderick Alleyn?' Chloris cried out. 'Why, of course!'

'I thought I'd put the whole thing before him. I thought that when I got upstairs I'd write it all down, everything I can remember from the time I got here. I don't know what the regulations are, but if I show what I've written to Alleyn, at least if *he* can't do anything he'll advise *me* what to do.'

'I think we should see your notes, Aubrey.'

'Of course, Jonathan. I hope you'll be able to add to them. It seems to me that when you write things out they have a way of falling into place. Perhaps when he reads our notes we may see a still wider gap in Hart's alibi. I think we should concentrate on the time Jonathan was in the downstairs cloakroom and the moment or two after Jonathan returned and before Lady Hersey went into the smoking room. I think we shall find that the gaps are there all right. If we don't, perhaps Alleyn will.'

'I'm afraid I don't believe he will,' said Chloris slowly. She reached out her hand and touched Mandrake's arm. 'Don't think I'm crabbing your idea. It's a grand idea. But somehow, I can't tell you how I hate to say it, somehow I don't believe we will find a big enough gap. I don't think there is one.'

'I won't have that,' said Jonathan loudly, 'there's plenty of time. There must be.'

He stood up and the others rose with him. At last they were going to bed. With dragging steps and heavy yawns they moved uncertainly about the room. The men had a last drink. Desultory suggestions were made. Nicholas, with a return of nervousness which contrasted strangely with his recent mood of heroic despondency, started an argument about leaving Hart's door unguarded. Hart might try to break out, he said. Mandrake pointed out that if they kept their own doors locked it wouldn't much matter if he did. He, as much as they, was a prisoner in the house. 'Anyway,' added Mandrake, 'we're not going to sleep through a door-smashing incident, I suppose. Here's your automatic, by the way, Compline.' And for the life of him Mandrake couldn't resist adding: 'You may feel more comfortable if you have it at your bedside.' Nicholas took it quite meekly.

'Well,' he said in a small desolate voice, 'I may as well go up, I suppose.' He looked towards the locked door into the smoking room and Mandrake saw his rather prominent eyes dilate. 'He offered to swap rooms with me,' said Nicholas. 'Decent of him, wasn't it? In case Hart tried anything during the night, you know. Of course, I wouldn't have let him. I'm glad we sort of got together a bit this evening.' He looked at his hands and then vaguely up at Jonathan. 'Well, goodnight,' said Nicholas.

'We'll come up with you, Nick,' said Hersey, and linked her arm in his.

'Will you? Oh, thank you, Hersey.'

'Of course we shall,' said Chloris. 'Come on, Nick.'

Jonathan and Mandrake followed, and as Mandrake, weary to death, limped up those stairs for the last time on that fatal day, he thought, and detested himself for so thinking: 'He *would* go up between the two women. I bet he's got hold of Chloris's hand.' Jonathan said goodnight on the halfway landing and turned off to his own wing.

Only then did it occur to Mandrake that since his flare-up with Hart, Jonathan had been unusually quiet. 'And no wonder,' he thought. 'They can say what they like, but after all if he hadn't thrown his fool party . . . '

They went with Nicholas to his room. Moved by an obscure mixture of contrition and genuine sympathy, Mandrake shook hands with him and instantly regretted it when Nicholas, with tears in his eyes, kissed the two women and said in a broken voice: 'Bless you. I'll be all right. Goodnight.'

'Goodnight,' said Hersey in the passage and stumped off to her room.

'Goodnight,' said Chloris to Mandrake, and then, rather defiantly: 'Well, I *am* sorry for him.'

'Goodnight,' said Mandrake, 'so am I.'

'You do look tired. We've all forgotten about your horrid plunge. You won't tackle those notes tonight?'

'I think so. While it's still seething, don't you know?'

'Well, don't treat the subject surrealistically or we'll none of us be able to contradict you. You ought not to have had all these games thrust upon you. Are you all right?'

'Perfectly all right,' said Mandrake. 'But I approve of you feeling sorry for me.'

So Chloris gave him a kiss, and in a state of bewildered satisfaction he went to his room.

II

It was one o'clock when he laid down his pen and read through his notes. At the end he had written a summary in which he attempted to marshal the salient facts of the three assaults. He re-read this summary twice.

'1. The incident of the Charter form. Hart wrote the message because he, and only he, handed his papers on to Nicholas. The letters resemble those in his note to Jonathan. The incident followed his picking a quarrel with Nicholas after dinner. NB – get an account of quarrel from Jonathan, who was the only witness.

'2. The incident by the pond. Motive apart, Nicholas didn't shove me over because he recognized me through the window and in any case knew I was wearing the cape. Besides he saved my life by throwing in the inflated bird. William didn't because he arrived at about the same time as Nicholas and had come down the terrace steps. Nicholas saw him come. Chloris didn't because she didn't. Jonathan arrived after Chloris, catching her up when she was nearly there. He had seen Hart leave by the front drive. Hart arrived by a path that comes out behind the pavilion. I had my back turned to him. He had seen Nicholas, wearing a cape that is the double of mine. I had the hood over my head. NB – who was the woman who came out of the house as far as the terrace? (Footprints in snow.) She may have seen who threw me overboard. If so, why hasn't she spoken? Her prints were close to the others. A small foot. Could she have gone down the steps inside my footprints?

Madame Lisse's window overlooks the terrace. Hart habitually wears a cape.

'3. The booby trap. Hart is the only member of the party who hasn't an alibi. Jonathan's alibi depends on me. I can't remember exactly how long he was in the drawing room before the crash, but anyway why should Jonathan want to kill Nicholas? Hart must have set the booby trap.

'4. The murder. On re-reading these notes I find that Madame Lisse, Lady Hersey and Mrs Compline have not got alibis. Madame Lisse and Mrs Compline could have come downstairs and entered the smoking room by the boudoir. But if either of them did it, how did she leave? Thomas was in the hall when William turned on the radio and remained there until the news. I suppose Madame Lisse or Mrs Compline might have actually hidden in the room and slipped out when Lady Hersey came to fetch Jonathan, but it seems more likely that they could have managed to dodge both Thomas and Jonathan. Mrs Compline is out of it. No motive. Madame Lisse had no motive in killing Nicholas, so if she did it she recognized William and her motive here . . . '

At this point Mandrake, remembering that the others would read his summary, lost his nerve and scored out the next three lines and the preceding words from 'No Motive' onwards. He then read on.

'Nicholas didn't do it because some time after he left the smoking room, the wireless was switched on. This must have been done by William, or conceivably by his murderer. We didn't see him although the door was open. The screen hid him. But someone did cross the room and turn on the wireless.

'Lady Hersey went in with the drink and of course, theoretically, could have killed William, and then come and called Jonathan. No motive.

'Hart came out of the boudoir and was seen by Thomas as he brought the drinks. When Thomas reappeared a few seconds later, Hart was on the stairs. No time to go back and kill William in the interim. He didn't return before the news because Thomas remained in the hall until then and because William turned on "Boomps-a-daisy" after Hart had gone. If Hart killed William, it was after Thomas left the hall. Could he have done it in the time and avoided meeting Jonathan?

'Jonathan himself left the library after the news began and returned before Hersey took in the drink. He says he crossed the hall to and from the cloakroom and saw nobody. Could Hart have dodged him? Possible.

'This seems to be the only explanation.'

Here the summary came abruptly to an end. Mandrake sat very still for perhaps a minute. Then he took out his cigarette case, put it down unopened, and reached again for his pen. He added seven words to his summary:

'Could Hart have set another booby trap?'

When he lifted his hand he saw that he had left a small red stain on the paper. He had washed his hands as soon as he came upstairs, but his mind jumped with a spasm of nausea to the memory of the red star that had fallen from William's mouth. Then he remembered that when he took out his cigarette case he had felt a prick and there, sure enough, on the tip of his middle finger was a little red globule. He felt again in his pocket and found the drawing-pin that had penetrated the sole of his shoe. He put it on the paper before him. Across the back of the drawing pin was a dry white ridge.

He heard William's voice speaking gravely in the drawing-room: '*Very* thick oil paint.'

He put the drawing-pin in a match-box and locked the box in his attaché case, together with the Charter form which he had got from Jonathan.

Then he went to bed.

III

It was some time before he slept. Several times he came to the borderland where conscious thought mingles fantastically with the images of the subconscious. At these moments he saw a Maori mere, like Damocles' sword, suspended above his head by a hair which was fixed to the ceiling by an old drawing-pin. 'It *might* hold,' said William, speaking indistinctly because his mouth was full of blood. 'It *might* hold, you know. I use *very* thick oil paint.' He couldn't move because the folds of the Tyrolese cape were wrapped round his limbs. A rubber bird, wearing a god-like leer, bobbed its scarlet beak at him.

'It's snowing harder than ever,' said the bird, and at that precise moment Hart cut the hair with a scalpel. *'Down* she comes, by Jupiter,' they all shouted, but Chloris, with excellent intentions, kicked him between the shoulder-blades and he fell with a sickening jolt back into his bed, and woke again to hear the rain driving against the windowpane.

At last, however, he fell into a true sleep, and was among the first of the seven living guests to do so. Dr Hart was the very first. Long before the others came upstairs to bed, Dr Hart's dose of proprietary soporific had restored his interrupted oblivion and now his mouth was open, his breathing deep and stertorous.

His wife was not so fortunate. She heard them all come upstairs, she heard them wish each other goodnight, she heard door after door close softly, and imagined key after key turning with a click as each door was shut. Sitting upright in bed in her fine nightgown she listened to the rain, and made plans for her own security.

Hersey Amblington, too, was wakeful. She kept her bedside lamp alight and absent-mindedly slapped 'Hersey's Skin Food' into her face with a patent celluloid patter. As she did this she tried distractedly to order her thoughts away from the memory of a figure in an armchair, from a head that was broken like an egg, and from a wireless cabinet that screamed 'Boomps-a-daisy'. She thought of herself twenty years ago, afraid to tell her cousin Jonathan that she would marry him. She thought of her business rival and wondered quite shamelessly if, with the arrest of Hart, Madame Lisse would carry her piratical trade elsewhere. Finally, hoping to set up a sort of counter-irritant in horror, she thought about her own age. But the figure in the chair was persistent, and Hersey was afraid to go to sleep.

Chloris was not much afraid. She had not seen William. But she was extremely bewildered over several discoveries that she had made about herself. The most upsetting of these was the discovery that she now felt nothing but a vague pity for Nicholas, and an acute pity for William. She had never pretended to herself that she was madly in love with William but she had believed herself to be very fond of him. It was Nicholas who had held her in the grip of a helpless attraction, it was from this bondage that she had torn herself on a climax of misery. She believed that when Nicholas had become aware of his brother's determined courtship, he had set himself to cut William out.

Having succeeded very easily in this project he had tired of her and, in the meantime, he had met Elise Lisse. She thought of the letter in which she broke off her engagement to Nicholas, and with shame of the new engagement to his brother; of how every look, every word that was exchanged between them, for her held only one significance; its effect upon Nicholas, of the miserable satisfaction she had known when Nicholas showed his resentment, of the exultation she had felt when, again, he began to show off his paces before her. And now it was all over. She had cried a little out of pity for William and from the shock to her nerves, and she had seen Nicholas once and for all as a silly fellow and a bit of a coward. A phrase came into her thoughts: 'So that's all about the Complines.' With an extraordinary lightening of her spirits she now allowed herself to think of Aubrey Mandrake. 'Of Mr Stanley Footling,' she corrected herself. 'It ought to be funny. Poor Mr Stanley Footling turning as white as paper and letting me in on the ground floor. It isn't funny. I can't make a good story of it. It's infinitely touching and it doesn't matter to me, only to him.' And she thought: 'Did I take the right line about it?' She had gone to her room determined to break Dr Hart's alibi, but a whole hour had passed and not once had she thought of Dr Hart.

Jonathan Royal clasped his hot-water bag to his midriff and stared before him into the darkness. If the top strata of his thoughts had been written down they would have read something like this: 'It's an infernal bore about Thomas but there must be some way out of it. Aubrey is going to be tiresome, I can see. He's half inclined to believe Hart. *Damn* Thomas. There must be some way. An ingenious turn, now. My thoughts are going round in circles. I must concentrate. What will Aubrey write in his notes? I must read them carefully. Can't be too careful. This fellow, Alleyn. What will he make of it? Why, there's motive, the two attempts, *our* alibis – he can't come to any other conclusion. *Damn* Thomas.'

Nicholas tossed and turned in the bed his brother had offered to take. He was unaccustomed to consecutive or ordered thinking, and across his mind drifted an endless procession of dissociated images and ideas. He saw himself and William as children. He saw William going back to school at the end of his holidays. Nicholas and his tutor had gone in the car to the station. There was Bill's face, pressed against the windowpane as the train went out. He heard Bill's adolescent voice breaking comically into falsetto: 'She'd like it to be you at Penfelton and me anywhere else. But I'm the eldest. You can't alter that. Mother will never forgive me for it.' He saw Chloris the first time she came to Penfelton as William's guest for a house-party. 'Mother, will you ask Chloris Wynne? She's my girl, Nick. No poaching.' And lastly he saw Elise Lisse, and heard his own voice: 'I never knew it could be like this. I never knew.'

Sandra Compline laid down her pen. She enclosed the paper in an envelope and wrote a single word of direction. Outside on the landing the grandfather clock struck two. She wrapped her dressing-gown more closely round her. The fire was almost dead and she was bitterly cold. The moment had come for her to get into bed. The bed-clothes were disordered. She straightened them carefully, and then glanced round the room which was quite impersonal and, but for the garments she had worn during the day, very neat. She folded them and put them away, shivering a little as she did so. She caught sight of her face in the glass and paused before it to touch her hair. On an impulse, she leant forward and stared at the reflection. Next, she moved to the bedside-table and for some minutes her hands were busy there. At last she got into bed, disposed the sheet careful-ly, and drew up the counterpane. Then she stretched out her hand to the bedside-table.

IV

It was an isolated storm that visited Cloudyfold that night. Over the greater part of Dorset the snow lay undisturbed, but here in the uplands it was drilled with rain, and all through the night hills and trees suffered a series of changes. In the depths of Jonathan's woods, branches, released from their burden of snow, jerked sharply upwards. From beneath battlements of snow, streams of water began to move and there were secret downward shiftings of white masses. With the diminution of snow the natural contours of the earth slowly returned. Towards dawn in places where there had been smooth depressions sharp furrows began to take form, and these were sunken lanes. In Deep Bottom, beneath the sound of rain was the sound of running water.

The guests, when at last they slept, were sometimes troubled in their dreams by strange noises on the roofs and eaves of the house where masses of snow became dislodged and slid into gutters and hollows. The drive and the road from Highfold down into Cloudyfold village and up into the hills began to find themselves. So heavy was the downpouring of rain that by dawn the countryside was dappled with streaks of heavy greys and patches of green. When Mandrake woke at eight o'clock his windows were blinded with rain and through the rain he saw the tops of evergreen trees, no longer burdened with snow.

He breakfasted alone with Jonathan, who told him that already he had seen some of the outdoor staff. His bailiff had ridden up from his own cottage on horseback and had gone out again on a round of inspection. Jonathan had told him of the tragedy. He had offered to ride over Cloudyfold. It meant twelve miles at a walking pace supposing he did get through.

'If I stick,' said Mandrake, 'he can try. If I'm not back in three hours, Jonathan, he had better try. What sort of mess is the drive, did he say?' The Bewlings, it seemed, had been down to the front gates and reported that the drive was 'a masterpiece of muck', but not, they thought, impassable. You could get over Cloudyfold on a horse, no doubt, but a car would never do it.

'How about the road down to the village?' asked Mandrake.

'That's in better case, I understand.'

'Then if I got through Deep Bottom I could drive down to Cloudyfold village and telephone from there to the rectory at Winton St Giles?'

'The lines may be down between the village and Winton. They go over the hills. I think it most probable that they are down. As far as the Bewlings went they found nothing the matter with my own line.'

'Can't I get to Winton St Giles by way of the village?'

'A venture that is comparable to Chesterton's journey to Birmingham by way of Beachy Head, my dear Aubrey. Let me see. You would have to take the main road east, turn to your right at Pen-Gidding, skirt Cloudyfold hills and – but Heaven knows what state those roads would be in. From Pen-Gidding there are only the merest country lanes.'

'I can but try.'

'I don't like it.'

'Jonathan,' said Mandrake, 'do you like the idea of leaving William Compline's body in your smoking room for very much longer?'

'Oh, my dear fellow, no. No, of course not. This is horrible, a nightmare. I shall never recover from this weekend, never.'

'Do you think one of the Bewling brothers could come with me? If I did come to a standstill it would be helpful to have someone, and if I don't he could direct me.'

'Of course, of course. If you must go.' Jonathan brightened a little and began to make plans. 'You must take a flask of brandy, my dear boy. James Bewling shall go with you. Chains now. You will need chains on your wheels, won't you?'

'There's not by any chance a police station at Cloudyfold village?'

'Good gracious, no. The merest hamlet. No, the nearest constable, I fancy, is at Chipping, and that's beyond Winton St Giles.'

'At any rate,' said Mandrake, 'I think I'd better see Alleyn first. I only hope he'll consent to run the whole show and come back with me, but I suppose I shall run into an entanglement of red-tape if I suggest such a thing.'

'Dear me, I suppose so. I scarcely know which prospect is more distasteful – the Chipping constabulary or your terrifying acquaintance.'

'He's a pleasant fellow.'

'Very possibly. Perhaps I had better send for old James Bewling before he plunges out of doors again.'

Jonathan rang the bell, which was answered by Thomas, who was unable to conceal entirely an air of covert excitement. He said that the Bewlings were still in the house and in a minute or two James appeared, very conscious of his boots.

'Now, James,' said Jonathan, 'Mr Mandrake and I want your advice and assistance. Dry your legs at the fire and never mind about your boots. Listen.'

He unfolded Mandrake's project. James listened with his mouth not quite shut, his eyes fixed upon some object at the far end of the room, and his brows drawn together in a formidable scowl.

'Now, do you think it is possible?' Jonathan demanded.

'Ah,' said James. 'Matter a twenty miles it be, that road. Going widdershins like, you see, sir. She'll be fair enough so furr as village and a good piece below. It's when she do turn in and up, if you take my meaning, sir, as us'll run into muck and as like as not, slip, and as like as not if there bean't no slips, there'll be drifts.'

'Then you *don't* think it possible, James?'

'With corpses stiffening on the premises, sir, all things be possible to a man with a desperate powerful idea egging him on.'

'My opinion exactly, Bewling,' said Mandrake. 'Will you come with me?'

'That I will, sir,' said James. 'When shall us start?'

'Now, if you will. As soon as possible.' And as he spoke these words Mandrake was moved by a great desire for his venture. Soon he would meet Chloris again, and to that meeting he looked forward steadily and ardently, but in the meantime he must be free of Highfold for a space. He must set out in driving rain on a difficult task. It would be with bad roads and ill weather that he must reckon for the next hour or so, not with the complexities of human conduct. His eagerness for these encounters was so foreign to his normal way of thinking that he felt a sort of astonishment at himself. 'But I don't like leaving her here. Shall I wait until she appears and suggest that she comes with us? Perhaps she would not care to come. Perhaps I have embarrassed her with my dreary confidences. She might be afraid I'd go all Footling at her on the drive.' He began to horrify himself with the notion that Chloris thought of him as under-bred and over-vehement, a man whom she would have to shake off before he became a nuisance. He went upstairs determined that he would not succumb to the temptation of asking her to go with him, met her on the top landing, and immediately asked her.

'Of course I'll come,' said Chloris.

'It may be quite frightful. We may break down completely.'

'At least we'll be out of all this. I won't be five minutes.'

'You'll want layers of coats,' cried Mandrake. 'I'll get hold of old James Bewling and we'll have the car round at the front door as soon as he's found me some chains.'

He went joyfully to his own room, put on an extra sweater, a muffler and his raincoat. He snatched up the attaché case containing his notes, the drawing-pin and the Charter form. He remembered suddenly that the others were to have gone over the notes before he took them to Alleyn. Well, if they wanted to do that they should have got up earlier. He couldn't wait about half the morning. They would have plenty of chances to argue over his account when he came back with Alleyn. Now for the car.

But before he went out of doors he found Jonathan and nerved himself to make a request. The thought of revisiting the smoking room was horrible, but he had promised himself that he would do so. He half hoped Jonathan would refuse, but he did not. 'I won't come with you, that's all. Don't ask it. Here are the keys. You may keep them. I simply can *not* accompany you.'

'I shan't touch anything. Please wait by the door.'

He was only a few minutes in that room. They had thrown a white sheet over the chair and what was in it. He tried not to look at that, but he was shaken when he came out and said goodbye quietly to Jonathan.

He went out by the west door and walked around the back of the house to the garages. The whole world seemed to be alive with the sound of rain and wind. Much of the snow lying in exposed places had gone, everywhere it was pocked and crenellated. From the eaves of Highfold it hung in strange forms that changed continually and tapered into falling water.

Using his stick vigorously, Mandrake reached the garages to find James Bewling, assisted by his brother, engaged in fitting chains to the car wheels. They seemed to Mandrake to be incredibly slow about this. The chains were improvised arrangements and one set kept slipping. At last, however, they were ready and he prepared to drive out.

'They'll hold now, certain sure. Lucky we had 'em,' said James. 'Us'll need 'em up along, never fear. Now then, sir, if you be agreeable I reckon car's ready to start. Us've filled her up with petrol and water and there's hauly-chains and sacks in the back.'

'Come on then,' said Mandrake.

James climbed in the back. As they left the garage his brother bawled at them: 'If 'er skiddles, rush 'er up.' He drove round to the front doors and found Chloris there. The collar of her heavy coat was turned up, and she had a gay scarf tied round her head so that he saw her face as a triangle. It was a very white triangle and her eyes looked horror-stricken. As soon as she saw the car she stumbled down the steps, and, leaning against the wind, ran round to the passenger's door. Before he could get it open she was struggling with the handle and in a moment had scrambled in beside him.

'What now?' asked Mandrake.

'I'd better tell you before we start, but Mr Royal says we're to go anyway. Another ghastliness. Mrs Compline. She's tried to kill herself.'

V

Mandrake turned with his hands on the driving-wheel and gazed at her. James Bewling cleared his throat stertorously.

'Please start,' said Chloris, and without a word Mandrake engaged his first gear. To the sound of slapping chains, driving wind and rain, and with a cold engine, they moved across the wide sweep and round the west side of the house.

'She did it herself,' said Chloris. 'One of the maids went up with her breakfast and found the door locked. The housekeeper thought she ought not to be disturbed, but the maid had seen lamplight under the door when she went up with early tea. So they told Mr Royal. It seemed queer, you see, for the lamps to be going after it was light. In the end they decided to knock. It was just after you went out. They knocked and knocked and she didn't answer. By that time Nicholas was there and in an awful state. He insisted on Mr Royal forcing the door. She'd left a note for him – for Nicholas. There's been a frightful scene, it seems, because Mr Royal said Nicholas should give the note to somebody. He won't let Nicholas keep it, but he hasn't read it himself. I don't know what was in the note. Only Nick knows. She's unconscious. They think she's dying.'

'But – how?'

'The rest of that sleeping draught and all the aspirins she'd got. She'd told Lady Hersey she had no aspirins. I suppose she wanted to get as much as possible. You'd feel sorry for Nicholas if you could see him now.'

'Yes,' said Mandrake sombrely. 'Yes, I do feel sorry for Nicholas now.'

'He's gone to pieces. No more showing-off for poor old Nick,' said Chloris with a catch in her voice. 'There couldn't be any doubt at all that it was suicide, and he agreed that Dr Hart should be asked to see her. Pretty queer, wasn't it? They all agree that he murdered Bill, and yet there he was working at artificial respiration and snapping out orders with everybody running round obeying them. I think the world's gone mad or something. He's given me a list of things we're to get at the chemist's in Chipping. It's not far beyond Winton St Giles. I could take the car on if you like while you see Mr Alleyn. And the police surgeon. We've got to try and find him, but the important thing is to get back as quickly as possible.'

'Does Hart think . . . ?'

'I'm sure he thinks it's pretty hopeless. I wasn't in the room. I waited by the door for orders. I heard him say something about two hundred grains of veronal alone. He was barking out questions to Lady Hersey. How much had she given? How dared she give it. If it wasn't so frightful it'd be funny. She's in a pretty ghastly state herself. She feels she's responsible.'

'I took the stuff away from Hart,' said Mandrake. 'God, that's a touch of irony for you! I was afraid he might try something on himself.'

'You needn't go all remorseful,' said Chloris quickly. 'Dr Hart said the aspirin alone would have been disastrous. I heard him say that to Lady Hersey.'

They had reached the woods, where the drive ran between steep banks. Here the surface, no longer gravelled, was soft, laced with runnels of water, and littered with broken twigs and with clods of earth that had carried away from the banks. In one place there was a miniature landslide across their route. Mandrake drove hard at it in second gear and felt his back wheels spin and then grip on the chains.

'That's a taste of what we may expect in Deep Bottom, I suppose,' he called to James Bewling.

''Twill be watter down-along, I reckon, sir.'

'If we stick . . . ' Chloris began.

'If we stick, my dear, they can damn' well produce a farm animal to lug us out on the far side.'

'It's dogged as does it,' said Chloris.

Beyond Highfold woods, the drive, where it crossed the exposed parklands, was furrowed and broken by pot-holes. James Bewling remarked that he and Thomas had been telling the master for a matter of ten years that he did ought to lay down a load of metal. The rain drove full on the windscreen, checking the wiper, splaying out in serrated circles and finding its way in above the dashboard. The thrust of the wind made the car fight against Mandrake's steering. He drove cautiously towards the edge of Deep Bottom, peering through the blear of water. He recognized in himself an exhilaration, and this discovery astonished him, for he had always thought that he loathed discomfort.

Snow still lay in Deep Bottom. When they reached the lip of the hollow and looked down, they saw the drive disappear under it and rise again on the far side like a muddy ribbon.

'She's be gone down a tidy piece,' said James. 'Not above two foot now, I reckon, but happen thurr'll be watter underneath. Happen us'll do better with sack over radiator, sir.'

Mandrake pulled up and James plunged out with his sack. Mandrake stumbled after him. He didn't want to sit in the car while James fixed up the sack. He wanted to be knowledgeable and active. He tied the sacking over the radiator cap, using his handkerchief to bind it. He looked critically at the way James had tied the corners of the sack. Swinging his heavy boot briskly, he came back to the car, smiling through the rain at Chloris. The warmth in her returning glance delighted him and he innocently supposed that it was inspired by his activity. It was the glance, he told himself, of the female, approving, dependent, and even clinging. He would never know that Chloris was deeply touched, not because she saw him as a protector, but because suddenly she read his thoughts. And from that moment, in her wisdom, she let herself be minded by Mandrake.

The car began its crawl down into Deep Bottom.

'For a tidy ten yurr and more,' said James Bewling in the back seat, 'my wold brother Thomas and me been telling master as 'ow 'ee did oughter put a dinky lil' bridge across this yurr bottom. Last winter 'er was in a muck with ranging torrents and floods. Winter afore, 'er fruz. Winter afore that 'er caved in sudden.' Here the car lurched in and out of a pot-hole and James was thrown about in the back seat. 'Winter afore that 'er flooded again. Bean't no proper entrance to gentleman's 'state, us tells 'un. Ay, and us tells bailiff tu.

Pull over to your right, sir, by this yurr puddlesome corner or us'll sink to our bottoms.'

The front wheels plunged deep into a welter of slush. The back wheels churned, gripped, skidded and gripped again. Now they were into the snow, with James Bewling roaring: 'To tha right and rush 'er up.' The bonnet dipped abruptly and a welter of snow spurted over the windscreen. Mandrake leant out of the driving window and took the whipping rain full in his eyes. 'Keep 'er going, sir,' yelled James.

'I'm in a blasted hole or something. Come *up.*'

The car moved bodily to the left, churned, crept forward in a series of jerks and stopped. 'Doan't stop in-gine fur Lawk's sake,' James implored, and was out and up to his knees. He disappeared in the rear of the car.

'What's he doing?' asked Mandrake. 'He's on your side.'

Chloris looked out on her side. 'I can only see his stern. He seems to be stuffing something under the back wheel. Now he's waving. He wants you to go on.'

Mandrake engaged his bottom gear, pulled out his choke a fraction, and tried. The car gripped somewhere, wallowed forward and stuck again. James returned for his shovel and set to work in front of the bonnet. Mandrake got out, leaving instructions with Chloris to keep the engine going. The noise of the storm met him like a physical blow, and the drive of rain on his face numbed it. He struggled round to the front of the car and found James shovelling with a will in three feet of snow. Mandrake wore heavy driving gloves, and set to work with his hands. In the centre the snow was still frozen, but at the bottom it had turned to slush and the earth beneath was soft and muddy. The front wheels had jammed in a cross-gut which, as they cleared it, began to fill with water. James roared out something that Mandrake could not understand, thrust his shovel into his hands, and plunged away behind the car. Mandrake toiled on, looking up once to see Chloris's face pressed anxiously against the windscreen. He grinned, waved his hand, and fell to again with a will. James had returned, dragging two great boughs after him. They broke them up as best they could, filled in the gut with smaller branches, and thrust the remaining pieces in front of the rear wheels.

The inside of the car seemed a different world, a world that smelt of petrol, upholstery, cigarettes and something that both Mandrake and Chloris secretly realized was peculiar to James Bewling, an aftermath of oilskin, elderly man, and agricultural activities. Mandrake slammed the door, sounded his horn as a warning to James, and speeded up his engine.

'Now then, you old besom,' Mandrake apostrophized his car, 'up with you.' With a great crackling of branches, an ominous sinking and a violent lurch, they went forward and up, with James's voice raised to an elderly screech, sounding like a banshee in the storm. The chains bit into firmer ground. They were going uphill.

'That's the first hurdle over, I fancy,' said Mandrake. 'We'll wait for James at the top.'

VI

In the rectory at Winton St Giles, Chief Detective-Inspector Alleyn put his head round the study door and said to his wife: 'I've been looking out of the top windows at the summit of Cloudyfold. I wouldn't be surprised if it's raining over there. What do you say, Rector?'

The Reverend Walter Copeland turned his head to look out of the window. The lady behind the large canvas muttered to herself and laid down her brushes.

'Rain?' echoed the rector. 'It's still freezing down here. Upon my word, though, I believe you're right. Yes, yes, undoubtedly it's pouring up round Highfold. Very odd.'

'Very odd indeed,' said Mrs Alleyn grimly.

'My angel,' said her husband. 'I apologize in fourteen different positions. Rector, for pity's sake resume your pose.'

With a nervous start the rector turned from the window, clasped his hands, tilted his fine head, and stared obediently at the top left-hand corner of the canvas.

'Is that right?'

'Yes, thank you,' said the lady. Her thin face, wearing a streak of green paint across the nose, looked round the side of the canvas at her husband.

'I suppose,' she said with a surprising air of diffidence, 'you wouldn't like to read to us?'

'Yes, I would,' said Alleyn. He came in and shut the door.

'Now that's really delightful,' said Mr Copeland. 'I hope I'm not a bad parish priest,' he added, 'but it *is* rather pleasant to know that there can be no more services today – Dinah and I had matins all to ourselves you know – and that for once the weather is *so* bad that nobody is likely to come and visit me.'

'If I were on duty,' said Alleyn, looking along the bookshelves, 'I should never dare to make those observations.'

'Why not?'

'Because, if I did, as sure as fate I'd be called out into the snow, like a melodrama heroine, to a particularly disagreeable case. However,' said Alleyn, taking down a copy of *Northanger Abbey*, 'I'm not on duty, thank the Lord. Shall we have Miss Austen?'

VII

'This yurr be Pen-Gidding,' said James Bewling. 'Just to right, sir. We'm half-way theer. A nasty stretch she'll be round those thurr hills, and by the looks of her thurr's bin no rain hereabouts.'

'What's the time?' asked Chloris.

Mandrake held out his wrist. 'Have a look.'

She pushed up his cuff. 'Ten past eleven.'

'With any luck we'll be ringing the rectory doorbell before noon.'

CHAPTER 11

Alleyn

'Nicholas,' said Madame Lisse, 'come here to me.'

He had been staring through the windows of the green sitting room at the rain, which still came down like a multitude of rods, piercing all that remained of snow on the drive, filling the house with a melancholy insistence of sound. After she had spoken, though not immediately, he turned from the window and slowly crossed the room.

'Well?' he asked. 'Well, Elise?'

She reached out her hand to him, touching his wrist, compelling him with her fingers to come nearer to her. 'I am deeply grieved for you. You know that?' she said.

He took the hand and rubbed it between his two palms as if he hoped to get some warmth from it. 'If she goes,' he said, 'I've no one else, no one at all but you.' He stood beside her, still moving her fingers between his hands and peering at her oddly, almost as if he saw her for the first time. 'I don't understand,' he said. 'I don't understand.'

Madame Lisse pulled him down to the footstool beside her chair. He yielded quite obediently.

'We have got to think, to plan, to decide,' said Madame Lisse. 'I am, as I have said, deeply grieved for you. If she does not live it will be a great loss, of course. Your mother having always favoured you, one is much puzzled that she should despair to extremity at the death of your brother. For myself I believe her action should rather be attributed to a morbid dread of publicity about the misfortune to her beauty.' Madame Lisse touched her hair with the tips of her fingers. 'The loss of beauty is a sufficient tragedy, but to that she had become resigned. Your brother's threat to expose Francis, as well as the shock she sustained on recognizing Francis, no doubt unhinged her. It is very sad.' She looked down at the top of his head. It was a speculative and even a calculating glance. 'Of course,' she said, 'I have not seen her letter.' Nicholas's whole body seemed to writhe. 'I can't talk about it,' he muttered.

'Mr Royal has taken it?'

'Yes. In case – he said . . . '

'That was quite sensible, of course.'

'Elise, did you know it was Hart who did it – to her – in Vienna?'

'He told me on Friday night that he had recognized her.'

'My God, why didn't you tell me?'

'Why should I? I was already terrified of the situation between you. Why should I add to your antagonism? No, my one desire was to suppress it, my one terror that she should recognize him and that we should be ruined.' She clenched her hands and beat the arms of her chair. 'And now what am I to do! It will all come out. That he is my husband. That you are my lover. He will say terrible things when they arrest him. He will bring me down in his own ruin.'

'I swear you won't suffer.' Nicholas pressed his face against her knees and began to mutter feverish endearments and reassurances. 'Elise – when it's over – it seems frightful to speak of it – everything different, now. Elise – alone together. *Elise?*'

She stopped him at last, pressing her hands on his head.

'Very well,' she said. 'When it's all over. Very well.'

II

Dr Hart leant back on his heels, looked at the prostrate figure on the mattress, bent forward again and slapped the discoloured and distorted face. The eyes remained not quite closed, the head jerked flaccidly. He uttered a disconsolate grunt, turned the figure on its face again, and placed his hands over the ribs. Sweat was pouring down his own face and arms.

'Let me go on,' said Hersey. 'I know what to do.'

He continued three or four times with the movements of artificial respiration, and then said suddenly: 'Very well. Thank you. I have cramp.'

Hersey knelt on the floor.

'It is so long,' said Hart, 'since I was in general practice. Twenty-three years. I cannot remember my poisons. The stomach should be emptied – that is certain. If only they can return soon from the chemist. If only they can find the police surgeon!'

'Is there any improvement?' asked Jonathan.

Hart raised his shoulders and arms and let them fall.

'Oh dear, oh dear!' cried Jonathan, and wrung his hands. 'What possessed her?'

'I cannot understand it. It is the other son to whom she gave her devotion.'

Hersey raised her head for a moment to give Dr Hart a very direct stare. 'Do not stop or hesitate,' he said at once, 'steady rhythmic movements are essential. Where is the other son now?'

'Nicholas is downstairs,' Hersey grunted. 'We thought it better to keep him out of this. All things considered.'

'Perhaps you are right.' He knelt again, close to Sandra Compline's head, and stooped down. 'Where is that woman? That Pouting, who was to prepare the emetic, and find me a tube. She is too long coming.'

'I'll see,' said Jonathan and hurried out of the room.

For a time Hersey worked on in silence. Then Hart took the patient's pulse and respiration. Jonathan came panting back with a tray covered by a napkin. Hart looked at the contents. 'A poor substitute,' he said. 'We can but try. It will be better perhaps if you leave us, Mr Royal.'

'Very well.' Jonathan walked to the door, where he turned and spoke in a high voice. 'We are trusting you, Dr Hart, because we have no alternative. You will remember, if you please, that you are virtually under arrest.'

'Ah, ah!' Hart muttered. 'Go away. Don't be silly. Go away.'

'*Honestly!*' said Hersey, and then: 'You'd better go, Jo.'

Jonathan went, but no farther than the passage, where he paced up and down for some ten minutes. It is a peculiarity of some people to sing when they are agitated or annoyed. Jonathan was one of these. As, with mincing steps, he moved about his guest-wing passage, he hummed breathily, 'Il Etait Une Bergère', and beat time with his fingertips on the back of his hand. Past the niche in the wall where the brass Buddha had stood, as far as the grandfather clock, and back down the whole length of the passage, he trotted, with closed doors on each side of him and his figure passing in and out of shadows. Once he broke off his sentry-go to enter Hart's room, where he stood at the window, tapping the pane, breathily humming, staring at the rain. But in a moment or two he was back and down the passage, pausing to listen outside Mrs Compline's door, and then on again to the grandfather clock. Hersey found him at this employment when she came out. She took his arm and fell into step with him.

'Well, Jo,' said Hersey, and her voice was not very steady, 'I'm afraid we're not doing much good. At the moment nothing's worked.'

'Hersey, she *must* recover. I – I can't believe – what's happening to us, Hersey? What's happening?'

'Oh, well,' said Hersey, 'it'll be worse in the air raids. Dr Hart's doing his best, Jo.'

'But *is* he? Is he? A murderer, Hersey. A murderer, to stand between our dear old friend Sandra and death! What an incredible – what a frightful situation!'

Hersey stood stock-still. Her hand closed nervously on Jonathan's arm and she drew in a long breath. 'I don't believe he is a murderer,' she said.

Jonathan pulled his arm away as violently as if she'd pinched it.

'My dear girl,' he said loudly, 'don't be a fool. Great Heaven . . . !' He checked himself. 'I'm sorry, my dear. I was discourteous. You will forgive me. But to suggest that Hart, *Hart*, who has scarcely attempted to conceal his guilt – '

'That's not true, Jo. I mean, if he did it he managed to provide himself with an alibi that none of us can easily break.'

'Nonsense, Hersey. We *have* broken it. He committed his crime after William had turned on the news or else he himself turned it on and waited his chance to dart out of the room.'

'Yes, I know. Why didn't you run into him?'

'Because he took very good care to avoid me.'

'He seems to have done a tidy lot of dodging,' said Hersey dubiously. Jonathan uttered an exasperated noise.

'What has come over you, Hersey? You agreed that he had done it. Of course he did it. Of course he killed William. Killed him brutally and deliberately, believing him to be his brother. Aubrey has made that much clear.'

'I don't believe he did it,' Hersey repeated, and added shakily, 'after all, it's not an easy thing to say. I don't enjoy facing the implication. But I – '

'*Don't say it again,*' whispered Jonathan, and took her by the wrists. 'Who else? Who else? What has come over you?'

'It's seeing him in there, working over Sandra. Why, I believe he'd even forgotten he was accused until you reminded him just now. It's the one or two things that he's said while I've been in there. I don't think he was saying them to me so much as to himself. I believe he's got an idea that if he can save Sandra it'll atone, in a queer sort of way, for what he did to her beauty.'

'Good God, what rubbish is this? He wants to save her because he thinks he'll impress us, as it seems he has impressed you, with his personal integrity. Of course he doesn't want Sandra to die.'

'If he was guilty of murdering her son? That's not good reasoning, Jo. Sandra would be one of the most damaging witnesses against him.'

'You must be demented,' Jonathan said breathlessly, and stood looking at her and biting his fingers. 'What does all this matter? I suppose you agree that whoever set the booby trap committed the murder? Only Hart could have set the booby trap. But I'll not argue with you, Hersey. You're distracted, poor girl, distracted as we all are.'

'No,' said Hersey. 'No, Jo, it's not that.'

'Then God knows what it is,' cried Jonathan, and turned away.

'I think I heard him,' said Hersey. 'I must go back.'

In a moment she had gone and Jonathan was left to stare at the closed door of Sandra Compline's room.

III

'Only five more miles to go,' said Mandrake. 'If the snow's frozen hard all the way I believe we'll do it.'

They were in a narrow lane. The car churned, squeaked and skidded through snow that packed down under the wheels, mounted in a hard mass between the front bumpers and the radiator, and clogged the axles. Their eyes were wearied with whiteness, Mandrake's arms and back ached abominably, James Bewling had developed a distressing tendency to suck his teeth.

'Queer though it may seem in these surroundings,' said Mandrake, 'the engine's getting hot. I've been in bottom gear for the last two miles. Chloris, be an angel and light me a cigarette.'

'Down hill now, sir, every foot of her,' said James.

'That may or may not be an unmixed blessing. Why the *hell* is she sidling like this? What happened to the chains? Never mind. On we go.'

Chloris lit a cigarette and put it between his lips. 'You're doing grand, dearie,' she said in Cockney.

'I've been trying to sort things out a little for a quick news bulletin when we get there, always adding the proviso, if we get there. What's best to do? Shall I, while you push on to the chemist, tell Alleyn in a few badly-chosen words, as few as possible, what's happened, and shall we implore him to come back at once, reading my notes on the way?'

'I suppose so. Perhaps he'll insist on our going on to Great Chipping for the local experts. Perhaps he won't play.'

'It's a poisonous distance to Great Chipping. He can ring up. Surely the lines won't be down all over this incredibly primitive landscape. We *must* get back with the things from the chemist.' The rear of the car moved uncannily sideways. 'She's curtsying again. Damn, there's a bad one. *Damn.*'

They were nearly into the hedgerow. Mandrake threw out his clutch and rammed on the brake. 'I'm going to have a look at those chains.'

'Don't 'ee stir, sir,' said James. 'I'll see.'

He got out. Chloris leant forward and covered her face with her hands.

'Hallo,' said Mandrake. 'Eye-strain?' She didn't answer, but some small movement of her shoulders prompted him to put his arm about them and then he felt her trembling. 'I'm so sorry,' he said, 'so terribly sorry. Darling Chloris, I implore you not to cry.'

'I won't. I'm not going to. It's not what you think, not sorrow. Though I am terribly sorry. It must be shock or something. I've been so miserable and ashamed about the Complines. I've so wanted to be rid of them. And now – look how it's happened. It was foul of me to get engaged to Bill on the rebound. That's what it was, no denying it. And I knew all the time what I was up to. Don't be nice to me, I feel like a sweep.'

'I can't be as nice as I'd like to because here, alas, comes Mr Bewling. Blow your nose, my sweet. There'll always be an England where there's a muddy lane, a hoarding by a cowslip field, and curates in the rain. Well, James, what have you discovered?'

'Pesky chain on off hind-wheel's carried away, sir. Which is why she's been skittering and skiddling the last mile or so.'

'No doubt. Well, get in, James, get in, and I'll see if I can waddle out of the hedgerow. On mature consideration, perhaps you'd better watch me.'

James hovered over the now familiar process of churning wheels, short jerks and final recoveries. He stood within view of Mandrake and made violent gyratory movements with his hands, while an enormous drop swung from the tip of his nose.

'I have never responded in the smallest degree to rustic charm,' said Mandrake. 'All dialects are alike to me. James seems to me to be an extremely unconvincing piece of *genre*. What does he mean by these ridiculous gestures?'

'He means you're backing us into the other ditch,' said Chloris, blowing her nose. 'Oh, do be careful. Don't you see, he's steering an imaginary wheel.'

'His antics are revolting. Moreover, he smells. There, you unspeakable old grotesque, is that right?'

James, capering in the snow and unable to hear any of this, innocently nodded and grinned.

'I think you're beastly about him,' said Chloris, 'he's *very* kind.'

'Well, he can get in again. Here he comes. Are you right, James? Have a cigarette.'

'No, thankee, sir,' said James, breathing hard. 'I've never smoked one of they since I was as high as yer elber. A pipe's my fancy, sir, and that be too powerful a piece of work for the lady.'

'Not a bit, James,' said Chloris. 'Do have a pipe. You've earned it.'

James thanked her, and soon the inside of the car smelt of nothing but his pipe. For some little time they lurched down the lane in silence, but presently Mandrake leant his head towards Chloris and said in a low voice: 'I hope you won't mind my mentioning it, but I never expected to lose my heart to a blonde. The darker the better hitherto, I assure you. Not pitch-black, of course. White faces and black heads have been my undoing.'

'If you're trying to cheer me up,' Chloris rejoined, 'you've hit on an unfortunate theme. I went ashen for Nicholas, and I certainly can't revoke for you.'

'There!' cried Mandrake triumphantly. 'I should have known my instinct was not at fault. You idiot, darling, why did you? Oh, all right, all right. What's the time?'

'It's five minutes to twelve. We shan't be there by midday after all.'

'We shan't be much later, I swear. I wonder – Have you ever known any one who took an overdose of a sleeping-draught?'

'Never. But we had something about them in my home-nursing course. I've been trying to remember. I think they're all barbitones, and I think the lecturer said that people who took too much sank into a coma and might keep on like that for hours or even days. You had to try and get rid of the poison and rouse them. I – I think it's terribly important that we should be quick. Dr Hart said so. Aubrey, we've got so much to say when we get there, and so little time for saying it.'

'I've tried to get it down to some sort of coherent form.'

'When you made your notes, did you think of anything new, anything that would help to explain about William?'

Mandrake did not answer immediately. They had reached a stretch of road where the snow was less thick and was frozen hard. They had left the Cloudyfold hills behind and to their right, and had come into a level stretch between downlands and within sight of scattered cottages, each with its banner of smoke, the only signals of warmth in that cold countryside. Hedges broke through the snow, like fringes of black coral in an immobile sea. There was no wind down here, and the trees, lined with snow, made frozen gestures against a sky of lead. Mandrake was visited by the notion that his car was a little world which clung precariously to its power of movement, and he felt as if he himself fought, not against snow and mud, but against immobility. He wrenched his thoughts round to Chloris's question.

'If you open that attaché case you'll find the notes,' he said. 'Would you get them out? I don't know if you can read in this state of upheaval. Try.'

Chloris managed to read the notes. They crept on with occasional wallowings in softer snow, and presently James Bewling said that the next turn in the road would bring them within sight of the spire of Winston St Giles parish church, and Mandrake himself began to recognize the countryside and distant groups of trees that he had passed on his way from Winton to Cloudyfold. That was on Thursday. And as he arrived at this point, through the open driving window came the faintest echo of a bell.

'Good Lord!' he thought, 'it's Sunday. Suppose they're all in church. James,' he called out, 'what time is morning service at St Giles?'

'Ah. Rector do set most store by early service,' James rejoined. 'She be at eight. T'other's at half-past ten. Reckon he'll have it to himself this morning.'

'That's all right, then. But what's that bell?'

'Rector do ring bell at noon.'

'The Angelus,' said Mandrake. Chloris looked up from her papers, and for a little while they listened to that distant clear-cold voice.

'They're friends of yours, aren't they?' said Chloris.

'The Copelands? Yes. Dinah's beginning to be quite a good actress. She's going to play in my new thing, if the blitzkrieg doesn't beat us to it. I suppose it won't seem odd to you, but for at least twelve hours I haven't thought about my play. What do you make of the notes?'

'There are some things I didn't know about, but not many.' Chloris caught her breath. 'You say at the end: 'Could Hart have set a second booby trap.' Do you mean could he have done something with that frightful weapon that would make it fall on . . . ? Is that what you mean?'

'Yes. I can't get any further, though. I can't think of anything.'

'A "Busman's Honeymoonish" sort of contraption? But there are no hanging flower-pots at Highfold.'

'Well, if you can think of anything! I must tell you I went into the room before we left. I looked all round, trying to see if some little thing was out of order in the arrangement of the room, unusual in any way. I – didn't enjoy it. I couldn't see anything remotely suggestive of booby traps. The ceiling's a high one. Anyway, how could Hart have dangled a stone weapon from the ceiling?'

As soon as these words had fallen from his lips, Mandrake experienced a strange fore-knowledge of how they would be answered. So vivid was this impression that when Chloris did speak, it was to him exactly as though she echoed his thoughts.

'Are you so certain,' she said, 'that it must be Dr Hart?'

And he heard his own voice answer, as if it spoke to a given cue: 'I thought I was. Aren't you?' She didn't reply, and a moment later he said with an air of conviction: 'It must be. Who else?' And as she still kept silence: 'Who else?'

'Nobody, I suppose. Nobody, of course.'

'If it was anybody else the original booby trap goes unexplained. We know that only Hart could have set it. Don't we?'

'I suppose so. Although, reading your notes, mightn't it be just possible that one of the ablibis – ? It's your evidence.'

'I know what you mean, but it's beyond all bounds incredible. Why? Not a motive in the wide world! Besides I can't believe it. It's monstrous.'

'Yes, I know. Well, then, what about a second booby trap? The detective stories tell you to look for the unusual, don't they?'

'I don't read them,' said Mandrake, with some slight return to his professional manner. 'However, I *did* look for the unusual.'

'And found nothing?'

'And found nothing. The room had a ghastly air of interrupted normality.'

They were ploughing through a small drift. The snow yielded, mounted in a wall in front of the radiator, and splashed across the windscreen. They felt a familiar and ominous quiver and in a moment had come to a standstill.

'Out comes wold shovel again,' said James cheerfully. 'She's not a bad 'un this time, sir.'

Mandrake backed out of the drift, and again James set to work.

'There's one detail,' said Mandrake. 'that for some reason annoys me. No doubt; there's nothing in it.'

'What's that?'

'You saw it. Do you remember the drawing-pin in the sole of my shoe? I picked it up in the smoking room. There's dried paint on it, and it's the same as the ones that are stuck in the lid of William's paint box.'

'I'm afraid I don't see . . . '

'I said there was nothing in it. The only thing is, why should William have had a drawing-pin in the study? He did no painting at Highfold.'

'Yes, he did,' Chloris contradicted. 'At least, he did a drawing of me yesterday before lunch. It was while he was doing it that we had our row. And the paper was pinned down to a bit of board. And he dropped one of the pins.'

'Oh,' said Mandrake flatly. 'Well, you might add that to the notes. That's a flop, then. What do we think of now?'

'Well, I can't think of anything,' said Chloris hopelessly.

'What the devil,' said Mandrake, 'is that old mountebank doing?'

James Bewling, having cleared a passage in front of the car, had, with great difficulty, climbed the bank under the buried hedgerow and now stood waving his arms and pointing down the road. Mandrake sounded his horn, and James instantly plunged down the bank and across the intervening snowdrift to the car. He climbed into the back seat, shouting excitedly as he came.

'Road's clear, down-along,' shouted James. 'There's a mort of chaps with shovels and one of they scrapers. On 'ee go, sir, us'll be there in ten minutes.'

'Thank God!' said Mandrake and Chloris sincerely.

IV

Dinah Copeland trudged down the side path and pressed her face against the french window, instantly obscuring it with her breath. Alleyn put down his book and let her in.

'You *do* look wholesome,' he said.

'Did you hear me ring the Angelus?' she demanded. 'Was it all right, Daddy?'

'Very nice, my dear,' said the rector out of the corner of his mouth, 'but I mustn't talk. Mrs Alleyn's doing my bottom lip.'

'I've finished,' said Troy.

'For the morning?'

'Yes. Would you like to look?'

Dinah kicked off her snow-boots and hurried round the easel. Troy grinned at her husband, who upon that signal joined her. She thrust her thin arm in its painty sleeve through his, and with Dinah they looked at the portrait.

'Pleased?' Alleyn asked his wife.

'Not so bad from my point of view, but what about Dinah?'

'It's heaven,' said Dinah emphatically.

'Not quite what the church-hen ordered, I'm afraid,' Troy murmured.

'No, thank the Lord. I *was* wondering if by any chance you'd gone surrealist and would mix Daddy up with some nice symbols. I've got rather keen on surrealism since I've been working with Aubrey Mandrake. But now I see it I'm quite glad you haven't put in any egg shells or phallic trimmings.'

'*Dinah!*'

'Well, Daddy, everybody recognizes the frightful importance – all right, darling, I won't. I do wish my young man was here to see it,' said Dinah. 'Daddy, aren't you glad we scraped acquaintance with Mr Alleyn over our murder?'

'I'm very glad, at all events,' said Troy. 'Do you know this is the only time since we were married that he's let me meet any of his criminal acquaintances?' She laughed, squinted at her work, and asked: 'Do you think it's all right, Roderick?'

'I like it,' said Alleyn gravely.

The rector, who wore the diffident simper of the subject, joined the group at Troy's easel. Alleyn, gripping his pipe between his teeth and humming gently to himself, began to roll up and put away his wife's tubes of paint. She lit a cigarette and watched him.

'For a long time,' said Troy, 'he endured my paint-box in silence, and then one day he asked me if dirt was an essential to self-expression. Since then it's got more and more like the regulation issue for investigating officers at C1.'

'Whereas before it was a test case for advanced students at Hendon. I found,' said Alleyn, 'characteristic refuse from Fiji, Quebec, Norway, and the Dolomites. Hallo! What's that?'

'What's what?' asked Troy.

'There's a car struggling outside in the church lane.'

'*Church lane!*' Dinah ejaculated. 'It must be driven by a lunatic if it's come from anywhere round Cloudyfold. They've cleared the lane up to the first turning, but above that it's thick snow. Your car must have come in from the main road, Mr Alleyn. It'll very soon have to stop.'

'It has stopped,' said Alleyn. 'And I fancy at your gate. Oh, dear me!'

'What's the matter with you?' asked his wife.

'By the pricking of my thumbs! Well, it can't be for me, anyway.'

'Somebody's coming up the side path,' cried Dinah, and a moment later she turned an astonished face upon the others.

'It's Aubrey Mandrake.'

'Mandrake?' said Alleyn sharply. 'But he ought to be on the other side of Cloudyfold.'

'It can't be Mandrake, my dear,' said the rector.

'But *it is*. And the car's driven away. Here he comes. He's seen me and he's coming to this window.' Dinah stared at Alleyn. 'I think there must be something wrong,' she said. 'Aubrey looks – different.'

She opened the french window, and in another moment Aubrey Mandrake walked in.

'Alleyn!' said Mandrake. 'Thank God you're here. There's been a most appalling tragedy at Highfold and we've come to get you.'

'You detestable young man,' said Alleyn.

V

'So you see,' Mandrake said, 'there really was nothing for it but to come to you.'

'But it's *not*,' Alleyn protested piteously, 'it's really *not* my cup-of-tea. It's the Chief Constable's cup-of-tea, and old Blandish's. Is Blandish still the Superintendent at Great Chipping, Rector?'

'Yes, he is. This is an appalling thing, Mandrake. I – I simply can't believe it. William Compline seemed such a nice fellow. We don't know them very well, they're rather beyond our country at Penfelton, but I liked what I saw of William.'

'Mrs Compline's in desperate case. If we don't get back quickly . . . ' Mandrake began. And to Alleyn cut in crisply: 'Yes, of course.' He turned to Mr Copeland. 'I've forgotten the name of your Chief Constable, sir.'

'Lord Hesterdon. Miles and miles away to the north, and if, as Mandrake says, the telephone wires over Cloudyfold are down, I'm afraid you won't get him.'

'I'll get Blandish if I have to wade to Great Chipping,' Alleyn muttered. 'May I use your telephone?'

He went into the hall.

'I'm sorry,' said Mandrake. 'He's livid with rage, isn't he?'

'Not really,' said Troy. 'It's only his pretty little ways. He'll do his stuff, I expect. He'll have to be asked, you know, by the local police. C1 people don't as a rule just nip in and take a case wherever they happen to be.'

'Red tape,' said Mandrake gloomily. 'I guessed as much. Murderers can ramp about country houses, women can kill themselves with overdoses of veronal, well-intentioned guests can wallow in and out of snowdrifts in an effort to help on an arrest, and when, after suffering the most disgusting privations, they win home to the fountain-head, it is only to become wreathed, Laocoön-like, in the toils of red tape.'

'I don't think,' said Troy, 'that it will be quite as bad as that.' And Dinah, who was listening shamelessly at the door, said: 'He's saying: "Well, you'll have to ring up C1, blast you." '

'Dinah, darling,' said her father, 'you really mustn't.'

'It's all right,' said Dinah, shutting the door. 'He's cursing freely and asking for Whitehall 1212. When do you think your girl-friend will get back, Aubrey?'

'She'll have to beat up the Little Chipping chemist. We only remembered it was Sunday when we heard your bell.'

'That was me,' said Dinah. 'Mr Tassy is our chemist, and he lives over his shop, so that'll be all right. The road from here to Chipping has been cleared pretty well, but I hear there are masses of frightful drifts beyond on the way to Great Chipping. So I don't see how you'll get the police surgeon or Mr Blandish.'

'If you'll excuse me,' said Troy, 'I believe I'll pack my husband's bag.'

'Then you think he'll come?' cried Mandrake.

'Oh yes,' said Troy vaguely, 'he'll come all right.'

She went out, and as the door opened they heard Alleyn's voice saying: 'I haven't got a damn' thing. I'll ring up the local chemist and get some stuff from him. Is Dr Curtis *there?* At the Yard? Well, get him to speak to me. You'd better find out . . . ' The door shut off the rest of his remarks.

'Daddy,' said Dinah, 'hadn't we better give Aubrey a drink?'

'Yes, yes, of course. My dear boy, forgive me; of course, you must be exhausted. I'm so sorry. You must have a glass of sherry. Or – '

'You'd better have a whisky, Aubrey. It's almost lunch-time, so why not eat while you're waiting? And if you can't wait for Miss Wynne, when she comes we can at least send something out to the car. I'll bustle them up in the kitchen. Bring him along to the dining room, Daddy.'

She hurried out, and met Alleyn in the hall. 'I'm so sorry,' Alleyn said. 'Nobody could want to go away less than I do, but here's Blandish gibbering at Great Chipping with a cracked water-tank in his car and a story of drifts six feet deep between us and him. He's going to get hold of a doctor, commandeer a car, and ginger up the road-clearing gang, but in the meantime he wants me to go ahead. I've rung up my atrocious superior, and he's all for it, blast his eyes. May Troy stay on as we originally planned, and finish her portrait?'

'Of course. We'd never forgive you if you put her off her stroke. I say, this *is* a rum go, isn't it?'

'Not 'alf,' said Alleyn. 'It's a damned ugly go by the sound of it.'

'Awful. Your wife's upstairs.'

'I'll find her.'

He ran to his dressing-room and found his wife on her knees before a small suitcase.

'Pyjamas, dressing-grown, shaving things,' Troy muttered. 'I suppose you'll be there tonight, won't you? What'll you do for all those things in the case bag? Squirts and bottles and powders, and stuff for making casts?'

'My darling oddity, I can't think. At least, I've got a camera, and I've rung up the chemist at Chipping. Miss Wynne was in the shop. He's going to give her some stuff for me – iodine and what-not. Can you lend me a soft brush, darling? One of the sort you use for watercolour. And scissors? And some bits of charcoal? For the rest, I'll have to trust to Fox and Co. getting through by train. They're looking out a route now. It'll be detecting in the raw, won't it? Case for the resourceful officer.'

'I'm a rotten packer,' said Troy, 'but I think that's all you'll want.'

'My dear,' said her husband, who was at the writing-table helping himself to several sheets of notepaper and some envelopes, 'almost you qualify for the rôle of clever little wife.'

'You go to the devil,' said Mrs Alleyn amiably.

He squatted down beside her, looked through the contents of the suitcase, refrained from improving on the pack and from saying that he did not think it likely he would need his pyjamas. 'Admirable,' he said. 'Now I'd better swathe myself in sweaters and topcoats. Give me a kiss and say you're sorry I'm going out on a beastly case.'

'Did you ever see such a change in any one as appears in the somewhat precious Mandrake?' asked Troy, hunting in his wardrobe.

'It takes murder to mould a man.'

'Do you think the statement he's written is dependable?'

'As regards fact, yes, I should say so. As regards his interpretation of fact, I fancy it wanders a bit. For a symbolic expressionist he seems to have remained very firmly wedded to a convention. But perhaps that's the secret of two-dimensional poetic drama. I wouldn't know. Is that a car?'

'Yes.'

'Then I must be off.' He kissed his wife, who was absently scrubbing at her painty nose with the collar of her smock. She looked at him, scowling a little.

'This is the worst sort of luck,' said Alleyn. 'It was being such a good holiday.'

'I hate these cases,' said Troy.

'Not more than I do, bless you.'

'For a different reason.'

'I'm so sorry,' he said quickly. 'I know.'

'No, you don't, Rorry. Not squeamishness, nowadays, exactly. I wish Br'er Fox was with you.'

She went downstairs with him and saw him go off with Mandrake, his hat pulled down over his right eye, the collar of his heavy raincoat turned up, his camera slung over his shoulder and his suitcase in his hand.

'He looks as if he was off on a winter sports holiday,' said Dinah. 'I don't mean to be particularly callous, but there's no denying a murder *is* rather exciting.'

'Dinah!' said her father automatically.

They heard the car start up the lane.

CHAPTER 12

Recapitulation

Alleyn sat in the back seat and read through Mandrake's notes. He was parted from Mr Bewling by a large luncheon basket provided by Dinah Copeland. 'We'll open it,' said Chloris Wynne, 'at our first breakdown. If The Others overheard me saying that I dare say they won't let me have a breakdown so that they can collar the lunch.'

'What *can* you mean?' asked Mandrake.

'Don't you know about The Others?' said Chloris in a sprightly manner. 'They're the ones that leave nails and broken glass on the road. They hide things when you're in a hurry. They've only got one arm and one leg each, you know. So they take single gloves and stockings, and they're frightfully keen on keys and unanswered letters.'

'My God, are you being whimsical?' Mandrake demanded, and Alleyn thought he recognized that particular shade of caressing rudeness which is the courtship note among members of the advanced intelligentsia. He was not mistaken. Miss Wynne made a small preening movement.

'Don't pretend you're not interested in The Others,' she said. 'I bet they take the top of your fountain-pen often enough.' She turned her beautifully arranged head to look at Alleyn. 'Bleached,' he thought automatically, 'but I dare say she's quite a nice creature.'

'Do they ever get into Scotland Yard, Mr Alleyn?' she asked.

'Do they not! They are the authors of most anonymous letters, I fancy.'

'There!' she cried. 'Mr Alleyn doesn't think I'm whimsical.' He saw, with some misgivings, that Mandrake had removed his left hand from the driving wheel, and reflected, not for the first time, that affairs of sentiment will flourish under the most unpropitious circumstances. 'But she's rattled all the same,' he thought. 'This brightness is all my eye. I wonder how well she knew the young man who is dead.' His reflections were interrupted by James Bewling, who cleared his throat portentously.

'Axcuse me, sir,' said James. 'I bin thinking.'

'Indeed?' said Mandrake apprehensively. 'What's the matter, James?'

'I bin thinking,' repeated James. 'Being this yurr is a lethal matter, and being this gentleman is going into the thick of it with his eyes only half-open like a kitten, and being he'll be burning in his official heart and soul to be axing you this and axing you that, I bin thinking it might be agreeable if I left the party along to Ogg's Corner.'

'Whatever do you mean, James?' asked Chloris. 'You can't just walk out into a snowdrift from motives of delicacy.'

'It's not so bad as that, Miss. My wold aunty, Miss Fancy Bewling, bides in cottage along to Ogg's Corner. Her's ninety-one yurs of age and so cantankerous an old masterpiece as ever you see. Reckon her'll be pleased as punch to blow me up at her leisure until Mr Blandish and his chaps comes along, when I'll get a lift and direct 'em best way to Highfold.'

'Well, James,' said Mandrake, 'it's not a bad idea. We'll be all right. I know the way, and we've ploughed a sort of path for ourselves. What do you think, Mr Alleyn?'

'If there's any danger of Blandish missing his way,' said Alleyn, 'I'd be very glad to think you were there, Bewling.'

'Good enough, sir. Then put me down if you please, souls, at next turning but one. Don't miss thicky little twiddling lane up to Pen Bidding, Mr Mandrake, sir, and be bold to rush 'er up when she skiddles.'

So they dropped him by his aunt's cottage, and it seemed to Alleyn that Miss Wynne watched him go with some regret. She said that Mandrake might despise James, but she considered he had shown extraordinary tact and forbearance. 'He must have died to know more about the disaster,' she said, 'but he never so much as asked a leading question.'

'We talked pretty freely without him having to bother,' Mandrake pointed out. 'However, I agree it was nice of James. Is there anything you want to ask us, Alleyn? By dint of terrific concentration I can manage to keep the car on its tracks and my mind more or less on the conversation.'

Alleyn took Mandrake's notes from his pocket, and at the rustle of paper he saw Chloris turn her head sharply. Something about the set of Mandrake's shoulders suggested that he, too, was suddenly alert.

'If I may,' said Alleyn, 'I should like to go over these notes with you. It's fortunate for me that you decided to make this very clear and well-ordered summary. I'm sure it gives the skeleton of events as completely as possible, and that is invaluable. But I should like with your help to clothe the bones in a semblance of flesh.'

This was spoken in what Troy called 'the official manner', and it was the first Chloris and Mandrake had heard of this manner. Neither of them answered, and Alleyn knew that with one short speech he had established an atmosphere of uneasy expectation. He was right. Until this moment Chloris and Mandrake had wished above all things for the assurance that Alleyn would take charge. Now that, with a certain crispness and a marked change of manner he had actually done so, each of them felt an icy touch of apprehension. They had set in motion a process which they were unable to stop. They were not yet nervous for themselves, but instinctively they moved a little nearer to each other. They had called in the Yard.

'First of all,' said Alleyn, 'I should like to go over the notes, putting them into my own words to make quite sure I've got hold of the right ends of all the sticks. Will you stop me if I'm wrong? The death of this young man, William Compline, occurred at about ten minutes past ten yesterday evening. He was sitting in a room which communicates with a library, a small sitting room, and a hall. Just before the discovery of his body, the library was occupied by his host, Mr Jonathan Royal, by Lady Hersey Amblington, by Miss Chloris Wynne, by Mr Aubrey Mandrake, and by Mr Nicholas Compline. The small sitting room had been occupied by Dr Francis Hart, but on his own statement and that of the footman, Thomas, it appears that Dr Hart left the sitting room – you call it a boudoir, I see – at the same time as Thomas came into the hall with a grog tray which he took into the library. That was some minutes after Nicholas Compline had left his brother and joined the party in the library, and quite definitely before you all heard the wireless turned on in the smoking room. The wireless was turned on after the drinks came in. You agreed you would like to hear it, and Nicholas Compline opened the door and called out to his brother. A screen hid William, but Nicholas heard someone cross the room, and a moment later the wireless struck up "Boomps-a-daisy".'

'That's it,' said Chloris. 'Nick left the door open.'

'Yes. You endured the dance music, and in a minute or so the news came on the air. At about this moment Mr Royal went out to reassure himself that Dr Hart was not in the boudoir. He states that he did not enter the boudoir, but saw there was no light under the door. He visited a cloakroom, and, having met no one in the hall, returned before the news ended.'

'Yes.'

'All right. Well, now, I understand that the wireless had been in use not long before. It's not likely, then, that the music was delayed by any warming-up process?'

'No,' said Chloris. 'I thought of that, but it seems that the radio had been switched on all the time and wouldn't need to warm up. As soon as Bill turned the volume control it'd come up.'

'As soon as the volume control was turned at all events,' said Alleyn, 'and it must have been turned.'

'By William,' said Mandrake, 'or his murderer. Exactly.'

'And you see,' Chloris added, 'we *asked* for it, and it was at once turned on. By *Somebody*.'

'Yes. We now come to the curious episode of the dancing footman. The music follows Thomas's re-entry into the hall when he saw Dr Hart on the stairs. Therefore, it seems, Dr Hart did not turn up the volume control. Now it appears that Thomas, arrested by the strains of a composition known as "Boomps-a-daisy", was moved to dance. As long as the music continued, Thomas, a solitary figure in the hall, capered, clapped his hands, slapped his knees, and stuck out his stern in a rhythmic sequence. When the music stopped, so did Thomas. He left the hall as the news bulletin began. Then we have Mr Royal's short excursion, and, lastly, some minutes later, Lady Hersey Amblington, carrying a tumbler, walked from the library into the smoking room, reappeared in the doorway, returned into the smoking room and switched off the radio. She then called out to her cousin, Mr Royal, who joined her. Finally she came back to the library and summoned you, Mr Mandrake. You went into the smoking room and found William Compline there, dead. It was somewhere about this time that you trod on a drawing-pin which stuck in the sole of your shoe.'

'Yes.'

'The instrument used by the assailant,' said Alleyn, with a private grimace over the police-court phrase, 'seems to have been a Maori mere which was one of a collection of weapons hanging on the smoking room wall. Which wall?'

'What? Oh, on the right from the library door. There's a red leather screen inside the door, and this unspeakable club was just beyond it.'

'I see you've given me a very useful sketch-plan. Would you mark the position on the wall? I'll put a cross, and you shall tell me if it's in the right place.'

Chloris took the paper and showed it to Mandrake, who slowed down, glanced at it, nodded, and accelerated. James Bewling had got hold of a set of chains in Chipping, and the wheels bit well into their old tracks.

'Right,' said Alleyn. 'During this time, two members of the party were upstairs. They were Mrs Compline and Madame Lisse, who you tell me is actually Mrs Francis Hart.' He paused. Neither Chloris nor Mandrake spoke.

'That's right, isn't it?'

'Yes,' said Chloris, 'that's it.'

'As far as we know,' said Mandrake unwillingly.

'As far as we know,' Alleyn agreed. 'At all events we know that neither of them could have come downstairs while Thomas was there. If it was anybody other than William Compline who turned up the wireless this person must have entered the room after Nicholas Compline left it and remained there until after Thomas left the hall. If, on the other hand, it was William himself who turned up the wireless, his murderer must have entered the room after Thomas left the hall, and made his getaway before Lady Hersey went in with the drink.'

'Avoiding Jonathan Royal,' added Mandrake. 'Don't forget he crossed the hall twice.'

'Oh,' said Alleyn vaguely. 'I hadn't forgotten that. Now, before we leave these, the crucial periods as I see them, I pause to remind myself that the communicating door between the smoking room and the boudoir was locked on the smoking room side.'

'Yes,' said Mandrake. 'I ought to have said, I think, that there is nowhere in the smoking room where anybody could hide. The screen's no good because of the door into the library. I think I'm right in saying the murderer must have come in by the hall door.'

'It looks like it,' Alleyn agreed. 'Avoiding the dancing footman and Mr Royal.'

'Somebody could hide in the hall,' said Chloris suddenly. 'We'd thought of that.'

'There's still the dancing footman. He defines the periods when it would have been possible for the murderer to enter or leave the smoking room.'

'Yes,' agreed Mandrake. 'Thomas continued his antics until the music stopped, and that leaves a margin of a few minutes before Lady Hersey entered the room. The boudoir's no good because the door was still locked. I know that.'

'Then,' said Chloris slowly, 'doesn't it look as if the crucial time is the time when the murderer *left* the room. Because whether he worked the wireless or not he could only have got away after Thomas had left the hall.'

'Top marks for deduction, Miss Wynne,' said Alleyn.

'It's a grim notion,' said Mandrake suddenly, 'to think of us all sitting there calling for the news. If it was Hart, imagine him having to pull himself together and turn up the wireless!'

'Don't!' said Chloris.

Alleyn had, with some difficulty in the jolting car, made a series of marginal notes. He now glanced up and found Chloris leaning her arm along the front seat and looking at him.

'I'd like to get Lady Hersey's movements fixed in my head,' he said. 'She went into the smoking room with the drink, disappeared round the screen, returned to the doorway, said something you couldn't hear, disappeared again, and called out to Mr Royal, who then joined her. Finally she re-entered the library and asked you, Mandrake, to go to your host.'

'That's it.' Mandrake changed down and crawled the car over its own skid marks. Chloris drew in her breath audibly. 'It's all right,' he said. 'No trouble this time.' But Alleyn, who had been watching her, knew that it was not their progress that had scared her. She looked quickly at him and away again. 'Lady Hersey,' she said, 'is an old friend of the Complines. She's terribly nice and she's been absolutely marvellous since it happened. She was helping Dr Hart with Mrs Compline. She couldn't be more sorry and upset about it all.'

These somewhat conventional phrases were shot out at nobody in particular, and were followed by an odd little pause.

'Ah,' Alleyn muttered, 'those are the sort of touches that help to clothe the bare bones of a case. We'll collect some more, I hope, as we go along. I'm working backwards through your notes, Mandrake, and arrive at the booby trap. A heavy brass Buddha, of all disagreeable objects, is perched on the top of a door so that when the door is opened it is bound to fall on the person who pushes the door. The room is Nicholas Compline's and it is upon his arm the Buddha falls. This trap was set, you say, during a visit Compline paid to Madame Lisse. You've worked out a time check on two clocks, the grandfather clock at the top of the stairs and the drawing room clock which agrees with it. On this reckoning it appears that the trap was set some time between half-past seven, which struck as Nicholas Compline left his room, and a minute or so past twenty-to-eight when you heard him cry out as the Buddha struck his arm. You suggest that you have found alibis during this period for everybody but Dr Hart who was in the bathroom. Lady Hersey gives Mrs Compline her alibi, Mr Royal gives you yours, Mandrake. Can you return the gesture?'

'I can say that I think he arrived in the drawing room some little time before the crash.'

'Ten minutes before?'

'I feel sure it must have been. I – we were talking. Yes, it must have been at least ten minutes.'

'There's no way by which you could come a little nearer to it? For example, did he light a cigarette when he came into the room?'

'Let me think. No. No, I don't believe he did. But I did. I'd forgotten to bring my case down and I was helping myself to one of his when he came into the room. I remember that,' said Mandrake, and Alleyn saw the back of his neck go red, 'because I felt – ' He stopped and made rather a business of adjusting his windscreen-wiper which at that moment was not needed.

'Yes?'

'What? Oh, I merely felt, very stupidly, a little embarrassed.' Mandrake's voice trailed off and then he said loudly: 'I was not born into the purple, Mr Alleyn. Until a few years ago I lived in the odour of extreme economy, among people who waited to be invited before they smoked other people's cigarettes.'

'I should call that a sign of courtesy rather than penury,' said Alleyn, and received a brilliant smile from Miss Wynne. 'Well, you lit your cigarette, then. That's a help. Was it still going when you heard Nicholas Compline yell?'

'Was it, now? Yes. Yes, I remember throwing it in the fire before I went upstairs, but it was almost smoked out, I'm sure. Yes, I'm sure of that.'

'Good. Well, now, Madame Lisse's alibi is vouched for by Nicholas Compline and looks pretty well cast-iron. William Compline was in the smoking room listening to the news bulletin. He heard Mr Royal speak to the butler in the hall, and was prepared to give the gist of the bulletin which does not come on until 7.30.'

'Surely that's of academic interest only,' said Mandrake, 'considering what happened to William Compline.'

'You are probably quite right, but you know what policemen are. Dr Hart has no alibi. Wait a bit, I must count up. Who haven't I got? Oh, there's you, Miss Wynne.'

'I haven't got one,' said Chloris quickly. 'I was in my room and I had a bath next door and I changed. But I can't prove it.'

'Oh, well,' said Alleyn, 'it'd be an odd state of affairs if everybody could prove all the things they hadn't done every minute of the day. Is there to be no privacy, not even in the bathroom? That leaves Lady Hersey Amblington.'

'But she was with Mrs Compline,' said Mandrake. 'Nicholas saw her go past his door on her way to Mrs Compline's room. It's there in the notes. We've been over that.'

'Have we? Then I've got myself into a muddle no doubt. Lady Hersey gives Mrs Compline an alibi. Does Mrs Compline do as much for Lady Hersey? I mean did Mrs Compline agree that Lady Hersey was in her room from 7.30 until the alarm?'

'Well, she – well, I mean she wasn't there when we talked about alibis. Lady Hersey saw her afterwards and may have spoken about it then.'

'But actually nobody else questioned Mrs Compline about it?'

'No, but of course it's all right. I mean it's out of the question that Lady Hersey – '

'I expect it is,' said Alleyn. 'But you see just at the moment we're dealing with hard facts, aren't we? And the actual fact, which may be of no importance whatever, is that Lady Hersey vouches for Mrs Compline but Mrs Compline doesn't happen to have corroborated her account. Is that it?'

'She can't,' said Chloris. 'She can't, now. She may never . . . '

'We won't jump that fence,' said Alleyn, 'until we meet it.'

II

So far the return journey had not presented many difficulties. The new set of chains worked well and Mandrake kept to his own tracks where the snow had packed down hard and was already freezing over again. They ran into desultory flurries of snow, but the rain had not crossed Cloudyfold. Beyond the hills the sky was still terraced with storm clouds, prolonged at their bases into down-pouring masses, as if some Olympian painter had dragged at them with a dry brush.

At Alleyn's suggestion they broached Dinah's luncheon hamper, and he continued his examination of Mandrake's notes in an atmosphere of ham and hard-boiled egg, plying Chloris with food and both of them with questions.

'The oddest thing about this beastly business,' he said, 'seems to be your plunge in the pond, Mandrake. You say here that Dr Hart had the best chance of bringing it off unobserved, and that he saw Compline leave the house wearing Mr Royal's cape, which is the double of your cape which incidentally seems to be Hart's cape. Having absorbed those fancy touches, I learn that Nicholas Compline saw you through the window of the pavilion where he was undressing in order to plunge into the ornamental waters in pursuance of a wager. He recognized you and you exchanged waves. Then comes your plunge attended by the Compline brothers, Hart, Miss Wynne, and Mr Royal, in that order. Again Mrs Compline, Madame Lisse and Lady Hersey are absent. The first two breakfasted in their rooms. Lady Hersey says she was in the smoking room. I understand you have read these notes, Miss Wynne?'

'Yes.'

'Have you formed any theory about the footprints which Mandrake says he saw in the snow? The small prints that led out to the top of the terrace from the house and returned to the house, suggesting that the person who made them stood on the terrace for a time at a spot from which she – apparently it must have been a woman – had a full view of the pond and the pavilion.'

'I?' said Chloris. 'Why, I've thought a lot about it ever since Aubrey told me, but I'm afraid I've no ideas at all. It might have been one the maids, even, though I suppose that's not very likely.'

'Did you notice these prints as you went down?'

'I'm not sure. I stood on the top of the terrace for a bit and noticed Aubrey's and some other big footprints – William's they must have been – and I thought I might walk down inside them, do you know? I've got a sort of feeling I did notice something out of the tail of my eye. I've got a sort of after-flavour of having fancied there must be someone else about, but it's much too vague to be useful. On the way back I was too concerned about Aubrey to notice.'

'Were you?' asked Mandrake with unmistakable fervour. Alleyn waited philosophically through an exchange of inaudible phrases, and remarked on the air of complacency that characterizes persons who have arrived at a certain stage of mutual attraction.

'The smoking room is on that side of the house, isn't it?' he said at last.

'Yes,' agreed Chloris uncomfortably, 'but so are the visitors' rooms upstairs.'

'Do they overlook the lake and pavilion?'

'Madame Lisse's room doesn't,' said Mandrake. 'I asked Jonathan that, and he said some tall evergreens on the bank would be in the way. I imagine they'd interrupt Mrs Compline's view too.'

'And you definitely connect these three strange events? You feel certain that the same person is behind all of them?'

'But – yes,' said Chloris blankly. 'Of course we do. Don't you?'

'It looks like it, certainly,' said Alleyn absently.

'Surely,' said Mandrake acidly, 'it would be too fantastic to suppose there has been more than one person planning elaborate deaths for Nicholas Compline during the weekend?'

'For Nicholas Compline,' Alleyn repeated. 'Oh, yes. It would, wouldn't it?'

'I assure you I had no enemies at Highfold. I'd never met a single one of the guests before.'

'Quite so,' said Alleyn mildly. 'Going back still farther we come to the first hint of trouble, the rather childish message on the Charter form which you say Dr Hart handed to Nicholas Compline, together with a form that had been correctly filled in. "You are warned. Keep off." You say that there is no question of any one else handing this paper to Compline.'

'No possibility of it. Nicholas simply took the paper from Hart,' said Mandrake, 'and on looking at it, found this second one underneath. Hart's explanation was that he must have torn two papers off at once. Nicholas didn't say at the time what was on the paper, but he was obviously very much upset and later that evening he told Jonathan he thought he ought to go. The following day, and good God it's only yesterday, he actually tried to go and nearly drowned himself in a drift.'

'Yes. And that completes the skeleton.' Alleyn folded the notes and put them in his pocket. 'As they used to say in Baker Street: "You are in possession of the facts." I'd like a little news about the people. You say that with the exception of your host you had met none of them before. That's not counting Miss Wynne, of course.'

'Yes, it is,' said Chloris, and with an air of great demureness she added: 'Aubrey and I are complete strangers.'

'I don't suppose I shall know her if I meet her again.' Alleyn sighed as Mandrake once more removed his left hand from the driving-wheel. 'He will resent everything I say to her,' thought Alleyn, 'and she will adore his resentment. Blow!' However, he introduced the subject of motive, which Mandrake, in his notes, had dealt with allusively, unconsciously supposing the reader would be almost as familiar as himself with the relationships of the eight guests to each other and to their host. In a very short time he discovered that these two were quite ready to talk about Madame Lisse and Lady Hersey, about Mrs Compline and Dr Hart, and about William's fury when he discovered that Hart was the author of his mother's disfigurement. They were less ready to discuss in detail Hart's enmity to Nicholas, though they never tired of stressing it. Hart had threatened Nicholas. Nicholas had goaded Hart until he completely lost control of himself. That was the burden of their song. It was on account of Nicholas's attentions to Madame Lisse, they said. When Alleyn asked if Nicholas knew that Madame Lisse was Madame Hart they said they hadn't asked him, and Chloris added, with a new edge to her voice, that it was highly probable. Alleyn said mildly that it appeared that Nicholas had acted like a fool. 'He seems to have baited Hart to the top of his bent and at the same time been rather frightened of him.'

'But that's Nicholas all over,' said Chloris. 'It was exactly that. The small boy tweaking the dog's tail. That's Nicholas.' Mandrake cut in rather hurriedly, but Alleyn stopped him. 'You know Compline well, Miss Wynne?' She took so long to answer that he was about to repeat the question which he was certain she had heard, when, without turning her head, she said: 'Yes. Quite well. I was engaged to him. You'd better hear all about it, I suppose.'

'I can't see . . . ' Mandrake began, but this time it was Chloris who stopped him: 'It hasn't anything to do with it, I know, but I think Mr Alleyn would rather see for himself.'

'An admirable conclusion,' said Alleyn lightly, and he heard without further comment the story of the two engagements. When she had finished he made her a little speech, saying he was sorry under such tragic circumstances to be obliged to pester her with questions. Nothing could have been more uncomfortable than their reception of this simple offer of sympathy. Their silence was eloquent of embarrassment. Chloris did not turn her head, and when Alleyn caught sight of Mandrake's face in the driving glass it was scarlet and scowling.

'You needn't bother,' said Chloris in a high voice. 'I wasn't in love with William. Didn't you guess that? As I have already explained to Aubrey I did it on the rebound from Nicholas.' In spite of herself her voice lost composure and she ended up shakily: 'That doesn't say I'm not terribly sorry. I liked old Bill. I liked him tremendously.'

'I liked him too,' said Mandrake. 'He was an oddity, wasn't he?' Chloris nodded, and Alleyn thought that in making this unemphatic comment on William Compline, Mandrake had shown sureness of touch and a certain delicacy of understanding. He went on quietly: 'He would have interested you, I believe, Alleyn. He was one of those people who speak a thing almost at the same time as they think it, and, as he had a curious simplicity about him, some of the things he said were odd and disconcerting. He was quite like his brother to look at. The shape of his head – ' Mandrake stumbled a little and then went on rather hurriedly. 'From behind, as I explained in those notes, it was difficult to tell them apart. But they couldn't have been more unlike in temperament, I should say.'

'And he painted?'

'Yes. I haven't seen any of the works.'

'They were queer,' Chloris said. 'You might like them, Aubrey. They might be quite your cup-of-tea, but most people thought his pictures too embarrassingly bad. I must say I always felt rather shy when I saw them. I never knew what to say.'

'What are they like?' asked Alleyn.

'Well, a bit as if a child had done them, but not quite like that.'

'*Very* thick oil paint,' said Mandrake under his breath.

'Why, have you seen one?' asked Chloris in astonishment.

'No. He told me. He said it rather quaintly. If there was something childlike in his painting it must have come from himself.'

'Yes, that's true,' said Chloris, and they began quite tranquilly to discuss William. Alleyn wondered how old they were. Miss Wynne was not more than twenty, he thought, and he remembered a critique of one of Mandrake's poetic dramas in which the author had been described as extremely young. Perhaps he was twenty-six. They were fortified with all the resilience that youth presents to an emotional shock. In the midst of murder and attempted suicide, they had managed not only to behave with address and good sense, but also to fall in love with each other. Very odd, thought Alleyn, and listened attentively to what they had to say about William Compline. They were discussing him with some animation. Alleyn was pretty sure they had almost forgotten his presence. This was all to the good, and a firm picture of the murdered and elder Compline began to take form. With owlish gravity Chloris and Mandrake discussed poor William's 'psychology' and decided that unconscious jealousy of Nicholas, a mother-fixation, an inferiority complex, and a particularly elaborate Œdipus complex were at the bottom of the lightest action and the sole causes of his violent outburst against Hart.

'Really,' said Mandrake, 'it's the Ugly Duckling and Cinderella themes. Extraordinarily sound, those folk tales.'

'And of course the painting was simply an effort to overcome the inferiority complex – er, on the pain-pleasure principle,' added Chloris uncertainly. Mandrake remarked that Mrs Compline's strong preference for Nicholas was extremely characteristic, but of what Alleyn could not quite make out. However, he did get a clear picture of two unhappy people dominated by the selfish, vain, and, according to the two experts in the front seat, excessively oversexed Nicholas. Shorn of intellectual garnishings it was still a sufficiently curious story. One phrase of Chloris's struck him as being particularly illuminating. 'I would have liked to be friends with her,' she said, 'but she hated me from the beginning, poor thing. First because I was engaged to Nick, and secondly and even more violently because, as she made herself suppose, I jilted him for William. I think she knew well enough that Nick hadn't been exactly the little gent, but she wouldn't let herself believe that he could do anything that wasn't perfect. For her he just *had* to be heroic, don't you know, and she had a fantastic hatred for anyone who made him look shabby.'

'Did she know about *l'affaire Lisse*, do you suppose?' asked Mandrake.

'I don't know. I dare say he kept it dark. He could be pretty quiet about his philanderings when it suited him. But even if she did know, I believe she would have taken it as a perfectly natural obsession on Madame Lisse's part. In her eyes Nicholas was really rather like one of those Greek gods who lolled about on clouds and said "I'll have *that* one!"'

Alleyn coughed, and Miss Wynne became aware of him. 'I suppose,' she said, 'you think it revolting of us to talk about them like this.'

'No,' he said, 'I would find a show of excessive distress much more disagreeable.'

'Yes, I know. All the same it's pretty ghastly not being able to get back quicker. I suppose you can't rush her up a bit, Aubrey, can you? It's terribly important that Dr Hart should get these things. I mean, in a sort of way, everything depends on us.'

'I'm banging along as fast as I dare. There's Pen-Gidding ahead. We're making much better time. Look, there's the rain still over the Highfold country. We'll be running into it again soon. If I stick in Deep Bottom it's only about half a mile from the house.'

'Return to horror,' said Chloris, under her breath.

'Never mind, my dear,' whispered Mandrake. 'Never mind.'

'There's one thing that strikes me as being very odd,' Alleyn said, 'and that is the house-party itself. What persuaded your host to collect such a gang of warring elements under his roof? Or didn't he know they were at war?'

'Yes,' said Mandrake, 'he knew.'

'Then why . . . ?'

'He did it on purpose. He explained it to me on the night I arrived. He wanted to work out his aesthetic frustration in a flesh-and-blood medium.'

'Good Lord!' Alleyn ejaculated, 'how unbelievably rum.'

III

There was no wind over Cloudyfold that afternoon, but the rain poured down inexorably. By half-past two the rooms at Highfold had begun to assume a stealthy dimness. The house itself, as well as the human beings inside it, seemed to listen and to wait. Highfold was dominated by two rooms. Behind the locked doors of the smoking room William Compline now sat as rigidly as if he had been made of iron, his hands propped between his feet and his head fixed between his knees. In the principal visitor's room his mother lay in bed, breathing very slowly, scarcely responding now to Dr Hart when he slapped the face he had marred twenty years ago, or when he advanced his own white face close to hers and called her name as if he cried for admittance at the door of her consciousness. Hersey Amblington, too, cried out to her old friend, and three times Nicholas had come. It had been difficult for Nicholas to obey Hart and call loudly upon his mother. At first his voice cracked grotesquely into a sobbing whisper. Hart kept repeating: 'Loudly. Loudly. To rouse her, you understand. She must be roused.' And Hersey: 'If she hears it's you, Nick, she may try. You must, Nick, you must.' Mrs Pouting in her sitting room, and Thomas in the hall, and Caper in the pantry, and Madame Lisse in the green boudoir, and Jonathan Royal on the stairs had all heard Nicholas shout as though across a nightmare of silence: *'Mother!* It's *Nicholas! Mother!'* They had all waited, listening intently, until his voice cracked into silence and they became aware once more of the hard beat of rain on the house. Jonathan, from his place on the stairs, had heard Nicholas leave his mother's room and cross the landing. He had seen him stop at the stairhead, raise his clasped hands to his lips, and then, as if some invisible cord had been released, jerk forward until his head rested on his arms across the balustrade. Jonathan started forward, but at the sound of harsh sobbing paused and finally stole downstairs, unseen by Nicholas. He crossed the hall, and after some hesitation entered the green boudoir.

Between Hersey Amblington and Dr Hart there had arisen a curious feeling of comradeship. Hersey had proved herself to be an efficient nurse, obeying Hart's instructions without question or fuss. There were certain unpleasant things that could be attempted and between them they had made the attempts. Hart had not pretended to any experience of veronal poisoning. 'But the treatment must be on general common sense lines,' he said. 'There we cannot go wrong. Unfortunately there has not been the response. We have not eliminated the poison. If only they would return from the chemist!'

'What's the time now?'

'Nearly two o'clock. They should have returned.'

He bent over the bed. Hersey watched him and in a minute or two she said: 'Am I mistaken, Dr Hart, or is there a change?'

'You are not mistaken. The pupils are now contracted, the pulse is 120. Do you notice the colour of the fingernails, a dusky red?'

'And her breathing.'

'It is gravely impeded. We shall take the temperature again. God be thanked that at least this old Pouting had a thermometer.'

Hersey fetched the thermometer and returned to the window where she waited, looking through rain across the terrace and down to the bathing pool. Cypress trees had been planted at intervals along the terrace and one of these hid the far end of the pool and the entrance to the pavilion. 'She could not have seen Mandrake go overboard,' thought Hersey, 'But she could have seen him leave the house and go down.' And she looked at the wardrobe where yesterday she had found a wet coat.

'The temperature is 102.8°,' said Hart. 'It has risen two points. Well, we must try the emetic again, but I am afraid she is now quite unable to swallow.'

Hersey rejoined him, and again they worked together to no avail. After a time she suggested that he should leave her in charge. 'You've eaten nothing and you haven't sat down since they brought you here hours ago. I can call you if there's any change.'

Hart glanced up with those prominent eyes of his and said: 'And where should I go, Lady Hersey? To my room? Should I not be locked up again? Ever since I came to the patient I believe there has been someone on guard in the passage or on the stairs. Is that not so? No, let me remain here until the car returns. If they have brought a medical man I shall go back to my cell.'

'I don't believe you killed William Compline,' Hersey said abruptly.

'No? You are a sensible woman. I did not kill him. There is no doubt, I am afraid, that the condition is less satisfactory. She is more comatose. The reflexes are completely abolished. Why do you look at me in that fashion, Lady Hersey?'

'You seem to have no thought for your own position.'

'You mean that I am not afraid,' said Dr Hart, who was again stooping over his patient. 'You are right. Lady Hersey, I am an Austrian refugee and a Jew who has become a naturalized Briton. I have developed what I believe you would call a good nose for justice. Austrian justice, Nazi justice, and English justice. I have learned when to be terrified and when not to be terrified. I am a kind of thermometer for terror. At this moment I am quite normal. I do not believe I shall be found guilty of a murder I did not commit.'

'Do you believe,' asked Hersey Amblington after a long pause, 'that the murderer will be arrested?'

'I do believe so.' He straightened his back, but he still watched his patient.

'Dr Hart,' Hersey said harshly, 'do you think you know who killed William Compline?'

'Oh, yes,' said Hart, and for the first time he looked directly at her. 'Yes. I believe I know. Do you wish me to say the name?'

'No,' she said. 'Let us not discuss it.'

'I agree,' said Dr Hart.

IV

Down in the green sitting room Jonathan Royal listened to Madame Lisse. An onlooker with a taste for irony might have found something to divert him in the scene, particularly if he liked his irony laced with a touch of macabre. A nice sense of the fitness of things had prompted Madame to dress herself in black, a dead crepey black that gloved her figure with adroitness. She looked and smelt most expensive. She had sent a message to her host by Mrs Pouting, asking for an interview. Jonathan, fresh from seeing Nicholas Compline's breakdown on the upstairs landing, eyed his beautiful guest with a certain air of wariness.

'It is so kind of you to see me,' said Madame Lisse. 'Ever since this terrible affair I have felt that of all our party you would remain the sanest, the best able to control events, the one to whom I must instinctively turn.'

Jonathan touched his glasses and said that it was very nice of her. She continued in this strain for some time. Her manner conveyed, as an Englishwoman's manner seldom conveys, a sort of woman-to-man awareness that was touched with camaraderie. With every look she gave him, and her glances were circumspect, she flattered Jonathan, and although he still made uncomfortable little noises in his throat, and fidgeted with his glasses, he began to look sleek and into his own manner there crept an air of calculation that would have astonished his cousin Hersey or Chloris Wynne. He and Madame Lisse were very polite to each other, but there was a hint of insolence in their civility. She began to explain her reasons for keeping her marriage to Hart a secret. It had been her idea, she said. She had not wished to give up her own business which was a flourishing one, but on the other hand Dr Hart, before they met, had, under his own name, published a book in which he exposed what he had called the 'beauty-parlour racket'. 'The book has had considerable publicity and is widely associated with his name,' she said. 'It would have been impossible for me as his wife to continue my business. Both of us would have appeared ridiculous. So we were married very quietly in London and continued in our separate ménages.'

'An ambiguous position,' Jonathan said with a little smile.

'Until recently it has worked quite well.'

'Until Nicholas Compline was transferred to Great Chipping, perhaps?'

'Until then,' she agreed, and for a time both of them were silent while Jonathan looked at her steadily through those blank glasses of his. 'Ah, well,' said Madame Lisse, 'there it is. I was quite powerless. Francis became insanely jealous. I should never have allowed this visit, but he guessed that Nicholas had been asked and he accepted. I had hoped that Nicholas would be sensible, and that Francis would become reassured. But, as it was, both of them behaved like lunatics. And now the brother and the disfigured mother too, perhaps – it is too horrible. I shall blame myself to the end of my life. I shall never recover from the horror,' said Madame Lisse, delicately clasping her hands, 'never.'

'Why did you wish to speak to me?'

'To explain my own position. When I heard last night of this tragedy I was shattered. All night I stayed awake thinking – thinking. Not of myself, you understand, but of that poor gauche William, killed, as it seems, on my account. That is what people will say. They will say that Francis mistook him for Nicholas and killed him because of me. It will not be true, Mr Royal.'

At this remarkable assemblage of contradictory data, Jonathan gaped a little, but Madame Lisse leant towards him and gazed into his spectacles, and he was silent.

'It will not be true,' she repeated. 'Do not misunderstand me. There can be no doubt who struck the blow. But the motive – the motive! You heard that unfortunate young man cry out that all the world should learn it was Francis who ruined his mother's beauty. Why did she try to kill herself? Because she knew that it was on her account that Francis Hart had killed her son.'

Jonathan primmed his lips. Madame Lisse leant towards him. 'You are a man of the world,' said this amazing lady, 'you understand women. I felt it the first time we met. There was *a frisson* – how shall I describe it. We were *en rapport*. One is never mistaken in these things. There is an instinct.' She continued in this vein for some time. Presently she was holding one of Jonathan's hands in both her own, and imperceptibly this state of affairs changed into Jonathan holding both hers in one of his. Her voice went on and on. He was to understand that she was the victim of men's passions. She could not help it. She could not stop Nicholas falling in love with her. Her husband had treated her exceedingly ill. But the murder had nothing to do with her or with Nicholas. There were terrible days ahead, she would never recover. But, and here she raised Jonathan's hand to her cheek, he, Jonathan, would protect her. He would keep their secret. 'What secret?' cried Jonathan in alarm. The secret of Nicholas's infatuation. Her name need never be brought into the picture. 'You ask the impossible!' Jonathan exclaimed. 'My dear lady, even if I – ' She wept a little and said it was evident he did not return the *deep, deep* regard she had for him. She swayed very close indeed and murmured something in his ear. Jonathan changed colour and spluttered: 'If I could . . . I should be enchanted, but it is beyond my power.' He wetted his lips. 'It's no good,' he said, 'Mandrake knows. They all know. It's impossible.'

While he still glared at her they both heard the sound of a car coming slowly up the last curve of the drive.

CHAPTER 13

Examination

Alleyn went alone to the smoking room. On their arrival Mandrake had gone at once to find Jonathan, and had returned to say he would be down in a minute or two. 'And in the meantime,' Mandrake said, 'I am deputed to show you anything you want to see. I suppose – I mean I've got the keys . . . ' Alleyn thanked him, took the keys, and let himself into the smoking room. He drew back the curtains from the windows and a very cold light discovered the body of William Compline. The greenstone blade lay on the floor about two feet from William's left shoe. The striking edge was stained. There was a short thong round the narrow grip. Alleyn had seen Maori meres in New Zealand museums and had reflected on the deadly efficiency of this beautifully shaped and balanced weapon. 'The nearest thing,' he murmured as he bent over it, 'to the deadly Gurkha kukri that is possible in stone, and that only in the extremely hard and tough New Zealand greenstone. Unless this expert is a lunatic, there'll be no prints, of course.' He looked very closely at the wireless. It was an all-wave instrument made by a famous firm. There were five bakelite control knobs under the dial. From left to right the knobs were marked Brilliance, Bass, Tuner, Wave-Band and Volume. The screws that attached them were sunk in small holes. The tuner control, placed above the others, was formed by a large quick-turning knob from the centre of which a smaller knob for more delicate tuning projected. The main switch was on the side facing the boudoir door. Alleyn noted the position of the tuning indicator and reflected that if a time check was needed he could get one from the BBC. He turned from the wireless to a writing-desk that stood against the same wall, between two windows. Above this desk was hung an array of weapons, a Malay kriss, a boomerang, a Chinese dagger, and a Javanese knife; the fruits, thought Alleyn, of some Royal tour through the East to Oceania. An empty space on the extreme left of the group suggested the position of the mere, and an unfaded patch on the wall gave a clear trace of its shape. It had been in full view of William as he sat fiddling with the radio controls and had hung immediately above and back from the volume control. This conjured up a curious picture. Was William so absorbed in the radio that he did not notice his assailant take the weapon from its place on the wall? That was scarcely credible. Had his assailant removed the weapon some time previously? Or did William notice the removal and see no cause for alarm? In that case the assailant could surely not have been Hart, since William's antagonism to Hart was so acute that it was impossible to imagine him regarding such a move with anything but the deepest suspicion. Had Hart, then, previously removed the mere? But when? Before Mandrake spoke to him in the boudoir? Not afterwards, because William was there with Nicholas, who locked the communicating door in Hart's face. Again he looked from the volume control to the space on the wall and wondered suddenly if Hart's ignorance of radio could possibly be assumed. But suppose Hart removed the mere? He had not been present at dinner. Had he taken it while the others were dining? Alleyn turned from the wall to the desk, a small affair with two drawers, one of which was not quite closed. He opened it with his fingernail. Inside were a number of small pads. 'Charter forms, by gum,' Alleyn muttered.

He had brought with him the parcel ordered by telephone from the chemist. He opened it and transferred the contents to his own attaché case. Among them were two pairs of tweezers. With these he took the Charter pads one by one from the drawer and laid them out on the desk. There were nine, and most of them were complete with their own small pencils. At the back of the drawer he found a number of india-rubbers.

'A little dreary labour,' he thought, 'should no doubt be expended. Later, perhaps.' And, taking great pains not to touch the pads, he transferred them, together with the pencils and india-rubbers, to an empty stationery box he found in another drawer. This he placed in his attaché case. He then moved on from the desk towards the library door. A four-fold red leather screen stood in front of the library door. It almost touched the outside wall and extended to an angle some five or six feet out into the room. Alleyn went round it and faced the door itself, which was in the corner of the room. The door-knob was on his right. He unlocked it, glanced into the library, and shut it again. As he stooped to the lock he noticed a small hole in the white paint on the jamb. It resembled the usual marks left by wood-rot. The one tool of his trade that Alleyn had about him was his pocket lens. He took it out, squatted down, squinted through it at the hole. He fetched a disgruntled sigh and moved to the fireplace. Above the mantlepiece the wall was decorated with an old-fashioned fishing-rod, complete with reel. Beneath it hung a faded photograph in an Oxford frame. It presented a Victorian gentleman wearing an ineffable air of hauteur and a costume which suggested that he had begun to dress up as Mr Sherlock Holmes, but, suddenly losing interest, had gone out fishing instead. With some success, it seemed, as from his right hand depended a large languid trout, while with his left hand he supported a rod. Across this gentleman's shins, in faded spidery letters, was written the legend: 'Hubert St John Worthington Royal, 1900. 4½ lbs. Pen-Felton Reach.' This brief but confusing information was supplemented by a label which hung from the old rod. 'With this rod,' said the label dimly, 'and this fly – an Alexandra – I caught a four-and-a-half pounder above Trott's Bridge in Pen-Felton Reach. It now enters an honourable retirement. H. St J.W. Royal, 1900.'

'Well done, H. St J. W. R.,' said Alleyn. 'Would you be Jonathan's papa, now, or his grandpapa? Not that it matters. I want to have a look at your reel.'

It appeared that somebody else had been interested in the reel. For whereas the rod and the reel itself had escaped the attention of Jonathan's housemaids, the mass of rolled line was comparatively free from dust, and, although on one side this roll of line was discoloured and faded, the centre and the other side were clean and new-looking. Alleyn saw that the loose end of the line that hung down had a clean cross-section. He caught this end in his tweezers, pulled out a good stretch of line, cut it off with Troy's nail scissors, which he had pocketed before leaving, and put it away in another envelope. Mandrake was an observant fellow, he thought, but evidently he had missed the trout line.

Alleyn now examined the fireplace, and, looking at the dead ash in the grate, sighed for his case bag and his usual band of assistants. It had been a wood fire, and in burning out had missed the two side logs, which had fallen apart, showing their charred inner surfaces. Between these was a heap of ash and small pieces of charcoal. Alleyn squatted down and peered through his pocket lens at this heap without disturbing it. Lying across the surface, broken at intervals, but suggesting rather than forming a thread-like pattern, trailed a fine worm of ash. It was the ghost of some alien substance that had been thrown on the fire not long before it died out. Alleyn decided to leave the ash for the moment and continued his prowl round the room. The door into the library was a massive affair, felted, and lined, on the library side, with shelves and dummy books, bearing titles devised by some sportive Royal.

'I fancy the radio'll have to blast its head off before you'd hear much of it in the library,' thought Alleyn. 'Damn, I'd like to try. Better not, though, till I've printed the knobs and trimmings.'

He hunted over the floor, using his torch and pressing his fingers into the pile of the carpet. He found nothing that seemed to him to be of interest. He completed his examination of the room and returned at last to the body of William Compline.

Alleyn's camera was a very expensive instrument. He had brought it with him to make records of his wife's work during its successive stages. He now used it to photograph William Compline's body, the area of floor surrounding his feet, his skull, the mere, the wireless cabinet, the ash in the fireplace, and the library door jamb. 'In case,' he muttered, 'Thompson and Co. don't get through tonight.' Detective-Sergeant Thompson was his photographic expert.

Having taken his pictures, he stood for a time looking down at William. 'I don't imagine *you* knew anything about it.' And he thought: 'Life's going to be pretty cheap when summer comes, but you've caught a blitzkrieg of your own, and so for you it's different. You've conjured up the Yard, you poor chap. You've cranked up the majesty of the law, and by the time *your* killer reaches the dock, Lord knows how many of your friends will be there to give evidence. There ought to be a moral lurking somewhere round this, but I'm damned if I know what it is.' He replaced the sheet, looked round the room once more, locked the two inner doors, gathered up his possessions and went into the hall. As he was locking the door he heard a sort of male twittering, and turning round saw on the stairs a small rotund gentleman dressed in plus fours and wearing thick-lensed glasses.

'I'm so awfully sorry to keep you waiting,' said this person. 'Mandrake looked after you?'

'Very well indeed, thank you.'

'Yes. He told me you were here,' said Jonathan. 'I begged him to – to give you the keys of that terrible room. I – I find myself very much upset. I'm quite ashamed of myself.'

'A very natural reaction, sir,' said Alleyn politely. 'May we have a word or two somewhere?'

'Eh? Yes. Yes, of course. Er – in the drawing room, shall we? This way.'

'I fancy Mandrake and Miss Wynne are in the drawing room. Perhaps the library?'

Jonathan nervously agreed to the library, and Alleyn had a notion that he would have preferred somewhere farther away from the smoking room. He saw Jonathan look quickly at the communicating door and then turn away abruptly to the fire.

'Before anything else,' Alleyn said, 'I must ask how Mrs Compline is. Mandrake will have told you that the local police are trying to find a doctor. In the meantime, I hope . . . '

'She's very ill indeed,' said Jonathan. 'That's why you find me so greatly upset. She – they think she's going to die.'

II

Jonathan was not easy to deal with. He was both restless and lugubrious, and it was with difficulty that Alleyn contrived to nail him down to hard facts. For five minutes he listened to a recital in which such matters as Jonathan's affection for the Complines, his bewilderment, the sacred laws of hospitality and the infamy of Dr Hart were strangely mingled. At last, however, Alleyn managed to pin him down to giving direct answers to questions based on Mandrake's notes. Jonathan gave a fairly coherent account of his own talks with Nicholas and laid great stress on the point of Hart's practically admitting that he had written threatening letters. 'And in *my* house, Alleyn, in *my* house he had the effrontery to make use of a round game . . . ' Alleyn cut short this lament with a direct question.

'Who is with Mrs Compline at the moment?'

'Hart!' Jonathan exclaimed. 'There it is, you see! Hart! I know it's a most improper, a monstrous arrangement, but what could we do?'

'Nothing else, sir, I'm sure. Is he alone?'

'No. No, my cousin, Lady Hersey Amblington, who is an experienced VAD, is there. I spoke to her on my way down. I did not go in. She came to the door. They – ah – they're doing something – I understand you brought – but Hart appears to think she is almost beyond help.'

'In that case,' said Alleyn, 'as soon as it's possible, I should like to see Dr Hart. At once, if he can leave his patient.'

'I don't think he can do so just yet. There's one other thing, Mr Alleyn.' Jonathan's hand went to the inside pocket of his coat. He drew out a long envelope.

'This,' he said, 'contains the letter she left behind for Nicholas. He has read it, but nobody else has done so. I persuaded him to place it in this envelope in the presence of my cousin, Hersey Amblington, and myself. We have signed a statement to that effect on the outside. I now,' said Jonathan, with a small bow to Alleyn, 'hand it to you.'

'That's very correct, sir,' said Alleyn.

'Oh, well, I'm a JP, you know, and if, as we fear, poor Sandra does not recover . . . '

'Yes, of course. I think I should see Mr Compline before I open the letter. It's more important at the moment that I should talk to Dr Hart. Perhaps we had better go upstairs. Dr Hart may be able to come out for a moment. Will you take me up, please?'

'But – is it absolutely necessary . . . ?'

'I'm afraid Mrs Compline's condition makes it imperative, sir. Shall we go?'

Jonathan pulled at his lower lip, eyed Alleyn over the top of his glasses, and finally made a little dart at him. 'In your hands,' he chattered, 'unreservedly. Come on.'

He led the way upstairs. They turned off to the left and came up to the visitors' wing. Alleyn paused at the stairhead. A little to his right, and facing the stairs, he saw an empty niche in the wall, and, remembering the plan Mandrake had sketched in the margin of his notes, he *recognized* this as the erstwhile perch of the brass Buddha. The men's rooms, then, would be down the passage. Madame Lisse's, he remembered, was opposite the stairhead, and Mrs Compline's next door to the left. Indeed, Jonathan now pointed to the door of this room, and, with a wealth of finicking gestures, indicated that Alleyn should wait where he stood. 'Just a moment, Alleyn,' he mouthed. 'Better just – if you don't mind – one doesn't know . . . '

He tiptoed to the door, and, staring apprehensively at Alleyn, tapped very gently, paused, shook his head and tapped again. In a moment or two the door opened. Alleyn saw a tallish woman, with a well-groomed head and a careful make-up on a face that wore an expression of extreme distress. Jonathan whispered, and the lady looked quickly over his shoulder at Alleyn. 'Not now, Jo,' she said. 'Surely, not now.' Jonathan whispered again, and she said with a show of irritation: 'There's no need to do that. *She* can't hear, poor dear.'

Alleyn moved towards them. 'I'm so sorry,' he said, 'but I'm afraid I must see Dr Hart as soon as possible.'

Jonathan said hurriedly and rather ludicrously: 'You don't know Mr Alleyn, Hersey. My cousin, Lady Hersey Amblington, Alleyn.'

'If he's still . . . ' Alleyn began, and Hersey said quickly: 'He's done everything possible. I'm afraid he doesn't think it's going to be any use. He's been rather marvellous, Mr Alleyn.'

Before Alleyn could reply to this unexpected tribute or to the petulant little cluck with which Jonathan received it, the door was suddenly pulled wide open from within and there stood a heavy, pale man wearing no jacket, his shirt-sleeves rolled up, his face glistening.

'What *is* all this?' demanded Dr Hart. 'What now! Lady Hersey, you have no business to stand chattering in doorways when perhaps I may need you.'

'I'm sorry,' said Hersey meekly, and disappeared into the room. Hart glanced at Alleyn. 'Well?' he said.

'I'm an officer of Scotland Yard, Dr Hart. May I speak to you?'

'Why in God's name haven't you brought a medical man with you? Well, well, come in here. Come in.'

So Alleyn went into the room and Hart very neatly shut the door in Jonathan's face.

III

The bed had been moved out from the wall and the light from a large window fell across it and directly upon the face of the woman who lay there. Her eyes were not quite closed, nor was her mouth, which, Alleyn saw, was crooked, dragged down on one side as though by an invisible cord. So strong was the light that, coming from the dark passage, he saw the scene as a pattern of hard whites and swimming blacks, and some moments passed before his eyes found, in the shadows round the bed, a litter of nursing paraphernalia which Hersey at once began to clear away. Alleyn became aware of a slow, deep, and stertorous rhythm, the sound of the patient's breathing.

'Is she deeply unconscious?' he asked.

'Profound coma,' said Hart. 'I have, I think, done everything possible in the way of treatment. Mr Mandrake gave me your notes, which, I understand, came from a surgeon at Scotland Yard. They confirmed my own opinion as regards treatment. I am deeply disappointed that you have not brought a medical man with you, not because I believe he could do anything, but because I wish to protect myself.'

'Was the stuff from the local chemist no use?'

'It enabled me to complete the treatment, but the condition has not improved. Have you pencil and paper?' demanded Dr Hart surprisingly.

'I have.' Alleyn's hand went to his pocket.

'I wish you to record the treatment. I am in a dangerous position. I wish to protect myself. Lady Hersey Amblington will be witness to my statement. I have administered injections of normal saline, and of Croton oil. Every attempt to obtain elimination – you are not taking notes,' said Dr Hart accusingly.

'Dr Hart,' said Alleyn, 'I shall take exhaustive notes in a little while, and you will be given every opportunity to make statements. At the moment I am concerned with your patient. Is there the smallest hope of her recovery?'

'In my opinion, none. That is why . . . '

'I think I understand your position. Has she, at any time since you have attended her, regained consciousness?'

Dr Hart turned down his shirt sleeves and looked about for his aggressively countrified coat. Hersey at once brought it and helped him into it, and Alleyn found a moment in which to appreciate Dr Hart's unconscious acceptance of her attention.

'At first,' he said, 'she could be made to wince by slapping the face. Twice she opened her eyes. The last time was when her son tried to rouse her. Otherwise there has been nothing.'

Hersey made a sharp movement and Alleyn said: 'Yes, Lady Hersey? You were going to say something, weren't you?'

'Only that she did speak once. Dr Hart was at the far end of the room, and I don't think he heard her.'

'What is this?' said Hart sharply. 'You should have told me immediately. When did the patient speak?'

'It was when Nicholas was here. You remember he shouted. You told him to. And he shook her. There was no response, she had closed her eyes again, and you – you sort of threw up your hands and walked away. Do you remember?'

'Of course I remember!'

'Nicholas leant forward and put his hand against her cheek – the disfigured cheek. He did it quite gently, but it seemed to rouse her. She opened her eyes and said one word. It was the faintest whisper. You couldn't have heard.'

'Well, well, well, what was this one word?' Hart demanded. 'Why did you not call me at once? What was it?'

'It was your name.' There was a short silence, and Hersey added: 'She didn't speak again.'

Alleyn said: 'Did you get the impression that she spoke with any intention?'

'I – don't think so. Perhaps she realized Dr Hart was attending her,' said Hersey, and Alleyn thought: 'You don't believe that.' He moved nearer to the bed and Dr Hart joined him there. 'How long?' Alleyn murmured.

'Not very long, I think.'

'Should I fetch Nicholas?' said Hersey.

'Does he wish to return?' asked Hart coolly.

'I don't think so. Not unless – I promised I would tell him when . . .'

'It will not be just yet, I think.'

'Perhaps I'd better tell him that. He's in his room. I shall be there if you want me.'

Alleyn opened the door for her. When he moved back into the room, Dr Hart was stooping over his patient. Without turning his head, but with a certain deepening of his voice, he said: 'I would have given much, I would have given something that I have struggled greatly to retain, if by doing so I could have saved this case. Do you know why that is?'

'I think perhaps I might guess.'

'Come here, Inspector. Look at that face. For many years I used to dream of those disfigurements, for a long time I was actually afraid to go to sleep for fear I should be visited by a certain nightmare, a nightmare of the re-enactment of my blunder, and of the terrible scene that followed her discovery of it. You have heard, of course, that she recognized me and that the elder son, who has been killed, reacted most violently to her story?'

'I've been given some account of it,' said Alleyn without emphasis.

'It is true that I was the Franz Hartz of Vienna who blundered. If I could have saved her life I would have felt it to be an atonement. I always knew,' said Dr Hart, straightening his back and facing Alleyn, 'I always knew that some day I should meet this woman again. There is no use in concealing these things from you, Inspector. These others, these fools, will come screaming to you, eager to accuse me. I have refused to discuss my dilemma with any one of them. I am ready to discuss it with you.'

Alleyn reflected with faint amusement that this, from a leading suspect, was just as well. He complimented Dr Hart on his decision, and together they moved away from the bed to a more distant window, where Jonathan's bouquet of everlasting flowers, papery little mummies, still rustled in their carefully chosen vase. And now Alleyn did produce a pocket notebook.

'Before we begin,' he said, 'is there any possibility that Mrs Compline will regain consciousness?'

'I should say there is not the remotest possibility. There may be a change. I expect, and your police surgeon's advice confirms my suspicion, that the respiration may change. I should prefer to remain in this room. We shall conduct the interview here, if you please.'

And, while the light from a rain-blurred window imperceptibly thickened and grew cold upon the face of Dr Hart's patient, he answered Alleyn's questions. Alleyn had had official dealings with aliens for many years. Since the onset of Nazidom he had learned to recognize a common and tragic characteristic in many of them, and that was a deep-seated terror of plain-clothes police officers. Dr Hart's attitude surprised him very much. As he carried forward his questions he found that in the face of what appeared to be an extremely nasty position Hart showed little nervousness. He answered readily, but with a suggestion of impatience. Alleyn was more than usually careful to give him the official warnings. Hart listened to them with an air of respect, nodding his head gravely but showing no inclination to consider his answers more carefully. If he was indeed innocent he was the ideal witness, but in this case his belief in his own safety was alarming. If he was guilty he was a very cool customer indeed. Alleyn decided to try him a little further.

'It comes to this, then,' he said. 'You can offer no explanation of how this extra Charter form containing the warning reached Captain Compline. Nor have you any theory as to who pushed Mr Mandrake into the pond, though you agree that you saw Mr Compline leave for the pond wearing precisely the same kind of cape. Is that right?'

'It is true that I do not know who pushed Mr Mandrake into the pond,' said Hart slowly. 'As for the Charter form, I suggested at the time that I might have torn two forms off together and that the bottom form had been written by somebody else.'

'Somebody who made letters reminiscent of your own writing?'

'I have not seen the form. I do not know what was written on it.'

'Five words. "You are warned. Keep off." '

A dull red crept into those heavy cheeks. For the first time he seemed disconcerted. For the first time Alleyn saw the nervous tic flutter under his lip.

'Dr Hart,' Alleyn said, 'of all the people in that room, who had most cause to send such a message to Nicholas Compline?'

'Two people had cause. His brother and myself. His brother had cause. Had he not practised his goat's tricks upon the girl, the brother's fiancée?'

'And only on her?' Hart was silent. 'Is it true,' Alleyn asked, 'that you had written to Nicholas Compline, objecting to his friendship with your wife and threatening to take certain steps if this friendship continued?'

'Did *he* tell you that?' Hart demanded.

'I haven't seen him yet, but if you wrote such letters he's not likely to keep it a secret.'

'I do not deny that I wrote them. I deny that I wrote this ridiculous message. And I object most strongly to the introduction into this affair of matters that concern only myself.'

'If they prove to be irrelevant they will not be made public. Dr Hart, you tell me you have nothing to fear and nothing to conceal from me. At the same time you don't deny that you threatened Nicholas Compline. I must tell you that I've had a very full account of this weekend from a member of your party. I've warned you that your statements, if relevant, may be used in subsequent proceedings. I'm going to ask you certain questions and I shall do my best to check your answers. We shall get on a good deal faster if you don't challenge my questions, but either refuse or consent to give plain answers to them.'

There was a pause and then Hart said hurriedly: 'Very well, very well. I do not seek to obstruct you. It is only that there is one matter that is most painful to me. Unendurably painful.'

'I'm sorry. Do you agree that you were at enmity with Compline?'

'I objected to his behaviour in regard to – my wife.'

'Did he know she was your wife?'

'I desired to tell him so.'

'But you didn't tell him?'

'No. My wife did not wish me to do so.'

'Have you quarrelled with him since you came to Highfold?'

'Yes. Openly. I have not attempted to conceal my mistrust and dislike of him. Would a man who was planning a murder behave in such a matter? Would he not rather simulate friendship?'

Alleyn looked at the pale face with its twitching lip. 'If he was in full command of his emotions, no doubt he would attempt to do so.' Hart found no answer to this, and he went on: 'Did you meet any one on your way from the house to the pond?'

'No.'

'I have had a very brief look at that part of the garden. You went by a path that comes out at the back of the pavilion?'

'Yes.'

'What did you see as you came round the pavilion?'

'I heard shouts and I saw William Compline, Nicholas Compline, Miss Wynne and Mr Royal gesticulating on the edge of the pond.'

'Yesterday evening when you came upstairs to dress, did you see anybody after you went to your room?'

'Nobody.'

'Have you ever touched the brass Buddha that injured Nicholas Compline?'

'Never. But – wait a moment – yes. Yes, my God, I have touched it.'

'When?'

'It was the first night. We went up to our rooms. I remember I drew back because I did not wish to accompany Nicholas Compline, who walked a little ahead with his brother. Mr Royal drew my attention to this Buddha. He asked me if I knew anything of Oriental art. As an excuse to delay I feigned an interest. I reached out my hands and touched it. Compline made some remark on the obesity of the Buddha. It was an insult to me. Whenever he could insult me he did so. So I have touched it.'

'Coming back to last night. Will you describe your movements from the time you entered the green boudoir until the time you went upstairs for the last time?'

Hart did this, and his description tallied with Mandrake's note. 'I felt I could not dine with them. They suspected me. It was an intolerable situation. I spoke to Mr Royal, and he suggested that I remain in that room. When, as I have told you, I finally left it, it was for the first time. I went straight to my room. The footman saw me.'

'Had you been into the smoking room at any time yesterday?'

'I do not think so. That insufferable machine was there.

In the morning he had driven me crazy with it. First one horrible noise, then another, and all of them distorted. I cannot endure radio. I have a radio-phobia. I did not go into the room at all yesterday.'

'But you have been there at some time?'

'Oh yes. The first night we played this Charter game in that room.'

'Will you describe the room to me?'

'Describe it? But you have seen it? Why should I?'

'I should like you to do so if you will.'

Hart stared at Alleyn as if he was insane and began a laborious catalogue. 'First then, if you must have it, there is this detestable radio close to the boudoir door. When I think of the room I think of the radio by which it is made hideous. There are English leather chairs. There is a red leather screen. There are pictures, English sportings, I think. And photographs, very old and faded. There is such a photograph above the mantelpiece of an old fellow with a fish. He wears an absurd costume. There is also hanging on the wall a fishing-rod. Surely this is a great waste of time, Inspector?'

'Are you a fisherman?'

Gott im Himmel, of what importance is it whether I fish or do not fish! I do not fish. I know nothing of fishing.' Hart stared irritably at Alleyn and then added: 'If I lose my temper you will forgive me. I have heard of the efficiency of Scotland Yard. No doubt there is some reason which I do not follow for these questions of interior decoration and fishing. I can tell you little more of the room. I did not particularly observe this room.'

'The colour of the walls?'

'A light colour. A neutral colour. Almost white.'

'And the carpet?'

'I cannot tell you – dark. Green, I think. Dark green. There are, of course, three doors. The one into the boudoir was locked by Nicholas Compline after I requested that he should not use that machine of hell.'

'What else did you see on the walls?'

'What else? Ah, the weapons, of course. Mr Royal drew our attention to the weapons, I remember, on Friday night. It was before dinner. Some of the men were in the room. He described the travels of his father in the antipodes where he collected some of them. He showed me – '

'Yes, Dr Hart?'

Hart paused with his mouth open and then turned away. 'I have just remembered,' he muttered. 'He took down the stone club from the wall, saying it was – I forget – a Polynesian or New Zealand native weapon. He gave it to me to examine. I was interested. I – examined the weapon.'

'Both the mere and the Buddha?' said Alleyn, without particular stress. 'I see.'

IV

It was twenty to four when Alleyn finished with Dr Hart. Hart made another examination of his patient. He said that her condition was 'less satisfactory'. Her temperature had risen and her respiration was more markedly abnormal. Alleyn would have been glad to escape from the rhythm of deep and then shallow breaths, broken by terrible intervals of silence. Hersey Amblington returned, and Hart said he thought that Nicholas should be warned of the change in his mother, and she went to fetch him. Obviously Hart expected Alleyn to go. He had told him there was no possibility of Mrs Compline's regaining consciousness before she died, but Alleyn did not feel justified in acting upon this assurance. He remained standing in shadow at the far end of the room, and Hart paid no more attention to him. The rain drove in sighing gusts against the closed windows, and found its way in through the open ones, so that Alleyn felt its touch upon his face. A vast desolation filled the room, annd still there came from the bed that sequence of deep breath, shallow breath, interval, and then again, deep breath, shallow breath.

The door opened and Hersey Amblington came in with Nicholas.

Alleyn saw a tall young man in uniform who carried his left arm in a sling. He noticed the lint-coloured hair, the blankly good-looking face with its blond moustache and faintly etched lines of dissipation, and he wondered if normally it held any trace of colour. He watched Nicholas walk slowly towards the bed, his gaze fixed, his right hand plucking at his tie. Hersey moved forward a chair, and without a word Nicholas sat beside his mother. Hersey stooped over the bed and presently Alleyn saw that she had drawn Mrs Compline's hand from under the sheets and laid it close beside Nicholas. It was so flaccid it seemed already dead. Nicholas laid his own hand over it, and at the touch broke down completely, burying his face beside their joined hands and weeping bitterly. For several minutes Alleyn stood in the shadow, hearing the wind and rain, the sound of distorted breathing, and the heavy sobs of Nicholas Compline. Then there was a lessening of sound. Hart moved to the head of the bed, looked at Hersey, and nodded. She had laid her hand on Nicholas's shoulder, but before he raised his head Alleyn had slipped out of the room.

It was darkish now, in the passage, and he almost collided with Jonathan Royal, who must have been standing close to the door. Jonathan had his finger to his lips. As they faced each other there they heard Nicholas, beyond the closed door, scream out: 'Don't touch her, you – ! Keep your hands off her. If it hadn't been for you she'd never have done it.'

'My God!' said Jonathan in a whisper. 'What now? What's he doing to her?'

'Nothing that can hurt her,' said Alleyn.

CHAPTER 14

Interrogation

At five o'clock the telephone in the library rang out. Alleyn, who was there, answered it. It was a police call from London for himself, and he took it with the greatest satisfaction. The Yard reported that Detective-Inspector Fox, together with a surgeon, a fingerprint expert, and a photographer, had left London at three o'clock and would reach Pen-Felton by way of a branch line at 7.30. The Chipping constabulary had arranged for a car to bring them on to Highfold.

'I'm damn' glad to hear it,' said Alleyn warmly. 'I'm here with a couple of bodies and seven lunatics. D'you know what's happened to the Chipping people?'

'They got stuck somewhere, sir, and had to walk back. We'd have reported before, but the line's only just fixed.'

'The whole thing's damn' silly,' said Alleyn. 'We might be marooned in Antarctica. Anyway, thank heaven for Fox and Co. Goodbye.'

He hung up the receiver, drove his hands through his hair, and returned to Mandrake's notes. As a postscript, Mandrake had added a sort of tabulated summary.

Alleyn shook his head over the last name. 'Industrious Mr Mandrake! But he's not to be trusted there,' he thought. 'We have a young woman who has been jilted by Nicholas, who attracted her. As soon as she engages herself to William, who does not attract her, Nicholas begins to make amorous antics at her all over again. A wicked young woman might wish to get rid of William. A desperate young woman might wish to get rid of Nicholas. And is it *quite* impossible that Miss Wynne darted down to the pond before making her official arrival with Jonathan? Perhaps it is. I'll have to go down to that pond.' He lit a cigarette and stared dolefully at the row of 'yes's' against Hart. 'All jolly fine, but how the devil did he rig a booby trap that neither Nicholas nor William noticed? No, it's not a bad effort on Master Mandrake's part. But I fancy he's made one error. Now, I *wonder.*' And, taking up his pen, he put a heavy cross against one of Mandrake's entries. He wandered disconsolately about the library, and finally, with a grimace, let himself into the smoking room. He went straight to the radio, passing behind the shrouded figure in the chair. This time he did not draw back the curtains from the windows, but turned up the lights and used his torch. The wireless cabinet stood on a low stool. Alleyn's torchlight crawled

	If the Murderer mistook William for Nicholas				If the Murderer recognized William	
	Motive	*Opp. 1st attempt*	*Opp. 2nd attempt*	*Opp. 3rd attempt*	*Motive*	*Reason for other attempts*
Dr Hart	Yes	Yes	Yes	Booby trap?	Yes	Made against Nicholas
Nicholas Compline	–	–	–	–	None	None
Jonathan Royal	None	Possibly	Improbable	Yes?	None	None
Lady Hersey	None	Yes	Yes?	Yes	None	None
Mrs C.	None	Yes	No	Yes	?	None
Aubrey Mandrake	None	Yes!	No	No	None	None
Madame Lisse	None	Yes	No	Yes	?	None
Chloris Wynne	None	No	Yes	No	None	None

over the front surface and finally came to rest on the bakelite volume control, which he examined through his lens. He found several extremely faint lines inside of the screw-hole. There were also some faint scratches across the surface outside the hole, making tracks in a film of dust.

The stillness of the room was interrupted by a small murmur of satisfaction. Alleyn got out his pair of tweezers, and introduced them delicately into the hole in the volume control. Screwing his face into an excruciating grimace, he manipulated his tweezers and finally drew them out. He squatted on the carpet quite close to the motionless folds of white linen that followed so closely the frozen posture of the figure they concealed that an onlooker might have been visited by the horrid notion that William imitated Alleyn and, under his shroud, conducted a secret scrutiny of the carpet. Alleyn had laid an envelope on the carpet, and on its surface he dropped the minute fragment he had taken in his tweezers. It was scarcely larger than an eyelash. He peered at it through his glass.

'Scarlet. Feather, I *think*. And a tiny scrap of green,' said Alleyn. And whistling soundlessly, he sealed his find up in the envelope.

Next he peered into the crevice between the large and small tuning controls. 'Not so much as a speck of dust,' he muttered, 'although there's plenty in the screw-hole. There's the actual shaft which rotates, of course. It's reminiscent of a pulley.' He found one or two scratches on the surface of the tuning control. It was just possible through the lens to see that each of these marks had a sharp beginning and a gentler tail, suggesting that some very fine pointed object had struck the surface smartly and fallen away. Alleyn re-examined the carpet. Below the wall where the mere had hung, and a little to the right, he found one or two marks that he had missed on his first examination. They occurred beneath the small desk that stood under the weapons. Here the pile of the carpet was protected and thick. Across its surface, running roughly parallel with the wall, were a series of marks which, when he examined them through his glass, looked like the traces of some sharp object that had torn across the surface of the pile. In one place he found a little tuft of carpet that had become detached. He photographed this area, fenced it in with chairs, and returned to the library.

Here he found a young footman with a tea-tray.

'Is that for me?' Alleyn asked.

'Yes, sir. I was to ask if there was anything further you required, sir.'

'Nothing, at the moment, thank you. Are you Thomas?'

'Yes, sir,' said Thomas with a nervous simper.

'I'd like a word with you.' Alleyn poured out a cup of tea. 'Still keen on Boomps-a-daisy?'

Thomas did not answer, and Alleyn glanced up at him.

'Never want to hear it again s'long as I live, sir,' said Thomas ardently.

'You needn't regret your burst of good spirits, you know. It may be very valuable.'

'Beg pardon, sir,' said Thomas, 'but I don't want to be mixed up in nothing unpleasant, sir. I've put my name down, sir, and I'm waiting to be called up. I don't want to go into the army, sir, with an unpleasantness hanging over me, like.'

Alleyn was only too familiar with this attitude of mind and was careful to reassure Thomas.

'There ought to be no unpleasantness about furthering the cause of justice, and that's what I hope you may be able to do. I only want you to repeat an assurance you have already given Mr Royal and Mr Mandrake. I'm going to put it this way, and I hope you'll agree that it couldn't be put more candidly. Would you be prepared to swear that between the time you passed through the hall to the library and the time when you left off dancing, Dr Hart could *not* have entered the smoking room?'

'Yes, sir, I would.'

'You've thought it over carefully, I expect, since Mr Royal spoke to you last night.'

'I have indeed, sir. I've been over and over it in my brain till I can't seem to think of anything else. But it's the same every time, sir. Dr Hart was crossing the hall when I took the tray in, and I wasn't above a few seconds setting it down, and when I come out, sir, he was halfway up the stairs.'

'Was there a good light on the stairs?'

'Enough to see him, sir.'

'You couldn't have mistaken somebody else for Dr Hart?'

'No, sir, not a chance, if you'll excuse me. I saw him quite distinct, sir, walking up with his hands behind his back. He turned the corner and I noticed his face looking sort of – well, it's difficult to describe.'

'Try,' said Alleyn.

'Well, sir, as if he was very worried. Well, kind of frantic, sir. Haunted almost,' added Thomas with an air of surprising himself. 'I noticed it particular, sir, because it was just the same as he looked when he was walking in the garden yesterday morning.'

Alleyn's cup was halfway to his lips. He set it down carefully.

'Did you see Dr Hart in the garden yesterday morning? Whereabouts?'

'Behind that bathing-shed – I mean that pavilion, sir. We'd heard about the bet Mr William Compline had on with his brother, sir, and I'm afraid I just nipped out to see the fun, sir. One of the maids kind of kidded me on, if you'll excuse the expression, sir.'

'I'll excuse it,' said Alleyn. 'Go on, Thomas. Tell me exactly what you did see.'

'Well, sir, I knew Mr Caper wouldn't be all that pleased if he knew, so I went out by the east wing door and walked round to the front of the house by a path in the lower gardens. It comes out a little way down the drive, sir.'

'Yes.'

'I dodged across the drive, sir, and up through the trees towards the terrace. I was just above the pavilion, sir, and I looked down and there was the doctor gentleman, with his hands behind his back, walking towards the rear of the pavilion. I'd seen him go out by the front door before I left, sir. Mr Royal saw him off.'

'Did you continue to watch him?'

'No, sir, not for long. You see, while I was looking at him I heard a splash and a great to-do, and I ran on to where I could see the pond, and there was Mr Nicholas throwing in one of them floating birds and yelling for help, and Mr Mandrake half drowning in the pond and Mr William running down the steps, with the young lady and Mr Royal just crossing the terrace. But the doctor must have come along as quick as he could, sir, because he got there just as they hauled Mr Mandrake out.'

'Did you see any one else on the terrace? A lady?'

'No, sir.' Thomas waited for a moment, and then said: 'Will there be anything further, sir?'

'I fancy not, Thomas. I'll get that down in writing and ask you to sign it. It'll do very nicely indeed to go on with.'

'Thank you, sir,' said Thomas primly, and withdrew.

II

'Dr Hart,' Alleyn muttered after a long cogitation. 'Opportunity for first attempt.' He altered the entry in Mandrake's tables and rang the bell. It was answered by Caper, a condescension that Alleyn imagined must have been prompted by curiosity. He divided butlers into two classes, the human and the inhuman. Caper, he thought, looked human.

'You rang, sir?' said Caper.

'To send a message to Mr Nicholas Compline. I don't want to worry him too much, but I should like to see him if he's free.'

'I'll make inquiries, sir,' said Caper. Inhuman butlers, Alleyn reflected, always ascertained.

'Thank you. Before you go, I'd like your opinion on the footman.'

'On Thomas, sir?'

'Yes. I expect he's told you all about his interviews with Mr Royal.'

'He has mentioned them, sir.'

'What's your opinion of him?'

Caper drew down his upper lip, placed Alleyn's cup and saucer on the tray, and appeared to deliberate. 'He's not cut out for service, sir,' he said finally. 'In a manner of speaking he's too high-spirited.'

'Ah,' Alleyn murmured, 'you've heard about Boomps-a-daisy.'

'I have, sir. I was horrified. But it's not that alone, not by any means. He's always up to something. There's no harm in the lad, sir. He's a nice, open, truthful lad, but not suitable. He'll do better in the army.'

'Truthful,' Alleyn repeated.

'I should say exceptionally so, sir. Very observant and bright in his ways, too.'

'That's a useful recommendation.'

"Will that be all, sir?'

'Not quite,' Alleyn waited for a moment and then looked directly at Caper. 'You know why I'm here, of course?'

'Yes, sir.'

'There is no doubt whatever that Mr William Compline has been murdered. This being so, it appears that his murderer is now at large in this house. I am sure that the members of Mr Royal's staff will want to give us all the help they can in a difficult and possibly even a dangerous situation.'

'I'm sure we'll all do our duty by the master, sir,' said Caper, and if this was not a direct answer Alleyn chose to regard it as one. He began, very delicately, to probe. He believed that the servants in a large household have a seventy per cent working knowledge of everything that happens on the other side of the green baize door. This uncanny awareness, he thought, was comparable to the secret communications of prisoners, and he sometimes wondered if it was engendered in the bad old days of domestic servitude. To tap this source of information is one of the arts of police investigation, and Alleyn, who did not care overmuch for the job, sighed for Inspector Fox, who had a great way with female domestics. Fox settled down comfortably and talked their own language, a difficult task and one which it was useless for Alleyn to attempt. Caper had placed him in Jonathan's class, and would distrust and despise any effort Alleyn made to get out of it. So he went warily to work, at first with poor results. Caper remembered speaking to Mr Royal in the hall before dinner on the previous evening. Mr Royal ordered the wine for dinner and asked the time, as there was some question of letting the port settle after it was decanted. It was twenty-five minutes to eight. It would be about five minutes later that Caper heard somewhere upstairs a heavy thud, followed by a shout from Mr Nicholas. Mr Royal had gone to the big drawing room when he left Caper. Alleyn tried for an account of the quarrel between Hart and Nicholas Compline on Friday night after dinner. Caper said he had heard nothing of it. Alleyn groped about, watching his man, and at last he found an opening. Caper, true to his class, disliked foreigners. Something in the turn of his voice when Hart's name was introduced gave Alleyn his cue.

'I suppose,' Alleyn said, 'Dr Hart and Madame Lisse have often visited Highfold?'

'No, sir. Only once previously. We had a ball in aid of the Polish refugees, and they both attended. That was in December, sir.'

'Has Mr Royal visited them?'

'I believe so, sir. I believe Mr Royal dined with Mrs Lisse, if that is the lady's name, not long after the ball. I understand the doctor was present on that occasion. Shortly afterwards he presented Mr Royal with That Garment, sir.'

'The Tyrolese cape?'

'Exactly so, sir,' said Caper, after closing his eyes for a second.

'It wouldn't be right, then, to say that the entire party was well known to the staff?'

'No, sir. Her ladyship and Mrs Compline and the two young gentlemen are old friends of Mr Royal's, and Mr Mandrake has often visited.'

'He's an old friend of Mr Royal's too, then?'

'I understand there is some business connection, sir,' said Caper, and a kind of quintessence of snobbery overlaid the qualification.

'Did it strike you that it was a curiously assorted party?' Alleyn ventured. 'Mr Royal tells me you've been with him since you were a boy. Frankly, Caper, have you ever known another weekend party quite like this one?'

'Frankly, sir,' said Caper, coming abruptly into the open, 'I haven't.' He paused for a moment, and perhaps he read a friendly interest in Alleyn's face. 'I don't mention the hall out of the hall as a rule, sir,' he said, 'but, as you say, this is different. And I will say that Mrs Pouting and myself never fancied them. Never.'

'Never fancied who, Caper?'

'The foreigners, sir. And what's been seen since they came hasn't served to change our opinion.'

With a certain distaste, Alleyn recognized his opening and took it. 'Well, Caper, what *has* been seen? Hadn't you better tell me?'

Caper told him. There had been stories of Dr Hart and Madame Lisse, stories that had percolated from Great Chipping. Caper digressed a little to throw out dark references to the Fifth Column and was led back gently to the burden of his song. There had been other stories, it seemed, of visits in the dead of night from Dr Hart to Madame Lisse, and Mrs Pouting had given it as her opinion that if they were not married they ought to be. From this it was an easy step to Nicholas. It was 'common knowledge' said Caper, that Mr Nicholas was paying serious court to Madame Lisse. 'If it had been the elder brother she'd have taken him, sir, and it's the opinion of some that if poor Mr William had come along first it would have been another story.' It was obvious that Nicholas passed the test of the servants' hall. Caper said they were always very pleased to hear he was coming. The impression Alleyn had got from Mandrake and Chloris Wynne was of a vain, shallow fellow with a great deal of physical attraction for women. The impression he had got from his own brief glimpse of Nicholas was of a young man bewildered and dazed by a profound emotional shock. Jonathan, when he spoke coherently, had sketched a picture of a somewhat out-of-date rip. Caper managed to suggest a spirited grandee. Mr William, he said, was the quiet one. Strange in his ways. But Mr Nicholas was the same to everybody, always open-handed and pleasant. He was very well liked in the district. Alleyn led him back to Madame Lisse, and soon discovered that Mrs Pouting and Caper believed she was out to catch Nicholas. That, in Caper's opinion, was the beginning of the trouble.

'If I may speak frankly, sir, we'd heard a good deal about it before Mrs Lisse came. There was a lot of talk.'

'What did it all add up to?'

'Why, sir, that the lady was taken up with this Dr Hart until she saw something a good deal better come along. Mrs Pouting says . . . '

'Look here,' said Alleyn, 'suppose you ask Mrs Pouting to come in for a moment.'

Mrs Pouting was fetched and proved to be a large, capable lady with a good deal of jaw and not very much lip. With her entrance it became clear that the servants had determined that Madame Lisse and Dr Hart, between them, were responsible for the whole tragedy. Alleyn recognized very characteristic forms of loyalty, prejudice and obstinacy. Jonathan and his intimate friends were not to be blown upon, they had been deceived and victimized by the foreigners. The remotest suggestion of Jonathan's complicity was enough to set Mrs Pouting off. She was very grand. Her manner as well as her skirts seemed to rustle, but Alleyn saw that she was big with a theory and meant to be delivered of it.

'Things have been going on,' said Mrs Pouting, 'which, if Mr Royal had heard of them, would have stopped certain persons from remaining at Highfold. Under this very roof, they've been going on.'

'What sort of things?'

'I cannot bring myself . . . ' Mrs Pouting began, but Alleyn interrupted her. Would it not be better, he suggested, for her to tell him what she knew, here in private, than to have it dragged out piecemeal at an inquest. He would not use information that was irrelevant. Mrs Pouting then said that there had been in-goings and out-comings from 'Mrs Lisse's' room. The housemaids had made discoveries. Dr Hart had been overheard accusing her of all sorts of things.

'What sorts of things?' Alleyn repeated patiently.

'She's a bad woman, sir. We've heard no good of her. She's treated her ladyship disgracefully over her shop. She made trouble between Mr Nicholas and his young lady. She's out for money, sir, and she doesn't care how she gets it. I've my own ideas about what's at the bottom of it all.'

'You'd better tell me what these ideas are, Mrs Pouting.'

Caper made an uncomfortable noise in his throat. Mrs Pouting glanced at him and said: 'Mr Caper doesn't altogether agree with me, I believe. Mr Caper is inclined to blame *him* more than *her*, whereas I'm quite positive it's *her* more than *him*.'

'What is?'

'If I may interrupt, sir,' said Caper, 'I think it would be best for us to say outright what's in our minds, sir.'

'So do I,' said Alleyn heartily.

'Thank you, sir. Yesterday evening, after the accident with the brass figure, Dr Hart came downstairs and sat in the small green room, the one that opens into the smoking room, sir. It happened that Mrs Pouting had gone into the smoking room to see if everything was to rights there, the flower vases full of water and the fire made up and so on. The communicating door was not quite closed and . . . '

'I hope it will be clearly understood,' Mrs Pouting struck in, 'that I had *not* realized anybody was in the boudoir. I was examining the radio for dust – the maids are *not* as thorough as I could wish – when quite suddenly, a few inches away, as it seemed, I heard Dr Hart's voice. He said: "Let them say what they like, they can prove nothing." And Mrs Lisse's voice said: "Are you sure?" I was very awkwardly placed,' continued Mrs Pouting genteelly. 'I scarcely knew what to do. They had evidently come close to the door. If I made my presence known they would think perhaps that I had heard more and – well, really, it was very difficult. While I hesitated they began to speak again, but more quietly. I heard Mrs Lisse say: "In that event I shall know what to do." He said: "Would you have the courage?" and she said: "Where much is at stake, I would dare much." And then,' said Mrs Pouting, no longer able to conceal her relish for dramatic values, *'then,* sir, he said, almost admiringly, sir: *"You devil, I believe you would."* And she said: "It's not *I would,* Francis, it's *I will."* Then they moved away from the door and I went out. But I repeat now what I said shortly afterwards to Mr Caper: she sounded murderous.'

III

'Well,' said Alleyn, after a pause, 'that's a very curious story, Mrs Pouting.' He looked from one to the other of the two servants, who still kept up their air of contained deference. 'What's your interpretation of it?' he asked.

Mrs Pouting did not reply, but she slightly cast up her eyes and her silence was ineffably expressive. Alleyn turned to Caper.

'Mrs Pouting and I differ a little, sir,' said Caper, exactly as if they had enjoyed an amiable discussion on the rival merits of thick and thin soup. 'Mrs Pouting, I understand, considers that Dr Hart and Mrs Lisse are adventurers who were working together to entrap Mr Nicholas Compline, but that Dr Hart had become jealous and that they had fallen out. Mrs Pouting considers that Mrs Lisse took advantage of Dr Hart's two attempts on Mr Nicholas to kill Mr William and make it look as if Dr Hart had done it, mistaking him for his brother. With a mercenary motive, sir.'

'Extremely Machiavellian!' said Alleyn. 'What do you think?'

'Well, sir, I don't know what to think, but somehow I can't fancy the lady actually struck the blow, sir.'

'That,' said Mrs Pouting vigorously, 'is because you're a man, Mr Caper. I hope I know vice when I see it,' she added.

'I'm sure you do, Mrs Pouting,' said Alleyn absently. 'Why not?'

Mrs Pouting clasped her hands together, and by that simple gesture turned herself into an anxious human creature. 'Whether it's both of them together or her alone,' she said, 'they're dangerous, sir. I know they're dangerous. If they'd heard me telling you what I have told you –! But it's not for myself, sir, but for Mr Royal, that I'm worried. He's made no secret of what he thinks. He says openly that Dr Hart (though why Doctor when he's no more than a meddler with Heaven's handiwork, I'm sure I don't know) – that Dr Hart struck down Mr William and that he'll see him hanged for it, and there they both are, free to deal another blow.'

'Not quite,' said Alleyn. 'Dr Hart, at his own suggestion, is once more locked in his room. I said I'd see Mr Compline next, Caper, but I've changed my mind. Will you find out if Madame Hart is disengaged?'

'Madame Hart!' they both said together.

'Ah, I forgot. You haven't heard that they are man and wife.'

'His wife!' whispered Mrs Pouting. 'That proves I'm right. She wanted to be rid of him. She wanted to catch the heir to Penfelton. That's why poor Mr William was killed, and if the man is hanged for it, mark my words, Mr Caper, she'll marry Mr Nicholas.'

And with this pronouncement, delivered with sibylline emphasis, Mrs Pouting withdrew, sweeping Caper away in her train.

Alleyn noted down the conversation, pulled a grimace at the result and fell to thinking of former cases when the fantastic solution had turned out to be the correct one. 'It's the left- and right theory,' he thought. 'A wishes to be rid of B and C. A murders B in such a fashion that C is arrested and hanged. Mrs Pouting casts Madame for the rôle of A. A murderess on the grand scale. What do murderesses on the grand scale look like?'

The next moment he was on his feet. Madame Lisse had made her entrance.

Nobody had told Alleyn that she was a remarkably beautiful woman, and for a brief moment he experienced the strange feeling of awed astonishment that extreme physical beauty may bring to the beholder. His first conscious thought was that she was lovely enough to stir up a limitless amount of trouble.

'You sent for me,' said Madame Lisse.

'I asked if I might see you,' said Alleyn. 'Won't you sit down?'

She sat down. The movement was like a lesson in deportment, deliberately executed and ending in stillness, her back held erect, her wrists crossed on her lap.

'I wonder,' thought Alleyn, 'if William ever wanted to paint her.' With every appearance of tranquillity she waited for him to begin. He took out his notebook and flattened it on his knee.

'First,' he said, 'I think I should have your name in full.'

'Elise Lisse.'

'I mean,' said Alleyn, 'your legal name, Madame. That should be Elise Hart, I understand.' And he thought: 'Golly! That's shaken her!' For a moment she looked furious. He saw the charming curve of her mouth harden and then compose itself. After a pause she said very sedately: 'My legal name. Yes, of course. I do not care to use it and it did not occur to me to give it. I am separated from my husband.'

'Ah, yes,' said Alleyn. 'Legally separated?'

'No,' she said placidly. 'Not legally.'

'I hope you will forgive me if I ask you questions that may seem irrelevant and impertinent. You are under no obligation to answer them: I must make that quite clear, and perhaps I should add that any questions which you refuse to answer will be noted.'

This uncompromising slice of the official manner seemed to have very little effect on Madame Lisse. She said: 'Of course,' and leant a little towards him. He got a whiff of her scent and recognized it as an expensive one.

'You are separated from your husband, but one supposes, since you go to the same house-parties, that it is an amicable arrangement.'

There was a considerable pause before she answered: 'Not precisely. I didn't care for accepting the same invitation but did so before I knew he had been invited.'

'Were his feelings in the matter much the same as yours?'

'I can't tell you,' said Madame Lisse. 'I think not.'

'You mean that you have not discussed the matter with him?'

'I don't enter into discussions with him if I can avoid doing so. I have tried as far as possible to avoid encounters.'

Alleyn watched her for a moment and then said: 'Did you drive here, Madame Lisse?'

'Yes.'

'In your own car?'

'No. My – my husband drove me. Mr Royal unfortunately made the suggestion and I couldn't very well refuse.'

'Could you not? I should have thought you might have found a way out.'

She surprised him by leaning still farther forward and putting her hand on the arm of his chair. It was a swift intimate gesture that brought her close to him.

'I see I must explain,' said Madame Lisse.

'Please do,' said Alleyn.

'I am a very unhappy woman, Mr – I do not know your name.'

Alleyn told her his name and she managed to convey with great delicacy a suggestion of deference. 'Mr Alleyn. I didn't know – I am so sorry. Of course I have read of your wonderful cases. I'm sure you will understand. It will be easy to explain to you, a relief, a great relief to me.' Her fingertips brushed his sleeve. 'There are more ways than one,' Alleyn thought, 'of saying: "Dilly, dilly, dilly, come and be killed." ' But he did not answer Madame Lisse, and in a moment she was launched. 'I have been so terribly unhappy. You see, although I had decided I could no longer live with my husband, it wasn't possible for either of us to leave Great Chipping. Of course it is a very large town, isn't it? I hoped we would be able to avoid encounters but he has made it very difficult for me. You will understand what I mean. He is still devoted to me.'

She paused, gazing at him. The scene was beginning to develop in the best tradition of the French novel. If the situation had been less serious and she had been less beautiful he might have found it more amusing, but he had a difficult job to do and there are few men who are able to feel amusement at overwhelming beauty.

'He has haunted me,' she was saying. 'I refused to see him but he lay in wait for me. He is insane. I believe him to be insane. He rang me up and implored that I should allow him to drive me to Highfold. I consented, hoping to bring him to reason. But all the way here he begged me to return to him. I said that it was impossible and immediately he began to rave against Mr Nicholas Compline. Nicholas Compline and I have seen a good deal of each other and he, my husband, became madly jealous of our friendship. I am a lonely woman, Mr Alleyn, and Mr Compline has been a kind and chivalrous friend to me. You do believe me, don't you?' said Madame Lisse.

Alleyn said: 'Is it true that some time ago you gave a dinner party to which you invited your husband and Mr Royal, who, by the way, did not know Dr Hart was your husband?'

He saw her eyes turn to flint but she scarcely hesitated: 'It was my one attempt,' she said, 'to try and establish friendly relations. I hoped that they would take pleasure in each other's company.'

'By gum!' thought Alleyn, 'You've got your nerve about you.'

'Madame,' he said, 'I am going to ask you a very direct question. Who, do you think, committed this murder?'

She clasped her hands over the arm of his chair. 'I had hoped,' she whispered, 'that I might be spared that question.'

'It is my duty to ask it,' said Alleyn solemnly.

'I must refuse to answer. How can I answer? I loved him once.'

By this remarkable statement Alleyn learned that if, as Mrs Pouting considered, Dr and Madame Hart were joint adventurers, the lady displayed a most characteristic readiness to betray her partner when the necessity arose.

'You will understand,' he said, 'that I must question each member of the party about his or her movements on three occasions. The first is the occasion when Mr Mandrake was thrown into the bathing pool. Where were you at that time, Madame Lisse?'

'In bed, in my room.'

'Was anybody else in your room?'

'I believe a maid came in with my breakfast. I remember it was a very little while after she left the room that I heard voices on the terrace beneath my window and not long after that I was told of the accident.'

'Who told you, please?'

She waited for a moment, and then, very delicately, shrugged her shoulders.

'It was Mr Compline,' she said. 'You will think it strange that I permitted the visit, but I have adopted the English custom in such matters. He was agitated and felt that he must warn me.'

'Warn you?'

'Of this exhibition on the part of my husband.'

'Suppose,' said Alleyn, 'that I told you I had convincing evidence that your husband was not responsible for this affair. What would you say?'

For the first time she looked frightened, and for a moment she had no answer to give him. Her hands were clenched and her arms rigid. 'I am afraid that I should not believe you,' she said. 'It is horrible to have to say such things. I find it unbearable. But one must protect oneself, and other innocent persons.'

Alleyn was beginning to get a sort of enjoyment out of Madame Lisse.

'I am to understand,' he said, 'that it was a very unusual event for Mr Compline to pay you such an informal visit?'

'The circumstances were extraordinary.'

'Were they extraordinary when he again visited you at half-past seven that same evening?'

'Of course. I had asked him to come. I was most anxious to see him alone. By that time I was convinced that my husband meant to do him an injury. My husband had told me as much.' Perhaps Alleyn looked a little incredulous, for she said quickly: 'It is quite true. He said that he had come to the end of his endurance and could not trust himself. I was terrified. I warned Mr Compline and begged him to be careful. When he left me I looked after him and I saw that horrible figure fall from the top of his door. His hand was almost on the door. I screamed out and at the same moment it struck his arm. It might have killed him.'

'No doubt,' said Alleyn, who had already taken possession of the Buddha. 'Then you and Mr Compline were together from the time he left his room and walked down the passage to yours, until he returned and received his injury?'

'Yes. He has told me he came straight to my room.'

'You were together,' Alleyn repeated slowly, 'the whole time?'

Again he thought he had frightened her. Again there was an odd little pause before she said: 'Yes, certainly. I never left my room until he went.'

'And did he?'

'He?' she said readily. 'Oh no, *he* didn't, of course. I had to send him away in the end.'

There was something here, Alleyn felt sure, that she had concealed from him, but he decided to leave it for the moment, and went on to the time of the murder. Again Madame Lisse had been in her room. 'I was in agony. I suffer from the *migraine* and this was a terrible attack, brought on, no doubt, by nervous suspense. I went to bed before dinner and remained there until I was told of the tragedy.'

'Who told you of the tragedy, Madame?'

'Nicholas Compline. He broke it to me after he had told his mother.'

'And what was your reaction?'

'I was horrified, of course.' She leant back again in her chair and it seemed to him that she marshalled a series of sentences she had previously rehearsed. 'At first I thought it was a mistake, that he had meant to kill Nicholas, but then it dawned upon me that it was William's threats to expose him that had driven him to do it. I realized that it had nothing to do with me, nothing at all. No other explanation is possible.'

'You believe that it was impossible that William could be mistaken for Nicholas?'

'Of course. They were not so alike. Even the backs of their heads. There was a small thin patch in William's hair, just below the crown of his head.'

'Yes,' said Alleyn, watching her trembling lips. 'There was.'

'Whereas Nicholas has thick hair, like honey. And the nape of William's neck – it was – ' She caught her breath and her voice seemed to die on her lips.

'You must have observed him very closely,' said Alleyn.

CHAPTER 15

Document

Alleyn's interview with Nicholas was an uncomfortable affair. They had not been together for two minutes before he realized that he had to deal with a man who had pretty well reached the end of his tether. Nicholas was bewildered and dazed. He answered Alleyn's questions abruptly and almost at random. Even when the question of the murderer's identity was directly broached, Nicholas merely flared up weakly like a damp squib, and went out. Alleyn became insistent and Nicholas made an effort to concentrate, saying that Hart must have done it and escaped after Thomas left the hall. When Alleyn asked if he thought it was a case of mistaken identity, he said he did and spoke incoherently of the two earlier attempts. 'It was me all along,' he said, 'that he was after. I thought at first Bill's fiddling about with the radio had sent him off his head, but Mandrake pointed out that Hart must have come in by the door from the hall, and that leaning over like that, the back of Bill's head and tunic would look like mine. And he must have heard me tell Bill to go to bed.'

'When was that?'

Nicholas passed his hand across his eyes, pressing down with his fingertips. 'Oh, God,' he said, 'when was it? I can't sort of think. It was when Hart turned bloody-minded over the radio. He and Mandrake were in the room they call the boudoir. He opened the door and raised hell about the wireless. I slammed the door in his face, and Mandrake yelled out that I was to turn off the radio. I got suddenly fed up with the whole show. I said to my brother something like: "Oh, all right, the wireless is no go. Get to bed, Bill."

Mandrake and Hart must have heard. I turned the radio down to a whisper. We didn't say anything and I suppose he thought Bill did go away. I heard him switch off the light. He must have done it as a blind or something, to make us think he had gone.'

'Was that long afterwards?'

'I don't know. I heard Mandrake go out. It was after that.'

'Did you and your brother not speak at all?'

'Yes. When, as I thought, I heard Hart go, I said it was all right now if Bill wanted to use the wireless. He was furious with Hart, you know. We both were, but I saw I'd been making a fool of myself. I was suddenly sick of the whole thing. I tried to calm Bill down. He'd turned pretty grim and wouldn't talk. I hung about a bit and then I came away.'

'Can you tell me exactly what he was doing when you left?'

Nicholas went very white. 'He was sitting by the fire. He didn't look up. He just grunted something, and I went into the library.'

'Did you shut the door?' Alleyn had to repeat this question. Nicholas was staring blankly at him. 'I don't remember,' he said at last. 'I suppose so. Yes, I did. They all began asking me about my brother. Whether he was still livid with Hart, kind of thing. I sort of tried to shut them up because of Bill hearing us, but I think I'd shut the door. I'm sorry, I'm not sure about that. Is it important?'

'I'd like an exact picture, you know. You are certain, then, that the door was shut?'

'I think so. Yes. I'm pretty sure it was.'

'Do you remember exactly at what moment Mr Royal left the library?'

'How the devil should I remember!' said Nicholas with a sort of peevish violence. 'He can tell you that himself. What is all this?' He stared at Alleyn and then said quickly: 'Look here, if you're thinking of Jonathan . . . I mean it'd be too preposterous. Jonathan! Good God, he's our greatest friend. God, what *are* you driving at!'

'Nothing in the world,' said Alleyn gently. 'I only want facts. I'm sorry to have to hammer away at details like this.'

'Well, all I can tell you is that some time during the news bulletin Jonathan went into the hall for a minute or two.'

'The red leather screen in the smoking room was stretched in front of the door, as it is now?'

'I suppose so.'

'Yes. To get back to the wireless. You tell me that you turned it down after the outburst from Dr Hart. Did you look closely at it?'

'Why the hell should I look closely at it,' demanded Nicholas, in a fury. 'I turned it down. You don't peer at a wireless when you turn it down.'

'You turned it *down*,' Alleyn murmured. 'Not off. Down.'

'You've grasped it. Down,' said Nicholas, and burst into hysterical laughter. 'I turned it down, and five minutes later somebody turned it up, and a little while after that Hart murdered my brother. You're getting on marvellously, Inspector.'

Alleyn waited for a moment. Nicholas had scrambled out of his chair and had turned away, half-weeping, half-laughing. 'I'm sorry,' he stammered, 'I can't help it. He's in there, murdered, and my mother – my mother. I can't help it.'

'I'm sorry, too,' said Alleyn. 'All this insistence on detail must seem unbearably futile, but I promise you it has its purpose. You see, this is unhappily a police matter, a matter, if you can stomach the phrase, of serving justice, and in that cause very many things must be sacrificed, including the nerves of the witnesses.'

'I'm all to pieces,' Nicholas mumbled: 'I'm no good. It must be shock or something.' His voice died away in a trail of inaudibilities. ' . . . can't concentrate . . . enough to send you mad . . . ' He pulled out his handkerchief and retired to the window where he blew his nose very violently, caught his breath in a harsh sob, and stared out at the teeming rain, beating his uninjured hand on the sill. Alleyn waited for a little while and presently Nicholas turned and faced him. 'All right,' said Nicholas. 'Go on.'

'I've nearly done. If you would rather, I can wait . . . '

'No, no. For God's sake, get it over.'

Alleyn went back to the incidents of the pond and the Buddha, and at first learnt nothing new from Nicholas. He had seen Mandrake through the pavilion window and they had waved to each other. He had then turned away and gone on with the dismal business of undressing. He had heard the sound of a splash but had not immediately looked out, thinking that Mandrake might have thrown something into the pond. When he did go out to the rescue he had seen nobody else, but the assailant would have had time to dodge behind the pavilion. He had not noticed any footprints. When Hart came upon the scene, Nicholas had already thrown the serio-comic lifebelt into the pond. As for his escape from the brass Buddha, it had fallen out exactly as Madame Lisse had described it. He had felt the door resist him and then give way suddenly. Almost simultaneously with this, he started back and immediately afterwards something had fallen on his forearm. 'It's damned sore,' said Nicholas querulously, and didn't need much persuasion to exhibit his injury which was sufficiently ugly. Alleyn said it should have a surgical dressing and Nicholas, with considerable emphasis, said he'd see Hart in hell before he let him near it.

'Madame Lisse watched you as you walked down the passage?'

It appeared that he had glanced back and seen her in the doorway. He said that but for this distraction he might have noticed the Buddha, but he didn't think he would have done so. Alleyn asked him the now familiar questions. Had he gone straight to her room on leaving his own and had they been together the whole time?

'Yes, the whole time,' said Nicholas, and looked extremely uncomfortable. 'We were talking. She wanted to see me, to warn me about him. I hope to Heaven you'll keep her name out of this as much as possible, Alleyn.'

Alleyn blandly disregarded this.

'You heard nothing suspicious? No noise in the passage outside?'

'We did, as a matter of fact. I thought it was somebody at the door. It was a very slight sound. We sort of – sensed it. You don't want to get a wrong idea, you know,' said Nicholas. 'I suppose. you've heard how he's made life hideous for her. She told me all about it.' For the first time Alleyn saw a wan shadow of Nicholas's old effrontery. He stroked the back of his head and there was a hint of complacency in the gesture. 'I wasn't going to be dictated to by the fellow,' he said.

'What did you do?' Alleyn inquired. Nicholas began to stammer again, and Alleyn had some little trouble in discovering that he had taken cover behind a screen while the lady looked into the passage.

'So, in point of fact, you were not together the whole time?'

'To all intents and purposes we were. She was away only for about a minute. Of course what we had heard was Hart going past the door with that blasted image in his hands. I suppose when Elise looked out he was in my room. She'll tell you it was only for a minute.'

Alleyn did not tell him that in giving her account of their meeting, Madame Lisse had made no mention of this incident.

II

Before he let Nicholas go, Alleyn asked him, as he had asked Hart, to give a description of the smoking room. Nicholas appeared to find this request suspicious and distressing and at first made a poor fist of his recital. '*I* don't know what's in the ghastly place. It's just an ordinary room. You've *seen* it. Why do you want to ask me for an inventory?' Alleyn persisted, however, and Nicholas gave him a list of objects, rattling it off in a series of jerks: 'The wireless. Those filthy knives. There are seven of them and the thing that did it' – he wetted his lips – 'hung on the left. I remember looking at it while we were talking. There were some flowering plants in pots, I think. And there's a glass-topped case with *objets d'art* in it. Medals and miniatures and things. And sporting prints and photographs. There's a glass-fronted cupboard with china and old sporting trophies inside, and a small bookcase with *Handley Cross* and *Stonehenge* and those sorts of books in it. Leather chairs and an occasional table with cigars and cigarettes. I can't think of anything else. My God, when I think of that room I see only one thing and I'll see it to the end of my days!'

'You've given me a very useful piece of information,' Alleyn said. 'You've told me that when you left your brother, the Maori mere was still in its place on the wall.'

Nicholas stared dully at him. 'I hadn't thought of it before,' he said. 'I suppose it was.'

'Are you quite certain?'

Nicholas passed his hand over his eyes again. 'Certain?' he repeated. 'I thought I was, but now you ask me again I'm not so sure. It might have been when Bill and I were in the smoking room in the morning. What were we talking about? Yes. Yes, we were talking about Mandrake in the pond. Yes, it *was* in the morning. Oh, hell, I'm sorry. I can't swear it was there in the evening. I don't think I looked at the wall, then. I can't remember.'

'There's only one other thing,' Alleyn said. 'I must tell you that Mr Royal has given me the letter that was found in your mother's room.'

'But,' said Nicholas, 'that's horrible. It was for me. There's nothing in it – can't you – must you pry into everything! There's nothing in it that can help you.'

'If that's how it is,' said Alleyn, 'it will go no further than the inquest. But I'm sure you will see that I must read it.'

Nicholas's lips had bleached to a mauve line. 'You won't understand it,' he said. 'You'll misread it. I shouldn't have given it to them. I should have burnt it.'

'You'd have made a really bad mistake if you'd done that.' Alleyn took the letter from his pocket and laid it on the desk.

'For God's sake,' Nicholas said, 'remember that when she wrote it she was thinking of me and how much I'd miss her. She's accusing herself of deserting me. For God's sake, remember that.'

'I'll remember,' Alleyn said. He put the letter aside with his other papers and said that he need keep Nicholas no longer. Now that he was free, Nicholas seemed less anxious to go. He hung about the library looking miserably at Alleyn out of the corners of his eyes. Alleyn wrote up his notes and wondered what was coming. He became aware that Nicholas was watching him. For some little time he went on sedately with his notes, but at last looked up to find, as he expected, those rather prominent grey eyes staring at him.

'What is it, Mr Compline?' said Alleyn quietly.

'Oh, nothing. It's just – there doesn't seem anywhere to go. It gets on your nerves wandering about the house. This damned mongrel rain and everything. I – I was going to ask you where he was.'

'Dr Hart?'

'Yes.'

'He's locked up at the moment, at his own request.'

'So long as he *is* locked up. Mandrake and Hersey seem to have gone silly over him. Because he attended my mother! God, she was at his mercy! Hart! The man who ruined her beauty and had just murdered her son. Pretty, wasn't it! How do I know what he was doing to her.'

'From what Lady Hersey tells me his treatment was exactly what the doctor I spoke to prescribed. I'm sure you need not distress yourself by thinking that any other treatment would have made the smallest difference.'

'Why didn't Mandrake get here sooner! They wanted the stuff from the chemist urgently, didn't they? What the hell was he doing! Nearly four hours to go sixty miles! My mother was dying and the best they could do was to send a bloody little highbrow cripple with a false name.'

'A false name!' Alleyn ejaculated.

'Yes. Didn't Jonathan tell you? He told me. He's as common as dirt, is Mr Aubrey Mandrake, and his name's Footling. Jonathan put me up to pulling his leg about it, and he's had his knife into me ever since.'

The door opened, and Aubrey Mandrake looked in.

'Sorry,' he said, 'I didn't know you were still engaged.'

'We've finished, I think,' said Alleyn. 'Thank you so much, Mr Compline. Come in, Mr Mandrake.'

III

'I only came in,' said Mandrake, 'to say Lady Hersey is free now, if you want to see her. She asked me to tell you.'

'I shall be glad to see her in a minute or so. I just want to get my notes into some sort of order. I suppose you can't do shorthand, can you?'

'Good heavens, no,' said Mandrake languidly. 'What an offensive suggestion.'

'I wish I could. Never mind. I've been going through your notes. They're of the greatest help. You haven't signed them, and I'll get you to do so, if you don't mind.'

'I don't mind, of course,' said Mandrake uneasily, 'but you must remember they're based on hearsay as well as on my own observation.'

'I think you've made that quite clear. Here they are.'

He gave Mandrake his pen and pressed the notes out flat for him. It was a decorative affair, the signature, with the tail of the y in 'Aubrey' greatly prolonged and slashed forward to make the up-stroke of the M in 'Mandrake'. Alleyn blotted it carefully and looked at it.

'This is your legal signature?' he said, as he folded the notes.

When Mandrake answered, his voice sounded astonishingly vicious. 'You've been talking to the bereaved Nicholas, of course,' he said. 'It seems that even in his sorrow he found a moment for one of his little pleasantries.'

'He's in a condition that might very well develop into a nervous crisis. He's lashing out blindly and rather stupidly. It's understandable.'

'I suppose he told you of the incident at dinner? About my name?'

'No. What was the incident at dinner?'

Mandrake told him. 'It's too squalidly insignificant and stupid, of course,' he ended rapidly. 'It was idiotic of me to let it get under my skin, but I happen to object rather strongly to that particular type of wholesome public-school humour. Possibly because I did not go to a public-school.' Before Alleyn could answer, he went on defiantly: 'And now, of course, you are able to place me. I'm the kind of inverted snob that can't quite manage to take the carefree line about my background. And I talk far too much about myself.'

'I should have thought,' said Alleyn, 'you'd have worked all that off with your writing. But then I'm not a psychologist. As for your name, you've had the fun of changing it, and all I want to know is whether you did it by deed poll or whether I've got to ask for the other signature.'

'I haven't, but I'm going to. "The next witness was Stanley Footling, better known as Aubrey Mandrake." It'll look jolly in the papers, won't it?'

'By the time this case comes off, the papers won't have much room for fancy touches, I believe,' said Alleyn. 'If you don't mind my mentioning it I think you're going to find that your particular bogey will be forgotten in a welter of what we are probably going to call "extreme realism". Now write your name down like a good chap, and never mind if it is a funny one. I've a hell of a lot to do.'

Mandrake said with a grin: 'How right you are, Inspector,' and resigned his notes. 'All the same,' he added, 'I could have murdered Nicholas.' He caught his breath. 'How often one uses that phrase! Don't suspend me, I implore you. I could have, but I didn't. I didn't even murder poor William. I liked poor William. Shall I fetch Lady Hersey?'

'Please do,' said Alleyn.

IV

Motive apart, Lady Hersey was, on paper, the likeliest suspect. She had opportunity to execute both attempts, if they had been attempts, as well as the actual murder. During the long journey in the car Alleyn had found his thoughts turning to this unknown woman, as a figure which, conjecturally, might be the key-piece in a complicated pattern. In all police investigations there is such a figure and sometimes, but not always, it is that of the criminal himself. Though none of the interviews had disclosed the smallest hint of a motive in Lady Hersey's case, he was still inclined to think she occupied a key position. She was the link common to the Complines, Jonathan Royal, and the two Harts. 'The one person who could have done it,' Alleyn muttered, 'and the one person who didn't want to.' This was an inaccurate statement but it relieved his feelings. The case was developing along lines with which Alleyn was all too familiar. He had now very little doubt as to the identity of William Compline's murderer, and also very little substantial proof to support his theory or to warrant an arrest. The *reductio ad absurdum* method is not usually smiled upon by the higher powers at New Scotland Yard, and it can be a joyous romping-ground for defending counsel. Alleyn knew that a bungling murderer can give more trouble than a clever one.

'And the murderer of William Compline is a bungler if ever there was one,' he thought. He was turning over Mrs Compline's letter to her son when he heard Lady Hersey's voice on the stairs. He hesitated, returned the letter to his pocket and fished out the length of line he had cut from the reel in the smoking room. When Hersey Amblington came in he was twisting this line through his long fingers and when he rose to greet her it dangled conspicuously from his hands.

'I'm sorry if I've kept you waiting, Mr Alleyn,' she said. 'there were things to do upstairs and nobody else to do them.'

He pushed forward a chair and she sat down slowly and wearily, letting her head fall back against the chair. A sequence of fine lines appeared about her mouth and eyes, and her hands looked exhausted. 'If you're going to ask me to provide myself with three nice little alibis,' said Hersey, 'you may as well know straightaway that I can't do it. I seem to remember reading somewhere that that makes me innocent and I'm sure I hope it's true.'

'It's in the best tradition of detective fiction, I understand,' said Alleyn with a smile.

'That's not very comforting. Am I allowed to smoke?'

Alleyn offered her his case and lit her cigarette for her, dropping his length of fishing line over her wrist as he did so. He apologized and gathered it into his hand.

'Is that a clue or something?' asked Hersey. 'It looks like fishing-line.'

'Are you a fisherman, Lady Hersey?'

'I used to be. Jonathan's father taught me when I was a child. He's the old party in the photograph in that ghastly room next door.'

'Hubert St John Worthington Royal who caught a four-and-a-half pounder in Pen-Felton Reach?'

'If I wasn't so tired,' said Hersey, 'I'd fall into a rapture over your powers of observation. That's the man. And the rod on the wall is his rod. Now I come to think of it, your bit of string looked very much like his line.'

Alleyn opened his hand. Without moving her head or her hands she looked languidly at it.

'Yes,' she said, 'that's it. It's been looped back from the point of the rod to the reel for years.' She looked up into Alleyn's face. 'There's something in this, isn't there? What is it?'

'There's a lot in it,' Alleyn said slowly. 'Lady Hersey, will you try to remember, without straining at your memory, when you last saw the line in its customary position.'

'Friday night,' said Hersey instantly. 'There was an old cast on it, shrivelled up with age, and a fly. I remember staring at it while I was trying to fit in a letter in that foul parlour-game of Jo's. It was the cast that caught the famous four-and-a-half pounder. Or so we've always been told.'

'You went into the smoking room last night some little time before the tragedy, but when the two brothers were there?'

'Yes. I went in to see if they had calmed down. That was before the row over the radio.'

'You didn't by any chance look at the old rod then?'

'No. No, but I did at lunch-time. Just before lunch. I was warming my toes at the fire and I stared absently at it as one does at things one has seen a thousand times before.'

'And there was the line looped from the tip to the reel?'

Hersey knitted her brows and for the first time her full attention seemed to be aroused. 'Now you ask me,' she said, 'it wasn't. I remember thinking vaguely that someone must have wound it up to something.'

'You are positive?'

'Yes. Yes, absolutely positive.'

'Suppose I began to heckle you about it?'

'I should dig my toes in.'

'Good!' said Alleyn heartily, and wrote it down.

When he looked up Hersey's eyes were closed, but she opened them and said: 'Before I forget or go to sleep there's one thing I must say. I don't believe the face-lifter did it.'

'Why?' asked Alleyn without emphasis.

'Because I've spent a good many hours working for him up there in Sandra Compline's room. I like him, and I don't think he's a murderer, and anyway I don't see how you can get over the dancing footman's story.' Alleyn dropped the coil of fishing line on the desk. 'That little man's no killer,' Hersey added. 'He worked like a navvy over Sandra, and if she'd lived she'd have done her best, poor darling, to have him convicted of homicidal lunacy. He knew that.'

'Why are you so sure she would have taken that line?'

'Don't forget,' said Hersey, 'I was the last person to see her alive. I gave her a half-dose of that stuff. She wouldn't take more, and she said she had no aspirin. I suppose she wanted – wanted to make sure later on. Nick had broken Bill's death to her. She seemed absolutely stunned, almost incredulous if that's not too strange a word to use. Not sorrowful so much as horrified. She wouldn't say anything much about it, although I did try gently to talk to her. It seemed to me it would be better if she broke down. She was stony with bewilderment. But just as I was going she said: "Dr Hart is mad, Hersey. I thought I could never forgive him, but I think my face has haunted him as badly as it has haunted me." And then she said: "Don't forget, Hersey, he's out of his mind." I haven't told any one else of this. I can't tell you how strange her manner was, and how astonished I was to hear her say all that so deliberately when a moment before she had seemed so confused.'

Alleyn asked Hersey to repeat this statement and wrote it down. When he had finished she said: 'There's one other thing. Have you examined her room?'

'Only superficially. I had a look round after Compline went out.'

'Did you look at her clothes?' asked Hersey.

'Yes.'

'The blue Harris tweed overcoat?'

'The one that is still very damp? Yes.'

'It was soaking wet yesterday afternoon, and she told me she hadn't stirred out of the house all day.'

V

Alleyn opened Mrs Compline's letter to her son in the presence of Jonathan Royal, Nicholas Compline, and Aubrey Mandrake. He did not read it aloud, but he showed it to Mandrake and asked him to make a copy. While they waited in an uncomfortable silence Mandrake performed this office, and at Alleyn's request re-sealed the original in a fresh envelope across the flap of which Jonathan was asked to sign his name. Alleyn then tied a string round the envelope and sealed the knot down with wax from his chemist's parcel. He said that he would be obliged if Jonathan and Nicholas would leave him alone with Mandrake. Jonathan seemed perfectly ready to comply with this request, but Nicholas treated them to a sudden and violent outbreak of hysteria. He demanded that the letter should be returned, stormed at Alleyn, threatened Hart, and at last, sobbing breathlessly, flung himself into a chair and refused to move. As the best means of cutting this performance short, Alleyn gathered up his possessions and, followed by a very much shaken Mandrake, moved to the green boudoir. Here he asked Mandrake to read over the copy of the letter.

'My Darling,' Mandrake read, 'you must not let this make you very sad. If I stayed with you even for the little time there would be left to me, the memory of these terrible days would lie between us. I think that during these last hours I have been insane. I cannot write a confession. I have tried, but the words were so terrible I could not write them. What I am going to do will make everything clear enough, and the innocent shall not suffer through me. Already Hersey suspects that I went out of the house this morning. I think she knows where I went. I cannot face it. You should have been my eldest son, my darling. If I could have taken any other way – but there was no other way. All my life, everything I have done has been for you, even this last terrible thing is for you, and, however wicked it may seem, you must always remember that. And now, darling, I must write down what I mean to do. I have kept the sleeping powders they took from that man's room and I have an unopened bottle of aspirins. I shan't feel anything at all. My last thoughts and my last prayers are for you. Mother. I sign this with my full name, because you will have to show it. SANDRA MARY COMPLINE.'

CHAPTER 16

Arrest

Alleyn had asked Mandrake to say nothing of the contents of the letter. 'Under ordinary circumstances,' he said, 'I would have had another officer with me when I opened it. I want you to fix the contents firmly in your mind, and I want you to be prepared, if necessary, to swear that it is the original letter which I have sealed in this envelope, the letter which I opened in your presence and from which you made this copy. All this may be quite unnecessary, but as the most detached member of the party I thought it well to get your assistance. I'll keep the copy, if you please.'

Mandrake gave him the copy. His hand shook so much that the paper rattled and he muttered an apology.

'It's horrible,' Mandrake said. 'Horrible. Mother love! My God!' He stared at Alleyn. 'This sort of thing,' he stammered, 'it can't happen. I never dreamed of this. It's so much worse – it's ever so much worse.'

Alleyn watched him for a moment. 'Worse than what?' he asked.

'It's real,' said Mandrake. 'I suppose you'll think it incredible, but until now it hasn't been quite real to me. Not even,' he jerked his head towards the smoking room door, 'not even – that. One works these things out in terms of an aesthetic, but for them to *happen* – ! God, this'll about kill Nicholas.'

'Yes.'

'To have it before him for the rest of his life! I don't know why it should affect me like this. After all, it's better that it should end this way. I suppose it's better. She's ended it. No horrible parade of justice.

She's spared him that. But I can't help suddenly *seeing* it. It's as if a mist had cleared, leaving the solid reality of a disfigured woman writing that letter, mixing the poison, getting into bed, and then, with God knows what nightmare of last memories, drinking it down.' Mandrake limped about the room, and Alleyn watched him. 'At least,' said Mandrake, 'we are spared an arrest. But Nicholas saw the letter. He *knew*."

'He still insists that Dr Hart killed his brother.'

'Let me see the copy of that letter again.'

Alleyn gave him the copy, and he muttered over the phrases. 'What else can it mean? "You should have been my eldest son." "Hersey suspects." "I cannot face it." "Everything I have done has been for you." What else but that she did it? But I can't understand. Why the other two attempts? It doesn't make sense.'

'I'm afraid it makes very good sense,' said Alleyn.

II

From five o'clock until seven Alleyn worked alone. First of all he inspected the Charter blocks, handling them with tweezers and wishing very heartily for Bailey, his fingerprint expert. The blocks were made of thinnish paper, and the impression of heavily pencilled letters appeared on the surface of the unused forms. The smoking room waste-paper baskets had been emptied, but a hunt through a rubbish bin in an outhouse brought to light several of the used forms. The rest, it appeared, had been thrown on the fire by the players after their scores had been marked. Mandrake had told him that after the little scene over the extra form Jonathan had suddenly suggested that they play some other game, and the Charter pads had been discarded. By dint of a wearisome round of questions, Alleyn managed to identify most of the used forms. Dr Hart readily selected his, admitting placidly that he had used 'threats' as a seven-square word. Alleyn found the ghost of this word on one of the blocks, which he was then able to classify definitely as Hart's. The doctor had used a sharp pencil and had pressed hard upon it, so that the marks persisted through two or three of the under papers. But neither on his used form nor on the rest of the pages did Alleyn find the faintest trace of the words: 'You are warned, keep off.' This was negative evidence. Hart might have been at pains to tear off that particular form and fill it in against the card back of the block, which would take no impression. At this stage Alleyn went to Jonathan and asked if he had a specimen of Hart's writing. Jonathan at once produced Hart's note accepting the invitation to Highfold. Alleyn shut himself up again and made his first really interesting discovery. The writing in the note was a script that still bore many foreign characteristics. But in his Charter form Dr Hart had used block capitals throughout, though his experimental scribblings in the margin were in his characteristic script. Turning to the warning message, which was written wholly in script, Alleyn discovered indications that the letters had been slowly and carefully formed, and he thought that it began to look very much like the work of someone who was familiar with Hart's writing and had deliberately introduced these characteristic letters.

Of the other players an exhaustive process of inquiry and comparison showed that Mrs Compline, Hersey, Nicholas and Jonathan had written too lightly to leave impressions, while William's and Mandrake's papers had been burnt after being marked. Alleyn could find no trace of the message on any of the blocks. At last he began to turn back the pages of each one, using his tweezers and going on doggedly, long after the faintest trace had faded, to the last leaf of each block. At the third block about halfway through he made his discovery. Here, suddenly, he came upon the indented trace of those five words, and a closer inspection showed him that the page before the one so marked had been torn away. Owing to its position the perforations had not been followed, and when he fitted the crumpled message to the torn edge the serrations tallied. This, then, was the block upon which the message had been written, and it was not Dr Hart's block. He turned back to the first pages and gave a little sigh. They held no impressions. Alleyn got a picture of the writer hurriedly using the mass of pages as a cover, scribbling his message on the central leaf and wrenching it free of the pad. Either this writer had written his legitimate Charters with a light hand, or else he had torn away the additional pages that held an impression. The pad had belonged neither to William nor to Mandrake, for theirs bore marks that Mandrake himself had identified. Two of the remaining pads were marked by certain faint traces, visible through the lens, and these, he thought, must have been used by Madame Lisse and Chloris Wynne, whose fingernails were long and pointed.

'Not so bad,' he murmured, and, whistling softly, put the Charter pads away again.

He went up to Mrs Compline's room, taking the not very willing Mandrake with him.

'I like to have a witness,' he said vaguely. 'As a general rule, we work in pairs over the ticklish bits. It'll be all right when Fox comes, but in the meantime you, as an unsuspected person, will do very nicely.'

Mandrake kept his back turned to the shrouded figure on the bed, and watched Alleyn go through the clothes in the wardrobe. Alleyn got him to feel the shoulders and skirts of a Harris tweed overcoat.

'Damp,' said Mandrake.

'Was it snowing when you went down to the pond?'

'Yes. My God, were they *her* footsteps? She must have walked down inside my own as Chloris suggested.'

Alleyn was looking at the hats on the top shelf of the wardrobe.

'This is the one she wore,' he said. 'It's still quite wettish. Blue tweedish sort of affair, with a salmon fly as ornament. No, two flies. A yellow and black salmon fly, and a rather jaded trout fly. Scarlet and green – an Alexandra. That seems excessive, doesn't it?' He peered more closely at the hat. 'Now, I wonder,' he said. And when Mandrake asked him peevishly what he wondered, sent him off to find the maid who had looked after Mrs Compline. She proved to be a Dorset girl, born and bred on the Highfold estate, a chatterbox, very trim and bright and full of the liveliest curiosity about the clothes and complexions of the ladies in Jonathan's party. She was anxious to become a ladies' maid, and Mrs Pouting had been training her. This was the first time she had maided any visitors to Highfold. She burst into a descriptive rapture over the wardrobes of Madame Lisse and Miss Wynne. It was with difficulty that Alleyn hauled her attention round to the less exciting garments of Mrs Compline. The interview took place in the little passage, and Alleyn held the tweed hat behind his back while the little maid chattered away about the wet coat.

'Mrs Compline hadn't worn that coat before, sir. She arrived in a Burberry like you see at the shooting parties, and when they took a walk on the first evening she wore it again, sir. It was yesterday morning she took out the tweed. When the two gentlemen was going to have that bet, sir,' said the little maid, turning pink. 'I was in madam's room, sir, asking what I should put out for her to wear, when poor Mr William called out in the passage, "It's worth a tenner to see him do it." She seemed very upset, sir. She got up and went to the door and looked after him. She called out, but I don't think he heard her, because he ran downstairs. She said she didn't require me. So I went out, and she must have followed him.'

'When did you see her again?'

'Well, after a minute or two, I saw her go downstairs wearing that coat, sir, and a tweed hat, and I called Elsie, the second housemaid, sir, and said we could slip in and make Mrs Compline's bed and do her room. So we did. At least – ' Here the little maid hesitated.

'Yes?' Alleyn asked.

'Well, sir, I'm afraid we *did* look out of the window because we knew about the bet. But you can't see the pond from that window on account of the shrubs. Only the terrace. We saw the poor lady cross the terrace. It was snowing very hard. She seemed to stare down towards the pond, sir, for a little while, and then she looked round and – and Elsie and I began to make the bed. It wasn't above two minutes before she was back, as white as a sheet and trembling. I offered to take away her wet coat and hat, but she said: "No, no, leave them," rather short, so Elsie and I went out. By that time there was a great to-do down by the pond, and Thomas came in and said one of the gentlemen had fallen in.'

'And while Mrs Compline was on the terrace, nobody joined her or appeared near her?'

'No, sir. I think Miss Wynne and poor Mr William must have gone out afterwards, because we heard their voices down there just before Mrs Compline got back.'

'Well done,' said Alleyn. 'And this,' he showed her the tweed hat, 'is this the hat she was wearing?'

'That's it, sir.'

'Looks just the same?'

The little maid took it in her hands and turned it round, eyeing it in a thoughtful bird-like manner. 'It's got two of those feathery hooks,' she said at last. 'Funny kind of trimming, *I* think. Two.'

'Yes?'

'It only had one yesterday. The big yellow and black one.'

'Thank you,' said Alleyn, and quite fluttered her by the fervency of his smile.

III

Detective-Inspector Fox and Detective-Sergeants Bailey and Thompson arrived at seven o'clock in a hired car from Pen-Gidding. Alleyn was delighted to see them. He set Bailey to work on the brass Buddha, the Charter forms, the Maori mere, and the wireless cabinet. Thompson photographed all the details that Alleyn had already taken with his own camera. And at last the body of William Compline was taken away from the armchair in the smoking room. There was a ballroom at Highfold. It had been added incontinently to the east side by a Victorian Royal, and was reached by a short passage. Here, in an atmosphere of unused grandeur and empty anticipation, Sandra Compline lay not far removed from the son for whom she had not greatly cared. Alleyn heard Jonathan issuing subdued but emphatic orders for flowers.

Fox and Alleyn went together to the library.

'Sit down, Br'er Fox,' said Alleyn. 'Sorry to have hauled you out, but I'm damn' glad to see you.'

'We had quite a job getting here,' said Fox, taking out his spectacle case. 'Very unpleasant weather. Nasty affair this, sir, by the looks of it. What's the strength of it? Murder followed by suicide, or what?'

'There's my report. You'd better take a look at it.'

'Ah,' said Fox. 'Much obliged. Thank you.' He settled his spectacles rather far down his nose and put on his reading face. Fox had a large rosy face. To Alleyn his reading expression always suggested that he had a slight cold in the head. He raised his sandy eyebrows, slightly opened his mouth and placidly absorbed the words before him. For some time there was no sound but the crackle of turning leaves and Fox's breathing.

'Um,' he said when he had finished. 'Silly sort of business. Meant to look complicated, but isn't. When do we fix this customer up, Mr Alleyn?'

'We'll wait for Bailey, I think. I'd like to arrest on a minor charge, but there isn't the smell of an excuse so far.'

'Assault on Mr Mandrake?'

'Well,' said Alleyn, 'we might do that. I suppose I haven't gone wrong anywhere. The thing's so blasted obvious I keep wondering if there's a catch in it. We'll have to experiment, of course, with the business next door. Might do that now, if Bailey's finished. They've taken that poor chap out, haven't they? All right. Come on, Foxkin.'

They went into the smoking room. Bailey, a taciturn officer with an air of permanent resentment, was packing away his fingerprint apparatus, and Thompson had taken down his camera.

'Finished?' asked Alleyn. 'Get a shot of the ash in the grate all right?'

'Yes, sir,' said Thompson. 'Made a little find there, Mr Alleyn. Bailey spotted it. You know this trace in the ash, the sort of coil affair?'

'Yes.'

'Well, sir, it's what you said all right. String or cord or something. There's a bit not quite burnt out up at the back. Charred-like, but still a bit of substance in it. Seems as if it was green originally.'

'We'll have it,' said Alleyn. 'Good work, Bailey. I missed that.'

The mulish expression on Sergeant Bailey's face deepened. 'We had a 500 watt lamp on it,' he said. 'Looks as if someone'd chucked this string on the fire and pulled those two side logs over it. They must have fallen apart, and the stuff smouldered out slowly. Tough, fine-fibred stuff, I'd say. Might be silk. It finishes with a trace of structureless, fairly tough black ash that has kept its form and run into lumps. What's the next job, sir?'

'We'll have to get their prints. I don't for a moment suppose they'll object. I warned Mr Royal about it. Thank the Lord I shan't have to use any of the funny things they brought me from the chemist. Anything to report?'

'There's a couple of nice ones on that brass image affair, sir. Latent, but came up nicely under the dust. Same as the ones on the stone cosh. There's something on the neck of the cosh, but badly blurred. As good a set as you'd want on the blade.'

'What about the wireless?'

'Regular mix-up, Mr Alleyn, like you'd expect. But there's a kind of smudge on the volume control.' Bailey looked at his boots. 'Might be gloves,' he muttered.

'Very easily,' said Alleyn. 'Now, look here. Mr Fox and I are going to make an experiment. I'll get you two to stay in here and look on. If it's a success I think we might stage a little show for a select audience.' He squatted down and laid his piece of fishing-line out on the floor. 'You might just lock the door,' he said.

IV

'This is a big house,' said Chloris, 'and yet there seems nowhere to go. I've no stomach for the party in the drawing room.'

'There's the boudoir,' Mandrake suggested.

'Aren't the police overflowing into that?'

'Not now. Alleyn and that vast red man went down to the pond a few minutes ago. Now they've gone back into the smoking room. Let's try the boudoir.'

'All right, let's.'

They went into the boudoir. The curtains were closed and the lamps alight. A cheerful fire crackled in the grate. Chloris moved restlessly about the room and Mandrake intercepted a quick glance at the door into the smoking room. 'It's all right,' he said. 'William's gone, you know, and the police seem to have moved into the library.' There was a sudden blare of radio on the other side of the door, and both Mandrake and Chloris jumped nervously. Chloris gave a little cry. 'They're in there,' she whispered. 'What are they doing?'

'I'll damn' well see!'

'No, *don't*,' cried Chloris, as Mandrake stooped to the communicating door and applied his eye to the keyhole.

'It's not very helpful!' he murmured. 'The key's in the lock. What *can* they be doing. God, the noise! Wait a minute.'

'Oh, *do* come away.'

'I'm quite shameless. I consider they are fair game. One can see a little past the key, but only in a straight line. Keyhole lurking is not what it's said to be in eighteenth-century literature. Hardly worth doing, in fact. I can see nothing but that red screen in front of the door into the library. There's no one . . . ' he broke off suddenly. 'What is it?' Chloris said, and he held up his hand warningly. The wireless was switched off. Mandrake got up and drew Chloris to the far end of the boudoir.

'It's very curious,' he said. 'There are only four of them. I know that, because I saw the others come. There's Alleyn and the red man and two others. Well, they've all just walked out of the library into the smoking room. *Who the devil turned on the radio?*'

'They must have gone into the library after they turned it on.'

'But they didn't. They hadn't time. The moment that noise started I looked through the keyhole and I looked straight at the door. Why should they turn on the wireless and make a blackguard rush into the library?'

'It's horrible. It sounded so like . . . '

'It's rather intriguing, though,' said Mandrake.

'How you *can!*'

He went quickly to her and took her hands. 'Darling Chloris,' he said, 'it wouldn't be much use if I pretended I wasn't interested, would it? You'll have to get used to my common ways, because I think I might want to marry you. I'm going to alter my name by deed poll, so you wouldn't have to be Mrs Stanley Footling. And if you think Mrs Aubrey Mandrake is too arty we could find something else. I can't conceive why people are so dull about their names. I don't suppose deed polls are very expensive. One could have a new name quite often, I dare say. My dear darling,' Mandrake continued, 'you're all white and trembly, and I really and truly believe I love you. Could you possibly love me, or shan't we mention it just now?'

'We shan't mention it just now,' said Chloris. 'I don't know why, but I'm frightened. I want to be at home, going to my WREN classes, and taking dogs for walks. I'm sick of horrors.'

'But you won't mix me up with horrors when you get back to your lusty girl-friends, will you? You won't say: "There was a killing highbrow cripple who made a pass at me during the murder"?'

'No. Honestly, I won't. I'll ask you to come and stay, and we might even have a gossip about the dear old days at Highfold. But at the moment I want my mother,' said Chloris, and her lower lip trembled.

'Well, I expect you'll be able to go quite soon. I fancy the police have finished with you and me.'

There was a tap on the door and Detective-Sergeant Bailey came in.

'Excuse me, sir,' he said sombrely. 'Chief Inspector Alleyn's compliments, and he'd be obliged if you'd let me take your fingerprints. Yours and the young lady's. Just a matter of routine, sir.'

'Oh,' said Chloris under her breath, 'that's what they always say to reassure murderers.'

'I beg pardon, miss?'

'We should be delighted.'

'Much obliged,' said Bailey gloomily, and laid his case down on a small table. Mandrake and Chloris stood side by side in awkward silence while Bailey set out on the table a glass plate, two sheets of paper, some cotton wool, a rubber roller, a fat tube and a small bottle, which, when he uncorked it. let loose a strong smell of ether.

'Are we to be anaesthetized?' asked Mandrake with nervous facetiousness. Bailey gave him a not very complimentary stare. He squeezed some black substance from the tube on to the plate and rolled it out into a thin film.

'I'll just clean your fingers with a drop of ether. If you please,' he said.

'Our hands are quite clean,' cried Mandrake.

'Not chemically,' Bailey corrected. 'There'll be a good deal of perspiration, I dare say. There usually is. Now, sir. Now, miss.'

'It's quite true,' said Chloris, 'there *is* a good deal of perspiration. Speaking for myself, I'm in a clammy sweat.'

Bailey cleaned their fingers and seemed to cheer up a little. 'Now, we'll just roll them gently on the plate,' he said, holding Mandrake's forefinger. 'Don't resist me.'

Chloris was making her last fingerprint, and Mandrake was cleaning the ink off his own fingers, when Fox came in and beamed upon them.

'Well, well,' said Fox. 'So they're fixing you up according to the regulations? Quite an ingenious little process, isn't it, sir?'

'Quite.'

'Yes. Miss Wynne won't care for it so well, perhaps. Nasty, dirty stuff, isn't it? The ladies never fancy it for that reason. Well, now that's very nice,' continued Fox, looking at Chloris's prints on the paper. 'You wouldn't believe how difficult a simple little affair like this can be made if people resist the pressure. Never resist the police in the execution of their duty. That's right, isn't it, sir?' Bailey looked inquiringly at him. 'In the drawing room,' said Fox in exactly the same tone of voice. Bailey wrote on the papers, put them away in his case, and took himself and his belongings out of the room.

'The Chief,' said Fox, who occasionally indulged himself by alluding to Alleyn in this fashion, 'would be glad if you could spare him a moment in about ten minutes' time, Mr Mandrake. In the library, if you please.'

'All right. Thanks.'

'Do I stay here?' asked Chloris in a small voice.

'Wherever you like, Miss Wynne,' rejoined Fox, looking mildly at her. 'It's not very pleasant waiting about. I dare say you'll find the time hangs rather heavy on your hands. Perhaps you'd like to join the party in the drawing room?'

'Not much,' said Chloris, 'but I can tell by your style that I'm supposed to go. So I'd better.'

'Thank you, miss,' said Fox simply. 'Perhaps Mr Mandrake would like to go with you. We'll see you in the library then, in about ten minutes, sir. As soon as Bailey has finished in the drawing room. He'll give you the word when to come along. You might quietly drop a hint to Mr Royal and Mr Compline to come with you, if you don't mind.'

He held the door open, and Mandrake and Chloris went out.

V

'Well, Br'er Fox,' said Alleyn, looking up from the library desk, 'did that pass off quietly?'

'Quite pleasantly, Mr Alleyn. Bailey's in the drawing room now, doing the rest of the party. I unloosed the doctor. It seemed silly him being up there behind a lock a moron could fix in two minutes. So he's in with the rest. His good lady doesn't much fancy being printed.'

Alleyn grinned. 'The expression "his good lady" as applied to La Belle Lisse-Hart,' he said, 'is perfect, Fox.'

'I put the young couple in with the others,' Fox continued. 'I've got an idea that Mr Mandrake was a bit inquisitive about what we were doing in the smoking room. He kept looking over at the door, and when he saw I'd noticed he looked away again. So I told him to come along and bring the other two with him as soon as we tip him the wink. You want independent witnesses, I suppose, sir?'

'Yes. What about Lady Hersey?'

'I haven't said anything. We can fetch her away when we want her.'

'We'll send Bailey to fetch her away, fetch her away, fetch her away,' Alleyn murmured under his breath. And then: 'I've never felt less sympathy over a homicide, Br'er Fox. This affair is not only stupid but beastly, and not only beastly but damn' cold-blooded and unnatural. However, we must watch our step. There's a hint of low cunning in spite of the mistakes. I hate the semi-public reconstruction stunt – it's theatrical and it upsets all sorts of harmless people. Still, it has its uses. We've known it to come off, haven't we?'

'We have so,' said Fox sombrely. 'I wonder how Bailey's getting on with that mob in there.'

'See here, Fox, let's make sure we've got it right.'

Fox looked benignly at his chief: 'It's all right, sir. You've worked it out to a hair. It can't go wrong. Why, we've tried it half a dozen times.'

'I meant the case as a whole.'

'You've got your usual attack of the doubts, Mr Alleyn. I've never seen a clearer case.'

Alleyn moved restlessly about the room. 'Disregard those two earlier farces and we've still got proof,' he said.

'Cast-iron proof.'

'In a funny sort of way it all hangs on this damned cheerful fellow Thomas. The dancing footman. He defines the limit of the time factor and the possible movements of the murderer. Add to this the ash, H. St J. W. R.'s fishing-line, the stuff on the wireless, and William's drawing-pin, and there's your case.'

'And a very pretty case, too.'

'Not so pretty,' Alleyn muttered. And then: 'I've never asked for your views on this war, Foxkin.'

Fox stared at him. 'On the war? Well, no, sir, you haven't. My view is that it hasn't started.'

'And mine. I believe that in a year's time we shall look back on these frozen weeks as on a strangely unreal period. Does it seem odd to you, Fox, that we should be here so solemnly tracking down one squalid little murderer, so laboriously using our methods to peer into two deaths, while over our heads are stretched the legions of guns? It's as if we stood on the edge of a crackling landslide, swatting flies.'

'It's our job.'

'And will continue to be so. But to hang someone – now! My God, Fox, it's almost funny.'

'I see what you mean.'

'It's nothing. Only one of those cold moments. We'll get on with our cosy little murder. Here comes Bailey.'

Bailey came in carrying his gear.

'Well,' said Alleyn, 'have you fixed that up?'

'Yes, sir.'

'Any objections?'

'The foreign lady. She didn't like the idea of blacking her fingers. Or that's what she said. Gave quite a bit of trouble in a quiet way.'

'And the rest of the party?'

'Jumpy,' said Bailey. 'Not saying much for stretches at a time and then all talking at once, very nervous and quick. Mr Royal and Compline seem unfriendly to the doctor and keep looking sideways at him. He's the coolest of the lot, though. You'd think he wasn't interested. He doesn't take any notice of the lady except to look at her as if he was surprised or something. Will you see the prints, Mr Alleyn?'

'Yes, we'll look at them and check them with what you found on the rest of the stuff. It won't be very illuminating, but it's got to be done. Then we'll have those four in here, and try for results. It'll do no harm to keep them guessing for a bit. Come on, Fox.'

VI

'What's the time?' asked Nicholas. Hersey Amblington looked at her wrist-watch. 'A quarter-past eight.'

'I have explained, haven't I,' said Jonathan, 'that there's a cold buffet in the dining room?'

'You have, Jo,' said Hersey. 'I'm afraid none of us feels like it.'

'I am hungry,' Dr Hart observed. 'But I cannot accept the hospitality of a gentleman who believes me to be a murderer.' Jonathan made an angry little noise in his throat.

'My dear Doctor Hart,' Hersey ejaculated, 'I really shouldn't let a point of etiquette hold you off the cold meats. You can't starve.'

'I expect to be released tomorrow,' said Hart, 'and a short abstinence will be of no harm. I habitually over-eat.' He looked at his wife, who was staring at him with a sort of incredulous wonder. 'Do I not, my dear?' asked Dr Hart.

Nicholas moved to her side. She turned to him and very slightly shrugged her shoulders.

'It is strange,' continued Dr Hart, 'that when my wife would not acknowledge our relationship I was plagued with the desire to make it known. Now that it is known I take but little satisfaction in the privilege.'

Nicholas produced a cliché. 'There is no need,' he said stiffly, 'to be insulting.'

'But whom do I insult? Not my wife, surely. Would it not be more insulting to deny the legal status?'

'This is too much,' Jonathan burst out, but Hersey said: 'Oh, let it go, for pity's sake, Jo.'

'I cannot expect,' said Madame Lisse, 'that Lady Hersey will neglect to find enjoyment in my humiliation.'

'I don't see that you are particularly humiliated.'

'A husband who had committed the most . . . ' began Madame Lisse, but Dr Hart interrupted her.

'Do you know what she has said, this woman?' he demanded of nobody in particular. 'She has told me that if she knew of a grain of evidence against me she would use it. I tell you this – if I was accused of the murder of this poor simpleton and if she, without doing harm to herself, could speak the word that would hang me, she would speak it. This is the woman for whom I have tortured myself. You are all thinking it is not nice to make a scene by speaking of her, it is not what an English gentleman would do. You are right. I am not English and I am not a gentleman. I am an Austrian peasant with a little of the south in my veins, and I have suddenly awakened. I am angry when I remember all the idiotic sorrow that I have wasted on this cold and treacherous wife.'

'*You bloody murderer!*' Nicholas burst out, and Madame Lisse seized his arm.

'No,' she said, 'no, Nicholas. For my sake.'

'For all our sakes,' said Mandrake suddenly, 'let's have no more scenes.' And a kind of murmur, profoundly in agreement, came from Hersey, Chloris, and Jonathan. Dr Hart smiled and made a little bow. 'Very well. By all means, no more scenes. But *you,*' he pointed a short white finger at Nicholas, 'will have cause to remember what I have said.'

The door opened and Bailey looked in. 'Mr Alleyn's compliments, sir,' he said to Jonathan, 'and he'd be glad to see you if you're free.' His glance travelled to Mandrake and Nicholas. 'Thank you, gentlemen,' he said, and held open the door. The three men went out. 'Mr Alleyn would be obliged if the rest of the party stayed where they are,' said Bailey. 'Sergeant Thompson is on duty in the hall.'

He closed the door gently, leaving the three women and Dr Hart together.

VII

'Before we go any further,' said Alleyn, 'I must explain that we have arrived at a definite conclusion in this case. It is therefore my duty to tell you that the questions I shall now put to you are of importance and that your answers may possibly be used in evidence. I have asked you to come into the library in order that we may go over the events immediately preceding the discovery of Mr William Compline's body in the next room. I have not asked those members of the party who were upstairs to be present. They cannot help us. I have left Miss Wynne out of the experiment. Her part was entirely negative and there is no need to distress her. I'm afraid that we shall have to ask Lady Hersey to come in, but I thought that first of all I should explain to you, sir, and to Mr Compline, exactly what we mean to do. You have all heard of police reconstructions. This very short experiment may be regarded as a reconstruction, and if we are at fault in the smallest detail we ask you to put us right. That's all quite clear, I hope. Now I must ask you if you have any objection to helping us in this way.'

'Do you mean,' asked Jonathan, 'that you want us to do everything we did last night?'

'Yes, if you will.'

'I'm – I'm not sure that I recollect precisely the order of events.'

'Mr Mandrake and Mr Compline will, I hope, help you.'

'God, I can remember!' said Nicholas.

'And I,' said Mandrake. 'I think I remember.'

'Good. Then, will you help us, Mr Royal?'

'Very well,' said Jonathan, and Mandrake and Nicholas said they too were ready to help.

'We'll begin,' said Alleyn, 'at the moment when Lady Hersey had returned from the smoking room where she had talked for a time with you, Mr Compline, and with your brother. Mr Mandrake is in the green boudoir beyond, talking to Dr Hart. Lady Hersey has left the two brothers together. The door into the boudoir is now locked on the smoking room side. The door from here into the smoking room is shut, as you can see. Right, Fox.'

Fox went out.

'Will you please take up your positions?' said Alleyn. 'Mr Mandrake, you are not here yet. Mr Compline, you are in the next room. Sergeant Bailey is there, and I'll get you to tell him as well as you can remember, exactly where you were and what you and your brother did.'

Alleyn opened wide the door into the smoking room. The red leather screen still hid the interior, which seemed to be very dimly lit. Nicholas hung back, white and nervous.

'Not too pleasant,' he muttered, and then: 'It wasn't dark like that.'

'The small shaded lamp by the fireside is turned on,' said Alleyn. 'There are no bulbs in the other lamps.'

'Why?' Nicholas demanded.

'Because we've removed them,' said Alleyn blandly. 'Will you go in?'

From behind the screen Bailey gave a slight cough. Nicholas said: 'Oh, all right,' and went into the smoking room. Alleyn shut the door. At the same moment Fox came in with Hersey Amblington. Evidently he had explained the procedure because she went straight to a chair opposite Jonathan's and sat down. 'That's what I did when I came in,' said Hersey. 'I'd left Nicholas and William in the smoking room and I came here by way of the hall. Is that what you wanted to know, Mr Alleyn?'

'The beginning of it,' said Alleyn. 'What next?'

'In a few minutes,' said Jonathan. 'Aubrey came in. He went to that chair on the far side of the fire. Miss Wynne was sitting there.'

Alleyn looked at Mandrake who at once walked to the chair. 'I'd come directly from the boudoir by way of the hall, leaving Dr Hart alone in the boudoir,' he said.

'And then?'

'We discussed the situation,' said Hersey. 'I reported that I'd left the two brothers talking quite sensibly, and then Mr Mandrake told us how Dr Hart and Nicholas had had a row over the wireless and how Nicholas had slammed the door between the boudoir and the smoking room in Dr Hart's face.'

'Next?'

'We talked for perhaps a minute and then Nicholas came in.' She looked from Jonathan to Mandrake. 'It wasn't longer, was it?'

'I should say about a minute,' Mandrake agreed.

Fox tapped on the door into the smoking room. There was a pause. Hersey Amblington caught her breath in a nervous sigh. Mandrake heard his own heart beat in the drums of his ears.

The door opened slowly into the smoking room and Nicholas stood on the threshold, his face like parchment against the dim scarlet of the screen. Bailey came past him and sat in a low stool just inside the door.

'Did you come straight in?' Alleyn asked Nicholas.

'I don't know. I expect I did.'

'Does any one else remember.'

'I do,' said Mandrake. 'I remember, Compline, that you came in and shut the door. I suppose you paused for a moment with your hand on the knob.'

'It is agreed that Mr Compline shut the door?' Alleyn asked.

'Yes, yes, yes,' Jonathan cried out shrilly, 'it was shut.'

'Then will you please go on?' said Alleyn quietly.

'Will somebody be very kind,' said Nicholas in a high voice, 'and tell me precisely what I did next? It would be a pity if I stepped off on the wrong foot, wouldn't it?'

'We may as well keep our tempers, Nick,' said Hersey. 'You made a face as if to say Bill was still pretty tricky. I did "Thumbs up?" and you did "Thumbs down", and then you sat in that chair by the door and we talked about Bill. After a bit Jo offered you a drink.'

'Agreed?'

'Agreed,' said Mandrake. Jonathan uttered an impatient sound and added very querulously: 'Yes. Oh yes.' Nicholas said: 'Oh, by all means, agreed,' and laughed.

'There's the chair,' said Alleyn.

Nicholas dropped into the armchair on the opposite side of the door from Bailey's stool.

'Jonathan asked me to ring for drinks,' said Mandrake, 'but before I could do so we heard a clink of glasses in the hall and . . . '

He stopped short. Fox had opened the door into the hall and in the complete silence that followed they all heard the faint jingling of glasses.

Thomas came in with the grog tray.

He set it on the table and went out, shutting the door behind him.

'He is now tidying the hall,' said Alleyn.

'I'm not enjoying this,' said Hersey Amblington loudly. 'I'm hating it.'

'It will not be much longer,' said Alleyn. Mandrake heard his own voice saying: 'But it *is* horrible. We're creating it all over again. It's as if we were making something take form – in there.'

'Oh, *don't,*' Hersey whispered.

'There's no one in the smoking room,' said Alleyn, and he spoke with unexpected emphasis. 'The other doors are locked. There is no one in there. Please go on. Did you have your drinks?'

Nobody answered. At last Mandrake forced himself to speak: 'Jonathan poured them out and then he said: "What about William?" '

'One moment. You should be at the table, then, Mr Royal.'

Jonathan went to the table. Mandrake's voice went on: 'He said: "What about William?" meaning would he like a drink, and Compline stuck his head in at the door and sang out: "Coming in for a drink, Bill?" '

'May we see that, Mr Compline?'

Nicholas reached out and opened the door. He made an attempt to speak, boggled over it, and finally said: 'I asked him to come in. I think he sort of grunted. Then I asked him to turn on the news. Jonathan and Mandrake had suggested that we might listen to it.'

'What exactly did you say?'

'I can't remember the precise words.'

'I can,' said Mandrake. 'Or pretty nearly. You said: "D'you mind switching on the wireless? It's time for the news and we'd like to hear it." Then there was a slight pause.'

Nicholas said: 'I waited and heard someone walk across the floor and I called out: "Thanks."'

Another heavy silence fell upon the room. Fox stood motionless by the door into the hall, Bailey by the door into the smoking room, Alleyn close to Jonathan by the table.

'And then?' Alleyn asked.

'And then we heard the wireless,' said Mandrake.

Bailey's hand moved.

And in the empty smoking room a voice roared:

> '... out the barrel,
> Roll out the barrel again.'

Jonathan Royal screamed out an oath and backed away from the table, his hand to his mouth.

He was almost knocked over. Nicholas had stumbled towards the door where he was checked by Bailey. He struck at Bailey, turned, and made for the door into the hall where Alleyn barred the way. Nicholas mouthed at him.

'Steady,' said Alleyn. Nicholas stretched out his uninjured arm, pointing back to the empty room: 'I didn't touch it,' he gabbled, 'I didn't touch it. Hart did it. It's the second booby trap. Don't look at me like that. You can't prove anything against me.' He fell back a pace. Alleyn made a move and Nicholas sprang at him. Bailey and Fox closed in on Nicholas Compline.

CHAPTER 17

Departure

The rain fell steadily over Highfold all through that night. When in the dead light of dawn Alleyn shaved and washed in the downstairs cloakroom, the house still drummed faintly to the inexorable onslaught of the rain. At five o'clock the Great Chipping police had telephoned to say they were coming through by the Pen-Gidding road and that an ambulance was already on its way. At half-past five Nicholas Compline lifted a blotched face from his arm and, breaking a silence of six hours, told Fox he wished to make a statement. At six o'clock Dr Francis Hart had an interview with Alleyn. He arrived fully dressed and said that with the permission of the authorities he would attempt to drive home by the long route. 'My wife has asked me to take her with me,' he said. 'I have agreed to do so if you allow.' Alleyn consented readily. Dr Hart then made him a formal speech, causing him acute embarrassment by many references to the courtesy and integrity of the British police.

'Never for a moment,' said Dr Hart, 'was I in doubt of the issue. As soon as I heard of William Compline's death I knew that it must be his brother.'

'You seem to have been the only member of the party who refused to be bamboozled by fancy touches,' said Alleyn. 'Why were you so certain?'

'I understand my wife,' said Dr Hart simply. He clasped his hands over his waistcoat, frowned judicially, and continued: 'My wife is extremely mercenary, and an almost perfect egoist. She was in love with Nicholas Compline. That I perceived, and with that knowledge

I tortured myself. She loved him as much as she could love any one other than herself, and obviously he was quite determined to have her. Whether she was his mistress or not I am unable to decide, but in any case my own suspicious attitude and the scenes I created so continually must have been very irksome. I have no doubt he wished her to break with me and if possible obtain a divorce. That, of course, she would refuse to do. A young man with little money would never persuade her to embark on a damaging scandal. But a young man with a large estate and fine prospects – how different! No doubt she told him so. I do not believe she was aware of his guilt, still less that she was a partner in his crime. She would never risk such a proceeding. No. She thought I killed William Compline and that when I was hanged she would wait for a discreet period and then marry his brother. She will now strain every nerve to disassociate herself with the brother.'

'I'm afraid,' said Alleyn grimly, 'that she will *not* succeed.'

'Of course not. But if you interview her she will try to persuade you that his motive was purely mercenary and that she was the victim of his importunities. She will also offer to return to me.'

Alleyn glanced up quickly. 'No,' said Dr Hart. 'I have recovered from that sickness. She would have betrayed me. In our last interview before the crime she told me that if anything happened to Compline she would accuse me. I said she would not have the courage and she replied that where much was at stake she would dare much. I felt as a man might feel if some possession he had treasured was suddenly proved to be worthless. I have lost all desire for my wife.'

'You have been very frank,' said Alleyn after a pause. 'When this is all over what do you mean to do?'

'I am a surgeon. I think in a little while there will be a need for many surgeons in England. Perhaps, who knows, I may do more admirable work than the patching-up of faded women's faces.' Dr Hart pulled at his lips with his short white finger. 'All the same,' he said, 'I wish I had been able to save her life.'

'It would have been no great service, you know.'

'I suppose not.' He held out his hand. 'Goodbye, Chief Inspector,' he said, and bowed stiffly from the waist. Alleyn watched him go, an almost arrogantly foreign figure in his English tweeds. A little while later he heard a car drive round the house. Bailey came in to say that Madame Lisse wished to see him before she left. Alleyn grimaced. 'I'm engaged,' he said. 'Tell her Mr Fox will see her. I think she'll say it doesn't matter.'

II

At half-past six Mandrake and Chloris came into the library with their top-coats over their arms, and asked if they too might leave Highfold.

'Yes,' Alleyn said. 'You'll be asked to attend the inquest, you know, so I'll have to keep in touch with you.'

'I know,' Mandrake agreed, 'we'd thought of that. When will it be?'

'Wednesday, I should think.'

'Jonathan's asked us to stay but we thought we'd like to go up to London for a slight change of scene. We might look in at the rectory. The road'll be all right now. Can we take a message for you?'

Alleyn gave his message. Mandrake and Chloris still hung off and on.

'We also thought,' said Mandrake at last, 'that we'd like a few of the worst knots unravelled by a master hand. Or doesn't one ask?'

'What knots?' said Alleyn with a smile.

'Well,' said Chloris, 'why Aubrey was shoved in the pond, for one. Did Nicholas shove him?'

'He did.'

'But he recognized Aubrey.'

'Because he recognized him.'

'Oh.'

'But,' said Mandrake. 'We'd worked that out quite differently. After the evidence of the footprints and her letter, we decided that Mrs Compline had followed out to stop Nicholas taking the plunge and had thought I was William gloating, and, on a wave of long pent-up resentment, had shoved me overboard.'

'And then,' said Chloris, 'we thought that when she heard Bill was dead she'd gone out of her mind and imagined that in some way she had killed him. That's how we read the letter.'

'It's a very ingenious reading,' said Alleyn with the ghost of a smile, 'but it doesn't quite fit. How could she have gone down the steps without you seeing her? And even suppose she did manage to do that, she would have had a very clear view of you as you stood facing the pond. Moreover she watched William go downstairs. And finally she had a full account of the whole affair afterwards and heard you being brought upstairs and all the rest of it. Even if she had pushed you overboard she must have very soon heard of her mistake, so how on earth could she think she'd killed William?'

'But the letter?' said Chloris.

'The letter is more tragic and less demented than you thought. The evidence of the footprints tells us that Mrs Compline stood on the terrace and looked down. A few moments later a housemaid saw her return, looking terribly upset. I believe that Mrs Compline saw her son Nicholas make his assault upon you, Mandrake. At the time she may have thought it a dangerous piece of horseplay, but what was she to think when she heard him declare that Hart had done it, believing the victim to be Nicholas himself? And what was she to think when the booby trap was set and again Nicholas accused Hart? Don't you think that, through the hysteria she displayed, ran some inkling of the truth? Last of all, when Nicholas went to her last night and told her William had been killed *in mistake for himself,* what was she to think then? With her secret knowledge how could she escape the terrible conclusion? Her adored son had murdered his brother. She made her last effort to save him and the legend she had made round his character. She wrote a letter that told him she knew and at the same time accused herself to us. She could not quite bring herself to say in so many words she had killed her son, but Nicholas understood – and so did we.'

'I never thought,' said Mandrake after a long silence, 'that Nicholas did it.'

'I must say I'd have thought you'd have guessed. Compline gave you the cape, Mandrake, didn't he? He looked out of the pavilion window and recognized you as you came down. He might have been looking at himself when you stood there in the other cloak. I think at that moment he saw his chance to bring off his tom-fool idea.'

'What tom-fool idea?'

'To stage a series of apparent attempts on his own life based on an idea of mistaken identity. He planted that idea in all your heads. He insisted on it. He shoved you in and rescued you and then went about shouting that Hart had tried to drown him. Evidently he'd some such plan in his head on the first night. Hart had written threatening letters and Compline followed up by writing himself a threatening message with a rather crude imitation of Hart's handwriting. Once we'd proved Hart didn't write the message on the Charter form it was obvious only Nicholas could have done so. Perhaps he chucked you that cape deliberately. Before the bathing incident he knew where you all were and no doubt he watched Hart set off alone down the drive. If the plan failed there wasn't much harm done. Next he staged his own flight over country that he knew damned well was impassable. If nobody had gone with him he'd have come back half-drowned in snow and told the tale. Next he rigged up his own booby trap, choosing a moment when you were all changing in your rooms. He hadn't bargained on Madame Lisse looking after him as he went down the passage. He was going to kick the door open and let the brass Buddha fall on the floor. But knowing that she was watching he had to go a bit further than was comfortable, and he mucked up the business. He chose the Buddha because he'd seen Hart handle it the night before. He chose the Maori mere for the same reason, but he smudged Hart's prints when he used it. He himself wore gloves, of course.'

'But the wireless?' asked Chloris.

'Do you remember that Hart had complained bitterly of the wireless? That appears in Mandrake's most useful and exhaustive notes. Compline knew Hart loathed radio. After the fiasco at the pond he shut himself up in the smoking-room, didn't he, until he was turned out by William who wanted to make his drawing. And discordant noises were heard? He was always at the radio? Yes, well, he was making himself very familiar with that wireless set. Do you remember the fishing rod above the mantelpiece in the smoking-room?'

'Yes,' they said.

'Complete with fly and cast and green line?'

'Yes.'

'Well, when we came on the scene there was no fly and the line had been freshly cut. On the screw-hole on the volume control I found a number of almost invisible scratches, all radiating outwards. I also found some minute fragments of red and green feather. The card on the rod tells us that the late Mr St J. Worthington Royal used that red-and-green fly when he caught his four-and-a-half pounder. There were other marks on the double tuning control which, at its centre, was free of dust. In the jamb of the door into the library there was a hole which accommodated the drawing-pin Mandrake picked up in the sole of his shoe. You say that William dropped one of his drawing-pins in the smoking room. I fancy Nicholas found and used it. In Mrs Compline's tweed hat I found two flies, one red-and-green, rather the worse for wear. The maid who looked after her swears there was only one, a yellow-and-black salmon fly, when she arrived. Who went straight to his mother's room after the murder? Right,' said Alleyn answering their startled glances. 'Well, yesterday evening we experimented. We found that if we used a length of fishing-line with a fly attached but without a cast, we could hook the fly in the screw-hole of the volume control, pass the green line under the wave band and over the tuning control axis which served as a sort of smooth-running pulley, and fix the other end of the line to the library door jamb with a drawing-pin. When you tweaked the line the hook pulled the volume control from zero to fairly loud, the line playing over the tuning control, which we had set in such a way that the slight pull turned it to the station. As the hook in the screw-hole reached the bottom of the circuit it fell out, and the wireless was giving tongue.'

There was a long silence, broken at last by Mandrake. 'But anybody could have fixed it,' said Mandrake.

'Only after William was dead. He would have seen it when he was tuning, wouldn't he? But this is the place, I see, to introduce Thomas, the dancing footman. Thomas set a limit to the time when the murderer departed. Incidentally, he also proved, by a little excursion, that Hart couldn't have shoved you in the pond. Thomas was Nicholas Compline's undoing. If it hadn't been for Thomas we would have had a job proving that Hart didn't do exactly what Nicholas said he did: creep in by the door from the hall into the smoking room and kill William. The mistaken identity stunt had to be supported by an approach from the rear. That was why Nicholas locked the door into the boudoir. But as things stood it was perfectly clear from the start that only Nicholas could have benefited by the wireless alibi. Mr Royal, whose trip into the hall looked rather fishy, left the library after the wireless started, and Dr Hart would have gained nothing whatsoever by the trick since he was alone for the entire time. Lady Hersey, who had no motive, is the stock figure of the thriller-fiction – the all-too-obvious suspect. Moreover the trout-line device would have been of no use to her either, since she went in after the noise started.'

'What *exactly* did he do, though?' asked Chloris.

'He killed his brother, rigged the wireless trick, came out and shut the door. Later, he opened the door, held a one-sided conversation with William, asked for the news, tweaked the string which he had pinned to the door jamb, and waited, with God knows what sensations, for someone to go into the smoking room.'

'What happened to the line?'

'You will remember, Mandrake, that while you and Mr Royal were together by the body, Nicholas came in. He had shut the door after him and was hidden from you by the screen. He had only to stoop and pull the line towards him. The drawing-pin had jerked away and he had no time to hunt for it. The line was in heavy shadow and the same colour as the carpet. It throws back well towards the screen when the trick is worked. He gathered it up and put it on the fire when he got the chance. You left him by the fire for a moment, perhaps?'

'He asked us to leave him to himself.'

'I'll be bound he did. But a trout line doesn't burn without leaving a trace, and we found its trace in the ashes.'

'I see,' said Mandrake.

'I can't help thinking about his mother,' said Chloris. 'I mean, it was Nicholas she adored.'

'And for that reason she killed herself. At the inquest you will hear the letter she wrote. Mandrake has already seen it. She hoped to save Nicholas by that letter. While seeming to make a confession it tells him that she knew what he had done. No wonder he was upset when he read it. It was her last gesture of love – a very terrible gesture.'

'I think,' said Chloris shakily, 'that he truly was fond of her.'

'Perhaps,' said Alleyn.

The library door opened and Hersey's face, very pale and exhausted, looked in. 'Is it an official party?' she asked. Alleyn asked her to come in: 'I have already been over a good deal of this with Lady Hersey and with Mr Royal,' he explained, and to Hersey: 'I have not got as far as your visit with Nicholas Compline to his mother.'

'Oh, yes. You asked me last night to tell you exactly what he did and I couldn't remember very clearly. That's why I've come in. I've remembered what happened after he'd tried to tell her about William. I'm afraid it's quite insignificant. He seemed frightfully upset, of course, and I suppose in a ghastly sort of way he was. He didn't make her understand, and turned away. I had to tell her. I knelt by her bed and put my arms round her. We were old friends, you know. I told her as best I could. I remember, now, hearing him walk away behind me and I remember that in the back of my head I was irritated with him because he seemed to be fidgeting about by the wardrobe. He must have been in a pretty awful state of mind. He was swinging the wardrobe door, I thought. I supposed he didn't know what he was doing.'

'I think he knew,' said Alleyn. 'The tweed hat was on the top shelf of the wardrobe. He was getting rid of a green-and-red Alexandra trout fly.'

III

'Wasn't that rather a mad thing to do?' asked Hersey wearily when Alleyn had explained about the trout fly.

'Not quite as mad as it sounds. The hook was not an easy thing to get rid of. He couldn't burn it or risk putting it in a waste-paper basket. He would have been wiser to keep the hook until he could safely dispose of it, or merely leave it on the mantelpiece, but no doubt he was possessed by the intense desire of all homicides to rid himself of the corpus delicti. In the shock of William's death his mother would have been most unlikely to notice a second and very insignificant trout fly in her hat-band.'

'And that's all,' said Mandrake after a long silence.

'That, I think, is all. You would like to go now, wouldn't you?'

'Shall we go?' Mandrake asked Chloris.

She nodded listlessly but didn't move. 'I think I should go if I were you,' said Alleyn, looking very directly at Mandrake.

'Come along, darling,' Mandrake said gently. They bade goodbye to Hersey and Alleyn and went out.

' "Darling"?' murmured Hersey. 'But it means nothing, nowadays, does it? Why do you want to get rid of them, Mr Alleyn?'

'We're expecting the police car and the ambulance. It won't be very pleasant. You would like to get away too, I expect, wouldn't you?'

'No, thank you,' said Hersey. 'I think I'll stay with my cousin Jo. He's pretty well cut up about this, you know. After all, he gave the party. It's not a pleasant thought.' She looked at the door into the smoking room, the door with its rows of dummy books. 'Mr Alleyn,' she said, 'he's a despicable monster, but I was fond of his mother. Would she perhaps have liked me to see him now?'

'I don't think I should if I were you. We can tell him you've offered to see him and we can let you know later on if he'd like it.'

'I must ask you – has he confessed?'

'He has made a written statement. It's not a confession.'

'But . . . ?'

'I can't tell you more than that, I'm afraid,' said Alleyn, and before his imagination rose the memory of sheets of paper covered with phrases that had no form, ending abruptly or straggling off into incoherence, phrases that contradicted each other and that made wild accusations against Hart, against the mother who had accused herself. He heard Fox saying: 'I've given him the warning over and over again, but he will do it. He's hanging himself with every word of it.' He felt Hersey's gaze upon him, and looking up saw that she was white to the lips. 'Mr Alleyn,' she said, 'what will happen to Nicholas?' And when he did not answer Hersey covered her face with her hands.

Through the sound of pouring rain Alleyn heard a car coming up the drive and out on the sweep before the house.

Fox came in. 'It's our people, Mr Alleyn.'

'All right,' said Alleyn, and he turned to Hersey. 'I must go.' Hersey walked to the door. He opened it and he and Fox followed her into the hall.

Jonathan was standing there. Hersey went straight to him and he took her by the hands. 'Well, dear,' said Jonathan, 'it – it's time, I think.'

Fox had gone to the front door and opened it. The sound of rain filled the hall. A large man in plain clothes came in, followed by two policemen. Alleyn met them and the large man shook hands. Jonathan came forward.

'Well, Blandish,' he said.

'Very sorry about this, sir,' said Superintendent Blandish. Jonathan made a small waving of his hands and turned back to Hersey.

'All ready for us, Mr Alleyn?'

'I think so,' Alleyn said, and they went into the green sitting room, shutting the door behind them.

'Hersey, my dearest,' said Jonathan, 'don't stay out here, now.'

'Would you rather I went away, Jo?'

'I – it's for your sake.'

'Then I'll stay.'

So Hersey saw Nicholas come out between Bailey and Fox, the senior officers keeping close behind him. He walked stiffly with short steps, looking out of the corners of his eyes. His unshaven cheeks were creased with a sort of grin and his mouth was not quite shut. His blond hair hung across his forehead in dishevelled streaks. Without turning his head he looked at his host. Jonathan moved towards him and at once the two men halted.

'I want to tell you,' Jonathan said, 'that if you wish me to see your solicitors or do anything else that I am able to do, you have only to send instructions.'

'There now,' said Fox, comfortably, 'that'll be very nice, won't it?'

Nicholas said in an unrecognizable voice: 'Stop them hanging me,' and suddenly sagged at the knees.

'Come along, now,' said Fox. 'You don't want to be talking like that.'

As they went out Jonathan and Hersey saw the ambulance van outside by the police car, and men with stretchers waiting to come in.

IV

'He'd made up his mind to do it somehow, Jo,' said Hersey that afternoon. 'You mustn't blame yourself too much.'

'I do blame myself dreadfully,' said Jonathan. He had taken off his glasses and his myopic eyes, blurred with tears, looked childlike and helpless. 'It's just as you said, Hersey. I had to learn my lesson. You see I thought I'd have a dramatic party.'

'Oh, *Jo,*' cried Hersey, with a sob that was almost a laugh. *'Don't.'*

'I did. That was my plan. I thought Aubrey might make a poetic drama out of it. I'm a mischievous, selfish fellow, trying to amuse myself and never thinking – just as you said, my dear.'

'I talk too much. I was cross. You couldn't know what was behind it all.'

'No. I think perhaps I do these things because I'm a bit lonely.'

Hersey reached out her hand and he took it uncertainly between both of his. For a long time they sat in silence, looking at the fire.

V

'What you've got to do,' said Mandrake, 'is to think about other things. Get a new interest. Me for instance.'

'But it isn't over. If it was over it wouldn't be so awful. I've been so mixed up with the Complines,' said Chloris. 'I wanted to be free of them and now – all this has happened. It sounds silly but I feel sort of lonely.'

Mandrake removed his left hand from the driving wheel.

Colour Scheme

To the family at Tauranga

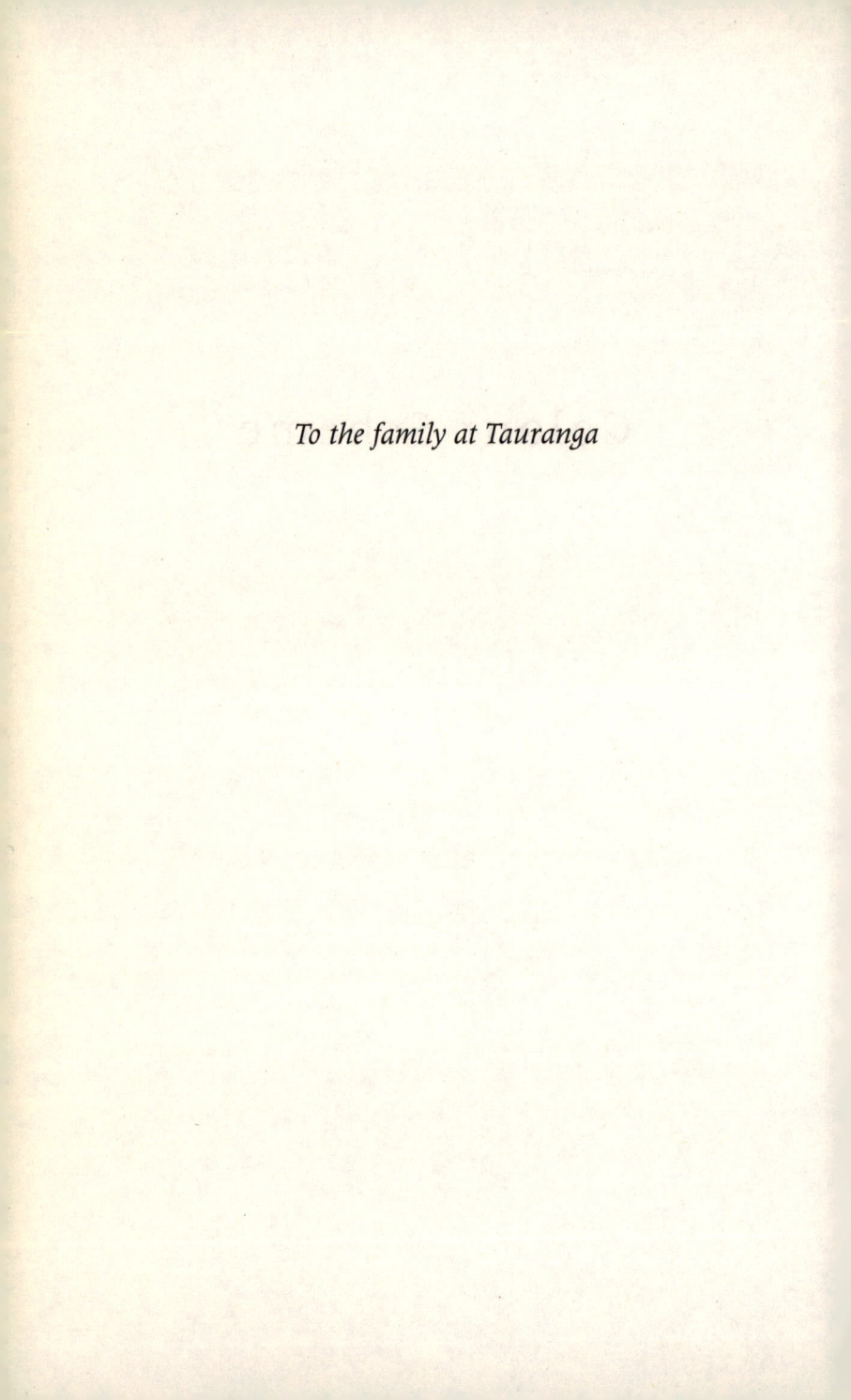

Contents

1	The Claires and Dr Ackrington	583
2	Mr Questing Goes Down for the First Time	601
3	Gaunt at the Springs	623
4	Red for Danger	637
5	Mr Questing Goes Down for the Second Time	655
6	Arrival of Septimus Falls	671
7	Torpedo	688
8	Concert	706
9	Mr Questing Goes Down for the Third Time	724
10	Entrance of Sergeant Webley	746
11	The Theory of a Put-Up Job	768
12	Skull	789
13	Letter from Mr Questing	804
14	Solo by Septimus Falls	822
15	The Last of Septimus Falls	836

Cast of Characters

Dr James Ackrington, MD, FRCS, FRCP
Barbara Claire — *His niece*
Mrs Claire — *His sister*
Colonel Edward Claire — *His brother-in-law*
Simon Claire — *His nephew*
Huia — *Maid at Wai-ata-tapu*
Geoffrey Gaunt — *A visiting celebrity*
Dikon Bell — *His secretary*
Alfred Colly — *His servant*
Maurice Questing — *Man of business*
Rua Te Kahu — *A chief of the Te Rarawas*
Herbert Smith — *Roustabout at Wai-ata-tapu*
Eru Saul — *A half-caste*
Septimus Falls
The Princess Te Papa
(Mrs Te Papa) — *Of the Te Rarawas*
Detective-Sergeant Webley — *Of the Harpoon Constabulary*
A Superintendent of Police

CHAPTER 1

The Claires and Dr Ackrington

When Dr James Ackrington limped into the Harpoon Club on the afternoon of Monday, January the thirteenth, he was in a poisonous temper. A sequence of events had combined to irritate and then to inflame him. He had slept badly. He had embarked, he scarcely knew why, on a row with his sister, a row based obscurely on the therapeutic value of mud pools and the technique of frying eggs. He had asked for the daily paper of the previous Thursday only to discover that it had been used to wrap up Mr Maurice Questing's picnic lunch. His niece Barbara, charged with this offence, burst out into one of her fits of nervous laughter and recovered the paper, stained with ham fat and reeking with onions. Dr Ackrington, in shaking it angrily before her, had tapped his sciatic nerve smartly against the table. Blind with pain and white with rage, he stumbled to his room, undressed, took a shower, wrapped himself in his dressing-gown and made his way to the hottest of the thermal baths, only to find Mr Maurice Questing sitting in it, his unattractive outline rimmed with effervescence. Mr Questing had laughed offensively and announced his intention of remaining in the pool for twenty minutes. He had pointed out the less hot but unoccupied baths. Dr Ackrington, standing on the hardened bluish mud banks that surrounded the pool, embarked on as violent a quarrel as he could bring about with a naked smiling antagonist who returned no answer to the grossest insults. He then went back to his room, dressed and, finding nobody upon whom to pour out his wrath, drove his car ruthlessly up the sharp track from Wai-ata-tapu Hot Springs to the main road for Harpoon. He left behind an atmosphere well suited to his mood, since the air, as always, reeked of sulphurous vapours.

Arrived at the club, he collected his letters and turned into the writing-room. The windows looked across the Harpoon Inlet whose waters on this midsummer morning were quite unscored by ripples and held immaculate the images of sky and white sand, and of the crimson flowering trees that bloom at this time of year in the Northland of New Zealand. A shimmer of heat rose from the pavement outside the club and under its influence the form of trees, hills and bays seemed to shake a little as if indeed the strangely primitive landscape were still taking shape and were rather a half-realized idea than a concrete accomplishment of nature.

It was a beautiful prospect but Dr Ackrington was not really moved by it. He reflected that the day would be snortingly hot and opened his letters. Only one of them seemed to arrest his attention. He spread it out before him on the writing-table and glared at it, whistling slightly between his teeth.

This is what he read:

> Harley Chambers,
> AUCKLAND, C.1
>
> My dear Dr Ackrington,
>
> I am venturing to ask for your advice in a rather tricky business involving a patient of mine, none other than our visiting celebrity the famous Geoffrey Gaunt. As you probably know, he arrived in Australia with his Shakespearean company just before war broke out and remained there, continuing to present his repertoire of plays but handing over a very generous dollop of all takings to the patriotic funds. On the final disbandment of his company he came to New Zealand, where, as you may not know (I remember your loathing of radio), he has done some excellent propaganda stuff on the air. About four weeks ago he consulted me. He complained of insomnia, acute pains in the joints, loss of appetite and intense depression. He asked me if I thought he had a chance of being accepted for active service. He wants to get back to England but only if he can be of use. I diagnosed fibrositis and nervous debility, put him on a very simple diet, and told him I certainly did not consider him fit for any sort of war service. It seems he has an idea of writing his autobiography. They all do it.

I suggested that he might combine this with a course of hydrotherapy and complete rest. I suggested Rotorua, but he won't hear of it. Says he'd be plagued with lion hunters and what-not and that he can't stand the tourist atmosphere.

You'll have guessed what I'm coming to.

I know you are living at Wai-ata-tapu, and understand that the Spa is under your sister's or her husband's management. I have heard that you are engaged on a *magnum opus* so therefore suppose that the place is conducive to quiet work. Would you be very kind and tell me if you think it would suit my patient, and if Colonel and Mrs Claire would care to have him as a resident for some six weeks or more? I know that you don't practise nowadays, and it is with the greatest diffidence that I make my final suggestion. Would you care to keep a professional eye on Mr Gaunt? He is an interesting figure, and I venture to hope that you may feel inclined to take him as a sort of patient extraordinary. I must add that, frankly, I should be very proud to hand him on to so distinguished a consultant.

Gaunt has a secretary and a manservant, and I understand he would want accommodation for both of them.

Please forgive me for writing what I fear may turn out to be a tiresome and exacting letter.

> Yours very sincerely,
> IAN FORSTER

Dr Ackrington read this letter through twice, folded it, placed it in his pocket book, and, still whistling between his teeth, filled his pipe and lit it. After some five minutes' cogitation he drew a sheet of paper towards him and began to cover it with his thin irritable script.

Dear Forster (he wrote),

Many thanks for your letter. It requires a frank answer and I give it for what it is worth. Wai-ata-tapu is, as you suggest, the property of my sister and her husband, who run it as a thermal spa. In many ways they are perfect fools, but they are honest fools and that is more than one can say of most people engaged in similar pursuits. The whole place is grossly mismanaged in my opinion, but I don't know that you would find anyone else who would agree with me. Claire is an army man and it's a pity he has failed so signally to absorb in the smallest degree the principles of system and orderly control that must at some time or another have been suggested to him. My sister is a bookish woman. However incompetent, she seems to command the affection of her martyred clients, and I am her only critic. Perhaps it is unnecessary to add that they make no money and work like bewildered horses at an occupation that requires merely the application of common sense to make it easy and profitable. On the alleged therapeutic properties of the baths you have evidently formed your own opinion. They consist, as you are aware, of thermal springs whose waters contain alkalis, free sulphuric acid, and free carbonic acid gas. There are also siliceous mud baths in connection with which my brother-in-law talks loosely and freely of radioactivity. This latter statement I regard as so much pious mumbo-jumbo, but I am alone in my opinion. The mud may be miraculous. My leg is no worse since I took to using it.

As for your spectacular patient, I don't know to what degree of comfort he is used, but can promise him he won't get it, though enormous and misguided efforts will be made to accommodate him. Actually there is no reason why he shouldn't be comfortable. Possibly his secretary and man might succeed where my unfortunate relatives may safely be relied upon to fail. I doubt if he will be more wretched than he would be anywhere else in this extraordinary country. The charges will certainly be less than elsewhere. Six guineas a week for resident patients. Possibly Gaunt would like a private sitting-room for which I imagine there would be an extra charge. Tonks of Harpoon is the visiting medical man. I need say no more. Possibly it is an oblique recommendation of the waters that all Tonks's patients who have taken them have at least survived. There is no reason why I should not keep an eye on your man and I shall do so if you and he wish it. What you say of him modifies my previous impression that he was one of the emasculate popinjays who appear to form the nucleus of the intelligentsia at home in these degenerate days. Bloomsbury.

My *magnum opus,* as you no doubt ironically call it, crawls on in spite of the concreted efforts of my immediate associates to withhold the merest necessities for undisturbed employment. I confess that the autobiographical outpourings of persons connected with the theatre seem to me to bear little relation to serious work, and, where I fail, Mr Geoffrey Gaunt may well succeed.

Again, many thanks for your letter,

> Yours,
> JAMES ACKRINGTON

PS. I should be doing you and your patient a disservice if I failed to tell you that the place is infested by as offensive a fellow as I have ever come across. I have the gravest suspicions regarding this person.

J.A.

As Dr Ackrington sealed and directed this letter a trace of complacency lightened the habitual austerity of his face. He rang the bell, ordered a small whisky and soda and with an air of relishing his employment began a second letter.

Roderick Alleyn, Esq., Chief Inspector, CID,
c/o Central Police Station,
Auckland.

Sir,

The newspapers, with gross indiscretion, report you as having come to this country in connection with scandalous leakages of information to the enemy, notably those which led to the sinking of SS *Hippolyte* last November.

I consider it my duty to inform you of the activities of a person at present living at Wai-ata-tapu Hot Springs, Harpoon Inlet. This person, calling himself Maurice Questing and staying at the local Spa, has formed the habit of leaving the house after dark. To my positive knowledge, he ascends the mountain known as Rangi's Peak, which is part of the native reserve and the western face of which looks out to sea. I have myself witnessed on several occasions a light flashing on the slopes of this face. You will note that *Hippolyte* was torpedoed at a spot some two miles out from Harpoon Inlet.

I have also to report that, on being questioned as to his movements, Mr Questing has returned evasive and even lying answers.

I conceived it my duty to report this matter to the local police authorities, who displayed a somnolence so profound as to be pathological.

I have the honour to be,
Yours faithfully,
JAMES ACKRINGTON, MD, FRCS, FRCP

The servant brought the drink. Dr Ackrington accused him of having substituted an inferior brand of whisky for the one ordered, but he did this with an air of routine rather than of rage. He accepted the servant's resigned assurances with surprising mildness, merely remarking that the whisky had probably been adulterated by the makers. He then finished his drink, clapped his hat on the side of his head and went out to post his letters. The hall porter pulled open the door.

'War news a bit brighter this morning, sir,' said the porter tentatively.

'The sooner we're all dead, the better,' Dr Ackrington replied cheerfully. He gave a falsetto barking noise, and limped quickly down the steps.

'Was that a joke?' said the hall porter to the servant. The servant turned up his eyes.

II

Colonel and Mrs Claire had lived for twelve years at Wai-ata-tapu Springs. They had come to New Zealand from India when their daughter Barbara, born ten years after their marriage, was thirteen, and their son Simon, nine years old. They had told their friends in gentle voices that they wanted to get away from the conventions of retired army life in England. They had spoken blithely, for they took an uncritical delight in such phrases, of wide-open spaces and of a small inheritance that had come to the Colonel. With most of this inheritance they had built the boarding house they now lived in. The remaining sums had been quietly lost in a series of timid speculations. They had worked like slaves, receiving good advice with well-bred resentment and bad advice with touching gratitude. Beside these failings, they had a positive genius for collecting impossible people, and at the time when this tale opens were at the mercy of a certain incubus called Herbert Smith.

On the retirement of her distinguished and irascible brother from practice in London, Mrs Claire had invited him to join them. He had consented to do so only as a paying guest, as he wished to enjoy complete freedom for making criticisms and complaints, an exercise he indulged with particular energy, especially in regard to his nephew Simon. His niece Barbara Claire had from the first done the work of two servants and, because she went out so little, retained the sort of English vicarage-garden atmosphere that emanated from her mother. Simon, on the contrary, had attended the Harpoon State schools and, influenced on the one hand by the persistent family attitude of poor but proud gentility and on the other by his schoolfellows' suspicion of 'pommy' settlers, had become truculently colonial, somewhat introverted and defiantly uncouth. A year before the outbreak of war he left school, and now was taking the preliminary Air Force training at home.

On the morning of Dr Ackrington's visit to Harpoon, the Claires pursued their normal occupations. At midday Colonel Claire took his lumbago to the radioactivity of the mud pool, Mrs Claire steeped her sciatica in a hot spring, Simon went into his cabin to practise Morse code, and Barbara cooked the midday meal in a hot and primitive kitchen with Huia, the Maori help, in attendance.

'You can dish up, Huia,' said Barbara. She brushed the locks of damp hair from her eyes with the back of her forearm. 'I'm afraid I seem to have used a lot of dishes. There'll be six in the dining-room. Mr Questing's out for lunch.'

'Good job,' said Huia skittishly. Barbara pretended not to hear. Huia, moving with the half-languid, half-vigorous grace of the young Maori, smiled brilliantly, and began to pile stacks of plates on a tray. 'He's no good,' she said softly.

Barbara glanced at her. Huia laughed richly, lifting her short upper lip. 'I shall never understand them,' Barbara thought. Aloud she said: 'Mightn't it be better if you just pretended not to hear when Mr Questing starts those – starts being – starts teasing you?'

'He makes me very angry,' said Huia, and suddenly she became childishly angry, flashing her eyes and stamping her foot. 'Silly ass,' she said.

'But you're not really angry.'

Huia looked out of the corners of her eyes at Barbara, pulled an equivocal grimace, and tittered.

'Don't forget your cap and apron,' said Barbara, and left the sweltering kitchen for the dining-room.

III

Wai-ata-tapu Hostel was a one-storeyed wooden building shaped like an E with the middle stroke missing. The dining-room occupied the centre of the long section separating the kitchen and serveries from the boarders' bedrooms, which extended into the east wing. The west wing, private to the Claires, was a series of cramped cabins and a tiny sitting-room. The house had been designed by Colonel Claire on army-hut lines with an additional flavour of sanatorium. There were no passages, and all the rooms opened on a partially covered-in verandah. The inside walls were of yellowish-red oiled wood. The house smelt faintly of linseed oil and positively of sulphur. An observant visitor might have traced in it the history of the Claires' venture. The framed London Board-of-Trade posters, the chairs and tables painted, not very capably, in primary colours, the notices in careful script, the archly reproachful rhyme sheets in bathrooms and lavatories, all spoke of high beginnings. Broken *passe-partout*, chipped paint and fly-blown papers hanging by single drawing pins traced unmistakably a gradual but inexorable decline. The house was clean but unexpectedly so, tidy but not orderly, and only vaguely uncomfortable. The front wall of the dining-room was built of glass panels designed to slide in grooves, but devilishly inclined to jam. These looked across the verandah to the hot springs themselves.

Barbara stood for a moment at one of the open windows and stared absently at a freakish landscape. Hills smudged with scrub were ranked against a heavy sky. Beyond them, across the hidden inlet, but tall enough to dominate the scene, rose the truncated cone of Rangi's Peak, an extinct volcano so characteristically shaped that it might have been placed in the landscape by a modern artist with a passion for simplified form. Though some eight miles away, it was actually clearer than the nearby hills, for their margins, dark and firm, were broken at intervals by plumes of steam that rose perpendicularly from the eight thermal pools. These lay close at hand, just beyond the earth-and-pumice sweep in front of the house. Five of them were hot springs hidden from the windows by fences of manuka scrub. The sixth was enclosed by a rough bath shed. The seventh was almost a lake over whose dark waters wraiths of steam vaguely drifted. The eighth was a mud pool, not hot enough to give off steam, and dark in colour with a kind of iridescence across its surface. This pool was only half-screened and from its open end protruded a naked pink head on top of a long neck. Barbara went out to the verandah, seized a brass schoolroom bell, and rang it vigorously. The pink head travelled slowly through the mud like some fantastic periscope until it disappeared behind the screen.

'Lunch, Father,' screamed Barbara unnecessarily. She walked across the sweep and entered the enclosure. On a brush fence that screened the first path hung a weather-worn placard: 'The Elfin Pool. Engaged.' The Claires had given each of the pools some amazingly insipid title, and Barbara had neatly executed the placards in poker work.

'Are you there, Mummy?' asked Barbara.

'Come in, my dear.'

She walked round the screen and found her mother at her feet, submerged up to the shoulders in bright blue steaming water that quite hid her plump body. Over her fuzz of hair Mrs Claire wore a rubber bag with a frilled edge and she had spectacles on her nose. With her right hand she held above the water a shilling edition of *Cranford*.

'So *charming*,' she said. 'They are all such dears. I never tire of them.'

'Lunch is nearly in.'

'I must pop out. The Elf is really wonderful, Ba. My tiresome arm is quite cleared up.'

'I'm so glad, Mummy,' said Barbara in a loud voice. 'I want to ask you something.'

'What is it?' said Mrs Claire, turning a page with her thumb.

'Do you like Mr Questing?'

Mrs Claire looked up over the top of her book. Barbara was standing at a curious angle, balanced on her right leg. Her left foot was hooked round her right ankle.

'Dear,' said Mrs Claire, *'don't* stand like that. It pushes all the wrong things out and tucks the right ones in.'

'But do you?' Barbara persisted, changing her posture with a jerk.

'Well, he's not out of the top drawer of course, poor thing.'

'I don't mind about that. And anyway what *is* the top drawer? It's a maddening sort of way to classify people. Such cheek! I'm sorry, Mummy, I didn't mean to be rude. But honestly, for *us* to talk about class!' Barbara gave a loud hoot of laughter. 'Look at us!' she said.

Mrs Claire edged modestly towards the side of the pool and thrust her book at her daughter. Stronger waves of sulphurous smells rose from the disturbed waters. A cascade of drops fell from the elderly rounded arm.

'Take *Cranford*,' she said. Barbara took it. Mrs Claire pulled her rubber bag a little closer about her ears. 'My dear,' she said, pitching her voice on a note that she usually reserved for death, 'aren't you mixing up money and breeding? It doesn't matter what one *does* surely . . . ' She paused.

'There is an innate something . . .' she began. 'One can always tell,' she added.

'Can one? Look at Simon.'

'Dear old Simon,' said her mother reproachfully.

'Yes, I know. I'm very fond of him. I couldn't have a kinder brother, but there isn't much innate something about Simon, is there?'

'It's only that awful accent. If we could have afforded . . .

'There you are, you see,' cried Barbara, and she went on in a great hurry, shooting out her words as if she fired them from a gun that was too big for her. 'Class consciousness is all my eye. Fundamentally it's based on money.'

On the verandah the bell was rung again with some abandon.

'I must pop out,' said Mrs Claire. 'That's Huia ringing.'

'It's not because he talks a different language or any of those things,' said Barbara hurriedly, 'that I don't like Mr Questing. I don't like *him*. And I don't like the way he behaves with Huia. Or,' she added under her breath, 'with me.'

'I expect,' said Mrs Claire, 'that's only because he used to be a commercial traveller. It's just his way.'

'Mummy, *why* do you find excuses for him? Why does Daddy, who would ordinarily loathe Mr Questing, put up with him? He even laughs at his awful jokes. It isn't because we want his board money. Look how Daddy and Uncle James practically froze out those rich Americans who were very nice, I thought.' Barbara drove her long fingers through her mouse-coloured hair, and avoiding her mother's gaze stared at the top of Rangi's Peak. 'You'd think Mr Questing had a sort of *hold* on us,' she said, and then burst into one of her fits of nervous laughter.

'Barbie darling,' said her mother, on a note that contrived to suggest the menace of some frightful indelicacy, 'I think we won't talk about it any more.'

'Uncle James hates him, anyway.'

'Barbara!'

'Lunch, Agnes,' said a quiet voice on the other side of the fence. 'You're late again.'

'Coming, dear. Please go on ahead with Daddy, Barbara,' said Mrs Claire.

IV

Dr Ackrington bucketed his car down the drive and pulled up at the verandah with a savage jolt just as Barbara reached it. She waited for him and took his arm.

'Stop it,' he said. 'You'll give me hell if you hurry me.' But when she made to draw away he held her arm in a wiry grasp.

'Is the leg bad, Uncle James?'

'It's always bad. Steady now.'

'Did you have your morning soak in the Porridge Pot?'

'I did not. And do you know why? That damned poisonous little bounder was wallowing in it.

'He never washes,' Dr Ackrington shouted. 'I'll swear he never washes. Why the devil you can't insist on people taking a shower before they use the pools is a mystery. He soaks his sweat off in my mud.'

'Are you sure . . . ?'

'Certain. Certain. Certain. I've watched him. He never goes near the shower. How in the name of common decency your parents can stomach him . . .'

'That's just what I've been asking Mummy.'

Dr Ackrington halted and stared at his niece. An observer might have been struck by their resemblance to each other. Barbara was much more like her uncle than her mother, yet while he, in a red-headed edgy sort of way, was remarkably handsome, she contrived to present as good a profile without its accompaniment of distinction. Nobody noticed Barbara's physical assets; her defects were inescapable. Her hair, her clothes, her incoherent gestures, her strangely untutored mannerisms, all combined against her looks and discounted them. She and her uncle stared at each other in silence for some seconds.

'Oh,' said Dr Ackrington at last. 'And what did your mother say?'

Barbara pulled a clown's grimace. 'She *reproved* me,' she said in sepulchral serio-comedy voice.

'Well, don't make faces at me,' snapped her uncle.

A window in the Claires' wing was thrown open, and between the curtains there appeared a vague pink face garnished with a faded moustache, and topped by a thatch of white hair.

'Hullo, James,' said the face crossly. 'Lunch. What's your mother doing, Ba? Where's Simon?'

'She's coming, Daddy. We're all coming. *Simon!*' screamed Barbara.

Mrs Claire, enveloped in a dark red flannel dressing-gown, came panting up from the pools, and hurried into the house.

'Aren't we going to *have* any lunch?' Colonel Claire asked bitterly.

'Of course we are,' said Barbara. 'Why don't you begin, Daddy, if you're in such a hurry? Come on, Uncle James.'

As they went indoors, a young man came round the house and slouched in behind them. He was tall, big-boned and sandy-haired, with a jutting underlip.

'Hullo, Sim,' said Barbara. 'Lunch.'

'Righto.'

'How's the Morse code this morning?'

'Going good,' said Simon.

Dr Ackrington instantly turned on him. 'Is there any creditable reason why you should not say "going well"?' he demanded.

'Huh!' said Simon.

He trailed behind them into the dining-room and they took their places at a long table where Colonel Claire was already seated.

'We won't wait for your mother,' said Colonel Claire, folding his hands over his abdomen. 'For what we are about to receive may the Lord make us truly thankful. Huia!'

Huia came in wearing cap, crackling apron and stiff curls. She looked like a Polynesian goddess who had assumed, on a whim, some barbaric disguise.

'Would you like cold ham, cold mutton, or grilled steak?' she asked, and her voice was as cool and deep as her native forests. As an afterthought she handed Barbara a menu.

'If I ask for steak,' said Dr Ackrington, 'will it be cooked . . .'

'You don't want to eat raw steak, Uncle, do you?' said Barbara.

'Let me finish. If I order steak, will it be cooked or tanned? Will it resemble steak or *biltong?*'

'Steak,' said Huia, musically.

'Is it cooked?'

'Yes.'

Thank you. I shall have ham.'

'What the devil are you driving at, James?' asked Colonel Claire, irritably. 'You talk in riddles. What *do* you want?'

'I want grilled steak. If it is already cooked it will not be grilled steak. It will be boot leather. You can't get a bit of grilled steak in the length and breadth of this country.'

Huia looked politely and inquiringly at Barbara.

'Grill Dr Ackrington a fresh piece of steak, please, Huia.'

Dr Ackrington shook his finger at Huia. 'Five minutes,' he shouted. 'Five minutes! A second longer and it's uneatable. Mind that!' Huia smiled. 'And while she's cooking it I have a letter to read to you,' he added importantly.

Mrs Claire came in. She looked as if she had just returned from a round of charitable visits in an English village. The Claires ordered their lunches and Dr Ackrington took out the letter from Dr Forster.

'This concerns all of you,' he announced.

'Where's Smith?' demanded Colonel Claire suddenly, opening his eyes very wide. His wife and children looked vaguely round the room. 'Did anyone call him?' asked Mrs Claire.

'Don't mind Smith, now,' said Dr Ackrington. 'He's not here and he won't be here. I passed him in Harpoon. He was turning in at a pub and by the look of him it was not the first by two or three. Don't mind him. He's better away.'

'He got a cheque from home yesterday,' said Simon, in his strong New Zealand dialect. 'Boy, oh boy!'

'Don't speak like that, dear,' said his mother. 'Poor Mr Smith, it's such a shame. He's a dear fellow at bottom.'

'Will you allow me to read this letter, or will you not?'

'Do read it, dear. Is it from home?'

Dr Ackrington struck the table angrily with the flat of his hand. His sister leant back in her chair, Colonel Claire stared out through the windows, and Simon and Barbara, after the first two sentences, listened eagerly. When he had finished the letter, which he read in a rapid uninflected patter, Dr Ackrington dropped it on the table and looked about him with an air of complacency.

Barbara whistled. 'I *say*,' she said – 'Geoffrey Gaunt! I *say*.'

'And a servant. And a secretary. I don't quite know what to say, James,' Mrs Claire murmured. 'I'm quite bewildered. I really don't think . . .

'We can't take on a chap like that,' said Simon loudly.

'And why not, pray?' his uncle demanded.

'He'll be no good to us and we'd be no good to him. He'll be used to posh hotels and slinging his weight about with a lot of English servants. What'd we do with a secretary and a manservant? What's he do with them anyway?' Simon went on with an extraordinary air of hostility. 'Is he feeble-minded or what?'

'Feeble-minded!' cried Barbara. 'He's probably the greatest living actor.'

'Well, he can have it for mine,' said Simon.

'For the love of heaven, Agnes, can't you teach your son an intelligent form of speech?'

'If the way I talk isn't good enough for you, Uncle James . . .'

'For pity's sake let's stick to the point,' Barbara cried. 'I'm for having Mr Gaunt and his staff, Sim's against it, Mother's hovering. You're for it, Uncle, I suppose.'

'I fondly imagined that three resident patients might be of some assistance to the exchequer. What does your father say?' He turned to Colonel Claire. 'What do you say, Edward?'

'Eh?' Colonel Claire opened his eyes and mouth and raised his eyebrows in a startled manner. 'Is it about that paper you've got in your hand? I wasn't listening. Read it again.'

'Great God Almighty!'

'Your steak,' said Huia, and placed before Dr Ackrington a strip of ghastly pale and bloated meat from which blood coursed freely over the plate.

During the lively scene which followed, Barbara hooted with frightened laughter, Mrs Claire murmured conciliatory phrases, Simon shuffled his feet, and Huia in turn shook her head angrily, giggled, and uttered soft apologies. Finally she burst into tears and ran back with the steak to the kitchen, where a crash of breaking crockery suggested that she had hurled the dish to the floor. Colonel Claire, after staring in surprise at his brother-in-law for a few seconds, quietly took up Dr Forster's letter and began to read it. This he continued to do until Dr Ackrington had been mollified with a helping of cold meat.

'Who is this Geoffrey Gaunt?' asked Colonel Claire after a long silence.

'Daddy! You *must* know. You saw him in *Jane Eyre* last time we went to the pictures in Harpoon. He's wildly famous.' Barbara paused with her left cheek bulging. 'He was *exactly* my idea of Mr Rochester,' she said ardently.

'Theatrical!' said her father distastefully. 'We don't want that sort.'

'Just what I say,' Simon agreed.

'I'm afraid,' said Mrs Claire, 'that Mr Gaunt would find us very humdrum sort of folk. Don't you think we'd better just keep to our own quiet ways, dear?'

'Mummy, you *are* . . .' Barbara began. Her uncle, speaking with a calm that was really terrifying, interrupted her.

'I haven't the smallest doubt, my dear Agnes,' he said, 'that Gaunt, who is possibly a man of some enterprise and intelligence, would find your quiet ways more than humdrum, as you complacently choose to describe them. I ventured to suggest in my reply to Forster that Gaunt would find few of the amenities and a good deal of comparative discomfort at Wai-ata-tapu. I added something to the effect that I hoped lack of luxury would be compensated for by kindness and by consideration for a man who is unwell. Apparently, I was mistaken. I also fancied that, having gone to considerable expense in building a Spa, your object was to acquire a clientele. Again, I was mistaken. You prefer to rest on your laurels with an alcoholic who doesn't pay his way, and a bounder whom I, for one, regard as a person better suited to confinement in an internment camp.'

Colonel Claire said: 'Are you talking about Questing, James?'

'I am.'

'Well, I wish you wouldn't.'

'May I ask why?'

Colonel Claire laid his knife and fork together, turned scarlet in the face and looked fixedly at the opposite wall.

'Because,' he said, 'I am under an obligation to him.'

There was a long silence.

'I see,' said Dr Ackrington at last.

'I haven't said anything about it to Agnes and the children. I suppose I'm old-fashioned. In my view a man doesn't speak of such matters to his family. But you, James, and you two children have shown so pointedly your dislike of Mr Questing that I'm forced to tell you that I – I cannot afford – I must ask you for my sake to show him more consideration.'

'You can't afford . . . ?' Dr Ackrington repeated. 'Good God, my dear fellow, what have you been up to?'

'Please, James, I hope I need say no more.'

With an air of martyrdom Colonel Claire rose and moved over to the windows. Mrs Claire made a movement to follow him, but he said, 'No, Agnes,' and she stopped at once. 'On second thoughts,' added Colonel Claire, 'I believe we should reconsider our decision about taking these people as guests. I – I'll speak to Questing about it. Please let the subject drop for the moment.' He walked out on to the verandah and past the windows, holding himself very straight, and, still extremely red in the face, disappeared.

'Of all the damned astounding how-d'ye-do's . . .' Dr Ackrington began.

'Oh, James, *don't,*' cried Mrs Claire, and burst into tears.

V

Huia slapped the last plate in the rack, swilled out the sink and turned her back on a moderately tidy kitchen. She lived with her family at a native settlement on the other side of the hill and, as it was her afternoon off, proposed to return there in order to change into her best dress. She walked round the house, crossed the pumice sweep, and set off along a path that skirted the warm lake, rounded the foot of Wai-ata-tapu Hill, and crossed a native thermal reserve that lay in the far side. The sky was overcast and the air oppressively warm and still. Huia moved with a leisurely stride. She seemed to be a part of the landscape, compounded of the same dark medium, quiescent as the earth under the dominion of the sky. White men move across the surface of New Zealand, but the Maori people are of its essence, tranquil or disturbed as the trees and lakes must be, and as much a member of the earth as they.

Huia's path took her through a patch of tall manuka scrub and here she came upon a young man, Eru Saul, a half-caste. He stepped out of the bushes and waited for her, the stump of a cigarette hanging from his lips.

'*Hu!*' said Huia. 'You. What *you* want?'

'It's your day off, isn't it? Come for a walk.'

'Too busy,' said Huia briefly. She moved forward. He checked her, holding her by the arms.

'No,' he said.

'Shut up.'

'I want to talk to you.'

'What about? Same old thing all the time. Talk, talk, talk. You make me tired.'

'You know what. Give us a kiss.'

Huia laughed and rolled her eyes. 'You're mad. Behave yourself. Mrs Claire will go crook if you hang about. I'm going home.'

'Come on,' he muttered, and flung his arms about her. She fought him off, laughing angrily, and he began to upbraid her. 'I'm not posh enough. Going with a *pakeha* now, aren't you? That's right, isn't it?'

'Don't you talk to me like that. You're no good. You're a no-good boy.'

'I haven't got a car and I'm not a thief. Questing's a ruddy thief.'

'That's a big lie,' said Huia blandly. 'He's all right.'

'What's he doing at night on the Peak? He's got no business on the Peak.'

'Talk, talk, talk. All the time.'

'You tell him if he doesn't look out he'll be in for it. How'll you like it if he gets packed up?'

'I don't care.'

'Don't you? *Don't you?*'

'*Oh*, you are silly,' cried Huia, stamping her foot. 'Silly fool! Now get out of my way and let me go home. I'll tell my great-grandfather about you and he'll *makutu* you.'

'Kid-stakes! Nobody's going to put a jinx on me.'

'My great-grandfather can do it,' said Huia and her eyes flashed.

'Listen, Huia,' said Eru. 'You think you can get away with dynamite. OK. But don't come at it with me. And another thing. Next time this joker Questing wants to have you on to go driving, you can tell him from me to lay off. See? Tell him from me, no kidding, that if he tries any more funny stuff, it'll be the stone end of his trips up the Peak.'

'Tell him yourself,' said Huia. She added, in dog Maori, an extremely pointed insult, and taking him off his guard slipped past him and ran round the hill.

Eru stood looking at the ground. His cigarette burnt his lip and he spat it out. After a moment he turned and slowly followed her.

CHAPTER 2

Mr Questing Goes Down for the First Time

'We've heard from Dr Forster, sir,' said Dikon Bell. He glanced anxiously at his employer. When Gaunt stood with his hands rammed down in the pockets of his dressing-gown and his shoulders hunched to his ears one watched one's step. Gaunt turned away from the window, and Dikon noticed apprehensively that his leg was very stiff this morning.

'Ha!' said Gaunt.

'He makes a suggestion.'

'I won't go to that sulphurous resort.'

'Rotorua, sir?'

'Is that what it's called?'

'He realizes you want somewhere quiet, sir. He's made inquiries about another place. It's in the Northland. On the west coast. Subtropical climate.'

'Sulphurous pneumonia?'

'Well, sir, we do want to clear up that leg, don't we?'

'We do.' With one of those swift changes of demeanour by which he so easily commanded devotion, Gaunt turned to his secretary and clapped him on the shoulder. 'I think you're as homesick as I am, Dikon. Isn't that true? You're a New Zealander, of course, but wouldn't you ten thousand times rather be there? In London? Isn't it exactly as if someone you loved was ill and you couldn't get to them?'

'A little like that, certainly,' said Dikon drily.

'I shouldn't keep you here. Go back, my dear chap. I'll find somebody in New Zealand,' said Gaunt with a certain melancholy relish.

'Are you giving me the sack, sir?'

'If only they can patch me up . . .'

'But they will, sir. Dr Forster said the leg ought to respond very quickly to hydrotherapy,' said Dikon with a prime imitation of the doctor's manner. 'They simply hated the sight of me in the Australian recruiting offices. And I fancy I should have little more than refuse value at home. I'm as blind as a bat, you know. Of course, there's office work.'

'You must do what you think best,' said Gaunt gloomily. 'Leave me to stagnate. I'm no good to my country. Ha!'

'If you can call raising twelve thousand for colonial patriotic funds no good . . .'

'I'm a useless hulk,' said Gaunt, and even Dikon was reminded of the penultimate scene in *Jane Eyre*.

'What are you grinning at, blast you?' Gaunt demanded.

'You don't look precisely like a useless hulk. I'll stay a little longer if you'll have me.'

'Well, let's hear about this new place. You're looking wonderfully self-conscious. What hideous surprise have you got up your sleeve?'

Dikon put his attache case on the writing-table and opened it.

'There's a princely fan mail today,' he said, and laid a stack of typed sheets and photographs on one side.

'Good! I adore being adored. How many have written a little something themselves and wonder if I can advise them how to have their plays produced?'

'Four. One lady has sent a copy of her piece. She has dedicated it to you. It's a fantasy.'

'God!'

'Here is Dr Forster's letter, and one enclosed from a Dr James Ackrington who appears to be a celebrity from Harley Street. Perhaps you'd like to read them.'

'I should hate to read them.'

'I think you'd better, sir.'

Gaunt grimaced, took the letters and lowered himself into a chair by the writing-desk. Dikon watched him rather nervously.

Geoffrey Gaunt had spent twenty-seven of his forty-five years on the stage, and the last sixteen had seen him firmly established in the first rank. He was what used to be called a romantic actor, but he was also an intelligent one. His greatest distinction lay in his genius for making an audience hear the sense as well as the music of Shakespearean verse. So accurate and clear was his tracing out of the speeches' content that his art had about it something of mathematical precision and was saved from coldness only by the apparent profundity of his emotional understanding. How far this understanding was instinctive and how far intellectual, not even his secretary, who had been with him for six years, could decide. He was middle-sized, dark, and not particularly striking, but as an actor he possessed the two great assets: his skull was well-shaped, and his hands were beautiful. As for his disposition, Dikon Bell, writing six years before from London to a friend in New Zealand, had said, after a week in Gaunt's employment: 'He's tricky, affected, clever as a bagful of monkeys, a bit of a bounder with the temper of a fury, and no end of an egotist, but I think I'm going to like him.' He had never found reason to revise this first impression.

Gaunt read Dr Forster's note and then Dr Ackrington's letter. 'For heaven's sake,' he cried, 'what sort of an antic is this old person? Have you noted the acid treatment of his relations? Does he call this letter a recommendation? Discomfort leavened with inefficient kindness is the bait he offers. Moreover, there's a dirty little knock at me in the last paragraph. If Forster wants me to endure the place, one would have thought his policy would have been to suppress the letter. He's a poor psychologist.'

'The psychology,' said Dikon modestly, 'is mine. Forster wanted to suppress the letter. I took it upon myself to show it to you. I thought that if you jibbed at the Claires, sir, you wouldn't be able to resist Dr Ackrington.'

Gaunt shot a suspicious glance at his secretary. 'You're too clever by half, my friend,' he said.

'And he *does* say,' Dikon added persuasively, 'he *does* say "the mud may be miraculous".'

Gaunt laughed, made an abrupt movement, and drew in his breath sharply.

'Isn't it worth enduring the place if it puts your legs right, sir? And at least we could get on with the book.'

'Certain it is I can't write in this bloody hotel. *How* I hate hotels. Dikon,' cried Gaunt with an assumption of boyish enthusiasm, 'shall we fly to America? Shall we do *Henry V* in New York? They'd take it, you know, just now. *"And Crispin, Crispian shall ne'er go by . . ."* God, I think I must play Henry in New York.'

'Wouldn't you rather play him in London, sir, on a fit-up stage with the blitz for battle noises off?'

'Of course I would, damn you.'

'Why not try this place? At least it may turn out to be copy for the Life. Thermal *divertissements*. And then, when you're fit and ready to hit 'em . . . London.'

'You talk like a nanny in her dotage,' said Gaunt fretfully. 'I suppose you and Colly have plotted this frightfulness between you. Where is Colly?'

'Ironing your trousers, sir.'

'Tell him to come here.'

Dikon spoke on the telephone and in a moment the door opened to admit a wisp of a man with a face that resembled a wrinkled kid glove. This was Gaunt's dresser and personal servant, Alfred Colly. Colly had been the dresser provided by the management when Gaunt, a promising young leading man with no social background, had made his first great success. After a phenomenal run, Colly accepted Gaunt's offer of permanent employment, but had never adopted the technique of a manservant. His attitudes towards his employer held the balance between extreme familiarity and a cheerful recognition of Gaunt's prestige. He laid the trousers that he carried over the back of a chair, folded his hands and blinked.

'You've heard all about this damned hot spot, no doubt?' said Gaunt.

'That's right, sir,' said Colly. 'Going to run mudlarks, aren't we?'

'I haven't said so.'

'It's about time we did something about ourself though, isn't it, sir? We're not sleeping as pretty as we'd like, are we? And how about our leg?'

'Oh, you go to hell,' said Gaunt.

'There's a gentleman downstairs, sir, wants to see you. Come in over an hour ago. They told him in the office you were seeing nobody and he said that's all right and give in his card. They say it's no use, you only see visitors by appointment, and he comes back with that's just too bad and sits in the lounge with a Scotch and soda, reading the paper and watching the door.'

'That won't do him much good,' said Dikon. 'Mr Gaunt's not going out. The masseur will be here in half an hour. What's this man look like? Pressman?'

'Noüe!' said Colly, with the cockney's singular emphasis. 'More like business. Hard. Smooth worsted suiting. Go-getter type. I was thinking you might like to see him, Mr Bell.'

'Why?'

'I was thinking you might. Satisfy him.'

Dikon looked fixedly at Colly and saw the faintest vibration of his left eyelid.

'Perhaps I'd better get rid of him,' he said. 'Did they give you his card?'

Colly dipped his finger and thumb in a pocket of his black alpaca coat. 'Persistent sort of bloke, sir,' he said, and fished out a card.

'Oh, get rid of him, Dikon, for God's sake,' said Gaunt. 'You know all the answers. I won't leer out of advertisements, I won't open fetes, I won't attend amateur productions, I'm accepting no invitations. I think New Zealand's marvellous. I wish I was in London. If it's anything to do with the war effort, reserve your answer. If they want me to do something for the troops, I will if I can.'

Dikon went down to the lounge. In the lift he looked at the visitor's card:

MR MAURICE QUESTING
Wai-ata-tapu Thermal Springs.

Scribbled across the bottom he read: 'May I have five minutes? Matter of interest to yourself. MQ.'

II

Mr Maurice Questing was about fifty years old and so much a type that a casual observer would have found it difficult to describe him. He might have been any one of a group of heavy men playing cards on a rug in the first-class carriage of a train. He appeared in triplicate at private bars, hotel lounges, business meetings and race courses. His features were blurred and thick, his eyes sharp. His clothes always looked expensive and new. His speech, both in accent and in choice of words, was an affair of mass production rather than selection. It suggested that wherever he went he would instinctively adopt the cheapest, the slickest and the most popular commercial phrases of the community in which he found himself. Yet though he was as voluble as a radio advertiser, shooting out his machine-turned phrases in a loud voice, and with a great air of assurance, every word he uttered seemed synthetic and quite unrelated to his thoughts. His conversation was full of the near-Americanisms that are part of the New Zealand dialect, but they, too, sounded dubious, and it was impossible to guess at his place of origin though he sometimes spoke of himself vaguely as a native of New South Wales. He was a successful man of business.

When Dikon Bell walked into the hotel lobby, Mr Questing at once flung down his paper and rose to his feet.

'Pardon me if I speak in error,' he said, 'but is this Mr Bell?'

'Er, yes,' said Dikon, who still held the card in his fingers.

'Mr Gaunt's private secretary?'

'Yes.'

'That's great,' said Mr Questing, shaking hands ruthlessly, and breaking into laughter. 'I'm very pleased to meet you, Mr Bell. I know you're a busy man, but I'd be very very happy if you could spare me five minutes.'

'Well, I . . .'

'That's fine,' said Mr Questing, jamming a flat pale thumb against a bell-push. 'Great work! Sit down.'

Dikon sat sedately on a small chair, crossed his legs, joined his hands, and looked attentively over his glasses at Mr Questing.

'How's the Big Man?' Mr Questing asked.

'Mr Gaunt? Not very well, I'm afraid.'

'So I understand. So I understand. Well, now, Mr Bell, I had hoped for a word with him, but I've got an idea that a little chat with you will be very very satisfactory. What'll you have?'

Dikon refused a drink. Mr Questing ordered whisky and soda. 'Yes,' said Mr Questing with a heartiness that suggested a complete understanding between them. 'Yes. That's fine. Well now, Mr Bell, I'm going to tell you, flat out, that I think I'm in a position to help you. Now!'

'I see,' said Dikon, 'that you come from Wai-ata-tapu Springs.'

'That is the case. Yes. Yes, I'm going to be quite frank with you, Mr Bell. I'm going to tell you that not only do I come from the Springs, but I've got a very considerable interest in the Springs.'

'Do you mean that you own the place? I thought a Colonel and Mrs Claire . . .'

'Well, now, Mr Bell, shall we just take things as they come? I'm going to bring you right into my confidence about the Springs. The Springs mean a lot to me.'

'Financially?' asked Dikon mildly. 'Therapeutically? Or sentimentally?'

Mr Questing, who had looked restlessly at Dikon's tie, shoes and hands, now took a furtive glance at his face.

'Don't make it too hot,' he said merrily.

With a rapid movement suggestive of sleight-of-hand he produced from an inner pocket a sheaf of pamphlets which he laid before Dikon. 'Read these at your leisure. May I suggest that you bring them to Mr Gaunt's notice?'

'Look here, Mr Questing,' said Dikon briskly, 'would you mind, awfully, if we came to the point? You've evidently discovered that we've heard about this place. You've come to recommend it. That's very kind of you, but I gather your motive isn't purely altruistic. You've spoken of frankness so perhaps you won't object to my asking again if you've a financial interest in Wai-ata-tapu.'

Mr Questing laughed uproariously and said that he saw they understood each other. His conversation became thick with hints and evasions. After a minute or two Dikon saw that he himself was being offered some sort of inducement. Mr Questing told him repeatedly that he would be looked after, that he would have every cause for personal gratification if Geoffrey Gaunt decided to take the cure. It was not by any means the first scene of its kind. Dikon was mildly entertained, and, while he listened to Mr Questing, turned over the pamphlets. The medical recommendations seemed very good. A set of rooms – Mr Questing called it a suite – would be theirs. Mr Questing would see to it that the rooms were refurnished. Dikon's eyebrows went up, and Mr Questing, becoming very confidential, said that he believed in doing things in a big way. He was not, he said, going to pretend that he didn't recognize the value of such a guest to the Springs. Dikon distrusted him more with every phrase he uttered, but he began to think that if such enormous efforts were to be made, Gaunt should be tolerably comfortable at Wai-ata-tapu. He put out a feeler.

'I understand,' he said, 'that there is a resident doctor.'

He was surprised to see Mr Questing change colour. 'Dr Tonks,' Questing said, 'doesn't actually reside at the Springs, Mr Bell. He's at Harpoon. Only a few minutes by road. A very, very fine doctor.'

'I meant Dr James Ackrington.'

Mr Questing did not answer immediately. He offered Dikon a cigarette, lit one himself and rang the bell again.

'Dr Ackrington,' Dikon repeated.

'Oh, yes. Ye-es. The old doctor. Quite a character.'

'Doesn't he live at the hostel?'

'That is correct. Yes. That is the case. The old doctor's retired now, I understand.'

'He's something of an authority on muscular and nervous complaints, isn't he?'

'Is that so?' said Mr Questing. 'Well, well, well. The old doctor, eh? Quite a character. Well, now, Mr Bell, I've a little suggestion to make. I've been wondering if you'd be interested in a wee trip to the Springs. I'm driving back there tomorrow. It's a six hours' run and I'd be very very delighted to take you with me. Of course the suite won't be poshed up by then. You'll see us in the raw, sir, but any suggestions you cared to make . . .'

'Do you live there, Mr Questing?'

'You can't keep me away from the Springs for long,' cried Mr Questing evasively. 'Now about this suggestion of mine . . .'

'It's very kind of you,' said Dikon thoughtfully. He rose to his feet and held out his hand. 'I'll tell Mr Gaunt about it. Thank you so much.'

Mr Questing wrung his hand excruciatingly.

'Goodbye,' said Dikon politely.

'I'm staying here tonight, Mr Bell, and I'll be right on the spot if . . .'

'Oh, yes. Perfectly splendid. Goodbye.'

He returned to his employer.

III

Late on the afternoon of Saturday the eighteenth, old Rua Te Kahu sat on the crest of a hill that rose in an unbroken curve above his native village. The hill formed a natural barrier between the Maori reserve lands and the thermal resort of Wai-ata-tapu Springs where the Claires lived. From where he sat Rua looked down to his right upon the sulphur-corroded roof of the Claires' house, and to his left upon the smaller hip-roofs of his own people's dwelling houses and shacks. From each side of the hill rose plumes of steam, for the native *pa* was built near its own thermal pools. Rua, therefore, sat in a place that became him well. Behind his head, and softened by wreaths of steam, was the shape of Rangi's Peak. At his feet, in the warm friable soil, grew manuka scrub.

He was an extremely old man, exactly how old he did not choose to say; but his father, a chief of the Te Rarawa tribe, had set his mark to the Treaty of Waitangi, not many years before Rua, his youngest child, was born. Rua's grandfather, Rewi, a chieftain and a cannibal, was a neolithic man. To find his European counterpart, one would look back beyond the dawn of civilization. Rua himself had witnessed the full impact of the white man's ways upon a people living in a stone age. He had in turn been warrior, editor of a native newspaper, and member of Parliament. In his extreme age he had sloughed his European habits and returned to his own sub-tribe and to a way of life that was an echo in a minor key of his earliest youth.

'My great-great-grandfather is a hundred,' bragged little Hoani Smith at the Harpoon primary school. 'He is the oldest man in New Zealand. He is nearly as old as God. *Hu!*'

Rua was dressed in a shabby suit. About his shoulders he wore a blanket, for nowadays he felt the cold. Sartorially he was rather disreputable, but for all that he had about him an air of greatness. His head was magnificent, long and shapely. His nose was a formidable beak, his lips thin and uncompromising. His eyes still held their brilliance. He was a patrician, and looked down the long lines of his ancestry until they met in one of the canoes of the first Polynesian sea rovers. One would have said that his descent must have been free from the coarsening of Melanesian blood. But for his colour, a light brown, he looked for all the world like a Jacobite patriot's notion of a Highland chieftain.

Every evening he climbed to the top of the hill and smoked a pipe, beginning his slow ascent an hour before sunset. Sometimes one of his grandchildren, or an old crony of his own clan, would go up with him, but more often he sat there alone, lost, as it seemed, in a long perspective of recollections. The Claires, down at the Springs, would glance up and see him appearing larger than human against the sky and very still. Or Huia, sitting on the bank behind the house when she should have been scrubbing potatoes, would wave to him and send him a long-drawn-out cry of greeting in his own tongue. She was one of his many great-great-grandchildren.

This evening he found much to interest him down at the Springs. A covered van had turned in from the main road and had lurched and skidded down the track which the Claires called their drive, until it pulled up at their front door. Excited noises came from inside the house. Old Rua heard his great-granddaughter's voice and Miss Barbara Claire's unmelodious laughter. There were bumping sounds. A large car came down the track and pulled up at the edge of the sweep. Mr Maurice Questing got out of it followed by a younger man. Rua leant forward a little, grasped the head of his stick firmly and rested his chin on his knotted hands. He seemed rooted in the hilltop, and part of its texture. After a long pause he heard a sound for which his ears had inherited an acute awareness. Someone was coming up the track behind him. The dry scrub brushed against approaching legs. In a moment or two a man stood beside him on the hilltop.

'Good evening, Mr Smith,' said old Rua without turning his head.

'G'day, Rua.'

The man lurched forward and squatted beside Te Kahu. He was a European, but his easy adoption of this native posture suggested a familiarity with the ways of the Maori people. He was thin, and baldish. His long jaw was ill-shaved. His skin hung loosely from the bones of his face and was unwholesome in colour. There was an air of raffishness about him. His clothes were seedy. Over them he wore a raincoat that was dragged out of shape by a bottle in an inner pocket. He began to make a cigarette, and his fingers, deeply stained with nicotine, were unsteady. He smelt very strongly of stale spirits.

'Great doings down at the Springs,' he said.

'They seem to be busy,' said Rua tranquilly.

'Haven't you heard? They've got a big pot coming to stay. That's his secretary, that young chap that's just come. You'd think it was royalty. They've been making it pretty solid for everybody down there. Hauling everything out and shifting us all round. I got sick of it and sloped off.'

'A distinguished guest should be given a fitting welcome.'

'He's only an actor.'

'Mr Geoffrey Gaunt. He is a man of great distinction.'

'Then you know all about it, do you?'

'I think so,' said old Rua.

Smith licked his cigarette and hung it from the corner of his mouth.

'Questing's at the back of it,' he said. Rua stirred slightly. 'He's kidded this Gaunt the mud'll fix his leg for him. He's falling over himself polishing the old dump up. You ought to see the furniture. Questing!' added Smith viciously. 'By cripes, I'd like to see that joker get what's coming to him.'

Unexpectedly Rua gave a subterranean chuckle.

'Look!' Smith said. 'He's got something coming to him all right, that joker. The old doctor's got it in for him, and so's everybody else but Claire. I reckon Claire's not so keen, either, but Questing's put him where he just *can't* squeal. That's what I reckon.'

He lit the cigarette and looked out of the corners of his eyes at Rua. 'You don't say much,' he said. His hand moved shakily over the bulge in his mackintosh. 'Like a spot?' he asked.

'No, thank you. What should I say? It is no business of mine.'

'Look, Rua,' said Smith energetically. 'I like your people. I get on with them. Always have. That's a fact, isn't it?'

'You are intimate with some of my people.'

'Yes. Well, I came up here to tell you something. Something about Questing.' Smith paused. The quiet of evening had impregnated the countryside. The air was clear and the smallest noises from below reached the hilltop with uncanny sharpness. Down in the native reserve a collection of small brown boys milled about, squabbling. Several elderly women with handkerchiefs tied over their heads sat round one of the cooking pools. The smell of steaming sweet potatoes was mingled with the fumes of sulphur. On the other side, the van crawled up to the main road sounding its horn. From inside the Claires' house hollow bumping noises still continued. The sun was now behind Rangi's Peak.

'Questing's got a great little game on,' said Smith. 'He's going round your younger lot talking about teams of *poi* girls and kids diving for pennies, and all the rest of it. He's offering big money. He says he doesn't see why the Arawas down at Rotorua should be the only tribe to profit by the tourist racket.'

Rua got slowly to his feet. He turned away from the Springs side of the hill to the east and looked down into his own hamlet, now deep in shadow.

'My people are well contented,' he said. 'We are not Arawas. We go our own way.'

'And another thing. He's been talking about having curios for sale. He's been nosing round. Asking about old times. Over at the Peak.' Smith's voice slid into an uncertain key. He went on with an air of nervousness. 'Someone's told him about Rewi's axe,' he said.

Rua turned, and for the first time looked fully at his companion.

'That's not so good, is it?' said Smith.

'My grandfather Rewi,' Rua said, 'was a man of prestige. His axe was dedicated to the god Tane and was named after him, Toki-poutangata-o-Tane. It was sacred. Its burial place, also, is sacred and secret.'

'Questing reckons it's somewhere on the Peak. He reckons there's a lot of stuff over on the Peak that might be exploited. He's talking about half-day trips to see the places of interest, with one of your people to act as guide and tell the tale.'

'The Peak is a native reserve.'

'He reckons he could square that up all right.'

'I am an old man,' said Rua affably, 'but I am not yet dead. He will not find any guides among my people.'

'Won't he! You ask Eru Saul. He knows what Questing's after.'

'Eru is not a satisfactory youth. He is a bad *pakeha* Maori.'

'Eru doesn't like the way Questing plays up to young Huia. He reckons Questing is kidding her to find guides for him.'

'He will not find guides,' Rua repeated.

'Money talks, you know.'

'So will the tapu of my grandfather's *toki-poutangata*.'

Smith looked curiously at the old man. 'You really believe that, don't you?' he said.

'I am a *rangitira*. My father attended an ancient school of learning. He was a tohunga. I don't believe, Mr Smith,' said Rua with a chuckle. 'I know.'

'You'll never get a white man to credit supernatural stories, Rua. Even your own younger lot don't think much . . .'

Rua interrupted him. The full magnificence of his voice sounded richly on the evening air. 'Our people,' Rua said, 'stand between two worlds. In a century we have had to swallow the progress of nineteen hundred years. Do you wonder that we suffer a little from evolutionary dyspepsia? We are loyal members of the great commonwealth; your enemies are our enemies. You speak of the young people. They are like voyagers whose canoes are in a great ocean between two countries. Sometimes they behave objectionably and are naughty children. Sometimes they are taught very bad tricks by their *pakeha* friends.' Rua looked full at Smith, who fidgeted. 'There are *pakeha* laws to prevent my young men from making fools of themselves with whisky and too much beer,' said Rua tranquilly, 'but there are also *pakehas* who help them to break these laws. The *pakehas* teach our young maidens that they should be quiet girls and not have babies before they are married, but in my own *hapu* there is a small boy whom we call Hoani Smith, though in law he has no right to that name.'

'Hell, Rua, that's an old story,' Smith muttered.

'Let me tell you another old story. Many years ago, when I was a youth, a maiden of our *hapu* lost her way in the mists on Rangi's Peak. In ignorance, intending no sacrilege, she came upon the place where my grandfather rests with his weapons, and, being hungry, ate a small piece of cooked food that she carried with her. In that place it was an act of horrible sacrilege. When the mists cleared, she discovered her crime and returned in terror to her people. She told her story, and was sent out to this hill while her case was discussed. At night she thought she would creep back, but she missed her way. She fell into Taupo-tapu, the boiling mud pool. Everybody in the village heard her scream. Next morning her dress was thrown up, rejected by the spirit of the pool. When your friend Mr Questing speaks of my grandfather's *toki,* relate this story to him. Tell him the girl's scream can still be heard sometimes at night. I am going home now,' Rua added, and drew his blanket about him with precisely the same gesture that his grandfather had used to adjust his feather cloak. 'Is it true, Mr Smith, that Mr Questing has said a great many times that when he takes over the Springs, you will lose your job?'

'He can have it for mine,' said Smith angrily. 'That'll do me all right. He doesn't have to talk about the sack. When Questing's the boss down there, I'm turning the job up.' He dragged the whisky bottle from his pocket and fumbled with the cork.

'And yet,' Rua said, 'it's a very soft job. You are going to drink? I shall go home. Good evening.'

IV

Dikon Bell, marooned in the Claires' private sitting-room, stared at faded photographs of regimental Anglo–Indians, at the backs of blameless novels, and at a framed poster of the Cotswolds in the spring. The poster was the work of a celebrated painter, and was at once gay, ordered, and delicate – a touching sequence of greens and blues. It made Dikon, the New Zealander, ache for England. By shifting his gaze slightly, he saw, framed in the sitting-room window, a landscape aloof from man. Its beauty was perfectly articulate yet utterly remote. Against his will he was moved by it as an unmusical listener may be profoundly disturbed by sound forms that he is unable to comprehend. He had travelled a great deal in his eight years' absence from New Zealand and had seen places famous for their antiquities, but it seemed to him that the landscape he now watched through the Claires' window was of an early age far more remote than any of these. It did not carry the scars of lost civilization. Rather, it seemed to make nothing of time, for it was still primeval and its only stigmata were those of neolithic age. Dikon, who longed to be in London, recognized in himself an affinity with this indifferent and profound country, and resented its attraction.

He wondered what Gaunt would say to it. He was to return to his employer next day by bus and train, a long and fatiguing business. Gaunt had brought a car, and on the following day he, Dikon and Colly would set out for Wai-ata-tapu. They had made many such journeys in many countries. Always at the end there had been expensive hotels or flats and lavish attention – amenities that Gaunt accepted as necessities of existence. Dikon was gripped by a sensation of panic. He had been mad to urge this place with its air of amateurish incompetence, its appalling Mr Questing, its incredible Claires, whose air of breeding would seem merely to underline their complacency. A bush pub might have amused Gaunt; the Springs would bore him to exasperation.

A figure passed the window and stood in the doorway. It was Miss Claire. Dikon, whose job obliged him to observe such things, noticed that her cotton dress had been most misguidedly garnished with a neck bow of shiny ribbon, that her hair was precisely the wrong length, and that she used no make-up.

'Mr Bell,' said Barbara, 'we were wondering if you'd advise us about Mr Gaunt's *rooms*. Where to *put* things. I'm afraid you'll find us very *primitive*.' She laid tremendous stress on odd syllables and words, and as she did so turned up her eyes in a deprecating manner and pulled down the corners of her mouth like a lugubrious clown.

'Comedy stuff,' thought Dikon. 'Alas, alas, she means to be funny.' He said that he would be delighted to see the rooms, and, nervously fingering his tie, followed her along the verandah.

The wing at the east end of the house, corresponding with the Claires' private rooms at the west end, had been turned into a sort of flat for Gaunt, Dikon and Colly. It consisted of four rooms: two small bedrooms, one tiny bedroom, and a slightly larger bedroom which had been converted into Mr Questing's idea of a celebrity study. In this apartment were assembled two chromium-steel chairs, one large armchair, and a streamlined desk, all of rather bad design, and with the dealer's tabs still attached to them. The floor was newly carpeted, and the windows in process of being freshly curtained by Mrs Claire. Mr Questing, wearing a cigar as if it were a sort of badge of office, lolled carelessly in the armchair. On Dikon's entrance he sprang to his feet.

'Well, well, well,' cried Mr Questing gaily, 'how's the young gentleman?'

'Quite well, thank you,' said Dikon, who had spent the greater part of the day motoring with Mr Questing, and had become reconciled to these constant inquiries.

'Is this service,' Mr Questing went on, waving his cigar at the room, 'or is it? Forty-eight hours ago I hadn't the pleasure of your acquaintance, Mr Bell. After our little chat yesterday, I felt so optimistic I just had to get out and get going. I went to the finest furnishing firm in Auckland, and I told the manager, I told him: "Look," I told him. "I'll take this stuff, if you can get it to Wai-ata-tapu, Harpoon, by tomorrow afternoon. And if not, not." That's the way I like to do things, Mr Bell.'

'I hope you have explained that even now Gaunt may not decide to come,' said Dikon. 'You have all taken a great deal of trouble, Mrs Claire.'

Mrs Claire looked doubtfully from Questing to Dikon. 'I'm afraid,' she said plaintively, 'that I don't really quite appreciate very up-to-date furniture. I always think a home-like atmosphere, no matter how shabby . . . However.'

Questing cut in, and Dikon only half listened to another dissertation on the necessity of moving with the times. He was jerked into full awareness when Questing, with an air of familiarity, addressed himself to Barbara. 'And what's Babs got to say about it?' he asked, lowering his voice to a rich and offensive purr. Dikon saw her step backwards. It was an instinctive movement, he thought, uncontrollable as a reflex jerk, but less ungainly than her usual habit. Its effect on Dikon was as simple and as automatic as itself; he felt a stab of sympathy and a protective impulse. She was no longer regrettable; she was, for a moment, rather touching. Surprised, and a little disturbed, he looked away from Barbara to Mrs Claire, and saw that her plump hands were clenched among sharp folds of the shining chintz. He felt that a little scene of climax had been enacted. It was disturbed by the appearance of another figure. Limping steps sounded on the verandah, and the doorway was darkened. A stocky man, elderly but still red-headed and extremely handsome in an angry sort of way, stood glaring at Questing.

'Oh, James,' Mrs Claire murmured, 'there you are, old man. You haven't met Mr Bell. My brother, Dr Ackrington.'

As they shook hands, Dikon saw that Barbara had moved close to her uncle.

'Have a good run up?' asked Dr Ackrington, throwing a needle-sharp glance at Dikon. 'Ever see anything more disgraceful than the roads? I've been fishing.'

Startled by this *non sequitur,* Dikon murmured politely: 'Indeed?'

'If you can call it fishing. Hope you and Gaunt aren't counting on catching any trout. What with native reserves and the damned infamous behaviour of white poaching cads, there's not a fish to be had in twenty miles.'

'Now, now, now, Doctor,' said Questing in a great hurry. 'We can't let you get away with that. Why, the greatest little trout streams in New Zealand . . .'

'D'you enjoy being called "Mister"?' Dr Ackrington demanded, so loudly that Dikon gave a nervous jump. Questing said uneasily: 'Not much.'

'Then don't call me "Doctor",' commanded Dr Ackrington. Questing laughed uproariously. 'That's just too bad,' he said.

Dr Ackrington looked round the room. 'Good God,' he said, 'what are you doing with the place?'

'Mr Questing,' began Mrs Claire, 'has very kindly . . .'

'I might have recognized the authentic touch,' said her brother, turning his back on the room. 'Staying here tonight are you, Bell? I'd like a word with you. Come along to my room when you've a moment.'

'Thank you, sir,' said Dikon.

Dr Ackrington looked through the doorway. 'The star boarder,' he said, 'is returning in his usual condition. Mr Bell is to be treated to a comprehensive view of our amenities.'

They all looked through the doorway. Dikon saw a shambling figure cross the pumice sweep and approach the verandah.

'Oh dear!' said Mrs Claire. 'I'm afraid . . . James, dear, could you . . . ?'

Dr Ackrington limped out to the verandah. The newcomer saw, stumbled to a halt, and dragged a bottle from the pocket of his raincoat.

To Dikon, watching through the window, the intrusion of a drunken white figure into the native landscape was at once preposterous and rather pathetic. A clear light, reflected from the pumice track, rimmed the folds of his shabby garments. He stood there, drooping and lonely, and turned the whisky bottle in his hand, staring at it as if it were the focal point for some fuddled meditation. Presently he raised his head and looked at Dr Ackrington.

'Well, Smith,' said Dr Ackrington.

'You're a sport, Doc,' said Smith. 'There's a couple of snifters left. Come on and have one.'

'You'll do better to keep it,' said Dr Ackrington quite mildly.

Smith peered beyond him into the room. His eyes narrowed. He lurched forward to the verandah. 'I'll deal with this,' said Questing importantly, and strode out to meet him. They confronted each other. Questing, planted squarely on the verandah edge, made much of his cigar; Smith clung to the post and stared up at him.

'You clear out of this, Smith,' said Questing.

'You get to hell yourself,' said Smith distinctly. He looked past Questing to the group in the doorway, and very solemnly took off his hat. 'Present company excepted,' he added.

'Did you hear what I said?'

'Is that the visitor?' Smith asked loudly, and pointed at Dikon. 'Is that the reason why we're all sweating our guts up? That? Let's have a better look at it. Gawd, what a sissy.'

Dikon wondered confusedly which of the party felt most embarrassed. Dr Ackrington made a loud barking noise, Barbara broke into agonized laughter, Mrs Claire rushed into a spate of apologies, Dikon himself attempted to suggest by gay inquiring glances that he had not understood the tenor of Smith's remarks. He might have spared himself the trouble. Smith made a plunge at the verandah step shouting: 'Look at the little bastard.' Questing attempted to stop him, and the scene mounted in a rapid crescendo. Dikon, Mrs Claire and Barbara remained in the room, Dr Ackrington on the verandah appeared to hold a watching brief, while Questing and Smith yelled industriously in each other's faces. The climax came when Questing again attempted to shove Smith away from the verandah. Smith drove his fist in Questing's face and lost his balance. They fell simultaneously.

The noise stopped as suddenly as it had begun. An inexplicable and ridiculous affair changed abruptly into a piece of convincing melodrama. Dikon had seen many such a set-up at the cinema studios. Smith, shaky and bloated, crouched where he had fallen and mouthed at Questing. Questing got to his feet and dabbed at the corner of his mouth with his handkerchief. His cigar lay smoking on the ground between them. It was a shot in Technicolor, for Rangi's Peak was now tinctured with such a violence of purple as is seldom seen outside the theatre, and in the middle distance rose the steam of the hot pools.

Dikon waited for a bit of rough dialogue to develop and was not disappointed.

'By God,' Questing said, exploring his jaw, 'you'll get yours for this. You're sacked.'

'You're not my bloody boss.'

'I'll bloody well get you the sack, don't you worry. When I'm in charge here . . .'

'That will do,' said Dr Ackrington crisply.

'What *is* all this?' a peevish voice demanded. Colonel Claire, followed by Simon, appeared round the wing of the house. Smith got to his feet.

'You'll have to get rid of this man, Colonel,' said Questing.

'What's he done?' Simon demanded.

'I socked him.' Smith took Simon by the lapels of his coat. 'You look out for yourselves,' he said. 'It's not only me he's after. Your dad won't sack me, will he, Sim?'

'We'll see about that,' Questing said.

'But *why* . . .' Colonel Claire began, and was cut short by his brother-in-law.

'If I may interrupt for a moment,' said Dr Ackrington acidly, 'I suggest that I take Mr Bell to my room. Unless, of course, he prefers a ring-side seat. Will you come and have a drink, Bell?'

Dikon thankfully accepted, leaving the room in a gale of apologies from Mrs Claire and Barbara. Questing, who seemed to have recovered his temper, followed them up with a speech in which anxiety, propitiation and a kind of fawning urgency were most disagreeably mingled. He was cut short by Dr Ackrington.

'Possibly,' Dr Ackrington said, 'Mr Bell may prefer to form his own opinion of this episode. No doubt he has seen a chronic alcoholic before now, and will not attach much significance to anything this particular specimen may choose to say.'

'Yes, yes. Of course,' Dikon murmured unhappily.

'As for the behaviour of Other Persons,' Dr Ackrington continued, 'there again, he may, as I do, form his own opinion. Come along, Bell.'

Dikon followed him along the verandah to his own room, a grimly neat apartment with a hideous desk.

'Sit down,' said Dr Ackrington. He wrenched open the door of a home-made cupboard, and took out a bottle and two tumblers. 'I can only offer you whisky,' he said. 'With Smith's horrible example before you, you may not like the idea. Afraid I don't go in for modern rot-gut.'

'Thank you,' said Dikon, 'I should like whisky. May I ask who he is?'

'Smith? He's a misfit, a hopeless fellow. No good in him at all. Drifted out here as a boy. Agnes, my sister, who is something of a snob, talks loosely about him being a public-school man. Her geese are invariably swans, but I suppose this suggestion is within the bounds of possibility. Smith may have originated in some ill-conducted establishment of dubious gentility. Sometimes their early habits of speech go down the wind with their self-respect. Sometimes they keep it up even in the gutter. They used to be called remittance men, and in this extraordinary country received a good deal of entirely misguided sympathy from native-born fools. That suit you?'

'Thank you, sir,' said Dikon, taking his drink.

'My sister chooses to regard him as a sort of invalid. Some instinct must have led him ten years ago to the Spring. It has proved to be an ideal battening ground. They give him his keep and a wage, in exchange for idling about the place with an axe in his hand and a bottle in his pocket. When his cheque comes from home he drinks himself silly, and my sister Agnes gives him beef tea and prays for him. He's a complete waster but he won't trouble you, I fancy. I confess that this evening I was almost in sympathy with him. He did what I have longed to do for the past three months.' Dikon glanced up quickly. 'He drove his fist into Questing's face,' Dr Ackrington explained. 'Here's luck to you,' he added. They drank to each other.

'Well,' said Dr Ackrington after a pause, 'you will doubtless lose no time in returning to Auckland and telling your principal to avoid this place like the devil.'

As this pretty well described Dikon's intention he could think of nothing to say, and made a polite murmuring.

'If it is of any interest, you may as well know you have seen it at its worst. Smith is not always drunk and Questing is not always with us.'

'Not? But I thought . . .'

'He absents himself. I rejoice in the event and deplore the motive. However.'

Dr Ackrington glared portentously into his glass and cleared his throat. Dikon waited for a moment, but his companion showed no sign of developing his theme. Dikon was to learn that Dr Ackrington could exploit with equal mastery the embarrassing phrase and the disconcerting silence.

'Since we have mentioned him,' Dikon began nervously, 'I confess I'm in a state of some confusion about Mr Questing. May I ask if he is actually the – if Wai-ata-tapu Springs is his property?'

'No,' said Dr Ackrington.

'I only ask,' Dikon continued in a hurry, 'because you see I was approached in the first instance by Mr Questing. Although I've warned him that Gaunt may decide against the Springs, he has been at extraordinary pains and really very considerable expense to – to alter existing arrangements and so on. And I mean – well, Dr Forster's note suggested that it was to Colonel and Mrs Claire that we should apply.'

'So it is.'

'I see. But – Questing?'

'If you decide against the Springs,' said Dr Ackrington, 'you should convey your decision to my sister.'

'But,' Dikon repeated obstinately, 'Questing?'

'Ignore him.'

'Oh.'

Steps sounded outside the window, and voices: Smith's voice slurred but vicious; Colonel Claire's high-pitched, perhaps a little hysterical; and Questing's the voice of a bully. As they came nearer, odd sentences separated out from the general rumpus.

'. . . if the Colonel's satisfied – it's not a fair pop.'

'. . . never mind that. You've been asking for it and you'll get it.'

'. . . sack me and see what you get, you – '

'. . . most disgraceful scene – force my hand . . .'

'. . . kick you out tomorrow.'

'This is too much,' Colonel Claire cried out. 'I've stood a great deal, Questing, but I must remind you that I still have some authority here.'

'Is that so? Where do you get it from? You'd better watch your step, Claire.'

'By God,' Smith roared out suddenly, 'you'd better watch yours.'

Dr Ackrington opened the door and stood on the threshold. Complete silence followed this move. Through the open door came a particularly strong wave of sulphurous air.

'I suggest, Edward,' Dr Ackrington said, 'that you continue your conversation in the laundry. Mr Bell has no doubt formed the opinion that we do not possess one.'

He shut the door. 'Let me give you another drink,' he said courteously.

CHAPTER 3

Gaunt at the Springs

'Five days ago,' said Gaunt, 'you dangled this place before me like some atrocious bait. Now you do nothing but bemoan its miseries. You are strangely inconsistent.'

'In the interval,' said Dikon, wrenching the car out of a pot hole, and changing down, 'I have seen the place. I implore you to remember, sir, that you have been warned.'

'You overdid it. You painted it in macabre colours. My curiosity was stimulated. For pity's sake, my dear Dikon, drive a little away from the edge of the abyss. Can this mountain goat track possibly be the main road?'

'It's the only road from Harpoon to Wai-ata-tapu, sir. You wanted somewhere quiet, you know, and these are not mountains. There are no mountains in the Northland. The big stuff is in the South.'

'I'm afraid you're a scenic snob. To me this is a mountain. When I fall over the edge of this precipice, I shall not be found with a sneer on my lips because the drop was merely five hundred feet instead of a thousand. There's a most unpleasant smell about this place.'

'It's the thermal smell. People are said to get to like it.'

'Nonsense. How are you travelling, Colly?'

Fenced in by luggage in the back seat, Colly replied that he kept his eyes closed at the curves. 'I didn't seem to notice it so much this morning in them forests,' he added. 'It's dynamite in the open.'

The road corkscrewed its way in and out of a gully and along a barren stretch of downland. On its left the coast ran freely northwards in a chain of scrolls, last interruptions in its firm line before it tightened into the Ninety Mile Beach. The thunder of the Tasman Sea hung like a vast rumour on the freshening air, and above the margin of the downs Rangi's Peak was slowly erected.

'That's an ominous-looking affair,' said Gaunt. 'What is it about these hills that gives them an air of the fabulous? They are not so very odd in shape, not incredible like the Dolomites or imposing like the Rockies – not, as you point out in your superior way, Dikon, really mountains at all. Yet they seem to be pregnant with some tiresome secret. What is it?'

'Perhaps it's something to do with the volcanic silhouette. If there's a secret the answer's in the Maori language. I'm afraid you'll get very tired of that cone, sir. It looks over the hills round the Springs.' Dikon waited for a moment. Gaunt had a trick of showing a fugitive interest in places, of asking for expositions, and of growing restless when they were given to him.

'Why is the answer in Maori?' he said.

'It was a native burial ground in the old days. They tipped the bodies into the crater. It's extinct, you know. Supposed to be full of them.'

'Good Lord!' said Gaunt softly.

The car climbed higher, and the base of Rangi's Peak, a series of broad platforms and slopes, came into sight. 'You can see quite clearly,' Dikon said, 'the route they must have followed. Miss Claire tells me the tribes used to camp at the foot for three days holding a *tangi*, the Maori equivalent of a wake. Then the body was carried up the Peak by relays of bearers. They said that if it was a chief who had died, and if the air was still, you could hear the singing as far away as Wai-ata-tapu.'

'Gawd!' said Colly.

'Can you look into the crater and see. . .?'

'I don't know. It's a native reserve, the Claires told me. Very tapu, of course.'

'What's that?'

'Tapu? Taboo. Sacred. Forbidden. Untouchable. I don't suppose the Maori people ever climb up the Peak nowadays. No admittance to the *pakeha*, of course; it would be much too tempting a hunting ground. They used to bury the chiefs' weapons with them. There is a certain adze inherited by the chief Rewi who died about a hundred years ago and was buried on the Peak. This adze, his favourite weapon, was hidden up there. It had featured prominently and bloodily in the Maori wars, and had been spoken of in their oral schools of learning for generations before that. Rewi's *toki-poutanga-ta*. It has a secret mark on it, and was said to be invested with supernatural power by the god Tane. There it is, they say, a collector's plum if ever there was one, somewhere on the Peak. The whole place belongs to the Maori people. It's forbidden territory to the white hunter.'

'How far away is it?'

'About eight miles.'

'It looks less than three in this uncanny atmosphere.'

'Kind of black, sir, isn't it?' said Colly.

'Black and clear,' said Gaunt. 'A marvellous back-drop.' They drove on in silence for some time. The flowing hills moved slowly about as if in a contrapuntal measure determined by the progress of the car. Dikon began to recognize landmarks. He felt extremely apprehensive.

'Hullo,' said Gaunt. 'What's that affair down on the right? A sort of doss-house, one would think.'

Dikon said nothing, but turned in at a ramshackle gate.

'You don't dare to tell me that we have arrived,' Gaunt demanded in a loud voice.

'Yes, sir.'

'My God, Dikon, you'll writhe for this. Look at it. Smell it. Colly, we are betrayed.'

'Mr Bell warned you, sir,' Colly said. 'I daresay it's very comfortable.'

'If anything,' said Dikon, 'it's less comfortable than it looks. Those are the Springs.'

'Those reeking puddles?'

'Yes. And there, on the verandah, I see the Claires assembled. You are expected, sir,' said Dikon. Out of the tail of his eyes he saw Gaunt's gloved fingers go first to his tie and then to his hat. He thought suddenly: 'He looks terribly like a famous actor.'

The car rocked down the last stretch of the drive and shot across the pumice sweep. Dikon pulled up at the verandah steps. He got out, and taking off his hat approached the expectant Claires. He felt nervous and absurd. The Claires were grouped after the manner of an Edwardian family portrait that had taken an eccentric turn. Mrs Claire and the Colonel were in deck chairs, Barbara sat on the steps grasping a reluctant dog. Dikon guessed that they wore their best clothes. Simon, obviously under duress, stood behind his mother's chair looking murderous. All that was lacking, one felt, was the native equivalent of a gillie holding a couple of staghounds in leash. As Dikon approached, Dr Ackrington came out of his room.

'Here we are, you see,' Dikon called out with an effort at gaiety. The Claires had risen. Impelled by confusion, doubt and apology, Dikon shook hands blindly all round. Barbara looked nervously over his shoulder and he saw with a dismay which he afterwards recognized as prophetic that she had gone white to her unpainted lips.

He felt Gaunt's hand on his arm and hurriedly introduced him.

Mrs Claire brought poise to the situation, Dikon realized, but it was the kind of poise with which Gaunt was quite unfamiliar. She might have been welcoming a bishop-suffragan to a slum parish, a bishop-suffragan in poor health.

'Such a long journey,' she said anxiously. 'You must be so tired.'

'Not a bit of it,' said Gaunt, who had arrived at an age when actors affect a certain air of youthful hardihood.

'But it's such a dreadful road. And you *look* very tired,' she persisted gently. Dikon saw Gaunt's smile grow formal. He turned to Barbara. For some reason which he had not attempted to analyse, Dikon wanted Gaunt to like Barbara. It was with apprehension that he watched her give a galvanic jerk, open her eyes very wide, and put her head on one side like a chidden puppy. 'Oh, hell,' he thought, 'she's going to be funny.'

'Welcome,' Barbara said in her sepulchral voice, 'to the *humble* abode.' Gaunt dropped her hand rather quickly.

'Find us very quiet, I'm afraid,' Colonel Claire said, looking quickly at Gaunt and away again. 'Not much in your line, this country, what?'

'But we've just been remarking,' Gaunt said lightly, 'that your landscape reeks of theatre.' He waved his stick at Rangi's Peak. 'One expects to hear the orchestra.' Colonel Claire looked baffled and slightly offended.

'My brother,' Mrs Claire murmured. Dr Ackrington limped forward. Dikon's attention was distracted from this last encounter by the behaviour of Simon Claire, who suddenly lurched out of cover, strode down the steps and seized the astounded Colly by the hand. Colly, who was about to unload the car, edged behind it.

'How are you?' Simon said loudly. 'Give you a hand with that stuff.'

'That's all right, thank you, sir.'

'Come on,' Simon insisted and laid violent hands on a pigskin dressing case which he lugged from the car and dumped none too gently on the pumice. Colly gave a little cry of dismay.

'Here, here, here!' a loud voice expostulated. Mr Questing thundered out of the house and down the steps. 'Cut that out, young fellow,' he ordered and shouldered Simon away from the car.

'Why?' Simon demanded.

'That's no way to treat high-class stuff,' bustled Mr Questing with an air of intolerable patronage. 'You'll have to learn better than that. Handle it carefully.' He advanced upon Dikon. 'We're willing,' he laughed, 'but we've a lot to learn. Well, well, well, how's the young gentleman?'

He removed his hat and placed himself before Gaunt. His change of manner was amazingly abrupt. He might have been a lightning impersonator or a marionette controlled by some pundit of second-rate etiquette. Suddenly, he oozed deference. 'I don't think,' he said, 'that I have had the honour – '

'Mr Questing,' said Dikon.

'This is a great day for the Springs, sir,' said Mr Questing. 'A great day.'

'Thank you,' said Gaunt, glancing at him. 'If I may I should like to see my rooms.'

He turned to Mrs Claire. 'Dikon tells me you have taken an enormous amount of trouble on my behalf. It's very kind indeed. Thank you so much.' And Dikon saw that with this one speech, delivered with Gaunt's famous air of gay sincerity, he had captivated Mrs Claire. She beamed at him. 'I shall try not to be troublesome,' Gaunt added. And to Mr Questing: 'Right.'

They went in procession along the verandah. Mr Questing, still uncovered, led the way.

II

Barbara sat on the edge of her stretcher bed in her small hot room and looked at two dresses. Which should she wear for dinner on the first night? Neither of them was new. The red lace had been sent out two years ago by her youngest aunt who had worn it a good deal in India. Barbara had altered it to fit herself and something had gone wrong with the shoulders, so that it bulged where it should lie flat. To cover this defect she had attached a black flower to the neck. It was a long dress and she did not as a rule change for dinner. Simon might make some frightful comment if she wore the red lace. The alternative was a short floral affair, thick blue colour with a messy yellow design. She had furbished it up with a devilish shell ornament and a satin belt and even poor Barbara wondered if it was a success. Knowing that she should be in the kitchen with Huia, she pulled off her print, dragged the red lace over her head and looked at herself in the inadequate glass. No, it would never become her dress, it would always hark back to unknown Aunty Wynne who two years ago had written: 'Am sending a box of odds and ends for Ba. Hope she can wear red.' But could she? Could she plunge about in the full light of day in this ownerless waif of a garment with everybody knowing she had dressed herself up? She peered at her face, which was slightly distorted by the glass. Suddenly she hauled the dress over her head, fighting with the stuffy-smelling lace. 'Barbara,' her mother called. 'Where are you? Ba!' 'Coming!' Well, it would have to be the floral.

But when, hot and desperate, she had finally dressed, and covered the floral with a clean overall, she pressed her hands together. 'Oh God,' she thought, 'make him like it here! Please dear God, make him like it.'

III

'Can you possibly endure it?' Dikon asked.

Gaunt was lying full length on the modern sofa. He raised his arms above his head. 'All,' he whispered, 'I can endure all but Questing. Questing must be kept from me.'

'But I told you – '

'You amaze me with your shameless parrot cry of "I told you so",' said Gaunt mildly. 'Let us have no more of it.' He looked out of the corner of his eye at Dikon. 'And don't look so tragic, my good ass,' he added. 'I've been a small-part touring actor in my day. This place is strangely reminiscent of a one-night fit-up. No doubt I can endure it. I *should* be dossing down in an Anderson shelter, by God. I do well to complain. Only spare me Questing, and I shall endure the rest.'

'At least we shall be spared his conversation this evening. He has a previous engagement. Lest he offer to put it off, I told him you would be desolated but had already arranged to dine in your rooms and go to bed at nine. So away he went.'

'Good. In that case I shall dine *en famille* and go to bed when it amuses me. I have yet to meet Mr Smith, remember. Is it too much to hope that he will stage another fight?'

'It seems he only gets drunk when his remittance comes in.' Dikon hesitated and then asked: 'What did you think of the Claires, sir?'

'Marvellous character parts. Overstated, of course. Not quite West End. A number-one production on tour, shall we say? The Colonel's moustache is a little too thick in both senses.'

Dikon felt vaguely resentful. 'You captivated Mrs Claire,' he said.

Gaunt ignored this. 'If one could take them as they are,' he said. 'If one could persuade them to appear in those clothes and speak those lines! My dear, they'd be a riot. Miss Claire! Dikon, I didn't believe she existed.'

'Actually,' said Dikon stiffly, 'she's rather attractive. If you look beyond her clothes.'

'You're a remarkably swift worker if you've been able to do that.'

'They're extraordinarily kind and, I think, very nice.'

'Until we arrived you never ceased to exclaim against them. Why have you bounced round to their side all of a sudden?'

'I only said, sir, that I thought you would be bored by them.'

'On the contrary I'm agreeably entertained. I think they're all darlings and marvellous comedy. What *is* your trouble?'

'Nothing. I'm sorry. I've just discovered that I like them. I thought,' said Dikon, smiling a little in spite of himself, 'that the tableau on the verandah was terribly sad. I wonder how long they'd been grouped up like that.'

'For ages, I should think. The dog was plainly exasperated and young Claire looked lethal.'

'It is rather touching,' said Dikon and turned away.

Mrs Claire and Barbara, wearing their garden hats and carrying trowels, went past the window on tiptoe, their faces solemn and absorbed. When they had gone a little way Dikon heard them whispering together.

'In heaven's name,' cried Gaunt, 'why do they stalk about their own premises like that? What are they plotting?'

'It's because I explained that you liked to relax before dinner. They don't want to disturb you. I fancy their vegetable garden is round the corner.'

After a pause Gaunt said: 'It will end in my feeling insecure and ashamed. Nothing arouses one's self-abasement more than the earnest amateur. How long have they had this place?'

'About twelve years, I think. Perhaps longer.'

'Twelve years and they are still amateurs!'

'They try so terribly hard,' Dikon said. He wandered out on to the verandah. Someone was walking slowly round the warm lake towards the springs.

'Hullo,' Dikon said. 'We've a caller.'

'What do you mean? Be very careful, now. I'll see no one, remember.'

'I don't think it's for us, sir,' Dikon said. 'It's a Maori.'

It was Rua. He wore the suit he bought in 1936 to welcome the Duke of Gloucester. He walked slowly across the pumice to the house, tapped twice with his stick on the central verandah post and waited tranquilly for someone to take notice of him. Presently Huia came out and gave a suppressed giggle on seeing her great-grandfather. He addressed her in Maori with an air of austerity and she went back into the house. Rua sat on the edge of the verandah and rested his chin on his stick.

'Do you know, sir,' said Dikon, 'I believe it might be for us, after all? I've recognized the old gentleman.'

'I won't see anybody,' said Gaunt. 'Who is he?'

'He's a Maori version of the Last of the Barons. Rua Te Kahu, sometime journalist and MP for the district. I'll swear he's called to pay his respects.'

'You must see him for me. We did bring some pictures, I suppose?'

'I don't think,' Dikon said, 'that the Last of the Barons will be waiting for signed photographs.'

'You're determined to snub me,' said Gaunt amiably. 'If it's an interview, you'll talk to him, won't you?'

Colonel Claire came out of the house, shook hands with Rua and led him off in the direction of their own quarters.

'It's not for us after all, sir.'

'Thank heavens for that,' Gaunt said but he looked a little huffy nevertheless.

In Colonel Claire's study, a room about the size of a small pantry and rather less comfortable, Rua unfolded the purpose of his call. Dim photographs of polo teams glared down menacingly from the walls. Rua's dark eyes rested for a moment on a group of turbaned Sikhs before he turned to address himself gravely to the Colonel.

'I have brought,' he said, 'a greeting from my *hapu* to your distinguished guest, Mr Geoffrey Gaunt. The Maori people of Waiata-tapu are glad that he has come here and would like to greet him with a cordial *Haere mai.*'

'Oh, thanks very much, Rua,' said the Colonel. 'I'll tell him.'

'We have heard that he wishes to be quiet. If however he would care to hear a little singing, we hope that he will do us the honour to come to a concert on Saturday week in the evening. I bring this invitation from my *hapu* to your guests and your family, Colonel.'

Colonel Claire raised his eyebrows, opened his eyes and mouth, and glared at his visitor. He was not particularly surprised, but merely wore his habitual expression for absorbing new ideas.

'Eh?' he said at last. 'Did you say a concert? Extraordinarily nice of you, Rua, I must say. A concert.'

'If Mr Gaunt would care to come.'

Colonel Claire gave a galvanic start. 'Care to?' he repeated. 'I don't know, I'm sure. We should have to ask him, what? Sound the secretary.'

Rua gave a little bow. 'Certainly,' he said.

Colonel Claire rose abruptly and thrust his head out of the window. '*James!*' he yelled. 'Here!'

'What for?' said Dr Ackrington's voice at some distance.

'I want you. It's my brother-in-law,' he explained more quietly to Rua. 'We'll see what he thinks, um?' He went out to the verandah and shouted, *'Agnes!'*

'Hoo-oo?' replied Mrs Claire from inside the house.

'Here.'

'In a minute, dear.'

'Barbara!'

'Wait a bit, Daddy. I can't.'

'Here.'

Having summoned his family, Colonel Claire sank into an armchair, and glancing at Rua gave a rather aimless laugh. His eye happened to fall upon a Wild West novel that he had been reading. He was a greedy consumer of thrillers, and the sight of this one lying open and close at hand affected him as an open box of chocolate affects a child. He smiled at Rua and offered him a cigarette. Rua thanked him and took one, holding it cautiously between the tips of his fingers and thumb. Colonel Claire looked out of the corners of his eyes at his thriller. He was long-sighted.

'There was another matter about which I hoped to speak,' Rua said.

'Oh yes?' said Colonel Claire. 'D'you read much?'

'My eyesight is not as good as it once was, but I can still manage clear print.'

'Awful rot, some of these yarns,' Colonel Claire continued, casually picking up his novel. 'This thing I've been dipping into, now. Blood-and-thunder stuff. Ridiculous.'

'I am a little troubled in my mind. Disturbing rumours have reached me . . .'

'Oh?' Colonel Claire, still with an air of absent-mindedness, flipped over a page.

'. . . about proposals that have been made in regard to native reserves. You have been a good friend to our people, Colonel . . .'

'Not at all,' Colonel Claire murmured abstractedly, and felt for his reading glasses. 'Always very pleased . . .' He found his spectacles, put them on and, still casually, laid the book on his knee.

'Since you have been at Wai-ata-tapu, there have been friendly relations between your family and my *hapu*. We should not care to see anyone else here.'

'Very nice of you.' Colonel Claire was now frankly reading, but he continued to wear a social smile. He contrived to suggest that he merely looked at the book because after all one must look at something. Old Rua's magnificent voice rolled on. The Maori people are never in a hurry, and in his almost forgotten generation a gentleman led up to the true matter of an official call through a series of polite approaches. Rua's approval of his host was based on an event twelve years old. The Claires arrived at Wai-ata-tapu during a particularly virulent epidemic of influenza. Over at Rua's village there were many deaths. The Harpoon health authorities, led by the irate and overworked Dr Tonks, had fallen foul of the Maori people in matters of hygiene, and a dangerous deadlock had been reached. Rua, who normally exercised an iron authority, was himself too ill to control his *hapu*. Funeral ceremonies lasting for days, punctuated with long-drawn-out wails of greeting and lamentation, songs of death and interminable after-burial feasts maintained native conditions in a community lashed by a European scourge. Rua's people became frightened, truculent and obstructive, and the health authorities could do nothing. Upon this scene came the Claires. Mrs Claire instantly translated the whole affair into terms of an English village, offered their newly built house as an emergency hospital and herself undertook the nursing, with Rua as her first patient. Colonel Claire, whose absence of mind had inoculated him against the arrogance of Anglo–Indianism, and who by his very simplicity had fluked his way into a sort of understanding of native peoples, paid a visit to the settlement, arranged matters with Rua, and was accepted by the Maori people as a *rangitira*, a person of breeding. He and his wife professed neither extreme liking nor antipathy for the Maori people, who nevertheless found something recognizable and admirable in both of them. The war had brought them closer together. The Colonel commanded the local Home Guard and had brought many of Rua's older men into his division. Rua considered that he owed his life to his *pakeha* friends, and, though he thought them funny, loved them. It did not offend him, therefore, when Colonel Claire furtively read a novel under his very nose. He rumbled on magnificently with his story, in amiable competition with Texas Rangers and six-shooter blondes.

'. . . there has been enough trouble in the past. The Peak is a native reserve and we do not care for trespassers. He has been seen by a certain rascal coming down the western flank with a sack on his shoulders. At first he was friendly with this no-good young fellow, Eru Saul, who is a bad *pakeha* and a bad Maori. Now they have quarrelled and their quarrel concerns my great-granddaughter Huia, who is a foolish girl but much too good for either of them. And Eru tells my grandson Rangi, and my grandson tells me, that Mr Questing is behaving dishonestly on the Peak. Because he is your guest we have said nothing, but now I find him talking to some silly young fellows amongst our people and putting a lot of bad ideas into their heads. Now that makes me very angry,' said Rua, and his eyes flashed. 'I do not like my young people to be taught to cheapen the culture of their race. It has been bad enough with Mr Herbert Smith, who buys whisky for them and teaches them to make pigs of themselves. He is no good. But even *he* comes to me to warn me of this Questing.'

The Colonel's novel dropped with a loud slap. His eyebrows climbed his forehead, his eyes and mouth opened. He turned pale.

'Hey?' he said. 'Questing? What about Questing?'

'You have not been listening, Colonel,' said Rua, rather crossly.

'Yes, I have, only I didn't catch everything. I'm getting deaf.'

'I am sorry. I have been telling you that Mr Questing has been looking for curios on the Peak and boasting that in a little while Wai-ata-tapu will be his property. I have to come to ask you in confidence if this is true.'

'What's all this about Questing?' demanded Dr Ackrington, appearing at the doorway in his dressing-gown. 'Evening, Rua. How are you?'

'It began by being about Gaunt and a concert party,' said the Colonel unhappily. 'It's only just turned into something in confidence about Questing.'

'Well, if it's in confidence, why the devil did you call me? There seems to be conspiracy in this house to deny my sciatica thermal treatment.'

'I wanted to ask you if you thought Gaunt would like to go to a concert. Rua's people have very kindly offered . . .'

'How the devil do I know? Ask young Bell. Very nice of you, Rua, I must say.'

'And then Rua began to talk about Questing and the Peak.'

'Why don't you call him Quisling and be done with it?' Dr Ackrington demanded loudly. 'It's what he is, by God.'

'James! I really must insist – You have no shred of evidence.'

'Haven't I? Haven't I? Very well. Wait and see.'

Rua stood up. 'If it is not troubling you too much,' he said, 'perhaps you would ask Mr Gaunt's secretary . . . ?'

'Yes, yes,' the Colonel agreed hurriedly. 'Of course. Wait a minute, will you?'

He stumbled out of the room, and they heard him thump along the verandah towards Geoffrey Gaunt's quarters.

Rua's old eyes were very bright and cunning as he looked at Dr Ackrington, but he did not speak.

'So he's been trespassing, has he?' asked Dr Ackrington venomously. 'I could have told you that when the *Hippolyte* was torpedoed.'

Rua made a brusque movement with his wrinkled hands but still he did not speak.

'He does it by night sometimes, doesn't he?' Dr Ackrington went on. 'Doesn't he go up by night, with a flash lamp? Good God, my dear fellow, I've seen it myself. Curios be damned.'

'Somehow,' Rua said mildly, 'I have never been able to enjoy spy stories. They always seem to me to be incredible.'

'Indeed!' Dr Ackrington rejoined acidly. 'So this country, alone in the English-speaking world, stands immune from the activities of enemy agents. And why, pray? Do you think the enemy is frightened of us? Amazing complacency!'

'But he has been seen digging.'

'Do you imagine he would be seen semaphoring? Of course he digs. No doubt he robs your ancestors' graves. No doubt he will have some infamous booty to exhibit when he is brought to book.'

Rua pinched his lower lip and became very solemn. 'I have felt many regrets,' he said, 'for the old age which compelled me to watch my grandsons and great-grandsons set out to war without me. But if you are right, there is still work in Ao-tea-roa for an old warrior.' He chuckled, and Dr Ackrington looked apprehensively at him.

'I have been indiscreet,' he said. 'Keep this under your hat, Rua. A word too soon and we shan't get him. I may tell you I have taken steps. But, see here. There's a certain amount of cover on the Peak. If your young people haven't altogether lost the art of their forebears – '

'We must arrange something,' said Rua composedly. 'Yes. No doubt something can be arranged.'

'What is it, dear?' said Mrs Claire, appearing abruptly in the doorway. 'Oh! Oh, I thought Edward called me, James. Good evening, Rua.'

'I *did* call you about half an hour ago,' said her husband crossly from behind her back, 'but it's all over now. Old Rua was here with some – oh, you're still there, Rua. Mr Gaunt's secretary says they'll be delighted.'

Barbara came running distractedly from the kitchen. She and her parents formed up in a sort of queue outside the door.

'What is it, Daddy?' she asked. 'What do you want?'

'Nobody wants anything,' shouted her father angrily. 'Everybody's delighted. Why do you all come running at me?'

'My people will be very pleased,' said Rua. 'I shall go now and tell them. I wish you all good evening.'

As he walked along the verandah his great-granddaughter, Huia, flew out and excitedly rang the dinner bell in his face. He gave her a good-natured buffet and struck for home. Dikon, looking startled, came out on the verandah followed by Gaunt. Huia, over-stimulated by her first view of the celebrity, flashed her eyes, laughed excitedly and continued to peal her bell until Barbara took it away from her.

'I think that must be dinner,' said Mrs Claire with a bright assumption of surprise, while their ears still rang with the din. She turned with poise towards Gaunt. 'Shall we go in?' she asked gently, and they formed up into a kind of procession, trailing after each other towards the dining-room door. At the last moment Simon appeared, as usual from the direction of the cabins, where he had a sort of workshop.

But the first night's dinner was not to go forward without the intrusion of that particular form of grotesque irrelevance which Dikon was learning to associate with the Claires, for, as Gaunt and Mrs Claire approached the front door, a terrific rumpus broke out in the kitchen.

'Where's the Colonel?' an agitated voice demanded. 'I've got to see the Colonel.'

Smith, dishevelled and with threads of blood crossing his face, blundered through the dining-room from the kitchen, thrust Gaunt and Mrs Claire aside, and seized the Colonel by his coat lapels. 'Here,' he said, 'you've got to do something. You've got to look after me. He tried to kill me.'

CHAPTER 4

Red for Danger

Dikon, mindful of his only other encounter with him and influenced by an exceedingly significant smell, came to the conclusion that Mr Smith was mad drunk. Perhaps a minute went by before he realized that he was merely terrified. It was obvious that the entire Claire family made the same mistake for they all, together and severally and entirely without success, tried to shut Smith up and hustle him away into the background. Finally it was Dr Ackrington who, after a sharp look at Smith, said to his brother-in-law: 'Wait a minute now, Edward, you're making a mistake. Come along with me, Smith, and tell me what it's all about.'

'I won't come along with anyone. I've just been along with someone and it's practically killed me. You listen to what I'm telling you! He's a bloody murderer.'

'Who is?' asked Simon from somewhere in the rear.

'Questing.'

'Smith, for God's sake!' said the Colonel, and tried to lead him away by the elbow.

'Leave me alone. I know what I'm talking about. I'm telling you.'

'Oh, Daddy, *not* here!' Barbara cried out, and Mrs Claire said: 'No, Edward, *please*. Your study, dear.' And, as if Smith were some recalcitrant schoolboy, she repeated in a hushed voice: 'Yes, yes, much better in your study.'

'But you're not listening to me,' said Smith. And, to the acute embarrassment of everybody except Gaunt, he began to blubber. 'Straight out of the jaws of death,' he cried piteously, 'and you ask a chap to go to the study.'

Dikon heard Gaunt give a little cough of laughter before he turned to Mrs Claire and said: 'We'll remove ourselves.'

'Yes, of course,' said Dikon.

The doorway, however, was blocked by Simon and Mrs Claire, and before they could get out of the way Smith roared out: 'I don't want anybody to go. I want witnesses. You stay where you are.'

Gaunt looked good-humouredly from one horrified face to another, and said: 'Suppose we all sit down.'

Barbara took her uncle fiercely by the arm. 'Uncle James,' she whispered, 'stop him. He mustn't. *Uncle James, please.*'

'By all means let us sit down,' said Dr Ackrington.

They filed solemnly and ridiculously into the dining-room and, as if they were about to witness a cabaret turn, sat themselves down at the small tables. This manoeuvre appeared to quieten Smith. He took up a strategic position between the tables. With the touch of complacency which must have appeared in the Ancient Mariner when he cornered the wedding guest, he embarked upon his story.

'It was over at the level crossing,' he began. 'I'd been up the Peak with Eru Saul and I don't mind telling you why. Questing's been nosing around the Peak and the Maoris don't like it. We'd seen him drive along the Peak road earlier in the evening. Eru and I reckoned we'd cut along by the bush track to a hideout in the scrub. We didn't see anything. He must have gone up the other face of the hill if he was there at all. We waited for about an hour and then I got fed up and came down by myself. I hit the railroad about a couple of chains above the level crossing.'

'By the railroad bridge?' said Simon.

'You're telling me it was by the bridge,' said Smith with extraordinary violence. 'I'll say it was by the bridge. And get this. The 5.15 from Harpoon was just about due. You know what it's like. The railroad twists in and out of the scrub and round the shoulder of the hill and then comes through a wee tunnel. You can't see or hear a thing. Before you know what's happening, she's on top of you.'

'She is, too,' agreed Simon, with an air of supporting Smith against unfair opposition.

'The bridge is the worst bit. You can't see the signals but you can see a bend in the Peak road above the level crossing. To get over the gully you can hop across the bridge on the sleepers, or you can wade the creek. I stood there wondering if I'd risk the bridge. I don't like trains. There was a Maori boy killed on that bridge.'

'There was, too.'

'Yes; well, while I was kind of hesitating I saw Questing's car come over the crest of the road and stop. He leant out of the driving window and saw me. Now listen. You've got to remember he could see the signal and I couldn't. It's the red and green light affair they put in after the accident. I saw him turn his head to look that way.'

Smith wiped his mouth with the back of his hand. He spoke quietly now, was no longer ridiculous, and held the attention of his audience. He sat down at an empty table and looked about him with an air of astonishment.

'He waved me on,' he said. 'He could see the signal and he gave me the all-clear. Like this. I didn't move at first and he did it again. See? A bit impatient, too, as much as to say: "What's eating you? Hop to it." Yes, well, I hopped. I've never liked the bridge. It's a short stride between sleepers and you can see the creek through the gaps. Look. I'd got halfway when I heard her behind me, blowing her whistle in the tunnel. It's funny how quick you can think. Whether to jump for it or swing from the end of a sleeper, or stand waving my arms and, if she didn't pull up in time, dive for the engine. I thought about Questing, too, and how, if she got me, nobody'd know he gave me the office. And all the time I was hopping like a bloody ballet dancer, with the creek below clicking through the gaps. Like one of those dreams. Look, she was on the bridge when I jumped. I was above the bank by then. I suppose it wasn't more than ten feet. I landed in a *matagouri* bush. Scratched all over, and look at my pants. I didn't even try to get out of it. She rumbled over my head, and muck off the sleepers fell in my eyes. I felt funny. I mean my body felt funny, as if it didn't belong to me. I was kind of surprised to find myself climbing the bank and it seemed to be someone else that was winded when I got to the top. And yet all the time I was hell-set on getting at Questing. And had he waited for me? He had not. 'Struth, I stood there shaking like a bloody jelly and I heard him tooting his horn away along the Peak road. I don't know how I'd have got home if it hadn't been for Eru Saul. Eru'd come down the hill and he saw what Questing swung across me. He's a witness to it. He gave me a hand to come home. Look, Eru's out there in the kitchen. You ask him. He knows.' He turned to Mrs Claire. 'Can I get Eru to come in, Mrs Claire?'

'I'll get him,' said Simon, and went out to the kitchen. He returned, followed by Eru, who stood oafishly in the doorway. Dikon saw, for the first time, a fleshy youth dressed in a stained blue suit. His coat was open, displaying a brilliant tie, and an expanse of puce-coloured shirt stretched tight across the diaphragm. He showed little of his Maori blood, but Dikon thought he might have served as an illustration of the least admirable aspect of colonization in a native country.

'Here, listen, Eru,' said Smith. 'You saw Questing swing it across me, didn't you?'

'Too right,' Eru muttered.

'Go on. Tell them.'

It was the same story. Eru had come down the hillside behind Smith. He could see the bridge and Questing's car. 'Questing leant out of the window and beckoned Bert to come on. I couldn't see the signal, but I reckoned he was crazy, seeing what time it was. I yelled out to Bert to turn it up and come back, but he never heard me. Then she blew her whistle.' Eru's olive face turned white. 'Gee, I thought he was under the engine all right. I couldn't see him, like, from where I was. The train was between us. Gee, I certainly expected the jolt. I never picked he'd jump for it. Crikey, was I relieved when I seen old Bert sitting in the prickles!'

'The engine driver pulled her up and they came back to inquire, didn't they, Eru?'

'Too right. They looked terrible. You know, white as a sheet. They'd got the shock of their lives, those jokers. We had to put it down in writing he'd blown the whistle. They had to protect themselves, see?'

'Yeh. Well, that's the whole works,' said Smith. 'Thanks, Eru.'

He rubbed his hands over his face and looked at them. 'I could do with a drink,' he said. 'You may think I've had some by the way I smell. I swear to God I haven't. It broke when I went over.'

'That's right,' said Eru. He looked round awkwardly. 'I'll say good day,' he added.

He returned to the kitchen. Mrs Claire glanced after him dubiously, and presently got up and followed him.

Smith sagged forward, resting his cheek on his hand as though he sat meditating alone in the room. Dr Ackrington limped across and put his hand on Smith's shoulder.

'I'll fix you up,' he said. 'Come along.'

Smith looked up at him, got to his feet, and shambled to the door.

'I could have him up, couldn't I, Doc?' he said. 'It's attempted murder, isn't it?'

'I hope so,' said Dr Ackrington.

II

Mrs Claire stood in the centre of her own kitchen looking up at Eru Saul. The top of her head reached no farther than his chin, but she was a plumply authoritative figure and he shuffled his feet and would not look at her. Huia, with an air of conscious virtue, was dishing up the dinner.

'You are going home now, Eru, I suppose,' said Mrs Claire.

'That's right, Mrs Claire,' said Eru, looking at Huia.

'Huia is very busy, you know.'

'Yeh, that's right.'

'And we don't like you waiting about. You know that.'

'I'm not doing anything, Mrs Claire.'

'The Colonel doesn't wish you to come. You understand?'

'I was only asking Huia what say we went to the pictures.'

'I'm not going to the pictures. I told you already,' said Huia loudly.

'There, Eru,' said Mrs Claire.

'Got another date, haven't you?'

Huia tossed her head.

'That will do, Eru,' said Mrs Claire.

'Too bad,' said Eru, looking at Huia.

'You'll go now, if you please,' Mrs Claire insisted.

'OK, Mrs Claire. But listen, Mrs Claire. You wouldn't pick Huia wasn't on the level, would you? I didn't pick it right away, but it's a fact. Ask Mr Questing, Mrs Claire. She's been over at the Bay with him this afternoon. I'll be seeing you, Huia.'

When he had gone Mrs Claire's round face was very rosy-red. She said: 'If Eru comes here again you must tell me at once, Huia, and the Colonel will speak to him.'

'Yes, Mrs Claire.'

'We are ready for dinner.' She walked to the door and hesitated. Huia gave her a brilliant smile.

'You know we trust you, Huia, don't you?'

'Yes, Mrs Claire.'

Mrs Claire went into the dining-room.

They dined in an atmosphere of repressed curiosity. Dr Ackrington returned alone, saying that he had sent Smith to bed, and that in any case he was better out of the way. Throughout dinner, Gaunt and Dikon, who had a small table to themselves, made elaborate conversation about nothing. Dikon was in a state of confusion so acute that it surprised himself. From where he sat he could see Barbara – her lamentable clothes, her white face, and her nervous hands clattering her knife and fork on the plate and pushing about the food she could not eat. Because he tried not to look, he looked the more and was annoyed with himself for doing so. Gaunt sat with his back to the Claires' table, and Dikon saw that Barbara could not prevent herself from watching him.

During the years of the association, Dikon's duties had included the fending away of Gaunt's adorers. He thought that he could interpret Barbara's glances. He thought that she was sick with disappointment, and told himself that only too easily could he translate her mortification and misery. He was angry and disgusted – angry with Gaunt, and, so he said to himself, disgusted with Barbara – and his reaction was so foreign to his habit that he ended by falling quite out of humour with himself. Presently he became aware that Gaunt was watching him sharply and he realized that he had actually been speaking at random. He began to stammer and was actually relieved when, upon the disappearance of Huia, Colonel and Mrs Claire embarked in antiphony upon an apologetic chant of which the theme was Smith's unseemly behaviour. This rapidly developed into a solo performance by Mrs Claire in the course of which she attempted the impossible feat of distributing whitewash equally between Questing and Smith. Her recital became rich in cliches: 'More sinned against than sinning . . . A dear fellow at bottom . . .

Means well but not quite . . . So sorry it should have happened . . .' She was encouraged by punctual ejaculations of 'Quite' from her distracted husband.

Gaunt was beginning to get out of an impossible situation as gracefully as might be when Dr Ackrington spared him any further recital.

'My dear Agnes,' said Dr Ackrington, 'and my dear Edward. I expect we are all agreed that attempted murder is not in the best possible taste and a vague distribution of brummagem haloes will not persuade us to alter our opinion. Suppose we leave it at that. I have one suggestion – let us call it a request – to make, and I should like to make it at once. That fellow may return at any moment.'

The Claires fidgeted. Simon, who seemed to be unable to speak in any mode but a truculent roar, said that he reckoned he was going to ask Questing what the hell he thought he was up to. 'It's crook, that's what it is,' Simon shouted angrily. 'By cripey, I reckon it's crook. I'm going to ask him flat out – '

'You will ask him nothing, if you'll be so good,' his uncle said briskly, 'and I shall be obliged if you will suffer me to finish.'

'Yes, but – '

'Simon, *please*,' his mother implored.

'I was about to ask,' Dr Ackrington went on, 'that you allow *me* to speak to Mr Questing when he arrives. I have a specific reason for making this suggestion.'

'I thought perhaps,' said Mrs Claire unhappily, 'Edward might take him to his study.'

'Is Edward's study the Ark of the Tabernacle of the Lord,' cried Dr Ackrington in a fury, 'that Questing should be subdued in it? Why this perpetual itch to herd people together in Edward's study, which, when all's said and done, is no bigger than a lavatory and rather less comfortable? Will you listen to me? Will you indulge me so far as to keep quiet while I speak to Questing, here, openly, in the presence of you all?'

Dikon's attention was momentarily diverted by Gaunt, who said in a fierce whisper: 'If you forget a syllable of that speech I shall sack you.'

The Claires were all speaking together again but their expostulations died out when Dr Ackrington cast himself back in his chair, turned up his eyes and began to whistle through his teeth. After an uncomfortable silence Mrs Claire said timidly: 'I'm sure there's been some mistake.'

'Indeed?' said her brother. 'Do you mean that Questing miscalculated and that Smith has no right to be alive?'

'No, dear.'

'What was Smith saying about lights?' asked Colonel Claire suddenly. 'I didn't catch all that about lights.'

'Will someone explain to Edward about railway signals?' Dr Ackrington asked dangerously, but Colonel Claire went on in a high complaining voice. 'I mean, suppose Questing didn't happen to notice the signals.'

'You, Edward,' his brother-in-law interrupted, 'are the only person of my acquaintance from whom I can conceive such a display of negligence, but even you could scarcely fail to glance at a signal some twenty-two yards in front of your nose before inviting a man to risk his life on a single-track railway bridge. I find it impossible to believe that Questing didn't act deliberately and I have good reason to believe that he did.'

There was another silence broken unexpectedly by Geoffrey Gaunt. 'In fact, Dr Ackrington,' said Gaunt, 'you think we have a potential murderer among us?'

'I do.'

'Strange. I've never thought of a murderer being an insufferable bore.'

Barbara gave a yelp of unhappy laughter.

'Wait on!' said Simon. 'Listen!'

They all heard Questing's car come down the drive. He drove past the windows and round the house to the garages.

'He'll come in here!' Barbara whispered.

'I implore you to leave him to me, Edward.'

Colonel Claire threw up his hands. 'Shall Barbie and I – ?' Mrs Claire began, but her brother silenced her with an angry flap of his hand. After that nobody spoke and Questing's footfall sounded loud as he came round the house and along the verandah.

Perhaps Dikon had anticipated, subconsciously, a sinister change in Questing. Undoubtedly he experienced a shock of anticlimax when he heard the familiar and detestable inquiry.

'Well, well, well,' said Mr Questing, beaming in the doorway, 'how's tricks? Any dinner left for a little feller? Am I hungry or am I hungry! Good evening, Mr Gaunt. And how's the young gentleman?'

He sat down at his own table, rubbed his hands together, and shouted: 'Where's the Glamour Girl? Come on, Beautiful. Let's have a slant at the me-and-you.'

It was at this moment that Dikon, to his unspeakable horror, discovered in himself a liking for Mr Questing.

III

To Dikon's surprise, Dr Ackrington did not go at once into the attack. Huia brought Mr Questing's first course and received an offensive leer with a toss of her head. Mrs Claire murmured something to Barbara and they went out together. With an air of secret exultation, Gaunt began to make theatrical conversation with Dikon. The other three men did not utter a word. To Dikon, the tension in the room seemed almost ponderable, but Questing did not appear to notice it. He ate a colossal dinner, became increasingly playful with Huia, and, on her final withdrawal, leant back in his chair, sucked his teeth, produced a cigar case and was about to offer it to Gaunt when at last Dr Ackrington spoke.

'You did not bring Smith back with you, Mr Questing?'

Questing turned indolently and looked at him. 'Smith?' he said. 'By gum, I meant to ask you about Smith. Hasn't he come in?'

'He's in bed. He's knocked about and is suffering from shock.'

'Is that so?' said Questing very earnestly. 'By gum, now, I'm sorry to hear that. Suffering from shock, eh? So he would be. So he would be.'

Dr Ackrington drew in his breath with a sharp whistle and by this manoeuvre seemed to gain control of himself.

'I bet that chap's annoyed with me,' Questing added cheerfully, 'and I don't blame him. So would I be in his place. It's the kind of thing that would annoy you, you know. Isn't it?'

'Smith appears to find attempted murder distinctly irritating,' agreed Dr Ackrington.

'Attempted murder?' said Questing, opening his eyes very wide. 'That's not a very nice way to put it, Doctor. We all of us make mistakes.'

Dr Ackrington uttered a loud oath.

'Now, now, now,' Questing chided, 'what's biting you? You come out on the verandah, Doc, and we'll have a little chat.'

Dr Ackrington beat his fist on the table and began to stutter. Dikon thought they were in for a tirade, but with a really terrifying effort at self-control Dr Ackrington pulled himself up, gripped the edge of the table and at last addressed Questing coherently and with a kind of calmness. He outlined the story of Smith's escape, adding several details that he had evidently gleaned after leaving the dining-room. At first Questing listened with the air of a connoisseur, but as Dr Ackrington went on he began to get restless. He attempted several interjections but was ruthlessly talked down. Finally, however, when his inquisitor enlarged upon his abominable behaviour in deserting a man who might have been fatally injured, Questing raised a cry of protest. 'Fatally injured, my foot! He came charging up the bank like a horse, don't you worry. It was me that looked like getting a fatal injury.'

'So you turned tail and bolted?'

'Don't be ridiculous. I didn't want a lot of unpleasantness, that's all. I wasn't deserting the chap. There was another chap there to look after him. He came bowling down the hill after it had happened. A chap in a blue shirt. And the train stopped. I didn't want a lot of humbug with the engine driver. Smith was all right. I could see he wasn't hurt.'

'Mr Questing, did you or did you not look at the signal before you beckoned Smith to cross the bridge?'

For the first time, Questing looked acutely uncomfortable. He turned very red in the face and said: 'Look, Doctor, we've got a very, very distinguished guest. We don't need to trouble Mr Gaunt – '

'Not at all,' said Gaunt. 'I'm enormously interested.'

'Will you answer me?' Dr Ackrington shouted. 'Knowing that the evening train was due, and seeing the fellow hesitated to cross the railway bridge, did you or did you not look at the signal before waving him on?'

'Of course I looked at it.' Questing examined the end of his cigar, glanced up from under his eyebrows and added in a curiously flat voice: 'It wasn't working.'

Dikon experienced that wave of personal shame with which an amateur reciter at close quarters can embarrass his audience. It was such a bad lie. It was so clearly false. Questing so obviously knew that he was not believed. Even Dr Ackrington seemed deflated and found nothing to say. After a moment Questing mumbled: 'Well, *I* didn't see it, anyway. They ought to have a wig-wag there.'

'A red light some ten inches in diameter and you didn't see it.'

'I said it wasn't working.'

'We can check up on that,' said Simon.

Questing turned on him. 'You mind your own business,' he said, but his voice missed the note of anger, and it seemed to Dikon that there was something he could not bring himself to say.

'Do you mind telling us where you have been?' Dr Ackrington continued.

'Pohutukawa Bay.'

'But you were on the Peak road.'

'I know I was. I thought I'd just take a run along the Peak road before I came home.'

'You'd been to Pohutukawa Bay?'

'I'm telling you I went there.'

'To see the trees in flower?'

'My God, why shouldn't I go to see the pootacows! It's a great sight, isn't it? Hundreds of people go, don't they? If you must know I thought it would be a nice little run for Mr Gaunt. I thought I'd take a look-see if they were in full bloom before suggesting he went over there.'

'But you must have heard that there is no bloom this year on the *pohutukawas*. Everybody's talking about it.'

For some inexplicable reason Questing looked pleased. 'I hadn't heard,' he said quickly. 'I was astonished when I got there. It's very, very disappointing. Just too bad.'

Dr Ackrington, also, looked pleased. He got up and stood with his back to Questing, his eyes fixed triumphantly on his brother-in-law.

'Yes, but I don't know what the devil you're getting at, both of you,' Colonel Claire complained. 'I've been –'

'Do me the extraordinary kindness to hold your tongue, Edward.'

'Look here, James!'

'Cut it out, Dad,' said Simon. He looked at his uncle. 'I reckon I'm satisfied,' he said roughly.

'I am obliged to you. Thank you, Mr Questing. I fancy we need detain you no longer.'

Questing drew at his cigar, exhaled a long dribble of smoke and remained where he was. '*Wait* a bit, *wait* a bit,' he said, speaking in the best tradition of the cinema boss. 'You're satisfied, huh? OK. That's fine. That's swell. What about me? Just because I've got an instinct about the right way to behave when we've distinguished guests among us, you think you can get away with dynamite. I've tried to save Mr Gaunt the embarrassment of this scene. I apologize to Mr Gaunt. I'd like him to know that when I've taken over this joint the resemblance to a giggle-house will fade out automatically.' He walked to the door. 'But we *must* have an exit line,' Gaunt muttered. Questing turned. 'And just in case you didn't hear me, Claire,' he said magnificently, 'I said *when* and not *if*. Good evening.'

He did his best to slam the door but true to the tradition of the house it jammed halfway and he wisely made no second attempt. He walked slowly past the windows with his thumbs in the armholes of his waistcoat, making much of his cigar.

As soon as he had passed out of earshot, Colonel Claire raised a piteous cry of protest. He hadn't understood. He would never understand. What was all that about Pohutukawa Bay? Nobody had told him anything about it. On the contrary –

With extraordinary complacency, Dr Ackrington cut in: 'Nobody told you it was a bad year for *pohutukawas,* my good Edward, for the conclusive reason that it is a phenomenally good year. The Bay is ablaze with blossom. I laid for your friend Questing, Edward, and, as Simon's intolerable jargon would have it – did he fall!'

IV

After the party in the dining-room had broken up, Gaunt suggested that he and Dikon should go for a stroll before night set in. Dikon proposed the path leading past the Springs and round the shoulder of the hill that separated them from the native settlement. Their departure was hindered by Mrs Claire, who hurried from the house, full of warnings about boiling mud. 'But you can't miss your way, really,' she added. 'There are little flags, white for safe and red for boiling mud. But you will take care of him, Mr Bell, won't you? Come back before dark. One would never forgive oneself if after all this . . .' The sentence died away as a doubt arose in Mrs Claire's mind about the propriety of saying that death by boiling mud would be a poor sequel to an evening of social solecisms. She looked very earnestly at Gaunt and repeated: 'So you *will* take care, won't you? Such a horrid place, really. When one thinks of our dear old English lanes . . .'

They assured her and set off. Soon after their arrival Gaunt had taken his first steep in the Elfin Pool. Whether through the agency of free sulphuric acid, or through the stimulus provided by the scene they had just witnessed, his leg was less painful than it had been for some time, and he was in good spirits. 'I've always adored scenes,' he said, 'and this was a princely one. They can't keep it up, of course, but really, Dikon, if this is anything like a fair sample, I shall do very nicely at Wai-ata-tapu. How right you were to urge me to come.'

'I'm glad you've been entertained,' Dikon rejoined, 'but honestly, sir, I regard the whole affair as an exceedingly sinister set-up. I mean, *why* did Questing lie like a flat-fish?'

'Several most satisfactory theories present themselves. I am inclined to think that Miss Claire is the key figure.'

Dikon, who was leading the way, stopped so suddenly that Gaunt walked into him. 'What can you mean, sir!' Dikon cried. 'How can Questing's relations with Smith have any possible connection with Barbara Claire?'

'I may be wrong, of course, but there is no doubt that he has his eye on her. Didn't you notice that? All that frightful line of stuff with the Maori waitress was undoubtedly directed at Barbara Claire. A display of really most unpalatable oomph. I must say she didn't seem to care for it. Always the young gentlewoman, of course.' They walked on in silence for a minute, and then Gaunt said lightly: 'Surely you can't have fallen for her?'

Without turning his head Dikon said crossly: 'What in the name of high fantasy could have put that antic notion into your head?'

'The back of your neck has bristled like a hedgehog ever since I mentioned her. And it's not such an antic notion. There are possibilities. She's got eyes and a profile and a figure. Submerged it is true in dressy floral *ninon*, but there nevertheless.' And, with a touch of the malice with which Dikon was only too familiar, Gaunt added: 'Barbara Claire. It's a charming name, isn't it? You must teach her not to hoot.'

Dikon never liked his employer less than he did at that moment. When Gaunt prodded him in the back with his stick, Dikon pretended not to notice, but cursed softly to himself.

'I apologize,' said Gaunt, 'in fourteen different positions.'

'Not at all, sir.'

'Then don't prance along at such a rate. Stop a moment. I'm exhausted. What's that noise?'

They had rounded the flank of the hill and now came in sight of the native settlement. The swift northern dusk had fallen upon the countryside with no suggestion of density. The darkening of the air seemed merely to be a change in translucence. It was very still, and as they stood listening Dikon became aware of a curious sound. It was as if a giant somewhere close at hand were blowing thick bubbles very slowly and complacently; or as if, over the brink of the hill, a vast porridge pot had just come to boiling point. The sounds were irregular, each one mounting to its point of explosion. Plop. Plop-plop . . . Plop.

They moved forward and reached a point where the scrub and grass came to an end and the path descended a steep bank to traverse a region of solidified blue mud, sinister mounds, hot pools and geysers. The sulphurous smell was very strong. The track, defined at intervals by stakes to which pieces of white rag had been tied, went forward over naked hillocks towards the hip-roofs of the native settlement.

'Shall we go farther?' asked Dikon.

'It's a detestable place, but I think we must see this infernal brew.'

'We must keep to the track, then. Shall I go first?'

They walked on and presently, through the soles of their feet, received a strange experience. The ground beneath them was unsteady, quivering a little, telling them that, after all, there was no stability in the earth by which we symbolize stability. They moved across a skin and the organism beneath it was restless.

'This is abominable,' said Gaunt. 'The whole place works secretly. It's alive.'

'Look to your right,' said Dikon. They had come to a hillock; the path divided and, where it turned to the right, was marked by red flags.

'They told me you used to be able to walk along there,' Dikon explained, 'but it's not safe now. Taupo-tapu is encroaching.'

They followed the white flags, climbed steeply, and at last from the top of the hillock looked down on Taupo-tapu.

It was perhaps fifteen feet across, dun-coloured and glistening, a working ulcer in the body of the earth. Great bubbles of mud formed themselves deliberately, swelled, and broke with the sounds which they had noticed a few minutes before and which were now loud and insistent. With each eruption unctuous rings momentarily creased the surface of the brew. It was impossible to escape the notion that Taupo-tapu had some idiotic purpose of its own.

For perhaps two minutes Gaunt looked at it in silence. 'Quite obscene, isn't it?' he said at last. 'If you know anything about it, don't tell me.'

'The only story I've heard,' Dikon said, 'is not a pretty one. I won't.'

Gaunt's reply was unexpected. 'I should prefer to hear it from a Maori,' he said.

'You can see where the thing has eaten into the old path,' Dikon pointed out. 'The red flags begin again on the other side and rejoin our track just below us. Just as well. It would be an unpleasant error to mistake the paths, wouldn't it?'

'Don't, for God's sake,' said Gaunt. 'It's getting dark. Let's go home.'

When they turned back, Dikon found that he had to make a deliberate effort to prevent himself from hurrying, and he thought he sensed Gaunt's impatience too. The firm dry earth felt wholesome under their feet as once more they circled the hill. Behind them, in the native village, a drift of song rose on the cool air, intolerably plaintive and lonely.

'What's that?'

'One of their songs,' said Dikon. 'Perhaps they're rehearsing for your concert. It's the genuine thing. You get the authentic music up here.'

The shoulder of the hill came between them and the song. It was almost dark as they walked along the brushwood fence towards Wai-ata-tapu. Steam from the hot pools drifted in wraiths across the still night air. It was only when she moved forward that Barbara's dress and the blurred patches of white that were her arms and face told them that she had been waiting for them. Perhaps the darkness gave her courage and balance. Perhaps any voice would have been welcome just then, but it seemed to Dikon that Barbara's had a directness and repose that he had not heard in it before.

'I hope I didn't startle you,' she said. 'I heard you coming down the path and thought I should like to speak to you.'

Gaunt said: 'What is it, Miss Claire? More excursions and alarms?'

'No, no. We seem to have settled down again. It's only that I wanted to tell you how very sorry we all are about that frightful scene. We shan't go on apologizing, but I did just want to say this: Please don't think you are under an obligation to stay. Of course you know you are not, but perhaps you feel it's rather difficult to tell us you are going. Don't hesitate. We shall quite understand.'

She turned her head and they saw her in profile against a shifting background of steam. The dusk, simplifying her ugly dress, revealed the beauty of her silhouette. The profile lines of her head and throat were well-drawn, delicate and harmonious. It was an astonishing change. Perhaps if Gaunt had not seen her so translated, his voice would have held less warmth and friendliness when he answered her.

'But there is no question of our going,' he said. 'We have not thought of it. As for the scene, Dikon will tell you that I have a lust for scenes. We are very sorry if you're in difficulties, but we don't in the least want to go.'

Dikon saw him take her arm and turn her towards the house. It was a gesture he often used on the stage, adroit and impersonal. Dikon followed behind as they walked across the pumice.

'It's awfully nice of you,' Barbara was saying. 'I – we have felt so frightful about it. I was horrified when I heard what Mr Questing had done, badgering you to come. We didn't know what he was up to. Uncle James and I were horrified.'

'He didn't badger *me*,' said Gaunt. 'Dikon attended to Questing. That's why I keep him.'

'Oh.' Barbara half turned her head and laughed, not with her usual boisterousness, but shyly. 'I wondered what he was for,' she said.

'He has his uses. When I start work again he'll be kept very spry.'

'You're going to write, aren't you? Uncle James told me. Is it an autobiography? I do hope it is.'

Gaunt moved his hand above her elbow. 'And why do you hope that?'

'Because I want to read it. You see, I've seen your Rochester, and once somebody who was staying here had an American magazine, I think it was called the *Theatre Arts*, and there was an article in it with photographs of you as different people. I liked the Hamlet one the best because – '

'Well?' asked Gaunt when she paused.

Barbara stumbled over her next speech. 'Because – well, I suppose because I know it best. No, that's not really why, I didn't know it at all well until then, but I read it again, lots of times and tried to imagine how you sounded when you said the speech in the photograph. Of course after hearing Mr Rochester it was easier.'

'Which photograph was that, Dikon?' asked Gaunt over his shoulder.

'It was Rosencrantz . . .' Barbara began eagerly.

'Ah, I remember.'

Gaunt stood still and put her from him, holding her by the shoulder as he had held the gratified small-part actor who played Rosencrantz in New York. Dikon heard him draw in his breath as he always did when he collected himself to rehearse. In the silence of that warm evening, amidst the reek of sulphur and against the nebulous thermal background, the beautiful voice spoke quietly:

' *"O God, I could be bounded in a nutshell and count myself a king of infinite space, were it not that I have bad dreams."* '

Dikon was irritated and disturbed by Barbara's rapturous silence and infuriated by the whispered 'Thank you' with which she finally ended it. 'She's making a perfect little ass of herself,' he thought, but he knew Gaunt would not find her attitude excessive. He had an infinite capacity for absorbing adulation.

'Can you go on?' Gaunt was saying. ' *"Which dreams – "* '

' *"Which dreams indeed are ambition, for the very substance of the ambitious is merely the shadow of a dream."* '

' *"A dream itself is but a shadow!"* Do you hear this, Dikon?' cried Gaunt. 'She knows the lines.' He moved forward again, Barbara at his side. 'You've got a voice, my child,' he said. 'How have you escaped the accent? Do you know what you've been talking about? You must hear the music, but you must also achieve the meaning. Say it again: thinking – *"Which dreams indeed are ambition."* ' But Barbara fumbled the second time, and they spoke the line backwards and forward to each other as they crossed the pumice to the house. Gaunt was treating her to an almost indecent helping of charm, Dikon considered.

The lights were up in the house and Mrs Claire was hurriedly doing the blackout. She had left the door open and a square of warmth reached across the verandah to the pumice. Before they came to its margin Gaunt checked Barbara again.

'We say goodnight here,' he said. 'The dusk becomes you well. Goodnight, Miss Claire.'

He turned on his heel and walked towards his rooms.

'Goodnight,' said Dikon.

She had moved into the light. The look she turned upon him was radiant. 'You're terribly lucky, aren't you?' said Barbara.

'Lucky?'

'Your job. To be with him.'

'Oh,' said Dikon, 'that. Yes, of course.'

'Goodnight,' said Barbara, and ran indoors.

He looked after her, absently polishing his glasses with his handkerchief.

v

Barbara lay in bed with her eyes wide open to the dark. Until this moment she had denied the waves of bliss that lapped at the edge of her thoughts. Now she opened her heart to them.

She passed the sequence of those few minutes in the dusk through and through her mind, examining each moment, feeling again its lustre, wondering at her happiness. It is easy to smile at such fervours, but in her unreasoned ecstasy she reached a point of pure enchantment to which she would perhaps never again ascend. The experience may appear more touching but its reality is not impugned if it is recorded that Gaunt, at the same time, was preening himself a little.

'Do you know, Dikon,' he said, 'that strange little devil quivered like a puppy out there in the dusk?' Dikon did not answer and after a moment Gaunt added: 'After all, it's pleasant to know that one's work can reach so far. The Bard and sulphuric phenomena! An amusing juxtaposition, isn't it? One lights a little flame, you know. One carries the torch.'

CHAPTER 5

Mr Questing Goes Down for the Second Time

The more blatant eccentricities of the first evening were not repeated during the following days, and the household at Wai-ata-tapu settled down to something like a normal routine. The Colonel fatigued himself to exhaustion with Home Guard exercises. His wife and daughter, overtaxed by the new standard they had set themselves, laboured incessantly in the house. Gaunt, following Dr Ackrington's instruction, sat at stated hours in the Springs, took short walks, and began to work steadily on his book. Dikon filed old letters and programmes which had to be winnowed for use in the autobiography. Gaunt dictated for two hours every morning and evening, and expected Dikon's shorthand notes to be translated into typescript before they began work on the following day. Dr Ackrington dealt austerely in his own room with the problems of comparative anatomy. On Wednesday he announced that he was going away for a week and, when Mrs Claire said gently that she hoped there was nothing the matter, replied that they would all be better if they were dead, and drove away. Colly, who had been a signaller in the 1914 war, recovered from the surprise of Simon's first advance, and spent a good deal of time in the cabin helping him with his Morse. Simon's attitude to Gaunt was one of morose suspicion. As far as possible he avoided encounters, but on the rare occasions when they met, his behaviour was remarkable. He was not content to remain altogether silent, but would suddenly roar out strange inquiries and statements. He asked Gaunt whether he reckoned the theatre did any good in the world and, when Gaunt replied with some heat that he did, inquired the price of seats. On receiving this information he said instantly that a poor family could live for a week on the price of a stall and that there ought to be a flat charge all over the house. Gaunt's book had gone badly that morning and his leg was painful. He became irritable and a ridiculous argument took place.

'It's selfishness that's at the bottom of it,' Simon shouted. 'The actors ought to have smaller wages, see? What I reckon, the thing ought to be run for the good of everybody. Smaller wages all round.'

'Including the stage staff? The workmen?' asked Gaunt.

'They all ought to get the same.'

'Then I couldn't afford to keep your friend Colly.'

'I reckon he's wasting his time anyway,' said Simon, and Gaunt walked away in a rage.

Evidently Simon confided this conversation to Colly, who considered it necessary to apologize for his new friend.

'You don't want to pay too much attention to him, sir,' Colly said, as he massaged his employer's leg that evening. 'He's a nice young chap. Just a touch on the red side. He's a bit funny. It's Mr Questing that's upset the apple cart, really.'

'He's an idiotic cub,' said Gaunt. 'What's Questing got to do with the price of stalls?'

'He's been talking big business, sir. Young Simon thinks he's lent a good bit to the Colonel on this show. He thinks the Colonel can't pay up and Mr Questing's going to shut down on them and run the place on his pat. Young Simon's that disgusted he's taken a scunner on anything that looks like smart business.'

'Yes, but – '

'He's funny. I had it out with him. He told me what he'd been saying to you, and I said he'd acted very silly. "I've been with my gentleman for ten years," I told him, "and there's not much we don't know about the show business. I seen him when he was a small-part actor playing a couple-of-coughs-and-a-spit in stock," I said, "and he may be getting the big money, but how long'll it last?"'

'What the hell did you mean by that?'

'We're not as young as we was, sir, are we? "You don't want to talk silly," I said. "Questing's one thing and my gentleman's another." But no. "You're no better than a flunkey," he says. "You're demeaning yourself." I straightened him up about that. "There's none of the blooming vally about me," I says, "I'm a dresser and make-up, and what I do on the side is done by me own choice. I'm in the game with my gentleman." "It's greed for money," he howls, "that's ruining the world. Big business started this war," he says, "and when we've won it us chaps that did the fighting are going to have a say in the way things are run. The Questings'll be wiped right off the slate." That's the way he talks, you see, sir. Mind, I feel sorry for him. He's got the idea that his dad and ma are going to just about conk out over this business and to his way of thinking Questing's as good as a murderer. He says Smith knows something about Questing and that's why he had to jump for it when the train come. You've had fifteen minutes on them muscles and that'll do you.'

'You've damned nearly flayed me alive.'

'Yes,' said Colly, flinging a blanket over his victim and going into the next room to wash his hands. 'He's morbid, is young Sim. And of course Mr Questing's little attempts at the funny business with Miss Barbara kind of put the pot on it.'

Dikon, who had been clattering his typewriter, paused.

'What's that?' said Gaunt, suddenly alert.

'Had you missed the funny business, sir?' said Colly from the next room. 'Oh, yes. Quite a bit of trouble she has with him, I understand.'

'What did I tell you, Dikon?'

'The way I look at it,' Colly went on, appearing in the doorway with a towel, 'she's capable. No getting away from it, and you can't get domestic labour in this country without you pay the earth, so Questing thinks he'll do better to keep her when the old people go.'

'But damn it,' Dikon said angrily, 'this is insufferable. It's revolting.'

'That's right, Mr Bell. That's what young Sim thinks. He's worked it out. Questing'll try putting in the fine work, making out he'll look after the old people if she sees it in the right light. Coo! It's a touch of the old blood-and-thunder dope, isn't it, sir? Mortgage and all. The villain still pursued her. Only the juvenile to cast, and there, as we say in *The Dream,* sir, is a play fitted. I used to enjoy them old pieces.'

'You talk too much, Colly,' said Gaunt mildly.

'That's right, sir. Beg pardon, I'm sure. Associating with young Mr Claire must have brought out the latent democracy in me soul. I tell him there's no call to worry about his sister. "It's easy seen she hates his guts," I said, if you'll excuse me.'

'I'll excuse you altogether. I'm going to work.'

'Thank you, sir,' said Colly neatly, and closed the door.

He would perhaps have been gratified if he had known how accurately his speculations about Barbara were to be realized. It was on that same evening, a Thursday, nine days before the Maori concert, that Questing decided to carry forward his hitherto tentative approach to Barbara. He chose the time when, wearing a shabby bathing dress and a raincoat, she went for her four-o'clock swim in the warm lake. Her attitude towards public bathing had been settled for her by her mother. Mrs Claire was nearly forty when Barbara was born, and her habit of mind was Victorian. She herself had grown up in an age when one ducked furtively in the ocean, surrounded by the heavy bell of one's braided serge. She felt apprehensive whenever she saw her daughter drop her raincoat and plunge hastily into the lake clad in the longest and most conservative garment obtainable at the Harpoon Co-operative Stores. Only once did Barbara attempt to make a change in this procedure. Stimulated by some pre-war magazine photographs of fashionable nudities on the Lido, she thought of sun-bathing, of strolling in a leisurely, even a seductive manner down to the lake, not covered by her raincoat. She showed the magazines to her mother. Mrs Claire looked at the welter of oiled limbs, glistening lips and greased eyelids. 'I know, dear,' she said, turning pink. 'So very common. Of course newspaper photographers would never persuade the really, really *quite* to be taken, so I suppose they are obliged to fall back on these people.'

'But Mummy, they're not "these people"! Look, there's . . .'

'Barbara darling,' said Mrs Claire in her special voice, 'some day you will understand that there are folk who move in rather *loud* and vulgar *sets*, and who may seem to be very *exciting*, and who I expect are all very *rich*. But, my dear,' Mrs Claire had added, gently, exhibiting a photograph of an enormously obese peer in bathing shorts, supported on the one hand by a famous *coryphée* and on the other by a fashionable prize fighter – 'my dear, they are not Our Sort.' And she had given Barbara a bright smile and a kiss, and Barbara had stuck to her raincoat.

On the occasion of his proposal, Mr Questing, who did not care for sitting on the ground, took a camp stool to the far end of the lake, placed it behind some manuka scrub near the diving board and, fortified by a cigar, sat there until he spied Barbara leaving the house. He then discarded the cigar, and stepped out to meet her.

'Well, well, well,' said Mr Questing. 'Look who's here! How's the young lady?'

Barbara clawed the raincoat about her and said she was very well.

'That's fine,' said Mr Questing. 'Feeling good, eh? That's the great little lass.' He laughed boisterously and manoeuvred in an agile manner in order to place himself between Barbara and the diving board. 'What's your hurry?' he asked merrily. 'Plenty of time for the bathing-beauty stuff. What say we have a wee chin-wag, You, Me and Co, uh?'

Barbara eyed him with dismay. What new and odious development was this? Since the extraordinary scene on the evening of Smith's accident, she had not encountered Questing alone and was almost unaware of the angry undercurrents which ran strongly through the normal course of life at Wai-ata-tapu. For Barbara was carried along the headier stream of infatuation. She was bemused with calf-love, an infant disease which, caught late, is doubly virulent. Since that first meeting in the dusk, she had not seen much of Gaunt. She was so grateful for her brief rapture and, upon consideration, so doubtful of its endurance, that she made no attempt to bring about a second encounter. It was enough to see him at long intervals, and receive his greeting. Of Questing she had thought hardly at all, and his appearance at the lake surprised as much as it dismayed her.

'What do you want to see me about, Mr Questing?'

'Well, now, I seem to have the idea there's quite a lot I'd like to talk to Miss Babs about. All sorts of things,' said Mr Questing, dropping his voice to a fruity croon. 'All sorts of things.'

'But – would you mind – you see I'm just going to . . .'

'What's the big hurry?' urged Mr Questing, in his best synthetic American. 'Wait a bit, wait a bit. The lake won't get cold. You ought to do some sun bathing. You'd look good if you bronzed, Babs. Snappy.'

'I'm afraid I really can't. . .'

'Look,' said Mr Questing with emphasis. 'I said I wanted to talk to you and what I meant was I wanted to talk to you. You've no call to act as if I'd made certain suggestions. What's the idea of all this shrinking stuff? Mind, I like it in moderation. It's old-world. Up to a point it pleases a man, but after that it's irritating and right now's the place where you want to forget it. We all know you're the pure-minded type by this time, girlie. Let it go at that.'

Barbara gaped at him. 'There's a camp stool behind that bush,' he continued. 'Come and sit on it. I'll say this better if I keep on my feet. Be sensible, now. You're going to enjoy this, I hope. It's a great little proposition when viewed in the correct light.'

Barbara looked back at the house. Her mother appeared hurrying along the verandah. She did not glance up, but at any moment she might do so and the picture of her daughter, tête-à-tête with Mr Questing instead of swimming in the lake, would certainly disturb her. Yet Mr Questing stood between Barbara and the lake and, if she tried to dodge him, might attempt to restrain her. Better get the extraordinary interview over as inconspicuously as possible. She walked round the manuka bush and sat on the stool; Mr Questing followed. He stood over her smelling of soap, cigars and scented *cachous*.

'That's fine and dandy,' he said. 'Have a cigarette. No? OK. Now, listen, honey, I'm a practical man and I like to come straight to the point, never mind whether it's business or pleasure and you might call this a bit of both. I got a proposition to put up which I think is going to interest you a whole lot, but first of all we'll clear the air of misunderstandings. Now I don't just know how far you're wise to the position between me and your dad.'

He paused, and Barbara, full of apprehension, hurriedly collected her thoughts. 'Nothing!' she murmured. 'I know nothing. Father doesn't discuss business with us.'

'Doesn't he, now? Is that the case? Very old-world in his notions, isn't he. Well, now, we don't expect ladies to take a great deal of interest in business so I won't trouble you with a lot of detail. Just the broad outline,' said Mr Questing making an appropriate gesture, 'so's you'll get the idea. Now, you might put it this way, you might say that your dad's under an obligation to me.'

'You might indeed,' Barbara thought, as Mr Questing's only too lucid explanation rolled on. It seemed that five years ago when he first came to Wai-ata-tapu to ease himself of lumbago, he had lent Colonel Claire a thousand pounds, at a low rate of interest taking the hotel and springs as security. Colonel Claire was behind with the interest and the principal was now due. Mr Questing clothed the bare bones of his narrative in a vestment of playful hints and nudges. He wasn't, he said, a hard man. He didn't want to make it too solid for the old Colonel, not he. 'But just the same – ' Cliché followed cliche, business continued to be business, and more and more dubious grew the development of his theme until at last even poor Barbara began to understand him.

'No!' she cried out at last. 'Oh, no! I couldn't. Please don't!'

'Wait a bit, now. Don't act as if I'm not making a straight offer. Don't get me all wrong. I'm asking you to marry me, Babs.'

'Yes, I know, but I can't possibly. Please!'

'Don't run away with the idea it's just a business deal. It's not.' Mr Questing's voice actually faltered and if Barbara had been less frantically distracted she might have noticed that he had changed colour. 'To tell you the truth I've fallen for you, kid,' he continued appallingly. 'I don't know why, I'm sure. I like 'em snappy and kind of wise as a general rule and if you'll pardon my candour you're sloppy in your dress and, boy, are you simple! Maybe that's exactly why I've fallen. Now don't interrupt me. I'm not dizzy yet and I know you're not that way about me. I don't say I'd have asked you if I hadn't got a big idea you'd run this joint damn well when I showed you how. I don't say I haven't put you on the spot where it's going to be hard to say no. I have. I knew where I could get in the fine work, seeing how your old folks are placed, and I got it in. I'll use it all right. But listen, little girl!' – Mr Questing on a sudden note of fervour breathed out his final cliché – 'I want you,' he said hoarsely.

To Barbara the whole speech had sounded nightmarish. She quite failed to realize that Mr Questing thought on these standardized lines and spoke his commonplaces from a full heart. It was the first experience of its kind that she had endured, and he seemed to her a terrible figure, half-threatening, half-amorous. When she forced herself to look up and saw him in his smooth pale suit, himself pale, slightly obese and glistening, and found his eyes fixed rather greedily upon hers, her panic mounted to its climax, and she thought: 'I shan't like to refuse. I must get away.' She noticed that his expensive watch chain was heaving up and down in an agitated rhythm about two feet away from her nose. She sprang to her feet and, as if she had released a spring in Mr Questing, he flung his arms about her. During the following moments the thing she was most conscious of was his stertorous breathing. She brought her elbows together and shoved with her forearms against his waistcoat. At the same time she dodged the face which thrust forward repeatedly at hers. She thought: 'This is frightful. This is the worst thing that has ever happened to me. I'm hating this.' Mr Questing muttered excitedly: 'Now, now, now,' and they tramped to and fro. Barbara tripped over the camp stool and rapped her shin. She gave a little yelp of pain.

And upon this scene came Simon and Dikon.

II

Gaunt had announced that he would do no work after all and Dikon, released from duty, decided to go for a walk in the direction of the Peak. He had an idea that he would like to see for himself the level crossing and the bridge where Smith had his escape from the train. He found Simon and asked him to point out the short cut to the Peak road. Simon, most unexpectedly, offered to go with him. They set out together along the path that ran past the springs and lake. They had not gone far before they heard a confused trampling and a sharp cry. Without a word but on a single impulse, they ran forward together and Barbara was discovered in Mr Questing's arms.

Dikon was an over-civilized young man. He belonged to a generation whose attitude of mind was industriously ironic. He could accept scenes that arose out of crises of the nerves; they were a commonplace of the circle into which his association with Gaunt had introduced him. It was inconceivable that any young woman of those circles would be unable to cope with the advances of a Mr Questing or, for a matter of that, fail to lunch and dine off such an attempt when she had dealt with it. Dikon's normal reaction to Barbara's terror would perhaps have been a feeling of incredulous embarrassment. After all they were within a few hundred yards of the house in broad daylight. It was up to her to cope. He could never have predicted the impulse of pure anger that flooded through him, and he had time actually to feel astonished at himself. It was not until afterwards that he recognized the complementary emotion which arose when Barbara ran to her brother. Dikon realized then that he himself was a lay figure and felt a twinge of regret that it was so.

Simon behaved with more dignity than might have been expected of him. He put his arm across his sister's shoulders and in his appalling voice said: 'What's up, Barbie?' When she did not answer he went on: 'I'll look after this. You cut along out of it.'

'Hey!' said Mr Questing. 'What's the big idea?'

'It's nothing, Sim. Sim, it's all right, really.'

Simon looked over her shoulder at Dikon. 'Fix her up, will you?' he said, and Dikon answered: 'Yes, of course,' and wondered what was expected of him. Simon shoved her, not ungently, towards him.

'Great hopping fleas,' Mr Questing expostulated, 'what's biting you now! There's not a damn thing a man can do in this place without you all come milling round like magpies. You're crazy. I try to get a little private yarn with Babs and you start howling as if it was the Rape of the What-have-you Women.'

'Go and boil your head,' said Simon. 'And Barbie, you buzz off.'

'I really think you'd better,' Dikon said, realizing that his function was to remove her. She murmured something hurriedly to Simon and turned away. 'All right, all right,' said Simon, 'don't you worry.' They left Simon and Questing glaring at each other in ominous silence.

Dikon followed her along the path. She started off at a great rate, with her head high, clutching her raincoat about her. They had gone some little way before he saw that her shoulders were quivering. He felt certain that all she wanted of him was to leave her to herself, but he could not make up his mind to do this. As they drew nearer to the house they saw Colonel and Mrs Claire come out on the verandah and begin to set up their deck chairs. Barbara stopped short and turned. Her face was stained with tears.

'I can't let them see,' she said.

'Come round by the other path.'

It was a track that skirted the springs and came out near the cabins. A brushwood fence screened it from the verandah. Halfway along, Barbara faltered, sat on the bank, buried her face in her arms and cried most bitterly.

'Oh God, I'm so sorry,' said Dikon confusedly. 'Have my handkerchief. I'll turn my back, shall I? Or shall I?'

She took the handkerchief with a woebegone attempt at a smile. He sat beside her and put his arm around her.

'Never mind,' he said. 'He's quite preposterous. A ridiculous episode.'

'It was *beastly*.'

'Well, confound the fellow, anyway, for upsetting you.'

'It's not only that. He – he – ' Barbara hesitated and then with a most dejected attempt at her trick of over-emphasis sobbed out: 'He's got a *hold* on us.'

'So Colly was right,' Dikon thought. 'It *is* the old dope.'

'If only Daddy had never met him! And what Sim's doing now, I can't imagine. If Sim loses his temper he's frightful. Oh dear,' said Barbara blowing her nose very loudly on Dikon's handkerchief, 'what have we all done that everything should go so hideously wrong with us? Really, it's exactly as if we dotted scenes about the place like booby traps for Mr Gaunt and you. And he was so heavenly about the other time, pretending he didn't mind.'

'It wasn't a pretence. He told you the truth when he said he adored scenes. He does. He even uses them in his work. Do you remember in the *Jane Eyre*, when Rochester, without realizing what he did, slowly wrung the necks of Jane's bridal flowers?'

'Of course I do,' said Barbara eagerly. 'It was terrible but sort of noble.'

'He got it from a drunken dresser who flew into a rage with the star she looked after. She wrenched the heads off one of the bouquets. He never forgets things like that.'

'Oh.'

'You're feeling a bit better now?'

'A bit. You're very kind, aren't you?' said Barbara rather as if she saw Dikon for the first time. 'I mean, to take trouble over our frightfulness.'

'You must stop being apologetic,' Dikon said. 'So far I've taken no trouble at all.'

'You listen nicely,' Barbara said.

'I'm almost ghoulishly discreet, if that's any recommendation.'

'I do so wonder what Sim's doing. Can you hear anything?'

'We've come rather far away from them to hear anything. Unless, of course, they begin to scream in each other's faces. What would you expect to hear? Dull thuds?'

'I don't know. *Listen!*'

'Well,' said Dikon after a pause, 'that *was* a dull thud. Do you suppose that Mr Questing has been felled to the ground for the second time in a fortnight?'

'I'm afraid Sim's hit him.'

'I'm afraid so too,' Dikon agreed. 'Look.'

From where they sat they could see the patch of manuka scrub. Mr Questing appeared, nursing his face in his handkerchief. He came slowly along the main path and as he drew nearer they saw that his handkerchief was dappled red. 'A dong on the nose, by gum,' said Dikon. When he arrived at the intersection, Mr Questing paused.

'I'm going – He'll see me. I can't – ' Barbara began, but she was too late. Mr Questing had already seen them. He advanced a short way down the side path and, still holding his handkerchief to his nose, addressed them from some considerable distance.

'Look at this,' he shouted. 'Is it a swell set-up, or is it? I like to do things in a refined way and here's what I get for it. What's the matter with the crowd around here? Ask a lady to marry you and somebody hauls off and half kills you. I'm going to clean this dump right up. Pardon me, Mr Bell, for intruding personal affairs.'

'Not at all, Mr Questing,' said Dikon politely.

Mr Questing unguardedly removed his handkerchief and three large red blobs fell on his shirt front. 'Blast!' he said violently and staunched his nose again. 'Listen, Babs,' he continued through the handkerchief. 'If you feel like changing your mind, I won't say the offer's closed, but if you want to do anything you'll need to make it snappy. I'm going to pack them up, the whole crowd of them. I'll give the Colonel till the end of the month and then *out*. And, by God, if I'd got a witness I'd charge your tough young brother with assault. By God, I would. I'm fed up. I'm in pain and I'm fed up.' He goggled at Dikon over the handkerchief. 'Apologizing once again, old man,' said Mr Questing, 'and assuring you that you'll very shortly see a big change for the better in the management of this bloody dump. So long, for now.'

III

Long after the events recorded in this tale were ended, Dikon, looking back at the first fortnight at Wai-ata-tapu, would reflect that they had suffered collectively from intermittent emotional hiccoughs. For long intervals the daily routine would be interrupted and then, when he wondered if they had settled down, they would be convulsed and embarrassed by yet another common spasm. Not that he ever believed, after Mr Questing's outburst, that there was much hope of the Claires settling back into their old way of life. It seemed to Dikon that Mr Questing had been out for blood. A marked increase in Colonel Claire's vagueness, together with an air of bewildered misery, suggested that he had been faced with an ultimatum. Dikon had come upon Mrs Claire on her knees before an old trunk, shaking her head over Edwardian photographs and aimlessly arranging them in heaps. When she saw him she murmured something about clinging to one's household gods wherever one went. Barbara, who had taken to confiding in Dikon, told him that she had sworn Simon to secrecy over the incident by the lake, but that Questing had been closeted with her father for half an hour, still wearing his blood-stained shirt, and had no doubt given the Colonel his own version of the affray. Dikon had described the scene by the lake to Gaunt and, halfway through the recital, wished he had left it alone. Gaunt was surprisingly interested. 'It really is most *intriguing*,' he said, rubbing his delicate hands together. 'I was right about the girl, you see. She *has* got something. I'm never mistaken. She's incredibly gauche, she talks like a madwoman, and she grimaces like a monkey. That's simply because she's raw, uncertain of herself. It's the bone one should look at. Show me a good bone, and a pair of eyes, give me a free hand, and I'll create beauty. She's roused the unspeakable Questing, you see.'

'But Questing has his eye on the place.'

'Nobody, my dear Dikon, for the sake of seven squalid mud puddles is going to marry a woman who doesn't attract him. No, no, the girl's got something. I've been talking to her. Studying her. I tell you I'm never mistaken. You remember that understudy child at the Unicorn? I saw there was something in her. I told the management. She's never looked back. It's a flair one has. I could . . .' Gaunt paused and took his chin between his thumb and forefinger. 'It would be rather fun to try,' he said.

With a sensation of panic, Dikon said: 'To try what, sir?'

'Dikon, shall I make Barbara Claire a present? What was the name of the dress shop we noticed in Auckland? Near the hotel? Quite good? You must remember. A ridiculous name.'

'I don't remember.'

'Sarah Snappe! Of course. Barbara shall have a new dress for this Maori concert on Saturday. Black, of course. It must be terribly simple. You can write at once. No, perhaps you should go to Harpoon and telephone, and they must put it on tomorrow's train. There was a dress in the window, woollen with a dusting of steel stars. Really quite good. It would fit her. And ask them to be kind and find shoes and gloves for us. If possible, stockings. You can get the size somehow. And underclothes, for God's sake. One can imagine what hers are like. I shall indulge myself in this, Dikon. And we must take her to a hairdresser and stand over him. I shall make her up. If Sarah Snappe doesn't believe you're my secretary you can ring up the hotel and do it through them.' Gaunt beamed at his secretary. 'What a child I am, after all, Dikon, aren't I? I mean this is going to give me such *real* pleasure.'

Dikon said in a voice of ice: 'But it's quite impossible, sir.'

'What the devil do you mean!'

'There's no parity between Barbara Claire and an understudy at the Unicorn.'

'I should damn well say there wasn't. The other little person had quite a lot to start with. She was merely incredibly vulgar.'

'Which Barbara Claire is not,' said Dikon. He looked at his employer, noted his air of peevish complacency and went on steadily. 'Honestly, sir, the Claires would never understand. You know what they're like. A comparative stranger to offer their daughter clothes!'

'Why the hell not?'

'It just isn't done in their world.'

'You've become maddenly class-conscious all of a sudden, my good Dikon. What is their world, pray?'

'Shall we say proudly poor, sir?'

'The suspicious-genteel, you mean. The incredibly, the insultingly stupid *bourgeoisie* who read offence in a kindly impulse. You wish me to understand that these people would try to snub me, don't you?'

'I think they would be very polite,' Dikon said, and tried not to sound priggish, 'but it would, in effect, be a snub. I'm sure they would understand that your impulse was a kind one.'

Gaunt's face had bleached. Dikon, who knew the danger signals, wondered in a panic if he was about to lose his job. Gaunt walked to the door and looked out. With his back still turned to his secretary he said: 'You will go into Harpoon and give the order over the telephone. The bill is to be sent to me, and the parcel to be addressed to Miss Claire. Wait a moment.' He went to his desk and wrote on a slip of paper. 'Ask them to write out this message and put it in the parcel. No signature, of course. You will go at once, if you please.'

'Very well, sir,' said Dikon.

Filled with the liveliest misgivings he went out to the car. Simon was in the garage. Gaunt had been granted a traveller's petrol licence and Simon had offered to keep the magnificent car in order. Gloating secretly, he would spend hours over slight adjustments; cleaning, listening, peering.

'I still reckon we might advance the spark a bit,' he said without looking at Dikon.

'I'm going into Harpoon,' said Dikon. 'Would you care to come?'

'I don't mind.'

Dikon had learned to recognize this form of acceptance. 'Jump in then,' he said. 'You can drive.'

'I won't come at that.'

'Why not?'

'She's not my bus. Not my place to drive her.'

'Don't be an ass. I've got a free hand and I'm asking you. You can check up the engine better if you're driving, can't you?'

He saw desire and defensiveness struggling together in Simon. 'Get on with it,' he said and sat firmly in the passenger's place.

They drove round the house and up the abominable drive. Dikon glanced at Simon and was touched by his look of inward happiness. He drove delicately and with assurance.

'Running well, isn't she?' asked Dikon.

'She's a trimmer,' said Simon. As the car gathered speed on the main road he lost his customary air of mulishness and gained a kind of authority. Bent on dismissing the scene with Gaunt from his thoughts, Dikon lured Simon into talking about his own affairs, his impatience to get into uniform, his struggles with Morse, his passionate absorption with the war in the air. Dikon thought how young Simon would have seemed among English youth of his own age and how vulnerable. 'I'm coming on with the old dah-dah-dit, though,' Simon said. 'I've made my own practice transmitter. It's got a corker fulcrum, too. I'm not so hot at receiving yet, but I can get quite a bit of the stuff on the shortwave. Nearly all code, of course, but some of it's straight English. Gosh, I wish they'd pull me in. It's a blooming nark the way they keep you hanging about.'

'They'll miss you on the place.'

'We won't be on the place much longer, don't *you* worry. Questing'll look after that. By cripey, I sometimes wonder if it's a fair pop, me going away when that bloke's hanging round.' They drove on in silence for a time and then, without warning, Simon burst into a spate of bewildered protest and fury. It was difficult to follow the progress of his ideas: Questing's infamy, the Colonel's unworldliness, Barbara's virtue, the indignation of the Maori people, and the infamy of big business and vested interests were inextricably mixed together in his discourse. Presently, however, a new theme appeared. 'Uncle James,' said Simon, 'reckons the curio business is all a blind. He reckons Questing's an enemy agent.'

Dikon made a faint incredulous noise. 'Well, he might be,' said Simon combatively. 'Why not? You don't kid yourself they haven't got agents in New Zealand, do you?'

'Somehow he doesn't strike me as the type.'

'They don't knock around wearing masks and looking tough,' Simon pointed out with an unexpected touch of his uncle's acerbity.

'I know, I know. It's only that one hears such a lot of palpable nonsense about spies that the whole idea is suspect. Like arrow poison in a detective story. Why does Dr Ackrington think – '

'I don't get the strength of it myself. He wouldn't say much. Only dropped hints that we needn't be sure Questing'd kick Dad off the place. Were you in this country when the *Hippolyte* was torpedoed?'

'No. We heard about it, of course. It was a submarine, wasn't it?'

'That's right. The *Hippolyte* put out from Harpoon at night. She went down in sight of land. Uncle James reckoned at the time that the raider got the tip from someone on shore.'

'Questing?' said Dikon, and tried very hard to keep the note of scepticism from his voice.

'Yeah, Questing. Uncle James dopes it out that it's been Questing's idea to get this place on his own ever since he lent Dad the money. He reckons he's been acting as an agent for years and that he'll use the Springs as his headquarters with bogus patients and as likely as not a secret transmitting station.'

'Oh, Lord!'

'Well, anyway he's acted pretty crook, hasn't he? I don't think it's so funny. And if the old dead-beats at home hadn't been too tired to take notice, perhaps we wouldn't have been looking so silly now,' Simon added vindictively. 'Chaps like Questing ought to be cleaned right up, I reckon. Out of it altogether. What'd they do with them in Russia? Look here,' Simon continued, 'I'll tell you something. The night before the *Hippolyte* went down there was a light flashing on the Peak. Some of the chaps over at the Kainga, Eru and Rewi Te Kahu and that gang, had gone out in a boat from Harpoon and they said they saw it. Uncle James has seen it since. Everybody knows there's a reinforcement sailing any time now. What's Questing doing, where does he go half the time? He's messing round on the Peak, isn't he? Why did he try to put Bert Smith under the train?' Dikon attempted to speak and was firmly talked down. 'Accident my foot,' said Simon. 'He ought to be charged with attempted murder. The police round here seem to think they amount to something. I reckon they don't know they're born.'

'Well,' Dikon said mildly, 'what action do you propose to take?'

'There's no need to be sarcastic,' Simon roared out. 'If you want to know what I'm going to do I'll tell you. I'm going to stay up at nights. If Questing goes out I'll slip after him and I'll watch the Peak. My Morse'll be good enough for what he does. It'll be in code, of course, but if it's Morse he's using I'll spot it. You bet I will, and by gum I'll go to the station at Harpoon and if they don't pull him in on that I'll charge him with attempted murder.'

'And if they don't care for that either?'

'I'll do *something*,' said Simon. 'I'll do *something*.'

CHAPTER 6

Arrival of Septimus Falls

Friday, the day before the concert, marked the beginning of a crescendo in the affairs of Wai-ata-tapu. It began at breakfast. The London news bulletin was more than usually ominous and the pall of depression that was in the background of all New Zealanders' minds at that time seemed to drag a little nearer. Colonel Claire, looking miserable, ate his breakfast in silence. Questing and Simon were both late for this meal, and one glance at Simon's face convinced Dikon that something had happened to disturb him. He had black marks under his eyes and an air of angry satisfaction. Mr Questing, too, looked as if he had not slept well. He spared them his customary sallies of matutinal playfulness. Since their drive to Harpoon two days ago, Dikon had tried to adjust his ideas of Mr Questing to that of a paid enemy agent. He had even kept awake for an hour or two beyond his usual time watching the face of Rangi's Peak. But, although Mr Questing announced his intention each night of dining at the hotel in Harpoon and had not returned when the rest of the party went to bed, the Peak changed from wine to purple and from purple to black outside Dikon's window and no points of light had pricked its velvet surface. At last he lost patience with watching and fell asleep. On both mornings he awoke with a dim recollection of hearing a car come round the house to the garages. Simon, he knew, had watched each night and he felt sure that the second vigil had been fruitful. Dikon fancied that Questing had delivered a final notice to the Claires, as at Friday's breakfast they bore an elderly resemblance to the Babes in the Wood. They ate nothing and he caught them looking at each other with an air of bewilderment and despair.

Smith, who seemed to be really shaken by his jump from the bridge, breakfasted early, a habit that kept up the tradition that he worked for his keep.

The general atmosphere of discomfort and suspense was aggravated by the behaviour of Huia, who, after placing a plate of porridge before Dr Ackrington, burst into tears and ran howling from the room.

'What the devil's the matter with the girl?' he demanded. 'I've said nothing.'

'It's Eru Saul,' said Barbara. 'He's been waiting for her again when she goes home, Mummy.'

'Yes, dear. Ssh!' Mrs Claire leant towards her husband and said in her special voice: 'I think, dear, that you should speak to young Saul. He's *not* the desirable type.'

'Oh, damn!' muttered the Colonel.

Mr Questing pushed his chair back and walked quickly from the room.

'That's the joker you ought to speak to, Dad,' said Simon, jerking his head at the door. 'You've only got to look at the way he carries on with – '

'Please, dear!' said Mrs Claire, and the party relapsed into silence.

Gaunt breakfasted in his room. On the previous evening he had been restless and irritable, unable to work or read. He had left Dikon to his typewriter and, on an unaccountable impulse, elected to drive himself along the appalling coastal road to the north. He was in a state of excitement which Dikon found ridiculous and disturbing. During six years of employment Dikon had found their association pleasant and amusing. His early hero-worship of Gaunt had long ago been replaced by a tolerant and somewhat detached affection, but ten days at Wai-ata-tapu had wrought an alarming change in this attitude. It was as if the Claires, muddle-headed, gentle, and perhaps a little foolish, had proved to be a sort of touchstone to which Gaunt had been brought and found wanting. And yet Dikon, distressed by this change, could not altogether agree with his own judgement. It was the business of the dress for Barbara, he recognized, that had irritated him most. He had accused Gaunt of a gross error in taste and yet he himself had learnt to mistrust and deride the very attitude of mind that the Claires upheld. Was it not, in fact, an ungenerous attitude that forbade the acceptance of a generous gift, an attitude of self-righteous snobbism?

And exploring unhappily the backwaters of his own impulses he asked himself finally if perhaps he resented the gift because he was not the author of it.

The rural mail car passed along the main highway at about eleven o'clock in the morning, and any letters for the Springs were left in a tin post box on the top gate. Parcels too big for the box were merely dumped beneath it. The morning was overcast and Gaunt was in a fever lest the Claires should delay the trip to the gate and the parcel from Sarah Snappe be rained upon. Dikon gathered that the gift was to remain anonymous but doubted Gaunt's ability to deny himself the pleasure of enacting the part of fairy godfather. 'He will drop some arch hint and betray himself,' Dikon thought angrily. 'And even if she refuses the blasted dress she'll be more besotted on him than ever.'

After breakfast Mrs Claire and Barbara, assisted in a leisurely manner by Huia, bucketed into their household duties with their customary air of laying back their ears and rushing their fences. Simon, who usually fetched the mail, disappeared and presently it began to rain.

'The oaf!' Gaunt fulminated. 'He will lurch up the hill an hour late and bring down a mess of repellent pulp.'

'I can go up if you like, sir. The man always sounds his horn if he has anything for us. I can go as soon as I hear it.'

'They would guess that we expected something. Even Colly – No, they must fetch their own detestable mail. She must receive her parcel at their hands. I want to see it, though. I can stroll out for my own letters. Good God, a second deluge is descending upon us. Perhaps, after all, Dikon, *you* had better go for a stroll and casually pick up the mail.'

Dikon looked at the rods of water that now descended with such force that they spurted off the pumice in fans, and asked his employer if he did not think it would seem a little eccentric to stroll in such weather. 'Besides, sir,' he pointed out, 'the mail car cannot possibly arrive for two hours and my stroll would be ridiculously protracted.'

'You have been against me from the outset,' Gaunt muttered. 'Very well, I shall dictate for an hour.'

Dikon followed him indoors, sat down, and produced his shorthand pad. He was dying to ask Simon if he had succeeded in his vigil.

Gaunt walked up and down and began to dictate. *'The actor,'* he said, *'is a modest warm-hearted fellow. Being, perhaps, more highly sensitized than his fellow man he is more sensitive . . .'* Dikon hesitated. 'Well, what's wrong with that?' Gaunt demanded.

'Sensitized, sensitive!'

'Death and damnation! . . . *he is more responsive*, then, *to the more subtle . . .'*

'More, sir, and *more.'*

'Then delete the second *more*. How often am I to implore you to make these paltry amendments without disturbing me? . . . *to the subtle nuances, the delicate halftones of emotion. I had always been conscious of this gift, if it is one, in myself.'*

'Do you mind repeating that, sir? The rain makes such a din on the iron roof I can scarcely hear you. I got the *subtle nuances.'*

'Am I, then, to compose at the full pitch of my lungs?'

'I could trot after you with my little pad in my hand.'

'A preposterous suggestion.'

'It's leaving off, now.'

The rain stopped with the abruptness of subtropical downpours, and the ground and roofs of Wai-ata-tapu began to steam. Gaunt became less restive and the dictation proceeded along lines that Dikon, in his new mood of open-eyed criticism, considered all too typical of almost any theatrical autobiography. But perhaps Gaunt would rescue his book by taking a line of defiant egoism. He seemed to be drifting that way. There was a growing flavour of: 'This is the life story of a damn good actor who isn't going to spoil it with gestures of false modesty'; a fashionable attitude and no doubt Gaunt had decided to adopt it.

At ten o'clock Gaunt went down to the Springs with Colly in attendance, and Dikon hurried away in search of Simon. He found him in his cabin, a scrupulously tidy room where wireless magazines and textbooks were set out on a working bench. He was in consultation with Smith, who broke off in the middle of some mumbled recital and with a grudging acknowledgement of Dikon's greeting sloped away.

In contrast to Smith, Simon appeared to be almost cordial. Dikon was not quite sure how he stood with this curious young man, but he had a notion that his passive acceptance of the role cast for him in the lake incident as the remover of Barbara, and his suggestion that Simon should drive the car, had given him a kind of status. He thought that Simon disapproved of him on general principles as a parasite and a freak, but didn't altogether dislike him.

'Here!' said Simon. 'Can you beat it? Questing's been telling Bert Smith he won't put him off *after* all, when he cleans us up. He's going to keep him on and give him good money. What d'you make of that?'

'Sudden change, isn't it?'

'You bet it's sudden. D'you get the big idea, though?'

'Does he want to keep him quiet?' Dikon suggested cautiously.

'I'll say! Too right he wants to keep him quiet. He's windy. He's had one pop at rubbing Bert out and he's made a mess of it. He daren't come at that game again so he's trying the other stuff. "Keep your mouth shut and it's OK by me." '

'But honestly – '

'Look, Mr Bell, don't start telling me it's "incredible". You've been getting round with theatrical sissies for so long you don't know a real man when you see one.'

'My dear Claire,' said Dikon with some heat, 'may I suggest that speaking in the back of your throat and going out of your way to insult everybody that doesn't is not the sole evidence of virility. And if real men spend their time trying to kill and bribe each other, I infinitely prefer my theatrical sissies.' Dikon removed his spectacles and polished them with his handkerchief. 'And if,' he added, 'you mean what I imagine you mean by "sissies", allow me to tell you you're a liar. And furthermore, don't call me Mr Bell. I'm afraid you're an inverted snob.'

Simon stared at him. 'Aw, Dickon!' he said at last, and then turned purple. 'I'm not calling you by your Christian name,' he explained hurriedly. 'That's a kind of expression. Like you'd say, "Come off it."'

'Oh.'

'And a sissy is just a chap who's kind of weak. You know. Too tired to take the trouble. English!'

'Like Winston Churchill?'

'Aw, to hell!' roared Simon, and then grinned. 'All right, all right!' he said. 'You win. I apologize.'

Dikon blinked. 'Well,' he said sedately, 'I call that very handsome of you. I also apologize. And now, do tell me the latest news of Questing. I swear I shan't boggle at sabotage, homicide, espionage, or incendiarism. What, if anything, have you discovered?'

Simon rose and shut the door. He then shoved a packet of cigarettes at Dikon, leant back with his elbows on his desk and, with his own cigarette jutting out of the corner of his mouth, embarked on his story.

'Wednesday night,' he said, 'was a wash-out. He went into Harpoon and had tea at the pub. You call it "dinnah." The pub keeper's a cobber of his. Bert Smith was in town and he says Questing was there all right. He gave Bert a lift home. Bert was half-shickered or he'd have been too windy to take it. He's on the booze again after that show at the crossing. It was then Questing put it up to him he could stay on after we'd got the boot. Yes, Wednesday night's out of it. But last night's different. I suppose he got his tea in town, all right, but he went over to the Peak. About seven o'clock I biked down to the level crossing – and, by the way, that light's working OK. I hid up in the scrub. Three hours later, along comes Mr Questing in his bus. Where he gets the juice is just nobody's business. He steams off up the Peak road. I lit off to a possie I'd taped out beforehand. It's a bit of a bluff that sticks out on the other side of the inlet. Opposite the Peak, sort of. At the end of a rocky spit. I had to wade the last bit. The Peak's at the end of a long neck, you know. The seaward side's all cliff, but you can climb up a fence line. But the near face is *easy* going. There's still a trace of track the Maori people used when they buried their dead in the crater. About halfway up it twists and you could strike out from there to the seaward face. There's a bit of a shelf above the cliff. You can't see it from most places, but you can from where I was. I picked that was where he'd go. From my possie you look across the harbour to it, see? It was a pretty solid bike ride, but I reckoned I'd make it quicker than Questing'd climb the Peak track. He's flabby. I had to crawl up the rock to get where I wanted. Wet to the middle, I was. Did I get cold! I'll say. And soon after I'd got there she blew up wet from the sea. It was lovely.'

'You don't mean to say you bicycled to that headland beyond Harpoon? It must be seven miles.'

'Yeah, that's right. I beat Questing hands down, too. I sat on that ruddy bluff till I just about froze to the rock, and I'll bet you anything you like I never took me eyes off the Peak. I looked right across the harbour. There's a big ship in and she was loading in the blackout. Gee I'd like to know what she was loading. I bet Bert Smith knows. He's cobbers with some of the wharfies, him and Eru Saul. Eru and Bert get shickered with the wharfies. They were shickered last night, Bert says. I don't think it's so hot going round with – '

'The Peak and Mr Questing,' Dikon reminded him.

'OK. Well, just when I thought I'd been had for a mug, it started. A little point of light right where I told you on the seaward face. Popping in and out.'

'Could you read it?'

'Neow!' said Simon angrily in his broadest twang. 'If it was Morse it was some code. Just a lot of *t*'s and *i*'s and *s*'s. He *wouldn't* use plain language. You bet he wouldn't. There'd be a system of signals. A long flash repeated three times at intervals of a minute. "Come in. I'm talking to you." Then the message. Say five short flashes: "Ship in port." That'd be repeated three times. Then the day when she sails. One long flash: "Tonight." Two short flashes: "Tomorrow." Three short flashes: "Tomorrow night." Repeat. Then a long interval, and the whole show over again. What I reckon,' Simon concluded, and inhaled a prodigious draught of smoke.

'But did you, in fact, see the sequence you've described?'

With maddening deliberation Simon ground out his cigarette, made several small backward movements of his head which invested him with an extraordinary air of complacency, and said: 'Six times at fifteen-minute intervals. The end signal was three flashes each time.'

'Was it, by George!' Dikon murmured.

'Course I haven't got the reading OK. May be something quite different.'

'Of course.' They stared at each other, a sense of companionship weaving between them.

'But I'd like to know what that ship's loading,' Simon said.

'Was there any answering flash out at sea? I couldn't know less about such things.'

'I didn't pick it. But I don't reckon she'd do anything. If it's a raider I reckon she'd come in close on the north side of the Peak, so's to keep it between herself and Harpoon, and wait to see. There's nothing but bays and rough stuff up the coast north of the Peak.'

'How long did you stay?'

'Till there was no more signalling. The tide was in by then. By heck, I didn't much enjoy wading back. He beat me to it coming home. Me blinking tyre had gone flat on me and I had to pump up three times. His bus was in the garage. By cripey, he's a beaut. Wait till I get him. That'll be the day.'

'What will you do about it?'

'Bike into town and go to the police station.'

'I'll ask for the car.'

'Heck, no. I'll bike. Here, you'd better not say anything to him.'

'Who?'

Simon jerked his head.

'Gaunt? I can't promise not to do that. You see we've discussed Questing so much, and Colly talks to Gaunt and you've talked to Colly. And anyway,' said Dikon, 'I can't suddenly begin keeping him in the dark about things. You've got a fantastic idea of Gaunt. He's – dear me, how embarrassing the word still is – he's a patriot. He gave the entire profit of the last three weeks' Shakespearean season in Melbourne to the war effort.'

'Huh,' Simon grunted. 'Money.'

'It's what's wanted. And I'd like to talk to him about last night for another reason. He took the car out after dinner. Once in a blue moon he gets a sudden idea he wants to drive. He may have noticed a light out to sea. He said he'd go up the coast road to the north.'

'And what he's done to the car is nobody's business. It's a terrible road. Have you looked at her? Covered in mud and scratched all over the wings. It's not his fault he didn't burst up the back axle in a pot hole. He's a shocking driver.'

Dikon decided to ignore this. 'What about Dr Ackrington?' he said. 'After all he was the first to suspect something. Oughtn't you to take his advice before you make a move?'

'Uncle James doesn't see things my way,' said Simon aggressively, 'and I don't see things his way. He thinks I'm crude and I think he's a nark and a dug-out.'

'Nevertheless I think I should tell him.'

'I dunno where he's got to.'

'He's returning tomorrow, isn't he? Wait till he comes before you do anything.'

A motor horn sounded on the main road.

'Is that the mail?' cried Dikon.

'That's right. What about it?'

Dikon looked out of the window. 'It's beginning to rain again.'

'What of it?'

'Nothing, nothing,' said Dikon in a hurry.

II

It was Barbara, after all, who went first to get the mail. Dikon saw her run out of the house with her mackintosh over her shoulders, and heard Mrs Claire call out something about the rain spoiling the bread. Of course. It was the day for the bread, thought Dikon, who had reached the secondary stage of occupation when the routine of a household is becoming familiar. With an extraordinary sensation of approaching disaster he watched Barbara go haring up the hill in the rain. 'But it's ridiculous,' he told himself, 'to treat a mere incident as if it was an epic. What the devil has come upon me that I can do nothing but fidget like an old woman over this damn girl's clothes? Blast her clothes. Either she refuses or she accepts them. Either she guesses who sent for them or she doesn't. The affair will merely become an anecdote, amusing or dull. To hell with it.'

The little figure ran over the brow of the hill and disappeared.

Dikon, obeying orders, went to tell his employer that the mail was in.

Barbara was happy as she ran up the hill. The rain was soft on her face; thin like mist, and warm. The scent of wet earth was more pungent than the reek of sulphur, and a light breeze brought a sensation of the ocean across the hills. Her spirit rose to meet it, and all the impending disasters of Wai-ata-tapu could not check her humour. It was impossible for Barbara to be unhappy that morning. She had received in small doses during the past week an antidote of unhappiness. With each little sign of friendliness and interest from Gaunt, and he had given her many such signs, her spirit danced. Barbara had not been protected against green-sickness by inoculations of calflove. Unable to compete with the few neighbouring families whom her parents considered 'suitable', and prevented by a hundred reservations and prejudices from forming friendships with the 'unsuitable', she had ended by forming no friendships at all. Occasionally, she would be asked to some local festivity, but her clothes were all wrong, her face unpainted, and her manner nervous and uneven. She alarmed the young men with her gusts of frightened laughter and her too eager attentiveness. If her shyness had taken any other form she might have found someone to befriend her, but as it was she hovered on the outside of every group, making her hostess uneasy or irritable, refusing to recognize the rising misery of her own loneliness. She was happier when she was no longer invited and settled down to her course of emotional starvation, hardly aware, until Gaunt came, of her sickness. How, then, could the financial crisis, still only half-realized by Barbara, cast more than a faint shadow over her new exhilaration? Geoffrey Gaunt smiled at her, quiet prim Mr Bell sought her out to talk to her. And, though she would never have admitted it, Mr Questing's behaviour, odious and terrifying as it had been at the time, was not altogether ungratifying in retrospect. As for his matrimonial alternative to financial disaster, she contrived to hide the memory of it under a layer of less disturbing recollections.

The parcel from Sarah Snappe lay under the mail box, half obscured by tussock and loaves of bread. At first she thought it had been left there by mistake, then that it was for Gaunt or Dikon Bell; then she read her own name. Her brain skipped about among improbabilities. Unknown Auntie Wynne had sent another lot of alien and faintly squalid cast-offs. This was the first of her conjectures. Only when she was fumbling with the wet string did she notice the smart modern lettering on the label and the New Zealand stamps and postmark.

It lay under folds of tissue paper, immaculately folded.

She might have knelt there in the wet grass for much longer if a gentle drift of rain had not dimmed the three steel stars. With a nervous movement of her hands she thrust down the lid of the box and pulled the wrapping paper over it. Still she knelt before it, haloed in mist, bewildered, her hands pressed upon the parcel. Simon came upon her there. She turned and looked at him with a glance half-radiant, half-incredulous.

'It's not meant for me,' she said.

He asked what was in the parcel. By this time she had taken off her mackintosh and wrapped the box in it. 'A black dress,' she said. 'With three stars on it. Other things, underneath. Another box. I didn't look past the dress. It's not meant for me.'

'Aunt Wynne.'

'It's not one of Aunt Wynne's dresses. It's new. It came from Auckland. There must be another Barbara Claire.'

'You're nuts,' said Simon. 'I suppose she's sent the money or something. Why the heck have you taken your mac off? You'll get wet.'

Barbara rose to her feet clutching the enormous package. 'It's got my name on it. Barbara Claire, Wai-ata-tapu Spa, via Harpoon. There's an envelope inside, too, with my name on it.'

'What was in it?'

'I didn't look.'

'You're dopey.'

'It can't be for me.'

'Gee whiz, you're mad. Here, what about the bread and the rest of the mail?'

'I didn't look.'

'Aw, hell, you're mad as a meat axe.' Simon opened the letter box. 'There's a postcard from Uncle James. He's coming back tonight. A telegram for Mum from Auckland. That's funny. And a whole swag for the boarders. Yes, and look at the bread kicking around in the dirt. No trouble to you. Wait on.'

But Barbara, clutching the parcel, was running down the hill in the rain.

Gaunt waited on the verandah in his dressing-gown; 'very dark and magnificent,' thought Dikon maliciously. Whatever the fate of the dress, whatever Barbara's subsequent reaction, Gaunt had his reward, Dikon thought, when she ran across the pumice and laid the parcel on the verandah table, calling her mother.

'Hullo,' said Gaunt. 'Had a birthday?'

'No. It's something that's happened. I can't understand it.' She was unwrapping the mackintosh from the parcel. Her hands, stained with housework but not yet thickened, shook a little. She unfolded the wrapping paper.

'Is it china that you handle it so gingerly?'

'No. It's – my hands!' She ran down the verandah to the bathroom. Simon came slowly across the pumice with the bread and walked through the house.

'Did you tell them what to write?' Gaunt asked Dikon.

'Yes.'

Barbara returned, shouting for her mother. Mrs Claire and the Colonel appeared looking as if they anticipated some new catastrophe.

'Barbie, not *quite* so noisy, my dear,' said her mother. She glanced at her celebrated visitor and smiled uncertainly. Her husband and her brother did not stroll about the verandah in exotic dressing-gowns but she had begun to formulate a sort of spare code of manners for Gaunt, who, as Dikon had not failed to notice, spoke to her nicely and repeatedly of his mother.

Barbara lifted the lid from her box. Her parents, making uncertain noises, stared at the dress. She took up the envelope. 'How can it be for me?' she said, and Dikon saw that she was afraid to open the envelope.

'Good Lord!' her father ejaculated. 'What on earth have you been buying?'

'I haven't, Daddy. It's – '

'From Auntie Wynne. How kind,' said Mrs Claire.

'That's not Wynne's writing,' said the Colonel suddenly.

'No.' Barbara opened the envelope and a large card fell on the black surface of the dress. The inscription in green ink had been written across it somewhat flamboyantly and in an extremely feminine script. Barbara read it aloud.

'If you accept it, then its worth is great.'

'That's all,' said Barbara, and her parents began to look baffled and mulish. Simon appeared and repeated his suggestion that the aunt had sent a cheque to the shop in Auckland.

'But she's never been to Auckland,' said the Colonel crossly. 'How can a woman living in Poona write cheques to shops she's never heard of in New Zealand? The thing's absurd.'

'I must say,' said Mrs Claire, 'that although it's very kind of dear Wynne, I think it's always nice not to make mysteries. You must write and thank her just the same, Barbie, of course.'

'But I repeat, Agnes, that it's not from Wynne.'

'How can we tell, dear, when she doesn't write her name? That's what I mean when I say we would rather she put in a little note as usual.'

'It's not her writing. Green ink and loud flourishes! Ridiculous.'

'I suppose she wanted to puzzle us.'

Colonel Claire suddenly walked away, looking miserable.

'Mayn't we see the dress?' asked Gaunt.

Barbara drew it from the box and sheets of tissue paper fell from it as she held it up. The three stars shone again in the folds of the skirt. It was a beautifully simple dress.

'But it's charming,' Gaunt said. 'It couldn't be better. Do you like it?'

'Like it?' Barbara looked at him and her eyes filled with tears. 'It's so beautiful,' she said, 'that I can't believe it's true.'

'There are more things in the box, aren't there? Shall I hold the dress?'

He took it from her and she knelt on the chair, exploring feverishly. Dikon, whose orders had been to give Sarah Snappe *carte blanche*, saw that she had taken him at his word. The shell-coloured satin was dull and heavy and the lace delicately rich. There seemed to be a complete set of garments. Barbara folded them back, lifted an extraordinarily pert and scanty object, turned crimson in the face and hurriedly replaced it. Her mother stepped between her and Gaunt. 'Wouldn't it be best if you took your parcel indoors, dear?' she said with poise. Barbara blundered through the door with her box and, to her mother's evident dismay, Gaunt followed, holding the dress. A curious scene was enacted in the dining-room. Barbara hesitated between rapture and embarrassment, as Gaunt actually began to inspect the contents of the box while Mrs Claire attempted to catch his attention with a distracted résumé of the distant Wynne's dual office of aunt and godmother, Dikon looked on, and Simon read the morning paper. The smaller boxes were found to contain shoes and stockings. 'Bless my soul,' said Gaunt lightly. 'It's a trousseau.'

Colonel Claire appeared briefly in the doorway. 'It must be James,' he said, and walked away again, quickly.

'Uncle James!' cried Barbara. 'Mother, could it be Uncle James?'

'Perhaps Wynne wrote to James,' began her mother, and Simon said from behind his paper: 'She doesn't know him.'

'She knows *of* him,' said Mrs Claire gravely.

'You've got that telegram in your hand, Mum,' said Simon. 'Why don't you read it? It might have something to do with Barbie's clothes.'

They all stared at her while she read the telegram. Her expression suggested astonishment, followed by the liveliest consternation. 'Oh, *no*,' she cried out at last. 'We *can't* have another. Oh dear!'

'What's up?' asked Simon.

'It's from a Mr Septimus Falls. He says he's got lumbago and is coming for a fortnight. What *am* I to do?'

'Put him off.'

'I can't. There's no address. It just says "Kindly reserve single room Friday and arrange treatment lumbago staying fortnight Septimus Falls." Friday. *Friday!*' wailed Mrs Claire. 'What *are* we to do? That's today.'

III

Mr Septimus Falls arrived by train and taxi at 4.30, within a few minutes of Dr Ackrington, who picked up his own car in Harpoon. By some Herculean effort the Claires had made ready for Mr Falls. Simon moved into his cabin, Barbara moved into Simon's room, Barbara's room was made ready for Mr Falls. He turned out to be a middle-aged Englishman, tall but bent forward at a wooden angle and leaning heavily on his stick. He was good-looking, well-mannered, and inclined to be bookishly facetious.

'I'm so sorry not to give you longer warning,' said Mr Falls, grunting slightly as he came up the steps. 'But this wretched incubus of a disease came upon me quite suddenly yesterday evening. I happened to see your advertisement in the paper and the doctor I consulted agreed that I should try thermal treatment.'

'But we have no advertisement in the papers,' said Mrs Claire.

'I assure you I saw one. Unless, by any frightful chance, I'm come to the wrong Wai-ata-tapu Hot Springs. Your name *is* Questing, I hope?'

Mrs Claire turned pink and replied gently: 'My name is Claire, but you have made no other mistake. May I help you to your room?'

He apologized and thanked her, but added that he could still totter under his own steam. He seemed to be delighted with the dubious amenities of Barbara's room. 'I can't tell you,' he said in a friendly manner, 'how deeply I have grown to detest suites. I have been living in hotels for six months and have become so moulded to the *en suite* tradition that I assure you I have quite a struggle before I can bring myelf to wear a spotted tie with striped suit. It makes everything very difficult. Now this – ' he looked at Barbara's pieces of furniture, which, under the brief influence of a domestic magazine, she had painted severally in the primary colours – 'this will restore me to normal in no time.'

The taxi driver brought his luggage, which was of two sorts. Three extremely new suitcases consorted with a solitary small one which was much worn and covered with labels. Mrs Claire had never seen so many labels. In addition to partially removed records of English and continental hotels, New Zealand place names jostled each other over the lid. He followed her glance and said: 'You are thinking that I am "Monsieur Traveller, one who would disable all the benefits of his own country", and so forth. The fact is the evil brute got lost and has followed some other Falls all over the country. Would you care for the evening paper? The news, alas, is as usual.'

She thanked him confusedly, and retired with the paper to the verandah where she found her brother in angry consultation with Barbara. Dikon stood diffidently in the background.

'Well, old boy,' said Mrs Claire, and kissed him warmly. 'Lovely to have you with us again.'

'No need to cry over me. I haven't been to the South Pole,' said Dr Ackrington, but he returned her kiss, and in the next second attacked his niece. 'Will you stop making faces at me? Am I in the habit of lying? Why should I bestow raiment upon you, you silly girl?'

'But truly, Uncle James? Word of honour?'

'I believe he knows something about it!' Mrs Claire exclaimed very archly. 'Weren't we silly-billies? We thought of a fairy god*mother*, but we never guessed it might be a fairy god*father* at work, did we? Dear James, and she kissed him again. 'But you *shouldn't*.'

'Merciful Creator,' apostrophized Dr Ackrington, 'do I look like a fairy! Is it likely that I, who for the past decade have urged upon this insane household the virtues of economy, and investment – is it likely that I should madly lavish large sums of money upon feminine garments? And pray, Agnes, why are you gaping at that paper? Surely you didn't expect the war news to be anything but disastrous?'

Mrs Claire gave him the paper and pointed silently to a paragraph in the advertisement columns. Barbara read over his shoulder:

THE SPA
WAI-ATA-TAPU HOT SPRINGS

Visit the miraculous health-giving thermal fairyland of the North. Astounding cures wrought by unique chemical properties of amazing pools. Delightful surroundings. Homelike residential private hotel. Every comfort and attention. Medical supervision. Under new management.

M. QUESTING

The paper shook in Dr Ackrington's hand, but he said nothing. His sister pointed to the personal column.

'Mr Geoffrey Gaunt, the famous English actor, is at present a guest at Wai-ata-tapu Spa. He is accompanied by Mr Dikon Bell, his private secretary.'

'James!' Mrs Claire cried out. 'Remember your dyspepsia, dear. It's so bad for you!'

Her brother, white to the lips and trembling, presented the formidable spectacle of a man transported by rage. 'After all,' Mrs Claire added timidly, 'it *is* going to be true, dear, we're afraid. He *will* be manager very soon. Of course it's inconsiderate not to wait. Poor Edward – '

'To hell with poor Edward!' whispered Dr Ackrington. 'Have you eyes! Can you read! Will you forget for one moment the inevitable consequences of poor Edward's imbecility, and tell me how I am to interpret THAT?' His quivering finger pointed to the penultimate phrase of the advertisement. 'Medical supervision. *Medical supervision!* My God, the fellow means ME!' Dr Ackrington's voice broke into a surprising falsetto. He glared at Barbara, who immediately burst into a hoot of terrified laughter. He uttered a loud oath, crushed the newspaper into a ball, and flung it at her feet. 'Certifiable lunatics, the lot of you!' he raged, and turned blindly along the verandah towards his own room.

Before he could reach it, however, Mr Septimus Falls, doubled over his stick, came out of his own room. The two limping gentlemen hurried towards each other. A collision seemed imminent and Dikon cried out involuntarily: 'Dr Ackrington! Look out, sir.'

They halted, facing each other. Mr Falls said mellifluously: '*Dr* Ackrington? How do you do, sir? I was about to make inquiries. Allow me to introduce myself. My name is Septimus Falls. You, I take it, are the medical superintendent.'

Mrs Claire, Dikon and Barbara drew in their breaths sharply as Dr Ackrington clenched his fists and began to stutter. Mr Falls, with the experimental wariness of those suffering from lumbago, straightened himself slightly and looked mildly into Dr Ackrington's face. 'I hope to benefit by your treatment,' he said. 'Can it possibly be Dr *James* Ackrington? If so I am indeed fortunate. I *had* heard that New Zealand was so happy as to – but I am sure I recognize you. The photograph in *Some Aspects of the Study of Comparative Anatomy*, you know. Well, well, this is the greatest pleasure.'

'Did you say your name was Septimus Falls?'

'Yes.'

'Good God.'

'I can hardly hope that my small activities have come to your notice.'

'Here!' said Dr Ackrington abruptly. 'Come to my room.'

CHAPTER 7

Torpedo

'It appears,' said Dikon later that evening, 'that Mr Falls is a sort of amateur of anatomy and that Ackrington is his god. I am convinced that the revelation came only just in time to avert bloodshed. As it is the doctor seems prepared to suffer the adulation of his rather affected disciple.'

'When is Falls going to appear?' asked Gaunt. 'Why didn't he dine?'

'I understand he took old Ackrington's advice, had a prolonged stew in the most powerful of the mud baths, and retired sweating to bed. Ackrington suspects a wrong diagnosis and is going to prod his lumbar region.'

'A terrifying experience. He tried it on my leg. Dikon, have you ever seen anything like the transformation in that child? She was almost beautiful with the dress in her hands. She will be quite beautiful when she wears it. How can we engineer a visit to the hairdresser before tomorrow evening? With any normal girl it would be automatic, but with Barbara Claire! I'm determined she shall dazzle the native audience. Isn't it a fantastic notion? Metamorphosis at a Maori concert!'

'Yes,' said Dikon.

'Of course, if you're going to be cantankerous.'

'I am not, I assure you, sir,' said Dikon, and forced himself to add: 'You have given her an enormous amount of pleasure.'

'And she suspects nothing.' Gaunt looked sharply at his secretary, seemed to hesitate, and then took him by the arm. 'Do you know what I'm going to do? A little experiment in psychology. I'm going to wait until she has worn her new things and everybody has told her how nice she looks, until she has been stroked and stimulated and enriched by good clothes, and then, swearing her to secrecy first, I shall tell her where they came from. What do you think she will do?'

'Break her heart and give them up?'

'Not she. My dear chap, I shall be much too charming and tactful. It is a little test I have set myself. You wait, my boy, you wait.' Dikon was silent. 'Well, don't you think it'll work?' Gaunt demanded.

'Yes, sir. On consideration, I'm afraid I do.'

'What d'you mean, *afraid?* We're not going to have this absurd argument all over again I hope. Damn it, Dikon, you're no better than a croaking old woman. Why the devil I put up with you I don't know.'

'Perhaps because I try to give an honest answer to an awkward question, sir.'

'I don't propose to make a pass at the girl, if that's what's worrying you. You've allowed yourself to become melodrama-minded, my friend. All this chat of spies and mortgages and sacrificial marriage has blunted your aesthetic judgement. You insist upon regarding a charming episode as a seduction scene on a robust scale. I repeat I have no evil designs upon Barbara Claire. I am not a second Questing.'

'You'd be less of a potential danger if you were,' Dikon blurted out. 'The little fool's not besotted on Questing. Don't you see, sir, that if you go on like this the resemblance to King Cophetua will become so marked that she won't know the difference and will half expect the sequel? She's gone all haywire over you as it is.'

'Nonsense,' said Gaunt. But he stroked the back of his head and small complacent dints appeared at the corners of his mouth. 'She can't possibly imagine that my attentions are anything but avuncular.'

'She won't know what to imagine,' said Dikon. 'She's in a foreign country.'

'Where the alpine ranges appear to be entirely composed of mole hills.'

'Where, at any rate, she is altogether too much i' the sun. She's dazzled.'

'I'm afraid,' said Gaunt, 'that you are dressing up a very old emotion in a series of classy, and, if I may say so, rather priggish phrases. My good ass, you've fallen for the girl yourself.' Dikon was silent, and in a moment Gaunt came behind him and shook him boisterously by the shoulders. 'You'll recover,' he said. 'Think it over and you'll find I'm right. In the meantime I promise you need have no qualms. I shall treat her like porcelain. But I refuse to be deprived of my mission. She shall awake and sing.'

With this unconvincing reassurance Dikon had to be content. They said goodnight and he went to bed.

II

At twenty minutes past twelve on that same night a ship was torpedoed in the Tasman Sea six miles northwest of Harpoon Inlet. She was the same ship that Simon, from his eyrie of Friday night, had watched loading in the harbour. Later, they were to learn that she was the *Hokianga*, outward bound from New Zealand with a cargo of bullion for the United States of America. It was a very still night, warm, with a light breeze off the sea, and many Harpoon people said afterwards that they heard the explosion. The news was brought to Wai-ata-tapu the following morning by Huia, who rushed in with her eyes rolling and poured it out. Most of the crew were saved, she said, and had been landed at Harpoon. The *Hokianga* had not yet gone to the bottom, and from the Peak it was possible, through field glasses, to see her bows pointed despairingly at the skies.

Simon plunged into Dikon's room, full of angry triumph, and doubly convinced of Questing's guilt. He was all for leaping on his bicycle and pedalling furiously into Harpoon. In his own words he proposed to stir up the dead-beats at the police station, and the local army headquarters. 'If I'd gone yesterday like I wanted to, it wouldn't have happened. By cripey, I've let him get away with it. That was your big idea, Belt, and I hope you're tickled to death the way it's worked out.' Dikon tried to point out that even if the authorities at Harpoon were less somnolent than Simon represented them to be they would scarcely have been able in twelve hours to prevent the activities of an enemy submarine.

'They might have stopped the ship,' cried Simon.

'On your story that you saw lights on the Peak? Yes, I know there was a definite sequence and that it was repeated. I myself believe you're on to something, but you won't move authority as easily as that.'

'To hell with authority!' poor Simon roared out. 'I'll go and knock Questing's bloody block off for him.'

'Not again,' said Dikon sedately. 'You really can't continue in your battery of Questing. You know, I still think you should speak to Dr Ackrington, who, you say yourself, already suspects him.'

In the end Simon, who seemed, in spite of his aggressiveness, to place some kind of reliance on Dikon's advice, agreed to keep away from Questing, and to tell his story to his uncle. When, however, he went to find Dr Ackrington, it was only to discover he had already driven away in his car saying that he would probably return before lunch.

'Isn't it a fair nark!' Simon grumbled. 'What's he think he's doing? Precious time being wasted. To hell with him anyway, I'll think something up for myself. Don't you go to talking, now. We don't want everyone to know.'

'I'll keep it under my hat,' said Dikon. 'Gaunt knows, of course. I told you – '

'Oh, hell!' said Simon disgustedly.

Gaunt came out and told Dikon he wanted to be driven to the Peak. He offered a seat in the car to anyone who would like it. 'I've asked your sister,' he said to Simon. 'Why don't you come too?' Simon consented ungraciously. They borrowed the Colonel's field glasses and set out.

It was the first time Dikon had been to Rangi's Peak. After crossing the railway line, the road ran out to the coast and thence along the narrow neck of land, at the end of which rose the great truncated cone. So symmetrical was its form that even at close quarters the mountain seemed to be the expression of some grossly simple impulse – the impulse, one would have said, of a primordial cubist. The road ended abruptly at a gate in a barbed-wire fence. A notice, headed *Native Reserve*, set out a number of prohibitions. Dikon saw that it was forbidden to remove any objects found on the Peak.

They were not the first arrivals. Several cars were parked outside the fence.

'You have to walk from here,' said Simon, and glanced disparagingly at Gaunt's shoes.

'Oh, God! Is it far?'

'*You* might think so.'

Barbara cut in quickly. 'Not very. It's a good path and we can turn back if you don't think it's worth it.'

'So we can. Come on,' said Gaunt with an air of boyish hardihood, and Simon led the way, following the outside of the barbed-wire fence. They were moving round the flank of the Peak. The turf was springy under their feet, the air fresh with a tang in it. Some way behind them the song of a lark, a detached pin-prick of sound, tinkled above the peninsula. Soon his voice faded into thin air and was lost in the mewing of a flight of gulls who came flapping in from seawards. 'I never heard those creatures,' said Gaunt, 'without thinking of a BBC serial.' He looked up the sloping flank of the mountain, to where its crater stood black against the brilliant sky. 'And that's where they buried their dead?'

Barbara pointed to the natural planes of ascent in the structure of the mountain. 'It looks as if they had made a rough road up to the top,' she said, 'but I don't think they did. It's as though the hill had been shaped for the purpose, isn't it? They believe it was, you know. Of course they haven't used it for ages and ages. At least, that's what we're told. There *are* stories of a secret burial up there after the *pakehas* came.'

'Do they never come here, nowadays?'

'Hardly at all. It's tapu. Some of the younger ones who don't mind so much wander about the lower slopes, but they don't go into the bush and I'm sure they never climb to the top. Do they, Sim?'

'Too much like hard work,' Simon grunted.

'No, it's not that, really. It's because of the sort of place it is.'

Simon gave Dikon a gloomily significant glance. 'Yeh,' he said. 'Do what you like up here and nobody's going to ask questions.'

'You refer to the infamous Questing,' said Gaunt lightly. Simon glared at him and Dikon said hurriedly: 'I told you I had spoken to Mr Gaunt of our little theory.'

'That's right,' Simon said angrily. 'So now we've got to gas about it in front of everybody.'

'If you mean me,' said Barbara, whom even the mention of Questing could not embarrass that morning, 'I know all about what he's supposed to do on the Peak.'

Simon stopped short. 'You!' he said. '*What* do you know?' Barbara didn't answer immediately, and he said roughly: 'Come on. What do you know?'

'Well, only what they're all saying about Maori curios.'

'Oh,' said Simon. 'That.' Dikon spared a moment to hope that if Simon did well in the Air Force they would not make the mistake of entrusting him with secret instructions.

'And I know Uncle James thinks it's something worse, and . . .' She broke off and looked from one to another of the three men. Dikon blinked, Gaunt whistled, and Simon looked inescapably portentous. 'Sim!' cried Barbara. 'You're not thinking . . . about *this* . . . the ship? Oh, but it couldn't possibly . . .'

'Here, you keep out of this, Barbie,' said Simon in a great hurry. 'Uncle James talks a lot of hooey. You want to forget it. Come on.'

The track, curving always to the right, now mounted the crest of a low hill. The seaward horizon marched up to meet them. In three strides their whole range of vision was filled with blue. Harpoon Inlet lay behind on their left; on their right Rangi's Peak rose from the sea in a sharp cliff. The fence followed the top of this cliff, leaving a narrow path between itself and the actual verge.

'If you want to see anything,' said Simon, 'you'll have to get up there. Do you mind heights?'

'Speaking for myself,' said Gaunt, 'they inspire me with vertigo, nausea, and a strongly marked impulse towards *felo-de-se*. However, having come so far I refuse to turn back. That fence looks tolerably strong. I shall cling to it.' He smiled at Barbara. 'If you should happen to notice a mad glint of suicide in my eye,' he said, 'I wish you'd fling your arms round me and thus restore me to my nobler self.'

'But what about your leg, sir?' said Dikon. 'How's it holding out?'

'Never you mind about my leg. You go ahead with Claire. We'll take it in our own time.'

Dikon, having gathered from sundry pieces of distressingly obvious pantomime on Simon's part that this suggestion met with his approval, followed him at a gruelling pace up the track. The ocean spread out blandly before them as they mounted. Dikon, unused to such exercise, very rapidly acquired a pain in the chest, a stitch, and a thudding heart. Sweat gathered behind his spectacles. The smooth soles of his shoes slipped on the dry grass, and Simon's hobnailed boots threw dust into his face.

'If we kick it in,' said Simon presently, 'we can get up to the place where I reckon I saw the signalling on Thursday night.'

'Oh.'

'The others won't come any farther than this.'

They had climbed to a place where the track widened and ran out to a short headland. Here they found a group of some ten or twelve men who squatted on the dry turf, chewed ends of grass and stared out to sea. Two youths greeted Simon. Dikon recognized one of them as Eru Saul.

'What d'you know?' Simon asked.

'She's out there,' said Eru. 'Going down quick, now. You can pick her up through the glasses.'

They had left the Colonel's glasses with Gaunt, but Eru lent them his. Dikon had some difficulty focusing them but eventually the hazy blue field clarified and in a moment or two he found a tiny black triangle. It looked appallingly insignificant.

'They've been out to see if they could salvage anything,' said Eru, 'but not a chance. She's packed up all right. Tough!'

'I'll say,' said Simon. 'Come on, Bell.'

Dikon returned the field glasses, thanked Eru Saul and with feelings of the liveliest distaste meekly followed Simon up the fence line which now rose precipitously before flattening out to encompass a higher shoulder of the Peak. At last they reached a very small platform, no more than a shelf in the seaward face of the mountain. Dikon was profoundly relieved to see Simon, who was well ahead, come to a halt and squat on his heels.

'What I reckon,' said Simon as Dikon crawled up beside him, 'he must have worked it from here.'

Dry-mouthed and still very short-winded, Dikon prepared to fling himself down on the ledge.

'Here!' said Simon. 'Better cut that out. Stay where you are. We don't want it mucked up. Pity it rained yesterday.'

'And what do you expect to find, may I ask?' asked Dikon acidly. Physical discomfort did not increase his tolerance for Simon's high-handedness. 'Are you by any chance building on footprints? My poor fellow, let me tell you that footprints exist only on sandy beaches and in the minds of detective fiction-mongers. All that twittering about bent blades of grass and imprints slightly defaced by rain! In my opinion, they do *not* occur.'

'Don't they?' returned Simon combatively. 'Somebody's been up this track ahead of us. Didn't you pick that?'

'How could I "pick" anything when you did nothing but kick dust in my glasses? Show me a footprint and I'll believe in it. Not before.'

'Good-oh, then. There. What's that?'

'You've just made it with your own flat foot,' said Dikon crossly.

'What if I have? It's a print, isn't it? Goes to show.'

'Possibly.' Dikon wiped his glasses and peered round. 'What are *those* things?' he said. 'Over by the bank. Dents in the ground?'

He pointed and Simon gave a raucous cry of triumph. 'What did I tell you? Prints!' He removed his boots and crossed to the bank. 'You better take a look,' he said. Dikon removed his shoes. He had a blister on each heel and was glad to do so. He joined Simon.

'Yes,' he said. 'The footprints after all, and I can tell you exactly how they would be described by the know-alls. Several confused impressions of the Booted Foot, two being more clearly defined and making an angle of approximately thirty degrees the one with the other. Distance between inside margins of heel, half an inch. Distance between position of outside margin of big toes, approximately ten inches. This latter pair of impressions was found in damp clay but had been protected from recent rain by a bank which overhung them at a height of approximately three feet. There's great virtue in the word "approximately".'

'Good-ow!' said Simon on a more enthusiastic inflection than he usually gave to this odious expression. 'Nice work, go on.'

'Nails in the soles and heels. Toes more deeply indented than heels. Right foot, four nails in heel; six in sole. Left foot, three in heel, six in sole. *Ergo*, he lost a nail.'

'How much, he lost a nail?'

'*Ergo*. I'm being affected.'

'Huh! Yeh, well, what sort of chap is he? Does he act like Questing? Stands with his heels close together and his toes apart.

Puts more weight on his toes than his heels. Say what you like, you can deduce quite a bit if you use your nut.'

'As, for instance, he must be a dwarf.'

'Eye?'

'The bank overhangs the prints at a height of three feet. How could he stand?'

'Aw heck!'

'Would squatting fill the bill? The other prints show where he scuffled round trying to settle.'

'That's right. OK, he squatted. For a long time.'

'With his weight forward on his toes,' Dikon suggested. He had begun to feel mildly stimulated. 'The clay was damp at the time. Yesterday's rain was easterly and hasn't got in under the bank. On Thursday night there was a light rain from the sea.'

'Don't I know it? I was away out there, don't forget.'

Dikon looked out to his left. The shoulder of the hill hid Harpoon and the harbour, but Simon's rock was just visible, a shapeless spot down in the blue. 'If you stand on the edge you can just see the other boulders leading out to it,' said Simon.

'Thanks, I'll take your word for them.'

'Gee, can't you see the sand spit under the water clearly from up here? That's what it'll be like from the air. Coastal patrol work. Cripey, I wish they'd get on with it and pull me in.'

Simon stood on the lip of the shelf and Dikon looked at him. His chin was up. A light breeze whipped his hair back from his forehead. His shoulders were squared. Human beings gain prestige when they are seen at a great height against a simple background of sea and sky. Simon lost his uncouthness and became a significant figure. Dikon took off his glasses and wiped them. The young Simon was blurred.

'I envy you,' said Dikon.

'Me? What for?'

'You have the right of entry to danger. You'll move out towards it. I'm one of the sort that sit pretty and wait. Blind as a bat, you know.'

'Tough luck. Still, they reckon this is everyone's war, don't they?'

'They do.'

'Lend a hand to catch this joker Questing. There's a job for you.'

'Quite so,' said Dikon, who already regretted his digression. 'What have we decided? That Questing climbed up here on Thursday night, wearing hobnailed boots? That he signalled to a U-boat information about a ship loading at Harpoon and sailing the following night? By the way, can you visualize Questing in hobnailed boots?'

'He's been mucking about on the Peak for the last three months. He must have learnt sense.'

'Perhaps they are hobnailed shoes. Was there moonlight on Thursday night?'

'Not after the rain came up, but he was here by then. There was, before that.'

'They'll have to look at all his shoes. Should we perhaps try to make a sort of record of these prints? Glare at them until they leave an indelible impression on our minds and we can take oaths about them hereafter? Or shall I try to make a sketch of them?'

'That's an idea. If they knew their business they'd take casts. I've read about that.'

'Who precisely are *they?*' asked Dikon, taking out his notebook and beginning to sketch. 'The police? The army? Have we got anything approaching a secret service in New Zealand? What's the matter!' he added angrily. Simon had uttered a loud exclamation and Dikon's pencil skidded across his sketch.

'There's some bloke out here from Scotland Yard. A big pot. There was something about him in the papers a week or two back. They reckoned he'd come here to investigate fifth columnists, and Uncle James said they ought to be put in jail for giving away official secrets. By cripey, he's the joker we ought to get hold of. Go to the top if you want to get things done.'

'What's his name?'

'That's the catch,' said Simon. 'I've forgotten.'

III

Barbara and Gaunt did not go up the hill after all. They watched Simon and Dikon clinging to the fence and slipping on the short grass and friable soil.

'I have decided that my leg jibs at the prospect,' said Gaunt. 'Don't you think it would be much pleasanter to go a little way towards the sea and smoke a cigarette? This morbid desire to look at sinking ships! Isn't it kinder to let her go down alone? I feel that it would be rather like watching the public execution of a good friend. And we know the crew is safe. Don't you agree?'

Barbara agreed, thinking that he was talking to her as if she herself was a good friend. It was the first time they had been alone together.

They found a place near to the sea. Gaunt flung himself down with an air of boyish enthusiasm which would have intensely annoyed his secretary. Barbara knelt, sitting back on her heels, the light wind blowing full in her face.

'Do you mind if I tell you you should always do your hair like that?' said Gaunt.

'Like this?' She raised her hand to her head. The wind flattened her cotton dress. It might have been drenched in rain, so closely did it cling to her. She turned her head quickly, and Gaunt, as quickly, looked again at her hair. 'Yes. Straight off your face and brushed fiercely back. No frizz or nonsense. Terribly simple.'

'Orders?' said Barbara. It was so miraculously easy to talk to him.

'Please.'

'I'm afraid I'll look very bony.'

'But that's how you should look when you have good bones. Do you know that soon after we met I told Dikon I thought you had – but I'm making you self-conscious, and that's bad manners, isn't it? I'm afraid,' said Gaunt with a sort of aftermath of the Rochester manner, 'that I'm accustomed to say pretty much what I think. Do you mind?'

'No,' said Barbara, suddenly at a loss.

It was years, Gaunt thought, since he had met a young woman who was simply shy. Nervous, or deliberately coy young women, yes; but not a girl who blushed with pleasure and was too well-mannered to turn away her head. If only she would always behave like this she would be charming. He was taking exactly the right line with her. He began to talk to her about himself.

Barbara was enchanted. He spoke so intimately, as if she were somebody with a special gift of understanding. He told her all sorts of things. How, as a boy in school, he had been set to read 'The Eve of Crispian' speech from *Henry V*, and had started in the accepted wooden style which he now imitated comically for her amusement.

Then, so he told her, something had happened to him. The heady phrases began to ring through his voice. To the astonishment of his English master (here followed a neat mimicry of the English master) and, strange to say, the enthralment of his classmates, he gave the speech something of its due. 'There were mistakes, of course. I had no technique beyond an instinctive knowledge of certain values. But – ' he tapped the breast pocket of his coat – 'it was *there*. I knew then that I must become a Shakespearean actor. I heard the lines as if someone else spoke them:

> *'And Crispin, Crispian shall ne'er go by*
> *From this day to the ending of the world,*
> *But we in it shall be remembered.'*

Gulls mewed overhead and the sea thudded and dragged at the coast, a thrilling accompaniment, Barbara thought, to the lovely words.

'Isn't there any more?' she asked greedily.

'Little ignoramus! There's a lot more.' He took her hand. 'You are my Cousin Westmoreland. Listen, my fair cousin.' And he gave her the whole speech. It was impossible for him to be anything but touched and delighted by her eagerness, by the tears of excitement that stood in her eyes when he ended. He still held her hand. Dikon, limping over the brow of the hill ahead of Simon, was just in time to see him lightly kiss it.

Dikon drove back with Simon, completely mum, beside him in the front seat. Gaunt and Barbara, after a few desultory questions about the wreck, were also silent, a circumstance that Dikon mistrusted, and with some reason, for Barbara was lost in enchantment. One glance at her face had been all too enlightening. 'Besotted,' Dikon muttered to himself. 'What has he been up to? Telling her the story of his life, I don't doubt, with all the trimmings. Acting his socks off. Kissing her hand. By heaven, if the place had a second floor, before we knew where we were he'd be treating her to the balcony scene. Romeo with fibrositis! The truth is, he's reached the age when a girl's ignorance and adulation can make a fool of a man. It's revolting.' But although he allowed himself to fume inwardly, he would have resented and denied such imputations against Gaunt from any outsider, for not the least of his troubles lay in his sense of divided allegiance. He reflected that, Barbara apart, he liked his employer too much to enjoy the spectacle of him making a fool of himself.

When they returned to the house they found Mr Septimus Falls and Mr Questing sitting in deck chairs side by side on the verandah, a singular association. Dikon had implored Simon to show no signs of particular animosity when he encountered Questing, but was nevertheless very much relieved when Simon grunted a word of thanks to Gaunt and walked off in the direction of his cabin. Barbara, with a radiant face, ran straight past Questing into the house. Gaunt, before leaving the car, leant forward and said: 'I haven't been so delightfully entertained for years. She's a darling and she shall certainly be told who sent the dress.'

Dikon drove the car round to the garage.

When he returned he found that Questing, having introduced Septimus Falls to Gaunt, had adopted the manner of a sort of referee or ring master. 'I've been telling this gentleman all the morning, Mr Gaunt, that you and he must get together. "Here's our celebrated guest," I said, "with nobody to provide him with the correct cultural stimulus until you came along." It seems this gentleman is a great student of the drama, Mr Gaunt.'

'Really?' said Gaunt, and contrived to suggest distaste of Questing without positively insulting Falls.

Falls made a deprecating and slightly precious gesture. 'Mr Questing is too generous,' he said. 'The merest tyro, I assure you, sir. Calliope rather than Thalia commands me.'

'Oh, yes?'

'There you are!' cried Mr Questing admiringly. 'And I don't even know what you're talking about. Mr Falls has been telling me that he's a great fan of yours, Mr Gaunt.'

His victims laughed unhappily and Falls, with an air of making the best of a bad business, said: 'That, at least, is true. I don't believe I've missed a London production of yours for ten years or more.'

'Splendid,' said Gaunt more cordially. 'You've met my secretary, haven't you? Let's sit down for pity's sake.' They sat down. Mr Falls hitched his chair a little nearer to Gaunt's.

'I've often thought I should like to ask you to confirm or refute a pet theory of mine,' he said. 'It concerns Horatio's very palpable lie in reference to the liquidation of Rosencrantz and Guildenstern. It seems to me that in view of your brilliant reading of Hamlet's account of the affair – '

'Yes, yes. I know what you're at. *"He never gave commandment for their death."* Pure whitewash. What else?'

'I have always thought the line refers to Claudius. Your Horatio – '

'No, no. To Hamlet. Obviously to Hamlet.'

'Of course the comparison is absurd, but I was going to ask you if you had ever seen Gustav Gründgen's treatment – '

'Gründgen's? But that's Hitler's tame actor, isn't it?'

'Yes, yes.' Mr Falls made a little movement, gave a little yelp, and clapped his hand to the small of his back. 'This odious complaint!' he lamented. 'Yes, that is the fellow. A ridiculous performer. You never saw anything like the Hamlet. Madder and madder and madder does he grow and they think he's marvellous. I witnessed it. Before the war, of course. Naturally.'

'Naturally!' said Questing with a loud laugh.

'But we were speaking of the play. I have always considered – ' And Mr Falls was off on an extremely knowledgeable discussion of the minor puzzles of the play. Six years' association with Shakespearean productions had not killed Dikon's passion for *Hamlet* and he listened with interest. Falls was a good talker if an affected one. He had all sorts of mannerisms, nervous movements of his hands that accorded ill with his face, which was tranquil and remarkably comely. He had taken out a pipe, but, instead of lighting it, emphasized the points in his argument by knocking it out against the leg of his deck chair. 'To make *three* acts where in the text there are *five!*' he said, excitedly, and the dottle from his pipe flew about Mrs Claire's clean verandah as he illustrated his theme with appropriate and angry raps on the chair leg: 'Three, mind you, three, three! In God's name, why not leave the play as he wrote it?'

'But we do play it in its entirety, sometimes.'

'My dear sir, I know you do. I am enormously grateful as all Shakespeareans must be. Do forgive me. I am riding my hobby horse to death, and before you of all people. Arrogant presumption!'

'Not a bit of it,' said Gaunt cheerfully. 'I've been off my native diet long enough to have developed an inordinate appetite for it. But I must say I fail to see your point about the acts. Since we must abridge . . .'

Barbara looked out of the dining-room door, saw Questing still there, and hesitated. Without pausing in his argument, Gaunt put out his hand, inviting her to join them. She sat beside Dikon on the step. 'This will be good for you, my child,' said Gaunt in parenthesis, and she glowed ardently. 'What on earth has happened to her?' Dikon wondered. 'That's the same dress, better than the others because it's simpler, but the same. She's brushed her hair back since we came in, and that's an improvement, of course, but what's happened to *her?* I haven't heard a hoot from the girl for days, and she's stopped pulling faces.' Gaunt had begun to talk about the more difficult plays, of *Troilus and Cressida,* of *Henry VI* and finally of *Measure for Measure.* Falls, still beating his irritating tattoo, followed him eagerly.

'Of course he was an agnostic,' he cried – 'the most famous of the soliloquies proves it. If further proof is needed this play provides it.'

'You mean Claudio? I played him once as a very young actor. Yes, that speech! It's death without flattery, isn't it? It strikes cold.

> *'Ay, but to die, and go we know not where:*
> *To lie in cold obstruction, and to rot . . .'*

Gaunt's voice flattened out to a horrid monotone and his audience stirred uneasily. Mrs Claire came to one of the windows and listened with a doubtful smile. Falls's pipe dropped from his hand and he leant forward. The door of Dr Ackrington's room opened and he stood there, attentive. 'Do go on,' said Mr Falls. The icy sentences went forward.

> *'To be imprison'd in the viewless winds . . .'*

Mr Questing, always polite, tiptoed across the verandah, and retrieved the pipe. Falls seemed not to hear him. Questing stood with the pipe in his hand, his head on one side, and an expression of proprietary admiration on his face.

> *'. . . to be worse than worst*
> *Of those that lawless and incertain thought*
> *Imagine howling.'*

A shadow fell across the pumice. Smith, unshaven and looking very much the worse for wear, appeared from the direction of the cabin, followed by Simon. They stopped dead. Smith passed a shaky hand across his face and pulled at his under lip. Simon, after a disgusted stare at Gaunt, watched Questing.

Gaunt drew to the close of the short and terrifying speech. Dikon reflected that perhaps he was the only living actor who could get away with Shakespeare at high noon on the verandah of a thermal spa. That he had not embarrassed his listeners but had made some of them coldly uneasy was very apparent. He had forced them to think of death.

Questing, after clearing his throat, broke into loud applause, tapping Mr Falls's pipe enthusiastically against the verandah post. 'Well, well, well,' cried Mr Questing. 'If that wasn't an intellectual treat! Quite a treat, Mr Falls, wasn't it?'

'My pipe, I believe,' said Mr Falls, politely, and took it. 'Thank you.' He turned to Gaunt. 'Of course you may lay the agnosticism of those lines at the door of character and set against them a hundred others that are orthodox enough, but my own opinion – '

'*As You Like It* has always been *my* favourite,' said Mrs Claire from the window. 'Such a pretty play. All those lovely woodland scenes. Dear Rosalind!'

Dr Ackrington advanced from his doorway. 'With all this modern taste for psychopathological balderdash,' he said, 'I wonder you get anyone to listen to the plays.'

'On the contrary,' said Gaunt stuffily, 'there is a renaissance.'

Huia came out – clanging her inevitable bell. The Colonel appeared from his study looking vaguely miserable.

'Is that lunch?' he asked. 'What have you been talking about? Sounded as if someone was making a stump speech or somethin'.'

Barbara whispered hurriedly in her father's ear.

'Eh? I can't hear you,' he complained. 'What?' He stared at Gaunt. 'Out of a play, was it? Good Lord.' He seemed to be faintly disgusted, but presently an expression of complacency stole over his face. 'We used to do quite a bit of theatrical poodle-fakin' when I was a subaltern in India,' he said. 'They put me into one of their plays once. Damn' good thing. D'you know it? It's called *Charley's Aunt.*'

IV

Throughout lunch it was obvious to Dikon that Simon was big with some new theory. Indeed, so eloquent were his glances that neither Questing nor anybody else, Dikon thought, could possibly mistake their meaning. Dikon himself was in a state of mind so confused that he seemed to be living in the middle of a rather bad dream. Anxiety about Barbara, based on an emotion which he refused to define, a disturbing change in his own attitude towards his employer, and an ever-increasing weight of apprehension which the war bred in all New Zealanders at that time – all these elements mingled in a vague cloud of uneasiness and alarm. And then there was Questing. In spite of Simon's discoveries, in spite, even, of the witness of the torpedoed ship, Dikon still found it difficult to cast Questing for the role of spy. Indeed, he was still enough of a New Zealander to doubt the existence of enemy agents in his country at all, still inclined to think that they existed only as bugaboos in the minds of tiresome old ladies and clubmen. And yet ... mentally he ticked off the points against Questing. Had he tried to bring about Smith's destruction, and if so, why? Why did he pretend that he had been to Pohutukawa Bay, when, as Dr Ackrington had proved by his pitfall, he hadn't been near the place? If he visited the Peak only to hunt for curios, why should he have six times flashed his signal of three, five, and three, from a place where obviously no curios could be buried? He couldn't help looking at Questing, at his smooth, rather naïve face, his business man's clothes, his not altogether convincing air of commercial acumen. Were these the outward casings of a potential murderer, who was quietly betraying his country? Irrelevantly, Dikon thought: 'This war is changing the values of my generation. There are all sorts of things that we have thought funny that we shall never think funny again.' For perhaps the first time he contemplated coldly and deliberately a possible invasion of New Zealand. As he thought, the picture clarified. An emotion long dormant, rooted in the very soil of his native country, roused in him, and he recognized it as anger. He realized, finally, that he could no longer go on as he was. Somehow, no matter how uselessly, he, like Simon, must go forward to danger.

It was with this new determination in his mind that he visited Simon in his cabin after lunch. 'Did you guess I wanted to see you?' asked Simon. 'I didn't like to drop the hint over there. He might have spotted it.'

'My dear old thing, the air was electric with your hints. What's occurred?'

'We've got him,' said Simon. 'Didn't you pick it? Before lunch? Him and his pipe?'

Dikon gaped at him.

'Missed it, did you?' said Simon complacently. 'And there you were sitting where you might have touched him. What beats me is why he did it. D'you reckon he's got it so much on his mind he's acting kind of automatically?'

'If I had the faintest idea what you were talking about, I might attempt to answer you.'

'Aren't you conscious yet? I was sitting in here trying to dope things out when I heard it. I snooped round to the corner. All through the hooey Gaunt and Falls were spilling about Shakespeare or someone. It was the same in every detail.'

'For pity's sake, what was the same in every detail?'

'The tapping. A long one repeated three times. Dah, dah, dah. Then five short dits. Then three shorts. Then the whole works repeated. The flashes from the cliff all over again. So what have you?'

They stared at each other. 'It just doesn't make sense,' said Dikon. 'Why? Why? Why?'

'Search me.'

'Coincidence?'

'The odds against coincidence are long enough to make you dizzy. No, I reckon I'm right. It's habit. He's had to memorize it and he's gone over and over it in his mind before he shot the works on Thursday night . . . '

'Hold on. Hold on. Whose habit?'

'Aw hell,' said Simon disgustedly. 'You're dopey. Who the heck are we talking about?'

'We're talking about two different people,' said Dikon excitedly. 'Questing had picked up that pipe just before you came on the scene. It wasn't Questing who tapped out your blasted signal. It was Mr Septimus Falls.'

CHAPTER 8

Concert

The telephone at Wai-ata-tapu was on a party line. The Claires' tradesmen used it, and occasionally weekend trippers who rang up to give notice of their arrival. Otherwise, until Gaunt and Dikon came, it was seldom heard. The result of housing a celebrity, however, had begun to work out very much as Mr Questing had predicted. During the first weekend, quite a spate of visitors had arrived, ostensibly for thermal *divertissements*, actually, so it very soon transpired, with the object of getting a close-up view of Geoffrey Gaunt. These visitors, with an air of studied nonchalance, walked up and down the verandah, delayed over their tea, and attempted to pump Huia as to the whereabouts of the celebrity. The hardier among them came provided with autograph books which passed, by way of Barbara, from Huia to Dikon and thence to Gaunt, who, to the astonishment of Mrs Claire, cheerfully signed every one of them. He kept to his room, however, until the last of the visitors, trying not to look baffled, had lost patience and gone home. Once, but only once, Mr Questing had succeeded in luring him on to the verandah, and on Gaunt's discovering what he was up to had been treated to such a blast of temperament as sent him back into the house nervously biting his fingers.

On this particular Saturday afternoon, though there were no trippers, the telephone rang almost incessantly. Was it true that there was to be a concert that evening? Was Mr Geoffrey Gaunt going to perform at it? Could one obtain tickets and, if so, were the receipts to go to the patriotic funds? So insistent did these demands become that at last Huia was dispatched over the hill for definite instructions from old Rua. She returned, laughing excitedly, with the message that everybody would be welcome.

The Maori people are a kindly and easy-going race. In temperament they are so vivid a mixture of Scottish Highlander and Irishman that to many observers the resemblance seems more than fortuitous. Except in the matter of family and tribal feuds, which they keep up with the liveliest enthusiasm, they are extremely hospitable. Rua and his people were not disturbed by the last-minute transformation into a large public gathering of what was to have been a private party between themselves and the Springs. Huia, who returned with Eru Saul and an escort of grinning youths, reported that extra benches were being hurriedly knocked up, and might they borrow some armchairs for the guests of honour?

'Py korry!' said one of the youths. 'Big crowd coming, Mrs Keeah. Very good party. Te Mayor coming too, all the time more people.'

'Now, Maui,' said Mrs Claire gently, 'why don't you speak nicely as you did when you used to come to Sunday school?'

Huia and the youths laughed uproariously. Eru sniggered.

'Tell Rua we shall be pleased to lend the chairs. Did you say the Mayor was coming?'

'That's right, Mrs Keeah. We'll be having a good party, all right.'

'No drink, I hope,' said Mrs Claire severely, and was answered by further roars of laughter. 'We don't want Mr Gaunt to go away thinking our boys don't know how to behave, do we?'

'No fear,' said Maui obligingly. Eru gave an offensive laugh and Mrs Claire looked coldly at him.

'Plenty of tea for everybody,' said Maui.

'That will be very nice. Well, now you may come in and get the chairs.'

'Grandfather's compliments,' said Huia suddenly, 'and he sent you this, please.'

It was a letter from old Rua, written in a style so urbane that Lord Chesterfield might have envied its felicity. It suggested that though the Maori people themselves did not venture to hope that Gaunt would come in any other capacity than that of honoured guest, yet they had been made aware of certain rumours from a *pakeha* source. If, in Mrs Claire's opinion, there was any foundation of truth in these rumours, Rua would be deeply grateful if she advised him of it, as certain preparations should be made for so distinguished a guest.

Mrs Claire in some perturbation handed the letter over to Dikon, who took it to his employer.

'Translated,' said Dikon, 'it means that they're burning their guts out for you to perform. I'm sure, sir, you'd like me to decline in the same grand style.'

'Who said I was going to decline?' Gaunt demanded. 'My compliments to this old gentleman, and I should be delighted to appear. I must decide what to give them.'

'You could fell me with a feather,' said Dikon to Barbara after early dinner. 'I can't imagine what's come over the man. As a general rule platform performances are anathema to him. And at a little show like this!'

'Everything that's happening's so marvellous,' said Barbara, 'that I for one can't believe it's true.'

Dikon rubbed his nose and stared at her.

'Why are you looking at me like that?' Barbara demanded.

'I didn't know I was,' said Dikon hastily.

'You're thinking I shouldn't be happy,' she said with a sudden return to her owlish manner, 'because of Mr *Questing* and *ruin* staring us in the *face.*'

'No, no. I assure you that I'm delighted. It's only . . .'

'Yes?'

'It's only that I hope it's going to last.'

'Oh.' She considered him for a moment and then turned white. 'I'm not thinking about that. I don't believe I mind so very much. You see, I'm not building on anything. I'm just happy.'

He read in her eyes the knowledge that she had betrayed herself. To forestall, if he could, the hurt that her pride would suffer when it recovered from the opiate Gaunt had administered, Dikon said: 'But you can build on looking very nice tonight. Are you going to wear the new dress?'

Barbara nodded. 'Yes. I didn't change before dinner because of the washing-up. Huia wants to get off. But that's not what I mean about being happy . . .'

He cut in quickly. She must not be allowed to tell him the true reason for her bliss. 'Haven't you an idea who sent it to you?'

'None. Honestly. You see,' said Barbara conclusively, 'we don't know anyone in New Zealand well enough. You'd have to be a great friend, almost family, wouldn't you, to give a present like that? That's what's so puzzling.'

Mr Questing appeared from the dining-room in all the glory of a dinner jacket, a white waistcoat and his postprandial cigar. As far as anybody at the Springs knew, he had not been invited to the concert, but evidently he meant to take advantage of its new and public character.

'What's all this I hear about a new dress?' he asked genially.

'I shall be late,' said Barbara, and hurried into the house.

Dikon reflected that surely nobody in the world but Mr Questing would have had the gall, after what had happened by the lake, to attempt another three-cornered conversation with Barbara and himself. In some confusion, and because he could think of nothing else to say, Dikon murmured something about the arrival of an anonymous present. Mr Questing took it very quietly. For a little while he made no comment, and then, with a foxy look at Dikon, he said: 'Well, well, well, is that so? And the little lady just hasn't got a notion where it came from? Fancy that, now.'

'I believe,' said Dikon, already regretting his indiscretion, 'that there is an aunt in India.'

'And the pretty things come from Auckland, eh?'

'I don't think I said so.'

'That's quite all right, Mr Bell. Maybe you didn't,' Mr Questing conceded. 'Between you and me, Mr Bell, I know all about it.'

'What!' cried Dikon, flabbergasted. 'You do! But how the devil . . . ?'

'Just a little chat with Dorothy Lamour.'

'With . . . ?'

'My pet name for the Dusky Maiden,' Mr Questing explained.

'Oh,' said Dikon, greatly relieved. 'Huia.'

'Where do you reckon it came from, yourself?' asked Mr Questing with an atrocious wink.

'The aunt, undoubtedly,' said Dikon firmly, and on the wings of a rapid flight of fancy he added: 'She's in the habit of sending things to Miss Claire who writes to her most regularly. A very likely explanation is that at some time or another Miss Claire has mentioned this shop.'

'Oh, yeah?' said Mr Questing. 'Accidental-done-on purpose, sort of?'

'Nothing of the kind,' said Dikon furiously. 'The most natural thing in the world . . . '

'OK, OK, Mr Bell. Quite so. You mustn't mind my little joke. India,' he added thoughtfully. 'That's quite a little way off, isn't it?' He walked away, whistling softly and waving his cigar. Dikon uttered a few very raw words under his breath. 'He's guessed!' he thought. 'Blast him, if he gets a chance he'll tell her.' He polished his glasses on his handkerchief and stared dimly after the retreating figure of Mr Questing. 'Or will he?' he added dubiously.

II

Although it had been built with European tools, the meeting house at the native settlement followed the traditional design of all Maori buildings. It was a single room surmounted by a ridged roof which projected beyond the gable. The barge boards and supporting pillars were intricately covered in the formidable mode of Polynesian art. Growing out of the ridge pole stood a wooden god with out-thrust tongue and eyes of shell, squat, menacing, the symbol of the tribe's fecundity and its will to do battle. The traditional tree-fern poles and thatching had been replaced by timber and galvanized iron, but nevertheless, the meeting house contrived to distil a quintessence of savagery and of primordial culture.

The floor space, normally left clear, was now filled with a heterogeneous collection of seats. The Claires' armchairs, looking mildly astonished at their own transplantation, were grouped together in the front row. They faced a temporarily erected stage which was decked out with tree-fern, exquisitely woven cloaks, Union Jacks and quantities of fly-blown paper streamers. On the back were hung coloured prints of three kings of England, two photographs of former premiers, and an enlargement of Rua as an MP. On the platform stood a hard-bitten piano, three chairs and a table bearing the insignia of all British gatherings, a carafe of untempting water and a tumbler.

The Maori members of the audience had been present more or less all day. They squatted on the floor, on the edge of the stage, on the permanent benches along the sides and all over the verandah and front steps.

Among them was Eru Saul. Groups of youths collected round Eru. He talked to them in an undertone. There was a great deal of furtive giggling and sudden guffaws. At intervals Eru and his following would slouch off together and when they returned the boys were always noiser and more excited. At seven o'clock Simon, Colly and Smith arrived with three more chairs from Wai-ata-tapu. Colly and Simon stood about looking self-conscious, but Smith was at once absorbed into Eru Saul's faction.

'Hey, Eru!' said Smith, who had a pair of pumps in his pocket. 'Do we wind up with a dance?'

'No chance!'

'No fear you don't wind up with a dance,' said a woman's voice. 'Last time you wind up with a dance you got tight. If you can't behave yourselves you don't have dances.'

'Too bad,' said Smith.

The owner of the voice was seated on the floor with her back against the stage. She was Mrs Te Papa, an old lady with an incredibly aristocratic head tied up in a cerise handkerchief. Over her European dress she wore, in honour of the occasion, a magnificent flax skirt. She was the leading great-grandmother of the *hapu* and, though she did not bother much about her title, a princess of the Te Rarawas. Being one of the last of the old regime she had a tattooed chin. From her point of vantage she was able to call full-throated greetings and orders to members of her clan as they drifted in and out or put the finishing touches to the decorations. She spoke always in Maori. If one of the younger fry answered her in English she reached forward and caught the offender a good-natured buffet. One of the oddities of contemporary Maori life may be seen in the fact that, although some of the people in outlying districts use a fragmentary and native-sounding form of English, yet they have only a rudimentary knowledge of their own tongue.

At half-past seven visitors from Harpoon and the surrounding districts began to appear. Old Rua Te Kahu came in wearing a feather cloak over his best suit and, with great urbanity, moved among his guests. Mrs Te Papa rose magnificently and walked with the correct swinging gait of her youth to her appointed place.

At a quarter to eight a party of five white gentlemen, unhappily dressed in dinner suits and carrying music, were ushered into a special row of seats near the platform. These were members of the Harpoon Savage Club, famous throughout the district for their rendering in close harmony of Irish ballads. The last of them, an anxious small man, carried a large black bag, for he was also a ventriloquist. They were followed by a little girl with permanently waved hair who was dressed in frills, by her fierce mother, and by a firmly cheerful lady who carried a copy of *One Day When We Were Young*. It was to be mixed entertainment.

An observer might have noticed that while the ladies of the district exchanged many nods and smiles, occasionally pointing at each other with an air of playful astonishment, their men merely acknowledged one another by raising their eyebrows, winking, or very slightly inclining their heads to one side. This procedure changed when the member for the district came in as he shook hands heartily with almost everybody. At five minutes to eight the Mayor arrived with the Mayoress and shook hands with literally anyone who confronted him. They were shown into armchairs. By this time all the seats except those reserved for the official party were full and there were Maoris standing in solid groups at the far end of the hall, or settling themselves in parties on the floor. With the arrival of their guests they became circumspect and quiet. Those beautiful voices, that can turn English into a language composed almost entirely of deep-throated vowels, fell into silence, and the meeting house buzzed with the noise made by white New Zealanders in the mass. It became very hot and the Maori people thought indulgently that it smelt of *pakeha*, while the *pakehas* thought a little less indulgently that it smelt of Maori.

At eight o'clock a premature wave of interest was caused by the arrival of Colonel Claire, Mr Questing and Mr Falls. They had walked over from the Springs, crossing the native thermal reserve by the short cut. Mrs Claire, Barbara, Dr Ackrington and Gaunt were to be driven by Dikon and would arrive by the main road. The three older men were ushered up to the official chairs, but Simon at once showed the whites of his eyes and backed away into a group of young Maoris where he was presently joined by Smith, who was still very puffy and pink-eyed, and by Colly.

Mrs Te Papa was heard to issue an order. A party of girls in native dress came through the audience and mounted the stage. They carried in each hand cords from which hung balls made from dry leaves. Rua took up his station outside the door of the meeting house. He was an impressive figure, standing erect in the half-light, his feather cloak hanging rigidly from his shoulders. So had his great-grandfather stood to welcome visitors from afar. Near to him were leading men among the clan and, in the offing, Mrs Te Papa and other elderly ladies. Most of the Maori members of the audience turned to face the back of the meeting house and as many as could do so leant out of the windows.

Out on the road a chiming motor horn sounded, and at least twenty people said importantly that they recognized it as Gaunt's. The conglomerate hum of voices rose and died out. In the hush that followed, Rua's attenuated chant of welcome pierced the night air.

'*Haere mai. E te ururangi! Na wai taua?*'

Each syllable was intoned and prolonged. It might have been the voice of the night wind from the sea, a primal voice, strange and disturbing to white listeners. Out in the dark Mrs Te Papa and her supporters leant forward and stretched out their arms. Their hands fluttered rhythmically in the correct half-dance of greeting. Rua was honouring Gaunt with the almost forgotten welcome of tradition. The mutations of a century of white men's ways were pulled like cobwebs from the face of a savage culture, and the Europeans in the meeting house became strangers.

As they moved forward from the car Gaunt said: 'But we should reply. We should know what he is saying and reply!'

'I'm not certain,' said Dikon, 'but I've heard at some time what it is. I fancy he's saying we've got a common ancestor, in the first parents. I think he asks us to say who we are.'

'It's not really very *sensible*,' Mrs Claire murmured. 'They *know* who we are. Some of their customs are not at all nice, I'm afraid, but they really mean this to be quite a compliment, poor dears.'

'As of course it is,' said Gaunt quickly. 'I wish we could answer.'

On a soft ripple of greeting from the Maori party he moved forward and shook hands with Rua. 'He's at his best,' Dikon thought. 'He does this sort of thing admirably.'

With Mrs Claire and Gaunt leading, they made a formal entrance and for the first time Dikon saw Barbara in her new dress.

III

She had been late and the rest of the party were already in the car when she ran out, huddled in a wrap of obviously Anglo–Indian origin. Apologizing nervously she scrambled into the back seat and Dikon had time only to see that her head shone sleekly. Gaunt had funked the hairdressing and make-up part of his plan, and when Dikon caught a glimpse of Barbara's face he was glad of this. She had paid a little timid attention to it herself. Mrs Claire sat beside Dikon, Barbara between Gaunt and her uncle in the back seat. When they had started, Dikon thought, unaccountably, of the many many times that he had driven Gaunt out to parties, of the things that were always said by the women who went with them, of how they so anxiously took the temperature of their own pleasure; of restaurants and night clubs reflecting each other's images like mirrors in a tailor's fitting room; of the end of such parties and of Gaunt's fretful displeasure if the sequel was not a success; of money pouring out as if from the nerveless hands of an imbecile. Finally he thought of how, very gradually, his own reaction to this routine had changed. From being excited and stimulated he had become acquiescent and at last an addict. He was roused from this unaccountable retrospect by Mrs Claire who, twisting her plump little torso, peered back at her daughter. 'Dear,' she said, 'isn't your hair rather odd? Couldn't you fluff it forward a little, softly?' And Gaunt said quickly: 'But I have been thinking how charming it looked.' Dr Ackrington, who up till now had not uttered a word, cleared his throat and said he supposed they were to suffer exquisite discomfort at the concert. 'No air, wooden benches, smells and caterwauling. Hope you expect nothing better, Gaunt. The natives of this country have been ruined by their own inertia and the criminal imbecility of the white population. We sent missionaries to stop them eating each other and bribed them with bad whisky to give up their land. We cured them of their own perfectly good communistic system, and taught them how to loaf on government support. We took away their chiefs and gave them trade-union secretaries. And for mating customs that agreed very well with them, we substituted, with a sanctimonious grimace, disease and holy matrimony.'

'James!'

'A fine people ruined. Look at the young men! Spend their time in . . .'

'*James!*'

Gaunt, with the colour of laughter in his voice, asked if the Maori Battalion didn't prove that the warrior spirit lived again.

'Because in the army they've come under a system that agrees with them. Certainly,' said Dr Ackrington triumphantly.

For the remainder of the short drive they had been silent.

It was too dark outside the meeting house for Dikon to see Barbara at all clearly. He knew, however, that she had left the cloak behind her. But when she walked before him through the audience, he saw that Gaunt had wrought a miracle. Dikon's connection with the theatre had taught him to think about clothes in terms of art, and it was with a curious mixture of regret and excitement that he now recognized the effect of Barbara's transformation upon himself. It had made a difference and he was not sure that he did not resent this. He felt as if Gaunt had forestalled him. 'In a little while,' he said, 'even though I had not seen her like this, I should have loved her. *I* ought to have been the one to show her to herself.'

She sat between Gaunt and her uncle. There were not enough armchairs to go round, and Dikon slipped into an extremely uncomfortable seat in the second row. 'Definitely the self-effacing young secretary,' he said to himself. In a state of great mental confusion he prepared to watch the concert, and ended by watching Barbara. The girls on the platform broke rhythmically into the opening dance. They were led by a stout lady who, turning from side to side, cast extraordinarily significant glances about her, and made Dikon feel rather shy.

Of all the Maori clans living in this remote district of the far North, Rua's was the least sophisticated. They sang and postured as their ancestors had done and their audience were spared Maori imitations of popular ballad mongers and crooners. The words and gestures that they used had grown out of the habit of a primitive people and told of their canoes, their tillage, their mating, and their warfare. Many of their songs, sacred to the rites of death, are not considered suitable for public performance, but there was one they sang that night that was to be remembered with a shudder by everyone who heard it.

Rua, in a little speech, introduced it. It had been composed, he said, by an ancestress of his on the occasion of the death of a maiden who unwittingly committed sacrilege and died in Taupo-tapu. He repeated the horrific legend that, one night on the hilltop, he had related to Smith. The song, he explained, was not a funeral dirge and therefore not particularly tapu. His eyes flashed for a moment as he glanced at Questing. He added blandly that he hoped the story might be of interest.

The song was very short and simple, a minor thread of melody that wavered about through a few plain phrases, but the hymn-like over-sweetness of some of the other songs was absent in this one. Dikon wondered how much its icy undercurrent of horror depended upon a knowledge of its theme. In the penultimate line a single girl's voice rang out in a piercing scream, the cry of the maiden as she went to her death in the seething mud cauldron. It left an uncomfortable and abiding impression, which was not dispelled by the subsequent activities of the Savage Club quartette, the ventriloquist, the infant prodigy, or the determined soprano.

Gaunt had said that he would appear last on the programme. With what Dikon considered ridiculous solicitude, he had told Barbara to choose for him and she had at once asked for the Crispian Day speech: 'The one we had this morning.' 'Then he *was* spouting the Bard by the sad sea waves,' thought Dikon vindictively. 'Good God, it's nauseating.'

Gaunt said afterwards that he changed his mind about the opening speech because he realized that his audience would demand an encore, and he thought it better to finish up with the *Henry V.* But Dikon always believed that he had been influenced in his choice by the echo of the little song about death. For after opening rather obviously with the Bastard's speech on England, he turned sombrely to Macbeth.

> *'I have almost forgot the taste of fears . . .'*

and continued to the end

> *'. . . it is a tale*
> *Told by an idiot, full of sound and fury,*
> *Signifying nothing.'*

It is a terrible speech and Gaunt's treatment of it, a deadly calm monotone, struck very cold indeed. When he had ended there was a second's silence, 'and then,' Dikon said afterwards to Barbara, 'they clapped because they wanted to get some warmth back into their hands.' Gaunt watched them with a faint smile, collected himself, and then gave them *Henry V* with everything he'd got, bringing the Maori members of his audience to their feet, cheering. In the end he had to do the speech before Agincourt as well.

He came down glowing. He was, to use a phrase that has been done to death by actors, a great artist, but an audience meant only one thing to him: it was a single entity that must fall in love with him, and, as a corollary, with Shakespeare. Nobody knew better than Gaunt that to rouse an audience whose acquaintance with the plays was probably confined to the first line of Anthony's oration was very nice work indeed. Rua, pacing to and fro in the traditional manner, thanked him first in Maori and then in English. The concert drew to an uproarious conclusion. 'And now,' said Rua, 'The King.'

But before the audience could get to its feet Mr Questing was on his and had walked up on the platform.

It is unnecessary to give Mr Questing's speech in detail. Indeed, it is almost enough to say that it was a *tour de force* of bad taste, and that its author, though by no means drunk, was, as Colly afterwards put it, ticking over very sweetly. He called Gaunt up to the platform and forced him to stand first on one foot and then on the other for a quarter of an hour. Mr Questing was, he said, returning thanks for a real intellectual treat but it very soon transpired that he was also using Gaunt as a kind of bait for possible visitors to the Springs. What was good enough for the famous Geoffrey Gaunt, he intimated, was good enough for anybody. Upon this one clear harp he played in divers keys while the party from Wai-ata-tapu grew clammy with shame. Dikon, filled with the liveliest apprehension, watched the glow of complacency die in his employer's face to be succeeded by all the signs of extreme fury. 'My God,' Dikon thought, 'he's going to throw a temperament.' Simultaneously, Barbara, with rising terror, observed the same phenomenon in her uncle.

Mr Questing, with a beaming face, at last drew to his insufferably fulsome conclusion, and the Mayor, who had obviously intended to make a speech himself, rose to his feet, faced the audience, and let out a stentorian bellow.

'*For-or* . . .' sang the Mayor encouragingly.

And the audience, freed from the bondage of Mr Questing's oratory, thankfully proclaimed Gaunt as a jolly good fellow.

But the party was not yet at an end. Steaming trays of tea were brought in from outside, and formidable quantities of food.

Dikon hurried to his employer and discovered him to be in the third degree of temperament, breathing noisily through his nostrils and conversing with unnatural politeness. The last time Dikon had seen him in this condition had been at a rehearsal of the fight in *Macbeth*. The Macduff, a timid man whose skill with the claymore had not equalled that of his adversary, continually backed away from Gaunt's onslaught and so incensed him that in the end, quite beside himself with fury, he dealt the fellow a swinging blow and chipped the point off his collarbone.

Gaunt completely ignored his secretary, accepted a cup of strong and milky tea, and stationed himself beside Barbara. There he was joined by Dr Ackrington, who, in a voice that trembled with fury, began to apologize, none too quietly, for Questing's infamies. Dikon could not hear everything that Dr Ackrington said, but the word 'horsewhipping' came through very clearly several times. It struck him that he and Barbara, hovering anxiously behind these two angry men, were for all the world like a couple of seconds at a prize fight.

Upon this ludicrous but alarming pantomime came the cause of it, Mr Questing himself. With his thumbs in the armholes of his white waistcoat he balanced quizzically from his toes to his heels and looked at Barbara through half-closed eyes.

'Well, well, well,' Mr Questing purred in a noticeably thick voice. 'So we've got 'em all on, eh? And very nice too. So she didn't know who sent them to her? Fancy that, now. Not an idea, eh? Must have been Auntie in India, huh? Well, well, well!'

If he wished to cause a sensation, he met with unqualified success. They gaped at him. Barbara said in a small desperate voice: 'But it wasn't . . .? It couldn't have been . . .?'

'I'm not saying a thing,' cried Mr Questing in high glee. 'Not a thing.' He leered possessively upon Barbara, dug Dr Ackrington in the waistcoat and clapped Gaunt on the back. 'Great work, Mr Gaunt,' he said. 'Bit highbrow for me, y'know, but they seemed to take it. Mind, I was interested. I used to do a bit of reciting myself at one time. Humorous monologues. Hope you liked the little pat on the back I gave you. It all helps, doesn't it? Even at a one-eyed little show like this,' he added in a spirituous whisper, and, laughing easily, turned to find Rua at his elbow. 'Why, hullo, Rua,' Mr Questing continued without batting an eyelid. 'Great little show. See you some more.' And, humming the refrain of the song about death, he moved forward to shake hands heartily with the Mayor. He made a sort of royal progress to the door and finally strolled out.

Later, when it was of enormous importance that he should remember every detail of the next few minutes, Dikon was to find that he retained only a few disconnected impressions. Barbara's look of desolation; Mr Septimus Falls in pedantic conversation with Mrs Claire and the Colonel, both of whom seemed to be wildly inattentive; the startling blasphemies that Gaunt whispered as he looked after Questing – these details only was he able to focus in a field of hazy recollections.

It was Rua, he decided afterwards, who saved the situation. With the adroitness of a diplomat at a difficult conference, he talked through Dr Ackrington's furious expostulations and, without appearing to hurry, somehow succeeded in presenting the Mayoral party to Gaunt. They got through the next few minutes without an actual flare-up.

It must have been Rua, Dikon decided, who asked a member of the glee club to strike up the National Anthem on the meetinghouse piano.

As they moved towards the entrance, Gaunt, speaking in a furious whisper, told Dikon to drive the Claires home without him.

'But . . .' Dikon began.

'Will you do as you're told?' said Gaunt. 'I'm walking.'

He remembered to shake hands with Rua and then slipped up a side aisle and out by the front door. The rest of the party became involved in a series of introductions forced upon them by the Mayor and, escaping from these, fell into the clutches of a very young reporter from the *Harpoon Courier* who, having let Gaunt escape him, seized upon Dikon and Mrs Claire.

At last Dr Ackrington said loudly: 'I'm walking.'

'But James, dear,' Mrs Claire protested gently. 'Your leg!'

'I said I was walking, Agnes. You can take Edward. I'll tell Gaunt.'

Before Dikon, who was separated from him by one or two people could do anything to stop him, he had edged between a row of chairs and gone out by the side aisle.

'Then,' said Dikon to Mrs Claire, 'perhaps the Colonel would like to come with us?'

'Yes, yes,' said Mrs Claire uneasily. 'I am sure . . . Edward! Where is he?'

He was some way ahead. Dikon could see his white crest moving slowly towards the door.

'We'll catch him when we get outside,' he said.

'Quite a crush, isn't it?' said Mr Falls at his elbow. 'More like the West End every moment.'

Dikon turned to look at him. The remark seemed to be not altogether in character. Mr Falls raised his eyebrow. A theatrical phrase in common usage came into Dikon's mind. 'He's got good appearance,' he thought.

'I'm afraid the Colonel has escaped us,' said Mr Falls.

As they moved slowly down the aisle Dikon was conscious of a feeling of extreme urgency, a sense of being obstructed, such as one sometimes experiences in a nightmare. Barbara's distress assumed a disproportionate significance. Dikon was determined that she should not be hoodwinked by Mr Questing's outrageous hint that he had sent the dress, yet he could not tell her that Gaunt had done so. And where was Gaunt? In his present state of mind he was capable of anything. It was highly probable that at this very moment he was hot on Questing's track.

At last they were out in the warm air. The night was clear and the stars shone brightly. The houses of Rua's *hapu* were dimly visible against the blackness of the hills. A tall fence of manuka poles showed dramatically against the night sky, resembling in the half-light the palisade that had stood there in the days when the village was a fort. Most of the visitors had already gone. From out of the dark came the sound of many quiet voices and of one, a man's, that seemed to be raised in anger. 'But it is a Maori voice,' Dikon said. In a distant hut one or two women broke quietly into the refrain of the little song. So still was the air that in the intervals between these sounds Taupo-tapu and the lesser mud pots could be heard, placidly working in the dark, out on the native reserve: *plop, plop-plop,* a monstrously domestic noise.

Dikon was oppressed by the sensation of something primordial in which he himself had no part. Three small boys, their brown faces and limbs scarcely discernible in the shadow of the meeting house, suddenly darted out in front of Barbara and Dikon. Striking the ground with their bare feet and slapping their thighs they sketched the movements of the war dance. They thrust out their tongues and rolled their eyes. *'Eee-e! Eee-e,'* they said, making their voices deep. A woman spoke out of the dark, scolding them for their boldness and calling them home. They giggled skittishly and ran away. 'They are too cheeky,' the invisible woman's voice said profoundly.

The Colonel and Mr Falls had disappeared. Mrs Claire was still by the meeting house, engaged in a long conversation with Mrs Te Papa.

'Let's bring the car round, shall we?' said Dikon to Barbara. He was determined to get a word with her alone. She walked ahead of him quickly and he followed, stumbling in the dark.

'Jump into the front seat,' he said. 'I want to talk to you.' But when they were in the car he was silent for a time, wondering how to begin, and astonished to find himself so greatly disturbed by her nearness.

'Now listen to me,' he said at last. 'You've got hold of the idea that Questing sent you those damned clothes, haven't you?'

'But of course he did. You heard what he said. You saw how he looked.' And with an air of simplicity that he found very touching she added: 'And I did look nice, didn't I?'

'You little ninny!' Dikon scolded. 'You did and you do and you shall continue to look nice.'

'You knew that wasn't true before you said it. Shall I have to give it back myself, do you imagine? Or do you think my father might do it for me? I suppose I ought to hate my lovely dress but I can't quite do that.'

'Really,' Dikon cried, 'you're the most irritating girl in a quiet way that I have ever encountered. Why should you jump to the conclusion he did it? The man's slightly tight anyway. See here, if Questing sent you the things, I'll buy Wai-ata-tapu myself and run it as a lunatic asylum.'

'How can you be so certain?'

'It's a matter of psychology,' Dikon blustered.

'If you mean he's not the sort of person to do a thing like that,' said Barbara with some spirit, 'I think you're quite wrong. You've seen how frightful his behaviour can be. He just wouldn't know it isn't done.'

Dikon could think of no answer. 'I don't know anything about that,' he said disagreeably. 'I merely think it's idiotic to say he had anything to do with it.'

'If you think I'm idiotic,' said Barbara loudly, 'I wonder you bother to mix yourself up in our affairs at all.' And she added childishly in a trembling voice: 'Anyway it's quite *obvious* that you think I'm *hopeless.*'

'If you want to know what I think about you,' Dikon said furiously, 'I think you deliberately make the worst of yourself. If you didn't pull faces like a clown and do silly things with your voice you'd be remarkably attractive.'

'Good Lord, that's absolutely impertinent!' cried Barbara, stung to anger. 'How *dare* you,' she added, 'how *dare* you speak about me like that!'

'You asked for an honest opinion . . .'

'I didn't. So you've no business to give it.' As this statement was true Dikon made no attempt to counter it. 'I'm uncouth and crude and I irritate you,' Barbara continued.

'Then stop talking!' Dikon shouted. He did not mean to kiss her, he was telling himself. He had not even thought of doing so. It was by some compulsion that it happened, some chance touch upon an emotional reflex. Having begun, there seemed to be no reason why he should stop, though an onlooker in his brain was saying quite distinctly: 'This is a pretty kettle of fish.'

'You *beast!*' Barbara muttered. '*Beast! Beast!*'

'Hold your tongue.'

'*Barbie!*' called Mrs Claire. '*Where are you?*'

'Here!' shouted Barbara at the top of her voice.

By the time Mrs Claire came up to them Barbara was out of the car.

'Thank you, dear,' said her mother. 'You needn't have moved. I'm sorry I was such a long time. Mr Falls has been looking for Edward but I'm afraid he's gone.' She got in beside Dikon. 'I don't think we need wait. Jump in, dear, we mustn't keep Mr Bell any longer.'

Barbara's hand was on the door and Dikon had reached out towards the self-starter. They were arrested by a cry which, though it endured for no longer than two seconds, filled the night so shockingly that it hung on the air as a sensation after it had ceased to be a sound.

An observer would have seen in the half-light that their faces were all turned in one direction as if their heads had been jerked by a wire. On the silence that followed upon the scream there came again the monstrously domestic noise of a boiling pot.

CHAPTER 9

Mr Questing Goes Down for the Third Time

They were not alone for more than two minutes. A subdued hubbub had broken out in the village around them. Doors were opened and slammed. A woman's voice – was it Mrs Te Papa's? – was raised in a long wail.

'What,' asked Mrs Claire steadily, 'was that dreadful noise?'

They began to protect themselves with improbabilities. It was the small boys trying to frighten them. It was someone repeating the death cry of the girl in the song. The last suggestion came from Dikon, and as soon as he had made it he felt its reflection in his hearers.

'Will you wait here by the car?' he said. 'I'd better go and see if anyone's in trouble out there.' He moved his hand towards the pools. The open space before the meeting house was filled with shadowy forms. The woman broke out again into a wail. Other voices joined hers: '*Aue! Aue! Taukiri e!*' Rua spoke authoritatively out of the darkness and the wailing stopped.

'Get into the car, Barbara, and wait,' said Dikon.

'You mustn't go out there by yourself.'

'I've got a torch in the car. In the rack above your head, Mrs Claire. May I have it?' Mrs Claire gave it to him.

'Not by yourself,' said Barbara. 'I'm coming too.'

'Please stay here. It's probably nothing at all, but I'd better look.'

'Stay here, dear,' said Mrs Claire. 'Keep to the white flags, Mr Bell, won't you?'

Dikon called into the darkness: 'Mr Te Kahu! What's wrong?'

'Who is that?' Rua's voice held a note of surprise. 'I know of nothing that is wrong. Someone cried out. Where are you?'

Mrs Claire put her head out of the car window. 'Here we are, Rua.'

Dikon switched on his torch, shouted that he was going to the thermal reserve, and set out.

The village was surrounded by a manuka fence. The only path across the thermal region started at a gap in this fence and Dikon found his way there easily enough. He could hear the pools working. The reek of sulphur grew stronger as he moved towards the gap. He felt and dimly saw wraiths of steam. When he put his hand to his face he found it was damp with condensed vapour. Now he was outside the hedge, his torch light found the white flags. He followed them. The ground beneath his feet quivered, alongside the path a mud pot no bigger than a saucepan worked industriously, forming ringed bosses that swelled and broke interminably. Out to his left an unseen vent hissed. He caught sight of a steaming pool. The path mounted and then encompassed the mound of an old geyser. A mass of whitish-grey sinter rose up in front of Dikon and his path veered sharply to the right.

He had felt himself to be very much alone and was startled to see the figure of a man, clearly silhouetted against a pale background of sinter. At first Dikon thought this man stood with his back towards him but as he moved forward he discovered that they were face to face. The man's head was bent forward. Some trick of shadow, or perhaps of Dikon's nerves, suggested that the stranger had turned sharply and now stood ready to defend himself. So vivid was this impression that Dikon halted.

'Who's that?' he said loudly.

'I was about to ask you the same question,' said Mr Septimus Falls. 'I see now that it is Mr Bell. I thought you were to drive back to the Springs.'

'We heard someone scream.'

'Yes?'

'It seemed to be in this direction. Has anything happened?'

'I have seen nothing.'

'But you must have heard it.'

'One could scarcely escape hearing it.'

'What are you doing here?' Dikon asked.

'I came to look for Colonel Claire.'

'Where is he?'

'As I have explained, I have seen nobody. I hope he has reached the hill and gone home.'

Dikon looked across to where the hill that separated them from the Springs stood black against the stars.

'You hope?' he said.

'Have you a good nerve?' asked Mr Falls. 'I think you have.'

'Why do you ask that, for God's sake!'

'Look here.'

Dikon moved towards him and he at once turned about and led the way to the base of a hillock. The eruptive noises were now much louder. Falls waited for Dikon and took him by the elbow. His fingers were like steel. Dikon saw that they stood at a junction of red-and-white-flagged tracks on the native side of the mound above Taupo-tapu. It was on the summit of this mound that Dikon and Gaunt had stood on the evening that they first saw Taupo-tapu.

'When I came to look for Colonel Claire,' said Falls, 'I stood for a moment in the gap in the fence. As I looked, a man's figure appeared against the skyline. He carried a torch and I saw him in silhouette. He must have been somewhere near the extinct geyser you passed a moment ago. I was about to hail him when I noticed that he wore an overcoat, and then I knew that it couldn't be the Colonel so I let him go. I'd looked for Colonel Claire all over the village and I now decided that he must have gone home by way of the reserve and by this time would have got too far for it to be worthwhile calling him back. I stood there idly waiting for the figure of the man in the overcoat to appear again on the skyline, as it was bound to do when he climbed this hillock. I knew that it would be a little time before you left so I paused long enough to take out my pipe and fill it. I remember thinking how ancient the half-seen landscape felt, and how alien. I don't know if it was long, perhaps it was half a minute, before I realized that the man in the overcoat was taking a long time to reach the hillock. I wondered if he, like myself, stood listening to the working of this hell-brew. Then I heard the scream.'

He paused. Dikon thought: 'There's no need for him to continue. I know what he's going to say.'

'I ran along this track,' said Mr Falls, 'until I reached the top of the hillock. There was nobody there. I ran down the far side and called. There was no answer.'

He paused again, and Dikon said: 'I didn't hear you.'

'The hillock was between us . . . I turned and looked back and it was then I remembered that the path on the crest of the hillock was broken. I was aware of it all the time, but I had attached no significance to it and had taken the small gap in my stride. I was flashing my torch here and there, you see, and at this moment it happened to catch the raw edge. I returned. As you see, the hillock falls away in a steep bank immediately above the big mud pot. Taupo-tapu, they call it, don't they? The path runs along the edge of this bank. Look.'

He flashed his torch light, a very powerful beam, on the crest of the hillock. Dikon could see clearly where the gap had eaten into the path. The inside of his mouth was dry. 'Then . . . it had happened?' he said.

'Of course I looked down. I suppose I expected to see something unspeakable. There was nothing, you understand. Nothing at all.'

'Yes – but . . .'

'Nothing. Nothing at all. The rings and blisters formed and broke. The mud has a kind of lustre at night. I then followed the path right over to the big hill above the Springs. I went almost to the house but there was nobody. I came back here and saw you walking towards me.'

Whether by accident or design, Mr Falls switched on his torch and its strong beam shone full in Dikon's eyes. He moved his head but the light followed him. He said thickly: 'I'm going up there. To look.'

'I think you had better not do that,' said Mr Falls.

'Why?'

'It should be left undisturbed. We can do nothing.'

'But you've already disturbed it.'

'Not more than I could help. Very little. Believe me, we can do nothing here.'

'It's all a mistake,' said Dikon violently. 'It means nothing. The path may have fallen in a week ago.'

'You forget that we came that way to the concert. It has fallen in since then.'

'Since you know all the answers,' said Dikon unevenly, 'perhaps you'll tell me what we do next. No, I'm sorry. I expect you're right. Actually, what *do* we do next?'

'Establish the identity of the man in the overcoat, don't you think?'

'You mean – find the members of the party. To see . . . Yes, you're quite right. For God's sake let's go back.'

'By all means let us go back,' said Mr Falls. 'But you know there was only one member of the party who wore an overcoat, and that was Mr Questing.'

II

They had agreed to tell Mrs Claire and Barbara that they had met nobody on the reserve and leave it at that. The short drive home was made ghastly by Mrs Claire's speculations on the origin of the scream. She was full of comfortable explanations which, Dikon felt, she herself did not altogether believe. The Maori people, she said, were so excitable. Always playing foolish pranks. 'I expect,' she ended on a note that was almost tranquil, 'they just thought they'd give us a good fright.'

Barbara, on the other hand, was completely silent. 'It was in another age,' Dikon thought, 'that I kissed her.' But he did not believe that it was because of the kiss that she was silent. 'She knows something has happened,' he thought. It was a relief to hear Mrs Claire say that after such a late night they'd just pop straight off to bed.

When they had returned to the Springs, Dikon let his passengers out and drove the car round to the garage. He saw Mrs Claire and Barbara walk along the verandah towards their rooms. He parked the car and returned to find Mr Falls waiting for him on the verandah.

They had agreed that Dr Ackrington should be consulted. It was not until now that Dikon remembered how scattered the various departures from the concert had been. Mr Questing's enormities, Gaunt's fury, and the Colonel's disappearance seemed now to be profoundly insignificant. But he knew a moment's unreasoning panic as they crossed the verandah to the dining-room. He didn't know what he had expected to find but it was extraordinarily disconcerting to hear Gaunt's voice, angrily scolding.

'I maintain, and anybody who knows me will bear this out, that I am an amazingly even-tempered man. But mark this: when I get angry I get *angry* and by heaven I'll give him hell. "Do you realize," I shall say, "that I – I whom you have publicly insulted – have refused to make a concert-platform appearance before royalty? Do you realize . . . " '

Dikon and Mr Falls walked into the dining-room. Gaunt was sitting on one of the tables. His hand was raised and his eyes flashed. Dikon had time to remark that his employer was now coasting on the down-grade of a bout of temperament. When he began to talk the worst was usually over. Beside him on the table stood a bottle of his own whisky to which he had evidently been treating Dr Ackrington and Colonel Claire. The Colonel sat with a tumbler in his hand. His hair was ruffled and his mouth was not quite closed. Dr Ackrington appeared to be listening with angry approval to Gaunt's tirade.

'Come and have a drink, Falls,' said Gaunt. 'I've just been telling them – ' He broke off and stared at his secretary. 'And may I ask what's the matter with you?'

They were all staring at Dikon. He thought: 'I suppose I look sick or something.' He sat at one of the tables and, resting his head on his hand, listened to Mr Falls giving an exact repetition of the story he had already told to Dikon. He was heard in utter silence and it was some time after he had finished that Dr Ackrington said in a voice that seemed foreign to him: 'He may, after all, have returned. How do you know that he hasn't returned? Have you looked?'

'By all means let us look,' said Falls. 'Bell, perhaps you wouldn't mind?'

Dikon went along the verandah to Mr Questing's room. The pearl-grey worsted suit was neatly disposed on a chair, ties that had a familiar look hung over the looking-glass, the bed was turned back and a suit of remarkably brilliant pyjamas with a violent puce motif was laid out. The room smelt strongly of the cream Mr Questing had used on his hair and, indefinably, of him. Dikon shut the door and went on to look, with an unhurried precision that surprised himself, through any other rooms where Questing might conceivably be found. He could hear Simon practising Morse in the cabin and through the open door saw that he and Smith were together there. On his return he saw Colly cross the verandah with a suit of Gaunt's over his arm. Dikon returned to the dining-room and again sat down at the table. Nobody asked him if he had seen Questing.

Colonel Claire said suddenly: 'Yes, but I don't understand why it should have happened.'

Mr Falls was very patient. 'A probable explanation might be that he walked too near the edge and it gave way.'

'The only explanation, surely,' said Dr Ackrington sharply.

'Do you think so?' asked Mr Falls politely. 'Yes, perhaps you are right.'

'Would it be possible,' asked Dikon suddenly, 'to branch off from the path and return to the *pa* by another route?'

'There you are!' cried Colonel Claire with childish optimism. 'Why didn't somebody think of that?'

'Utterly impossible, I should say,' said Dr Ackrington crisply. 'Where's that boy? And Smith? They ought to know.'

'Dikon will find them,' said Gaunt. 'God, this can't be true! It's monstrous, it's unthinkable. I – I won't have it.'

'You'll have to lump it,' thought Dikon as he went off to the cabin.

They were still there. Dikon interrupted Simon in the middle of a heated dissertation on fifth columnists in New Zealand. The sinking of the ship, together with all other crises of the past week, had been forgotten in this new and supreme horror, but now Dikon thought suddenly that if Questing had indeed been an agent, it would have been better for him to have faced discovery and a firing squad than to have met his fate in Taupo-tapu. He told Simon briefly what they believed to have happened, and was inexpressibly shocked by the way he took it.

'Packed up, is he?' said Simon angrily. 'Yeh, and now they'll *never* believe me. What a bastard!'

'Cursing and swearing about the poor bastard when he's dead,' said Mr Smith reproachfully. 'You ought to be bloody well ashamed of yourself.' He stirred uneasily and disseminated a thick spirituous odour. 'What a death!' he added thickly. 'Give you the willies to think about it, wouldn't it?' He shivered and rubbed the back of his hand across his mouth. 'I had one or two over at the *pa* with the boys,' he explained needlessly.

Dikon was disgusted with both of them. He said shortly that they were wanted in the dining-room, and walked out, leaving them to follow. Simon caught up with him. 'Bert's not so good,' he said. 'He's had a couple.'

'Quite obviously.'

Smith lurched between them and took them by the arms. 'That's right,' he agreed heavily, 'I'm not so good.'

When Dr Ackrington questioned them about a possible means of returning to the Maori settlement by any route other than the flagged path, they said emphatically that it could not be done. 'Even the Maoris,' said Smith, staring avidly at the whisky bottle, 'won't come at that.'

'You can forget it,' said Simon briefly. 'He couldn't do it.'

Gaunt, with a beautifully expressive gesture, covered his eyes with his hands. 'This will haunt me,' he said, 'for the rest of my life. It's in here.' He beat the palms of his hands against his temples. 'Indelibly fixed. Hag-ridden by a memory.'

'Fiddlesticks,' said Dr Ackrington briskly.

Gaunt laughed acidly. 'Perhaps I am exceptional,' he said with a kind of tragic airiness.

'Well,' said the Colonel most unexpectedly, 'if you don't mind, James, I think I'll go to bed. I feel rather sick.'

'Good God, Edward, are you demented? Is it possible that you have ever been in a position of authority? When, as we are forced to believe, you were responsible for the conduct of a regiment, did you meet the threat of native uprisings by feeling sick and taking to your bed?'

'Who's talking about native uprisings? The natives of this country don't do that sort of thing. They give concerts and mind their own business.'

'You deliberately misconstrue my meaning. The threat of danger – '

'But,' objected Colonel Claire, opening his eyes very wide, 'we aren't threatened with danger at the moment, James. Either Questing has fallen into a boiling mud cauldron, poor feller, in which case we can do nothing, or else, you know, he hasn't, in which case there is nothing the matter with him.'

'Good God, man, we've an extremely grave responsibility.'

Colonel Claire said loudly: 'What in heaven's name do you mean?'

Dr Ackrington beat the air with both hands. 'If this appalling accident has happened – I say, *if* it has happened, then the police must be informed.'

'Very well, James,' said the Colonel. 'Inform them. I am all for handing over to the proper authorities. Falls would be the one to do that, you know, because he almost saw it happen. Didn't you?' he asked, gazing mournfully at Mr Falls.

'I was not as close as that, I think,' said Mr Falls. 'But you are perfectly right, sir. I should inform the police. In point of fact,' he added after a pause, 'I have already done so. While Bell was parking the car.'

They gaped at him. 'I felt,' he added modestly, 'that the responsibility of taking this step devolved upon myself.'

Dikon expected Dr Ackrington to bristle at this disclosure, but it appeared that his enormous capacity for irritation was exhausted by his brother-in-law, upon whom he now turned his back.

'Is it remotely possible,' he asked Mr Falls, 'that the fellow came on here and has made off somewhere or another?' He looked hard at his nephew. 'Such a proceeding,' he said, 'would not be altogether out of character.'

'His car's in the garage,' said Simon.

'Nevertheless he may have gone.'

'I'm afraid it's impossible,' said Falls precisely. 'If he followed the path I must have seen him.'

'And there was the scream,' Dikon heard himself say.

'Exactly. But I agree that we should form a search party. Indeed, the police have suggested that we do so before they take any steps in the matter. I make one stipulation. Let us avoid the path past Taupo-tapu.'

'*Why?*' demanded Simon, instantly truculent.

'Because the police will wish to make an examination.'

'You talk as if it was murder,' said Gaunt loudly. Smith gave a violent snuffle.

'No, I assure you,' said Mr Falls politely. 'I only talk as if there will be an inquest.'

'You can't have an inquest without a body,' said Simon.

'Can't you? But in any case – '

'Well!' Simon demanded. 'What?'

'In any case there may be a body. Later on. Or part of one,' Mr Falls added impassively.

'And now I'm afraid I really am going to be sick,' said the Colonel. He hurried out to the verandah and was.

III

The search party was formed. The Colonel, having recovered from his nausea, astonished them all by offering to go to the Maori settlement and make inquiries.

'If they've got wind of it, as you seem to suggest, Bell, they'll work themselves up into a state. In my experience, half the trouble with native people is not lettin' them know what you're up to. The poor feller's been killed on their property, you know. That makes it a bit tricky. I think I'd better have a word with old Rua.'

'Edward,' said his brother-in-law, 'you are incomprehensible. By all means go. The Maori people appear to understand you. They are to be congratulated.'

'I'll come with you, Dad,' said Simon.

'No, thank you, Sim,' said the Colonel. 'You can help with the search party. You know the terrain, and may prevent anyone else falling into a geyser or somethin'.' He gazed in his startled fashion at Mr Falls. 'I don't catch everything people say,' he added, 'but if I understand you, he must be dead. I mean, why scream? And you say there was nobody else about. Still, you'd better have a look round, I suppose. I think before I go over to the *pa*, I'd better tell Agnes.'

'Need Agnes be told yet?'

'Yes,' said the Colonel, and went away.

As Mr Falls still insisted that the section of the path above Taupo-tapu was not to be used, the only way to the native settlement was by the main road. It was agreed that the Colonel should drive there in Dr Ackrington's car, satisfy the Maori people, and organize a thorough search of the village. Meanwhile the rest of the party would explore the hills, thermal enclosures and paths round the Springs. Dikon felt sure that none of them had the smallest expectation of finding Questing. The search seemed futile and horrible but he welcomed it as something that staved off for a time the moment when he would have to think closely about Questing's death. He was busy shoving away from his thoughts the too vivid picture that formed itself about the memory of a falsetto scream.

It was decided that Dr Ackrington should take the stretch of kitchen garden and rough paddock behind the house, Dikon the hill, Smith and Simon the hot springs, their surrounding path, and the rough country round the warm lake. Mr Falls proposed to follow the path across the native thermal reserve until he came within a short distance of Taupo-tapu. The Colonel had suggested that Questing might have broken his ankle and fallen. Nobody believed in this theory. Gaunt said hurriedly that there seemed nowhere for him to go. 'I am ready to do anything, anything possible, anything in reason,' he said, 'but I am deeply shaken and if you can manage without me I shall be grateful.' They decided to manage without him. Dikon was uncomfortably aware that the other men had dismissed Gaunt as useless and that Simon, at least, had done so with contempt. He watched Simon speak in an undertone to Smith and was miserably angry when Smith glanced at Gaunt and sniggered. So far from being an understatement, Gaunt's description of himself was, Dikon realized, accurate. Gaunt was profoundly shocked. His hands were unsteady and his face pinched. Lines, normally dormant, netted the corners of his eyes. It was not in Gaunt to conceal emotion but it was an error to suppose that, because his distress was unchecked, it was not authentic.

Dikon set out along the path by the Springs to the hill. While they were indoors the moon had risen. Its light brought into strange relief the landscape of Wai-ata-tapu. Plumes of steam stood erect above the pools. Shadows were graved like caverns in the flanks of the hill, but while the higher surfaces, as if drawn in wood by an engraver, were strongly marked in passages of silver and black, the lower planes were wreathed in vapour through which rose manuka bushes, stiffly pallid. These, when Dikon brushed against them, gave off an aromatic scent. As always, in moonlight, there was a feeling of secret expectancy in the air.

Simon caught up with Dikon by the brushwood fence. 'Here,' he said. 'I want you.'

Dikon felt unequal to Simon but he waited. 'Don't you reckon we're dopey if we let that bloke go off on his pat?' Simon demanded.

'Who are you talking about?' asked Dikon wearily.

'Falls. He seems to think he amounts to something, shooting out orders. Who is he anyway? If I got him right this morning when he did his stuff with the pipe he's the bird that knows the signals. And if he knows the signals he was in with Questing, wasn't he? He's just a bit too anxious about his cobber, in my opinion. We ought to watch him.'

'But if Questing's dead what can Falls, if he *is* an agent, do about it?'

'I'm not a mathematician,' said Simon obscurely, 'but I reckon I can add up the fifth column when the answer's two plus two.'

'But he telephoned the police.'

'*Did* he? *He* says he did. The telephone's in Dad's office. You can't hear it from the dining-room. How do we know he used it?'

'Well, stop him if you like.'

'He's lit off. Streaked away before we got started. Where's his lumbago?'

'How the hell do I know! He's shed it in your marvellous free sulphuric-acid baths,' said Dikon, but he began to feel uneasy.

'OK, call me a fool. But you're doing the hill. If I were you I'd keep a lookout across the reserve while you're at it. See what Mr Falls's big idea is when he goes along the path. Why does he want to keep everyone off it except himself? How do we know he won't go over the ground above the mud pot? Know what I reckon? I reckon he's dead scared Questing dropped something when he took the toss. He's going to look for it.'

'Pure conjecture,' Dikon muttered. 'However, I'll watch.'

Smith, like some unattractive genie, materialized out of a drift of steam. 'Know what I reckon?' he began and Dikon sighed at the repetition of this persistent phrase. 'I reckon it's blind justice. After what he tried on me. I'd rather a train killed me than Taupo-tapu, by God. Give you the willies, wouldn't it? What's the good of looking for the poor bastard when he's been an hour in the stock pot?'

Dikon swore at Smith with a violence that surprised himself. 'It's no good howling at me,' said Smith, 'you can't get away from the facts. C'mon, Sim.'

He moved on towards the lake.

'He reeks of alcohol,' said Dikon. 'Is it wise to let him loose?'

'He'll be OK,' said Simon, 'I'll keep the tags on *him*. You look after Falls.'

Dikon stood for a moment watching them fade into wraiths as they turned into the Springs' enclosure. He lit a cigarette and was about to strike out for the hill when he heard his name called softly.

'Dikon!'

It was Barbara in her red flannel dressing-gown and felt slippers, running across the pumice in the moonlight. He went to meet her. 'You called me by my first name,' he said, 'so perhaps you've forgiven me. I'm sorry, Barbara.'

'Oh, that!' said Barbara. 'I expect I behaved stupidly. You see it hasn't happened to me ever before.' And with an owlish imitation of somebody else's wisdom she quoted: 'It's always the woman's fault.'

'You little goat,' said Dikon unsteadily.

'I didn't come out to talk about that. I wanted to ask you what's happened.'

'Hasn't your father – ?'

'He's talking to Mummy. I know by his voice that it's something frightful. They won't tell me, they never do. I must know. What are you all doing? Why are you out here? Uncle James has brought his car round and I saw Sim and Mr Smith go out together. And when I met *him* on the verandah he looked so terrible. He didn't answer when I spoke to him – just walked away to his room and slammed the door. It's something to do with what we heard, isn't it? Please tell me. Please do.'

'We think there may have been an accident.'

'To whom?'

'Questing. We don't know yet. He may have just wandered off somewhere. Or sprained his ankle.'

'You don't believe that.' Barbara's arm in its red flannel sleeve shot out as she pointed to the hill. 'You think something's happened, out there. Don't you? Don't you?'

Dikon took her by the shoulders. 'I'm not going to conjure up horrors,' he said, 'before there are any to conjure. If you take my tip you'll follow suit. Think what a frightful waste of the jim-jams if we find him cursing over a fat ankle, or if he merely went home to supper with the Mayor. I'm sure he adores mayors.'

'And so, who screamed?'

'Seagulls,' said Dikon, shaking her gently. 'Banshees, Maori maidens. Go home and do your stuff. Make cups of tea. Go to bed. Men must search and women must sleep and if you don't like me kissing you you don't look at me like that.'

He turned her about and shoved her away from him. 'Flaunting about in your nightgown,' he said. 'Get along with you.'

He watched her go and then, with a sigh, set out for the hill.

He thought he would climb high enough to get a comprehensive view of the native thermal reserve and the land surrounding it. If anything stirred down there he should stand a good chance of seeing it in the bright moonlight. He found the track that Rua used on his evening walks and felt better for the stiff climb. Someone had suggested half-heartedly that they should at intervals call out to Questing but Dikon could not bring himself to do this. A vivid imagination stimulated by the conviction that Questing was most horribly dead made the idea of shouting his name quite appallingly stupid. However, he had promised to search so he climbed steadily until he reached a place where the reserve was spread out before him in theatrical relief. It had the curious and startling unreality of an infra-red photograph. 'If it wasn't so infernally alive,' he thought, 'it would be like a lunar landscape.' He could see that the reserve was more extensive than he had imagined it to be. It was pocked all over with mud pots and steaming pools. Far out toward its eastern border he caught a glimpse of a delicate jet that spurted from its geyser and was gone. 'It's a lost world,' Dikon thought. He reflected that a man lying in one of the inky shadows would be quite invisible and decided that he had had his climb for nothing. He looked at the slopes of the hill immediately beneath him. The short tufts of grass and brush were motionless. He wandered about a little and was going to turn back when he sensed, rather than saw, that beneath him and out to his left something had moved.

His heart and his nerves were jolted before his eyes had time to tell him that it was only Mr Septimus Falls, moving quietly along the white-flagged path across the reserve. As far as he could make out, Mr Falls was bent forward. Dikon remembered Simon's theory and wondered if, after all, it was so preposterous. But Mr Falls was still well within the bounds that he himself had set, though he walked fairly rapidly towards the forbidden territory. Dikon realized with a sudden pang of interest that he was moving in a very singular manner, running when he was in the moonlight and dawdling in the shadows. The mound above Taupo-tapu was easily distinguishable; Mr Falls had almost reached the limit of his allotted patrol. 'Now,' Dikon said, 'he must turn.'

At that moment a cloud passed before the face of the moon and Dikon was alone in the dark. The reserve, the path and Mr Falls had all been blotted out.

Clouds must have come up from the south while Dikon climbed the hill, for the sky was now filled with them, sweeping majestically to the northeast. A vague sighing told him that a night wind had arisen and presently his hair lifted from his forehead. He had brought his torch but he was unwilling to disclose himself. He had told nobody of his intention to climb high up the hill. He saw that in a minute or two the moon would reappear and he waited, peering into darkness, for the moment when Mr Falls would be revealed.

It was not long, perhaps no more than a minute, before the return of the moonlight. After its brief eclipse the strange landscape seemed to be more sharply defined; mounds, craters, pools and mud pots all showed clearly. He could even see the white flags along the path. But Mr Falls had completely disappeared.

IV

'Really,' Dikon thought, 'if I go all jitter-bug after the problematical death of a man who was almost certainly an enemy agent, I'm not likely to be a howling success in the blitz. No doubt Mr Falls is pottering about in the shadows. In a moment he will reappear.'

He waited and watched. He could hear his watch tick. Away to the east a night bird cried out twice. He saw a light moving about in the village and wondered if it was Colonel Claire's. Two or three more sprang up. They were searching about the village. Once, far below on the other side of the hill, he heard Simon and Smith call to each other. An interval in the vast procession of clouds left the face of the moon quite clear. But still Mr Falls remained invisible.

'I can't stand this any longer,' Dikon thought. He had taken three strides downhill when a brilliant point of light flashed on the mound above Taupo-tapu and was gone, but not before the image of a stooping man had darted up in Dikon's brain. The flash was not repeated but in a little while the faintest possible glow of reflected light appeared behind the mound. 'Why, damn and blast the fellow,' thought Dikon, 'he's messing about on forbidden territory!'

His only emotion was that of fury; his impulse, to plunge downhill, cross the path and catch Falls red-handed. He had actually set out to do this when a shattering fall taught him that he could not run downhill and at the same time keep his eye on a distant spot on the landscape. When he had picked himself up and recovered his torch, which had rolled downhill, he heard a thin sweet whistle threading its way through an air that transported Dikon with astounding vividness into the wings of a London theatre.

> *'Come away, come away, Death,*
> *I am slain by a fair cruel maid.'*

Mr Septimus Falls was walking briskly back along the path, whistling his way home.

He had reached the foot of the hill and turned its flank before Dikon, cursing freely, was halfway down. The thin whistle changed into a throaty baritone and the last Dikon heard of the singer was a doleful rendering of the song which begins: *'Fear no more the heat of the sun.'*

The jolts and stumbles of his journey downhill took the fine edge off his temper and by the time he had reached the bottom he was telling himself that he must go warily with Falls. He paused, lit a cigarette and made some attempt to sort out the jumble of events, suspicions and conjectures that had collected about the person and activities of Maurice Questing.

Questing had visited Rangi's Peak and the Maori people believed he had gone there to collect forbidden curios. When Smith attempted to spy on Questing he had narrowly escaped death under a train and at the time had believed Questing had done his best to bring about the accident. Had Smith, then, been on the verge of stumbling across evidence which would incriminate Questing? Subsequently Questing had offered to keep Smith on at the Springs and pay him a generous wage. This sounded like bribery on Questing's part. Simon and Dr Ackrington were convinced that Questing's main object in visiting the Peak was to flash signals out to sea. This theory was strongly borne out by Simon's investigations on the night before the ship went down. Questing had manoeuvred to get possession of Wai-ata-tapu and, when he was about to take over, Septimus Falls had arrived, making certain that he would not be refused a room. Mr Falls had made himself pleasant. He had talked comparative anatomy with Dr Ackrington, and Shakespeare with Gaunt. He had also tapped out something that Simon declared was a repetition of the signal flashed from the Peak. Had this been an intimation to Questing that Falls himself was another agent? Why had Falls been at such pains to ensure that nobody inspected the path above Taupo-tapu? Was it because he was afraid that Questing might have left some incriminating piece of evidence behind him? If so, what? Papers? Some object that might be recovered from the cauldron? For the first time Dikon forced himself to consider the possibility of anything being recovered from the cauldron, and was sickened by a procession of unspeakable conjectures.

He decided that as soon as he returned he would tell Dr Ackrington what he had seen. 'I shan't tell Simon,' he decided. 'His present theory will lead him to behave like the recording angel's off-sider whenever he sets eyes on Falls.'

And Gaunt? His first impulse was not to tell Gaunt. It was an impulse based on some instinctive warning which he did not care to recognize. He told himself that knowledge of this new development would only add to Gaunt's nervous distress and that no good purpose would be served by speaking to him.

As he walked briskly along the path towards the Springs, he was conscious of a feeling of extreme dissatisfaction and uneasiness. There was at the back of his mind some apprehension which he had not yet acknowledged. He felt that a further revelation was to come and that within himself, unadmitted to his thoughts, was the knowledge of what it would be. The air of the little Maori song came back to him and with it, like a chain jerked out of dark waters, sprang the sequence of ideas he was so loath to examine.

It was with a sense of extreme depression that he finally reached the house.

The dining-room was in darkness but a light shone faintly round the edge of the study window. The Colonel's blackout arrangements were not entirely successful. Dikon could hear the drone of voices – the Colonel's, he thought, and Dr Ackrington's – and he tapped at the door and the Colonel called out in a high voice: 'Yes, yes, yes? Come in.'

They sat together, portentously, after the manner of elderly gentlemen in conclave. They seemed to be distressed. With a trace, or so Dikon thought, of his old regimental manner, the Colonel said: 'Come to report, Bell? That's right. That's right.'

Feeling rather like a blushing subaltern, Dikon stood by the desk and gave his account. The Colonel, as usual, stared at him with his eyes wide open and his mouth not quite closed. Dr Ackrington looked increasingly perturbed and uncomfortable. When Dikon had finished there was a long silence and this surprised him, for he had anticipated that from Dr Ackrington, at least, there would be a display of wrath in the grand manner. Dikon waited for a minute and then said: 'So I thought I'd better come straight back and report.'

'Exactly so,' said the Colonel. 'Perfectly correct. Thank you, Bell.' And he actually gave a little nod of dismissal.

'This,' thought Dikon, 'is not good enough,' and he said: 'The whole affair seemed so very suspicious.'

'No doubt, no doubt,' said Dr Ackrington very quickly. 'I'm afraid, Bell, you've merely been afforded a momentary glimpse into a mare's nest.'

'Yes, but look here, sir . . .'

Dr Ackrington raised his hand. 'Mr Falls,' he said, 'has already informed us of this incident. We're satisfied that he acted advisedly.'

'Quite. Quite!' said the Colonel, and touched his moustache. Again with that air of dismissal, he added: 'Thank you, Bell.'

'This is *not* the army,' Dikon thought furiously, and stood his ground.

Dr Ackrington said: 'I think, Edward, that perhaps Bell is entitled to an explanation. Won't you sit down, Bell?'

With a sense of bewilderment Dikon sat down and waited. These two amazing old gentlemen appeared to have effected a swap of their respective personalities. As far as his native mildness would permit, the Colonel had now assumed an air of austerity; Dr Ackrington's manner, on the contrary, was almost propitiatory. He glanced sharply at Dikon, looked away again, cleared his throat, and began.

'Falls,' he said loudly, 'had no intention of infringing the bounds that he himself had set upon the extent of his investigation. You will remember that the area between the two points where the red-flagged path deviated from the white-flagged one was to be regarded as out of bounds. He had arrived at the first red flag on this side of Taupo-tapu and was about to turn back when he was arrested by a suspicious noise.'

Dr Ackrington paused for so long that Dikon felt obliged to prompt him.

'What sort of noise, sir?' he asked.

'Somebody moving about,' said Dr Ackrington, 'on the other side of the mound. Under the circumstances Falls decided – rightly, in my opinion – that he'd go forward and establish the identity of this person. As quietly as possible and very slowly, he crept up the mound and looked over it.'

With a sudden dart that made Dikon jump, Colonel Claire thrust a box of cigarettes at him, muttering the preposterous phrase: 'No need for formality.' Dikon refused a cigarette and asked what Mr Falls had discovered.

'Nothing!' said the Colonel opening his eyes very wide. 'Nothing at all. Damned annoyin'. What!'

'The fellow had either heard Falls coming,' said Dr Ackrington, 'or else he'd finished whatever game he was up to and bolted while Falls was climbing the mound; in my opinion the more likely explanation. He'd a good start and although Falls went some way down the other side and flashed his torch, there wasn't a sign of anybody. Fellow had got clean away.'

Dikon felt foolish and therefore rather annoyed.

'I see, sir,' he said. 'Obviously, I've been barking up the wrong tree. But Simon and I had some further cause for believing Mr Falls to be a rather mysterious person.'

He paused, wishing he had held his tongue.

'Well,' said Dr Ackrington sharply, 'what was it, what was it?'

'I thought perhaps Simon had told you.'

'Simon hasn't honoured me with his theories which, I have no doubt, constitute a plethora of wildcat speculations.'

'Not quite that, I think,' Dikon rejoined and he related the story of Mr Falls and his pipe. To this recital they listened with ill-concealed impatience; indeed it had the effect of restoring Dr Ackrington to his customary form. 'Damn and blast that cub of yours, Edward,' he shouted. 'What the devil does he mean by concocting these fables and broadcasting them in every quarter but the right one? He knew perfectly well that I regarded Questing's visits to the Peak with the gravest suspicion, he goes haring off by himself, picks up what may prove to be vital information, and tells me nothing whatever about it. In the meantime a ship goes down and an agent from whom we should have got valuable information goes and gets lost in a mud pot. Of all the blasted, self-sufficient young popinjays . . .' He broke off and glared at Dikon. 'As a partner in this conspiracy of silence, perhaps you will be good enough to offer an explanation.'

Dikon was in a quandary. Though he had refused to be bound to secrecy by Simon he felt that he had betrayed a trust. To tell Dr Ackrington that he had urged a consultation and that Simon had refused it would be to present himself as an insufferable prig. He said he understood that Simon had every intention of going to the police with his story. Far from pacifying Dr Ackrington this statement had the effect of still further inflaming him, and Dikon's assurances that so far as he knew Simon had not yet consulted an authority did little to calm him.

The Colonel bit his moustache and apologized to his brother-in-law for Simon's behaviour. Dikon attempted to lead the conversation back to Mr Falls and was instantly snubbed for his pains.

'Sheer twaddle and moonshine,' Dr Ackrington fumed. 'The young ass had his head full of this precious signal and no doubt heard it in everything. What was it?' he demanded. Fortunately Dikon remembered the signal and repeated it.

'Makes no sense in Morse,' said the Colonel unhappily. 'Four *t*'s, four 5's, a *t*, a 1 and an *s*. Ridiculous, you know, that sort of thing.'

'My good Edward, I don't for an instant doubt the significance of this signal as flashed from the Peak. Do you imagine that Questing would communicate in intelligent Morse code to an enemy raider: "Ship sails tomorrow night kindly sink and oblige yours Questing"?' He gave an unpleasant bark of laughter. 'It's this tarradiddle about Falls and his pipe that I totally discredit. The man's full of nervous mannerisms. I've observed him. He's forever fiddling with his pipe. And will you be good enough to tell me, Mr Bell, how one distinguishes between a long and a short tap? Pah!'

Dikon thought this over. 'By the intervals between the taps?' he suggested timidly.

'Indeed? Would Simon be able, without warning, so to distinguish?'

'The *t*'s would sound very like a collection of *o*'s and *m*'s,' said the Colonel.

'I never heard such high-falutin' piffle in my life,' added Dr Ackrington.

'I don't profess to read Morse,' said Dikon huffily.

'And you never will if you take lessons from Falls and his pipe. He's a reputable person and not altogether a fool on the subject of comparative anatomy. I may add that we have discovered friends in common. Men of some standing and authority.'

'Really, sir?' said Dikon demurely. 'That, of course, completely exonerates him.'

Dr Ackrington darted a needle-sharp glance at Dikon and evidently decided that he had not intended an impertinence. 'I consider,' he said, 'that Falls has behaved with admirable propriety. I shall speak to Simon tonight. It's essential that he should not go shouting about this preposterous theory to anyone else.'

'Quite,' said the Colonel. 'We'll speak to him.'

'As for the interloper at Taupo-tapu, it was doubtless one of your Maori acquaintances, Edward, disobeying orders as usual. By the way, you must have been there at the time. Did you notice any suspicious behaviour?'

The Colonel rubbed his hair and looked miserable. 'Not to say suspicious, James. Odd. They see things differently, you know. I don't pretend to understand them. Never have. I like them, you know. They keep their word and so on. But of course they're a superstitious lot. Interestin'.'

'If you found their behaviour this evening so absorbing,' said Dr Ackrington acidly, 'perhaps you will favour us with a somewhat closer description of it.'

'Well, it's difficult, you know. I expected to find they'd all gone to bed, but not a bit of it. They were hangin' about the *marae* in groups and a good many of them seemed to be in the hall; not tidyin' up or anything – just talkin'. Old Mrs Te Papa seemed to be in a great taking-on. She was in the middle of a long speech. Very excited. Some of them were at that beastly wailin' noise. Rua was on the verandah with a lot of the older men. Funny thing,' said the Colonel and stared absently at Dikon without completing his sentence.

'What, my dear Edward, was a funny thing?'

'Eh? Oh! I was going to say, funny thing he didn't seem surprised to see me.' The Colonel gave a rather mad little laugh and pointed at his brother-in-law. 'And funnier still,' he said, 'when I told them what we thought had happened to Questing, they didn't seem surprised about that, either.'

CHAPTER 10

Entrance of Sergeant Webley

Dikon was dispatched with orders to find Simon and send him to his father in ten minutes' time. He had Simon rather heavily on his conscience. Thinking longingly of his bed he went once more to the cabin. The sky was overcast and a light drizzle was falling. Dikon was assailed by a feeling of profound depression. He found Simon still up and still closeted with Smith, in whom the effect of alcohol had faded to a condition of stale despair.

'My luck all over,' Smith said lugubriously as soon as he saw Dikon. 'I land a permanent job with good money and the boss fades out on me. Is it tough or is it tough?'

'You'll be OK, Bert,' said Simon. 'Dad'll keep you on. I told you.'

'Yeah, but what a prospect. I'm not saying anything against your dad, Sim, but he's on to a good thing with me and he knows it. If I liked to squeal on him your dad'd be compelled by law to give me hotel wages. I'm not complaining, mind, but that's the strength of it. I'd have done good with Questing.'

Dikon said: 'I find it difficult to reconcile your disappointment with your former statement that Questing tried to run a train over you.'

Smith stared owlishly at him. 'He satisfied me about that,' he said. 'It wasn't like he said at the time. The signal was working OK but his car's got one of them green talc sun screens. He was looking through it and never noticed the light turn red. He took me along and showed me. I went crook at the time. Him and me hadn't hit it off too well and I taped it out he'd tried to fix me up for keeps but I had to hand it to him when he showed me. He was upset, you know. But I said I'd overlook it.'

'With certain stipulations, I fancy,' said Dikon drily.

'Why not!' cried Smith indignantly. 'He owed it to me, didn't he? I was suffering from shock and abrasions. You ask the Doc. My behind's like one of them monkeys', yet. I'd got a lot to complain about, hadn't I, Sim?' he added with an air of injury.

'I'll say.'

'Yeh, and what's Mr Bell's great idea talking as if it was me that acted crook?'

'Not a bit of it, Mr Smith,' said Dikon soothingly. 'I only admire your talents as an opportunist.'

'Call a bloke names,' said Smith darkly, 'and never offer him a drink even though he *is* supposed to be a blasted guest.' He brooded, Dikon understood, on Gaunt's bottle of whisky.

'All the same, Bert,' said Simon abruptly, 'I reckon you were pretty simple to believe Questing. He was only trying to keep you quiet. You wouldn't have seen your good money, don't you worry.'

'I got it in writing,' shouted Smith belligerently. 'I'm not childish yet. I got it in writing while he was still worried I'd turn nasty over the train. Far-sighted. That's me.'

Dikon burst out laughing.

'Aw, turn it up and go to hell,' roared Smith. 'I'm a disappointed man. I'm going to bed.' He gave an indignant belch and left them.

'He'd be all right,' said Simon apologetically, 'if he kept off the booze.'

'Have you told him about your views on Questing?'

'Not more than I could help. You can't be sure he won't talk when he's got one or two in. He still reckons Questing went up to the Peak for curios. I didn't say anything. You want to keep quiet about the signals.'

'Yes,' agreed Dikon and rubbed his nose. 'On that score I'm afraid you're not going to be very pleased with me.' And he explained that he had told the whole story to the Colonel and Dr Ackrington. Simon took this surprisingly well, reserving his indignation for Mr Falls's behaviour at Taupo-tapu which Dikon now revealed to him. In Simon's opinion Falls had no right, however suspicious the circumstances, to exceed the limit that he himself had set. 'I don't like that joker,' he said. 'He's a darned sight too plausible.'

'He's no fool.'

'I reckon he's a crook. You can't get away from those signals.'

Rather apprehensively Dikon advanced Dr Ackrington's views on the signals. 'And I must confess,' he added, 'that to me it seems a likely explanation. After all, why on earth should Falls take such an elaborate and senseless means of introducing himself to Questing? All he had to do was to take Questing on one side and present his credentials. Why run the danger of someone spotting the signal? It doesn't make sense.'

Unable to answer this objection, Simon angrily reiterated his own views. 'And if you think I'm dopey,' he stormed, 'there are others that don't. You may be interested to hear I went to the police station this afternoon.' He observed Dikon's astonishment with an air of satisfaction. 'Yes,' he said, 'after you'd told me it was Falls tapped out the signal, I hopped on my bike and got going. I know the old sergeant and I got on to him. He started off by acting as if I was a kid but I convinced him. Well, anyway,' Simon amended, 'I stuck to it until he let me in to see the super.'

'Well done,' Dikon murmured.

'Yes,' Simon continued, stroking the back of his head. 'I was an hour in the office. Talking all the time, too. And they were interested. They didn't say much, you know, but they took a lot of it down in writing and I could see they were impressed. They're going to make inquiries about this Falls. If Uncle James and Dad reckon they know better than the authorities why should I worry? Wait till the police pull in their net. That'll be the day. They're not as dumb as I thought they were. I'm satisfied.'

'Splendid,' said Dikon. 'I congratulate you. By the way, I was to ask you to go and see your father and I may as well warn you that you're going to be bound over to secrecy about your theory of Falls's signals with the pipe. And now I think I shall go to bed.'

He had reached the door when Simon stopped him. 'I forgot to tell you,' said Simon. 'I asked them the name of this big pot out from home. They looked a bit funny on it and I thought they weren't going to tell me but they came across with it in the end. It's Alleyn. Chief Detective-Inspector Alleyn.'

II

Dikon's notions as to the legal proceedings arising out of the circumstances of Questing's disappearance were exceedingly vague. Half-forgotten phrases about presumption of death after a lapse of time occurred to him. He had speculated briefly about Questing's nationality and next of kin. He had never anticipated that on the following morning he would wake to find several large men standing about the Claires' verandah, staring at their boots, mumbling to each other, and exuding the unmistakable aroma of plain-clothes policemen.

This, however, was what he did find. The drone of voices awakened him; the light was excluded from his room by a massive back which actually bulged through the open window. Dikon put on his dressing-gown and went to see his employer. He had looked in on Gaunt before going to bed and had discovered him to be in a state of nervous prostration, undergoing massage from Colly. Dikon, having been told for God's sake to let him alone, had left the room followed by Colly. 'Oh, my aunt!' Colly whispered, jerking his thumb at the door. 'High strikes with bells on. A fit of the flutters with musical honours. We're in for a nice helping of ter-hemperament, sir, and no beg pardons. Watch out for skids, and count your collars. We'll be out on tour again tomorrow.' He turned down his thumbs. 'Colly!' Gaunt had yelled at this juncture. 'Colly! Damnation! *Colly!*' And Colly had darted back into the bedroom.

Remembering this episode, Dikon approached his employer with some misgivings. He listened at the door, caught a whiff of Turkish tobacco, heard Gaunt's cigarette cough, tapped and walked in. Gaunt, wearing a purple dressing-gown, was propped up in bed, smoking. When Dikon asked how he had slept he laughed bitterly and said nothing. Dikon attempted one or two other little opening gambits all of which were received in silence. He was about to make an uncomfortable exit when Gaunt said: 'Ring up that hotel in Auckland and book rooms for tonight.'

With a feeling of the most utter desolation Dikon said: 'Then we are leaving, sir?'

'I should have thought,' said Gaunt, 'that it followed as the night the day. I do not book rooms out of sheer elfin whimsy. Please settle with the Claires. We leave as soon as possible.'

'But, sir, your cure?'

Gaunt shook his finger at him. 'Are you so grossly lacking in sensibility,' he asked, 'that you can blandly suggest that I, with the loathsome picture of last night starting up before my eyes when ever I close them, should steep my body, *mine*, in seething mud?'

'I hadn't thought of it like that,' said Dikon lamely. 'I'm sorry. I'll tell the Claires.'

'Pray do,' said Gaunt and turned his shoulder on him.

Dikon went to find Mrs Claire and encountered Colly on the way. Colly turned his eyes up and affected to dash a tear from them. The phrase, 'He's too cheeky,' formed itself in Dikon's thoughts and instantly reminded him of the small brown boys who had grimaced in the moonlight. He continued on his way without an answering gesture. He ran the Colonel to earth in his study where he was closeted with a large dark man with a high colour, wearing an uneventful suit and a pair of repellent boots. This person turned upon Dikon a hard speculative stare.

'Sergeant Webley,' said the Colonel. Sergeant Webley rose slowly.

'How do you do, sir?' he said in a muffled voice. 'Mr . . . ?'

'Bell,' said the Colonel.

'Ah, yes. Mr Bell,' repeated Sergeant Webley. He half-opened his hand which was broad, flat and flabby with lateral creases. He seemed to peer into its palm. Dikon realized with a stab of alarm that he was consulting a small notebook. "That's right,' repeated Sergeant Webley heavily. 'Mr Dikon Bell. Would that be a kind of nickname, sir?'

'Not at all,' said Dikon. 'It was given me in my baptism.'

'Is that so, sir? Very unusual. Old English perhaps.'

'Perhaps,' said Dikon coldly. Webley cleared his throat and waited.

'Sergeant Webley,' said the Colonel uncomfortably, 'is making some inquiries . . .'

'Yes, of course,' said Dikon hurriedly. 'I'm sorry I interrupted, sir. I'll go.'

'No need for that, Mr Bell,' said Webley with a sort of fumbling cordiality. 'Very glad you looked in. Quite an unfortunate affair. Yes. Take a seat, Mr Bell, take a seat.'

With a claustrophobic sensation of something closing in upon him, Dikon sat down and waited.

'I understand,' said Webley, 'that your movements last night were as follows.' He flattened his notebook on his knees and began to read from it. 'But I've heard all this before,' Dikon thought. 'I've read it a hundred times in airliners, on the decks of steamers, in hotel bedrooms.' And he saw yellow dust jackets picturing lethal weapons, clutching hands, handcuffs, and men like Mr Webley squinting along the barrels of revolvers. More in answer to his thoughts than to Webley's questions he cried aloud: 'But it was only an accident!'

'In a case of this sort, Mr Bell, disappearance of the party concerned under circumstances pointing to demise, we make inquiries. Now, you were saying?'

His heavy interrogation began to take on a kind of lifeless rhythm: question, answer, pause, while Sergeant Webley wrote and Dikon fidgeted, and again, question. It was a colourless measure reiterated drearily with variations. Under its burden Dikon walked again down a narrow track, through a gap in a hedge, and across a barren place where white flags showed clearly. Beyond the drone of Webley's voice a single scream rose and fell like a jet from a geyser.

Webley was very insistent about the scream. Was Dikon positive that it had come from the direction of the mud cauldron? Sounds were deceptive, Webley said. Might it not have come from the village? Dikon was quite positive that it had not and, on consideration, said he would swear that it had arisen close at hand in the thermal region. Where precisely had he been when he first saw Mr Falls? Here Webley unfolded a large-scale and extremely detailed map of the district. Dikon was able to find his place on the map and, a punctual wraith, Mr Falls walked again towards him in the starlight. 'Then you'd say he was about halfway between you and the mud pot?' The sense of impending horror which had haunted Dikon ever since he woke was now intensified and translated physically into a dryness of the throat. 'About that,' he said.

Webley looked up from the map, his pale finger still flattened on the point where Dikon had stood. 'Now, Mr Bell, how long would you say it was from the time you left Mrs and Miss Claire until the moment you first saw Mr Falls?'

'No longer than it takes to walk fairly briskly from the car to the point under your finger. Perhaps a couple of minutes. No more.'

'A couple of minutes,' Webley repeated, and stooped over his notebook. With his head bent, so that his voice sounded more muffled than ever, he said much too casually: 'You're in young Mr Claire's confidence, aren't you, Mr Bell?'

'In what sense?'

'Didn't he tell you about his ideas on Mr Questing?'

'He talked to me about them. Yes.'

'And did you agree with him?' asked Webley, raising his florid face for a moment to look at Dikon.

'At first I considered them fantastic.'

'But you got round to thinking there might be something in it? Did you?'

'I suppose so,' said Dikon, and then, ashamed of answering so guardedly, he said firmly: 'Yes, I did. It seems to me to be inescapable.'

'Is that so?' said Webley. 'Thank you very very much, Mr Bell. We won't trouble you any more just now.'

Dikon thought: 'I seem to be forever getting my *congé*.' He said to the Colonel: 'I really came to tell you, sir, that Mr Gaunt has been very much upset by this appalling business and thinks he would like to get away, for a time at least. He's most anxious that you should know how much he appreciates all the kindness and consideration that he has been shown and . . . and,' Dikon stammered, 'and I hope that after a little while we may return. I'm so sorry to bother you now but if I might settle up . . . ?'

'Yes, yes, of course,' said the Colonel with obvious relief. 'Quite understandable. Sorry it's happened like this.'

'So are we,' said Dikon. 'Enormously. I'll come back a little later, shall I? We'll be leaving at about eleven.' He backed away to the door.

'Just a minute, Mr Bell.'

Webley had been stolidly conning over his notes, and Dikon, in his embarrassment, had almost forgotten him. He now rose to his feet, a swarthy official in an ugly suit. 'You were thinking of leaving this morning, were you, Mr Bell?'

'Yes,' said Dikon. 'This morning.'

'You and Mr Geoffrey Gaunt and Mr Gaunt's personal vally?' He wetted his thumb and turned a page of his notebook. That'd be Mr Alfred Colly, won't it?'

'Yes.'

'Yes. Well, now, we'll be very sorry to upset your arrangements, Mr Bell, but I'm just afraid we'll have to ask you to stay on a bit longer. Until we've cleared up this little mystery, shall we say?'

With a sense of plunging downwards in a lift that was out of control, Dikon said: 'But I've told you everything I know, and Mr Gaunt had nothing whatever to do with the affair. I mean he was nowhere near. I mean . . .'

'Nowhere near, eh?' Webley repeated. 'Is that so? Yes. He didn't drive home in his car, did he? Which way did Mr Gaunt go home, Mr Bell?'

And now Dikon was back in the meeting house, and Gaunt, shaking with rage, was pushing his way along the side aisles as if propelled by an intolerable urge. He was engulfed in a crowd of people who stared curiously at him. He showed for a moment in the doorway and was gone.

Dikon was recalled by Webley's voice. 'I was asking which way Mr Gaunt went home from the concert, Mr Bell.'

'I don't know,' said Dikon. 'If you like I'll go and ask him.'

'I won't trouble you to do that, Mr Bell. I'll ask Mr Gaunt myself.'

III

We are slow to recognize disaster, quick to erect screens between ourselves and a full realization of jeopardy. Perhaps the idea of something more ominous than accident had lain dormant at the back of Dikon's thoughts. As there are some diseases that we are loath to name, so there are crimes with which we refuse consciously to associate ourselves. Though Dikon was oppressed by the sense of an approaching threat, his conscious reaction was to wonder how in the world under these new restrictions he was to cope with Gaunt. Thus, by a process of mental juggling, the minor was substituted for the major horror.

He said: 'If you're going to see Mr Gaunt perhaps I may come with you. I don't know if he's up yet.'

Webley looked thoughtfully at him and then with an air of heartiness which Dikon found most disconcerting he said: 'That'll do very very nicely, Mr Bell. We like to do things in a friendly way. If you don't mind introducing me to Mr Gaunt, I'll just explain the position to him. I'm quite sure he'll understand.'

'Are you, by God!' thought Dikon, and led the way along the verandah.

As they approached Gaunt's rooms, Colly came out staggering under the weight of a wardrobe trunk. Webley gave him that hard stare with which Dikon was to become so familiar. 'You'd better take that thing away, Colly,' said Dikon.

'Take it away?' asked Colly indignantly. 'I've only just brought it out. What am I supposed to be, sir? Atmosphere in the big railway-station scene or what?' He glanced shrewdly at Webley. 'Pardon me, Chief Inspector,' he said. 'There's no corpse in this trunk. Take a look if you don't believe me, and don't muck up our underwear, We're fussy about details.'

'That'll be quite all right, Colly,' said Webley. 'Stay handy, will you? I'd like to have a yarn with you.'

'Rapture as expressed in six easy poses,' said Colly. 'Yours to command.' He winked at Dikon. 'If you're looking for His Royal Serenity, sir,' he said, 'he's in his barf.'

'We'll wait,' said Dikon. 'In here, will you, Mr Webley?' They waited in Gaunt's sitting-room. Colly, whistling limpidly, staggered away under the trunk.

'That kind of joker's out of our line in New Zealand,' said Webley. 'He's different from what you'd have thought. A bit too fresh, isn't he? Not my idea of a vally.'

'Colly's a dresser,' said Dikon, 'not a valet. He's been a long time with Mr Gaunt, and I'm afraid he's got into the way of thinking he's a licensed buffoon. I'm sorry, Sergeant. I'll just go and tell Mr Gaunt you're here.'

He had hoped to get one word in private with Gaunt, but Webley thanked him and followed him out on the verandah. 'Going in for the treatment, is he?' he asked easily. 'Just across the way, isn't it? I've never taken a look at these Springs. Been here ten years and never taken a look at them. Fancy that!'

He followed Dikon across the pumice.

It was Gaunt's custom before breakfast to soak for fifteen minutes in the largest of the pools, that which was enclosed by a rough shed.

Evidently, Dikon thought, his new abhorrence of thermal activities did not extend to this particular bath.

Closely followed by Webley, Dikon went up to the bath house and tapped at the door.

'Who the hell's out there!' Gaunt demanded.

'Sergeant Webley to see you, sir.'

'Sergeant *who?*'

'Webley.'

'Who's he?'

'Harpoon police force, sir,' said Mr Webley. 'Very sorry to trouble you.'

There was no reply to this. Webley made no move. Dikon waited uncertainly. He heard a splash as Gaunt shifted in the pool. He had the idea that Gaunt was sitting up, listening. At last, in a cautious undertone, the voice beyond the door called him. 'Dikon?'

'I'm here, sir.'

'Come in.'

Dikon went in quickly, closing the door behind him. There was his employer as he had expected to find him, naked, vulnerable, and a little ridiculous, jutting out of the vivid water.

'What *is* all this?'

Dikon gestured. 'Is he there?' Gaunt muttered.

Dikon nodded violently and, with an attempt at cheerfulness that he felt rang very false, said aloud: 'The Sergeant would like to have a word with you, sir.'

He groped in his pocket, found an envelope and a pencil and wrote quickly: 'It's about Questing. They won't let us go.' He went on talking as he showed it to Gaunt: 'Shall I send Colly in, sir?'

Gaunt was staring at the paper. Water trickled off his shoulders. His face was pinched and looked old, the skin on his hands was waterlogged and wrinkled. He began to swear under his breath.

On the other side of the door Webley cleared his throat. Gaunt, his lips moving, looked at the door. He grasped the rail at the edge of the bath and stood upright, a not very handsome figure. 'He ought to say something,' Dikon thought. 'It looks bad to say nothing.' Gaunt beckoned and Dikon stooped towards him but he seemed to change his mind and said loudly, 'Ask him to wait. I'm coming out.'

The morning was warm and humid and the pool Gaunt had left was a hot one, but even when he was wrapped in his heavy bathrobe he seemed to be cold. He asked Dikon for a cigarette. Conscious always of Webley on the other side of the thin wooden wall Dikon forced himself to talk. 'I'm afraid this appalling business is going to hold us up a bit, sir. I should have thought of it before.' Gaunt suddenly joined in. 'Yes, a damned nuisance, of course, but it can't be helped.' It all sounded horribly false.

They came out of the bath house and there was Webley. 'Hanging about,' thought Dikon, 'like Frankenstein's monster.' He walked up with them to the house and stayed outside Gaunt's window while he dressed. Dikon sat on the edge of the verandah and smoked. The clouds that had blown up in the night were gone and the wind had dropped. Rangi's Peak was a clear blue. The trees on its flanks looked as if they had been blobbed down by a water-colourist with a full and generous brush. The hill by the Springs basked in the sun and high above it the voices of larks reached that pinnacle of shrillness that floats on the outer margin of human perception. The air seemed to hold a rumour of notes rather than an actual song. Three men came round the path by the lake. One of them carried a sack which he held away from him, the others, rakes and long manuka poles. They walked in Indian file, slowly. When they came near, Dikon saw that a heavy globule hung from the corner of the sack. It swung to and fro, thickened, and dropped with a splat of sound on the pumice. It was mud. The rake and the ends of the poles were also muddy.

He sat still, his cigarette burning down to his fingers, and watched the men. They came over the pumice to the verandah, and Webley moved across to meet them. The man with the sack opened it furtively and the others moved between him and Dikon. Webley pushed his black felt hat to the back of his head and squatted, peering. They mumbled together. A phrase of Septimus Falls's came into Dikon's mind and nauseated him. Inside the house Barbara called to her mother. At once the group broke up. The three men disappeared round the far end of the house, carrying their muddy trophies, and Webley returned to his post by Gaunt's window.

Dikon heard the creak of a door behind him. His nerves were on edge and he turned quickly; but it was only Mr Septimus Falls on the threshold of his room.

'Good morning, Bell,' he said. 'A lovely day, isn't it? Quite unsullied and in strong contrast to the events associated with it. "Only man is vile." It is not often that one goes to hymns A and M for profundity of observation but I remember the same phrase occurred to me on the night that war broke out.'

'Where were you then, Mr Falls?'

' "Going to and fro in the earth",' said Mr Falls lightly. 'Like the devil, you know. In London, to be precise. I didn't see you after your return last night but hear that your vigil on the hill was an uneventful one.'

'So they *haven't* told him I was watching him,' thought Dikon. 'And how did you get on?' he asked.

'I? I was obliged to trespass, and all to no avail. I thought you must have seen me.' He smiled at Dikon. 'I heard you falling about on your hill. No injuries, I trust? But you are young and can triumph over such mishaps. I, on the contrary, have played the very devil with my lumbar region.'

'I thought last night that you seemed remarkably lively.'

'Zeal,' said Mr Falls. 'All zeal. Wonderful what it will do, but one pays for it afterwards, unhappily.' He placed his hand in the small of his back and hobbled towards Webley. 'Well, Sergeant,' he said, 'any new developments?'

Webley looked cautiously at him. 'Well, yes, sir, I think we might say there are,' he said. 'I don't see any harm in telling you we're pretty well satisfied that this gentleman came by his death in the manner previously suspected. My chaps have been over there and they've found something. In the mud pot.'

'Not – ?' said Dikon.

'No, Mr Bell, not the remains. We could hardly hope for them under the circumstances, though of course we'll have to try. But my chaps have been there on the lookout ever since it got light. About half an hour ago they spotted something white working about in the pot. Sometimes, they said, you'd see it and sometimes you wouldn't. One of them who's a family man passed the remark that it reminded him of the week's wash.'

'And . . . was it?' asked Falls.

'In a manner of speaking, sir, it was. We raked it out and are holding it. It's a gentleman's dress waistcoat. One of those backless ones.'

IV

Dikon, at his employer's request, was present at the interview between Gaunt and Webley. Gaunt was at his worst, alternately too persuasive and too intolerant. Webley remained perfectly civil, muffled and immovable.

'I'm afraid I'll have to ask you to stay, sir. Very sorry to inconvenience you but there it is.'

'But I've told you a dozen times I've no information to give you. None. I'm unwell and I came here for a rest. A rest! My God! You may have my address and if I should be wanted you'll know where to find me. But I know nothing that can be of the smallest help to you.'

'Well, now, Mr Gaunt, we'll just see if that's so. I haven't got round yet to asking you anything, have I? Now, perhaps you wouldn't mind telling me just how you got home last night.'

Gaunt beat the arms of his chair and with an excruciating air of enforced control said in a whisper: 'How I got home? Very well. Very well. I walked home.'

'Across the reserve, sir?'

'No. I loathe and abominate the reserve. I walked home by the road.'

'That's quite a long way round, Mr Gaunt. I understand you had your car at the concert.'

'Yes, Sergeant, I had my car. That did not prevent me from wishing to walk. I walked. I wanted fresh air and I walked.'

'Who drove the car, sir?'

'I did,' said Dikon.

'Then I suppose, Mr Bell, that you overtook Mr Gaunt?'

'No. It was some time before we left.'

'Longer than fifteen minutes after the concert was over, would you say?'

'I don't know. I haven't thought.'

'Mr Falls puts it at about fifteen minutes. It's a mile and a quarter by the main road, sir,' said Webley, shifting his position in order to face Gaunt. 'You must be a smart walker.'

'The car can't do more than crawl along that road, you know. But I walked fast on this occasion, certainly.'

'Yes. Would that be because you were at all excited, Mr Gaunt? I've noticed that when people are kind of stimulated or excited they're inclined to step out.'

Gaunt laughed and adopted mistakenly, Dikon thought, an air of raillery. 'I believe you're a pressman in disguise, Sergeant. You want me to tell you about my temperament.'

'No, sir,' said Webley stolidly. 'I just wondered why you walked so fast.'

'You have guessed why. I was stimulated. For the first time in months I had spoken Shakespearean lines to an audience.'

'Yes?' Webley opened his notebook. 'I understand you left before the other members of your party. With the exception of Mr Questing, that is. Mr Questing left before you, didn't he?'

'Did he? I believe he did.' Gaunt put his delicate hand to his eyes and then shook his head violently as though he dismissed some unwelcome vision. Next he smiled sadly at Mr Webley, extended his arms and let them flop. It was a bit of business that he used in *Hamlet* during the penultimate duologue with Horatio. Mr Webley watched it glumly. 'You must forgive me, Sergeant,' said Gaunt. 'This thing has upset me rather badly.'

'It's a terrible affair, sir, isn't it? Was the deceased a friend of yours, may I ask?'

'No, no. It's not that. For it to happen to anyone!'

'Quite so. You must have seen him, I suppose, after you left the hall.'

Gaunt took out his cigarette case and offered it to Webley, who said he didn't smoke. Dikon saw a tremor in Gaunt's hand and lit his cigarette for him. Gaunt made rather a business of this, and as they were at it, said something not so much in a whisper as with an almost soundless articulation of tongue and teeth. Dikon thought it was: 'I've got to get out of it.'

'I was saying – ' said Webley heavily, and repeated his question.

Gaunt said that as far as he could remember he had caught a glimpse of Questing outside the hall. He wasn't positive. Webley kept him to this point and he grew restive. At last he broke off and drew his chair closer to Webley.

'Look here,' he said. 'I've honestly told you all I know about this poor fellow. I want you to understand something. I'm an actor and an immensely well-known one. Things that happen to me are news, quite big news, at home and in the States. Bell, as my secretary, will tell you how tremendously careful I have to be. The sort of things that are said about me in print matter enormously. It may sound far-fetched, but I assure you it is not, when I tell you that a few sentences in the hot-news columns, linking my name up with this accident, would be exactly the wrong kind of publicity. We don't know much about this unfortunate man but I've heard rumours that he wasn't an altogether savoury character. That may come out, mayn't it? We'll get hints about it. "Mystery man dies horribly after hearing Geoffrey Gaunt recite at one-eyed burg in New Zealand." That's how the hot-columnists will treat it.'

'We don't get much of that sort of thing in this country, Mr Gaunt.'

'Good Lord, man, I'm not talking about this country. As far as I'm concerned this country doesn't exist. I'm talking of New York.'

'Oh,' said Mr Webley impassively.

'See here,' said Gaunt, 'I know you've got your job to do. If there's anything more you want to ask, why, ask it. Ask it now. But for God's sake don't keep me hanging on here. I can't invite you to come out and have a drink with me but – '

Dikon, appalled, saw Gaunt's hand go to the inside pocket of his coat. He got behind Webley and shook his head violently, but Gaunt's note case was now in his hand and Webley on his feet.

'Now, Mr Gaunt,' Webley said with no change whatever in his uninflected and thick voice. 'You should know better than to think of that. If you're as careful of your reputation as you've been telling me, you ought to realize that anything of this nature looks very bad indeed if it gets known. Put that case away, sir, We'll let you go as soon as possible but until this black business is cleared up nobody's leaving Wai-ata-tapu. Nobody.'

Gaunt drew back his head with a certain characteristic movement which Dikon always associated with an adder.

'I think you're making a mistake, Sergeant,' he said with elaborate indifference. 'However, we'll leave it as it is for the moment. I'll telephone to Sir Stephen Johnston and ask him to advise me what steps to take. He's a personal friend of mine. Isn't he your Chief Justice or something?'

'That'll be quite in order, Mr Gaunt,' said Webley tranquilly. 'His Honour may make some special arrangement. In the meantime I'll ask you to stay here.'

'*Great God Almighty!*' Gaunt screamed out. 'If you say that again I'll lose all control of my temper. How dare you take this attitude with me! The man has been killed by a loathsome accident. You behave, my God, as if he'd been murdered.'

'But,' said a voice in the doorway, 'isn't it almost certain that he has?'

It was Mr Septimus Falls, standing diffidently on the threshold.

V

'Do forgive me,' said Mr Falls in his rather spinster-like fashion. 'I *did* tap on the door, I promise you, but you didn't notice. I came to tell Sergeant Webley that he is wanted on the telephone.'

'Thank you, sir,' said Webley, and went out.

'May I come in?' asked Falls, and came in. 'As that large efficient man has tramped away, it seems a propitious moment to review our position.'

'Why did you say that – *that* – about Questing?' asked Gaunt. 'Why in heaven's name?'

'That he has been murdered? Because of several observations I have made. Let me enumerate them. *A*, the attitude of the police seems to me to be more consistent with a homicide investigation than with an inquiry into an accident. *B*, the circumstances surrounding the affair appear to be suspicious; as, for instance, the bite out of the path. Have you ever tried to dislodge a piece of that solidified mud? My dear sir, you couldn't do it unless you positively danced on the spot. *C*, I observed by the light of my torch that the displaced clod had fallen to the foot of the bank. It held the impression of a nailed boot or shoe. Questing was the only man in evening dress at the concert. *D* (and, dear me, how departmental I sound), the clod had contained a white flag which lay beside it, the only white flag on that side of the mound. As far as I could see the grooves on the edge of the gap and down the sides of the clod must have been the hole made by the flag standard. I am certain Webley and his satellites have discovered these not inconsiderable phenomena. Which would account for their somewhat implacable attitude towards ourselves, don't you feel? I too have been forbidden to leave Wai-ata-tapu. A tiresome restriction.'

'I fail utterly,' said Gaunt breathlessly, 'to see why these ludicrous details should suggest that there has been foul play.'

'Do you? And yet when Hamlet felt the point unbated did he not smell villainy?'

'I haven't the slightest idea what you mean. I still think it monstrous that I, who after all am a guest in this country, should be subjected to this imbecile entanglement in red tape. If the position continues,' said Gaunt, speaking very rapidly and looking down his nose at Mr Falls, 'I shall appeal directly to the Governor-General whom I have the honour to know personally.'

'This is frightful,' thought Dikon. 'First a Chief Justice and now a Governor-General. We shall be cabling to the Royal Family if Webley remains unshaken.'

At this point Dr Ackrington appeared in the doorway.

'May I come in?' he asked.

Gaunt waved his hand.

'I don't know whether you realize it,' said Dr Ackrington, taking them all in with a comprehensive glare, 'but we are under suspicion of homicide, every man jack of us.' He gave an angrily triumphant laugh.

'I refuse to believe it!' Gaunt shouted. 'I refuse to be entangled. It was an accident. He was drunk and he stumbled. Nobody is to blame, I least of all. I refuse to be implicated.'

'You can refuse till you're black in the face, my good sir,' said Dr Ackrington. 'Much good will it do you. You liked him no better than the rest of us, a fact that even this purple monument to inefficiency must stumble across sooner or later.'

'Do you mean Sergeant Webley?' asked Falls.

'I do. I'm sorry to say I regard the man as a moron.'

'That, if you will forgive me, Dr Ackrington, is a mistake. I feel sure that we should be extremely ill-advised to dismiss Webley as a person of no intelligence. And in any case, if, as I am persuaded, Questing has been deliberately sent to an unspeakable death, do we not wish his murderer to be discovered?'

With a faint smile Mr Falls looked from one face to another. After an uncomfortable interval, Gaunt, Dr Ackrington and Dikon all spoke together. 'Yes, of course,' they said impatiently. 'Of course,' Dr Ackrington added. 'But I must tell you at the outset, Falls, that if you concur with the official view of this case, I utterly disagree with you. However, I merely wish to warn you of the possible, the almost inevitable blunders that will be perpetrated by this person. If he is to be in charge of this case I consider that none of us is safe.'

'And what are you going to do about it?' asked Gaunt offensively.

'I intend to call a meeting.'

'Good God, how perfectly footling!'

'And why, may I ask you? Why?'

'Does somebody propose somebody else as a murderer? Or what?'

'You are facetious, sir,' said Dr Ackrington furiously. 'I confess that I did not expect to find you so confident of your own immunity.'

'I should like to know precisely what you mean by that, Ackrington.'

'Come,' said Falls. 'Nothing is gained by losing our tempers.'

'Nor by the merciless introduction of clichés,' Gaunt retorted, darting his head at him.

'Are you in there, James?' asked Colonel Claire. His face, slightly distorted, was pressed against the window pane.

'I'm coming.' Dr Ackrington surveyed his audience of three, it is my duty,' he said grandly, 'to inform you that Webley has apparently been recalled to Harpoon. His men have returned to the reserve. At the moment we are not under direct supervision and I suggest that we lose no time in discussing our position. We are meeting in the dining-room in ten minutes. After this conversation I cannot, I imagine, expect to see you there.'

'On the contrary,' said Falls, 'I shall certainly attend.'

'And I,' said Dikon.

'Obviously,' said Gaunt, 'I had better be there, if only to protect myself.'

'I am delighted that you recognize the necessity,' said Dr Ackrington. 'Coming, Edward.' He joined his brother-in-law on the verandah.

Mr Falls did not follow him. To Dikon's embarrassment he stayed and listened with the air of a connoisseur to Gaunt's renewed display of temper. Gaunt had never been averse to an audience at these moments but on this occasion he seemed to be unaware of anyone but Dikon, who received the full blast of his displeasure. He was told that he had bungled the whole affair, that he should never have allowed Webley an interview, that he was totally indifferent to Gaunt's agony of mind. Never before had Dikon found his employer so unreasonably abusive. His own feeling of apprehension mounted with each intemperate phrase. He was ashamed of Gaunt.

This uncomfortable display was brought to an end by a sudden and unnerving clangour outside the window. Huia was performing with vigour upon the dinner bell. Gaunt, abominably startled, uttered a loud oath.

'Is that lunch?' exclaimed Dikon, who had himself been shaken. 'Now I come to think of it,' he added, I forgot to have breakfast.'

'I fancy it is a summons to the conference,' said Falls placidly. 'Shall we go in?'

VI

Three of the small dining tables had been shoved together and at the head of them sat Dr Ackrington with the Colonel, looking miserable, on his right hand. Simon and Smith sat together at the far end. Simon looked mulish and Smith foggily disgusted. Dr Ackrington pointed portentously to the chairs on his left. Dikon and Falls sat together; Gaunt, like a sulky schoolboy, took the chair farthest removed from everyone else. The Colonel, evidently feeling that the silence was oppressive, suddenly ejaculated: 'Rum go, what?' and seemed alarmed at the sound of his own voice.

'Very rum,' agreed Mr Falls sedately.

Mrs Claire and Barbara came in. They wore their best dresses, together with hats and gloves, and they carried prayer books. They contrived to disseminate an atmosphere of English Sunday morning. There was a great scraping of chairs as the men got up. Smith and Simon seemed to grudge this small courtesy, and looked foolish.

'I'm so sorry if we are late, dear,' said Mrs Claire. 'Everything was a little disorganized this morning.' She began to peel the worn gloves from her plump little hands and looked about her with an air of brisk expectancy. Dikon remembered with a start that she conducted a Sunday school in the native village. 'We had to come and go by the long way,' she explained.

Barbara went off with the prayer books and returned, without her hat, looking scared.

'Well, sit down, Agnes, sit down,' Dr Ackrington commanded. 'Now that you *have* come. Though why the devil you elected to traipse off . . . However! I imagine that you had no pupils.'

'Not a *very* good attendance,' said Mrs Claire gently, 'and I'm afraid they *were* rather inattentive, poor dears.'

Dikon was amazed to see that she was quite unruffled. She sat beside her husband and looked brightly at her brother. 'Well, dear?' she asked.

Dr Ackrington grasped the edge of the table with both hands and leant back in his chair.

'It seems to me,' he began, 'it is essential that we, as a group of people in extraordinary circumstances, should understand one another. I, and I have no doubt all of you, have been subjected to a cross-examination from a person who, I am persuaded, is grossly unfit for his work. I am afraid my opinion of the local police force has never been a high one and Sergeant Webley has said and done nothing to alter it. I may state that I have formed my own view of this case. A brief inspection of the scene of the alleged tragedy would possibly confirm this view but Sergeant Webley, in his wisdom, sees fit to deny me access to the place. Ha!'

He paused, and Mrs Claire, evidently feeling that he expected an answer, said: 'Fancy, dear! What a pity, yes.'

Dr Ackrington looked pityingly at his sister. 'I said "the *alleged* tragedy",' he pronounced. 'The *alleged* tragedy.' He glared at them.

'We heard you, James,' said Colonel Claire mildly, 'the first time.'

'Then why don't you say something?'

'Perhaps, dear,' said his sister, 'it's because you speak so loudly and look so cross. I mean,' she went on with an apologetic cough, 'one thinks to oneself: "How cross he is and how loudly he speaks," and then, you know, one forgets to listen. It's confusing.'

'I was not aware,' Dr Ackrington shouted, and checked himself. 'Very well, Agnes,' he said, dropping his voice to an ominous monotone. 'You desire a continuation of the mealy-mouthed procedure of your Sunday school. You shall have it. With a charge of homicide hanging over all our heads, I shall smirk and whisper my way through this meeting and perhaps you will manage to listen to me.'

' "*I will roar you*" 'thought Dikon, '"*as 'twere any nightingale."*'

'You said *alleged*,' Mr Falls reminded Dr Ackrington pacifically.

'I did. Advisedly.'

'It will be interesting to learn why. Undoubtedly,' said Mr Falls mellifluously, 'the whole affair is not to be described out of hand as murder. I don't pretend to understand the, shall I call it, technical position of a case like this. I mean, the absence of a body . . .'

'*Habeas corpus?*' suggested Colonel Claire dimly.

'I fancy, sir, that *habeas corpus* refers rather to the body of the accused than to that of the victim. Any one of us, I imagine,' Mr Falls continued, looking amiably round the table, 'may be a potential *corpus* within the meaning of the writ. Or am I mistaken?'

'Who's going to be a corpse?' Smith roared out in a panic. 'Speak for yourself.'

'Cut it out, Bert,' Simon muttered.

'Yeh, well, I want to know what it's all about. If anyone's going to call me names I got a right to stick up for myself, haven't I?'

'Perhaps I may be allowed to continue,' said Dr Ackrington coldly.

'For God's sake get on with it,' said Gaunt disgustedly. Dikon saw Barbara look wonderingly at him.

'As I came along the verandah just now,' said Dr Ackrington, 'I heard you, Falls, giving a tolerably clear account of the locale. You, as the only member of our party who has had the opportunity of seeing the track, are at an advantage. If, however, your description is accurate, it seems to me there is only one conclusion to be drawn. You say Questing carried a torch and was using it. How, therefore, could he miss the place where the path has fallen in? You yourself saw it a few moments later.'

Mr Falls looked steadily at Dr Ackrington. Dikon found it impossible to interpret his expression. He had a singularly impassive face. 'The point is quite well taken,' he said at last.

'The chap was half shot,' said Simon. 'They all say he smelt of booze. I reckon it was an accident. He went too near the edge and it caved in with him.'

'But,' said Dikon, 'Mr Falls says the clod that carried away has got an impression of a nailed boot or shoe on it. Questing wore pumps. What's the matter!' he ejaculated. Simon, with an incoherent exclamation, had half risen. He stared at Dikon with his mouth open.

'What the devil's got hold of *you?*' his uncle demanded.

'Sim, dear!'

'All right, all right. Nothing,' said Simon and relapsed into his chair.

'The footprint which you say you noticed, my dear Falls,' said Dr Ackrington, '*might* have been there for some time. It may be of no significance whatever. On the other hand, and this is my contention, it may have been put there deliberately, to create a false impression.'

'Who by?' asked the Colonel. 'I don't follow all this. What did Falls see? I don't catch what people say.'

'Falls,' said Dr Ackrington, 'is it too much to ask you to put forward your theory once more?'

'It is rather the theory which I believe the police will advance,' said Falls. With perfect urbanity he repeated his own observations and the conclusions which he thought the police had drawn from the circumstances surrounding Questing's disappearance. Colonel Claire listened blankly. When Falls had ended he merely said: 'Oh, that!' and looked faintly disgusted.

Gaunt said: 'What's the good of all this? It seems to me you're running round in circles. Questing's gone. He's dead in a nightmarish, an unspeakable manner and I for one believe that, like many a drunken man before him, he stumbled and fell. I won't listen to any other theory. And this drivelling about footprints! The track must be covered in footprints. My God, it's too much. What sort of country is this that I've landed in? A purple-faced policeman to speak to me like that! I can promise you there's going to be a full-dress thumping row when I get away from here.' His voice broke. He struck his hand on the table. 'It was an accident. I won't have anything else. An accident. An accident. He's dead. Let him lie.'

'That is precisely where I differ from you,' said Dr Ackrington crisply. 'In my opinion Questing is very far from being dead.'

CHAPTER 11

The Theory of a Put-Up Job

The sensation he had created seemed to mollify Dr Ackrington. After a moment's utter silence his hearers all started together to exclaim or expostulate. Dikon was visited by one of those chance notions that startle us by their vividness and their irrelevancy. He actually thought for a moment that Ackrington, of all people, had suggested some return from death. A horrific picture of a resurrection from the seething mud rose in his mind and was violently dismissed. From this fantasy he was aroused by Gaunt, who cried out with extraordinary vehemence: 'You're demented! What idiocy is this!' and by Falls who, with an air of concentration, raised his hand and succeeded, unexpectedly, in quelling the rumpus.

'I assure you,' he said, 'if he was uninjured and moving, I must have seen him. But perhaps, Dr Ackrington, you think that he was uninjured and still.'

'I see you take my point,' said Ackrington, who, as usual, seemed ready to tolerate Falls. 'In my opinion the whole thing was an elaborately staged disappearance.'

'Do you mean he's still hangin' about?' cried the Colonel, looking acutely uncomfortable.

'Of course,' Mrs Claire said, 'we should all be only too thankful if we could believe . . .'

'Gosh!' said Simon under his breath. 'I wish to God you were right.'

'Same here,' agreed Smith fervently. 'Suit me all right, never mind what happened before.' His hand moved to the breast pocket of his coat. He opened the coat and looked inside. An unpleasant thought seemed to strike him. 'Here!' he said angrily. 'Do you mean he's hopped it altogether?'

'I mean that taking into consideration the profound incompetence of the authorities, he has every chance of doing so,' said Ackrington.

'Aw, hell!' said Smith plaintively. 'What do you know about that!' He laughed bitterly. 'If he's hooked it,' he said, 'that's the finish. I'm not interested.' The corners of his mouth drooped dolorously. He looked like an alcoholic and disappointed clown. 'I'm disgusted,' he said.

'Perhaps we should let Dr Ackrington expound,' Falls suggested.

'Thank you. I have become accustomed to a continuous stream of interruptions whenever I open my mouth in this household. However.'

'Do explain, dear,' said his sister. 'Nobody's going to interrupt you, old boy.'

'For some time,' Dr Ackrington began, pitching his voice on a determined note, 'I have suspected Questing of certain activities; in a word, I believe him to be an enemy agent. Some of you have been aware of my views. My nephew, apparently, has shared them. He had not seen fit to consult me and has conducted independent investigations of the nature of which I was informed, for the first time, last night.' He paused. Simon kicked his legs about and said nothing. 'It appears,' Dr Ackrington continued, 'that my nephew has had other confidants. It would be strange under these circumstances if Questing, undoubtedly an astute blackguard, failed to discover that he was in some danger. How many of you, for instance, knew of his real activities on the Peak?'

'I know what he was up to,' said Smith instantly. 'I told Rua, weeks ago. I warned him.'

'Of what did you warn him, pray?'

'I told him Questing was after his grandfather's club. You know, Rewi's adze. I was sorry later on that I'd spoken. I got Questing wrong. It was different afterwards. He was going to treat me all right.' Again, his hand moved to the inside pocket of his coat.

'I too had spoken to Rua. I had received no satisfaction from the police or from the military authorities, and, wrongly perhaps, I conceived it my duty to warn Rua of the true significance of Questing's visits to the Peak. Don't interrupt me,' Dr Ackrington commanded, as Smith began a querulous outcry. 'I told Rua the curio story was a blind. I gather that unknown to myself, at least three other persons' – he looked from Simon to Dikon and Gaunt – 'were aware of my suspicions. Simon had actually visited the police. As for you, Edward, I tried repeatedly to convince you . . .'

'Yes, but you're always goin' on about somethin' or other, James.'

'My God!' said Dr Ackrington quietly.

'Please, dear!' begged Mrs Claire.

'Is it too much,' asked Gaunt on a high note, 'to ask that this conversation should grow to a point?'

'May I interrupt?' murmured Falls. 'Dr Ackrington suggests that Questing, feeling that the place was getting too hot for him, has staged his own disappearance in order to make good his escape. We have got so far, haven't we?'

'Certainly. Further, I suggest that he was lying in the shadows when you hunted along the path last night after the scream, and that as soon as you had gone he completed a change of garments. Doubtless he had hidden his new clothes in some suitable cache. He threw the ones he was wearing into Taupo-tapu and made off under cover of the dark. In support of this theory I draw your attention to a development of which Falls has acquainted me. They have salvaged Questing's white waistcoat from Taupo-tapu. How could a waistcoat detach itself from a body?'

'It was a backless waistcoat,' Dikon muttered. 'The straps might have gone. And anyway, sir, the chemicals in the thing . . .'

But Dr Ackrington swept on with his discourse. 'It is even possible that the person you, Falls, heard moving about when you returned was Questing himself. Remember that he could only get away by returning through the village or by coming on round the hill. No doubt he waited for everything to settle down. He acted, of course, under orders.' Dr Ackrington coughed slightly and looked complacently at Falls. 'My theory,' he said with a most unconvincing air of modesty, 'for what it is worth.'

'If you don't mind my saying so, Uncle James,' said Simon instantly, 'in my opinion it's not so much a theory as a joke.'

'Indeed! Perhaps you'll be kind enough . . .'

'You're trying to tell us that Questing wanted to make a clean getaway. What was his big idea letting out a screech you could hear for miles around?'

'I had scarcely dared to hope that I would be asked that question,' said Dr Ackrington complacently. 'What better method could he employ if he wished to protect himself from interruption from the Maori people? Do you imagine that after hearing that scream, there was a Maori on the place who would venture near Taupo-tapu?'

'What about us?'

'It was sheer chance that kept Bell and your mother and sister and Mr Falls behind. And, most important, please remember that it had been arranged that we should *all* pack into Gaunt's car for the return journey. All, that is, except Questing himself, Simon and Smith. It was an unexpected turn of events when Gaunt, Edward, Falls and I all decided, separately, to walk. He had expected to be practically free from disturbance. The audience was leaving when Questing himself went out.'

'And what about this print?' Simon continued exactly as if his uncle had not spoken. 'I thought the idea was that somebody had deliberately kicked the clod away. Bell's pointed out that Questing wore pansy pumps.'

'Ah!' cried Dr Ackrington triumphantly. 'Aha!' Simon looked coldly at him. 'Questing,' his uncle went on, 'wished to create the impression that he fell in. If my theory is correct he will have made as great a change as possible in his appearance. Rough clothes. Workmen's boots. He waits until he has changed his evening shoes for these boots and then stamps away the edge of the path.' Dr Ackrington slapped the table and flung himself back in his chair. 'I invite comment,' he said grandly.

For a moment nobody spoke, and then, to Dikon's profound astonishment, one after another, Gaunt, Smith, the Colonel and Simon, the last somewhat grudgingly, said that they had no comments to offer. It seemed to Dikon that the listeners round the table had relaxed. There was a feeling of expansion. Gaunt touched his forehead with his handkerchief and took out his cigarette case.

Obviously gratified, Ackrington turned to Falls. 'You say nothing,' he said.

'But I am filled with admiration nevertheless,' said Falls. 'A most ingenious theory and lucidly presented. I congratulate you.'

'What *is* it about the man?' Dikon wondered. 'He looks all right, rather particularly so. His voice is pleasant. One keeps thinking he's going to be an honest-to-God sort of fellow and then he prims up his mouth and talks like an affected pedagogue.' Out of patience with Falls, he turned to look at Barbara. He had tried not to look at her ever since she came in. Her pallor, her air of bewilderment and the painful attentiveness with which she listened to everybody and said nothing seemed to Dikon almost unbearably touching. She was watching him now, anxiously, asking him something. She answered his smile with a shadowy one of her own. There was an empty chair beside hers.

'Dikon!'

Gaunt had shouted at him. He jumped and looked round guiltily. 'I'm sorry, sir. Did you say something to me?'

'Dr Ackrington has been waiting for your answer for some considerable time. He wants your opinion on his solution.'

'I'm terribly sorry. My opinion?' Dikon thrust his hands into his pockets and clenched them. They were all watching him. 'Well, sir, I'm afraid I've been completely addled by the whole affair. I can't pretend to have any constructive theory to offer.'

'Then I take it you are prepared to accept mine?' said Ackrington impatiently.

Why had he got the feeling that they were bending their wills upon him, that they sat there boring into his mind with theirs, trying to compel him to something?

'What the devil's the matter with you?' Gaunt demanded.

'Come, come, Bell, if you've nothing to say we must conclude you've no objection.'

'But I have,' said Dikon, rousing himself. 'I've every objection. I don't believe in it at all.'

II

He knew that his explanations sounded hopelessly inadequate. He heard himself stumbling from one feeble objection to another. 'I can't disprove it of course, sir. It might be true. I mean, it's all sort of logical but I mean it's not based on anything.'

'On the contrary,' said Dr Ackrington and his very mildness seemed to Dikon to be most disquieting, 'it is based on the man's character, on the circumstances surrounding him, and upon the undisputed fact that no body has been found.'

'It sounds so sort of bogus, though,' Dikon floundered about through a series of slangy phrases which he was quite unaccustomed to use. 'I mean it's the kind of thing that they do in thrillers. I mean he wouldn't know there was going to be all that chat at the concert about the girl who fell in Taupo-tapu. Would he? And if he didn't know that then he wouldn't know about the scream keeping the Maoris away.'

'My good fool,' said Gaunt, 'can't you understand that the scream was introduced *because* of the legend? An extra bit of atmosphere. If he hadn't heard the legend and the song he wouldn't have screamed.'

'Precisely,' said Dr Ackrington.

'Well, Mr Bell?' asked Falls.

'Yes, that fits in, of course, but I'm afraid it all sort of fits too neatly for me. As if it was concocted, don't you know? Like china packed too closely. No lee-way for jolts. I'm afraid my objections are maddeningly vague but I simply cannot *see* him hiding a disguise in an extinct geyser and tossing his boiled shirt into a mud pot. And then going off – where?'

'It is highly probable that a car was waiting for him somewhere along the road,' said Ackrington.

'There's a goods train goes through at midnight,' suggested Smith. 'He might of hopped on to that. Geeze, I hope you're right, Doc. It'd give you the willies to think he was stewing over there, wouldn't it?'

Mrs Claire uttered a cry of protest and Ackrington instantly blasted Smith.

'Cut it out, Bert!' advised Simon. 'You don't put things nicely.'

'Hell, I said I hoped he *wasn't*, didn't I? What's wrong with that?'

'If you are not satisfied with Dr Ackrington's theory, Mr Bell,' said Falls, 'can you suggest any other explanation?'

'I'm afraid I can't. I haven't seen the print on the clod of mud, of course, but it seems to me it can't be an old one if it suggests that somebody kicked the clod loose. If that's so, it looks as if there has been foul play. And yet I'm afraid I don't think Questing was drunk enough to fall in or even that it's at all likely, if he did put his foot into the gap, that he would go right over. And it seems to be a very chancy sort of trap for a murderer to set, doesn't it? I mean Simon might have gone over, or anybody else who happened to walk that way. How could a murderer reckon on Questing being the first to leave the concert?'

'You don't think it was an accident. You can't advance any tenable theory of homicide. You find my theory logical and yet cannot accept it. I think, Mr Bell,' Dr Ackrington summed up, 'you may be excused from any further attempts to explain yourself.'

'Thank you very much, sir,' said Dikon sincerely. 'I think I may.'

He walked round the table and sat down by Barbara.

From that moment the other men treated Dikon as an onlooker. It was impossible, they agreed, that in a homicide investigation the police could regard him as a suspect. He was with Mrs Claire and Barbara when Questing screamed, he drove to the hall and had no opportunity to enter the thermal reserve either before, after, or during the concert. The fact that the path had been intact when the other men walked over to the village excluded him from any suspicion of complicity as far as the displaced clod was concerned. 'Even the egregious Webley,' said Dr Ackrington, 'could scarcely blunder where Bell is concerned.' Dikon realized with amusement that in a way he lost caste by his immunity.

'As for the rest of us,' said Dr Ackrington importantly, 'I have no doubt that Webley, in the best tradition of the worst type of fiction, will suspect each of us in turn. For this reason I have thought it well that we should consult together. We do not know along what fantastic corridors his fancy may lead him but it is quite evident from certain questions that he has already put to *me* that he has crystallized upon the footprint. Now, did any of us wear boots or shoes with nails in them?'

Only Simon and Smith, it appeared, had done so. 'I got them on now,' Smith roared out. 'In my position you don't wear pansy shoes. I wear working boots and I wear them all the time.' He hitched up his knee and planked a most unlovely boot firmly against the edge of the table. 'Anybody's welcome to inspect my feet,' he said.

'Thank you so much,' Gaunt murmured. 'No. Definitely no.'

'That goes for me,' said Simon. 'I've got three pairs. They can look at the lot for mine.'

'Very well,' said Dr Ackrington. 'Next, they require to know our movements. Perhaps each of us has already been asked to account for himself. You, Agnes, and you, Barbara, are naturally not personally involved. Nevertheless you may be questioned about us. You should be prepared.'

'Yes, dear. But if we are asked any questions we tell the truth don't we? It's so simple,' said Mrs Claire, opening her eyes very wide, 'just to tell the truth, isn't it?'

'Possibly. It's the interpretation this incubus may put upon the truth that should concern us. When I tell you that he has three times taken me through a recital of my own movements and has not made so much as a single note upon my theory of disappearance, you may understand my anxiety.'

'Won't he listen to the idea?' asked Gaunt anxiously and then added at once: 'No. No. He questioned me in the same way. He suspects one of us. We're in danger.'

'I think you underrate Webley,' said Falls. 'I must confess that I cannot see why you are so anxious. He is following police procedure, which, of necessity, may be a little cumbersome. After all Questing *has* gone and the manner of his going must be investigated.'

'Quite right,' said the Colonel. 'Very sensible. Matter of routine. What I told you, James.'

'And in the absence of motive,' Mr Falls continued, and was interrupted by Dr Ackrington.

'Motive!' he shouted. 'Absence of motive! My dear man, he will find the path to Taupo-tapu littered with alleged motives. Even I – *I* am suspect if it comes to motive.'

'Good Lord,' said the Colonel, 'I suppose you are, James! You've been calling the chap a spy and saying shootin' was too good for him for the last three months or more!'

'And what about you, my good Edward? I imagine your position is fairly well known by this time.'

'James! Please!' cried Mrs Claire.

'Nonsense, Agnes. Don't be such an ostrich. We all know Questing had Edward under his thumb. It's common gossip.'

Gaunt shook a finger at Simon. 'And what about you?' he said. 'You come into the picture, don't you?' He glanced at Barbara, and Dikon wished most profoundly that he had never confided in him.

Simon said quickly: 'I've never tried to make out I liked him. He was a traitor. If he's cleared out I hope they get him. The police know what I thought about Questing. I've told them. And if I'm in the picture so are you, Mr Gaunt. You looked as if you'd like to scrag him yourself after he'd finished his little speech last night.'

'That's fantastically absurd, I'm afraid. I wouldn't wish my worst enemy to – God, I can't even bear to think of it.'

'The police won't worry about how you think, Mr Gaunt. It's the way you acted that'll interest them.'

'Too right,' said Smith rather smugly. Gaunt instantly turned on him.

'What about you and your outcry?' said Gaunt. 'Three weeks ago you were howling attempted murder and breathing revenge.'

'I've explained all that,' shouted Smith in a great hurry. 'Sim knows all about that. It was a misunderstanding. Him and me were cobbers. Here, don't you go dragging that up and telling the police I threatened him. That'd be a nasty way to behave. They might go thinking anything, mightn't they, Sim?'

'I'll say.'

'Naturally, they'll have their eye on you,' said Gaunt with some enjoyment. 'I should say they'll be handing you the usual warning in less than no time.'

Smith's eyes filled with tears. He thrust a shaking hand into the breast pocket of his coat and pulled out a sheet of paper which he flung on to the table. 'Look at it!' he cried. 'Look at it. Him and me were cobbers. Gawd spare me days, we buried the bloody hatchet, Morry Questing and me. That's what he was going to do for me. Look at it. Written out by his own hand in pansy green ink. Pass it round. Go on.'

They passed it round. It was a signed statement written in green ink. The Colonel at once recognized the small businesslike script as Questing's. It undertook, in the event of Questing becoming the proprietor of Wai-ata-tapu, that the bearer, Herbert Smith, would be given permanent employment as outside porter at a wage of five pounds a week and keep.

'You must have made yourself very unpleasant to extract this,' said Gaunt.

'You bet your boots I did!' said Smith heartily. 'I got him while my bruises were still bad. They were bad, too, weren't they, Doc?'

Dr Ackrington grunted. 'Bad enough,' he said.

'Yeh, that's right. "You owe it to me, Questing," I said, and then he drove me over to the level crossing and showed me how it happened, him looking through the coloured sun screen at the light. "That may be a reason but it's no excuse," I said. "I could make things nasty for you and you know it." So then he asks me what I want and after a bit he comes across with this contract. After that we got on well. And now, what's it worth? Dead or bolted it makes no odds, me contract's a washout.'

'I should keep it, nevertheless,' said Dr Ackrington.

'Too right, I'll keep it. If Stan Webley starts in on me – '

'I had an idea,' said Mr Falls gently, 'that we were going to discuss alibis.'

'You're perfectly right, Falls. It's utterly beyond the power of man, in this extraordinary household, to persuade any single person to keep to the point for two seconds together. However. Now, we left this infernal concert severally. Questing went out first. You followed him, Gaunt, after an interval of perhaps three minutes. Not more.'

'What of it?' Gaunt demanded, at once on the offensive. He added immediately, 'I'm sorry, Ackrington. I'm behaving badly, I know.' He looked at Mrs Claire and Barbara. 'Will you forgive me?' he said. 'I don't deserve to be forgiven, I know, but this business has jangled my nerves to such an extent I hardly know what I'm saying. I'm a bit run-down, I suppose, and – well, it's hit me rather hard, for some stupid reason.'

Mrs Claire made soft consolatory noises. For the life of him Dikon could not stop himself looking at Barbara. Until now, Gaunt had completely disregarded her but the famous charm had suddenly reappeared and he was smiling at her anxiously, pleading with her to understand him. Barbara met this advance with a puzzled frown and turned away. Then, as if ashamed of this refusal, she raised her head and, finding that he was still watching her, blushed. 'I'm so sorry,' said Gaunt and Dikon thought he made his last apology indecently personal. Barbara answered it with an unexpected gesture. She gave an awkward little bow. 'She's got good manners,' thought Dikon. 'She's a darling.' He saw that her hands were working together under the edge of the table and wished he could tranquillize them with his own. When he listened again to the conversation he found that Gaunt was giving an account of his movements after the concert.

'I don't pretend I wasn't angry,' he said. 'I was furious. He'd behaved abominably, using my name as a blurb for his own squalid business. I thought the best thing I could do was to go out and apply fresh air to the famous temperament. That's what I did. There was nobody about. I lit a cigarette and walked home by the road. I don't think I can prove to the strange Mr Webley that I did precisely that, but it happens to be the truth. I regained my temper in the process. When I arrived here I went to my room. Then I heard voices in the dining-room and thought that a drink might be rather pleasant. I came to the dining-room bringing a bottle of whisky with me. I found Colonel Claire and Dr Ackrington. That's all.'

'Quite so,' said Dr Ackrington. 'Thank you. Now, Gaunt, your best move, obviously, is to find some witness to your movements. You say there is none.'

'I'm positive. I've told you.'

'But it's more than possible some of the Maori people hanging round the doorway saw you walk away. The same observers might already have seen Questing go off in the opposite direction. I myself followed close after you but you had already disappeared. However, I heard distant voices that seemed to me to come from the far side of the village, the side nearest the main road. Possibly the owners of these voices saw you. It was with the object of collecting such data that I suggested we should call this meeting.'

'I saw nobody,' said Gaunt, 'and I heard no voices.'

'Did you hear the scream?' asked Simon.

'No, I heard nothing,' said Gaunt easily and smiled again at Barbara.

'Then,' said Dr Ackrington importantly, 'I may proceed with my own statement.'

'No, wait a bit, James.'

Colonel Claire drove his fingers through his hair and gazed unhappily at his brother-in-law. 'I'm afraid we can't let things go like this. I mean, since you've insisted on us thrashing the thing out between us one mustn't keep back anything, must one? Gaunt's statement may be quite all right. I don't know. But at the same time . . .'

Dikon saw Gaunt turn white while his lips still held their smile. Gaunt did not look at the Colonel, his eyes still rested on Barbara, but they stared blankly, now. He did not speak and after glancing uncomfortably at him the Colonel went on.

'You remember,' he said, 'I went back to the *pa* last night.'

'Well?' said Dr Ackrington sharply as he paused.

'Well, I think I told you that they were all excited. They said a lot of things that at the time I felt I'd better keep to myself. I used to take that line in India, pretty much, when there was trouble with the natives. Wait a bit before handin' on anything they tell you or you may land yourself in a mess. It's the best way in my opinion. But when we agree to give full reports on our movements and there's evidence that a report may *not* be full, well then it's one's duty to speak. That's my view.'

'Your ethics, my dear Edward, may be admirable. No doubt they are. But having decided to reveal that which you formerly held locked in your bosom, will you be kind enough to come to the point and, in fact, reveal it.'

'All right, James. Don't start rattlin' me, there's a good chap. It's only this. One of the boys over there said that during Questing's speech he went up to a *whare* near the road. I'm afraid they'd got a keg of beer there stowed away for the evening. Young Eru Saul, it was. He said that some minutes later he heard a couple of *pakehas* having a fearful row. At least, one of them was abusin' the other like a pickpocket and the other seemed to be half laughin' and half jeerin'. "Made him get very angry" was the way Saul put it. He didn't understand what it was all about but he listened to it until he heard one of them call the other a bloody liar (please forgive me, Agnes, I have been against your attendin' this meetin' from the beginnin') and threatened to do something or another that Saul couldn't catch. Then there was a long pause. He got tired of it and went back to the beer. He heard someone walk past the *whare* and went out to see who it was. Of course it was dark but he left the door open. They're very careless about the blackout over there, my dear. I think we ought – '

'*Will you get on, Edward?*'

'Very well, James. The light from the door showed up this person and Saul said it was Gaunt. He said he'd recognized the angry voice as Gaunt's as soon as he heard it and he's quite certain the other man was Questing.'

III

During the next five minutes Dikon underwent as many changes of temperament as Gaunt himself at his worst. Incredulity, panic, sympathy, shame and irritation in turn possessed him as Gaunt first denied, then admitted and finally explained away his interview with Questing. He began by suggesting that the Colonel's informant had either made up his story of a quarrel or else mistaken the principals. The Colonel remained unshaken.

'I'm sorry,' he said gently. 'I don't think there was any mistake, you know.'

'The youth was probably tight. Isn't he the fellow you've had to get rid of, Mrs Claire?'

'Eru Saul? Yes, I'm afraid he really *is* an unsatisfactory boy. No home influence, alas. One of those *unfortunate* cases,' said Mrs Claire meaningly. 'We've tried to give him a good start but he's drifted back. Such a pity, yes.'

Gaunt shook his finger at the Colonel: 'You say yourself he'd been at the beer.'

'Yes, I know I do, but he wasn't a bit tight and I'm sure he believed he was speaking the truth.'

'All right, Colonel.' Gaunt raised his hands and let them fall on the table. 'I give up. I met the man and told him precisely what I thought of him. I'm sorry it's had to come out. Another bit of most undesirable publicity. If my agent was here he'd give me absolute hell, wouldn't he, Dikon? My one desire was to keep out of this extremely distasteful affair. I'm perfectly certain that Dr Ackrington is right and that the whole thing's a put-up job. Frankly, I'm tremendously anxious that my name should not appear and that is precisely why I hoped to avoid any mention of this encounter. I've been foolish. I realize that. I apologize.'

'It's just too bad about you,' said Simon. 'You're in it with the rest of us. Why the heck should *you* get away with a pack of lies!'

'You're perfectly right, of course,' said Gaunt. 'Why should I?'

'If people start talking about murder – ' began Smith confusedly, and Gaunt at once interrupted him.

'If there's talk of murder,' he said, 'I fancy this story gives *me* a complete alibi. Young Saul says that he saw me walking up to the main road. As a matter of fact I remember passing the lighted hut. I distinctly noticed a smell of beer. The thermal region's in the opposite direction. I suppose I should be grateful to the dubious Mr Saul.'

'You should be thankful you haven't landed yourself in a damned equivocal position,' said Dr Ackrington, staring at Gaunt. 'I pass over the more serious view, which we should be perfectly justified in taking, of your attempt to keep us in the dark. I merely advise you to make quite sure of this alibi you have just thought of.'

'It is quite genuine, I promise you,' said Gaunt easily. 'Might we get on with someone else's movements?'

'Well, of all the bloody nerve – ' began Simon.

'Simon!' said his parents together and the Colonel added, 'You'll apologize to your mother and sister, immediately, Simon. And to Mr Gaunt.'

Dikon, in his distress, had time to reflect that the Claires were a little too good to be true. Simon muttered his apology.

'Suppose,' Mr Falls suggested, 'we get on with the other narratives. Yours, for instance, Ackrington.'

'By all means. I shall begin by stating flatly that if I could have got at Questing last night I should have certainly have given him fits. I left the hall with every intention of giving him fits. I couldn't find him. I heard voices in the distance; in the light of Gaunt's amended statement, I presume they were his and Questing's voices but I did not recognize them. I had it in my head that Questing would be halfway across the thermal reserve and I hurried along with the idea of catching him up. I did not find him. I carried on and came home.'

'May one know why you wanted to tackle him?' asked Falls.

'Certainly. His behaviour at the concert. It was the final straw. Any questions?' asked Dr Ackrington loudly.

'Too right. Doc, there's a question,' said Smith with an air of the deepest acumen. 'Can you prove it?'

'No.'

'Oh.'

'Any other questions?'

'I should like to know,' said Falls, 'if you noticed the gap in the path.'

'I am glad, Falls, that you at least have had the intelligence to ask the only question that can possibly have any useful bearing on our problem. I did not. I must confess I don't actually remember seeing the flag, which I admit is curious. But I'm perfectly certain there was no gap in the path.'

'Might you have missed it, Uncle?' asked Barbara suddenly and Dikon noticed how the men all looked at her as if a domestic pet had given utterance.

'Conceivably,' said Dr Ackrington. 'I don't think so. However. Now you, Edward.'

'It's unfortunate,' said Gaunt airily, 'that nobody saw the doctor whizzing past the geysers.'

'I am aware of that. I realize my position. The purple policeman has doubtless put some fantastic interpretation upon the circumstance. I agree that I am unfortunate in that I was unobserved.'

'But you *were* observed, James,' said the Colonel, opening his eyes very widely. 'I observed you, you know.'

IV

The Colonel seemed to be mildly gratified by his brother-in-law's reception of this news. He smiled gently and nodded his head at Ackrington, who gaped at him, opened and shut his mouth once or twice, and finally swore softly under his breath.

'I was behind you, you know,' Colonel Claire added. 'Walkin'.'

'I didn't suppose, Edward, that you cycled through the thermal region. May I ask why you have not mentioned this before?'

Colonel Claire returned the classic answer: 'Nobody asked me,' he said.

'Were you hard on his heels the whole way, Colonel?'

'Eh? No, Falls. No, you see he went so fast. I caught sight of him when I got to that gap in the hedge round the village and then the bumps in the ground hid him. Then I saw him again when I got to the top of the mound. He was nearly over at the hill by then.'

'I must say it's not my idea of a cast-iron alibi,' said Gaunt, who seemed to welcome the chance of scoring off Dr Ackrington. 'Two little peeps in the dark with craters and mounds between you.'

'Oh, he had a torch,' said the Colonel. 'Hadn't you, James? And, by the way, the scream was *much* later. I was nearly home when I heard the scream. I thought it was a bird,' added the Colonel.

'What sort of bird, for God's sake?'

'A mutton bird, James. They make beastly noises at night.'

'There are no mutton birds round here, Edward.'

'Does it matter?' asked Dikon wearily.

'Not two hoots, I should have thought,' said Gaunt bitterly. 'I've always detested nature study.'

'He *is* sure of himself all of a sudden,' thought Dikon.

They ploughed on with the Colonel's story. When asked if he had noticed the gap in the path he became distressingly vague and changed his mind with each question as it was put to him. Falls took a hand. 'You say you had a pocket torch, Colonel. Now my recollection of the gap is that it showed rather sharp and dark in the torchlight, like a shadow or even a stain across the outer edge of the path.'

'Yes!' the Colonel exclaimed. 'That's a jolly good way of describin' it. Like a black stain.'

'Then you did see it?'

'I only said it was a good way of *describin'* it. Vivid.'

'Didn't you notice that the white flag at the top was missing?'

'Ah! Now, did I? You'd notice a thing like that, wouldn't you?'

Dr Ackrington groaned and executed a rapid tattoo with his fingers on the table.

'But then again,' the Colonel said, 'one saw the *red* flags going off at the *foot* of the mound, so naturally one wouldn't follow *them*. And the path is quite sharply defined and that. One would just follow it up the mound, wouldn't one, Agnes?'

'What, dear?' said Mrs Claire, startled by this sudden demand upon her attention. 'Yes, of course. Naturally.'

'The hole!' Dr Ackrington shouted. 'The gap! For pity's sake pull yourself together, Edward. Throw your mind, a courtesy title for your cerebral arrangements, I fear, back to your walk up the path. Visualize it. Think. Concentrate.'

Colonel Claire obediently screwed up his face and shut his eyes tightly.

'Now,' said Dr Ackrington, 'you are climbing the path, using your torch. Do you see the white flag on the top of the mound?'

Colonel Claire, without opening his eyes, shook his head.

'Then, as you reach the top, what *do* you see?'

'Nothing. How can I? I'm flat on my face.'

'What!'

'I fell down, you know. Flat.'

'What the devil did you do that for?'

'I don't know,' said Colonel Claire, opening his eyes very wide. 'Not on purpose, of course. I caught sight of you some way ahead and I thought to myself, "Hullo, there goes James," and there, at that moment, went I. It gave me quite a fright because after all one is close to the edge up there. However, I picked myself up and carried on.'

'Did you fall into the hole, dear?' asked Mrs Claire, solicitously.

'What hole, Agnes?'

'James seems to think there was a hole,' she muttered.

'Did you look to see why you'd fallen? Did you examine the path with your torch?'

'How could I, James, when the torch had gone out? I fell on it and it wouldn't go on again. But I could see the flags dimly so I was all right.'

'I'm glad you weren't hurt, dear,' said his wife.

'And so there, in effect,' said the Colonel quite cosily, 'we are.'

'Precisely nowhere,' said Dr Ackrington. 'I take it you can't produce a witness to your movements, Edward?'

'Not unless Questing saw me. And even if he's alive, as we all seem to have agreed, he's vanished into thin air, so that's no good, is it?'

Dr Ackrington pointed at his nephew. 'You,' he said.

'Bert and Colly and I were together,' said Simon. 'A chap from Harpoon gave us a lift back. Ernie Priest, it was. Some of the boys over there wanted us to stay for a drink but I don't think it's so hot getting dragged in on those parties. It was Eru Saul's gang and I draw the line there. Ernie had a bottle of beer in the car. We had one with him and he dropped us up at the front gate. That's right, isn't it, Bert?'

'I'll say,' said Smith moodily.

'Did any of you leave the hall during the performance?' asked Falls.

'You did, didn't you, Bert?'

'What if I did!' cried Smith, instantly on the defensive. 'Sure, I did. I went out with two of the boys for a quick one. There's some people when they've got a drink on the place has the decency to offer you one.' He looked accusingly at Gaunt. '*Some* people, I said,' he added. 'Not everyone.'

'Who were the two youths?' Dr Ackrington demanded.

'Eru Saul and Maui Matai.'

'Did you separate at all, Mr Smith?' asked Falls.

'That's right, pick on me. We did *not*. We stuck together and we got back in time to hear his nibs screeching his socks off.'

'Are you talking about me?' asked Gaunt bristling.

'That's right.'

'I should be glad to know at what point in my performance I could be said, even by a drunken Philistine, to screech.'

' "*Once more into the blasted breeches, pals,*" ' said Smith in a shrill falsetto. ' "*Once more*" We could hear you all the way down the path. Does it hurt you much?'

'Cut it out, for Pete's sake, Bert,' whispered Simon and stifled a laugh.

'I resent this,' said Gaunt, breathing noisily.

'My dear Gaunt, surely not?' soothed Mr Falls. 'A piquant incident! You will dine off it when the undesirable publicity has subsided. I should like to ask Mr Smith and Mr Claire,' he went on, 'if they and Mr Gaunt's man remained in the hall until the general exodus.'

'Yes,' said Simon, glaring at him.

'Did you see Questing go out?' asked Dr Ackrington.

'Too right we did,' said Smith. 'He was talking to us. Well, to me. Very pleased with his bit of a speech and skiting about it. It was while we were with some of the Maori gang, wasn't it, Sim? Outside the hall.'

'That's right. And d'you know what I reckon he was doing?'

'You're asking me!' said Smith. 'He was passing over the doings. Had a bottle in his overcoat pocket. One of those flatties.'

'Brandy,' said Simon.

'Yeh. I saw him slip it to young Maui Matai. It's like what I told Rua. He was keeping in with the young lot. That's why Maui asked us to have one. I could of done with it, too,' confessed Smith.

'Well, and then Ernie Priest came along,' Simon explained, 'and the four of us sloped off up to his car.'

'Leaving Questing with those Maori youths?' asked Falls.

'That's right,' said Smith.

'Interesting!' Falls murmured. 'And your Maori friends said nothing to you of this, Colonel?'

'They wouldn't. They know what we think about the whole business of giving spirits to the natives.'

'It would be after this that you met Questing, Mr Gaunt?'

'I suppose so. Yes, yes,' said Gaunt in an exhausted voice.

'Ah, yes,' said Mr Falls blandly. 'Quite so. Afterwards. I take it,' he went on with his air of precision, 'that this meeting doesn't wish for a repetition of my own extremely inconclusive statement? I understand that you have all become acquainted with it.'

'That's right,' said Simon before anyone else could answer. 'We know you were just about on the spot when he yelled. We know you took pretty good care to keep us off the path while you went back there yourself. We know you wouldn't have had to say anything if Bell hadn't come along and found you. You're the only one of the lot of us except Uncle James that's seen this gap in the path. You seem to have got hold of the idea that everything you say goes for gospel. Well, by cripey, it doesn't for mine. By my idea you've had a free run of the hot air round here for a bit too long. There's one other thing we know about you. What about that stuff with your pipe?'

'*Simon!*' said his father and uncle together.

'What about it? Come on. What about it?'

'Simon, will you . . .'

'No, no, please!' begged Falls. 'Do let us hear about this. I'm completely baffled, I assure you. Did you say my *pipe?*'

'I'm not saying another thing, Uncle. Keep your shirt on.'

Colonel Claire looked coldly at his son and said: 'You'll come and speak to me afterwards, Simon. In the meantime you will be good enough to say nothing. I am ashamed of you.'

'Damned young cub,' Dr Ackrington began, and his sister at once said: 'No, James, please. It's for his father to speak to him, dear, if he's done wrong.'

'*I'm* sorry,' Simon muttered ungraciously. 'I didn't mean to . . .'

'That will do,' said his father.

'Well,' said Falls, 'since this seems to be another little mystery that is to remain unsolved, perhaps, Ackrington, you would sum up for us.'

'Certainly. I'm afraid,' said Dr Ackrington, clearing his throat, 'that beyond establishing a species of alibi in three cases, and also clarifying the situation generally, we do not appear at first glance to have attained very much.'

'Hear, hear,' said Gaunt.

'Nevertheless,' continued Dr Ackrington, quelling him with an acid stare, 'there are certain valuable points to be noted. The gap in the path was not there before the concert. I didn't see it on my return and as Claire was close behind me it seems most unlikely, indeed impossible, that it could have appeared before he got there or that even he could have missed it. We are agreed that the clod of mud could only have been dislodged by considerable force and we know that it bears the deep impression of a nailed boot. The only two members of our party wearing nailed shoes or boots appear to have alibis. Questing must have entered the thermal reserve after Claire and I had crossed it and after his scene with Gaunt. What was he doing in the interim?'

'Having one with the boys?' Simon suggested.

'Possibly. That can be checked. Now, we have discovered nothing to contradict my theory of a put-up job. On the other hand we've narrowed down the margin for murder. If the clod was dislodged with the idea of Questing putting his foot into the gap and falling over, this fictitious murderer must have dodged out after you, Edward, had gone by. He must have danced and stamped about, revealing himself on the skyline if you'd happened to glance back and, having completed his work, come on here or returned to the *pa*. During this period Gaunt had quarrelled with Questing, and gone up to the main road; Simon and Smith were drinking in somebody's car after consorting for a time with certain Maoris; while Bell, Agnes and Barbara had gone to Gaunt's car.' Dr Ackrington looked triumphantly round the table. 'We are completely covered for the crucial time. What's the matter, Agnes?'

Mrs Claire was weaving her small plump hands. 'Nothing really, dear,' she said gently. 'It's only – I know nothing about such things, of course, nothing. But I do read some of Edward's thrillers, and it always seems to me that in the stories they make everything rather more elaborate than it would be in real life.'

'This is not a discussion on the dubious realism of detective fiction, Agnes.'

'No, dear. But I was wondering if perhaps we were not a little inclined to be too elaborate ourselves? I mean, it's very clever of you to think of all the other things, and I don't pretend I can follow them; but mightn't it be simpler if somebody had just hit poor Mr Questing?'

Dikon broke a dead silence by saying: 'Mrs Claire, you make me want to stand up and cheer.'

CHAPTER 12

Skull

Dikon's was the only voice lifted in praise of Mrs Claire's unexpected theory. Her brother, after looking at her in blank astonishment, told her roundly that she was talking nonsense. He explained, as if to a child, that a blow from a hidden assailant would not account for the displaced clod of mud and that even in a struggle, which could scarcely have taken place without Falls hearing it, the path was altogether too firm for any portion of it to give way. The Colonel supported him, saying that when the iron standards for the flags were driven in, the Maoris had used a sledge hammer. Mrs Claire said that of course they were right, and they looked uneasily at her.

Barbara said: 'Even if the police *do* think someone attacked him, haven't we proved that none of us could have been there at the time?'

'Bravo!' cried Gaunt. 'Of course we have.'

'As far as that goes,' said Simon, 'there is one of us who could have knocked him over.' He looked at Falls.

'I?' said Falls. 'Dear me, yes. So I could. So I could.'

'After all,' said Simon, 'they'll only have your word for it that you didn't know what happened. Bell heard Questing scream and went out there. And what did he find? You. Alone.'

'I was not wearing hobnail boots, however.'

'Lucky for you, I reckon. And talking about these boots, there's something else I've got to tell you. Questing owned a pair of boots with sprigs. I can prove it.'

Dikon had seen enough of Simon by this time to know that a piece of portentous information burnt holes in the pockets of his reticence.

He frowned at Simon. He even tried to stave him off by an effort of the will but it was no good. Out came the story of their climb up Rangi's Peak, out came a description of the hobnailed footprints.

'And if the police show me this clod of mud I reckon I can tell if it's the same print. Anyway, they can go up the Peak and look for themselves. With any luck the prints'll still be there.'

With this recital he bounded into popular favour. Dr Ackrington, after a comparatively mild blast on the danger of withholding information, declared that Simon, by his vigil on the rock, had gone far towards proving that Questing was the signaller. If Questing was the signaller it was almost certain, said Dr Ackrington, that the prints on the ledge were his prints. If these corresponded with the impression on the detached clod then they might well prove to be a determining factor.

'You may depend upon it,' cried Dr Ackrington, 'the damned blackguard's a hundred miles away if he hasn't got clean out to sea, and wherever he is, he's wearing these blasted boots.'

Steps sounded outside, followed by a muffled grumble of voices. Dikon turned to look. Through the wide windows of the dining-room the men at the table watched Webley's three assistants cross the pumice and come towards the verandah. Dikon was visited by a sensation of unreality, a feeling that the mental and physical experiences of this interminable morning were repeating themselves exactly. For the men walked in the same order that they had adopted when he last saw them. They carried again their muddy rakes and poles, and one of them held away from him a heavy sack from which a globule of mud formed and dropped. And just as before, his heart had jolted against his ribs, so it jolted again: As the men drew near the verandah they saw the party in the dining-room. They paused and the two groups looked at each other through the open windows. A car came down the drive. Webley and an elderly man got out. The men with the sack moved towards them and again there was a huddled inspection.

Mrs Claire and Barbara, who sat with their backs to the windows, followed the direction of their companions' gaze, and half turned.

'Wait a moment, Agnes,' said Dr Ackrington loudly. 'Will you attend to me? Never mind the windows now. Mind what I say. Barbara, will you listen!'

'Yes, James.'

'Yes, Uncle James.'

They turned back dutifully. Dikon, sharing Dr Ackrington's desire that Barbara should not see the men outside, got to his feet and moved behind her chair. Dr Ackrington spoke loudly and rapidly. Colonel Claire and his wife and daughter looked at him. The others made no pretence of doing so, and Dikon tried to read in their faces the progress of the men beyond the window.

'... I repeat,' Dr Ackrington was saying, 'that it's as clear as daylight. Questing, having changed into workman's clothes and heavy boots, stamped away the clod from the path, threw his evening clothes into the cauldron and bolted. We were meant to presume accidental death.'

'I still think it was incredibly stupid of him to forget that he would leave prints,' said Dikon. He saw Simon's eyes widen as he watched the men beyond the windows.

'He thought the clod would fall into the cauldron, Bell. It must be by the merest fluke that it did not do so.'

Simon's hands were clenched. Falls raised an eyebrow. Dr Ackrington himself, looking, as they did, beyond the windows, paused and then added rapidly: 'If Questing is found before he gets clean away, he will be wearing hobnail boots. I'll stake my oath on it.'

Simon was on his feet pointing. 'Look!'

Now they all turned.

The group of men outside the window parted. Webley had taken something from the sack. He held it up. It was a heavy boot and it dripped mud.

II

They were all shown the boot. Webley brought it into the dining-room and displayed it, standing on a sheet of newspaper in the middle of the table, and exuding a strong smell of sulphur. He wiped away most of the mud. The surface of the leather was pulpy and greatly disfigured, some of the metal eyelets had fallen out and the upper had become detached in places from the sole. There were, however, still two hobnails in the heel, though the others had fallen out.

Webley wiped his large flat hands on a piece of rag and looked woodenly at his trophy.

'I'd be obliged,' he said, 'if any of you ladies or gentlemen could put an owner on this. We've got its mate outside.'

Nobody spoke.

'We fished them out with a hay fork,' Webley said. 'Don't any of you gentlemen recognize it?'

Dr Ackrington made a brusque movement. 'Yes, Doctor?' Webley said at once. 'You were going to say something?'

'I believe – I think that quite possibly they were Questing's.'

'His? But you told me he wore evening shoes, Doctor.'

'Yes. There's a new development, however. My nephew – perhaps he should explain.'

Dikon wondered if for a fraction of a second Webley had looked resigned, if his singularly inexpressive face had been blurred momentarily with the glaze of boredom. He passed his flat fingers over his jowl, stared at Simon and said: 'Oh, yes?' Simon embarked with a great air of consequence upon an account of their visit to the Peak. He forgot to include Dikon in his recital. 'The night before when I was out on the rock, I picked that Questing was signalling from this ledge on the Peak. That's why I went straight up there yesterday morning. Soon as I got there I looked for footprints and did I find them! Two beauties. Squatting on his heels, he'd been, under the lee of the bank. Here! You let me have a look at the soles of the boots and I reckon I'll tell you if they made these prints on the Peak. That's a fair pop, isn't it?'

Webley went out and returned with the second boot. It was further advanced in disintegration than its mate. He laid them on their sides with the soles towards Simon.

'Some of the sprigs are gone,' he said. 'You can see where they've been, though. How about it?'

Simon leant forward portentously and stared at the boots. He counted under his breath and his face grew redder and redder.

'How about it?' repeated Webley.

'Give us a chance,' said Simon. He laughed uncomfortably. 'I've just got to think. You know. You have to concentrate on a thing like this.'

'That's right,' said Webley impassively.

Simon concentrated.

Gaunt lit a cigarette. 'The young investigator seems to be going into a trance,' he said. 'I don't think I shall wait for the revelation. May I be excused?'

'Don't you start being funny,' said Simon angrily. 'This is important. You stay where you are.' Dikon took out his notebook and Simon pounced on it. 'Here! Why didn't you give me that before?' He ruffled the pages. 'This is what I wanted all the time, Mr Webley. I saw the significance of these prints right away and I got Bell to make a sketch of them. Wait till I find it.'

'Was Mr Bell up there with you?'

'That's right. Yes, I took him along as a witness. Here,' cried Simon in triumph, 'here it is. Look at that.'

Dikon, having made the sketch, had a pretty clear recollection of the prints. He decided that they might have been made by the boots on the table. Such hobnails as remained, as well as the scars left by those that had fallen out, corresponded, he thought, with the impressions he had copied. Webley, breathing placidly through his mouth, shielded the sketch with his hand and compared it with his muddy exhibits. He looked at Dikon.

'Would you have any objection, Mr Bell, to my taking possession of this page?'

'None.'

'That'll be quite OK, Mr Webley,' said Simon magnificently.

'Much obliged, Mr Bell,' said Webley and neatly detached the page.

Gaunt said: 'And in what condition is our fugitive Questing now, Dr Ackrington? Is he galloping away to some hideout, dressed in dungarees and patent-leather pumps, or is he capering about in the rude nude?'

Dr Ackrington darted a glance of loathing at Gaunt and said nothing.

Webley said: 'You've been telling them about your theory, have you, Doctor? Disappearance, eh? You'll find it difficult to fit in these boots, won't you?'

'The difficulty,' said Dr Ackrington, 'is not insuperable. Isn't it at least possible that Questing realized he had left recognizable footprints and threw the boots he had intended to wear into the cauldron?'

'You are as nimble in the concoction of unlikelihoods,' said Gaunt, 'as a Baconian nosing in the plays of Shakespeare.'

'An utter irrelevancy, Gaunt. A little while ago you supported my contention. I find your change of attitude incomprehensible.'

'I'm afraid that on consideration I find all your theories equally irrelevant *and* incomprehensible. I'm afraid that for me, however selfishly, the point of interest lies in the fact that whether Questing slipped, was pushed, or escaped, I cannot, in the wildest realms of conjecture, be supposed to have had anything to do with the event. If I'm wanted, Sergeant Webley, I shall be in my room.'

'That'll be quite OK, thank you, Mr Gaunt,' said Webley and watched him go.

III

When Gaunt had gone, the meeting dissolved into a series of mumbled duologues. Dikon heard Webley say that he wanted to look through their rooms. Mrs Claire said that he would find them dreadfully untidy. It appeared that Huia, stimulated to the point of hysteria by the events of the last twelve hours, was incapable of performing her duties. She slept over at the native village which, Mrs Claire explained, she reported to be seething with terrified speculations.

'They get such strange ideas, you know,' said Mrs Claire to Webley. 'One tries to tell them that all their old superstitions are wrong but still they are there – underneath.'

Dikon thought that Webley pricked up his ears at this. However the Sergeant merely said in his sluggish way that he would rather the rooms were not touched and that he hoped nobody would object to his looking through them. He added the ominous request that they should all remain on the premises as he would like to see them again. He went off with the Colonel in the direction of the study. Mr Falls looked after them meditatively.

Dikon went to see his employer and found him on the sofa with his eyes closed.

'Well?' said Gaunt, without opening his eyes.

'Well, sir, the meeting's dissolved.'

'I've been thinking. The Maori youth must be found. The youth who saw me go up the main road.'

'Eru Saul?'

'Yes. They must get a statement from him. It will establish my alibi.' He opened his eyes. 'You'd better tell the empurpled sergeant.'

'He's not to be approached at the moment, I fancy,' said Dikon, who did not care at all for this suggestion.

'Well, don't leave it too long. After all it's of some slight importance since it protects me from a charge of homicide,' said Gaunt bitterly.

'Is there anything else I can do?'

'No. I'm utterly prostrated. I want to be left alone.'

Hoping that this mood would persist, Dikon went outside. There was no one about. He crossed the pumice sweep and wandered up and down the path by the warm lake. Wai-ata-tapu was unusually silent. The familiar morning sounds of housework were not to be heard or the voices of Mrs Claire and Barbara screeching companionably to each other from different rooms. He could see Huia moving about in the dining-room. Presently Smith and Simon walked round the house, Simon discoursing magnificently. Webley came out of the study, unlocked the door of Questing's room and went in. Dikon was overstimulated and so restless that he was unable to think closely about Questing's disappearance or indeed about anything. He was conscious that he had been frustrated at the moment of departure upon an emotional journey; he was both dissatisfied and apprehensive.

Presently Barbara came out of the house. She looked about her in desultory fashion and, after a moment, caught sight of him. He waved vigorously. She hesitated and then, with a backward glance, came to meet him.

'What have you been doing all this time?' he asked.

'I don't know. Nothing. I ought to be seeing about lunch but I can't settle down.'

'Nor can I. Couldn't we sit down for a moment? I've been pounding to and fro like a sentry until I feel quite worn out.'

'I feel I ought to be doing something or another,' said Barbara. 'Not just sitting.'

'Well, perhaps we could march up and down together.'

'Oh, Dikon,' Barbara said, 'what is it that's waiting for us? Where are we going?'

He had no answer to this and after a moment she said: 'You don't think he's alive, do you?'

'No.'

'Do you think somebody killed him?' She looked into his face. 'Yes, that is what you think,' she said.

'Not for any logical reason. I can't work it out. I'm like your mother, I can't go all elaborate over it. I certainly can't believe in Dr Ackrington's theory. He's so hell-bent on making everything fit into the mould of his own idea. Intellectually he's as obstinate as a mule, it seems to me.'

'Uncle James turns everything into a kind of argument. Even terribly serious things. He can't help it. The most ordinary conversation with Uncle James can turn in the twinkling of an eye into a violent argument. But, though you mightn't think it, he *is* open to conviction. In the end. Only by that time you're so exhausted you've forgotten what it's all about.'

'I know. The verdict goes by default.'

'Would that be the way the scientific mind works?'

'How should I know, my dear?'

'I should like to ask you something,' said Barbara after a silence. 'It's nothing much but it's been worrying me. Suppose this does turn out to be – ' She hesitated.

'Murder? One feels rather shy about uttering that word, doesn't one? Do you prefer the more classy "homicide"?'

'No, thank you. Suppose it is murder, then. The police will want to know every tiny little thing about last night, won't they?'

'I suppose so. It's what one imagines. A prolonged and dreary winnowing.'

'Yes. Well now, please don't fly into another rage with me because I really couldn't bear it, but ought I to tell them about my new dress?'

Dikon gaped at her. 'Why on earth?'

'I mean, about him coming up to me and talking as if he'd given it to me.'

Appalled by the possible implication of the project Dikon said roughly: 'Good Lord, what tomfoolery is this!'

'There!' said Barbara. 'You're livid again. I can't think why you lose your temper every time I mention the dress. I still think he did it. He's the only person we knew who wouldn't see that it was an impossible sort of thing to do.'

Dikon took a deep breath. 'Listen,' he said. 'I told Questing the blasted clothes were almost certainly a present from your Auntie Whatnot in India. He remarked that India was a long way away and I've no doubt he thought he'd take a gamble and pretend he was the little fairy godfather. He was simply trying to make capital. And anyway,' Dikon added, hearing his voice turn flat, 'you must see that all this can have no possible bearing on the case. You don't want to go trotting to the police with tatty little bits of gossip about your clothes. Answer any questions that are put to you, you silly child, and don't muddle the poor gentlemen. Barbara, will you promise?'

'I'll think about it,' said Barbara gravely. 'It's only that I've got a notion in my head that somehow or another my dress does fit into the picture.'

Dikon was in a quandary. If Gaunt was forced to acknowledge the authorship of the present to Barbara, his fury against Questing would be brought out in stronger relief, an unpleasant development. Dikon scolded, ridiculed, and pleaded. Barbara listened quietly and at last promised that she would say nothing of the dress without first telling him of her intention. 'Though I must say,' she added, 'that I can't see why you're getting into such a tig over it. If, as you say, it's completely irrelevant, it wouldn't matter much if I did tell them.'

'You might put some damn-fool idea into their thick heads. The mere fact of you lugging the wretched affair into the conversation would make them think there was something behind it. Let it alone, for pity's sake. What they don't know won't hurt them.'

He kept her with him a little longer. He had an idea that she'd substituted this nonsense about the dress for a more important discussion which, at the last moment, she had funked. He saw her look unhappily at the door into Gaunt's rooms. At last, twisting her hands together, she said very solemnly: 'I suppose you've had a lot of *experience*, haven't you?'

'I must say you do astonish me,' cried Dikon. 'What sort of experience? Do you imagine I'm dyed deep in strange sins?'

'Of course not,' said Barbara, turning pink. 'I meant you must have had a good deal of experience of the Artistic Temperament.'

'Oh, that. Well, yes; we come at it rather strong in our line of business, you know. What about it?'

Barbara said rapidly: 'People who are very sensitive – ' she corrected herself – 'I mean, highly sensitized, are terribly vulnerable, aren't they? Emotionally they're a skin short. Sort of. Aren't they? Things hurt them more than they hurt us.' She glanced doubtfully at Dikon. 'This,' he thought, 'is pure Gaunt; a paraphrase, I shouldn't wonder, of the stuff he sold her while I was sweating up that mountain.'

'I mean,' Barbara continued, 'that it would be wrong to expect them to behave like less delicately adjusted people when something emotionally disintegrating happens to them.'

'Emotionally . . . ?'

'Disintegrating,' said Barbara hurriedly. 'I mean you can't treat porcelain like kitchen china, can you?'

'That,' said Dikon, 'is the generally accepted line of chat.'

'Don't you agree with it?'

'For the last six years,' said Dikon cautiously, 'part of my job has been to act as a shock absorber for temperaments. You can't expect me to go all dewy-eyed over them at my time of life. But you may be right.'

'I hope I am,' said Barbara.

'The thing about actors, for instance, that makes them different from ordinary people is that they are technicians of emotion. They are trained not to suppress but to flourish their feelings. If an actor is angry, he says to himself and to everyone else, "My God, I am angry. This is what I'm like when I'm angry. This is how I do it." It doesn't mean he's angrier or less angry than you or I, who bite our lips and feel sick and six hours later think up all the things we might have said. He says them. If he likes someone, he lets them know it with soft music and purring chest notes. If he's upset he puts tears in his voice. Underneath he's as nice a fellow as the next man. He just does things more thoroughly.'

'You do sound cold-blooded.'

'Bless me soul, I take pinches of salt whenever I enter a stage door. Just a precautionary measure.'

Barbara's eyes had filled with tears. Dikon took her hand in his. 'Do you know why I've said all this?' he asked. 'If I was a noble-minded young man with gentlemanly instincts, I should go white to the lips and in a strangulated voice agree with everything you say. Since I can't pretend we're not talking about Gaunt I should add that it is our privilege to sacrifice ourselves to a Great Artist. Because I'm Gaunt's secretary I should say that my lips were sealed and stand on one side like a noble-minded dumb-bell while you made yourself miserable over him. I don't behave like this because I'm not such a fool, and also because I'm falling very deeply in love with you myself. There are Webley and your father going into a huddle on the verandah so we can't pursue this conversation. Go back into the house. I love you. Put that on your needles and knit it.'

IV

Somewhat shaken by his own boldness, Dikon watched Barbara run into the house. She had given him one bewildered and astonished glance before she turned tail and fled. 'So I've done it,' he thought, 'and how badly! No more pleasant talks with Barbara. No more arguments and confidences. After this she'll fly before me like the wind. Or will she think it her duty to hand me a lemon on a silver salver and tell me nicely that she hopes we'll still be friends?' The more he thought about it the more deeply convinced did he become that he had behaved like a fool. 'But it's all one,' he thought. 'She's never even looked at me. All I've done is to make her rather more miserable about Gaunt than she need have been.'

Webley and the Colonel were still huddled together on the verandah. They moved and Dikon saw that between them they held a curious-looking object. Seen from a distance, it resembled a gigantic wishbone adorned with a hairy crest. It was by this crest that they held it, standing well away from the two shafts, one of which was wooden while the other glinted dully in the sunlight. It was a Maori adze.

Webley looked up and saw Dikon, who instantly felt as though he had been caught spying on them. To dispel this uncomfortable illusion, he walked over and joined them.

'Hullo, Bell,' said the Colonel. 'Here's a rum go.' He looked at Webley. 'Shall we tell him?' he asked.

'Just a minute, Colonel,' said Webley, 'just a minute. I'd like to ask Mr Bell if he's ever seen this object before.'

'Never,' said Dikon. 'To my knowledge, never.'

'You were in Questing's room last night, weren't you, Mr Bell?'

'I glanced in to see if he was there. Yes.'

'You didn't look in any of his boxes?'

'Why should I?' cried Dikon. 'This isn't a corpse-in-a-trunk mystery. Why on earth should I? Anyway,' he added lamely after a glance at Webley's impassive face, 'I didn't.'

Webley, still holding the adze by its hairy crest, laid it carefully on the verandah table. The haft, intricately carved, was crowned by a grimacing manikin. The stone blade, which had been worked down to a double edge with a rounded point, projected, almost at right angles to the haft, from beneath the rump of the manikin.

'They used to dong one another with those things,' said Dikon. 'Did you find it in Questing's room?'

The Colonel glanced uncomfortably at Webley, who merely said: 'I think we'll let old Rua take a look at this, Colonel. Could you get a message over to him? My chaps are busy out there. I'd rather nobody touched this axe affair and anyway it'd be as well to get Rua away from the rest of his gang.'

'I'll go,' Dikon offered.

Webley looked him over thoughtfully. 'Well, now that's very kind of you, Mr Bell,' he said.

'Trophies of the chase, Sergeant?' asked Mr Falls, suddenly thrusting his head out of his bedroom window which was above the verandah table. 'Do forgive me. I couldn't help overhearing you. You've found a magnificent expression of a savage art, haven't you? And you wish for an expert opinion? May I suggest that Bell and I go hand-in-hand to the native village? We can, as it were, keep an eye on each other. A variant of the adage that one should set a thief to catch a thief. Do you follow me?'

'Well, sir,' said Webley, watching him carefully, 'there's no call to put it like that. At the same time, if you two gentlemen care to stroll over to the *pa*, I'm sure I'd be much obliged.'

'Splendid!' cried Mr Falls gaily. 'May we go by the short route? It will be much quicker and since, as I imagine, the cauldron is all set about with your myrmidons, neither of us will have an opportunity to add articles of evening dress to the seething mud. You could give us a chit to your men, no doubt.'

Greatly to Dikon's astonishment, and somewhat to his dismay, Webley raised no objection to this project. Dikon and Mr Falls set out, by the all too familiar path, for the native reserve. Mr Falls led the way, limping a little it is true, but not, it seemed, greatly inconvenienced this morning by his lumbago.

'I must congratulate you,' he said pleasantly, 'on the attitude you adopted at our rather abortive conference. You felt that our anatomist's flights into the realms of conjecture were becoming fantastic. So, I must confess, did I.'

'You did!' Dikon ejaculated. 'Then, I must say . . .' He stopped short.

'You were about to say that I didn't contradict him. My dear sir, you saved me the trouble. You propounded my views to a nicety.'

'I'm afraid I find that difficult to believe,' said Dikon drily.

'You do? Ah, yes, of course. You regard me as the prime suspect. Very naturally. Do you realize, Mr Bell, that if I'm tried for murder, you will be the chief witness for the prosecution? Why, bless my soul, you almost caught me red-handed. Always presuming that my hands were red.'

Mr Falls's face was habitually inscrutable and naturally the back of his head was entirely so. Dikon was walking behind him and felt himself to be at a loss. He tried to keep his voice as colourless as Mr Falls's own. 'Quite so,' he said. 'But I tell myself that as a guilty person you might have shown more enthusiasm for Dr Ackrington's theory. No murder, no murderer.'

'Unbounded enthusiasm would hint at a lack of artistry, don't you feel?'

'The others exhibited it,' said Dikon. Mr Falls gave a little chuckle. 'Yes,' he agreed, 'their relief was almost tangible, wasn't it? Now you, as the only one of the men with a really formidable alibi, were also the only man to exhibit scepticism.'

'Mr Falls,' said Dikon loudly, 'what's your idea? Do you think he's dead?'

'Yes.'

'Murdered?'

'Oh, yes. Rather. Don't you?'

By this time they had reached the borders of the thermal region. Remembering the lunar landscape of last night Dikon thought that by day it looked only less strange. There, in the distance, the geyser's jet was, for a flash of time, erected like a plume in the air. Here, the path threaded its way between quaking ulcers; there, the white flags drooped from their iron standards. There, too, on the crest of the mound above Taupo-tapu, were Mr Webley's men, black figures against a sombre background, figures that stooped, thrust downwards, and then laboriously lifted.

'One can't believe in things like this,' said Dikon under his breath.

Mr Falls had very sharp ears. 'Horrible, isn't it?' he said. And again it was impossible to find in his voice the colour of his thoughts. He waved his stick. 'The whole place,' he said, 'is impossibly Doréesque, don't you feel?'

'I find it so difficult to believe that it's entirely impersonal.'

'The Maori people make no attempt to do so, I understand.'

Now they had drawn close to the mound. Dikon said to himself: 'It is nothing. Falls will hand over Webley's authority and we shall walk quickly over the mound. I shall look at the path between Falls's feet and my feet and in a moment it will begin to lead downhill. And then I shall know that my back is turned to Taupo-tapu. It is nothing.'

But as they climbed the mound the distance between them widened and Dikon didn't hear what Falls said to the men. Why were they waiting? Why this long mumbled colloquy? He looked up. The path was steep on that side of the mound and his eyes were on a level with the men's knees.

'Can't we get on with it?' he heard himself say angrily.

One of the men pushed past him and stumbled down the path. Falls said: 'Wait a moment, Bell.' The man who had blundered down the path began to make retching noises.

The men on the top of the mound – there were two of them now beside Falls – squatted close to each other as if they held a corroboree. One of them let go a pitchfork he held and it rattled down the path. Falls stood up. His back was towards the light but Dikon saw that his face had bleached. He said: 'Come on, Bell.' Although Dikon desired most passionately to turn and escape by the path along which they had come, his muscles sent him forward.

It would have been much worse, of course, if they hadn't covered it, but, though the sack was thick, it was wet. It followed the shape beneath it in a hard eloquent curve. Dikon's imagination found sockets in the shadows beneath the curve. One of the men must have pushed him forward.

Falls waited for him on the far side at the foot of the mound, but as soon as Dikon reached him he turned and led the way onwards to the gap in the manuka hedge. Here a man stood on guard.

Even when they were beyond the fence he could still hear the sound of Taupo-tapu, the grotesquely enlarged domestic sound of a boiling pot.

CHAPTER 13

Letter from Mr Questing

Strangely enough the sensation that was uppermost in Dikon's mind was one of embarrassment. He would have to speak to Falls about what they had seen, and like a man who hesitates before making a speech of condolence he did not know how to form his phrases. Should he say: 'I suppose that was Questing's head under the sack'? Or, 'That settles it'? Or, 'That disposes of Ackrington's theory, doesn't it?' It was impossible to find the right phrase. He was so occupied with his preposterous difficulty and, at the same time, suffered such a violent feeling of nausea that he didn't notice Eru Saul and was startled when Falls spoke to him.

'Hullo,' said Mr Falls. 'Can you direct me to Mr Rua Te Kahu's house?'

Dikon thought that Eru must have been standing in a recess in the hedge, perhaps peering through the twigs, and that he had turned quickly as they came up to him. He was coatless, and wore his puce-coloured shirt. Bits of dry manuka stuck to it and to the front of his waistcoat.

Mr Falls pointed the ferrule of his stick at the recess. 'Can you see the working party from here?' He squinted through an opening in the manuka. 'Ah, yes. Quite clearly.' He picked a twig off the front of Eru's waistcoat. 'Terrible affair, isn't it?' he said. 'And now, as we have a message for Mr Te Kahu from the police, would you mind directing us?'

Eru said: 'Have they found him?'

' "A part of him." Forgive the inadvertent quotation. His skull, to be exact.'

"Struth!' Eru whispered and showed his teeth. He turned and walked quickly up the path to the *marae* and they followed him. Old Mrs Te Papa sat on the verandah floor with her back against the meeting-house wall. When she saw them she shouted something in Maori and Eru replied briefly. Her response was formidable. She flung up her hands and pulled her shawl over her face.

'*Aue! Aue! Aue! Te mamae i au!*' wailed Mrs Te Papa.

'Good God!' cried Mr Falls nervously. 'What's she doing?'

'I've told her,' said Eru sulkily. 'She's going to *tangi.*'

'To wail,' Dikon translated. 'To lament the dead. Think of an Irish wake.'

'Really? Extraordinarily interesting.'

Mrs Te Papa continued to wail like a banshee while Eru led them to the largest of the cottages that stood round the *marae*. Like its fellows it was shabby. Its galvanized iron roof was corroded by sulphur.

'That's it,' said Eru, and made off.

Attracted by Mrs Te Papa's cries, other women came out of the houses and, calling to each other, trooped towards the meeting house. Eru was joined by three youths. They stood with their hands in their pockets, watching Mr Falls and Dikon. Dikon still felt very sick, and hoped ardently that he would not disgrace himself before the youths.

Mr Falls was about to tap on the door when it opened and old Rua stood upon the threshold. Mrs Te Papa shouted agitatedly. He answered her in Maori and waited courteously for his visitors to announce their errand. Falls delivered Sergeant Webley's message and Rua at once said that he would come with them. He shouted, and a small girl ran out of the house, bringing the grey blanket he wore on his shoulders. 'It is as well,' he said tranquilly, but with a faint glint in his eyes, 'to give instant obedience when it is a policeman who asks. Let us go.' He turned off as if to follow the track that led to the main road.

'We've got the Sergeant's permission to cross the reserve,' said Mr Falls.

'It will be better by the road,' said Rua.

'It's very much farther,' Falls pointed out.

'Then we should take Mrs Te Papa's car.' Again Rua shouted and Mrs Te Papa broke off in the middle of a desolate wail to say prosaically: 'All right, you take him but he won't go.'

'We shall take him,' said Rua, 'and perhaps he will go.'

'Eru can make him go,' Mrs Te Papa remarked and she hurled an order across the *marae*. Eru detached himself from the group of young men and slouched off behind the houses.

'Thank you so much, Mrs Te Papa,' said Falls, taking off his hat.

'You are very welcome,' she replied, and composed herself for a further lamentation.

Mrs Te Papa's car was not so much a car as a mass of wreckage. It stood in a back yard in a little pool of oil, sketchily protected by the remains of its own fabric hood. One of its peeling doors hung disconsolately from a single hinge. It was markedly bandy and had that look of battered gentility that belongs to very old-fashioned vehicles.

Rua opened the only door that was shut and said: 'Do you prefer front or back?'

'I shall sit in the back with you, if I may,' said Falls.

Dikon climbed into the front. Eru wrenched at the starting handle and, as though he had dug a thumb in her ribs, the old car gave a galvanic start and set up a terrific commotion. 'Ah!' Rua shouted cheerfully. 'She goes, you see.' Having been left in gear, she almost ran over her driver. However, Eru flung himself in as she passed, and in a moment they were jolting up the hill. The noise was appalling.

'I see no reason,' Mr Falls began in a stentorian voice, 'why you should not be told the object of Sergeant Webley's message.'

Dikon slewed round in his seat to gaze in consternation at Mr Falls. He met the unwinking glare of old Rua, huddled comfortably in his blanket.

'Webley wants your opinion on a native weapon,' Falls continued. 'A beautiful piece, it seems to me, a collector's piece.' Rua said nothing. 'I should call it an adze but perhaps that is incorrect. Let me describe it.'

He described it with extraordinary accuracy and in such detail that Dikon was first amazed at his faculty of observation and then extremely suspicious of it. Could Mr Falls possibly have seen all these things through his window during the brief time that the adze was on the verandah table?

'One thing struck me very forcibly,' Mr Falls was saying. 'The figure at the head of the haft has got, not one protruding tongue, but two. Two long protruding tongues, side by side. The little god, if indeed he is a god, holds one in each of his three-fingered hands.

Between the fingers there are small pieces of shell and beneath them the tongues are encircled by a narrow band.'

'You are driving too fast, Eru,' said old Rua, to Dikon's profound relief. Mrs Te Papa's car, bucketing down a steep incline, had developed a curious flaunting movement which, he felt certain, its back axle could sustain no longer. Eru checked her with a jerk.

'The band itself,' Mr Falls continued mellifluously in the comparative silence, 'is most delicately carved. One marvels at the skill of your ancient craftsmen, Mr Te Kahu. When one considers that their tools were those of a stone age – what did you say?'

Rua had made some ejaculation in his native tongue.

'Nothing,' he said. 'Drive carefully, Eru. You are too impetuous.'

'But it seems to me that across this band some other hand has graved three vertical furrows. The design is repeated all over the weapon, but in no other place do these three lines occur. Now how do you explain that?'

Rua did not answer at once. Eru trod violently on the accelerator, and Dikon repressed a cry of dismay as Mrs Te Papa's car responded with a shattering leap. Rua's words were lost in the din of progress. 'Wait . . . impossible . . . until I see . . .'

He roared at Eru and at the same time Dikon turned to protest against this new turn of speed. He saw, with astonishment, that the half-caste's lips were trembling, that his face was livid. 'He must be feeling like I feel,' thought Dikon. 'He must have seen everything through the hole in the manuka hedge.'

Mr Falls leant forward and tapped Eru on the shoulder. He started violently.

'I hear you missed the star turn at the concert last night,' said Mr Falls.

'We heard some of it,' said Eru. 'It was all right, too!'

'Mr Smith tells me you missed the earlier speeches. I do hope you returned in time for the magnificent Saint Crispin's Eve.'

'Was that when he said something about the old dugouts being asleep while him and the boys was waiting for the balloon to go up?'

'*And gentlemen in England now a-bed?*'

'Yeh, that's right. We heard that one. It was good, too.'

'Marvellous,' said Mr Falls, and sat back in his seat. 'Marvellous, wasn't it?'

They arrived intact at Wai-ata-tapu. The adze had been removed evidently to the Colonel's study, as Rua was at once taken there, Falls, rather unnecessarily, ushering him in. Dikon was left alone with Eru Saul in Mrs Te Papa's palpitating car. 'Hadn't you better turn off your engine?' he suggested. Eru jumped and switched back the key. 'Have a cigarette?' said Dikon.

'*Ta*.' He helped himself with trembling fingers.

'This is a bad business, isn't it?'

'It's terrible all right,' said Eru, staring at the study window.

Dikon got out and lit his own cigarette. He was feeling better.

'Where did they find it?' Eru demanded.

'What? Oh, the axe. I don't know.'

'Did they find it in *his* stuff?'

'Whose?' said Dikon woodenly. He was determined to know nothing. Eru electrified him by jerking his head, not at Questing's room but at Gaunt's.

II

'That's where he hangs out, isn't it?' said Eru. 'Your boss?'

'What the hell do you think you're talking about?' said Dikon violently.

'Nothing, nothing!' said Eru, showing the whites of his eyes. 'I was only kidding. You don't want to go crook over a joke.'

'I can't see anything amusing in your extraordinary suggestion that a Maori axe should be discovered in Mr Gaunt's room.'

'OK, OK, I only wondered if he was one of these collectors. They'll come at anything, if they're mad on it. You know. Lose their respect for other people's property.'

'Let me assure you that Mr Gaunt is not a collector.'

'Good-oh. He's not. Let it go.'

Dikon turned on his heel and walked toward his own room. It was in his mind to go straight to Gaunt. His idea of Gaunt, by no means an unrealistic one, had been defaced by the events of the day. He felt a strange necessity to see Gaunt for himself, alone, to try if it was possible to re-establish their old relationship. He had not gone more than six paces when he was arrested by a terrific rumpus which seemed to come from the Colonel's study. It was old Rua. His voice was raised in a roar as formidable as any with which his ancestors had led their clans to battle. The words at first were indistinguishable. Dikon thought that he made out ejaculations in Maori and occasional words of English. A babble of consolatory phrases broke out. The Colonel, Sergeant Webley and Mr Falls seemed to be making an attempt to placate him. He roared them down. 'It is the Toki-poutangata-o-Tane. It is the weapon of my grandfather, Rewi. It is a matter of offence against a most sacred and tapu possession. It must be returned immediately. *Immediately!*'

'Wait on, wait on,' Dikon heard Webley mumble. 'You'll get it back all right.'

'I shall have it back immediately. I shall appeal to the native land courts. I shall go to the Minister for Native Affairs,' Rua stormed and Dikon was reminded vividly of his employer. The rumpus broke out with renewed enthusiasm. Mrs Claire came out from the dining-room.

'Oh, Mr Bell,' she whispered, '*what* now?' She laid a plump hand on his arm, a hand which he thought the more touching for its calluses and stains. 'It's Rua, isn't it?' she said.

'Something about his grandfather's axe,' Dikon muttered. 'He's very cross with Webley for holding on to it.'

'Oh dear! One of those *silly* superstitions. Sometimes one almost loses hope. And yet, you know, he's a regular communicant.'

The regular communicant, at this moment, came charging out of the study roaring like a bull and flourishing the ancestral adze. Webley and the Colonel were hot on his heels. Mr Falls followed in a more leisurely manner.

'He's raining the prints,' Webley shouted in great agitation. 'It's most irregular.'

Rua plunged blindly along the verandah. Mrs Claire moved forward to meet him. He fetched up short. He was breathless, and his eyes flashed. He stamped twice with his heavy boot and shook the adze. 'It is an outrage!' he panted.

'Now, Rua,' said Mrs Claire placidly. 'It's not at all good for you to work yourself up like this and it's not a nice way to behave in somebody else's house. I'm ashamed of you.'

Webley approached cautiously and Rua backed away from him.

'I obey the gods,' said Rua. 'He robbed the grave of my ancestor. The fury of Tane has fallen upon him. My grandfather Rewi is avenged.' It occurred to Dikon that all this grandiloquence would have sounded more impressive in the native tongue. Mrs Claire seemed to be of this opinion. She administered a crisp scolding, her hands folded at her waist, while Rua, still clutching his preposterous trophy, rolled his eyes and seemed to be in two minds whether to go for Webley or beat a retreat.

Upon this scene, half comic, half ominous as all scenes at Waiata-tapu seemed fated to appear, came Huia, nervously twisting her hands. She edged her way round the dining-room door and along the back of the verandah. Her gaze was fixed upon her great-grandfather. At the same time Simon appeared round the corner of the house and Barbara, carrying a tray, drifted through the dining-room and paused at the windows. Dr Ackrington loomed up behind her, peered through the window and, seeing what was afoot, limped out to the verandah. A moment later Dikon heard a movement in Gaunt's rooms. It was as though the characters in a loosely constructed drama had begun to converge upon a focal point.

Huia's face had lost its warmth of colour. She and the old man stared at each other, seeming to communicate. He raised the adze. The crest of hair quivered. *'Haere ami,'* said Rua. 'Come here to me.'

She crept a little nearer. He began to speak to her in their own tongue but soon checked himself. 'You do not understand me. You know little of the speech of the children of Tane. Very well. Let your shame be made known in the tongue of the *pakeha.*' He looked about him, commanding the attention of his hearers. 'Many months ago, feeling myself draw near to the path that goes down to the final abode, I spoke with my eldest grandson who now fights with our battalions in a strange country. To him I confided the secret hiding place of this weapon, a secret which has been known only to the *ariki*, the first-born, of each generation of my family. Beyond the manuka bushes where we spoke, unknown to me, this girl lay dreaming. I discovered her when my grandson had left me. I questioned her and she told me that since I had spoken in our own tongue she had not understood me. Look at her now and judge if she deceived me.' He moved towards her. She pressed herself against the wall and watched him. 'To whom did you betray the resting place of Rewi's *toki?* Answer me. To whom?'

She made a timid abortive gesture, half raising her hand. Then as if Rua had menaced her, she shot out her arm and pointed at Eru Saul.

III

Throughout the scenes that followed Dikon had the feeling that he was peering into some room which at first seemed to be quite dark. But, he thought, out of the shadow nearer objects presently appeared so that first the figure of Huia and then that of Eru were distinguishable, while behind these, in deeper shadow, more significant forms awaited the slow adjustment of his vision.

Eru faced old Rua with an air strangely compounded of terror and effrontery. Dikon fancied that a struggle was at work in the half-caste, between his European and his native impulses. If this was so the Maori, under Rua's dominance, was the more potent agent. A shabby attempt at defiance soon broke down. Eru began with protestations and ended with a confession.

'I never touched it. I never took it. I never seen it before.'

'You knew where it rested. Huia, answer me. You told him where it was hidden?'

Huia nodded and burst into tears. Eru threw a venomous glance at her.

'So you, Eru, stole it and took money for it from this man Questing?'

'I never! I never knew he'd got it. I hadn't got any time for him.'

'Huia, did you tell Questing?'

'No! *No!* Never, I never tell anyone but Eru. It was long time ago. I told Eru for fun when we go together. Nobody else. Eru told him.'

'If I'd thought it was for that bastard,' said Eru, 'I'd never of told nobody.' And with extraordinary venom he added: 'You and your fancy *pakeha*. I might've picked Questing was at the back of it. Why the hell didn't he say it was for Questing?'

'To whom *did* you speak of this matter? Answer me.'

'Come on, Eru,' said Webley. 'You won't do yourself any good by holding out on it. There's a serious charge mixed up in this business, don't forget. You want to put yourself right, don't you?'

'I told Bert Smith,' Eru muttered and Dikon thought he saw a little farther into the darkness of that shrouded room: not to the end, he thought, but a little farther. Webley moved forward and said to Simon, 'Find Bert, will you?'

'OK,' said Simon.

When he appeared Smith was querulous and uneasy. 'Can't a bloke have *any* time to himself?' he demanded and then saw the adze in Rua's hand. 'By cripey!' he said. 'By cripey, it's Rewi's axe.' He looked at Rua and drew a deep breath. 'So he stuck to it, *after* all,' he said.

'Who stuck to what?' asked Webley. 'Take a look at that axe, Bert. Have you ever seen it before? Come on.'

Smith cautiously approached Rua, who drew back. 'You'll have to let him see it, Rua,' said Webley. 'Come on, now.'

'It's all right,' said Smith. 'I've never seen it but I know what it is all right. I'd heard all about it.'

'You stole it – ' Rua began and Smith, in a great hurry, interrupted him. 'Not on your life, I didn't! You haven't got anything on me. I might have known where it was and I might of told him but I never went curio hunting on the Peak. No bloody fear, I didn't.'

'You told Questing where it was?' Dr Ackrington demanded. 'Why?'

'Just a minute, Doctor, if *you* please,' Webley intercepted. 'Now then, Bert. What was the idea, telling Questing?'

'He asked me.' And now it was Questing's large face that showed in the dark.

'Asked you to find out? *And* paid you for your trouble, eh?' said Webley.

'All right. Put it that way. Nothing criminal in passing on a bit of information, is there? He asked me to find out and I found out. Eru told me. Come on, Eru. You told me, you know you did.'

'You said it was for the other bloke,' Eru said breathlessly.

'What other bloke?' Webley demanded. Eru once again jerked his head at Gaunt's rooms. 'Him,' he said. And Dikon now saw into the farthest corner of his imaginary room.

In the silence that followed Mr Falls said: 'There seems to be a multiplicity of blokes all passing on information like a hot potato. Are we to understand, Sergeant Webley, that the deceased, on behalf of Mr Gaunt, bribed Mr Smith to bribe Mr – Saul, is it? Thank you – Mr Saul, to obtain information as to the *locale* of this exquisite weapon?'

'It looks as if that's about the strength of it, sir.'

'You damn well choose your words!' said Smith indignantly. 'Who's talking about bribes? It was between friends. Him and me were cobbers, weren't we, Sim?'

'I thought he tried to put you under the train, Bert,' said Webley.

'Oh, my Gawd, do I have to go into that again!' apostrophized Mr Smith with evident fatigue. 'We got it all ironed out. Here. Take a look.' He lugged out his written agreement with Questing and thrust it at Webley.

'Let it go,' said Webley. 'You've showed me that before. We won't trouble you any more just now, Bert.'

'So *you* say,' Smith grumbled and, carefully folding his precious document, wandered morosely into the dining-room.

Webley turned to Rua. 'Look, Rua. You can see by what's been said that we've got to keep hold of your granddad's axe. We'll give you a receipt for it. You'll get it back all right.'

'It should not be touched. You do not understand. I myself, holding it, am now tapu.'

'Rua, Rua!' chided Mrs Claire softly.

'Sergeant Webley,' said Falls, 'please correct me if I am wrong, but suppose Mr Te Kahu gave you his undertaking that when the adze is needed by the police he will allow them to have it? Could it not in the meantime be entrusted to the Colonel? The Colonel is your friend, Mr Te Kahu, isn't he? Suppose you went with him to his bank and left it there for safe-keeping? How would that be? Colonel, what do you say?'

'Eh?' said the Colonel. 'Oh, certainly, if Webley agrees.'

'Sergeant?'

'I'll be satisfied, sir.'

'Well, then?' Falls turned to Rua.

The old man looked at the weapon in his hands. 'You will think it strange,' he said, 'that I, who have in my time led my people towards the culture of the *pakeha*, should now grow quarrelsome over a silly savage notion. Perhaps in our old age we return to the paths of our forebears. The reason may put on new garments but the heart and the blood are constant. From the haft of the weapon there flows into my blood an influence darker and more potent than all the *pakeha* wisdom I have stored in my foolish old head. But, as you say, Colonel Claire is the friend of my people. To him I submit.'

Falls went into his room and came out with that heavily belabelled case which Mrs Claire had noticed on his arrival. He placed it, open, upon the table, and Rua laid the adze in it.

'If it remains in Colonel Claire's hands,' he said, 'I am satisfied.' He turned to Eru. 'You are not of the Maori people. In the days when this *toki* was fashioned your breed was unknown. Yet the punishment of Tane shall reach you. It were better that you had died in Taupo-tapu. I forbid you to return to our people.' After this final burst of magnificence Rua added placidly, 'I myself can drive Mrs Te Papa's car.'

And drive it he did, sitting upright at the wheel, his blanket about his shoulders, bouncing slightly as he negotiated the inequalities of the pumice track.

Huia, sobbing noisily, ran into the house followed by the gently clucking Mrs Claire. Eru moistened his lips and, without another word, set off up the track.

'That's a very embarrassing old gentleman.'

Gaunt had strolled along the verandah, smoking a cigarette. He had dressed that morning in a travelling suit and looked an extraordinarily incongruous figure. His clothes, his hands and his hair were as little in harmony with Wai-ata-tapu as would have been those of Sergeant Webley at the Ritz. Webley at once fastened on him.

'Now, Mr Gaunt.'

'Well, Sergeant?'

'You must have heard what's been said. Is it correct that you wanted to get hold of this weapon?'

'I should have liked to buy it, certainly. I have a taste for barbaric ornament.'

'Did you offer to buy it?'

'I told Questing I should like to see it first. Not unnaturally. My secretary had related the story of Rewi's axe. When Questing came to me a few nights ago and littered the place up with obscure hints that he could if he would and so on, I confess my curiosity was stimulated. But I assure you that I did not commit myself in any way.'

'Do you realize that the removal of property from a native reserve is a criminal offence?' Dr Ackrington demanded.

'No. Is it really? Questing told me the old gentleman was prepared to sell but that he didn't want the rest of his tribe to know. He said we should have to be very hush-hush.'

'Did you know anything about this, Mr Bell?' asked Webley, turning his dark face towards Dikon.

'Oh, no,' said Gaunt easily. 'I didn't mention it to anybody. Questing was rather particular about that.'

'I'll be bound he was,' said Webley with a nearer approach to bitterness than Dikon had thought him capable of expressing.

'It was really too bad of him to involve me in a dubious transaction, you know. I resent it,' said Gaunt. 'And I must say, Sergeant, you seem to me to be working yourself into a tig over an abortive attempt at theft while an enemy agent bustles into obscurity. Why not deny yourself your passion for curios and catch Mr Questing?'

Dikon opened his mouth and shut it again. He was looking at Mr Falls, upon whose lips were painted the faintest trace of a smile.

'But we have found Mr Questing,' said Webley dully. Gaunt's hands contracted and he gave a sharp exclamation. Dikon saw again the hard curve of an orb under wet sacking.

'Found him?' said Gaunt softly. 'Where?'

'Where he was lost, Mr Gaunt. In Taupo-tapu.'

'My God!'

Gaunt looked at his fingers, seemed to hesitate, and then turned on his heel and walked back along the verandah. As he reached his own rooms he said loudly with a sort of sneer: 'That takes the icing off old Ackrington's gingerbread, doesn't it! I beg your pardon, Doctor. Do forgive me. I'd forgotten you were here.'

He went into his room and they heard him shout for Colly.

Mr Falls broke an awkward silence by saying: 'What a very gay taste in shirts Mr Eru Saul displays, doesn't he?'

Eru, a desolate figure, had plodded up the drive as far as the last turn that was visible from the house. His puce-coloured sleeves were vivid in the sunlight.

Barbara leant out of the window and said nervously: 'He always wears that shirt. One wonders if it's ever washed.'

Dikon, expecting Dr Ackrington's outburst to come at any moment, said hurriedly: 'I know. He wore it on the day of Smith's accident.'

'So he did.'

'No, he didn't,' said the Colonel unexpectedly.

They stared at him. 'But, Daddy, he *did,*' said Barbara. 'Don't you remember he came into the dining-room to sort of confirm Mr Smith's account and he was wearing the pink shirt? Wasn't he, Sim?'

'What the heck's it matter?' Simon asked. 'He was, as a matter of fact.'

'He couldn't have been,' said the Colonel.

Dr Ackrington began in a high voice, 'In the name of all that's futile, Edward, will you – ' and stopped short. 'The shirt was pink,' he said loudly.

'No.'

'It was pink, Edward.'

'It couldn't have been, James.'

Webley said heavily: 'If you'll excuse me I'll get on with it,' and casting a disgusted look at the Colonel he returned to Questing's room.

'I know it wasn't pink,' the Colonel went on.

'Did you *see* the fellow's shirt?'

'I suppose I must have, James. I don't remember that, but I have it in my head it was blue. People talked about the feller's blue shirt.'

'Well, it wasn't blue, Dad,' said Simon. 'It was the same godalmighty affair he's got on now.'

'I don't catch what people say, but I did catch that. Blue.'

'This is extremely interesting,' said Mr Falls. 'Here are three people swearing pink and one blue. What about you, Bell?'

'I'm on both sides,' said Dikon. 'It was puce but I agree with the Colonel that Questing said it was blue.'

'It is extraordinary to me,' said Dr Ackrington, 'that you can all moon about, arguing like magpies over a perfectly footling affair, when the discovery of Questing's body puts us all in a damned equivocal position.'

'I am interested in the man in the ambiguous shirt. Could we not have Mr Smith's opinion?' suggested Mr Falls. 'Where is he?'

Without moving, Simon yelled: 'Hey, Bert!' and in due course Smith reappeared.

Mr Falls said: 'I wonder if you can settle an argument. Do you remember that on the evening of your escape from the train, Mr Questing said that he left you to the attentions of a man in a blue shirt?'

'Uh?'

Mr Falls repeated his question.

'That'd be Eru Saul. He brought me home. What of it?'

'Wearing a blue shirt?'

'Yeh, that's right.'

'It was pink,' said Dr Ackrington and Simon together.

'If Questing said it was blue it must've been blue,' said Smith crossly. 'I was that knocked about I wouldn't notice whether the man was wearing a pansy shirt or a pair of rompers. Yeh, I remember. It was blue.'

'You're colour blind,' said Simon. 'It was pink.'

He and Smith argued hotly. Smith walked away muttering and Simon shouted after him. 'You're making out it was blue because he said it was blue. You'll be telling us next he went to Pohutukawa Bay that afternoon, like he said he did.'

Smith stopped short. 'So he did go to the Bay,' he yelled.

'Yeh? And when Uncle James said wasn't it a pity the pootacows weren't in bloom he said yes, too bad. And they were blazing there all the time.'

'He did go to the Bay. He took Huia. You ask Huia. Eru told me. So get to hell,' added Smith and disappeared.

'What do you know about that!' Simon demanded. 'Here, do you reckon Eru changed his shirt in our kitchen? Or was it another man on the hill that Questing saw?'

'He did *not* go to Pohutukawa Bay,' said his uncle. 'I bowled him over. I completely bowled him over. *Huia!*'

After a short delay Huia, still weeping, appeared in the doorway.

'What you want?' she sobbed.

'Did you go in Mr Questing's car to Pohutukawa Bay on the day when Smith was nearly run over?'

'I never do anything bad with him,' roared poor Huia, relapsing into pidgin English. 'Only go for drive to te Bay and come back. Never stop te engine, all time.'

'Did you see the pootacows?' said Simon.

'How can we go to Pohutukawa Bay and not see *pohutukawas?* Of course we see *pohutukawas* like blazes all over te shop.'

'Did Eru Saul change his shirt in the kitchen that night?'

'What te devil you ask me nex'! Let me catch him change his shirt in my kitchen.'

'Oh, gee!' said Simon disgustedly and Huia plunged back into the house.

'It must be nearly lunch time,' the Colonel remarked vaguely. He followed Huia indoors and shouted for his wife.

'This is a madhouse,' said Dr Ackrington.

Webley came out of Questing's room. 'Mr Bell,' he said, 'may I trouble you, please?'

IV

'I couldn't feel more uncomfortable,' Dikon thought as he walked along the verandah, 'if I'd killed poor old Questing myself. It's extraordinary.'

Webley stood on one side at the door, followed Dikon inside and shut it. The blind was pulled down and the light was on so that Dikon was vividly reminded of his visit of the previous night. The pearl-grey worsted suit was still neatly disposed upon a chair. The ties and the puce-coloured pyjamas were in their former positions. Webley went to the dressing-table and took up an envelope. Dikon saw with astonishment that it was addressed to himself in the neat commercial script of Smith's talisman.

'Before you open this, Mr Bell, I'd like to have a witness.' He put his head round the door and mumbled audibly. Mr Falls was cautiously admitted.

'A witness before or after the fact, Sergeant?' he asked archly.

'A witness to the fact, shall we say, sir?'

'But why in heaven's name did he write to me?' Dikon murmured.

'That's what we'll find out, Mr Bell. Will you open it?'

It was written in green ink on a sheet of business paper on which printed titles were set out, representing Mr Questing as an indent agent and representative of several firms. It bore the date of the previous day and was headed: 'Private and Confidential'.

Dear Mr Bell [Dikon read],

You will be somewhat surprised to receive this communication. An unexpected cable necessitates my visiting Australia and I am leaving for Auckland first thing tomorrow morning to see about a passage by air. I shall not be returning for some little while.

Now, Mr Bell, I should commence by telling you that I appreciate the very very happy little relationship that has obtained since I first had the pleasure of contacting you. The personal antagonism that I have encountered in other quarters has never entered into our acquaintance and I take this opportunity of thanking you for your courtesy. You will note that I have endorsed this letter p and c. It is rather particularly so and I am sure I can rely upon you to keep the spirit of the endorsement. If you are not prepared to do so I will ask you to destroy this letter unread.

'I can't go on with this,' said Dikon.
'If you don't, sir, we will. He's dead, remember.'
'Oh, hell!'
'You can read it to yourself if you like, Mr Bell,' said Webley, keeping his eyes on Mr Falls, 'and then hand it over.'
Dikon read on a little way, made an ejaculation and finally said: 'No, by George, you shall hear it.' And he read the letter aloud.

Now, Mr Bell, I am going to be very frank with you. You may have understood from remarks that have been passed that I have become interested in certain possibilities regarding a particular district not ten miles distant from where you are located.

Mr Falls murmured: 'Enchanting circumlocution.'
'That'll be the Peak,' said Webley, still watching him.
'Quite.'

I have in the course of my visits made certain discoveries. To put it bluntly, on Friday last, the evening before the SS *Hokianga* was torpedoed off this certain place, I was on the latter and I observed certain suspicious occurrences. They were as follows. Being on the face overlooking the sea, my attention was arrested by a light which flashed several times from a spot some way farther up the slope. For personal reasons I was undesirous of contacting other persons: I therefore remained where I was, some nine feet off the track, lying behind some scrub. From here I observed a certain person, who passed by and was recognized by myself but who did not notice me. This morning, Saturday, I learnt of the sinking of the *Hokianga* and at once connected it with the above incident. I sought out the person in question and accused him straight out of being an enemy agent. He denied it and added that if I went any further in the matter he would turn the tables on myself. Now, Mr Bell, this put me in a very awkward spot. My activities in this particular place have leaked out and there are some who have not hesitated, as I am well aware, to put a very very nasty interpretation on them. I am not in a position to right myself against any accusations this person might bring and in *his* position he is more likely to be believed than I am. I was forced to give an undertaking that I would not say that I had seen him. He adopted a very threatening attitude. I do not think he trusts me. I don't mind admitting I'm uneasy. He seemed to think I had inside information about his code of signals, which is not the case.

Now, Mr Bell, I am a man of my word but I am also a patriot. I venerate the British Commonwealth of Nations and the idea of a spy in God's Own Little Country gets my goat good and proper. Hence this letter.

So it seems to me, Mr Bell, that the best thing I can do is to fix up this little matter of business across the Tasman right away. I shall tell Mrs C I am going in the morning.

So I drop you this line which I shall post before taking the air for Aussie. You will note that I have kept my undertaking to this person and have not mentioned his name. I trust you, Mr Bell, not to communicate the matter of this letter to anyone else, but to take what action you think best in all other respects.

Again expressing my appreciation for our very pleasant association.

> With kind regards,
> Yours faithfully
> MAURICE QUESTING

Dikon folded the letter and gave it to Webley.

' *"I do not think he trusts me"* ' quoted Mr Falls. 'How right he was!'

'Yes,' Dikon agreed and added, 'He was right about another thing too. He was an appalling scamp, but I always rather liked him.'

Huia rang the luncheon bell.

CHAPTER 14

Solo by Septimus Falls

Before they left the room Webley showed Dikon how Questing had already packed most of his clothes. Webley had forced open a heavy leather suitcase and found it full of pieces of greenstone, implements, and weapons; the fruits, he supposed, of many nights' digging on the Peak. Rewi's adze, Webley said, had been locked apart in another case. Dikon guessed that Questing had planned to show it to Gaunt when they returned from the concert and had kept it apart for that purpose.

'Do you suppose he meant to try and sell the other stuff in Australia?' he asked.

'That might be the case, Mr Bell, but he would never have got it past the Customs examination. The export of such things is strictly prohibited.'

'Or perhaps,' Mr Falls suggested, 'he was merely a passionate collector. There are men, you know, who, without any real appreciation for such things, become obsessed with a most imperative desire to acquire them. Scrupulous in other things they are entirely unscrupulous in that.'

'He was a pretty keen man of business,' Dikon said.

'I'll say he was,' said Webley. 'We've found blueprints for a new Wai-ata-tapu hotel and grounds that'd make Rotorua look like Shanty-town. Wonderful place he'd planned to make of it.'

He put Questing's letter in a large envelope, made a note of its contents across the back, and asked Dikon and Falls to sign it. They went out and he locked the door after them.

'Well,' said Dikon as they walked along the verandah, 'I never quite believed he was a spy.'

'It seems to leave the field wide open again, doesn't it?' Mr Falls murmured.

'For an enemy agent who is also a murderer?'

'It is a strong presumption. Have you any objection, Webley, to our making this new development known to the rest of our party?'

Webley was close behind them. Mr Falls stopped and turned to await his answer. It was a long time coming.

'Well, no,' said Webley at last. 'There's no objection to that. I can't exactly stop you, can I, Mr Falls?'

'I mean, with an enemy in our midst, isn't it a wise policy to put everyone on the alert as it were? Will you go in, Bell?'

'After you,' said Dikon.

'Mr Falls and I,' said Webley, 'are going to wash our hands. Don't wait for us, Mr Bell.'

Upon this sufficiently broad hint, Dikon went in to lunch.

The rest of the party was already seated. Dikon joined his employer. Dr Ackrington and the Claires, with the exception of Simon, were at the large family table. Simon sat apart with his friend Mr Smith. Mr Falls, when at last he and Webley came in, went to his own table close by.

'Do you mind if I join you, sir?' said Webley and did so.

'But I am honoured, Sergeant. As my guest, I hope?'

'No, no, sir, thanking you, all the same,' said Webley. I see there's a place laid, that's all.'

He had made a mistake, it seemed. There was no second place laid at Mr Falls's table but Huia, still very woebegone, rectified this, and he sat down.

'Nice of you to join me, Dikon,' said Gaunt loudly. 'I appear to be in disgrace.'

Barbara turned her head swiftly and as swiftly looked away again.

'I forgot to say,' Gaunt added, 'that Questing asked fifty guineas for the adze. I shall wonder if the price was excessive. I must ask the embarrassing old gentleman.'

Nobody answered this sally. Gaunt thrust out his chin and gave Dikon one of his hard bright glances.

Luncheon went forward in a silence that was only broken by Sergeant Webley's conscientious attention to his food. At an early stage of this uncomfortable meal Dikon, who faced the windows, saw two of Webley's men come round the shoulder of the hill carrying a covered stretcher between them. They disappeared behind the manuka hedge, taking a roundabout path to the cabins. This unmistakable incident killed what little appetite he had. In a minute or two the men, without their burden, appeared on the verandah. Here they were joined by a young man in grey flannel trousers and a sports coat whom Dikon had no difficulty in recognizing as a representative of the press. This new arrival, with an air of innocent detachment, stared in at the windows. Webley looked at him with lack-lustre eyes and shook his head. The two plain-clothes men hung about near the door. The pressman sat on the verandah step and lit his pipe. The party in the dining-room, though aware of these proceedings, paid no attention to them. 'The resemblance to the monkey house at feeding time grows more pronounced every second,' thought Dikon. Huia collected the plates and, when Mrs Claire was not watching her, tipped uneaten pieces of cold meat on to one dish. As if by agreement, Mrs Claire and Barbara went out together. Smith sucked his teeth savagely, muttered 'Excuse me', and slouched out to the verandah. The pressman looked up hopefully and spoke to him but evidently got an uncompromising answer. He let Smith move off, looking wistfully after him.

In heavy silence the remaining seven men finished their meal.

'One can hardly hear oneself speak for the buzz of gay inconsequent chatter,' said Gaunt. 'I think I shall relax for half an hour.'

He pushed back his chair.

'There is, after all, sufficient reason for our silence,' said Mr Falls.

Something in his attitude, though he had not risen, and some new quality in the tone of his voice, which was a deep one, brought sudden stillness upon his hearers.

'When one is in danger of arrest,' said Mr Falls, 'one does not feel disposed for chatter. May I, however, claim the attention of the company for a moment? Sergeant Webley, will you indulge me?'

Webley, who had made a brusque movement when Gaunt's chair scraped on the floor, leant the palms of his hands on the table and, looking attentively at Falls, said: 'Go ahead, sir.'

'I don't know,' said Mr Falls, 'whether you are all devotees of detective fiction. I must confess that I am. It is argued, in respect of these tales, that they bear little or no relation to fact. Police investigation, we protest, is not a matter of equally balanced motives, tortuous elaborations, and a final revelation in the course of which the investigator's threat hangs like an *ignis fatuus* over first one and then another of the artificially assembled suspects. It is rather the slow amassment of fact sufficient to justify the arrest of someone who has been more or less suspect from the moment that the crime was discovered. Sergeant Webley,' said Mr Falls, 'will correct me if I am wrong.'

Sergeant Webley cleared his throat sluggishly. One of the men outside the window looked over his shoulder into the room, turned away again, and moved out of sight.

'However that may be,' Falls continued, and they listened to him with confused attention as if he had, without warning, thrust an embarrassing ceremony upon them, 'however that may be, I detect some resemblance in our present assembly to those arbitrary musters, and with the permission of Sergeant Webley I should like, before we break up, to clear the memory of Mr Maurice Questing. Mr Questing was *not* an enemy agent.'

Here Dr Ackrington broke out with some violence and was not silenced until an account of Questing's letter had, by a sort of forcible feeding, been rammed down the gullet of his understanding. He took it rather badly. The recovery of Questing's skull had evidently been broken to him but this final blow to the very corner stone of all his theories seemed literally to horrify him. He turned quite pale, his protestations ceased, and he waited in silence for Falls to go on.

'Not only was Questing innocent of espionage but, if we are to believe his letter, he actually recognized and accused the real culprit, who adopted a threatening attitude and, by a species of blackmail, extracted an undertaking from Questing that he would not betray him. Questing suggests that when they parted they were mutually distrustful of one another, and I suggest that fright, rather than business, prompted his sudden decision to go to Australia. He felt himself to be in danger just as we now feel ourselves to be in danger and, in a figure that he himself might have used, he passed the buck to Mr Bell. I think he must have written that letter just before we left for the concert. I happened to pass his open door and saw him with his elbows squared on his table. As you know, some three hours later he was killed.'

'Will you excuse me,' said Gaunt. 'I don't want to be difficult but, as I've tried to point out before, I've been extremely upset by this unspeakably horrible affair and I'm afraid I just haven't got the kind of mind that revels in *post mortems*. I'm sorry. I shall leave you to it.'

'One moment, Mr Gaunt,' said Falls. 'You're upset, I fancy, not so much by the knowledge that Questing died very horridly, as by the fear that you yourself might be implicated.'

'I won't have this!' cried Gaunt, and sprang to his feet. 'I resent this, bitterly.'

'Do sit down. You see,' said Mr Falls, looking amiably about him, 'in spite of ourselves we are becoming the orthodox muster of suspects. Here is Mr Gaunt who quarrelled with Mr Questing because Mr Questing used his name as an advertisement, and because he pretended he was the author of a gift that Mr Gaunt himself had made.'

Barbara started galvanically. Gaunt began to accuse Dikon. 'So I've got you to thank – '

'No,' said Falls. 'My dear Gaunt, who but you could have made this gift? A quotation from Shakespeare on the card? Written by the shop assistant? You see I have heard all about it. And, if that was not enough, your very expressive face betrayed you most completely last night, when Questing spoke of her enchanting dress to Miss Barbara. You looked – please forgive the unhappy phrase – positively murderous. Was it not the memory of this that led you to conceal your subsequent quarrel with Questing? It seems to me you had quite a lot to agitate you when Questing was killed.'

'I have explained to the point of hysteria that I was anxious to avoid publicity. Good God, who ever committed murder for such a motive? Sergeant Webley, I beg that you – '

'I quite agree,' said Falls. 'Who ever did? May I pass on, for the moment, to another of our suspects? Mr Smith.'

'Here, you lay off Bert!' shouted Simon. 'He's right out of this. He's got his agreement.'

'His motive,' Mr Falls continued precisely, 'appears at first to be revenge. Revenge for an attempt on his life.'

'Revenge, my foot. They buried the hatchet.'

'In order to resurrect a much more valuable one in the form of Rewi's adze. Yes, yes, I agree that the revenge motive breaks down but it does well enough for a red herring. Dr Ackrington: your motive, at first, would seem to be a kind of quintessence of fury. You believed Questing to be a traitor and you could find little support in your efforts to bring him to book.'

'It's perfectly obvious to me now, Falls, that the man was done to death by someone from the native settlement. No doubt some wretched youth in the pay of the enemy.'

'Ah! The Maori theme. Shall we leave that for the moment? Now, in your case, Colonel, the motive is much more credible. Forgive me for introducing a painful theme but your position was, I'm afraid, only too clear. Questing's extraordinary assumption of proprietorship alone would have betrayed it. He was, as Mr Bell remarked a little while ago, a keen man of business. Have you not benefited greatly by his death . . .'

'Cut that out!' Simon cried out angrily. 'You damn well lay off my father.'

'Be quiet, Simon,' said the Colonel.

'. . . as indeed,' Mr Falls completed his sentence, 'have all the members of your family?' He looked at his hands, lightly clasped on the table. 'The Maori element,' he said, and paused. 'Revenge for the violation of a sacred object? Not an inconsiderable motive. To my mind, a perfectly credible motive. But did anybody beside Mr Gaunt, outside the Old Firm, as I feel tempted to call the Smith-Questing-Saul link-up, know of the disappearance of the adze? And beyond that there seems to be a jealousy theme centring round your mind, Colonel. Questing appears to have supplanted the man with the debatable shirt. Eru. Eru Saul.'

'But my dear Falls,' said Dr Ackrington, 'you seem to accept Questing's letter. Surely, then, the murderer is the spy?'

'Certainly. It is most probable. The point I am leading up to is this. It seems to me that in this case motive should, for the moment, be disregarded. There are too many motives. Let us look instead at circumstances. At fact.'

'Oh, for God's sake,' Gaunt said wearily.

'Four apparent inexplicable points have interested me enormously. The railway signal. Eru Saul's shirt. The *pohutukawa* trees. The misplaced flag. It seems to me that if an explanation is found that will apply equally to these four parts, then we shall have gone a long way towards solving the whole. These are factual things.'

'How about yourself?' Simon demanded abruptly. 'If it comes to facts you look pretty fishy, don't you?'

'I am coming to myself,' said Mr Falls modestly. 'I look extremely fishy. I have left myself to the last because what I have to say, or part of it, is in the nature of a confession.'

Webley looked up quickly. He moved his chair back a little and shifted the position of his great feet.

'When I left the hall,' said Mr Falls, 'I went immediately into the thermal reserve. I have stated that I saw Questing ahead of me and recognized him by his overcoat. I have also stated that I paused and lit my pipe, that then I heard Questing scream, and that a few moments later Bell came along from the direction of the village. I had no alibi. Later, having insisted that none of us should return to the scene of the crime, I myself returned there. You saw me from the hill, did you not, Bell? I was obliged, by the nature of my errand, to use my torch. I heard you plunging down the hillside and realized that you must have seen me. On my return I informed Colonel Claire and Dr Ackrington of my visit to the forbidden territory. Later, I believe, they told you I had given, as an excuse, a story that I had heard someone moving about on the other side of the mound. This was untrue. There was nobody there. And now,' Falls continued, 'I come to the last episode in my story.' With a swift movement he thrust his hand inside his jacket.

Simon scrambled to his feet with an inarticulate cry.

'Grab him!' he shouted. 'Grab him! Quick! Before he takes it! *Poison!*'

II

But it was not a phial or deadly capsule that Mr Falls drew from the inner pocket of his coat, but a strip of semi-transparent yellow substance which he held up before Simon, who was already halfway across the floor.

'You alarm me terribly,' said Mr Falls. 'What on earth are you up to?'

'Sit down, boy,' said Dr Ackrington, 'you're making a fool of yourself.'

'What the blazes are you gettin' at, Sim?' asked his father. 'Plungin' about like that?'

Gaunt laughed hysterically and Simon turned on him.

'All right, laugh! The man stands there and tells you he lied and you think it's funny. All along, I've said there was something fishy about him.' His face was scarlet. He addressed his father and uncle. 'I told you. I told you he tapped out the code signal. It's there under your noses and you won't do anything.'

'Ah!' said Mr Falls. 'You noticed my experiment on the verandah, did you? I thought as much. You have what used to be called a speaking countenance, Claire.'

'You admit it was the code signal? You admit it?'

'Certainly. An experiment to test Questing. It had an unfortunate result. He picked up the pipe. Quite innocently, of course, but it conveyed an unhappy impression, not only to you but to someone much more closely interested. His murderer.'

'That's right,' said Simon. 'You.'

'But I see,' Mr Falls continued urbanely, 'that you are looking at this piece of yellow celluloid which I hold in my hand. I cut it off Questing's sun screen on his car. Its colour is important. Colour, indeed, plays a significant part in our story. If you look at a red object through this celluloid it becomes a different shade of red, but it is still red. If you look at a green object through it, a similar phenomenon occurs. A blue-green, such as one may see on a railway signal, merely becomes slightly warmer yellowish-green. If Questing said that he mistook the red signal because he saw it through this celluloid, he lied.'

'Yes, but damn it all . . .' Simon began, and got no further.

'Questing stated that on the occasion of his almost fatal signal to Mr Smith at the railway bridge, Eru Saul wore a blue shirt, but we know that he wore a pink one. Did he lie again? That same evening he fell into Dr Ackrington's trap, and agreed that there was no bloom on the trees at Pohutukawa Bay, when, as a matter of fact, the Bay was, and still is, scarlet with blossom. Again, did he lie? Dr Ackrington, most naturally, concluded that he had not been to the Bay, but we know now that he had. Here I should tell you, in parenthesis, that Mr Questing's pyjamas and ties exhibit a recurrent theme of the peculiar shade of puce which it seems he did not recognize in Eru Saul's shirt. Now we come to the final scene.'

Webley got quickly to his feet. One of the men on the verandah opened the door and came in. He, too, moved quietly. Dikon thought that only he and Gaunt had seen him and his manoeuvre. Gaunt looked quickly from this man to Webley.

'Questing,' said Mr Falls, 'carried a torch when he crossed the thermal reserve. The moon was not yet up and he flashed his torchlight on the white flags that marked the path he must follow. When he reached the mound above Taupo-tapu, over which the track passes, he would see no white flags ahead of him for the one on the top had been displaced. He would, however, see the faded red flags marking the old path on which Taupo-tapu has now encroached. There are several mounds on both sides of Taupo-tapu and they look much alike by torchlight.

'My contention is that Questing followed the red flags and so came to his death. My contention is that Questing's murderer is the man who knew that he was colour blind.'

III

A sharp flick to that fascinating toy, the kaleidoscope, will transfer a jumble of fragments into symmetrical design. To Dikon, it seemed that Mr Falls had administered just such a flick to the confused scraps of evidence that had collected about the death of Maurice Questing. If the completed pattern was not yet fully visible it was because there was some defect, not in the design but in Dikon's faculty of observation. The central motif, the pivot of the system, was still hidden from him but it began to emerge as Falls, disregarding the sharp exclamations that broke from his listeners, and the emphatic slap with which Dr Ackrington brought his palm down on the table, went on steadily with his exposition. The affectations, and the excessive urbanity of manner, were no longer noticeable in his speech. He was grave and relentlessly methodical.

'Now, it is a characteristic of persons afflicted with colour blindness that they are most reluctant to admit to this defect. The great Hans Gross has noted this curious attitude and says that a colour-blind person, if he is forced to confess to his affliction, will behave as if guilty of some crime. Questing, when challenged by Dr Ackrington with an attempt to cause the death of Mr Smith, instead of admitting that he could not distinguish the red signal from the green, said that the signal was not working. Mr Smith told you that, later on, Questing gave him the story of the celluloid sun screen.'

'Yes, but look here . . .' Simon began and stopped short. 'On your way,' he said.

'Thank you. It is also characteristic of these people that they confuse green with red and they have a predilection for that peculiar shade of pink, kaffir pink or puce as it is sometimes called, which, apparently, seems to them to be blue. A patch of red if seen by green torchlight might appear to these people to be colourless. At any rate, with the white flag removed, Questing, if colour blind, would have no standard of comparison and would most certainly expect the red flag to be white and accept it as such. Accepting for the moment my theory of Questing's colour blindness, let us see how it squares up with the evidence of the track. Sergeant Webley,' said Mr Falls with a slight return of his old mellifluous style, 'will correct me if I am wrong. My own investigation took place by torchlight, remember.'

He smiled apologetically and took the tip of his nose between his thumb and forefinger. 'I saw,' he said, 'that the clod of displaced earth, or solidified mud as I believe it to be, had split away from the iron flag standard. I could see the groove made by the standard in the broken section of the bank. The heel marks made by the famous nailed boot were immediately behind it, as well as on the clod itself. These suggested a possibility that the heel stabs had been used with the object of loosening the standard rather than dislodging the clod. If one kicked at such a standard in the dark one would make a few dud shots. The standard itself lay a little distance away from the clod. They had both fallen on a narrow shelf of firm ground at the edge of the cauldron.

'Both flag and path were intact when we went to the concert. Of the returning party nobody remembers seeing the flag but, on the other hand, nobody remembers seeing the gap in the path. But Colonel Claire, who was the last to go through before the tragedy, tells us he fell when he reached the top of the mound.'

'Eh?' said the Colonel with one of his galvanic starts. 'Fell? Yes. Yes, I fell.'

'Is it possible, Colonel, that you trod on the clod already loosened by the removal of the flag and that it gave way beneath you, causing you to stumble forward?'

'Wait a bit,' said the Colonel. 'Let's think.'

'While Edward is lost in contemplation,' said Dr Ackrington, 'I should like to point out to you, Falls, that if your theory was correct, the flag was removed after we had entered the hall.'

'Yes.'

'And it was intended, originally, that we should all crowd into Gaunt's car for the return journey.'

'A point well taken,' said Mr Falls.

'And then the half-caste fellow left the hall during the performance.'

'Returning in time to hear Mr Gaunt's masterly presentation of the Saint Crispin's Eve speech.'

'The speech before Agincourt, wasn't it?'

'We shall see. Yes, Colonel?'

The Colonel had opened his eyes, and relaxed his moustache. 'Yes,' he said. 'That's what it was. Astonishin' I didn't think of it before. The ground gave way. By George, I might have gone over, you know. What?'

'A most fortunate escape,' said Mr Falls gravely. 'Well now, gentlemen – I have almost done. It seems to me that only one explanation will agree with all the facts I have mentioned. Questing's murderer was a man with hobnailed boots. He threw the boots into Taupotapu. He had visited the Peak, for the boots correspond with Bell's sketch of the prints. He had access to the reserve during the concert. He knew Questing was colour blind, and was most anxious that we should not discover this fact. He was an enemy agent and Questing knew it. Now what figure in our cast fits all these conditions?'

'Eru Saul,' said Dr Ackrington.

'No,' said Falls. 'Herbert Smith.'

IV

It was Simon who was making the greatest outcry: Simon protesting that Bert Smith wouldn't hurt a fly, that he couldn't have done it, that he had tried to join up, that he was all right as long as he kept off the liquor. It was Simon who, with a helpless slackening of his voice, repeated that Falls had no right to bring this accusation and, finally, that Falls did it to protect himself. The Colonel and Dr Ackrington tried to silence him, Webley attempted to get him out of the room, but he held his ground and in the end he talked himself to a standstill. His lips trembled, he made a gesture of relinquishment. Like an exhausted child, he stumbled clumsily to a seat, beat the table with his fists, and at last was silent.

'Smith!' said Gaunt. 'Lord, what an anticlimax! They must be hard-up for cogs in the fifth column set-up in this country if they found a job for Smith.'

'I'm afraid he is a very small cog,' replied Falls.

The Colonel said: 'He's been with us for years.'

'I am not entirely convinced,' said Dr Ackrington importantly. 'How are you so damned positive that Smith knew Questing was colour blind? He may have *believed* the story of the sun screen.'

'He was never told that story. According to Smith, Questing drove him to the crossing and showed him the light through the screen, which Smith said was green but which, as you see, is yellow. *He's* not colour blind, you know; he knew Questing wrote with green ink. The sun screen story was invented after the murder, for our benefit. He had to explain why he had suddenly become friendly with Questing. He had to produce his precious letter. Above all things, we mustn't know of Questing's defective sight. His insistence, this morning, that Questing must have been right about the colour of Eru Saul's shirt is only explicable in that light. Of course Questing gave Smith the real explanation of his failure to see the signal. Questing agreed to keep him quiet, and incidentally used him as a go-between in his curio hunts. All went well until Questing discovered him on the Peak and accused him of espionage. The goose that laid the golden eggs had to be killed.'

'Then the Maori theme,' said Dikon. 'Eru Saul, the stolen adze, and the violation of tapu, were all subsidiary factors?'

'In a way, yes. Eru Saul told me that when he returned to the concert, after going for a drink with Smith, he heard Mr Gaunt recite a speech about *"old dug-outs being asleep while him and the boys waited for the balloon to go up"*. This seemed to me to be a recognizable paraphrase of *"gentlemen in England now a-bed"*, which is part of the

Saint Crispin speech. But Smith told us that as he returned to the hall he heard Mr Gaunt shout a sentence which he rendered as: "*Once more into the blasted breeches, pals.*" Unmistakably the opening line of the Agincourt speech, the last item in Mr Gaunt's recital, which he gave only after prolonged and enthusiastic demands for an encore.'

'Bert wouldn't know,' Simon said. 'He wouldn't know. It's all one to Bert.'

'There is a time lag of some five or six minutes between the beginning of the Crispian speech and the beginning of the Agincourt speech. Would you put it at that, Gaunt?'

'I think so,' said Gaunt automatically.

'Time enough for Smith to re-enter the doorway with his companions and, while all eyes were focused on you, to slip out again and run to the reserve. Time enough, when he could not wrench it out, for him to kick the standard until it was loosened, and then drop it over the edge. Time enough to think of the evidence left by his boots and throw them overboard. Time enough to run back to the hall and be standing there, close by his friends, when the lights went up.' He turned to Simon. 'You were with him after the concert?' Simon nodded. 'Did you notice his feet?' Simon shook his head.

'Mr Gaunt's man was with you, wasn't he?'

'Yes.'

'Could we speak to him, I wonder?'

Webley nodded to the man at the door. He went out and returned with Colly.

'Colly,' said Mr Falls. 'What sort of boots was Mr Smith wearing when you went home last night?'

'Not boots at all, sir,' said Colly instantly. 'Soft shoes.'

'Did you walk over to the hall with him before the concert?'

'Yessir. We went over early with extra chairs.'

'Was he wearing shoes then?' Webley demanded.

Colly jumped and said: 'You're that small, Inspector, I never see you. No, he was wearing boots then. 'E took 'is shoes in 'is pocket 'case we finished up with a dance.'

'Did he carry his boots home?' asked Webley.

'I never see them,' said Colly, and looked uneasy.

'OK.'

Colly glanced unhappily at Simon and went out.
Webley walked over to the man at the door.
'Where is he?' he asked.
'In his room, Mr Webley. We're watching it.'
'Come on, then,' said Webley, and they went out, their boots making a heavy tramping sound that died away in the direction of Smith's room.

CHAPTER 15

The Last of Septimus Falls

'It's no good asking me to work up a grain of sympathy for him,' said Dikon. 'There's no capital punishment in this country now. He'll spend the rest of his life in jail, and a damned lucky let-off it is for him. He's a dirty little spy and a still dirtier murderer. It's poor old Questing I can't bear to think about.'

'Oh, *don't.*'

'I'm sorry, Barbara darling. No, I won't call you "Barbara darling". In our giddy theatrical circles we call people "darling" when we can't remember their names. I shall call you something calmly Victorian. Barbara, love. Barbara, my dear. Now, don't take umbrage. It doesn't hurt you, and it gives me a certain hollow satisfaction. How far shall we walk?'

'To the sea?'

'My feet will turn into smouldering sponges, but I'm game. Come on.'

They walked on in silence under a pontifical sky.

'It seems more like a week ago than two days,' said Barbara at last.

'I know. Exit Smith in custody. Exit Mr Septimus Falls in a trail of glory and soon, alas, exit us.'

'How soon?'

'He talks about next week. We've got to stay for the inquest. He's much better, you know. Your anatomical uncle says he doesn't think there will be a recrudescence of the fibrositis, which is, I consider, a magic phrase.'

'Where will he go?' asked Barbara in a flat voice.

'To London. He wants to take a company out on tour. The Bard in the blitz. Fit-ups. Play anywhere. It's a grand idea,' said Dikon and added, 'I'm leaving him.'

'*Leaving* him? But why?'

'To have one more shot at enlisting. If they won't like me any better here than they did in Australia I shall return with Gaunt. There must be *something* for a blind bat to do. They say they use everybody at home. I shall wear battle dress, and sit in a black little cellar at the end of the longest passage of an obscure building typewriting memoranda for a Minor Blimp. Will you write to me?'

Barbara didn't answer. 'Will you?' he insisted and she nodded.

'Fancy!' Dikon said after a moment. 'There are tears in your eyes because he's going and here am I, ready to howl like a banshee at the notion of leaving you. There's no sense in it.'

Barbara stopped short and glared at him. 'It's not for that,' she said. 'You're not as sharp as I thought you were. It's because, well, it's partly because I've been living in a *hollow mockery*.' She brought this out in her old style, turning her eyes up and the corner of her mouth down.

'Don't do that to your nice face,' said Dikon.

'I'll do what I like with my face,' said Barbara with spirit. 'If my face irritates you, you needn't look at it. You talk about being fond of me but all you want to do is fiddle about with me until you've made me into a bad imitation of some beastly glamour girl.'

'No, honestly. Honestly not. I wouldn't mind if you screamed at me because I sniff when I read and bite my nails. You can make one face after another with the virtuosity of a Saint Vitus and I shall still love you. Why have you been living in your "hollow mockery"?'

'I've been such a frightful fool. Slopping all over him because I thought he was like Mr Rochester and all the time he's just vain and selfish and rather common. Pretending his soul was lacerated by what happened and all the time he was just afraid he'd be mixed up in it. I'm so ashamed of myself.'

'Oh,' said Dikon.

'And for him to give me those things. And look at me as if I was a *cheap plaything* – I didn't make a face. You can't say I made a face.'

'You never batted an eyelash. But you're too hard on him. He's kind-hearted, and he gives presents like you'd shell peas. Model dresses are no more than a couple of rosebuds to him.'

'And when Daddy told him, very nicely, that I couldn't possibly accept them he behaved *frightfully*. He said: "She can etc. well turn an etc. nudist if it amuses her." Sim heard him.'

'That,' said Dikon, controlling his voice, 'is because he'd been dealt rather a stiff smack in his pride. It's a bit galling to have your presents returned with quiet dignity. He felt like two-penn'orth of dirt and that made him angry and bewildered.'

'Well, I'm sorry, but he really ought to have known better. And don't let's talk any more about the things because, however much I try, I can't pretend I didn't like them.' Barbara looked at Dikon. 'Which makes the whole thing rather comic, I suppose.'

'Bravo, Miss Claire,' said Dikon. He took her arm and to his great astonishment felt her hand slip into his own.

'You will write to me, won't you?' said Dikon. 'If the war lasts a long time you will forget what I'm like, but I shall come back.'

'Yes,' said Barbara. 'Come back.'

II

'That,' said Mr Falls, 'is about all, I fancy. I'm going down to Wellington as soon as the inquest's over. Hush-hush conversations with the PM and the commissioner and so on. I'm afraid we've only caught a sprat, but at least it will show the seriousness of the position.'

'Yes,' said the Superintendent. 'We'd got into the way of thinking these things don't reach us down here. The boys go away, reinforcement after reinforcement, and then it gets a bit closer and we begin building up our home forces, but we don't somehow think in terms of fifth columnists. Or the general public don't. We've been very fortunate to have you.'

'I'll say!' said Mr Webley. 'You know, sir, there was the old doctor writing in and writing in and yet the thing looked somehow ridiculous. He had hold of the wrong end of the stick, of course, but the idea was right.'

'Yes,' said the Superintendent heavily, 'the idea was right.'

Mr Falls said: 'Dr Ackrington behaved very well. As you know I got him to come and see me in Auckland. That was after I'd had his letter. But I didn't decide to go to Wai-ata-tapu until the next day when you people suggested it. There was no time to warn him and we met face to face on the verandah while I was doing my decrepit dilettante stuff. He didn't turn a hair. He backed me up nobly. We had to take the Colonel into our confidence, of course, and that *was* a bit tricky. And while I'm handing out bouquets I should like to say how very grateful I am to Webley. He was extraordinarily good over the whole show.'

'There you are, Sergeant!' said the Superintendent.

'He insisted on my doing the summing up business. We both thought that as the espionage aspect of the thing was an open secret among them, it was best to let them know the truth. Simon Claire, for one, would have raised a hell of a dust if there had been any doubt left in his mind. As it is, they have all undertaken to say nothing. If you can adjourn the inquest and hold things over for a little it will give me a chance to dig a bit deeper before the principals realize quite how much we know.'

'You don't want to appear at all, I gather?'

'Mr Septimus Falls will have to give evidence, I'm afraid, but he will not return to Wai-ata-tapu.'

Sergeant Webley passed his hand over his face and gave a low chuckle.

They all stood up and the Superintendent held out his hand. 'It's been a real privilege,' he said. 'I'm sure Webley has felt like that about it.'

'I'll say! A great day for me, sir.'

'We'll meet again, I hope, with a bigger catch.'

They shook hands. 'I'll warrant we do,' said the Superintendent, 'with you on the job. Goodbye, Mr Alleyn. Goodbye.'

A Fool About Money

A Fool About Money was first published in
Esquire magazine (USA) in 1973.

'Where money is concerned,' Harold Hancock told his audience at the enormous cocktail party, 'my poor Hersey – and she won't mind my saying so, will you, darling? – is the original dumbbell. Did I ever tell you about her trip to Dunedin?'

Did he ever tell them? Hersey thought. Wherever two or three were gathered did he ever fail to tell them? The predictable laugh, the lovingly coddled pause, and the punchline led into and delivered like an act of God – did he, for pity's sake, ever tell them!

Away he went, mock-serious, empurpled, expansive, and Hersey put on the comic baby face he expected of her. Poor Hersey, they would say, such a goose about money. It's a shame to laugh.

'It was like this – ' Harold began . . .

It had happened twelve years ago when they were first in New Zealand. Harold was occupied with a conference in Christchurch and Hersey was to stay with a friend in Dunedin. He had arranged that she would draw on his firm's Dunedin branch for money and take in her handbag no more than what she needed for the journey. 'You know how you are,' Harold said.

He arranged for her taxi, made her check that she had her ticket and reservation for the train, and reminded her that if on the journey she wanted cups of tea or synthetic coffee or a cooked lunch, she would have to take to her heels at the appropriate stations and vie with the competitive male. At this point her taxi was announced and Harold was summoned to a long-distance call from London.

'You push off,' he said. 'Don't forget that fiver on the dressing table. You won't need it but you'd better have it. Keep your wits about you. 'Bye, dear.'

He was still shouting into the telephone when she left.

She had enjoyed the adventurous feeling of being on her own. Although Harold had said you didn't in New Zealand, she tipped the taxi driver and he carried her suitcase to the train and found her seat, a single one just inside the door of a Pullman car.

A lady was occupying the seat facing hers and next to the window.

She was well-dressed, middle-aged and of a sandy complexion with noticeably light eyes. She had put a snakeskin dressing case on the empty seat beside her.

'It doesn't seem to be taken,' she said, smiling at Hersey.

They socialized – tentatively at first and, as the journey progressed, more freely. The lady (in his version Harold always called her Mrs X) confided that she was going all the way to Dunedin to visit her daughter. Hersey offered reciprocative information. In the world outside, plains and mountains performed a grandiose kind of measure and telegraph wires leaped and looped with frantic precision.

An hour passed. The lady extracted a novel from her dressing case and Hersey, impressed by the handsome appointments and immaculate order, had a good look inside the case.

The conductor came through the car intoning, 'Ten minutes for refreshments at Ashburton.'

'Shall you join in the onslaught?' asked the lady. 'It's a free-for-all.'

'Shall you?'

'Well – I might. When I travel with my daughter we take turns. I get the morning coffee and she gets the afternoon. I'm a bit slow on my pins, actually.'

She made very free use of the word 'actually'.

Hersey instantly offered to get their coffee at Ashburton and her companion, after a proper show of diffidence, gaily agreed. They explored their handbags for the correct amount. The train uttered a warning scream and everybody crowded into the corridor as it drew up to the platform.

Hersey left her handbag with the lady (an indiscretion heavily emphasized by Harold) and sprinted to the refreshment counter where she was blocked off by a phalanx of men. Train fever was running high by the time she was served and her return trip with brimming cups was hazardous indeed.

The lady was holding both their handbags as if she hadn't stirred an inch.

Between Ashburton and Oamaru, a long stretch, they developed their acquaintanceship further, discovered many tastes in common, and exchanged confidences and names. The lady was called Mrs Fortescue. Sometimes they dozed. Together, at Oamaru, they joined in an assault on the dining room and together they returned to the carriage where Hersey scuffled in her stuffed handbag for a powder compact. As usual it was in a muddle.

Suddenly a thought struck her like a blow in the wind and a lump of ice ran down her gullet into her stomach. She made an exhaustive search but there was no doubt about it.

Harold's fiver was gone.

Hersey let the handbag fall in her lap, raised her head, and found that her companion was staring at her with a very curious expression on her face. Hersey had been about to confide her awful intelligence but the lump of ice was exchanged for a coal of fire. She was racked by a terrible suspicion.

'Anything wrong?' asked Mrs Fortescue in an artificial voice.

Hersey heard herself say, 'No. Why?'

'Oh, nothing,' she said rather hurriedly. 'I thought – perhaps – like me, actually, you have bag trouble.'

'I do, rather,' Hersey said.

They laughed uncomfortably.

The next hour passed in mounting tension. Both ladies affected to read their novels. Occasionally one of them would look up to find the other one staring at her. Hersey's suspicions increased rampantly.

'Ten minutes for refreshments at Palmerston South,' said the conductor, lurching through the car.

Hersey had made up her mind. 'Your turn!' she cried brightly.

'Is it? Oh. Yes.'

'I think I'll have tea. The coffee was awful.'

'So's the tea actually. Always. Do we,' Mrs Fortescue swallowed, 'do we really want anything?'

'I do,' said Hersey very firmly and opened her handbag. She fished out her purse and took out the correct amount. 'And a bun,' she said. There was no gainsaying her. 'I've got a headache,' she lied. 'I'll be glad of a cuppa.'

When they arrived at Palmerston South, Hersey said, 'Shall I?' and reached for Mrs Fortescue's handbag. But Mrs Fortescue muttered something about requiring it for change and almost literally bolted. 'All that for nothing!' thought Hersey in despair. And then, seeing the elegant dressing case still on the square seat, she suddenly reached out and opened it.

On top of the neatly arranged contents lay a crumpled five pound note.

At the beginning of the journey when Mrs Fortescue had opened the case, there had, positively, been no fiver stuffed in it. Hersey snatched the banknote, stuffed it into her handbag, shut the dressing case, and leaned back, breathing short with her eyes shut.

When Mrs Fortescue returned she was scarlet in the face and trembling. She looked continuously at her dressing case and seemed to be in two minds whether or not to open it. Hersey died a thousand deaths.

The remainder of the journey was a nightmare. Both ladies pretended to read and to sleep. If ever Hersey had read guilt in a human countenance it was in Mrs Fortescue's.

'I ought to challenge her,' Hersey thought. 'But I won't. I'm a moral coward and I've got back my fiver.'

The train was already drawing into Dunedin station and Hersey had gathered herself and her belongings when Mrs Fortescue suddenly opened her dressing case. For a second or two she stared into it. Then she stared at Hersey. She opened and shut her mouth three times. The train jerked to a halt and Hersey fled.

Her friend greeted her warmly. When they were in the car she said, 'Oh, before I forget! There's a telegram for you.'

It was from Harold.

It said: YOU FORGOT YOUR FIVER, YOU DUMBBELL. LOVE HAROLD.

Harold had delivered the punchline. His listeners had broken into predictable guffaws. He had added the customary coda: 'And she didn't know Mrs X's address, so she couldn't do a thing about it. So of course to this day Mrs X thinks Hersey pinched her fiver.'

Hersey, inwardly seething, had reacted in the sheepish manner Harold expected of her when from somewhere at the back of the group a wailing broke out.

A lady erupted as if from a football scrimmage. She looked wildly about her, spotted Hersey, and made for her.

'At last, at last!' cried the lady. 'After all these years!'

It was Mrs Fortescue.

'It *was* your fiver!' she gabbled. 'It happened at Ashburton when I minded your bag. It was, it was!'

She turned on Harold. 'It's all your fault,' she amazingly announced. 'And mine of course.' She returned to Hersey. 'I'm dreadfully inquisitive. It's a compulsion. I – I – couldn't resist. I looked at your passport. I looked at everything. And my own handbag was open on my lap. And the train gave one of those recoupling jerks and both our handbags were upset. And I could see you,' she chattered breathlessly to Hersey, 'coming back with that ghastly coffee.'

'So I shovelled things back and there was the fiver on the floor. Well, I had one and I thought it was mine and there wasn't time to put it in my bag, so I slapped it into my dressing case. And then, when I paid my luncheon bill at Oamaru, I found my own fiver in a pocket of my bag.'

'Oh, my God!' said Hersey.

'Yes. And I couldn't bring myself to confess. I thought you might leave your bag with me if you went to the loo and I could put it back. But you didn't. And then, at Dunedin, I looked in my dressing case and the fiver was gone. So I thought you knew I knew.' She turned on Harold.

'You must have left *two* fivers on the dressing table,' she accused.

'Yes!' Hersey shouted. 'You did, you did! There were two. You put a second one out to get change.'

'Why the hell didn't you say so!' Harold roared.

'I'd forgotten. You know yourself,' Hersey said with the glint of victory in her eye, 'it's like you always say, darling, I'm such a fool about money.'